FALL FROM GRACE

by
J. L. SABA

J. L. SABA

Cover photo courtesy of Nan Burger at http://youcouldmakethat.blogspot.com

To C.J., Bron, and Mom
thanks for all the comments, encouragement, and even the dreaded deadlines—without all of you, there wouldn't be all of this; your faith in me made it possible.

Prologue

The darkness is his ally. It envelopes him, body and soul. Under its velvety cover he is a god and death is his disciple.

Concealed within the shadows of a stand of pine trees he watches and waits.

The humid air clings to his already damp skin and he can hear the sounds of a dog barking several blocks away in the stillness of the summer night. The only sound he can hear nearby is the incessant drip, drip, drip of water from the upper branches of the trees that arch above him like the dome of a cathedral.

As headlights sweep around the corner, his heartbeat leaps and speeds up. Although the lights pass by his breathing continues to accelerate until he is almost panting. Reaching down, his right hand grasps the uneven bulge in his jacket pocket.

"Not long, not long," he chants over and over again, calming.

Finally, after another quarter hour has passed, a second car rounds the corner and pulls into the driveway across the street from where he crouches.

His Angel has arrived.

Straining forward slightly he sees her gather her purse from the seat next to her and step out of the car. Not daring to breathe, he listens and hears her soft curses over the thundering of his heart as she steps off the path and sinks her high heel into grass still damp from a late afternoon thunderstorm.

Stiffening at her words, the wild elation that had filled him when he had seen her car is stripped away. Grinding his teeth he waits as she unlocks the front door, goes in, and turns to shut the door giving him one last glimpse of his Angel.

The sharp scent of pine fills his nose, and looking down he sees that he has dug his fingernails into the course bark of the tree that he is hiding behind.

Whore. Slut. Betrayer.

Tonight is the night.

It is not for another two hours that the last light turns out. After waiting another hour he creeps out from underneath the darkness of his hiding place.

1

A dark smear against an inky backdrop, he soundlessly makes his way along the street to the alley that runs behind his Angel's house and into her yard. As he slithers along the side of the house to the basement window he has already broken the lock on, the tension eases from his body.

Easing past the darkened living room he slowly climbs the stairs, stepping over the third step from the top to avoid the squeak he knows will disturb the silence of the night.

Stopping just outside of the Angel's room, he eases his instruments out of his backpack and once more reaches his right hand into his jacket pocket.

Click, click, click.

His Angel stirs slightly in her bed.

Click, click, click.

With a start she jerks awake. Her eyes open, trying to focus in the enveloping darkness. With the drum of her pulse in her ears it takes a moment for her heart to slow down enough so she can hear—there's nothing.

But that's wrong.

As her pulse skyrockets again she realizes that the window she always left open to let in the night air is closed and the room is stifling. Reaching slowly towards her bedside lamp her hand freezes in midair.

Click, click, click.

Screaming she lunges forward only to be thrown back onto the bed, a leather glove smothering her nose and mouth.

Chest heaving, she feels his damp breath on her cheek and hears over her muffled screams his guttural whisper, "You were my Angel, but you are no longer worthy."

Struggling fruitlessly against his hold she feels a sharp blow against her head, and as the room recedes she hears again—click, click, click.

He is a god, and death is his disciple.

ONE

Whoever said that breaking up was hard to do was wrong. Clearly Bradley Whiteside had no problem breaking up with her—or with going to bed with his amply endowed secretary. What a cliché. A sordid, embarrassing cliché.

"Bastard." Running a hand through her wind-blown hair, Maggie Sullivan slammed the door to her car and ran up the steps to her apartment building.

Just two stories tall, the apartment building sits on a quiet, tree-lined street, a few blocks from the beach. The spectacular view and the restful hominess of the neighborhood had drawn her from the first.

Taking the steps two at a time, the feeling of well-being that had filled her the very first time she'd entered the apartment calmed her once more.

Despite the small rooms and the old plumbing, the quaint two-bedroom apartment welcomed her today, just as it had nearly two years ago when she decided that it was finally time to move out of her parent's house.

Because she understood herself, she had known that she needed the quiet and *aloneness* of her own place after a lifetime of constantly sharing, of constantly being surrounded by her large, raucous family. And because she understood herself very well, she had known that she would miss the chaos and the camaraderie, the constant noise and affection of her family, and had moved less than a mile away from them.

Dropping her keys on the small table next to the door and blowing out a noisy breath, she kicked off her shoes and dropped into the big comfy chair that had passed down from some aunt or uncle to her brother, and then to her. "Maggie, m'girl, you're in for it now," she muttered.

Thinking that it was better to get it over with quickly, she picked up the phone, and once again running a hand through a dark tumble of auburn curls, she hit the speed dial. "Hi, Mom."

"What's wrong?"

"What do you mean, what's wrong?" Rolling her hazel eyes Maggie bit back another sigh.

3

"Something's wrong."

"Mom, there's noth…"

"I know that voice, Margaret Elizabeth."

Cringing at the use of her full name Maggie reflexively checked that her hands were clean before shrugging off the involuntary reaction to her mother's voice, "It's nothing, really."

"Come to dinner, you'll tell me everything."

And if she went, Maggie knew she would spill it all. Not only the fact that Bradley had cheated on her, but that she'd found out in such a humiliating way.

After weeks of waiting she'd finally received a copy of her very first professional article published in *The Art Bulletin*. Maggie had been so excited to see her name printed in the periodical that she had read religiously all while earning her degree and graduate degree in Art History.

Finally, she had made it.

It was all there in black and white on the printed page before her. *The Religious and Social Impact of Pieta Imagery throughout the Twentieth Century* by Margaret E. Sullivan.

She hadn't even stopped to call his office before she'd rushed over to show him. Thinking Bradley would be as happy as she was she'd burst right into his office holding up the journal triumphantly. She had gotten all the way into the room before realizing that Bradley was not behind the ruthlessly neat and polished antique captain's desk she had spent more than a month helping him find when he got his job at the accounting firm. Instead, he was sprawled out on his equally impressive Persian rug with his blond, buxom, secretary, Trixie. The bastard hadn't even had the gall to look guilty. He'd simply drawled, "Well, I guess we need to talk."

"Talk? You want to *talk*?"

Maggie had literally seen red. Sure that steam had to be pouring out of her ears, she had stalked right up to them, and with narrowed eyes, spit out, "Stay away from me, you low-lying scum sucker." Turning her eyes from Bradley to Trixie, who flinched back into him, Maggie growled, "You can have the cheating bastard." And turning on the heel of the Christian Louboutin heel that had cost her more than a month's wages, she had marched out, slamming the door with a crack of finality.

4

Nobody could get anything past Elizabeth Sullivan, particularly when it came to her children, and Maggie just wasn't up to reliving the day from hell—not even to share her small victory.

"Mom...really, I can't tonight, I just wanted to let you know that Bradley's not coming to dinner with me next weekend," holding her breath, Maggie continued in a falsely bright tone, "In fact, we broke up."

"Hmmm."

"What do you mean, 'Hmmm'?"

"Nothing, nothing. Are you okay?"

"I'm fine, Mom, really. I just want to relax tonight, but I'll see you Saturday, okay?"

"Are you sure you won't come for dinner? I'm making your favorites; meatloaf and mashed potatoes and apple pie."

The thought of her favorite meal was awfully tempting, but Maggie held firm. "I'm sure, but thanks, Mom. I'll see you Saturday."

"All right, but if you change your mind..."

"Thanks, Mom, I love you."

"Oh, Honey, I love you too. Goodnight."

"Night."

Hanging up the phone, Maggie settled further into the chair and let her head fall back.

Looking up at the cheery yellow walls that her brothers had helped her to paint just last month she willed away the tension of the day's events. Gripping the forearms of the chair she ordered herself not to let the tears pressing against her eyelids fall. *I will not cry over that jerk. He is* so *not worth it.*

It wasn't that she thought that crying was bad. In fact, she believed that crying was an important and necessary release—one that she enjoyed on a regular basis, whether from temper, joy, or sadness—it just galled her to squander one more iota of emotion on the pathetic excuse for a man she had wasted more than six months of her life on.

Shrugging off the tension with a lift of her shoulders, Maggie heaved herself up out of the chair and through her tiny dining room and into her bedroom. Filled with bold colors and soft fabrics, her bedroom was her retreat. Warm and inviting, it boasted a beautiful sleigh bed she'd found in an estate sale and lovingly refinished along with a collection of similar pieces passed on from various family members or carefully selected in antique shops and sales over the past two years.

Briskly slipping out of her skirt and blouse and into her most comfortable sweats, Maggie crammed her riot of curls up into a semblance of order with a clip.

Padding past the stacks of books that littered her floor on her way back towards the kitchen she paused to flip the stereo on. With the hopes that the heavy pulsing of rock would drown out any thoughts of the state of her love life, Maggie got a mini pizza from the freezer. If she could just zone out for a couple of hours in front of the TV, maybe she would be ready to face the confusing jumble of emotions that had been racing through her mind since walking in on Bradley.

As the oven preheated, she walked to the fridge and brought out the bottle of champagne that she'd been saving for a special occasion—like getting her article published.

"Of course, I thought I'd be celebrating *with* someone. All right, Maggie, talking to yourself is the first sign that you're loosing your marbles—just get a grip."

Angry with herself for letting her thoughts stray back in that direction, she ripped the foil from the top of the bottle with a little more force that was necessary. With a celebratory pop, the cork flew out and a waterfall of foam flowed out of the bottle and into the champagne flute she had dug out of the back of her cupboard. As she lifted the glass in a mock salute, she muttered grimly, "To new beginnings."

When the timer beeped she dished up the pizza, dug a couple of her mom's homemade chocolate chip cookies from the freezer, grabbed her drink and settled into the deep cushions of her couch to watch a movie. Reaching for the remote she mused, there's nothing like Humphry Bogart or Cary Grant or even Mel Gibson to restore a girl's faith in romance. When the FBI warning came up on the screen she settled back with a contented sigh and let the opening credits push the last stray thought of the real world from her mind.

When the alarm went off at its usual time the next morning, Maggie lifted her head off of the pillow with a muffled oath and practically knocked the clock off her bedside table before she managed to turn it off. The feel of her tongue stuck to the roof of her mouth had her swearing that she'd never "celebrate" again.

With a whimper she got out of bed and managed to drag her protesting body into the bathroom to splash a few gallons of cold water on her face.

It can't be as bad as I think it is, she prayed before she steeled herself to look up. She looked into the mirror and gasped at the pasty-faced reflection staring back at her. Taking stock, she bypassed the small, straight nose, high cheek bones and lips she'd always thought too small for her oval face and saw dark circles, hair stuck up in every direction and bloodshot eyes. "Now, that's attractive."

After pulling on running shorts and a tank top Maggie rushed past her cozy-looking bed before she could succumb to the urge to crawl back under the covers for the next three days and headed out the front door for her daily three mile run.

Running was not something that came naturally to her. When she ran, Maggie never experienced that magical endorphin rush she'd read so much about. Maggie breathed hard. She sweated. She counted the miles until she could be done.

So why do you do this to yourself?

With a scowl she answered herself, because you love to eat.

She also loved the way her whole body felt warm and strong and loose after she'd exercised. Running was simply the easiest and fastest way to get that exercise out of the way as quickly as possible.

She headed towards the beach. This early in the day it was almost always deserted, and she loved the fact that her footprints were the first to mar the small stretch of sand that she considered hers. The lonely cry of seagulls winging high above the calm gray waters of the bay filled her mind with a soaring feeling of freedom.

The first mile was torture, but the memory of an empty bottle of champagne and the serious dent she'd made in her emergency chocolate chip cookie stash pushed her on.

Turning at her half-way point, she pounded back over the imprints her shoes had made in the sand. Although she oftentimes

7

used her run to think and plan, she deliberately kept her mind blank, focusing instead on the steady beat of her footfalls.

By mile three her body was responding fluidly despite her labored breathing and the stitch in her side.

With a sigh of relief, she rounded the corner onto her block and saw her older brother, Steven sitting on her front stoop, two coffee cups steaming next to him.

Stumbling to a halt in front of him, Maggie bent at the waist to catch her breath before collapsing onto the stairs.

"Should I call the paramedics?" Holding out a steaming cup of coffee, Steven leaned over to look down at her, a small smirk on his face. Dressed in dark jeans and a battered brown leather bomber jacket that flared out over a black three-button shirt he looked relaxed and casual. But a careful observer would note the sharp awareness in dark brown eyes that missed little and saw much.

Snatching the cup, Maggie inhaled a deep breath, and with a groan gulped down a third of the coffee before replying. Steven winced and shook his head at her willingness to scald her mouth to get her first shot of caffeine.

"Ha, ha, you're *so* funny, Steven. What, are you giving up your illustrious career as a cop to become a comedian? I'd ask you what brought you here so early in the morning but it would be a waste of breath. Mom called, right?" Raising her eyebrows Maggie looked over her shoulder at her overprotective big brother and took another sip.

With a twinkle in his eye he tugged a stray curl that had fallen out of her bedraggled ponytail.

"She didn't have to, I was there when you called—you're lucky she was able to talk me out of stopping by last night."

"While I admire your tremendous restraint," she said sarcastically, "I can't really talk right now. If I don't get my butt inside in the next five minutes to get showered and dressed I will be totally late for work." With an insincere smile she handed him the empty cup and slipped quickly past him into the house.

"Not so fast, Mags," Steven followed her into the kitchen all humor gone from his face.

He crushed the empty coffee cups and two-pointed them into the garbage can, "Mom said you were close to tears on the phone last night, and I want to know what's going on." As immovable as the Sphinx, he stood rooted to the floor in the center of the kitchen with arms crossed.

Growing up in a house with four older brothers had taught her many things, not the least among them that the best defense was a good offense. Gathering herself, she turned to face off with him.

"Listen, Steven, I don't have time to go into this right now. I'm fine. I broke up with Bradley. It's over. End of discussion." Frustration making her tone sharper than intended, she punctuated each statement with a sharp wave of her hands.

Steven looked past the anger in her eyes and saw a weariness and vulnerability that worried him. "It's nowhere near the end of discussion, little sister, but I'll drop it…for now."

Maggie opened her mouth to deliver a scathing retort but before she could think of a good one he continued, "Do you want me to wait and give you a ride in to work?"

The love and caring in his voice brought the swift sting of tears to her eyes and swept away the remnants of her frustration with him. She closed her eyes and stepped into him. She felt his strong arms come around and resting her chin on his chest she smiled up into his concerned eyes. "I'll get there okay, Steven. Thanks for bringing the coffee."

Relieved to see that her smile reached her eyes, he gave her a quick squeeze and headed for the door. "I'll see you real soon, Maggie, and if you don't tell me what's going on, I'll go and have a little discussion with Brad myself."

All warm thoughts of brotherly concern fled, and drawing herself up as far as her petite 5'4" frame allowed she yelled at his retreating back, "Stay out of my business, Steven Michael, or I'll tell Mom that it was *you* that ran over her prize roses when you were fifteen."

With a satisfied smile she watched him freeze in his tracks before swinging back towards her, a look of stunned disbelief on his face.

"You wouldn't."

Gleefully she noted the panicked tone of voice. "Wouldn't I? I'm 27 years old, Steven, and I won't be held accountable to you or anyone else."

9

Now glowering, he turned and walked out the door, "This isn't over, Maggie."

Relieved that she had managed to stall Steven at least temporarily, Maggie sagged against the counter, exhausted from the exchange. With the echo of his parting shot and the slamming door still ringing in her ears, Maggie looked at the clock and swore violently.

She was going to be late.

TWO

Anyone who looked at Grant Evans knew he was a dangerous man. When men looked at him they saw a tall rangy man about 6'4" with dark hair and dark eyes. The danger they sensed was not in his outward appearance, but in the aura of repressed violence he exuded that had nothing to do with the fact that his job as a cop required that he carry a gun.

When women looked at him they did not fear what he would do to their body, but what he could do to their hearts. They saw a tight, well-toned body wide of shoulder and lean of hip, and the dark sculpted face of an angel fallen to earth worth a second, and often a third or fourth, look.

One look into his eyes and all thoughts of angels fled.

There weren't many women that didn't think, even fleetingly, that it might be worth getting burned to play with that fire.

While not entirely unaware of his effect on the fairer sex, it was something Grant had spent little to no time thinking about for the past year and half. Instead he had focused all his energy into recovering, body and soul, from the night both he and his partner Lou were gunned down in a dark alley behind a convenience store.

He had survived. Lou had not.

They had just gone off duty when they'd witnessed two men in ski masks brandishing guns run out of the store and head down the alley.

Refusing to go back down that alley again, even in his mind, Grant shook off the feelings of depression that seemed to hover, ready to invade his thoughts at the least provocation.

Drawing in a deep breath and rolling shoulders stiff from too many hours in the same position, he pulled his focus back to his surroundings in time to pass a sign proclaiming that he was only five miles from his destination. After spending most of the past three days in his Tahoe, it was a relief to know that his journey across most of the country was almost over.

A whine from the passenger seat drew his gaze from the road, and he reached over to give Jake, his 93 pound German Shepherd, a scratch.

"We're almost home, Boy. Almost home…"

Taking the next exit, he drove the dusty SUV up over a rise. As he reached the summit, the pine trees that had lined the roadside and sent the damp woodsy smell of pine and soil through his open car windows for the past several hours swept back dramatically leaving him with a panorama of the city of Hope, Minnesota, nestled along the shores of Ascension Lake. The view was just like the picture on the town's website, except the glory of autumn had painted broad brush strokes of gold, umber, and vibrant red where there had only been shades of green.

The early afternoon sun reflected off of the deep blue surface of the lake into his eyes as he descended into the heart of Hope. Within minutes, he had lost sight of the water and started passing by the sun-dappled tree-lined streets of the quiet city he had chosen to be his new home after spending the first 32 years of his life in the urban hustle and bustle of Seattle.

He had desperately needed a change, and Grant had a strong feeling that living in Hope would be as different from living in Seattle as he was from the man his mother, sister, and ex-fiancé had expected him to be. They had wanted him to be a lawyer, an accountant, a fisherman—anything except the cop he had always known he was destined to be.

The quick response to his email of interest in the job opening at the Hope Police Department had been exactly what he needed after months of medical leave, physical therapy and increased pressure from the women in his life to change careers. So, here he was, just three weeks later, his entire life packed into the back of a once-shiny new SUV, ready to make a new start in a small town.

"What the hell were you thinking?" he muttered, and with a last roll of his shoulders he pulled into an open parking space just two doors down from the police station. He turned off the engine and stepped out onto the pavement, telling Jake to stay.

Rubbing his hand along the rough stubble on his unshaved face, Grant walked into the small brick building that housed the local police and took a moment to investigate his new place of employment.

Immediately to his left sat a receptionist behind a huge wooden desk perched like a sentinel guarding her kingdom. Dwarfed by the big desk, she eyed him with shrewd interest from bright blue eyes in a round face topped by a tight cap of gray curls. Her pleasantly round body was encased in a fluffy pink sweater. Her nameplate declared that she was Ms. Shirley Larson.

Sending her a fleeting smile, Grant quickly scanned the rest of the squad room that stretched out behind her. The room was painted a soft creamy yellow instead of the institutional beige he'd been expecting. A row of metal filing cabinets lined one wall while a fax machine, copier, and coffee pots lined the facing wall. Instead of the standard cubicles there were perhaps eight desks set up in groups of twos scattered throughout the room and three doors leading to private offices on the back wall.

"May I help you?"

Grant returned his attention to Ms. Shirley Larson hiding his surprise at the distinctly Southern drawl that flowed from her mouth as smoothly and slowly as molasses on a hot day.

"I've an appointment with Chief Banyon, name's Grant Evans. He's expecting me, Ma'am."

Confronted with the bright flash of teeth in a charming smile and warm twinkling eyes the color of whiskey, Shirley found herself blushing and smiling back, instantly won over—no mean feat for a newcomer making the attempt to enter the inner sanctum of what she considered *her* territory.

Lifting one hand up to grasp the small golden cross necklace she wore, Shirley lifted the other to point back at the far wall, "Well then, you just head right on back to his office. It's the one in the back in the right hand corner."

Flashing another quick smile, Grant replied, "Thank you, Ma'am," and headed back towards the office.

Dropping her necklace Shirley fanned her flushed cheeks and watched Grant walk towards the Chief's office with a sigh of pure female appreciation before she turned back to buzz the Chief to let him know a visitor was on his way back.

As he walked back towards the far wall, Grant was all too aware of the interest he was garnering from the four officers busily working at the desks, and took the opportunity to observe the people he hoped to spend the next several years working with.

A sharp-faced woman with short cropped fire-engine-red hair talked into the phone in a calm, placating tone while her intense green eyes drilled into Grant. As he walked by Grant heard her murmur, "Yes, Mrs. Lee. I understand….of course he should keep the dog chained in his yard…absolutely. Officer McKenzie and I will be by within the hour, and we'll speak with Mr. Miner. Right. Yes, alright, Mrs. Lee."

Facing the female officer from the desk butted up to her desk a tall, bald black man quietly chuckled and shook his head as he glanced away from the redhead and acknowledged Grant's passing with a tip of the head.

Moving past the first duo Grant glanced to his right and saw another set of officers working at the far desks. The first was a short man with thinning blond hair hunched over a computer keyboard mumbling and cursing under his breath as he pecked out a sentence using two fingers. His uniform stretched over the extra ten pounds he'd apparently gained since first getting it.

Sitting on the edge of the desk was a fourth officer with dark chestnut brown hair and intelligent brown eyes. He was relaxed, sipping a cup of coffee and trying to smother a smile as he watched the other man struggle to type. Although he wasn't standing Grant judged him to be about the same height as he was.

"Jeez, Simmons, are you going to finish that report some time this century?" the tall officer cracked.

"Cripes sake, Sullivan, you nag worse than my Ma does. You'll get it when you get it, alright?"

Glancing up from his scrutiny the humor in Sullivan's eyes faded to curiosity as he assessed Grant. With a short nod Grant passed by to knock on the Chief's slightly open door.

From within the office a gruff voice called, "Come on in."

Grant pushed through the doorway and reached forward to shake Chief Banyon's hand. Chief Robert Banyon unfolded his long limbs and stood with slightly rounded shoulders to offer a calloused palm. Deep creases bracketed shrewd blue eyes when he smiled.

Instinct warned Grant not to be fooled by the Chief's laid back appearance—he suspected that underneath the well-worn jeans and casual tan chambray button-down shirt laid a cunning brain.

"Afternoon, Chief Banyon."

"Welcome to Hope, Detective Evans. Have a seat, have a seat," Chief Banyon gestured to two wooden visitor's chairs angled in front of his massive wooden desk before resuming his seat. "I hope the drive was good and you found us alright."

"Thank you, sir," Grant continued as he sat down, "The trip was great. I appreciate the information you sent me about the town and I'm looking forward to settling in."

As he eased back into the chair, Grant took a moment to take a look around. Once again he was surprised at the cheerful color on the walls—pale blue this time—and the overall orderliness of the office.

His old boss's office had been so cluttered with files, periodicals, and assorted flotsam there hadn't even been a place to sit. Shaking his head slightly to rid himself of the memory, Grant leaned back in the chair, one hand unconsciously rubbing his right thigh, and continued his survey.

Although not tremendously large, a set of windows flanking the desk gave the office an airy, open feel. One wall was devoted to plaques, photographs of the Chief shaking various peoples' hands, and framed certificates while the other held an assortment of filing cabinets and a large dry erase board filled with information on current cases. The desk itself was neat and orderly, the only files out of place those currently being worked on.

While he'd been cataloging the office, the Chief had been carefully scrutinizing Grant. Impressed with the quiet, composed man seated in front of him, the Chief did not miss—as many others had—the haunted look carefully disguised by a charming smile in a handsome face. Many other men would have handled this situation differently. Instead of acting like a big shot detective in a small town, Grant seemed more inclined to let his record speak for itself. And, having carefully read said record, the Chief was doubly impressed with him—despite, or perhaps because of, the incident that immediately preceded his leaving the Seattle P.D.

Grant turned his attention back to the man in time to hear him say, "Good, good. If you need any help finding anything or getting settled, you just let me know. I know we discussed all the particulars of the job on the phone last week, I just wanted to make sure that I got the chance to welcome you to town in person, and to tell you how pleased we are to have someone with your experience on the team," leaning forward with a serious look on his face, the Chief continued briskly, "There are a few papers we need to go over, but they can wait until next week when you officially start."

"I appreciate that, Chief. I need to get a few things settled, and then I'll be looking forward to getting back on the job."

Noting the weary set to Grant's shoulders, the Chief stood up saying, "Sounds good. If you'd like, I can quick introduce you to a couple of the guys before I let you get started on unpacking."

"Thank you, sir. I'd appreciate that," Grant stood and turned to leave the office. Once back in the main workplace, Grant noted that just two of the officers were left, and he assumed that the sharp redhead and her tall partner were off helping Mrs. Lee handle the chainless dog.

Simmons still sat hunched over his report and Sullivan had crossed to refill two mugs with coffee. The Chief paused by Simmons's desk first, saying, "Hey Dusty, meet our new detective, Grant Evans. Grant this is Officer Reginald Simmons."

"Nice to meet ya, Detective Evans," Dusty half stood to shake his hand, looking relieved to be interrupted.

"Grant."

Shifting swiftly from a pained look to a smile, Dusty blushed slightly and quickly inserted, "And you can call me Dusty, only my mama calls me Reginald."

"That's not what I heard, Dusty. I heard that there's a certain Miss Katie Bell that's been calling you Reginald pretty regularly…" an amused voice broke in.

Grant glanced back over his shoulder to watch the tall detective walk up with the steaming mugs before he handed one to the now beet red Dusty. Grant almost didn't catch the Chief's lightning quick smile, but there was no mistaking the sly grin and the look of devilish humor in the other detective's eyes. Clearly Dusty's new lady love was a hot topic in the squad room right now.

Shifting his attention from Dusty to Grant, the smiling detective extended his hand saying, "Hi, I'm Steve Sullivan."

Grant shook hands once more as the Chief spoke up, "Grant Evans, Detective Sullivan here is who you will be pairing up with. You'll be sitting at the open desk across from him." He gestured towards the desk in the far left corner of the room.

"Nice to meet you, Detective Sullivan," Grant nodded cautiously towards Steve, trying to get a quick read on him."

Before Grant could say anything else, the Chief was saying, "I know that you have a lot you need to get accomplished before you start work on Monday, Grant. I'm looking forward to working with you," shaking Grant's hand one more time, the Chief nodded at all three men and turned to go back into his office.

Leaning back against Dusty's desk, Steve gave Grant a measuring look, "So, the Chief told us you're from out west."

Prepared to see animosity, Grant was pleasantly surprised to find only curiosity in Steve's eyes. Nodding, he replied, "Yes, I was with the Seattle P.D. for the last nine years." Once again, memories of Lou flashed into his mind and were immediately banished.

When he didn't volunteer any more information Steve just nodded back and noted the stiffening of Grant's shoulders. Clearly a touchy subject for some reason—a reason that Steve would have to discover if he were going to be working side-by-side with Grant. "Have you found somewhere to live yet?"

"No. I have a hotel booked for the next couple a days, but I'm hoping to find a house to rent or buy quickly."

His expression thoughtful, Steve said slowly, "I *may* know about something that might interest you. There's a small house for rent across the street from where my sister lives. It's a nice neighborhood, kinda quiet, but it's only a couple of miles from here. If you'd like, I could take you by after my shift."

Surprised but pleased, Grant grinned and replied, "That would be great. I'm down at the Northern Lodge, I have a big dog and they were the only place in town that I could find that would allow him to stay with me."

"Alright. How about I swing by around 6. We can catch a quick dinner after you get a chance to take a look at the house."

"I really appreciate it," Grant replied as he stretched out his hand for one more shake with both men, "It was nice to meet both of you. I'll see you at six, Detective Sullivan."

"Steve."

"Alright, Steve." Grant turned and walked past the receptionist, nodding to her as he swept out the door and walked back to his SUV.

THREE

A whirlwind of motion, Maggie hurried into the small university office she shared with the two graduate students currently working with her boss carrying a tray with four coffees in it.

Cloë Sanders sat behind a small steel desk facing the door and glanced up from her typing to send Maggie a quick grin before answering the ringing phone at her elbow. Petite with short-cropped mouse brown hair streaked with saucy red highlights and cat-eye glasses framing large brown eyes slightly turned up on the ends, Cloë looked like a pert pixie with attitude.

Sweeping up to Cloë's desk, Maggie set a steaming mocha latte at her elbow before moving forward to a second desk and setting down another cup—coffee, black—in front of the tall, gaunt man with shaggy black hair more than a couple weeks past due for a haircut staring intently through a magnifying glass at a sheath of photo slides on a light box.

"Hey, Tony."

"Mmm," Tony Malone mumbled absently as he reached out unerringly to grab the coffee and take a big sip. As he looked up, his dark eyes blurred and refocused behind thick lenses set in dark black frames, "Mornin', Maggie." A slow stain of pink climbed his neck turning his ears bright red.

"Good morning," she replied as she leaned to set the tray down with her left arm on her scarred wooden desk. At the same time she stretched down with her right hand to open the bottom drawer and dropped her purse in. Straightening up, her right foot kicked the drawer shut with a bang as she collapsed with a big sigh into her chair to face Cloë and Tony.

"I can't believe how late I am. Is he in yet? How are you guys doing? Any messages for me? Any news yet on the Stanisleski slides?" Her hands moving quickly over her desk, Maggie opened a large purple leather day planner bursting with papers and flipped it open to the right day before looking up with a smile.

Looking like a deer caught in headlights Tony cleared his throat, opened his mouth and shut it again, before grabbing his cup of coffee with an air of desperation to take another gulp.

Recognizing the warning signs of an impending crush, Maggie's brow furrowed. She opened her mouth to say something reassuring before closing it again with a snap.

Although she'd had her share of students flirt with her, Tony was the first she had to work with in a professional capacity. Figuring out exactly what to say to him to let him know she was not interested in anything other than friendship without damaging their professional relationship was going to be tricky enough without attempting to do it after the night she'd just had.

I don't even know what to do about my own love life, what am I going to say to him? Shaking her head to shrug off the mood Maggie smiled softly and smoothed her brow.

Raising a finger in the air to catch their attention Cloë spoke quietly into the phone before hanging up and swiveling in her chair to face Maggie fully.

"Hey, Maggie, thanks for the coffee. Let me see, he is, fine, yes on your desk under your turtle paperweight, and we're supposed to get them in this afternoon's FED EX shipment."

Sitting back with a satisfied air Cloë grabbed her cup and took a small sip, her impish eyes sparkling at Maggie over the rim.

Grinning back at her Maggie reached out to move the heavy silver turtle her older brother Jack had given her for her last birthday to slide out the small pile of pink telephone messages. Flipping silently through them her face closed down completely before she crumpled them all into a ball and threw them into the trash bin under her desk.

Every one of them was from Bradley.

Maggie grabbed a file folder from the inbox basket perched on the front corner of her desk and stared blindly at it, not noticing the look of speculation and raised eyebrows Cloë shot at Tony before turning back to her computer.

After Maggie had flown out of the office to go see Bradley yesterday, Cloë had been sure that Maggie would be absolutely happy this morning. With a worried glance back at Maggie's still unmoving form, Cloë began typing again, wondering just what that creep Brad had done to upset Maggie so badly and calculating how long it was until lunch so she could pry it out of her.

19

His brows drawn down, Tony slowly turned back to the light box when he realized that Maggie was not going to look up at him again. Something was wrong. *If only she would share it with me*, he thought to himself, *she would see how good I could be to her.*

Blissfully unaware of what her officemates were thinking, Maggie rubbed her temples with both hands before telling herself— again—that she would *not* let her work, or any other part of her life, be disrupted by what had happened with Bradley. Rolling her shoulders one last time before standing, she grabbed her planner and the tray with the last two cups of coffee on them and strode to the inner office door just to the left of her desk with dry eyes and chin held high.

Juggling the planner and tray with one arm, she lifted the other to knock quietly on the door before walking through it to the small office beyond. The door closed behind her with a quiet click and she weaved her way through stacks of books and files to settle comfortably into a padded leather chair wedged between a bank of filing cabinets covered in dust, piles of books, papers, and sheets of slides and a second chair completely covered in papers, magazines, and what appeared to be about a month's worth of newspapers piled haphazardly together.

Leaning back in his chair in a rumpled white dress shirt and khakis, Professor Holden St. John talked intently into the phone, passing a small ball from one hand to the other as he spoke.

Although it was just past nine in the morning his suit coat was already on the back of his chair, his tie had been loosened, and his shirt sleeves were rolled up to his elbows exposing tanned, well-muscled forearms. Tracks showed where he had run his hands through sun-tipped hair and, as Maggie watched, his hand reached up to sweep through his hair once again in a gesture she knew to be habitual. Resuming the slow toss of the ball, Holden's eyes focused on Maggie's face and he nodded once before going back to his conversation.

Knowing that it could be anywhere from a few minutes to a half hour before the Professor finished up his call Maggie reached out to take the coffees from the tray before throwing it out and settling back to enjoy her first truly peaceful moment of the morning.

Soaking in the musty smell of academia and the low soothing tone of the Professor's voice as he talked, Maggie's eyes wandered around the cluttered office before staring out the open window at the clear blue sky filtered through the vibrantly green leaves of an ancient oak tree. With a start she realized the office was silent and she turned to see piercing green eyes boring into her.

Recognizing the look Maggie quickly straightened in her chair before relaxing again. Making a face she said, "I hate that look—you always used that look whenever you skewered some unsuspecting student with an unanswerable question."

With a sharp laugh Holden smiled, transforming his intense expression into one of warmth and humor and making him look much younger than his 46 years.

"That never seemed to faze you, Maggie," he chuckled, "You always were my star pupil." Relaxing back into his chair once more, his eyes narrowed when he noted her shadowed eyes and a too-pale face but he didn't comment, knowing it would only put her back up. Instead he reached over to pick up the small cardboard cup she'd placed on the corner of his overflowing desk and continued lightly, "I guess some things never change—I read your article, Maggie. It's superb."

"It really is, isn't it?" Maggie replied, laughing.

Faint lines fanned from the corners of his eyes as Holden joined in her laughter. "Don't be so modest, Maggie."

Relieved to see the color wash into her face and the bright humor in her eyes he went on, "Thanks for the coffee, by the way. So, what's on the agenda today? Anything I need to address before this morning's class?"

"Not really," Maggie replied and crossed her legs. Briskly opening her ever-present planner she continued, "You have a department heads meeting on Friday at five with the Dean and a couple of minor functions coming up next week, but I wanted to let you know that the Stanisleski slides are *finally* arriving this afternoon, thank God, so they will be ready for Thursday's lecture as long as everything you wanted is in the shipment."

"Sounds good." Abruptly abandoning his relaxed position he leaned forward, setting the cup aside and folding his hands together on the desk before pinning her with his intent gaze again, "So, are

21

you going to fill me in on what's going on with you, or are you going to make me guess?"

Blowing out a sigh Maggie flipped her planner closed with a snap and crossed her arms as if to ward off her emotions. "There's nothing wrong, I just celebrated the article with a little too much champagne last night, that's all."

When he simply continued to watch her patiently she dropped the planner on his desk, leapt to her feet to pace and, faced with the stacks of files and books littering the floor, dropped back into the chair in frustration.

Maggie knew he would let it go at that—temporarily—if she asked him to, but after more than six years of friendship she knew that eventually he would continue to chip away at her until she told him.

Looking into those calm green eyes she shrugged and, lowering her eyes, said in a resigned voice, "I brought the article over to show Bradley last night. He wasn't alone."

If she'd been looking up Maggie would have seen the quick flash of comprehension before fury darkened his eyes.

The viciousness of the single word Holden spit out had her eyes widening as they jerked up to meet his furious ones.

Before she could stop it, a snort of laughter escaped before she said, "Not anymore!" She clapped her hand to her mouth to stop another laugh from bubbling out.

Startled, for a long moment he could only stare at her before his wrath faded to humor and he snickered, appreciating her.

The snicker set her off again, and she laughed until she cried. To her dismay, she couldn't stop crying and after a moment or two of trying she just let it all out.

Holden watched, his humor replaced by the first stirrings of panic at the sight of her tears and almost desperately he handed her a wad of Kleenex when she eventually stopped.

"Thanks. I guess I needed that," Maggie said while she mopped up her face, "Sorry to drop all this on you, Holden, but I do feel much better having cried it out."

"No problem. Is there anything I can do—give you the afternoon off? Get you a drink of water? Kick his sorry ass?" Holden asked dryly.

Stifling a watery giggle, Maggie glanced up again, and her breath caught when she saw the anger that still hardened his eyes despite the light tone of his voice.

"I appreciate the thought, but it's going to be hard enough keeping my brothers from killing him, I don't need another white knight riding to the rescue."

"If you ever change your mind, darlin', you be sure to let me know."

Startled at the silky tone and with the flash of something foreign in his eyes, Maggie smiled uncertainly and cautiously re-opened her planner.

"So…I think that that's all I needed to fill you in on." Maggie looked up straight into Holden's eyes and seeing only the cool, unruffled demeanor she'd come to expect of her friend, dismissed the thought that the flash of emotion she'd seen in his eyes had been desire.

Relief washed through her and her smile brightened as she added, "Thanks again, Holden. I'm sorry I cried all over you."

"Anytime, Maggie."

As Maggie stood and turned to walk out, Holden swiveled in his chair to blindly face his computer, his shoulders slumping when he heard the click of the door as it shut behind her.

"Anytime."

Maggie slipped into the washroom to do a quick makeup repair before heading back to her desk. Tony would be gone at a class, but Cloë was almost as adept at reading people as Maggie's mother, and the fewer questions the better.

Dampening a paper towel, Maggie pressed the cool compress to her eyes before carefully reapplying mascara and concealer. The emotional purge had been therapeutic, if ill-timed. Maggie had known it would happen sooner or later, but she'd been counting on it happening later—much later.

What amazed her was just how much better she actually felt. God knew she was still furious at the betrayal, but Maggie was unnerved, and perhaps even a little ashamed, to discover that her pride was more damaged than her heart.

She had truly believed that what she felt for Bradley was love. After all, they'd had so much in common—a love of art and antiques, a strong need to advance their careers, they enjoyed many of the same restaurants, driving into the Cities to go to the opera. The past six months had been comfortable and enjoyable, and Maggie had thought she'd finally found someone she was compatible with.

"Compatible." Maggie rolled her eyes and stuck her tongue out at her reflection and muttered, "Maggie, you are such an idiot."

The idea that she could stop loving him so quickly was a shock, but what really troubled her was the little voice in the back of her mind that wouldn't shut up that kept whispering that she'd never loved him at all.

If her head hadn't already felt like an entire marching band was banging away in her skull, the crying jag and this lovely realization would have guaranteed it. She popped open a bottle of aspirin and swallowed three with a shudder.

Looking up into the mirror one last time, Maggie slashed on a vivid coating of lipstick, smoothed the front of her jade green silk blouse and black linen trousers, and concluded that the cold compress and makeup should do the trick.

Armed and ready, she lifted her chin and strode out to face the rest of her day.

It couldn't get any worse, right?

It could, and it did.

It had been a rhetorical question, Maggie thought angrily twelve hours later. *Not* a dare to the forces of Nature.

She was alone in the office. Cloë had left two hours earlier after giving up on getting Maggie to come out for a drink. Maggie felt a bit guilty, she had begged off of lunch, and what she was sure would have been an interrogation about Bradley. Cloë was a good friend, but Maggie just didn't have the energy to go through it all again. So, she'd used the excuse that she was swamped. Knowing Cloë, though, Maggie was sure that Cloë would corner her at some point tomorrow.

Dragging her hand through her hair for what felt like the thousandth time that day Maggie sighed and shut down her computer. Thank God that that was tomorrow. Maggie would deal with it then, she was beyond dealing with it now.

She had had about as much as she could handle for one day.

Just as she had dreaded, the archivist from the Stanisleski estate had sent the wrong slides, and that had taken more than three hours of calls, faxes, and threats before the situation had been resolved.

Holden would have his slides tomorrow, Maggie thought with grim satisfaction, and that imbecile from the archives had gotten a major chewing out.

Maggie shook off the twinge of guilt for having caused it and shut off the office lights before locking the office door. Catching movement out of the corner of her eye Maggie jumped stifling the scream that rose in her throat before realizing it was just Moe Swanson, the building custodian.

"Staying late again, Miz Sullivan?"

Smiling brightly, Maggie replied, "Someone's got to keep this place from falling apart. How's your mother doing, Moe? I hope she's feeling better."

"She's doing much better. Doc says it was just a touch of pneumonia, and that she should be fit as a fiddle in a week. It's real kind of you to ask."

"I so glad to hear that. Well, I better get headed home. You have a nice night, Moe."

"Would you like me to walk you out to your car, Miz Sullivan? It's getting dark out."

"I'm right outside the side door, but thanks," Maggie walked past him to the stairs.

She was home within ten minutes and in bed within twenty, too exhausted to feel anything.

FOUR

While Maggie had been busy dealing with her uncooperative archivist, just a few miles across town her brother Steve walked into O'Neil's Pub with Grant to celebrate the day's success.

After picking him up at the hotel that evening, Steve had taken Grant to look at the house.

It had been perfect—exactly what Grant had been looking for—and a quick call to the realtor later he was inside.

It had sparked an immediate and visceral reaction, a feeling of belonging, the moment he stepped through the front door.

The small brick bungalow with a fenced back yard and a two-car garage connected to the house by a breezeway was located just a couple blocks from Ascension Lake on a quiet tree-lined street. Looking past the tiny kitchen and the sloping ceilings on the second floor, Grant had fallen in love with the details—cove ceilings, built-in corner hutches in the dining room, a small fireplace and hardwood floors. With two decent-size bedrooms on the first floor, and two more on the second floor—although the minute size of the fourth suggested it would be better suited as an office—there was more than enough space.

A handshake and a few signatures later, the realtor was holding an earnest check and beaming, promising to have the closing papers ready for signing by the end of the next day and a lifelong of living in apartments was over.

Instead of simply renting it, he was buying it. He was going to own a home.

His head still reeling from the speed with which the events of the past two hours had happened, Grant simply nodded when Steve suggested going to the bar to celebrate with a couple of pints and some burgers.

As they walked out of the late evening sunshine into the bar, both men took a moment to let their eyes adjust to the dim lighting of the pub's main room. As he followed Steve to the bar, Grant's sharp eyes swept the room with interest.

What he saw could have been taken right out of a movie about an Irish pub—a huge stone fireplace, a long gleaming mahogany bar, a cozy grouping of wooden tables and chairs next to a tiny dance floor, and deep booths with dark green leather benches well-worn from countless people sliding in and out of them.

Although it was clearly not at peak occupancy—dinner was long over and it was far too early for the nightlife to begin—there was a fair amount of people scattered throughout the room. Grant mused that they must be the regulars.

Turning his attention back to Steve as he introduced the man behind the bar, Grant's only thought was that the bartender—and owner—Tom O'Neil was the very picture of an Irish pub owner—or at least how Grant had always imagined one would be.

O'Neil was short with thinning sandy red hair, ruddy cheeks, and merry blue eyes framed by permanent laugh lines. It was no surprise to Grant that when O'Neil stretched out a beefy hand to grab his in an enthusiastic handshake and welcomed Grant to the pub that he spoke in a voice that brought to mind rolling fields of vibrant green.

"Welcome to Hope and to O'Neil's Mr. Evans. I hope that you'll be happy with us."

Sitting down onto a barstool Grant smiled and replied, "Thank you, Mr. O'Neil. If today is any indication, I'm sure that I'm going to be very happy here. Everyone's been incredibly welcoming to me."

"Aye, and that's as it should be, then. Now, what can I get for you gents on this fine evenin'?" Eyebrows rising expectantly, O'Neil looked from Grant to Steve.

Steve reached over to slap a hand on Grant's shoulder as he said, "Well, it's a sad state of affairs, it is, Tom. A very sad state of affairs." Shaking his head sadly from side to side he continued in a hushed voice, "What you have here is a clean slate. I learned just this evening that Grant here has *never* had a Guinness."

"No!" O'Neil exclaimed in genuine shock and dismay.

"I'm afraid it's true," Grant hung his head in mock shame, eye's laughing, "will you pour me one, Mr. O'Neil."

"Pour a Guinness?" O'Neil said faintly, shaking his head in denial before roaring, "Jesus, Mary and Joseph, Son, you don't *pour* a Guinness, you *build* one!"

27

And turning to grab two mugs he commenced doing just that, the entire time muttering under his breath about the ignorance of youth.

Silently laughing Steve and Grant looked at each other in perfect accord. For Grant it was a revelation. He had never felt this immediate kinship and easy friendship with anyone before.

Lou had been like a brother to him, but it had taken months before he'd felt this at ease with his former partner.

For the first time in over a year, Grant felt truly happy.

O'Neil turned and slapped the pints of richly black beer in front of them and leaned forward onto the bar, his worn face wreathed in a smug smile to watch as both men lifted the frosty mugs.

"Here's to cold beer and new friends," Steve lifted his pint and grinned at Grant.

"I'll drink to that," Grant returned cheerfully and lifted his own pint before taking a long satisfying pull of the first, of what he was sure would be many, carefully built drafts of Guinness.

"Well, Mr. O'Neil, that's the best damn beer I've ever tasted," Grant said sincerely, and felt home at last when O'Neal pushed back from the bar, crossed his arms across his chest and beamed.

"Call me Tom."

Hours later, as he lay awake in the unfamiliar hotel bed, Grant thought back over the day's events and once again felt the satisfaction of having gotten so much accomplished. He'd never suspected that he'd find someplace to live—someplace where he felt that he could *belong*—so quickly.

Tomorrow he'd go to the furniture store Steve had recommended to pick out some basic furnishings. He'd need a bed and a couch to start with, but he'd like to look around for some antiques to really fill his new home.

When he'd decided to move it had been painfully obvious that very little of what he owned would be worth moving cross country. He had sold almost everything. None of it had meant anything to him, and he'd figured it would be easier to simply buy what he needed once he'd found a permanent place to live.

The only piece of furniture of any value to him was a beautiful oak partner desk with a deep brown leather top that his grandmother had given him when his grandfather had passed away.

Grant never sat behind that desk without picturing his grandfather leaning back in his chair with a big smile on his face, his feet propped up on the desk, and a cigar in his hand. He'd spent countless hours in his grandfather's office listening to him telling wild stories of adventure from his years on the force.

When he had been young, his grandfather had slipped him licorice whips and bottles of cold root beer from the fridge he kept next to the desk. By the time the candy had been replaced with a cigar of his own and the root beer with the real thing, the vigor and drive that had always made his grandfather seem larger-than-life had begun to drain away day by day.

And then one day he was just gone.

Sometimes, Grant swore he could still catch a hint of rich tobacco when he opened its drawers, and the smell never failed to comfort him.

Sighing, Grant shook off the grief that still managed to sneak up on him despite the years since his grandfather's death and tried to concentrate on tomorrow. Tomorrow he'd have to deal with getting the desk, along with his books and a few boxes of personal items, out of storage.

Other than the dog's supplies, his clothing, a TV, and some work files, he'd left it all behind.

With a feeling of dread, followed by a twinge of guilt, he realized that he would have to call his sister, Valerie, to see if she would send on the few things he'd stored. That call, he mused, would not be any more pleasant than the one he'd made earlier this afternoon to his mother to let her know he'd made it to Hope safely.

It wasn't that they didn't love him. They did. They had just never been able, or perhaps willing, to understand him.

The death of his father in the line of duty when Grant was just twelve had polarized them all, he supposed.

For his mother, it had been a loss so great, so enormous, that she had never looked past her own grief to really see that that same devastating event had turned Grant's vague dream of following in his father's footsteps into his vocation.

29

For Val, the anger of losing her father when she was fourteen had turned to anger at her younger brother for his relentless pursuit of what she believed would be the same end.

Neither one of them had ever forgiven him. He could never decide which was worse—his mother's vague confusion and constant fear for his choice of occupations or his sister's outright anger over it.

He was going to drive himself crazy if he kept this up—and that was the last thing he needed. He hadn't left behind everything and everyone he'd ever known just to slip back into the same self-destructive depression he had moved more than 1,600 miles to escape.

What he needed, he decided grimly, was to get a grip.

It was going to take everything he had to make this new beginning a good one, and he was determined to do just that.

Finding a friend in Steve, finding a place he could maybe belong in a small brick house on a tree-lined street—they were only the beginning. He *would* make it work.

With a groan Grant grabbed his hair in both hands and growled, "Judist Priest, Evans, you sound like a frickin' motivational speaker. Go to sleep, you idiot."

He rolled over, punched the pathetically flat pillow into a more comfortable shape and proceeded to do just that.

When Grant managed to drag himself out of bed the next morning it only took one glance at the clock on the bedside table to make him grateful that the kennel was taking care of Jake's food schedule. Had Jake been able to stay in the room with him, Grant would never have been able to sleep this late.

Grant rubbed a hand against a day's worth of beard before yanking on jeans and walking barefoot into the bathroom to splash cold water on his face. He straightened, ran both hands through his damp hair and stared intently into bloodshot eyes.

"Evans, you look like shit," he said and digging the heels of his hands into gritty eyes, then continued wearily, "And, you're talking to yourself again."

In the light of the new day, last night's euphoria had drained away and Grant gathered his courage to take a closer look at what was left behind in its absence. He was relieved to discover that he felt cautiously optimistic about his new job and partner and excited about his new house.

The relief that he felt was so great it was ridiculous. It had been so long since he'd felt truly happy it had taken him a moment to understand that that was what he was feeling.

He rubbed his hand down his face and turned to walk back into the bedroom to get dressed. He had a lot of details to see to in a short amount of time.

He grabbed the truck keys and his wallet and headed over to the kennel in the rear of the hotel to pick up Jake. Greeted with enthusiastic barking, Grant knelt down on one knee to give Jake a good rub and was rewarded with a vigorous licking.

"How ya doing, Boy?" Grant stood up and hooked a leash onto Jake's collar as he continued, "Let's go get some exercise."

They went for a long walk, beginning in the pleasant commercial area the hotel was located in and then winding through a residential area that had clearly been built in recent years.

Each gently curving street was lined by spindly trees just a few years old, and behind them sat house after house painted bland shades of cream and tan that were sure, Grant thought, to offend no one. Every once in a while some adventurous soul had shaken things up and gone with light blue or green.

Each house was beautiful and, while he could certainly see their appeal, it seemed just a little too "Stepford Wives" to Grant. When he compared them to his new little bungalow he was thrilled all over again.

As he walked along, Grant told Jake all about the house and about his evening at the bar with Steve. Talking to Jake had become a habit in the three years since he'd brought him home from the pound. Especially since he'd lost his best friend and the one person who had seemed to understand him, or at least accept him as he was.

There was nothing like a dog to make a person feel unconditional love. It was no exaggeration to say that Jake had helped save his life—or at least his sanity—when Lou had died.

Although he'd never consciously thought of it that way before, it was knowing that Jake needed him, was counting on him, that had helped him through some of his darkest days after the

31

shooting.   No matter what he was feeling, when Jake looked at Grant with his big brown eyes filled with adoration, listening intently to whatever he said, it had been—and still was—a comfort.

No, Grant reflected, there was nothing like a dog.

Which is probably why the twenty minute walk he'd intended to give Jake turned into one that lasted more than an hour.   When Grant locked a whining Jake back into the kennel with one last rub he reassured him, "Tonight I'm taking you home, buddy. Just a few more hours in this cage and you'll be outta here."

Hurrying back out to the truck Grant whistled cheerfully. There was a lot to get done, but he was eager to get started.

It was time to move forward.

FIVE

When she woke up to the ringing of her alarm clock the next morning Maggie took careful stock before she dared to sit up. She felt a little hungry—and since she'd only had the crumbling remains of a granola bar she'd dug out of the bottom of her desk drawer for dinner that was not a surprise—but otherwise, she felt normal.

"Thank you, God," she said fervently, and jumped out of bed before she muttered self-depreciatively, "I guess that's what getting a decent night's sleep and *not* drinking an entire bottle of champagne by yourself can do for you."

Out the door for her run within five minutes, and showered, dressed and ready to face another day within an hour, Maggie was right on schedule when she got into her cute red Cobalt for the drive to work.

The sporty little two-door had not really been in her price range, but one of her uncles worked at the dealership and was able to find a two-year-old model with just a few thousand miles on it. Because it had been used by the dealership her uncle had been able to get it for her at a price she could live with—as long as she didn't spend any money on little luxuries like designer shoes or food.

Glancing guiltily down at the brand new suede boots she'd just *had* to have when she found them at Macy's last week, Maggie rationalized to herself that since she ate at her parents' house several times a week, and never left without a large bag of leftovers, that she could afford them. Almost.

And besides, they'd been on sale.

When she pulled into the staff parking lot Maggie waved to the lot attendant and thought briefly that it looked like they had yet another new person.

Their old attendant, Manny, had been there for as long as Maggie had been coming to the college, but he'd retired six months ago and they'd had four different people in the position since.

This one looked to Maggie like he should still be in high school. Laughing at herself Maggie rolled her eyes at the thought. Clearly she was getting old when she started thinking that the college students looked like kids to her.

She just hoped that this one wouldn't ticket her car like the last one had. It had taken her weeks to correct that blunder. Just to be careful, Maggie made sure her parking sticker was easily visible on the dash before she locked her car.

"Maggie, wait up"

Still grinning at herself, Maggie turned, her smile growing bigger when she saw Holden getting out of his beat up Volkswagen Beetle juggling a battered leather briefcase and a tray of coffees.

"Morning, Holden. You're in early today."

"I had a couple of things I need to see to before my morning classes," he replied. Which was not really a lie, he assured himself, he just didn't tell her that what he needed to see to was her.

After yesterday he wanted to make sure Maggie was okay, and Wednesday's schedule was his busiest. If he didn't talk to her before his nine o'clock class he wouldn't see her until almost six, and that was only if she stayed late.

"Mmm, coffee, too. What's the occasion?" Maggie asked with a laugh as they turned towards the building.

"Well, you always bring in something for the rest of us and I thought since I was coming in early anyway, I might as well…" trailing off with a self-conscious shrug, Holden kept his eyes forward.

"You're just a big softie, Professor," Maggie teased. When Holden just kept his head down, a faint blush creeping over his face, she continued, "Don't worry, Boss, I won't tell anyone your secret."

Maggie reached to open the door for Holden, but a large hand came from behind her and grabbed the handle before she could. With a soft gasp Maggie turned and broke into a relieved grin when she saw Tony, followed closely by Cloë, behind her.

"Hey guys, looks like the gang's all here," Cloë chirped cheerily, almost drowning out Tony's quiet, "Mornin', Maggie."

While Cloë chattered brightly about her date the night before and Tony turned the radio on his desk to the jazz station he habitually tuned in to, Maggie listened to Holden's grumpy mutterings as he searched his overflowing desk for yet another "lost" paper.

She had just settled behind her desk when the office door opened again and the overnight deliveryman walked in with a

package for her. The Stanisleski slides had made it right on time—
exactly as Maggie had insisted they *must* be.

Sitting back with a satisfied smile on her face, Maggie sipped
her latte. Her smile slipped just a bit when she picked up her phone
to check her voicemail and heard Bradley's mild voice on the
recording.

With a few vicious pokes she deleted the message from her
phone—and his presence from her mind—and turned her attention
back to the ever-present pile of work in her In-Box.

Ratcheting up her smile once more she lectured herself—the
sun was shining, she loved her job, and she loved her friends and
family.

Everything was right with her world again. And she swore
that she'd never let it *not* be right again.

Hours later, as Maggie sat eating her meager dinner of
popcorn and an apple, she thought back with satisfaction over her
day.

After having avoided having lunch with Cloë the day before,
Maggie had not been able to put her off any longer. And to be
completely honest with herself, Maggie had to admit that she was
glad to be able to vent her roller coaster emotions to a sympathetic,
female, ear—one she was sure would take her side no matter what
the situation, but that would not threaten to beat her ex to a bloody
pulp.

No matter how much the thought of that happening made her
secretly smile.

They had taken their lunch out onto the small garden right
next to the Arts Building they worked in. It was something Maggie
did whenever the always unpredictable Minnesota weather allowed.

The gorgeous warm fall day had been perfect—warm and
sunny despite the vividly colored trees that warned that winter would
descend upon the state before she knew it.

After 27 years of living in Minnesota, Maggie had learned to
savor every last drop of sunshine, each soft warm breeze, once the
trees started turning because winter could plunge the state into a
frozen wasteland with no warning. And once winter was here, it

would be months before she would be able to spend her lunch, or any amount of time, outdoors comfortably.

Cloë had been the perfect audience for her recital of Bradley's betrayal; gasping in outraged shock and calling him every name her considerable imagination could come up with. By the time they had plotted his long, painful demise, Maggie was laughing and much of the weight she'd been carrying on her shoulders since finding Bradley horizontal on his office floor melted away.

As Maggie set the empty popcorn bowl in her dishwasher she was more convinced than ever that her feelings for Bradley had been no more than a flash in the pan.

Maybe she was just not cut out for love, Maggie mused.

Disgusted with her self-pity Maggie shut the dishwasher with a snap and shook off the depression that threatened to envelope her.

She'd be damned if she'd ever get that upset over a man again. She was a strong, successful woman, darn it, and what the heck did she need a man for, anyway?

Determinedly ignoring the snotty little voice in the back of her mind reminding her that she was a sucker for romance and really didn't mind the whole sex thing that much either, Maggie shook her head once and continued her pep talk.

She'd be Cool Aunt Maggie to her brothers' kids and push all her excess energy into becoming a world-famous authority on art history and premier art historian for the University. She would have everything she'd ever dreamed of having.

Everything except someone to share her successes and dreams with. Everything but someone who loved her.

Groaning in frustration Maggie slammed the door in the face of that irritating little voice and cried, "Shut up!"

Maggie pressed her fingers into her eyes and ran them through her ruffled hair.

Clearly she was driving herself insane. How many times in the past two days had she ended up in an argument—with *herself.*

"Get a grip, Maggie."

Almost desperate, Maggie headed to the bookshelf she had put right next to her bed and grabbed for one of the well-read romance novels she loved, and re-read over and over.

More than simple entertainment, the stories and characters brought to life on those tattered and well-read pages were an escape for Maggie. Whenever she was angry or sad, frustrated or stressed out—which, Maggie admitted ruefully, was often—she could dive into one of her favorite authors' stories and emerge a few hours later with a smile on her face.

And tonight, Maggie decided, was definitely a Nora night.

Settling back into a deep, comfy chair Maggie opened her selection to the first page and let the real world fade away, if only for a while.

When Grant walked out of the realtor's offices several hours after his pleasant walk with Jake he felt dazed. Only a couple of signatures—make that a couple hundred signatures he thought wryly—and suddenly he was further in debt than he could have ever imagined just a few weeks, hell, even just a few days before.

What had he been thinking?

He hadn't even started his job. What if he hated it? What if he couldn't hack it anymore? What if…

"What if you are a complete wuss?" Grant let out an exasperated oath and climbed into his truck. "Jesus, Evans, snap out of it." Raising an unsteady hand to wipe his suddenly very dry mouth, Grant laughed weakly at himself.

Grant had never considered himself to be set in his ways, but he'd always been reluctant to make big changes. The thought had him shifting uncomfortably in his seat his hand half way to the ignition before it dropped and he slumped back into the cushions.

Grant reached for the ignition again and with a determined air started the SUV. No more second guessing himself, he decided. He was going to go get Jake, check out of the hotel, and spend the first night in his very own house.

As he drove down the darkening streets of the quieting city he decided he was only human to be getting cold feet after changing so much of his life.

It wasn't that he was afraid of change, he assured himself, it was just that he was comfortable with things just as they were—or he had been until recently.

Just because he'd never owned a house or a car (or furniture or had more than one serious, long-term committed relationship a small voice in the back of his mind added) didn't mean he was afraid.

He was just…cautious.

"Yeah, and de Nile ain't just a river in Egypt," he quipped, then laughed at the ridiculous phrase. He could hear the exact tone of voice his grandmother had always used when she'd said it.

Arguing with himself, he told himself that he had never owned a car because he'd never needed one in the city. He'd never owned a house or nice furniture because he'd been content using the basics in an apartment.

Up until this point of his life, his focus had been on his career. He simply hadn't had the time needed, nor wanted the distractions of trying to upkeep a house—or serious relationships for that matter.

It wasn't that he didn't enjoy the company of women—just the opposite. He loved women—how they looked, how they smelled, how they walked and talked. Short or tall, big or small, serious or silly, loud and brash or quiet and shy, they all had an appeal.

He'd just never found one that appealed to him for the long term.

And what the hell was he doing waxing poetic about women, Grant thought with a groan and rolled his eyes.

He was loosing his grip on reality—spending too much time alone and talking to himself.

Again.

When the sign for a liquor shop nestled next to a pizza parlor caught his eye Grant didn't hesitate. He simply pulled over.

Tonight was a big night that called for celebration. And damn it, he was going to celebrate it in style.

A six pack of beer, a hot sausage and onions pizza and his best friend in the world—what could be better than that?

SIX

Sitting in the makeshift darkroom he'd rigged up under the staircase, he looked down at the developing image of her. He'd only had a moment to capture her before she'd turned to see him. He had only managed to get the two shots of her, but there was no mistaking it. She was his.

His Angel.

He'd caught her mid-laugh, her radiant hair floating around her beautiful face like an auburn halo. It was like she smiled just for him, he thought dreamily.

When the others had approached her, she'd greeted them politely, but her true warmth—her passion and her purity—seemed to flow directly from her eyes into his soul like a blessing.

God had sent her to him and she would be his—only his—always.

She would be better than the others. She would *never* betray him. Not like his fallen Angels.

Standing stiffly he twisted to rip picture after picture of the fallen Angel from the walls. Hands shaking he tore each picture into shreds. His breath pitched until it screamed in and out of his open mouth as flecks of spittle collected on his lips and sprayed over the torn images.

She had seemed so perfect, so untainted, so right.

But she was nothing but a whore. Tears streamed down his face as he lit a match and held it to the large pile of pictures.

The acrid smell of burning photographs filled the small enclosure and his breathing leveled as his eyes closed and he dreamed of how he would punish her for her unfaithfulness.

It would be soon, he thought, and opening his eyes he looked down into the burning images of his fallen Angel as fire blackened and distorted her features. A blissful smile spread across his now calm face. She would pay for her betrayal, and when he was through she would thank him for saving her.

He could almost hear her screams of gratitude.

Humming he took the two new pictures and hung them on the wall.

It had to be soon.

39

SEVEN

As Maggie trotted down her front steps to begin her morning jog, she noticed a new blue SUV parked in the driveway of the old Johnson house. *They must have finally sold it*, she thought as she started off slowly.

With a shrug, she began her three miles, and by the first half mile the sweat was flowing and all thoughts of new neighbors had been effectively erased from her mind.

She hit the beach just as the sun began to start its daily climb into the cool morning sky. Streaks of peaches and yellows turned the grayness of the predawn into a glorious canvas of glowing colors that bled into one another.

Breathing in the damp cool air, Maggie closed her eyes and blew out a long steady breath. Every sore muscle, every lost hour of sleep, every stitch in her side was worth experiencing this single perfect moment every morning.

A feeling of contentment flowed through her as she stepped from the paved path onto the soft wet sand and increased her pace.

Something was wrong.

Her brows swept down and her pace faltered when she noticed there were footprints already in the sand.

But, this was *her* beach.

Rolling her eyes, Maggie let out a short huff of laughter and picked up her pace again. *You're being ridiculous, Maggie, this is a public beach and anyone who wants to can run here.*

But it was a kind of tradition that she be the first one to mar the mile long stretch of pristine sand each day. Not once in the almost two years she'd been coming here had there been any sign of other early risers. *Well, you'll just have to share.*

She shook off the absurd sense of disappointment that had settled onto her heart when she'd noticed the prints and raised her head, determined to ignore the unknown interloper. There was no reason she should let it ruin her day.

The water was a moody gray this morning, and it seemed to slap crossly at the shore as if trying to beat it back. If she let her imagination go, the foam the waves deposited along the shore began to look like glistening lace draped over driftwood and sand.

40

Maggie turned at the end of the cove, and felt the full power of the sun warm her face despite the brisk breeze that blew the curling strands of her hair away from her damp skin.

With regret, she noted that most of the vibrantly colored leaves had been blown off of the trees that lined the beach and the path leading to her street.

Traffic began to pick up on the road nearby, and the whoosh of air each passing car created caused mini-tornadoes of dry rustling leaves to swirl across the pavement of the road. The swish of sound was a reminder that another season had died—fall was here, and another year was almost at an end.

Fall was normally Maggie's favorite season with its sunny days and crisp breezes, brilliant colors and relief from the humid days of late summer. She loved the sounds and smells of this time of year—the smell of leaves burning, the sound of kids as they walked to school, the appearance of pumpkins and hay bales, corn stalks and scarecrows as they popped up to decorate the yards and porches of her neighbors' houses.

But this year, she just couldn't seem to capture her usual enthusiasm. The season seemed more of an ending than usual—a kind of death, she supposed. *Well*, Maggie thought, *it doesn't take a trained psychologist to figure out why.*

Another year was nearing its end, and she was probably going to be spending it alone.

Again.

Her brows drew down once more and her thoughts darkened as they had been doing all week. Deliberately focusing on what she *did* have, Maggie thought of all of her friends and her family.

Thank goodness tomorrow was Saturday and she was going to be spending the day with them. She'd spent far too much time alone this week, and obviously it was not doing her any good—she was getting maudlin, and she really needed to move forward once and for all.

What she really needed was to talk to her mom.

They'd always been able to talk about anything. And, although it still drove her crazy sometimes that her mother seemed to be able to read her mind, it was a comfort to Maggie as well. That someone could know her that well, love her that much, and care enough to be there, no matter what, was a rare gift.

Maybe other moms wouldn't find it so extraordinary, Maggie mused. For them, the unconditional and boundless love for a child was something that just was. But after a few years out in the "real" world, Maggie had come to realize that not everyone was as fortunate as she was.

Maggie had always been able to count on her mom—both her parents, really. They had always been there. They were her rock, her foundation, and Maggie knew that without them her life would have been far more difficult, not to mention much less happy.

Perhaps she had once taken them for granted, assuming that that was just the way it *was*. Parents were always there to love you and support you. But no longer.

By the time she'd graduated from high school many, if not most, of her friends' parents had divorced. She'd heard too many stories about broken homes and feuding families in the years since.

Just look at Cloë. Her mom had left her family before Cloë was a teenager. Sure, her dad had stepped up to the plate and they were incredibly close, but it couldn't have been easy for her growing up without a mom.

Cloë's situation was just one that Maggie knew about that had helped her to truly appreciate her parents.

Maggie hadn't really thought about it before, but she'd never seemed to go through the "I hate you" faze that so many of her friends had gone through with their parents. Oh, sure, there'd been lots of times when she'd gotten into trouble—and even one or two times when she or one of her brothers had managed to "get away" with something, like the rose bushes Steven had run over—but she'd never been at war with her parents. There had just been too much genuine affection and *fun* in her house growing up.

Maggie knew how lucky she was, and she thanked God each day for her family.

And that, Maggie decided, *was what was important.* No more moping about the end of things, it was time to focus on what was coming next.

Soon, she knew, she would be breaking a path through the snow each morning.

Maybe this year she would splurge on a treadmill for those really cold and snowy mornings. *Yeah right. You say that every year, and every year you blow all your money on a new outfit or a pair of shoes.*

Amused at herself Maggie slowed to a walk. As she approached her stoop she took a few minutes to stretch and relax before the craziness of the coming day could begin.

She could hear a dog bark and a door opening across the street—apparently her new neighbor had a dog. She just hoped he wouldn't be a barker.

The Johnsons had had two small terriers, and it had seemed to Maggie as if every moment of the day and night had been filled with ceaseless yipping and yapping. The family had moved more than two months ago, and although Maggie missed the friendly family, she couldn't honestly say she missed those dogs, no matter how cute she'd thought they'd been.

She leaned back with her elbows on the step behind her and let her head fall back, her eyes sliding closed to let the sun bathe her face with warmth. As she let the quiet of the morning seep into her, her thoughts strayed to the upcoming weeks. It would be Halloween soon, and that was always one of her favorite times of the year.

This year, she promised herself, she'd have to carve a couple of big Jack-o-lanterns and decorate the front of the building.

And, it went without saying that she'd have to come up with a kick-ass costume to scare the kids with.

She had always loved picking out the perfect costume, getting to be someone, or something, totally different for just one day of the year. Over the years the kids in her parent's—and now her own—neighborhood had come to expect something really awesome from her.

Her senior year of high school she'd dressed up like Michael Jackson and recreated the entire Thriller dance in the front yard—to this day, that performance was the one that people started talking about around the beginning of each October.

Maggie grinned when she remembered that she'd nagged and harped on her brothers for more than two months before they'd agreed to dress up like zombies and dance back-up for her, but the end result had been so fantastic someone had called the local news and it had ended up on TV.

Each year the kids—and a lot of adults—looked forward to seeing just what crazy costume the "legendary" Maggie would come up with. So, each year it got more and more difficult to live up to the high expectations.

It had become a challenge for Maggie, and Maggie had never been able to back down from a challenge.

After years of coming up with unique ideas it had gotten to be a struggle to find something truly spectacular, and it had been a race to the finish to come up with something she felt would be worthy of the hype. Sure, it was all in good fun, but Maggie hated to disappoint the kids.

Not this year, Maggie thought smugly. This year she already knew exactly what she was going to do, and it was going to be great. Her only problem would be deciding which brother she would co-op into helping her out this year.

All four of her brothers usually ended up helping her decorate and prepare her sets (yes, God help her, she had sets), but this year she'd need a little extra something from one or two of them. She'd have to see which one of them "deserved" to help her after she told them about Bradley.

She'd originally planned on asking Bradley to be her partner for this year's big production, but the few times she'd talked about what she'd done in the past and brought up her plans for this one he'd seemed less than enthusiastic to discuss it.

The first time she'd brought it up to him, they'd gone out to dinner to celebrate his winning some big account and had gone back to her apartment to watch a movie and open a bottle of wine. When they'd gotten there, Maggie had found that the first part of her costume had come in the mail that day.

She'd been so excited, and had torn the package open, bubbling over with her plans for the coming holiday. It had taken a few moments before she'd realized that Bradley had walked away into the kitchen.

At the time she'd dismissed his indifference as tiredness and had let it drop. But the next few times she'd tried to bring it up, he'd simply changed the subject until one day he'd said that he thought

44

she was too old to be acting so childishly. Stung, Maggie had stopped talking about it with him and, she was now furious to remember, had actually started thinking that maybe it *was* time for her to stop dressing up each year.

Well, no more, Maggie thought. This year would go down in the books as the best one ever. Especially if she could count on her brothers helping her—and she knew she could.

No matter how often they argued and disagreed with one another, Maggie knew that all four of her brothers would do anything for her—just like she'd do anything for each of them.

Maggie never doubted the love and support she would get from her brothers, but it was her mother that was her compass, her true north.

Maggie knew that she would be able to tell her mother what had happened between her and Bradley, and how she felt about it, and Elizabeth Sullivan would know what to say and do to make it all better—or at least get Maggie started in the right direction.

Her mother was the only one that could keep her brothers and her dad in line, and Maggie would need all the help she could get in that direction if any of them ever found out exactly why she'd broken up with Bradley.

Someone had to keep them from ending up in jail for murder. Well, maybe just assault, Maggie snickered once. All vestiges of humor left her face when she thought seriously about what would happen if any one of the men in her life found out about Bradley's betrayal.

Shaking off a shiver, Maggie pushed herself to her feet and brushed off her clothes before heading up the stairs to get ready for work. There was no more time for sitting and thinking. She needed to get moving if she was going to make it in to work on time.

Thank goodness it was Friday. She was tired and needed a few days off. There was no point in worrying about tomorrow. Tomorrow would be here soon enough.

A cold nose burrowing into his neck woke Grant up at the ungodly hour of six in the morning. Clearly Jake didn't care that Grant did not have to be up early this morning.

45

"Get off me, you big jerk," Grant mumbled sleepily as he pushed the offending nose away and rolled over, "it's not even light out, for the love of Pete."

Jake simply stood there, his head cocked to one side a moment longer before letting out an ear-shattering bark directly into his master's ear.

"Alright, alright. Jesus. I'm up," Grant rasped out as he eased himself gingerly onto his elbows and was rewarded with a wet slurp across his face.

"Jeez, Jake, ever heard of oral hygiene?" Grant half-gagged, half-laughed and looked around the empty room through barely opened eyes. It took him a moment to remember exactly why he was currently laying in his old childhood sleeping bag on the rock-hard floor of an empty house before the events of the last twenty-four hours rushed back.

After picking up dinner and a six-pack to celebrate his new home, Grant had brought Jake to the house to see if he approved. He had.

After a thorough tour of the entire house—with Jake poking his nose into each and every nook and cranny to sniff inquisitively—Grant had let Jake out into the big back yard. Then, Grant had simply stood there as a pleased smile crossed his face and watched his normally quiet dog bark madly and gambol around like he was a puppy again.

It was in that moment that Grant had been sure—really sure for the first time in his heart, not just in his head—that he'd made the right choice in moving here.

They had headed back inside where Jake had gone straight back to the living room and settled down in front of the large window that faced the front yard with a satisfied grumble.

Grant had grabbed his pillow and the thin pad and sleeping bag he'd brought along to camp with on his drive out of the car and set them up in front of the fireplace. The rest of his stuff—and the many bags of new house supplies he'd bought at the local Target—would have to wait until morning, he'd decided.

After getting a small fire started and devouring most of the large pizza and six-pack, Grant had crashed out on the floor of his first house and had fallen instantly, and contentedly, to sleep.

"Until I was so rudely woken," Grant sighed and got slowly and stiffly to his feet. He let Jake out in the back yard to take care of business and headed into the bathroom to take care of his own before quickly changing into his running clothes and shoes.

Grant grabbed Jake's leash, whistled to call Jake, and they headed out the front door for their morning run. After pausing to stretch Grant headed down the quiet, tree-lined street in the direction of the lake.

The day that Steve had shown the house to him they'd talked about all manner of things—one of them that they both loved running. Grant preferred doing his running outside as much as possible. Steve did as well, and he'd recommended a few different parks with good running paths and had also shown Grant the path that led to the beach where his sister liked to run.

Grant headed down the block and turned west starting out at a brisk pace. The crisp dampness of the predawn air stung his face as he ran. He'd only run about a half mile when he saw the sign for the walking path Steve had pointed out to him.

Fully warmed up, Grant paused just long enough to let Jake off his line before stepping onto the sand and lengthening his strides.

Looking around him, Grant saw a short stretch of beach that was deserted, washed in tones of gray and brown that lightened incrementally as dawn approached. But it was clear to Grant that when the sun rose it would reveal a small paradise—an unblemished sand beach marred only by driftwood and small clumps of grasses and surrounded by pine and birch trees that would provide a full palate of colors year round.

The only fault Grant could find with it was that it was too short, and to get his usual five miles in, he knew he'd have to run its length several times. *Well*, he mused philosophically, *that was probably the reason it's not mobbed with other runners*. A big point in its favor. And, since it was so short he had no problem keeping an eye on Jake while he ran, which he considered another bonus.

Smiling, Grant cleared his mind and let his senses take in the quiet beauty around him.

With each step Grant listened to the pulse of the surf as it beat the shore, and unconsciously his footsteps began to fall in rhythm with the waves as they washed onto the sand beside him.

By the time he'd made his third circuit of the small cove it was getting fairly light out. He whistled for Jake and as soon as he was secured once again they headed back to the path for the short trip home.

Grant would be sure to check out the other running routes Steve had recommended, but he already knew that this one was going to be a favorite of his.

He couldn't wait to see how beautiful it would look in the winter.

After a quick shower in his tiny bathroom Grant stopped to look in the mirror over the pedestal sink. He ran his hand over his heavily whiskered face and contemplated a shave before dismissing the idea with a shrug.

Whistling cheerfully, he pulled on clean jeans and tucked a white t-shirt into them before heading into the kitchen to have a breakfast of cold pizza.

Standing at the bay window that looked out over his back yard Grant watched Jake sunning himself on the patio as he went over all he needed to get done today in his mind. He glanced at the silver divers watch on his left wrist and saw that it wasn't even eight yet.

He had more than three hours to kill before his new furniture was scheduled to be delivered, and that was if they were on time. *And the odds of that happening where slim to none,* he thought with a grimace.

Well, I guess that gave him time to run to the supermarket to pick up some decent food—he'd eaten all of the pizza, and he didn't think a lunch of beer was a smart idea. Especially for the newest cop in town.

Whistling once more, Grant grabbed his keys and cell phone and was halfway to the truck when he remembered that he still hadn't unpacked it. He stopped in his tracks, his eyes closed in frustration and swore quietly before shaking his head as he started forward once more.

It took him more than twenty minutes to unload all the various bags of purchases he'd made the day before and to dump the handful of luggage and boxes he'd brought on his trip cross country into the living room next to his makeshift bed.

He'd sort through it all after the furniture was delivered— after all, he had nowhere to put anything until it was.

That task complete, Grant walked through the breezeway to yell out the back door for Jake and was rewarded with a couple of sharp barks and a leap that almost knocked him on his ass.

Laughing, Grant pushed Jake back down and tried, unsuccessfully, to brush the dusty paw prints from his once clean shirt. After a quick shirt change, Grant left a snoozing Jake in his new spot in front of the living room window and was in the Tahoe and on his way to the Foodmart he'd driven by on the way home last night.

Two hours and two heaping shopping carts later, Grant put his beleaguered credit card back into his wallet and pasted a semblance of a smile on his face to thank the cashier and accept his three-foot-long receipt.

Well, you won't starve, Evans, he thought to himself as he led the helpful employee helping him push his carts to his truck.

The kid helped him toss all the bags into the back of the truck and then wheeled the carts off, a big smile on his face as he pocketed the five bucks Grant had slipped him.

Grant had just pulled the truck into the driveway when his cell phone rang.

"Evans."

"Hey, Grant, it's Steve. Whatcha up to?"

"Hey, man. I just got done cleaning out Foodmart. I've gotta unload my haul and then I got some furniture coming in about an hour. Thanks for recommending Sylvester's, by the way. I found exactly what I needed and they had no problem with delivering my stuff next day."

"No problem. Say, are you going to be tied up most of the day, or do you think you'll have some down time later?"

Grant glanced at the mountain of bags in his rearview mirror and grimaced before saying slowly, "Well…once I get these groceries put away it won't be too bad. I didn't really bring all that much with me. As long as the furniture is delivered on time I should be pretty set by about two or so. What did you have in mind?"

"My family is having a barbeque this afternoon and you're welcome to come over."

"Man, I don't wanna intrude on a family thing…"

"You wouldn't be intruding. Really. You don't know my family—there'll be a bunch of us running around and one more will be no problem. We're just grilling and my mom will have a ton of food," Steve replied casually, "It's no big deal."

"Sounds like a lot of people," Grant hedged, and picturing his own mother's horrified reaction if an uninvited guest showed up to one of her parties he added, "I'm sure your Mom wouldn't appreciate having to worry about another guest."

"She won't care. One of us is always bringing someone along. The more the merrier is what we always say. Seriously, Grant, it'll be a lot of fun, and I can personally guarantee some incredible food and probably a pick-up game of basketball or volleyball or something."

"Sounds like fun—as long as you're sure your parents won't mind, I'd love to come."

"Great. I'll give you directions and you can just come by whenever you can."

After noting the directions and getting one more assurance that his coming wouldn't be problem, Grant hung up.

Squaring his shoulders, Grant opened the back of the truck up to face unloading the daunting pile of food he'd bought like a man.

He'd barely finished putting the last bag away when the doorbell rang.

His furniture had arrived.

EIGHT

Her arms laden down with a large Tupperware salad bowl, Maggie burst through her parents' kitchen door, letting the screened door snap closed with a loud slam at her back.

"One of my lovely, well-bred children must be here," Elizabeth Sullivan quipped, her dark auburn eyebrows raised over humor-filled eyes. She managed to keep a stern expression on her face and stood in the kitchen doorway with her hands placed firmly on ample hips.

Elizabeth Colleen Sullivan stood just over five feet tall. Despite her diminutive stature, no one in her family disputed the fact that she ruled the Sullivan clan with a velvet fist. Her warm chocolate brown eyes forever seemed to sparkle with humor, intelligence and, most of all, with love for her family.

Her broad, freckled face was still as clear and smooth as a woman half her age—its only concession to the passing years were fine lines that radiated like delicate fans from the corners of her eyes.

If Maggie had been looking, she would have seen the affectionate smile her mother gave her before rearranging her face into a stern expression of disapproval.

"Sorry, Mom," Maggie sang out from inside the refrigerator, closing the door as she turned to face her mother. She wisely held back the grin that wanted to cross her face and placed a look of repentance on her face as she met her mother's eyes across the kitchen.

Hazel eyes met brown for a moment before both women broke into identical grins. Maggie crossed the small space, leaned down, and was enfolded in her mother's soft embrace.

The scent of Chanel no. 5 washed over her, and Maggie's eyes slid closed as she breathed in the familiar and comforting smell of home.

Drawing back, Maggie looked back down into her mom's face as Elizabeth reached up to frame Maggie's face with her hands.

"Where's Daddy?"

Elizabeth dropped her hands and replied, "Oh, you know your father," she rolled her eyes and grinned, "he's out in the back yard firing up the grill."

"Alone?" Maggie said in a horrified voice, "Did you notify the fire department?" she added, only half joking as she remembered the charred grass and burned out hunk of steel that was all that had been left of her parents' last grill.

"No," Elizabeth laughed, "You don't really think I'd let him near the new grill without one of your brothers there to supervise, do you? No. I made sure that Jack and Dillon would be here well before he'd have to get that thing started."

Relieved, Maggie settled down onto a well worn chair at the kitchen table and asked, "Is there anything left to do?"

"Steven called this morning to let me know he's bringing a friend—apparently Robert has assigned the new detective from out West to be Steve's partner. They seemed to hit it off and Steven wanted to make him feel at home his first weekend here. And, I guess Katie and Aaron are both bringing friends, so I decided to make some more potato salad. You can peel," Elizabeth dropped a new five pound bag of finger potatoes in front of Maggie, and settled across the table with onions and a knife.

Thinking of her niece and nephew erased the automatic grimace that peeling five pounds of potatoes had caused as Maggie got up to fetch a peeler and pan to hold the peeled potatoes.

Katie was a mischievous eight-year-old more likely to be found in ragged cut-offs, her honey blonde hair stuffed up in a ball cap, climbing trees and riding her bike than in a dress playing with dolls.

And, ten-year-old Aaron, with his unkempt copper hair and serious gray eyes that solemnly stared out from behind glasses, was the spitting image of her brother, Seth. He spent hours reading and daydreaming—when he wasn't out playing baseball with his friends.

Settling down to her task, Maggie smiled as she thought about seeing her brother and his family for the first time in over two months. Seth was a teacher, and he'd spent most of the summer participating in an exchange program that had sent him, and his family, to New Zealand.

The opportunity to go had come up right at the end of his usual school year, and they'd leapt at the chance for Seth to teach somewhere other than in the U.S., and to give the kids the opportunity to experience life in a foreign country.

Seth's wife Sybil's job as a writer for a local magazine allowed her the flexibility of working wherever she was, and she had been able to arrange things so that they'd get the chance to go.

Maggie had missed them immensely, and couldn't wait to see them.

"When are Seth and Sybil and the kids getting here?"

"Anytime now. It's been a crazy couple of days getting the kids back in school and settled in at home. Wait 'til you see how they've grown. I stopped by to drop off dinner their first night home and I hardly recognized them."

"I'm so glad they're home safe."

"Me, too. I must have said a hundred rosaries over the last two months," shaking her head Elizabeth continued, "Well, they're home now. When I stopped in, they were so exhausted from all the travel I didn't stay."

"I wanted to stop by, but I figured they'd be beat."

"Hmmm," Elizabeth paused to get some celery from the refrigerator before continuing as she sat down again, "So, are you going to tell me what happened between you and that boy to make you so unhappy, or should I just send your father out to take care of him?"

Startled at the repressed fury she heard in her usually laid back mother's voice, Maggie's head jerked up and looked into her mother's glittering eyes and sighed wearily.

"I never could fool you, could I," Maggie replied ruefully, "The short story is I caught him with another woman—a term I use for lack of a better one."

The self depreciative smile slowly slipped from Maggie's face as her mother simply watched her, "But the real truth is he just wasn't the One."

When her mother just sat silently, calmly waiting for Maggie to continue, the band of tension that had kept a stranglehold on Maggie's heart for the past six days eased and she breathed easier for the first time since finding Bradley on his office floor.

"Oh, God, Mom, I was so furious and hurt," Maggie leaned on the table and closed her eyes, missing the way Elizabeth's eye's narrowed dangerously and her mouth pinched tightly before she could smooth them again.

53

"I was so excited about my article being published I didn't even think, I just drove straight to his office to show him and walked in on them. I was so shocked and then I just saw red—I mean I didn't think that *actually* happened, but I swear it did.

"So I dumped him and left," heaving another sigh, Maggie ran both hands through her hair before she dropped them limply to the table, "It took me a day or two of wallowing before I realized that my pride was more hurt than my heart."

When Elizabeth simply reached out to hold her hand Maggie felt her eyes burn and blinked quickly to keep the tears she felt building once more from falling.

"I don't know how I could have been so *stupid* to think he was the right one for me. I mean we had a lot in common, but there were so many of the little things where we were like total opposites.

"After years of watching you and Daddy, I should have known what was real and what was just illusion. I guess I just wanted to be in love so badly that I let him be enough. Logically, he seemed so right. Mom, how will I be able to trust myself, let alone another guy again? What is *wrong* with me?"

"Enough of that, Margaret Elizabeth," Elizabeth squeezed Maggie's hand one last time before continuing briskly, "It is not your fault that that *man*, and I use the term loosely, betrayed you. To trust someone you love, or believe you love, is not foolish or stupid. It is right and natural. It is a gift—a blessing—that should be appreciated and cherished.

"Your only mistake was in using your head instead of your heart. Love is many things—some of them wonderful, some of them painful—but it is very rarely logical."

Maggie looked at her mother sitting across the table from her, calmly chopping vegetables and felt a huge upwelling of love and affection for that miracle that was her mother.

It never occurred to Maggie that Elizabeth would be picturing Bradley as she calmly sliced her knife through one vegetable after another.

Completely ignorant of her mother's fierce thoughts, Maggie thought to herself that she could always count on her mother to cut to the heart of any situation and respond in exactly the right way—

either with sympathy, sage advice, with a painfully honest opinion, or even a kick in the proverbial ass.

"Thanks, Mom," Maggie started to speak and stopped abruptly when she heard her father's and brothers' voices as they approached the back door.

"Um, Mom? Do you think we could just keep the details of why we broke up from Daddy and the guys? They'd go nuts if they knew why…" Maggie said quickly and quietly, her eye's darting towards the door.

"Maggie, your brothers love you, and I'm sure anything they would feel or do would be reasonable, but I'll leave what, and how much, you want to tell them up to you."

"And Daddy."

"I have no secrets from your father, Maggie, and I don't plan on starting to keep them now."

At Maggie's slightly panic stricken look Elizabeth continued confidently, a smug smile on her face, "You just leave your father to me. I'll take care of him."

When Maggie's face remained doubtful, she went on, "Don't worry so much, Sweetheart, it's not as if your father's going to get out his guns and hunt Bradley down."

Even if it's what the bastard deserves, Elizabeth thought darkly, barely managing to keep her features bland.

Reassured, Maggie relaxed and went back to peeling the forgotten potatoes, "I suppose."

"For goodness sakes, he's not some maniac, Maggie."

"Who's not a maniac?" Bram Sullivan asked cheerfully as he walked in the door.

Standing just 5'11", Brian Patrick Sullivan—Bram to his friends and family—had thick dark black hair graying at the temples and gray eyes that seemed to always be laughing at some secret joke. His craggy face was lined from years in the sun and with permanent laugh lines that bracketed his eyes and mouth. Despite a slightly stocky frame, Bram was a powerfully built man.

Grinning broadly he spotted Maggie sitting at the table and exclaimed, "There's my girl!" before sweeping her up in a bone-crushing hug.

After setting Maggie down on the floor once more Bram held her at arm's length to take a good look at one of the two most important women in his life. After her worrisome phone call last Monday he wanted to make sure that his girl was really alright.

When he looked down at Maggie's upturned face he was struck all at once with just how beautiful and grown up his little girl really was.

Dressed in white linen Capri's and a striped pink and white top, her long auburn hair curling in disarray around her smiling face, she was the spitting image of her mother at this age (except for the nose, she had his nose). It was a stab to Bram's heart to realize that his baby girl was a woman now.

Standing there, her shoulders held firmly in her father's large, work-callused hands, Maggie again felt an overwhelming wave of emotion wash through her.

"Oh, Daddy, I love you!" Maggie cried and threw her arms around his neck again.

Hearing the raw emotion in his normally fearless, outgoing daughter's voice, Bram held on tight and threw a worried, perplexed glance at his wife. Raising his eyebrows questioningly, Bram opened his mouth to ask what was wrong but shut it again when his wife shook her head slightly.

Tucking his questions away for later when he could be alone with Elizabeth, Bram replied simply, "I love you, too, Maggie m'girl."

"Look what the cat dragged in," Jack drawled from the doorway and elbowed Dillon in his side, a big smile on his face.

The humor that often laced his voice never reached his dark hazel eyes when they met Dillon's measured gaze. Both brothers had heard the almost unheard of tears in their little sister's voice, but with one look at each other came to the unspoken agreement not to bring it up.

"Yeah—one published article and suddenly, she's too important to mingle with the 'little people'," Dillon cracked and got the desired reaction when Maggie's eyes lit with laughter and she turned to place her hands on slim hips, one sandal-clad foot tapping.

"That's right, peons. I'm *far* too famous to be caught socializing with uncultured cretins like you two. Now, which one of you knuckleheads is going to fetch me something to drink—I'm absolutely *parched*."

Once again, the brothers' eyes met, this time in devilish glee. Both nodded once and they turned in unison back to grin devilishly at Maggie before striding quickly across the kitchen towards her.

A moment too late, Maggie caught the gleam in their eyes, and began to back up, both hands held up as if to stop them.

"Don't you dare…" The rest of her sentence cut off in a scream as she turned to run.

She never stood a chance. Maggie had only gone two steps before Jack grabbed her under the arms and Dillon grabbed for her feet. With satisfaction Maggie landed a quick elbow into Jack's stomach that elicited a pained grunt and she felt at least one of her kicking feet connect with Dillon's shins before they managed to hoist her into the air.

They almost dropped her twice they were laughing so hard at the constant stream of curses and threats she—ever conscious of her mother standing nearby—whispered viciously out of the corner of her mouth as she struggled to free herself.

They managed, despite her frantic attempts to get loose, to make it out the door, across the back yard, and onto the dock before heaving her in.

Her bitter, "I'll get both of you sons of…" ended in a scream quickly cut off with an impressive splash.

They were still laughing like loons when she surfaced, shivering in the late September water. Jack stood bent over, his hands on his knees while Dillon used the back of his hand to swipe at the blood on his lip from where Maggie had landed a lucky blow.

"Idiots," she yelled, shoving her dripping hair out of her face to glare at her unrepentant brothers. Affection warred with anger for a moment before it won out and she started laughing, too.

Both brothers backed a cautious distance away from the edge of the dock as Maggie heaved herself out of the frigid water. Their older brother Steven had made the foolish mistake of helping her out the last time they'd given her an impromptu dunking and had ended up in the lake with her.

That had been more than five years ago, but neither brother was willing to take the risk. Despite her laughter, both Jack and

Dillon knew that Maggie could, and would, turn on them in an instant. Neither of them underestimated her ability to kick their butts, and despite the pride they felt in her ability to look after herself, neither of them wanted to end up in the lake to prove it.

"Jack, Dillon, get out of the way, she'll catch her death," pushing past them Elizabeth draped a warm towel around Maggie's shoulders and bustled her towards the house, muttering under her breath the entire way.

"Idiots…raised a bunch of lunatics…water must be in the 50's…should be ashamed…"

Maggie wisely bit her lip to hold back the giggles that threatened to burst out and raised laughing eyes to meet her father's as he held the back door for them. He'd discreetly wiped the grin off his own face before his livid wife had turned back to the house with Maggie.

"Before you start grinning like a fool again you may want to tell those two baboons you call sons that they are now in charge of peeling the potatoes and chopping the rest of the vegetables. AND, they can have the pleasure of K.P. duty after dinner, too," she finished furiously before she swept her dripping daughter upstairs to get dried off.

Bram turned back to face the baboons, his eyebrows raised.

Still trying to stop laughing they both finally managed to rearrange their faces into identical looks of insincere chagrin before Jack leaned forward and whispered loudly, "It was *totally* worth it."

And all three men burst into laughter again.

Standing beneath the almost painfully hot spray of water in her parents' bathroom, Maggie closed her eyes, letting the water beat against her cold body. She raised her hands to shove her streaming hair away from her face and coolly, calmly contemplated the murder of the two idiots she called her brothers.

After a moment or two of careful deliberation, Maggie reluctantly admitted to herself that she probably owed them a big thank you—not that she'd ever let *them* know it.

It had felt liberating to release the rising tide of emotions that had been building in her over the preceding week in a purifying surge of anger that had burned away the last of her sadness. The emotional purge of baring her soul to her mother followed by the cleansing burst of anger with her brothers had left little room for pain or bitterness—a clean slate of sorts, she supposed.

Too weary to examine her current state of emotions any more closely, Maggie turned her thoughts to the happy task of coming up with a way to get even with the idiots for throwing her into the freezing lake and ruining her favorite pair of Jimmy Choo sandals.

It would have to be something devious—something they'd really hate—something truly humiliating. When the simple solution came to her, her eyes popped open and a gleeful smile spread across her face as she yelled, "Yes!"

She had her "volunteers" for this year's Halloween performance. And for a long moment, Maggie simply basked in the knowledge that despite the fact that both of her brothers would *really* hate what she was going to make them do, they would do it.

With a quick flick of the wrist, Maggie turned the water off and drew back the shower curtain to towel off. Wrapped in one terry cloth towel and using another as a turban for her hair, she stepped into the bedroom and found a neat pile of clothes waiting for her. Maggie had assumed her mother would give her some of her clothes to wear, but she was amused to see that Elizabeth had somehow unearthed some old things Maggie had apparently left at her parents when she moved out.

Maggie shrugged and pulled the bright yellow and white striped shirt over her head and worked well-worn cut-off jean shorts over hips that had definitely filled out since the summer of her freshman year of college when she'd worn these shorts practically every day. After finally tugging the zipper all the way up, Maggie turned to see how she looked in the shorts she'd thought essential that particular summer, only to be completely discarded the following year.

With one last rueful look in the full-length mirror her mother kept nailed to the inside of her closet door, Maggie muttered a few choice expletives under her breath and closed the closet door with a sharp snap before she turned to the smaller mirror on her mother's dresser to attempt to tame her unruly mop of hair. She dragged the wildly curling locks up into a high ponytail and secured it with a clip before borrowing some of her mother's mascara, all the while cursing her brothers for making the half hour she'd spent on her hair and makeup this morning a complete waste of time.

"Oh, well. It's just family," she mumbled, taking one last look before going to rejoin her family.

Maggie had just started down the stairs when she heard the front door fly open and the clamor of voices that could only mean that her brother Seth and his family where finally here. Eager to see them after so long, Maggie leapt down the rest of the stairs and, laughing, launched herself at her Seth. He caught her easily and swung her around once before setting her down to look into her upturned face.

A huge smile spread across his face and he murmured quietly, "Hello, Princess," before turning to his wife and saying loudly, "Lookey what we have here, Syb. It's little Maggie."

Socking him on the shoulder, Maggie rolled her eyes dramatically before she leaned around Seth to speak to Sybil, "Hey Syb. I'm glad *you're* here, but why'd you have to drag this cretin along with you? I thought you were going to take advantage of all those uninhabited, completely unknown locations in the outback to ditch this big guy."

Dark, slightly exotic looking eyes gleamed with amusement as Sybil replied, "I tried. Honestly. But he was just too cute and I couldn't let him go."

"That's right, Baby," Seth smiled smugly and draped an arm around his petite wife's shoulders. Gagging noises and coughing burst out of the gangly boy who walked through the door in a t-shirt and cutoffs similar to what Maggie was wearing. "Oh, man. I think I'm gonna ralph. Jeez, Dad do you have to call Mom that?"

"Aaron! " Maggie grabbed her nephew and gave him a big smacking kiss and a hug that muffled his embarrassed, "Jeez, Auntie Maggie," before reaching arms out to Katie, who had come in with a young boy and girl—clearly the friends the kids had invited over for the day.

"Katie, you look so beautiful and grown up. You both do," Maggie beamed at them both before leaning down to challenge them to a race to the dock.

With a sigh and a grimace that almost hid the smile that was trying to burst free on his face, Aaron just declared, "Races are for babies. Right, Randy?" and sneered at his friend, who sneered back in manly agreement. This time it was Katie who rolled her eyes.

"Just ignore him, Auntie Maggie. He's been a stick-in-the-mud all summer. This is my friend, Sarah."

"Nice to meet ya. Now, how about it—last one to the lake is a big *baby*," Maggie drawled the last word out teasingly and winked at her nephew before turning and sprinting towards the kitchen.

With a whoop and a laugh, all four kids stampeded in her wake leaving an amused Sybil and Seth staring after them.

"Some things never change," Seth grinned and took advantage of their rare solitude to yank his wife around and into his arms for a thorough kiss. Drawing back they smiled into each other's faces and, completely content, Seth sighed, "It's good to be back."

NINE

It was nearly three by the time Grant had finished arranging his new furniture and ushered the last deliveryman out the door. A quick shower later and he and Jake were on the way to Steve's parents' house, making one quick stop on the way.

It ended up being less than a mile from his house—so close they could have just walked. Grant brushed nervous fingers through his still-damp hair and glanced over at Jake and the package he'd just picked up—he just hoped that Steve's mother wouldn't be too upset he was late.

Steve had assured him that his parents wouldn't mind another mouth to feed, and that it wouldn't matter what time he showed up, but in Grant's experience with mothers—and women, for that matter—that had never held true.

And that was where the present came in.

It would surely appease any negative first impressions he may make. He was pretty sure. He hoped.

"What's the worst that could happen, right?" He asked Jake, who cocked his head to one side and grumbled in, what seemed to Grant, and entirely too sarcastic way.

"I don't know why I even give a damn," Grant breathed under his breath and pulled the SUV over to park in front of a completely normal looking two story A-frame house painted a bright white with black shutters.

Set on the corner of a street lined with similar houses painted or sided in a rainbow of colors, the Sullivan's house managed to stand out because of the amazing flower beds that seemed to surround the house and fill the yard with vibrant splashes of color despite the lateness of the season.

Grant could only imagine how incredible the gardens would look in the spring and summer months. The fairly pathetic flower beds that flanked his own house flashed into his mind and Grant's awestruck expression turned to one of contemplation as he thought maybe the artist in charge of the Sullivan gardens could give him some pointers.

Jumping out of the truck, Grant grabbed the present and gave a sharp whistle to get Jake to follow as he walked up the sidewalk and up onto the front porch that wrapped invitingly around the front of the building. He glanced at the comfortable looking white wicker swing with flowered cushions that seemed to tempt him to sit sown and swing a while. Cheerful clay pots of potted flowers—mums he thought—lined the porch and flanked the bright red door.

Somewhat more at ease in the welcoming surroundings Grant reached out and pushed the doorbell.

"Maggie, can you grab the last of the food, please? There's one more salad and a tray of condiments in the fridge."

"Sure, Mom."

Maggie climbed the three steps to the kitchen door and as she stepped out of the bright sunlight into the cool recesses of the kitchen the doorbell chimed. The house was laid out shotgun style with a hallway that led straight back from the front door past the living and dining rooms to the kitchen. From where she stood she could see the outline of a head of the person through the gauzy white curtain her mother had sewn and hung on the front door.

She padded barefoot down the dark hallway to the foyer and opened the door, thinking maybe Aaron or Katie had invited another one of their friends.

Confronted with over six feet of tall, dark, and gorgeous male dressed in snug, well-worn blue jeans and a black t-shirt and a ninety pound German Shepherd Maggie stopped dead in her tracks, her welcoming expression freezing on her face.

For what seemed like an eternity her mind scrambled to come up with something more coherent than "Oh my" to say as her stomach took one giant leap before settling down again. Unconsciously pressing a hand to her fluttering midsection Maggie's manners kicked in and, blushing, she cleared her throat nervously, smiled, and said, "Hi. Can I help you?"

Expecting to see Steve's mother or father, Grant's mind also blanked before he remembered that Steve had a little sister—but Steve had said she lived on her own and worked at the local university and this girl was far too young, Grant thought as he took in bright hazel eyes shining out from a face devoid of make-up and sporting a freckled, slightly sunburned nose.

"Hi. I'm looking for Steve Sullivan? I'm Grant. Grant Evans." Feeling like an idiot standing there holding a wrapped present and Jake's collar Grant offered up a blinding smile that made Maggie's breath stop for a second before she could speak.

"You've found him. I'm Maggie, Steven's sister," she replied, stepping back to let him into the house before continuing, "Come on in. Everyone's out in the backyard."

Jake followed Grant over the threshold and sat down in front of Maggie to lift a paw. Charmed, Maggie dropped to her knees to shake the proffered paw, "Nice to meet you…" and looked questioningly up at Grant.

When Maggie had knelt down to greet his dog Grant took a moment to reevaluate—Maggie may look like a teenager, but on closer examination it was clear she was not. Her petite frame boasted some clearly womanly features that made his eyes darken in appreciation before he remembered where he was.

Clearing his suddenly dry throat he replied, "Sorry. This is Jake," before tearing his eyes away from the enticing image of her shapely legs encased in snug worn denim cutoffs and a T-shirt that dipped and clung in all the right places.

"Hi, Jake," Maggie murmured before she pushed up again, and smiled uncertainly at the intent look in Grant's eyes that made her acutely aware of her careless appearance. Without her pretty little outfit, her stylish hairdo and makeup she felt exposed and unsophisticated. In her mind Maggie cursed her brothers again for forcing her to appear less than her very best. Out loud she calmly said, "Your timing is just about perfect. We were just about ready to eat.

Grant followed Maggie back down the hall and into the kitchen, watching her as she pulled open the refrigerator and bent over to grab a large bowl holding enough potato salad to feed a small army.

"I just need to grab a couple of things out of the fridge— would you like a beer or a soft drink?"

Grant's eyes had automatically drawn down to take in the alluring picture she made framed in the open door of the refrigerator, and in his mind he pictured grabbing her, yanking her around and devouring her mouth—and her sweet little body—in one big gulp.

The wave of desire nearly swept his reason away and he'd taken one step forward before his brain kicked in. *Whoa, Evans. Just slow the hell down and get a grip.*

Grant took a literal and figurative step back when Maggie turned clutching the bowl and raised questioning eyebrows when he didn't reply. Taken aback by the fierce look on his face she scrambled to fill the suddenly taut silence, "We have some iced tea or lemonade if you'd rather…"

Shaking his head Grant replied quickly, "No, no. A beer sounds great."

Relieved when Maggie turned back to the refrigerator Grant set his present on the table and sank back against the counter. "So. Steve told me you worked at the university. Which department do you work in?"

"I'm in the art history department. I work with the department head, helping him research and put together lectures and run the office for him."

Accepting the bottle Maggie held out to him, Grant nodded his thanks. "Sounds interesting. How did you end up in art history?"

Mirroring his pose, Maggie leaned back against the counter across from Grant, and taking in his relaxed bearing—his feet crossed in front of him as he took a long pull on the bottle she'd just handed to him—slowly she felt the tension that had built in her shoulders over the preceding few minutes recede. Clearly, she must have mistaken the look on his face.

When she'd first turned around, the look in his eyes had been so intense, so predatory; she had had the urge to flee. Looking at the friendly, interested look on his face now, she could easily dismiss her earlier thoughts, assigning them as an overactive imagination.

Except for one thing. Her heart was still racing.

And despite his otherwise calm demeanor Grant's left hand was gripping the countertop so hard his knuckles where white.

Well, I guess that's two things, she thought, amused at herself. Trying to slow her racing pulse, she focused on what Grant had just said.

"I've always loved art—looking at it, appreciating it, and creating it. That was what I had dreamed of doing—painting and showing my work in museums all over the world."

Maggie smiled a little wistfully, lost in thought. She shook her head once as if to clear it and started loading a serving tray with bottles of condiments from the refrigerator as she continued, "But it wasn't meant to be. I love painting, but I was missing that something, that spark I guess, that makes a painter an artist and a painting a work of art." Silent for a moment Maggie struggled to let go of the old ache before shaking her head again.

"And you were being polite and I'm babbling nonsense," Maggie grinned, embarrassed and a little shocked that she'd bared her soul to a virtual stranger, and turned back to fill her tray, hoping to hide the blush she could feel creeping into her cheeks.

"Well I'm no expert, but it sounds to me that maybe you can truly appreciate the art others have created because you really know the emotional price they've paid to create them. You must be very good at your job."

Startled and a little flustered at the seriousness of his quiet response, Maggie paused what she was doing and turned to face him, her arms at her side. "I've never thought of it that way before. Thank you," she replied softly, gratitude shining out from her eyes.

Their earlier discomfort forgotten, they fell into a comfortable silence that soothed as well as surprised them both.

When Maggie had finished filling her tray Grant pushed away from the counter and said, "Can I help you carry all this out?"

Holding the tray Maggie turned to meet him in the middle of the kitchen, a big smile on her face. "Sure. Just grab that salad bowl and we're all set," she replied cheerfully.

Steve burst through the door calling, "Mags, are you making the ketchup from scratch or something—we're starving out here…," he trailed off when he spotted Maggie and Grant standing in the middle of the kitchen grinning at each other like a couple of loons. "Evans! Hey, man, I'm glad you could make it. Perfect timing—the steaks and burgers are just coming off the grill now. Obviously you've met my baby sister and this must be Jake."

"Hey, Steve," Grant reached out to meet the hand Steve held out, "Yep, that's Jake. I hope it's okay I brought him along. I hated

66

to leave him alone again. If anyone's uncomfortable around dogs I brought along a rope so I can tie him up if need be."

"The kids will be ecstatic—it's no problem at all. Come out back and I'll introduce you to the rest of the family."

"I was just gonna grab this bowl for Maggie."

"I'll get it," Steve grabbed the bowl and held open the screen door to let Grant and Jake precede him into the yard.

Alone once more, Maggie half listened as Steven introduced Grant to the family and took the rare moment of solitude to ponder her own inexplicable behavior. She couldn't *believe* she'd just poured her soul out to a man she'd known less than an hour. Her only consolation was that he'd seemed to understand how she felt about what she did for a living.

Too embarrassed to fully take in the significance, Maggie instead thought about her brother's reaction to finding Grant here. Steven's obvious pleasure had been another surprise.

Steven was by far the most cautious of her brothers—slow to make friends and even slower to trust. Although he'd always been like this, his job and all the crap that came with it had ensured that his instinctive emotional barriers had been strengthened.

Somehow Grant had broken through those barriers to gain Steven's friendship and was well on the way to gaining his trust in just a matter of days. Maggie trusted her brother's instincts, and it eased some of her embarrassment and apprehension to discover that the instant ease she'd felt in Grant's presence was probably a reaction she could trust.

Looking back, Steven had never greeted Bradley with the openness and genuine pleasure that he'd just greeted Grant with.

"Just another warning sign you missed," Maggie muttered. Gathering up her tray Maggie dismissed her musings and swung out the door to join her family. It was time to have a little fun.

Grant stood across the yard talking about the Minnesota Twins' chances of winning the pennant race this year with Steve, Steve's father, and his brothers, Jack and Dillon. Although he'd been to tons of ball games as a boy, the time constraints and pressure of his job had ensured that Grant had not paid much attention to his old team, the Seattle Mariners, since he'd joined the force. But, he was making a fresh start here, and he might as well take the opportunity to get back into some of his old interests.

He'd loved the game when he was younger—had even dreamed of playing it professionally as young boys did. His father had taken him to countless games when he was a boy, but when he'd died, their shared love of the sport had seemed to die with him.

Grant turned his attention back to the conversation in time to hear Dillon begin furiously defending a pitcher that Jack had apparently called a "second rate hack." Bram and Steve looked on with bemused smiles on their faces despite the fact that the brothers were now standing nose to nose and shouting extremely creative insults at one another. Grant raised his eyebrows and grinned at Bram and Steve before taking a step back to enjoy the show.

As Grant lifted his beer to take a swallow, he glanced across the yard and was pleased and relieved to find Jake rolling around on the ground with the four kids in the doggy version of heaven.

Bram had walked back over to the grill and was leering down into his wife's eyes as he pulled steaks, hotdogs, and hamburgers off the grill and placed them onto the platter Elizabeth held for him. As he watched, Elizabeth walked past Bram, pausing a brief moment to give her husband a fast pinch on the rear before putting the platter on a picnic table covered with a gaily colored tablecloth.

Grant choked on his beer in amused surprise, just barely able to hold back a laugh. As he looked past the couple he met Maggie's delighted stare as she stepped down off the steps and onto the grass. She winked saucily before strolling over to place her tray on the table and leaning down to listen to her sister-in-law. Whatever it was she heard, Maggie leaned her head back and laughed before looking back to meet his gaze once more.

"So, Grant, what do you think about small town living so far?"

Grant dragged his attention back away from Maggie to find that Jack and Dillon had stopped fighting and were looking at him expectantly.

While Grant talked with Dillon and Jack he was fortunately unaware of the way Steve watched him, brown eyes narrowed. Although everyone else had missed Grant's exchange with Maggie, Steve had not. Despite the fact that he really liked Grant, Steve was unable to hold back his instinctive protective feelings for his baby sister—a term, he thought with amusement, she would *not* appreciate. But, she had just broken up with that asshole, Brad, and the last thing she needed, he thought indignantly, was some city slicker swooping in to take advantage of her fragile emotions.

Automatically relaxing, Steve smoothed his expression and called himself an idiot—Grant had no idea what was going on in Maggie's life right now, and he couldn't blame the guy for simply *looking* at his sister, could he?

No, no matter how much he disliked any man looking at his sister the way he'd just seen Grant looking at her, Steve knew he had no right to feel that way. Maggie was all grown up and Grant at least seemed like a decent guy. Grant had a sister himself, and surely knew that if he messed with Maggie he'd have not one, but four brothers to answer to.

Calm again, Steve tuned back into the conversation going on around him in time to hear Grant's reply.

"So far, so good. I wasn't sure what I expected when I left Seattle, but I really like it so far. Everyone I've met has gone out of their way to be friendly and helpful."

As he was speaking Seth walked up to join them.

"Food's all set if you guys want to grab a seat—better get a move on or the human garbage disposals I call my children and their friends will clean us out," Seth cracked as he led them back toward the picnic tables.

When Maggie had stepped out of the kitchen and seen the exchange between her parents she'd felt a rush of affection for them—no matter how long they'd been married, Bram and Elizabeth still showed each other (and anyone who happened to catch them in the act) that they truly loved each other.

It had been a surprise that it had been Grant who had witnessed the same act of affection and that a virtual stranger had seemed to find the same humor and delight in the moment that she had. For that single moment in time they had been in complete accord with one another.

"Hey, Maggie, what's up with the hottie?" Sybil called to Maggie before lowering her voice and forcing Maggie to lean down to hear her. She continued, "Talk about a *fine* looking form, girl. So, did you get his number yet? Is he single?"

Her eyebrows wiggled suggestively at Maggie causing Maggie to lean her head back and laugh before she looked back over to where Grant was talking with her brothers.

Laughing hazel eyes met deep brown eyes for what seemed to Maggie like an eternity before Grant turned away to speak with one of her brothers.

"Well," annoyed with herself for being slightly breathless, Maggie's eyebrows drew downward as she cleared her throat and turned her attention back to Sybil. Sitting down Maggie replied lightly, "He certainly isn't hard to look at."

Hiding her concern at her normally bold sister-in-law's timid tone, Sybil filed her concerns away to talk about with Seth later and replied as if she hadn't noticed anything wrong, "He certainly isn't. He fills out that T-shirt just fine if you ask me."

Maggie laughed again before settling in for a nice long chat. She'd really missed having her sister around to talk with.

"You are shameless, Syb. A married woman like you drooling over an unsuspecting male…," Maggie shook her head solemnly, trying hard to keep from cracking a grin, "And my poor sap of a brother completely in the dark."

"Which sap is that? Surely you wouldn't be talking about *me*, would you?" Seth came up behind Maggie and placed his hands on her shoulders, making Maggie jump in surprise before she grabbed hold of his hands and squeezed.

"Of *course* she doesn't mean *you*, darling," Sybil smiled wickedly at Seth, "She meant one of the other saps you call brothers—say isn't that them over there?" Sybil gestured at the group of men clustered around Grant.

"Yeah, right. I get the message. You guys want to talk alone," Seth said resignedly before adding sternly, "But, Maggie, I want to talk to you, too. *Before* you leave today."

Maggie fired off a mock salute before rolling her eyes at Sybil. When Seth was safely out of earshot she groaned, "God, save me from overprotective, well-meaning, macho-boy big brothers!"

It was Sybil's turn to lean back her head and laugh.

"Whatever happened between you and Bradley, you might as well spill, 'cause those four boys will not stop until they know *exactly* what happened—especially Steven."

When Maggie's face closed down Sybil leaned forward and placed her hand on Maggie's, a look of concern on her face.

"Maggie, if you don't fill them in soon, I doubt it will take long before Steven confronts Bradley directly."

"Aaargh! I wish, just this once, that I was an only child!" Maggie exclaimed in frustration and continued angrily, "I can handle this, and them butting their testosterone-laden heads in is only going to make a painful and embarrassing situation even worse for me."

Taking a deep breath she continued more calmly, "They all just need to back off and let me deal with him the way I need to."

"They love you," Sybil said simply and quietly.

Shoulders slumping in surrender, Maggie sighed, "I know. I know. I just wish they wouldn't be so annoyingly overprotective sometimes—I'm not a little girl anymore, and none of them seem to realize that I'm a grown up now and can take care of myself."

"Deep down, they know you can. They just hate to see you hurting, Maggie—we all do."

"I'm fine. *Really.* My pride is hurt far more than my heart, I promise."

Searching her face for a long moment Sybil saw the truth of her statement and felt genuine relief.

"I'm glad, Maggie, and that will probably be enough to satisfy Jack and Dillon. But Seth and Steven will not be so easily appeased. I can see what I can do to help with Seth—to a point—but Steven's going to be a problem."

"I know, but I've taken care of him for the time being," Maggie replied smugly, a wicked gleam of amusement in her eyes.

"Spill," Sybil leaned forward eagerly.

"I blackmailed him," Maggie whispered dramatically. She continued in barely contained hushed tones of glee, "I told him I'd tell Mom the truth about the Rose Bush Incident of the summer of 1989."

"You are devious, sister. Brilliant, but devious."

"I learned from the best," Maggie watched as the men turned to walk over to the picnic tables.

71

"Looks like it's time to eat."

Grant was acutely aware of Maggie as she sat across the picnic table from him eating and talking with her niece and nephew and their friends. Watching her ever-changing face as it shifted from sincere interest to indignation to utter delight to seriousness and back again, Grant was fascinated.

Seated between Elizabeth and Jack, Grant struggled to focus on Elizabeth as she spoke to him, but his attention was drawn time and again back to Maggie.

Maggie used her hands, often filled with a fork or knife, to gesture emphatically as she talked. Her ringing laugh sounded freely, and often, as she chatted about everything from the kids' trip to New Zealand to the upcoming school year, and it was easy to see that the kids adored her.

Pulling his attention back to the question Elizabeth was asking him, Grant heard the tail end of what she was saying, "...always interested in gardening?"

"I've never had a real garden before. When I lived at home, my mother's gardens were meticulously planted and arranged, and I was not allowed near them. And, there's no real place for a garden in apartments. I managed to grow a handful of herbs in some containers in my kitchen, but now that I have a house with a yard I really want to try my hand at a full-size garden.

"*If* I have the time with my new job," he added ruefully.

"Well, an herb garden is a wonderful start and if you want to put in a full bed I have quite a few plants I can divide in the spring. It's late in the season for doing much planting, but you could get some bulbs in the ground yet this year and have something colorful blooming by next spring. Are there any established beds at the house?"

"There are three small beds around the house, and the previous owners left a detailed description of what's planted in each. But, to be honest, I only recognized a handful of names—knowing what I know, I'm bound to mistake half the flowers for weeds, and vice versa. I'm gonna have to get some books."

"Books are always a great reference, but any time you have questions or need a hand, let me know. There's nothing better than digging into a new garden bed," Elizabeth said, her eyes shining with true satisfaction.

"If I were you," she continued, "I would put in a new bed that was all yours—established beds are great and something you can enjoy over the next year, but there's nothing better than planting exactly what you picked out yourself exactly where you want and seeing it grow and prosper."

"Ah, man, don't get her going," Jack groaned dramatically before leaning closer to Grant and lowering his voice, "Next she'll be talking about seedlings and soil PH levels and climate zones. Stop now, I beg you." With a full body shudder Jack whispered one last desperate "Please", his eyes sparkling with mischief.

Grant laughed, shaking his head, and Elizabeth added archly, "At least Grant is a man of intelligence and interests, which is more than I can say for *some* people." She raised one eyebrow at Jack before turning a warm smile on Grant again.

Continuing, she said, "Seth is the only one of my children who has any talent and appreciation for gardening."

"That's not true, Mom," Maggie called from across the table, a laugh in her voice, "I always liked gardening, I just never seemed to be able to keep anything alive."

"We call her 'The Reaper'," Jack whispered ominously to Grant who just managed to cut off his chuckles when Maggie skewered him with a pointed look before turning to her younger brother.

"Oh, are we sharing nicknames now, Puddles?" Maggie said sweetly, a nasty grin on her face.

Jack flushed and replied quickly, "No! No. That won't be necessary, Mags."

"Puddles?" Grant asked innocently, eyebrows raised above laughing brown eyes.

Jack opened and shut his mouth twice, trying to come up with a reply as Maggie jumped in with a question of her own.

"So. Grant, Steven said you are from Seattle? Hope must seem like another planet to you." Out of the corner of her eye Maggie caught Jack's relieved expression as she stared deeply into brown eyes that made her think of delicious warm melted chocolate.

Equally caught up in her eyes Grant lost his train of thought for one long moment before smoothly covering up the awkward pause by answering calmly, "That's right. But the city I grew up in was really a suburb on the outskirts of Seattle. It wasn't such a big step from a neighborhood like this—it just happened to be surrounded by a bunch of other cities just like it. Once I moved into an apartment downtown I discovered just how different life in the city really was."

"Well, I hope you will be happy here."

"The more I see, the better I like it."

Something in his voice made Maggie's cheeks heat, and in defense, she turned away to ask Katie a question.

Hours later, after several rounds of bocce and a couple of games of one-on-one on the front driveway, Maggie was in the kitchen getting packed up to go. Seth and his brood had left, as had Jack and Dillon.

She had successfully managed to avoid any interrogations by her brothers, and she wanted to get going before Steven got a chance to corner her alone—it would be best if she left while Grant was still here. Bram, Steven, and Grant were sprawled out on the front porch nursing beers and taking in the quiet peacefulness of the evening.

It wouldn't be long before fall gave way to winter, and then they would no longer be able to enjoy sitting outside as twilight descended turning the vibrant colors of the neighborhood into a myriad of shades of gray.

As Elizabeth swept in the back door, the last of the dessert dishes in her hands she said, "Maggie, don't forget to take some of those leftovers."

"I won't, Mom." Maggie grabbed some empty Tupperware containers and then began the seemingly futile search for matching lids in the chaotic mess of a drawer where her mother kept them. "I don't know how you can ever find anything in here, Mom," Maggie said setting aside a handful of lids that she'd selected and discarded as wrong.

"Let me look…there. Here you go."

Shaking her head, Maggie brought the containers—each with a corresponding lid—to the table and started filling them with enough food to feed her for most of the week.

"Grant sure seems like a nice guy," she said casually as she reached for another container.

"Mmmm hmmm. He certainly is. Did you see the present he brought for me?"

"No. What was it?"

"I had your father hang it up for me on the front porch right away—it's a beautiful brass wind chime with the sweetest little faeries. Said they would help guard my garden. I was so surprised—there aren't that many men who would think of something so thoughtful or charming to bring someone he'd never even met before."

"His mother must have raised him right."

"Hmmm," was all Elizabeth said, but she thought that Grant's mother probably had very little to do with the man she'd met today. Too many things that he'd said about his family and childhood had struck Elizabeth as *wrong*. Nothing terrible, really, just off.

"Well, I'm glad that he and Steven are going to be partners," Maggie replied absently, missing her mother's speculative tone. "It sure didn't take them long to become friends. I think it was more than six months before Steven brought home Charlie, and he only just met Grant this week."

"I have a feeling Grant could use a good friend or two," Elizabeth said brusquely as she placed the last container of food into a large paper bag before continuing, "It's so nice that he's living just across the street from you."

"He's *what*?"

"He's living right across the street from you. He bought the old Johnson house. Steven offered to help Grant find a place, and when Grant told him what kind of neighborhood he was looking for Steven immediately thought of the Johnson's old house. I guess Grant took one look and just fell in love with it, so he bought it."

"I'm surprised. I figured he'd get an apartment or rent a place. I guess I must have heard his dog barking the other morning."

"Now that you're neighbors, maybe you could invite Grant over for dinner or something."

Maggie rolled her eyes, "Mom. I *just* broke up with Bradley. Believe me, a setup with a guy is the last thing I need."

"Did I say anything about a setup? I raised you to be polite and friendly, Margaret Elizabeth, and it would be neighborly for you to stop by or have him over for a nice home-cooked meal. After all, he's new to town and I have this feeling that he could use as many friends as he can get."

Cringing at the use of her full name, Maggie smiled. Her mother had to be the all-time champ for making her children, and Maggie in particular, feel guilty—even if there was no real reason to feel that way.

Shrugging off the uncomfortable feeling Maggie said determinedly, "Well, Steven can be his friend. I've got nothing against him, but I'm just not up for any complicated relationships right now."

"Who said anything about complicated?"

Picturing deep brown eyes Maggie gave a single shake to her head before she replied dryly, "Trust me, Ma. It would be complicated."

Elizabeth let it drop, but inwardly she thought *maybe complicated is just what you need.* Outwardly she simply said, "All right, Honey. Why don't you see if your father can give you a lift home. This food is far too heavy to carry, and I don't think your sandals are completely dry yet."

Relieved that Elizabeth had dropped the subject without demanding an explanation of Maggie's last statement, Maggie said, "I'm sure I'll be fine, it's only about a mile and I would enjoy the walk.

"Thanks for the food," Maggie gave Elizabeth a fast hug, grabbed the paper bag and headed down the hall and out the front door to say goodbye to her father and brother.

"I'm heading out, Daddy," Maggie leaned down to plant a big kiss on Bram's cheek before she straightened and turned to face Grant. "It was nice to meet you, Grant. And you, too, Jake," she added as she reached down to give the shepherd sprawled on the floor in front of Grant's chair a quick scratch before facing the swing where Bram and Steven sat.

"See you later, Steven," Maggie trotted down the stairs carrying the paper bag with her food in it and a plastic bag with her now dry clothes.

"Where's your car? You aren't walking are you?" Worried disapproval colored Steven's voice when he called out to Maggie as she started down the walk.

Amused, Maggie just waved a hand and kept walking.

"Maggie…"

Still trying to keep things light Maggie simply said, "Steven. I'll be *fine*—it's less than a mile and it's barely dark."

"Maggie, you shouldn't walk so far by yourself, especially after dark," Bram put in, "I can drive you home, Baby."

Mortified, she replied, "Daddy, I'll be just fine."

"You're being a stubborn idiot, Mags. I can give her a lift, Dad," Steven got up and turned to Grant, "I'll just be a couple minutes."

Maggie stood, one hand on a cocked hip, her bags forgotten on the ground at her feet. A mutinous look covered her face, making her look even younger than he'd mistakenly thought she was when he first saw her that afternoon to Grant. When she opened her mouth to argue further he took pity on her and started talking before she could.

"It's getting late and Jake and I should be getting on home. If you'd like, I can give you a lift."

"I'll walk," she replied bluntly and inwardly wincing hastily added, "But thanks."

"Alright," he replied casually, then turned to make his goodbyes.

Mortified and flustered by the glint of amusement she saw in his eyes Maggie stood frozen in place, watching as he turned to shake her father's hand. Blessed anger spiked leaving no room for the unwelcome emotions she'd been feeling. Gathering her bags in her hands and her pride around her like a shield she spoke coldly.

"Fine. I'd *love* a ride home."

"Maggie," Bram said warningly. Maggie simply smiled, baring her teeth.

Holding his grin in check, Grant whistled for Jake and said one last goodbye to Steve. "Thanks again for inviting me, Steve. I really enjoyed meeting your family." Grant glanced over to Maggie again before saying, "I guess I'll see you Monday morning."

"Sounds good," Steven had not missed the look, nor had he mistaken Maggie's apparent calm for anything other than what it was. It was this that reassured him more than anything—if Maggie was as mad as he knew she probably was, there was no way Grant would be able to make a move on her. With this in mind he called out in a voice heavy with humor, "Good luck."

Grinning, Grant simply said, "Thanks," before he reached out and grabbed Maggie's bags. "All set?"

Still fuming Maggie simply nodded and stalked after Grant to his SUV, climbed in and, arms and legs crossed, stared stonily forward as Grant stowed the bags and Jake in the back.

When Grant slid behind the wheel he seemed to fill the small enclosed space with his presence. The homey scents of grass, dog, and the new leather smell of the SUV mingled with the spicy smell Maggie had come to associate with Grant throughout the afternoon.

Maggie drew in several deep breaths, her shoulders relaxing slightly. Smiling, Grant took in her stiff posture and flushed cheeks and raised one eyebrow at Jake in the back seat before shifting into gear. After two blocks Grant broke the silence.

"So, Red, is it just me, or do all men make you this nervous?"

"Please. Don't flatter yourself," Maggie smiled stiffly to cover the fact that she *was* nervous and turned to face him in the darkness.

The flash of passing lights illuminated the car's interior and the planes of his face, causing deep shadows to appear. The effect made his chiseled features appear fierce, like a living chiaroscuro work of art. The sight of his wide palmed hands gripping the wheel confidently made her already nervous stomach take one slow roll. She pressed a hand to her stomach and dragged her eyes back up to his face to find his head turned toward her, an amused half-smile on his mouth.

She flushed and quickly dropped her hand. Even though his eyes were cast deep in shadows, Maggie suspected that they were laughing at her. With a huff she turned forward again, relieved when they turned onto their block.

She was acting absolutely ridiculous, like some spoiled little girl pouting because she didn't get her way, and that was just not like her.

When Grant pulled the SUV into his driveway and turned off the engine Maggie turned back towards him and said, "Look, I'm sorry, I didn't mean to seem so ungrateful for the ride. I appreciate it, I do. I'm not usually such a jerk—it's just, my brothers and my father can be really overprotective, and they've been on my case all week, and you got caught in the crossfire. Truce?"

"Truce."

Relived, Maggie's smile flashed then froze when Grant reached out to tuck a stray curl behind her ear, brushing her cheek lightly as he drew his hand away.

"Um, Grant?"

"Um, Maggie?" He imitated her serious tone, eyes twinkling.

"Nothing. I better get in. Thanks again for the ride," Maggie reached for the handle but turned back when Grant grabbed her other hand.

"Maggie, just stay put for a minute, will ya?" Grant ran a hand through his dark hair once and leaned his arm on the steering wheel before continuing, "I know we just met, but I'd really like to get to know you better. Have dinner with me."

When she just stared at him he added with a charming smile, "After all, *I* don't make you nervous, so you've nothing to fear, right?"

Laughing she replied, "Just because you don't make me nervous doesn't mean I'm interested in going out with you." *Liar, liar* she chanted in her mind, grateful that he couldn't read her thoughts.

"Take pity on the new guy in town and show me around, then."

Sighing Maggie replied, "Look, Grant you seem like a really nice guy…"

"Ouch," Grant muttered and grimaced making her smile again.

"…and it's great that you and Steven have hit it off so quickly—believe me, that's rare. Steven is not one to trust easily, and the fact that he invited you over today…well, he wouldn't have if he didn't already. But…"

"But."

"But, I'm just not ready for any kind of relationship right now. I literally broke up with someone *this week*, and I'm no fun right now," she said and got out of the SUV.

Grant paused for one moment before jumping out and grabbing her bags from the back of the truck. As they crossed the street to her apartment building he spoke quietly.

"Maggie, I'm sorry you're hurting right now, although I'd be lying if I said I was sorry you're no longer seeing someone. I'm not looking for a serious commitment here, either. I mean, I just moved here and have no idea how I'll like my new job or living in a small town."

Because he sounded so sincere, Maggie kept silent. She simply unlocked the door to the building and climbed the short flight of stairs to her front door.

"I just want to spend some time with you. I want to know you better."

The fact that she wanted to say "yes" so badly only made Maggie more reluctant to agree. "I'm sorry, but I just don't think that would be a smart idea for me right now, and I know it wouldn't be fair to you."

"Whoever said being smart was any fun. C'mon, Red, let's be stupid together," Grant cajoled with a winning grin on his face.

Maggie laughed again, shaking her head reluctantly, "Tempting. You don't know just *how* tempting that is, but I think I need to say no."

"Fair enough. If you change your mind, you know where to find me."

"I do. Thanks for the ride."

"No problem."

Grant watched as Maggie went inside. When she turned to shut the door their eyes met and he said, "Be seeing you, Red. Real soon."

Maggie froze for a long moment, her hand on the door, before tearing her eyes from his and closing the door quietly. Turning she let herself collapse back against the door, her hand on her fluttering stomach again.

The image of intense brown eyes and a well sculpted mouth filled her mind and the only thing she could think to say was a weak, "Oh, boy."

After watching to make sure a light in Maggie's apartment came on, Grant headed back down to the SUV to let Jake out and together they went into the house. An hour later he clicked off the TV and threw the remote controller back on the side table with a clatter.

There was no point in trying to watch the old Bogart movie when all he kept seeing in front of him was a pair of haunting hazel eyes—sparkling with humor, one moment and drenched with sadness the next.

She was such an intriguing combination of innocence and strength, playfulness and seriousness, and he just couldn't seem to get her out of his head—and if he was being honest with himself, he didn't want to.

"Well, Evans, you'll just have to get over it."

Jake raised his head at the sound of his master's voice, but when Grant simply headed toward the bedroom he settled back down onto his bed.

Grant prepared for sleep knowing that the next few days would be exciting and exhausting. Starting a new job was never easy, no matter how much you looked forward to it. After months on the sidelines, he was finally getting back out on the streets again.

Expecting to stay awake for hours, it was a surprise when, despite the jumble of thoughts and emotions coursing through his busy mind, Grant managed to drift off to sleep almost immediately.

And when he dreamed, he dreamed of a pair of hazel eyes darkened with restrained passion, glowing skin dusted with freckles, and a long tumble of auburn curls that turned to fire in the sunlight.

ELEVEN

It would be tonight.

Since the first time he'd punished one of his Angels, he had put a lot of thought into what he needed in his supply kit, and he had packed it neatly. He always hoped that he wouldn't need it, but he also knew that it was better—and safer—to be prepared should his new Angel fall.

And she had.

After more than four months of devoted worship, four months of adoration. Four months wasted on that *woman*, that Jezebel.

His hands were shaking so hard, he could barely put the car key into his ignition. He gripped the steering wheel so tightly that his knuckles turned white and he felt shooting pains up his arms. The pain calmed him, and after taking several slow breaths he was able to start the truck and pull out into the deep darkness of the early morning.

As he drove the short distance to her apartment building, his heartbeat began to quicken, his breathing coming faster and faster as he visualized all the ways he'd make her pay for her sins. As he pictured how he'd make her repent, and how he'd save her in the end—*if* she proved worthy.

He pulled onto the quiet, tree-lined street two blocks down from her apartment building and grabbed the duffel bag containing his kit, locked the car and began walking swiftly and quietly down the shadowed street. Only the harsh rasping of his strained breathing marred the stillness of the cool morning.

He reached one hand into his jacket pocket to grasp the object that always calmed him. As his breathing slowed and softened, a muffled clicking could just be heard.

He searched the darkness, sweeping his head constantly from side to side, searching for any signs of any early risers. He'd specifically chosen this time of day because it was early enough he'd have come and gone before anyone should be up and about, but late enough that no night owls should disturb him.

Taking one last look around, he slunk behind the apartment building and slowed his pace as he approached the darkened building. He headed straight to the far right corner of the structure and slipped through the small basement window he'd jimmied open months ago.

People were so careless—they never checked their basement windows.

He landed in a dark, damp utility room and paused, holding his breath to listen for any signs of people in the adjacent laundry room—despite the hour, he knew that people sometimes did unusual things, and he hadn't gotten this far by being careless.

When he heard nothing but the clinks and moans of the old building settling around him, his hand returned to his pocket and the quiet clicking resumed, breaking the silence once more.

He glided across the floor, as silent as a ghost, and walked up the stairs and quickly across the hall to the janitor's closet where he'd found a master key on one of his previous nighttime visits.

With practiced ease he reached behind a stack of cleaners into a rusted coffee can for the precious key before making his way up one flight of stairs to the second floor apartment his Angel occupied.

Turning the key soundlessly in the lock—he'd oiled it himself—he let himself into the darkened apartment and wound his way silently through the maze of furniture, setting down his duffel to draw out the instruments of his art.

He slid the object from his jacket before taking the jacket off and placing it with the duffel. He crept forward once again.

After he slithered through the partially opened door to his Angel's bedroom, he glanced quickly around the room and noted that the windows were shut as usual and all but one of the shades where drawn.

Good. Less work for him to do.

Soundlessly, he shut the door behind him and locked it with a soft snick, causing him to pause for a full minute to ensure that she hadn't awoken at the soft noise before he continued his journey across the room to her bed. There he paused a moment to take in her soft, peaceful features.

In sleep she looked like the Angel he'd fallen in love with.

But as his gaze left her resting features they roamed down her body. She'd thrown her covers half off of her legs and torso while

83

she slept revealing a satin nightgown that had ridden up almost to her waist. A long expanse of thigh was exposed to his predatory gaze while one bare arm was draped loosely over her head, thrusting one breast forward to strain against the thin material of her nightgown.

His dark eyes swept hungrily over every exposed inch of her before they hardened and chilled to ice. With a soft sigh she stirred in her sleep, angling her face towards him.

His heartbeat leapt with anticipation when he saw her eyelids flutter. When she simply sighed and settled more deeply to sleep he grasped the object in his left hand more tightly.

Click, click, click.

Click, click, click.

Click, click, click.

And, again, his heartbeat slowed and regulated itself.

Dragged from her dreams with a start, she froze. This time it's her heartbeat that races. Staring blindly into the darkness of her bedroom, she searches for what woke her.

Click, click, click.

Screaming, she kicks out and connects with something solid.

"Angel," he croons in a sing-song voice as he comes closer, "There's nowhere to fly to now that you've fallen."

Whimpering she curls up against the headboard, her knees bent to her chest, and looks frantically around as her eyes adjust to the darkened room. Reaching slowly towards the bedside table, she knocks over a lamp and the book she'd set beside her bed before finding what she was looking for. Closing a shaking hand around a metal nail file she leaps from the bed and races across the room to the door and slams right into him.

A leather clad hand grips her by the neck as she struggles and plunges the nail file into his arm. With a howl like an animal he falls back, clutching his forearm before pushing off of the wall and coming at her again.

Frantically, she turns the door knob, yanking, the breath sobbing in and out of her tortured lungs as tears stream down her face. Before it fully registers that the door is locked, he's on her.

"Bitch!" He backhands her across the room and into the bed.

Holding her cheek, she struggles to stand and he pushes her down, straddling her to kneel on her arms and laughing cruelly.

She frantically thrashes, trying to buck him off, her heels pounding furiously against the floor.

"You were my Angel, but you are no longer worthy. You are *nothing*. Nothing but a whore, and you will be punished."

"Please," she whispers hoarsely, still sobbing desperately, "Please."

Looking into her pleading eyes, the cruel look of pleasure freezes for a moment, for just one shining moment, before the fury returns and her last sliver of hope disappears.

"Oh, God, help me," she whispers, making him throw back his head and laugh a terrible thin, high-pitched laugh.

"*I* am your god now, Bitch."

Picking up the object from the floor where he'd dropped it in the struggle, he places it around her throat, and when she tries to scream again, he pulls back a hand and swings again and again.

Panting heavily, he sits back in the sudden silence and smiles down at his Fallen Angel. Brushing her dark blonde hair back from her battered face, he's surprised by the amount of damage he sees.

The rush of power that had surged through him while she fought ebbs away, and his fury doubles.

She had failed him again.

His arms swing, slamming over and over again. Panting harder, tears run down his face as, once again, he seizes the object and pulls, pulls, pulls, until he can pull no more.

Scrambling to his feet, he stands looking down at her broken body. At some point she must have regained consciousness—at what point he had no idea. Her once brilliant blue eyes stare lifelessly up at him.

As he gathers his object, checking to make sure he is leaving nothing else behind, his eyes dart time and again to her still face and her staring eyes.

"Stop looking at me," he whispers, "Stop it, stop it, stop it!" he screams before seizing the object once more.

Click, click, click.
Click, click, click.
Click, click, click.

As he calms he begins to think more clearly, nodding once and striding forward to begin his work.

Less than an hour later he lay naked on his bed, freshly showered. Moving slowly in the darkness, he relives the encounter with his Fallen Angel over and over again.

Filled with joy, he knows that he has saved his Angel from Hell. That it was he that had rescued her soul. To do that he'd had to punish her severely, but he knew she was safe now, and he was certain she was grateful for what he'd done.

He was a god, and death was his disciple.

TWELVE

Grant's eyes snapped open five minutes before his alarm was set to go off on Monday morning. Before his mind could fill with worries about the job he would start in just a couple of hours he flung back his brand new green sheets and pulled on running shorts and shoes to head out into the still-dark morning.

As he stepped out onto the front walk to stretch, Jake at his side, Grant's eyes were invariably drawn across the street to Maggie's building. When he found himself searching for signs of life in her second floor windows he shook his head and turned away starting out in a slow jog.

The damp gray of the morning slowly lightened, revealing the white vapor clouds that bloomed from his mouth with each breath he expelled into the chill fall air. October had descended, and though the days were still sun-drenched, the predawn hours had become dark and cold.

If it got any colder—*when* it got colder Grant corrected himself—he would be forced to consider what to do when the temperatures plummeted in the coming winter months. Maybe he'd invest in a treadmill and convert one of the upstairs bedrooms into a workout room to be used over the winter.

When he stepped off the pavement onto the firmly packed sand of the beach and released Jake from his leash, Grant noted that many of the trees had been stripped of their vibrant foliage in the previous week. The winds and rains that had battered his cozy home had clearly wreaked their damage on the trees.

Turning at the end of the crescent shaped cove, Grant increased his pace, still thinking of the coming season. He'd read of the infamous snowfalls that regularly blanketed Minnesota in *feet* of snow—not inches, but feet of snow—and marveled at the idea. It was not as if he'd never experienced snow before, but the idea of feet of snow falling in a day or two was still mind-boggling to a West coast boy.

The sun broke over the horizon as he approached the path and prepared to do his second lap of the beach. The rhythmic slap of shoes on asphalt reached him a split second before he saw another runner rounding the corner before stopping dead at the end of the path.

"Mornin', Red," Grant drawled, a huge smile spread across his scruffy face when Maggie let out a muffled scream.

She swallowed twice before she could force the racing heart that had lodged itself in her throat at the sight of a large man running straight at her back where it belonged. Maggie took a deep breath and managed to reply weakly, "Grant. You startled me—I usually have the beach to myself this time of day, and I couldn't tell who you were with the sun at your back..."

Stopping abruptly, Maggie's face turned a bright red as she squatted to receive an enthusiastic greeting from Jake.

Smile gone, Grant turned suddenly serious brown eyes to stare down at her from where he stood above her crouched form. "I don't mind making you nervous, Maggie, but I never meant to scare you—I'm sorry."

"Don't be ridiculous..." Avoiding Grant's eyes Maggie stood and added swiftly, "I'll just let you get back to your run," before taking off across the sand at a brisk pace letting the cold air cool her burning cheeks.

When Grant simply fell in step with her, Maggie's shoulders stiffened. But when he stayed silent Maggie slowly relaxed and let the rhythm of their synchronized footsteps lull her.

After several minutes of silence, Maggie let out a heartfelt sigh, let her eyes close for just a moment and raised her face to the warmth of the newly-risen sun.

Turning his head to look at her, Grant watched as her eyes slid shut and took a moment to enjoy the way the dawning sunlight bathed her porcelain skin in a golden wash and lit her messily drawn up hair into a halo of burning curls surrounding her face.

And in that perfect moment he felt his heart stutter and his feet faltered momentarily. At the break in the rhythm her eyes opened and flashed to his and the intense look on his face caused her eyebrows to draw down in confusion.

Their perfect moment was over.

Grant smiled a strange half-smile and faced forward again. In unison once again they turned at the end of the cove to make their way back across the now thoroughly disturbed sand one last time.

Maggie glanced quickly back over at Grant's face again, and the tension that had slammed into her belly at the look she'd seen in his dark eyes a moment ago released when she saw a relaxed look back on his face.

She paused, running in place, when Grant stopped to reattach Jake's lead before the sand stopped, and together they headed back onto the path that led them away from their early morning retreat and back into the real world.

Each waved as they separated—Grant to jog up his driveway and into his breezeway, and Maggie up the stairs to her apartment building—to shower, dress and face the upcoming day.

Despite the single terror-filled moment when Grant had first loomed up in her path and that strange moment of tension, the morning had been oddly comfortable for Maggie.

Dismissing the thought as random, Maggie hummed along to the songs that played on her car's radio, and then blasted the volume when Katrina and the Waves came on the radio and began belting out "I'm Walking on Sunshine" as she drove along.

She was still humming the song when she pulled into the University's parking lot. Locking up she smiled to herself, picturing Grant's sweaty face as it broke into a broad smile and, still daydreaming, relieved that moment on the beach when she'd first opened her eyes to find him staring so intently at her.

Only *this* time, instead of turning away, *he stops, dragging her roughly against his chest while his lips devour hers with a desperate hunger. Her hands fist on his shirt and a throaty moan breaks the silence of the still morning when his arms tighten like a band around her, crushing her aching breasts to his chest. Nipping at his bottom lip, she angles her head...*

"Someone's pretty cheerful this morning."

"What? Nothing. What?" Maggie stammered as she jerked from her fantasy, blushing furiously. Stopping abruptly, she looked around in confusion.

"Hey, Cloë,"

"Not only cheerful, but guilty, too. Hmmmm. Who's the guy?"

"There's no guy."

"There's *always* a guy."

"There's no guy that I'm seeing."

"So, is there a guy you're *not* seeing?"

Laughing, Maggie rolled her eyes, "Cloë!"

"Maggie!"

"Fine, there's a guy that asked me out—my brother Steven's new work partner—but of course, I told him 'no'."

"Why 'of course'?"

"Because," Maggie replied slowly, as if to a small child, "I *just* broke up with someone."

"So?"

"So, I'm not ready."

"The dreamy smile I just saw on your face says differently."

"Dreamy smile? You're *crazy*, Cloë."

"Crazy like a fox!" Cloë grinned over at her friend.

"What does that mean? Where does that phrase come from anyway? I've never understood that saying."

"Nice try, Mags. You can't distract me—spill it. Tell me about this guy. Is he hot? He's got to be hot, right?"

Looking down at her friend's sparkling green eyes Maggie had to smile. "Yes. He's definitely hot," Maggie said.

"Hot damn! I *knew* it," Cloë chortled, breaking into a quick jig.

Laughing again, Maggie shook her head at Cloë and opened the door to their building.

As they walked up the stairs Cloë continued her interrogation, her voice full of mischief, "C'mon, Mags. I need the detes. You know I'm not seeing anyone right now—I need some vicarious thrills here."

"Well, his name is Grant and he just moved here from Seattle. He's already bought a house. He's Steven's new partner— oh, yeah, I already told you that. Oh! He has this gorgeous German Shepherd named Jake."

"Maggie," Cloë said pityingly, shaking her head slowly from side to side, "Maggie, that's just sad. I said *thrill*, girl. What does he *look* like?"

"I'm sorry," Maggie said, managing to keep a straight face, but only just. "Let's see. He's about 6' 4", has rich dark brown hair with just a touch of chestnut, deep brown eyes and an amazing smile."

Forgetting Cloë, Maggie sighed and continued, "His face is amazing—gorgeous—but not in a perfect pretty-boy way. More in a dangerous, fallen angel kind of way. His hands are strong and wide and just a little rough-looking, and his forearms are totally perfect—strong but not over-muscled." Maggie looked at Cloë for understanding before continuing, "He listens really well—with his whole attention—like whatever you're saying is the most important thing in the world, and he has this low, sexy voice that makes my palms sweat. He has broad shoulders and long, lean legs. And a terrific butt, if you want to know the truth."

Tapping one manicured red fingernail against matching red lips Maggie added, almost to herself, "He was so sweet with my parents, and the kids just *loved* him. He brought a present for my mom—which proves he has good manners and he was a perfect gentleman when he drove me home on Saturday. He has a great sense of humor and got along great with *all* of my brothers—which is a minor miracle."

By the time she stopped talking they had reached the office and Maggie turned to find Cloë standing with her mouth open.

"What?" Maggie asked.

"Let me get this straight. He's gorgeous, funny, a good listener, won over your *entire* family—including the four overprotective guard dogs you call brothers—and last, but certainly not least, has a great ass. And you said *no* when he asked you out?" Ending on a squeak, her eyes wide, Cloë raised her eyebrows at Maggie.

"Yes?" Maggie replied weakly. Then, she spotted the neat pile of pink messages from Bradley she had yet to throw out and the blinking light on her phone and her resolve hardened. Maggie squared her shoulders, grabbed the stack of messages, ripped them up and threw them out.

"Yes," she said firmly, all the dreaminess gone from her voice. Maggie sat down, turning away from her friend's gaze, and picked up her phone to make the first call of the day.

Taking one last look at Maggie's rigid shoulders and set face, Cloë turned to her own desk with a sigh before saying softly,

"Maggie. Timing aside, chances like this don't come along too often. Sometimes you have to risk it all to get it all. Don't let what one bastard did ruin your future happiness. I'm not saying that this guy is *the* guy, but you'll never know if you never give him a chance. If he asks you again, say yes."

Meeting Cloë's eyes for a brief moment Maggie's face softened for a moment and she opened her mouth to reply, but before she could, the person on the other end of her phone line answered, and she said instead, "Yes. Hello. Can I please speak with Mr. Anderson?"

The moment lost, Cloë sighed again and turned back to her own phone when it rang.

The work day had begun.

THIRTEEN

At a quarter to eight Grant found himself once again facing down the Hope Police Department's gate keeper, Ms. Shirley Larson, in the entrance to the station.

Flashing a polite smile Grant said, "Good morning, Ms. Larson. I'm a bit early, but Chief Banyon asked that I meet with him first thing this morning. Is it okay if I head on back, Ma'am?"

"Now, Detective Evans, you call me Shirley," Pleased that Grant had remembered her name, Shirley blushed and said, "And you head right on back—you don't have to check in with me."

"Thank you, Ms. Shirley. I appreciate it," Grant said and then walked through the bustling squad room to Chief Banyon's office and knocked.

"Enter."

Grant walked in to witness Chief Banyon hanging up the phone before he stood to shake Grant's hand. "Evans, good mornin'. Have a seat," Chief Banyon gestured at an empty chair before sitting himself back down behind the desk. "So are you getting settled in alright? Sullivan told me you'd found a nice house—that was quick work."

"Yes, Sir. It was a bit quick, but the house is exactly what I was looking for. I was lucky Detective Sullivan was able to help me out as much as he did. Without his help, I'm sure things wouldn't have gone nearly as smoothly."

Chief Banyon nodded once and said, "Are you ready to get back on the job?"

"Absolutely, Chief. I appreciate you giving me the time to get settled in here, but I am anxious to get back to work."

Smiling, Chief Banyon nodded again, this time in approval. "We have a few papers for you to fill out, and then we can get you situated at your new desk.

"As you know, you'll be partnering with Detective Sullivan. He'll be showing you the ropes these first few weeks, and should be able to answer any questions you may have. But I want you to know that my office is always open. If you have *any* problems or questions, I will be happy to address them.

"This partnership will have a trial period of let's say thirty days. If, during that time, you, Detective Sullivan, or I have any major problems with the situation, we will discuss an alternative. I do not foresee any problems, but we want you to be happy here in Hope. Any questions so far?"

"No, Sir."

"Good. Get started on these papers and..."

"Chief?"

Eyebrows drawn down at the interruption, Chief Banyon looked up at the door. He took one look at the expression on the face of the man Grant recognized as Officer Simmons from his first visit to the station and the Chief's look of irritation was quickly replaced with one of concern.

"What is it?" At Chief Banyon's calm question, Officer Simmon's face lost a fraction of its tension.

"It's Jessie Daniels, Chief," the visibly upset officer blurted out shakily. "The call just came in—it, it sounds real bad, Sir."

"Is she..."

Shaking his head Officer Simmons just said, "It sounded *real* bad, Sir. I think so, Sir. I looked for Sullivan, but he's not in yet."

"I want you and McKenzie, Jones and Sylvester over at her apartment building immediately. Secure the scene and keep anyone—especially the press—from going in."

Officer Simmons nodded jerkily once and hurried out. Chief Banyon swiveled his chair around to stare out one of his windows for a long moment before turning back to face Grant.

"It looks like that paperwork is going to have to wait, Evans. I need your experience on this case right away," Chief Banyon said.

Grant had silently watched the exchange between Officer Simmons and the Chief, and his long-unused instincts had interpreted—correctly—precisely what was going on.

A young girl—one both officers knew—was dead. Her death had not been an accident, it had not been due to a long illness, and it most assuredly had been violent.

What he didn't know was why the girl's death had caused the degree of tension he'd sensed between Simmons and the Chief.

Despite the fact that a death—accidental or otherwise—was rare for a town the size of Hope, it would *not* be unheard of. Every town—no matter the size—would experience its share of crime. People were people no matter where you went.

But the extreme nature of the men's reactions had Grant's instincts humming. Something more was going on here.

All of this flashed through Grant's mind in the seconds it took for Chief Banyon to turn back to meet Grant's eyes. Grant nodded once and Chief Banyon continued.

"As soon as Sullivan gets in, I want you and him to head over to the scene. I'm putting you two in as leads on this investigation. Doc Clayton is the local ME and will most likely be at the scene before you get there. Sullivan can fill you in on the way. I'm sorry to throw you in the deep end on your first day, but we have a limited number of detectives qualified to handle a case like this."

Running a hand through his hair, Chief Banyon leaned back in his chair, the only outward sign of stress his fingers tapping out an impatient tattoo on the desk top.

"How many other murders have there been?" Grant asked quietly, his dark eyes staring intently at the Chief.

Chief Banyon's fingers stopped drumming and his eyes sharpened and narrowed as he considered Grant's question.

"What makes you think there are more?" Chief Banyon asked, his voice calm and low despite the fact that his hands clenched tightly together betraying his true reaction.

"It's my job to know, Chief. I've spent too many years on the force—the majority of them in homicide—to *not* know, or at the least to suspect."

At Chief Banyon's continued silence Grant continued.

"My guess is there have been just one, maybe two other unsolved murders. Now that would not be all that unusual in Seattle, but in a town the size of Hope..." Grant trailed off with a shrug.

Chief Banyon leaned back in his chair, letting his hands fall to the desktop before speaking slowly, "Your Lieutenant Gere said your instincts were spot on, and as much as I'd like to say he was wrong in this instance, I cannot," Chief Banyon paused and sighed deeply once before continuing, "Jessie Daniels is the second—possibly the third violent murder we've had in the past two years.

"The first was more than eighteen months ago—and I'm still not convinced it is related to the second murder—and the second was

95

just six months ago. Obviously it's presumptuous to link any of these murders with the investigation barely even begun, but..."

Chief Banyon again paused to rub one large hand at the base of his neck as if to rub away tension before it could settle there.

"Do you now how many unsolved murders have occurred in Hope before these? Exactly two—the last of which happened in 1896."

The intercom on Chief Banyon's desk crackled and Ms. Larson's voice scratched out, "Detective Sullivan is here, Chief."

Chief Banyon reached forward and replied, "Thanks, Shirley," before turning back to Grant. He said, "Obviously I'm making this your number one priority."

Standing, Chief Banyon walked around the desk and Grant stood to meet him.

"Lieutenant Gere also said he was sorry to see you go, and that you were one hell of an investigator who, no matter the circumstances, refused to give up."

"I'm counting on it. So is Jessie Daniels."

"I won't let you down, Chief, and I won't let her down either," Grant said and turned away from Chief Banyon's assessing blue gaze and walked out of the office.

Less than one hour back on the job and Grant found himself facing a case of the likes he had believed he'd left behind when he'd left Seattle for Hope.

Grant looked around the room and spotted Steve standing at the grouping of desks he knew included his own and quickly strode over to greet him.

"Hey, Steve."

"Grant. Hey—a hell of a way to spend your first day, huh? I'd hoped to spend most of the morning introducing you around and getting you all set up, but we've got to hit it. I had Simmons pull a weapon and badge for you," Steve pointed to where both sat on the desk butted up to his own. Grant grabbed both, and after checking to make sure the weapon was secure, slid it into the holster he'd strapped around his waist that morning.

"Obviously, we don't have time for you to officially get certified right now, but we can hit the range after our shift tonight."

"Don't worry about it man, I stopped by the range a couple a days after I got to town and re-certified with one of my personal weapons," Grant said.

Steve replied, "Good. That's one less thing for us to worry about."

The two men made their way through the now-empty squad room and climbed into an ordinary looking maroon Chevy sedan that had Grant grinning. Even though it was cleaner and less beat up that any other work car he'd ever had, it still screamed cop car.

Steve reached over to activate the flashers and Grant leaned back, breathing in the familiar blend of smells—fast food, coffee, and stale sweat. Despite the seriousness of the circumstances, and the fact that any plans he might have had for easing back onto the job had been completely destroyed, Grant could not stop the thought that filled his mind as Steve accelerated and sped through town.

Grant was right where he was meant to be—and exactly where he wanted to be.

"Why don't you fill me in on the pertinent details of the first two murders," Grant said.

"The first victim was Anna Martin. Twenty-two years old, found inside her apartment bedroom twenty months ago. Cause of death was strangulation. She was found lying face down, naked. Looks like a single blow to the head knocked her out and then a thin cord was used to strangle her. No signs of sexual assault.

"The second victim was Natalie Roberts. Twenty-four years old, found beaten and strangled in the bedroom of her house six and a half months ago. There was considerable damage done to her bedroom and her body was beaten severely. A thin, ridged cord of undetermined type was used to strangle and kill her. Her body was also found naked, face down. However, this time a stylized picture was drawn on her back along with the word 'Angel'. Again, there are no signs of sexual assault. As of today, there have been no major suspects in either case. Both remain unsolved and open."

As Grant listened to the cool, detached voice of his new partner he filed away the facts of each case—including the fact that Steve's hands were clenching the steering wheel despite his calm demeanor. Clearly the unsolved status of the cases upset him.

"Is there any forensic evidence connecting the two victims?" Grant asked as they turned down a street filled with squad cars, flashers on. An ambulance sat silently at the corner, its lights turned off and a small crowd of people watched the apartment building where Jessie Daniels had lived from across the street.

"No. So far it's just my gut instinct that the two are connected. The Chief isn't convinced, I don't think he wants to believe it, but…I don't know, the two just *feel* the same to me."

"I can understand that. I mean, if the Chief agrees that the two—possibly three—cases are connected, he has to accept the fact that there is a monster loose somewhere in Hope.

"To even *think* that, let alone acknowledge it openly, opens himself and the entire department to a degree of scrutiny and public anxiety that, I'm sure, has rarely been experienced in Hope before. At the first hint of the word 'serial' you'll have the eyes of the entire country on you, and the press and federal pressure that goes along with it."

"Look, Evans, I know you have a lot of experience, but I've been on these cases for almost two years now, and I *know* they are connected," Steve began in a sharp voice.

Holding up a placating hand Grant jumped in quickly, "Steve, I believe you. I learned long ago to trust my instincts, particularly on the job. All I'm saying is that I can understand *why* the Chief may not want to believe you—even if he already does."

Steve nodded once as they parked.

Grant could see officers McKenzie and Jones flanking the entrance to the building, and he was sure that Simmons was inside on the door of the apartment itself. Without any more time to get filled in, Steve and Grant exited the Chevy and approached the small brick building.

As he passed the gathering crowd Grant scanned the faces, looking for someone just a little too eager, a little too excited, but saw nothing beyond the usual looks ranging from mild curiosity to distress.

He opened his mouth to recommend that one of the officers flanking the door begin to photograph or film the crowd and take down license plate numbers from any passing vehicles when he heard Steve tell McKenzie to do just that.

Together, the two men made their way through the lobby and up the stairs to the second floor. As Grant had guessed, Simmons was leaning against the wall across the hall from the open door of Jessie Daniel's apartment.

Grant again stayed silent as Steve spoke.

"Dusty, fill us in."

Pushing up from his position against the wall Simmons shook his head mournfully and pulled out a notebook to read from his notes.

"7:08 this morning Michael Peters came upstairs to see why Ms. Daniels had not come out to meet him for their drive to work as expected at 6:45. Peters says that the vic gave him the building code a few months ago and when she didn't show up he got impatient and headed up to get her. She's known for oversleeping.

"When he got to her door, he found it ajar and he walked in and found her in the bedroom. He immediately left the apartment and called it in on his cell phone. He claims he doesn't remember touching anything except the front door knob and the center of her bedroom door to push them open.

"Talked with the manager and there's no log of who enters the front door, no video either. According to him, the people in the apartment next door are on vacation and won't be back until Saturday. The apartment below Ms. Daniels is currently empty— apparently someone threw a rock through a window two days ago and set fire to the place. I've got a call in to the department to see who's handling the case and should hear back in about ten minutes. The current occupants are staying with a relative for the week until a crew can get in to clean it up."

Pausing, Simmons ran a hand through his already mussed hair before continuing, "Doc got here a half hour ago and Sam Prestin is inside taking photos." He nodded towards the open doorway where the three policemen could hear a low murmur of voices and see the intermittent flashes from a camera.

Steve reached out and grabbed Simmons's shoulder and said, "Thanks, Dusty. I'm sorry about Jessie."

When Simmons just nodded, looking down at the carpet Steve continued, "Why don't you start a canvass of the neighboring buildings, see if anyone saw or heard anything unusual. You know the drill."

"Sure, Sully, I'll get it started."

Grant nodded at Simmons as he passed and waited until Simmons had disappeared down the hall before he turned to Steve to ask, "How did he know the victim?"

"His little sister went to school with her. The two were inseparable and spent a lot of time at each other's houses, so Dusty got to know her really well—like another little sister, you know? Well, let's get this done," Steve said and walked through the doorway, Grant at his heels.

The familiar smell of death rolled over Grant in a wave forcing him to pause just inside the doorway. Flashes of gunfire and darkened alleys flickered through his mind like strobe lights before he forcibly returned his attention to the scene at hand.

Looking around the neat living room Grant saw bright colors, cheap furniture and a large collection of books lining the walls. The room was tidy, but not overly so. There were several books on various tables with book marks in them. Grant leaned down to read their titles finding *The Secret* side by side with Stephen King's latest novel and a nonfiction title on ways to help save the planet.

Walking over to the television he found a stash of DVD's in the attached cabinet. Again, he found an eclectic selection of subjects ranging from romantic comedies and action movies to documentaries and horror.

Scattered throughout the surfaces of the tiny apartment were an abundance of pictures of a pretty blonde mugging at the camera with a variety of people and knick-knacks, the majority of which were pigs.

He could see a small kitchen, barely big enough to fit two people, over the open counter separating the rooms. Two doors led off of the living room to a tiny bathroom and the apartment's single bedroom.

While Grant walked slowly through the apartment making notations in a small notebook Steve walked over to talk to a short, balding man in a light tan pant suit.

Despite the chilly breeze blowing in through an open window in the living room, the man had neatly folded the crisp white arms of his dress shirt up past his plump forearms. Round spectacles perched on a round face more suited to a department store Santa than to a medical examiner.

Through the open bedroom door Grant could see a skinny, freckle-faced redheaded man wielding a large camera, careful to keep it in front of his face at all times. Looking closer Grant noted the gray cast to the photographer's skin, and the light sheen of sweat covering his face.

Either he was new to the job, Grant thought grimly, or he'd never seen a crime scene like this one. Grant's hope that it was the former faded when he looked into the bedroom.

The scene before him was as horrific as any he'd seen in his years on the Seattle PD. His first impressions on viewing the room were of colors and unrecognizable shapes—it took him a few moments to understand just exactly what it was he was seeing.

What he saw was a grisly display of overturned furniture and blood that splattered everything with rust-colored spots and streaks in a repulsive impersonation of a Jackson Pollock painting.

Grant approached the body making careful notes on its position and surroundings. Jessie Daniels' body was stripped naked, posed in a chair holding what looked like a second body.

Upon closer examination Grant could tell that it was not a body, but clothing stuffed with other clothes to simulate a human being. He also saw what looked like fishing line being used to hold the body in its gruesome pose.

"Grant," Steve walked over to where Grant was squatting next to the body, "Let me introduce you to Dr. Alvin Clayton. He's acting medical examiner for Hope and the surrounding areas. Doc, this is Detective Grant Evans."

Grant stood quickly nodding once and holding up hands encased in latex gloves. He said, "Nice to meet you Dr. Clayton."

"Likewise, Detective," Doc Clayton said, "Are you new to the area?"

"Yes sir. I just moved here from Seattle," Grant replied.

Letting the polite interest fade from his voice, Doc Clayton continued brusquely. "So, I've done an initial cursory examination of the body. According to liver temp, it appears she's only been dead for 4-8 hours. I won't be able to narrow that down until I get the body back to the office. Cause of death is inconclusive at this point, and I'd hesitate to hazard a guess at this point. There's simply too much damage that's been done to the body…"

Doc Clayton trailed off, shaking his head before he continued in a low voice, "It's a terrible thing. Just terrible." Sharp blue eyes clouded behind round spectacles briefly before they turned back to Steve.

"I'll have a preliminary report for you by the end of the day, Detective Sullivan. As you may recall, the toxicology screens and DNA testing will, of course, take more time," Doc Clayton said, brusque once again.

"Thanks, Doc," Steve said as the doctor turned to go before turning back towards Grant.

"So, what do you think?" Steve asked quietly.

Grant looked carefully around the room, taking in the overturned furniture and the position of the body. "She put up a hell of a fight. This took some time," Grant paused to strip off his gloves and crossed his arms before continuing.

"Officer outside says there's no sign of forced entry to the apartment, but there was a basement window with a broken lock that leads to the boiler room. That appears to be the probable point of entry. Nothing else in the apartment appears to be disturbed and nothing seems to be missing—there's a TV and stereo, some nice pieces of jewelry, none of which were touched."

Grant sighed and rubbed one hand across the back of his neck. Silently he waited as the photographer packed his camera away and made a fast retreat out of the room.

When the detectives were alone Grant turned troubled eyes to Steve, "Steve, this is *not* good. Worst case scenario, this murder is tied to the previous murders and there will be no denying that Hope has a very serious problem on its hands. Best case, we have two separate, vicious killers on the loose."

"Shit."

"You can say that again."

After hours spent processing the body and scene, talking to the crime scene technicians and the ME about the pathology and autopsy reports, it was long past dinner time.

Leaning back in his new chair, Grant looked around the now-quiet squad room and used both hands to rub vigorously over his face. Grant leaned forward to plant both elbows on the edge of his desk and looked over to where Steve was finishing up a phone call.

"I got it. Yes. Yes. No. All right, we'll be there. That long? I know, I know. All right, thanks, Doc," Steve said.

As Steve hung up the phone he looked up at Grant. "Okay, Doc says he'll light a fire under the techs and try to get us the lab reports ASAP, but some of the tests they do just take time. So, nothing new there, but we should be able to get a good start with the preliminary autopsy report Doc had faxed over earlier. He asked that we come by tomorrow morning for the finished file."

Grant simply nodded tiredly, then said quietly, "I think we need to talk a few things over somewhere quieter—and more private—before we get too much further into the investigation, and definitely before we meet with the Chief in the morning to update him."

"Agreed. Why don't we head back to your place. You can box up these files and I'll go grab a pizza and meet you there."

"You read my mind."

"Anything you don't like on your pizza?" Steve asked as he pulled on a beat up brown leather bomber jacket.

"No fish," Grant shuddered, "I had an incident once. Suffice it to say I no longer eat *any* type of fish on my pizza."

"Got it. No fish," Steve grinned for the first time in what seemed like days to him. "See you back at the house."

Grant watched as Steve strode out the door before making a large pile of files to bring home. He quickly shrugged into his faded gray jean jacket, grabbed the files and headed out to climb slowly into his truck.

Driving through the darkened streets of his new hometown, Grant thought over his first day back at work. Despite the terribleness of the crimes he was currently investigating he couldn't help but feel good about being back on the job again, doing what he loved best.

After months of stagnant inactivity, here he was smack dab in the middle of the biggest case of his career. He just hoped that he was ready.

After he parked the truck in the garage and deposited the box of files on his brand new dining room table Grant headed out back to check on Jake. He had just settled the German shepherd down in the living room with a large milk bone when he saw the headlights from Steve's car sweep across the living room wall.

Grant opened the door for Steve and looked across the street to Maggie's apartment building. A stab of disappointment coursed through Grant when he noted her darkened windows. Shaking off the bothersome emotion, Grant turned his attention back to his partner, having completely missed the look Steve gave him when his attention was focused on Maggie's building.

"Smells good."

When Steve didn't reply Grant raised his eyebrows in silent inquiry.

"I got the works," Steve said abruptly and shrugged out of his coat.

"Perfect. I threw the files into the dining room. I'll grab a couple of beers and we can read while we eat," Grant replied.

Three hours later the pizza was gone and the men sat across from each other, the table between them strewn with opened files, carefully labeled evidence and a grisly array of crime scene photographs.

Grant now knew as much about the previous murders as Steve did and was convinced that the three cases were connected. The more he had read, the more his gut had told him they were in serious trouble.

"When I said before that this was a very bad situation, I may have understated things by quite a large margin. Steve, I'm no expert, but I'd say that the same killer murdered all three of these women," Grant stated quietly and rubbed slowly at his tired eyes.

"We can't even *think* the word serial unless we're absolutely sure—there's no faster way to get the Feds down here and the case taken over. I've spent too much time, put too much effort into these cases to just hand them over and hope that some outsider will care enough about them to give it their all.

"I *knew* these women, Grant," Steve tossed his pen down onto the table and sat back.

"I know. Look, I worked a serial case in Seattle on a joint task force with the State and Federal boys. I know a little bit about how they work, and their specialists are very good."

At Steve's snort Grant grinned and held up both hands. "I'm not saying we call them up and hand them the case on a silver platter, but it may be worth considering contacting this forensics guy I met to see if we can't have some of our evidence processed through their labs. No one does it better. No one.

"It would also be extremely helpful to get a profiler to take a look at the case files. A profiler could confirm or rule out the connections that I see between the cases. I may not have personally known these women, Steve, but I will *not* let them down. You have my word that they'll get my best—whatever that may be."

Steve stared into Grant's eyes for a long moment, carefully weighing Grant's words, noting the fierce passion that burned in his eyes. Steve relaxed and said, "I'm counting on it. I only pray that together, we're enough.

"You said that you're convinced all three were murdered by the same killer, but the M.O..."

"I know the M.O.'s don't match exactly on the surface, but at the core they are essentially the same. In each case the perp enters the building through a ground level window—usually in the basement. There are no other signs of forced entry. No witnesses so far. All three women died in their bedrooms—seemingly attacked while they slept. All three were struck on the head, strangled, and in the last two victims' cases, posed. The differences are also significant."

"In what way?" Steve asked.

Sighing, Grant leaned back in his chair and took a long drought of beer before stating roughly, "He's evolving. Making little improvements to suit his needs—adding to the scenarios with the posing, the slight changes in the materials he's using.

"He's probably doing this primarily to increase the level of satisfaction he gets out of the kills, but I'm betting that there are practical reasons as well. He's learning from his mistakes and shifting the things that aren't working well for him, changing the things that go wrong. This guy is seriously smart."

"And seriously pissed off."

Nodding Grant agreed, "Absolutely. He is supremely angry with women in general, and with these women specifically. Somehow or some way, they've said or done something that shifts them from objects of love or adoration to things that must be destroyed."

"You actually think that he *loves* them? And then slaughters them for no reason?" Steve asked, a look of incredulity on his face.

"Not for no reason. There would be a reason—at least in his mind. Some thing they said to him, or he overheard them saying. Something he witnessed them doing—it could be just about anything. As long as it violated whatever code of conduct, whatever standards he expected them to live up to.

"The point is there was never any way they would ever live up to his expectations. Sooner or later he's compelled to eliminate them."

"And if we're right and he's killed all three of these women," Steve began.

"Oh, this is one guy, Steve," Grant interrupted softly, "and that means that he's getting more and more dissatisfied with his kills. There was almost two years between the first two women's deaths and just six months between the last two."

"There's no real pattern here, Grant," Steve said, frustration ringing in his voice.

"There *is* a pattern. But until we know what it is, it will be almost impossible to identify. What *is* clear is that he's escalating."

Steve leaned back in his chair once more and combed both hands through his hair, "Shit. What a mess."

"A mess that may be beyond our capabilities. I was only on the periphery of that serial case and what I learned was that these cases grow out of control quickly. Any help we can get, any resources we can tap, well, it could mean all the difference catching this bastard."

When Steve remained silent Grant persisted, "Look, Man, I'm not saying we hand over the case or anything, just that we use my contacts to get a working profile done on this creep, and maybe outsource some of the more complicated lab work."

Steve nodded finally and said, "Okay. We'll talk it over with the Chief first thing and then we can get some sort of working group going on this."

Too exhausted to feel any real relief Grant smiled a brief half smile at Steve before gesturing to the jumble of case files, photographs, and notes spread over the table between them. "Let's get started then."

Another two hours later Steve sat back and said, "God, I'm glad you're here Grant."

"Me, too."

"You sound surprised."

"I guess I am. It wasn't that long ago I didn't care about much of anything," Grant stopped, thinking back over the months of bleakness and depression that had followed that night in the alley.

Steve watched as Grant rubbed his thigh, lost in thought. Grant stopped rubbing abruptly and clenched his hand into a fist before slowly relaxing it again. Grant lifted his eyes to look up into Steve's and continued in a low, gruff voice, "I lost my partner."

When Steve simply listened, Grant let out a shaky breath and, eyes falling to the table once again, continued, "We were both shot during an attempted robbery. I lived. He didn't.

"You want to know the funny thing about it? We weren't even supposed to be there—just happened to be nearby when it all went down."

Shaking his head again Grant looked up at Steve and said, "I thought you should know."

Steve nodded again. "Alright. I'm sorry about your partner. I can't imagine what that must have been like," Steve paused and when Grant didn't say anything further Steve changed the subject.

"Well, if we're going to be awake to present all this to the Chief first thing in the morning I'd better get going."

Relieved Steve had left it at that, Grant stood and walked him to the door.

"Do you think the Chief will go along with what we're proposing?" Grant asked as they walked down his drive to Steve's car.

"The Chief's a good guy. He may not like the idea of a multiple murderer, but when push comes to shove, he'll have your back. Don't let his laid-back demeanor fool you. He may be good at playing the political game, but he would never allow it to take precedence over solving a case. He's still one of us."

As he was talking Steve glanced across the street to his sister's apartment building and his eyebrows drew down with concern when he noted that her lights were still on. He knew that Maggie tended to be a night owl, but 2:30 in the morning was late even for her.

"Looks like Maggie's still up," Grant said as he, too, looked up at the lighted windows.

Turning to face Grant, Steve's eyes narrowed as he said, "Look, Grant, Maggie's going through a kinda tough time right now. She just broke up with the asshole she was dating and she doesn't need to deal with anyone else right now."

"As a big brother, I get why you're saying this, but you have nothing to worry about from me."

After a short pause Steve grinned and said, "She turned you down, huh?"

"Yep."

"Are you going to try again?"

"Yep. Is that going to be a problem for you?"

Sighing, Steve ran a hand through his mussed hair, "She's my baby sister. I don't want to see her hurt again. I don't know exactly *what* happened between her and that prick bastard, but she's more hurt than she lets on."

Steve paced back and forth as he spoke, "And, she won't tell me what happened, oh, no. Says it's none of my business. Frickin' *blackmails* me to keep me from doing anything about it. I mean, she's my sister, so *of course* she's my business, right?"

Grant opened his mouth to reply but Steve continued without pausing, "Not according to her—oh, no, she's a grown up. She can handle *anything*. I'm a big overprotective ape. She expects me to simply sit back and watch her get hurt, is that right?"

When Grant stayed silent, an amused grin on his face, Steve turned on him, "Well. *Is* it?"

"Uh…"

"Of *course* it's not right. Jesus, Evans back me up here."

Holding back a laugh Grant replied dryly, "I don't know where she got the idea that you were an overprotective ape, you seem completely reasonable to me."

When Steve glared at him Grant laughed and held up both hands in surrender. "Seriously, Steve, I can understand why you are upset. Any asshole hurt my little sister like that and I'd be upset, too. But Maggie seems to be handling things better than you give her credit for."

When Steve opened his mouth again, Grant simply talked over him, "Maggie strikes me as very confident and capable of handling just about any guy—I mean it seems to me that she handled you and presumably your three other brothers as well. What makes you think she can't handle any guy—even an asshole—without breaking a sweat?"

Steve had stopped pacing and stood leaning against the car, a thoughtful look on his face.

"Besides," Grant went on calmly, "She seemed more embarrassed and upset than truly hurt to me when she mentioned the creep. In fact, she seemed more concerned about handling you and the rest of her brothers than the asshole."

Almost as an afterthought Grant continued, his face darkening, "I got the distinct impression she dumped him unexpectedly, and that can only mean one or two things."

Fresh fury leapt onto Steve's face and his hands clenched into fists. As he turned to march across the street to *demand* an explanation from Maggie Grant grabbed his arm.

"You'll just piss her off, and probably wake her up, if you go charging over there now."

Turning back abruptly, Steve opened his mouth to rip into Grant when he took a close look at the banked fury that matched—perhaps even surpassed—his own in Grant's eyes. The look gave him pause and calmed Steve down long enough to think. A quick pain pierced his heart before he grinned, openly amused.

"It's that way is it?"

Now it was Grant's turn to spin away and pace furiously. When he simply glared at Steve, Steve dropped his head back and laughed, tucking his hands into his jeans pockets.

Delighted humor sounded in Steve's voice as he said, "Well, you seem to understand her, at least about this situation. And, you're smart enough not to let *her* know how you feel about it"

"Why would I do that? It would just tick her off."

Steve's voice turned serious as he added, "Take care of her. I'd hate to have to kill you."

Steve grinned once more and hopped into the car to drive away. "See you bright and early, partner."

"Fine," Grant spit out in exasperation, "That's just fine."

Grant watched as Steve pulled away before his eyes were drawn upwards once again to Maggie's windows. Standing there for several minutes, he watched as the lights in her apartment turned off one by one before he turned to go inside to collapse.

"Whole family's more trouble than it's worth," he muttered grumpily to himself as he undressed and climbed into bed.

What he couldn't understand was how any of them could matter as much as they seemed to matter to him so quickly.

Grant turned and punched his pillow twice before closing his eyes. When Maggie's smiling face appeared before his closed eyes he sighed deeply and muttered, "Shit. You are in *so* much trouble, Evans." before he dropped off into a deep, exhausted sleep.

FOURTEEN

Across the street Maggie lay in bed, unable to fall to sleep. Despite a fairly typical day of work Maggie could not get the fact that another young woman was not able to toss and turn sleeplessly out of her mind.

She hadn't known Jessie Daniels, but Maggie knew several people who had—including Tony. Maggie would never forget the look on Tony's face when they had told him the news.

Cloë had come back from lunch looking distressed, having heard the news that a woman had been killed violently. Although the news report she'd seen had not released the name of the victim, Cloë had run into a friend who worked at the station and found out who had died.

Maggie had been shocked when Cloë had told her some of the details her friend had divulged. She was still struggling to process the information when Tony had walked into the office.

As he walked in the door Cloë turned away from Maggie and asked, "Have you heard the terrible news yet, Tony?"

"No. What's going on?" Tony looked from Cloë to Maggie and back to Cloë. His look of unconcern slipped slowly from his face when he took in the looks on the women's faces.

"Jessie Daniels was found murdered in her apartment this morning."

Tony sat abruptly in one of the guest chairs in front of Maggie's desk before he managed to stutter, "M-murdered? Jessie? But, how? Why?"

"I don't know all the details yet; just that someone broke into her apartment and strangled her in her bedroom. I guess there was a terrible scene," Cloë trailed off, her large eyes bright in her too-pale face.

"Did you know her?" Maggie asked Tony, her tone gentle.

Tony stared at the floor and nodded silently. Maggie knelt down next to his chair and placed her hand on his arm. "Tony, are you going to be okay? Do you need to go home?"

Tony shook his head as if to clear it and looked blankly into Maggie's eyes. "N-no. I'll be okay, Maggie. Thanks." When Tony continued to stare at the floor Maggie's eyes met Cloë's, both at a loss as to how to handle the distraught man.

Cloë filled a glass of water and brought it to Tony, wrapping his hands around the cup. "Now you drink that, Tony," she said softly and patted his knee.

Maggie stood up and said, "I'm going to go find Holden, Tony. He can give you a lift home."

After searching unsuccessfully for Holden in his office and classroom, Maggie had ended up driving Tony home herself. As they sat in front of his apartment building Maggie turned off the engine and turned to face him.

"Tony, if there's anything that we can do to help you out, just let me know. Take as much time as you need, okay?"

Tony nodded and quickly turned to grasp her hands tightly causing Maggie to gasp in surprise. "Maggie, it means *so* much to me that you *really* care." Tony leaned forward to kiss her and Maggie jerked her hands from him, using them to press against his chest.

"Tony, I'm sorry. I *do* care about you, really," Maggie stopped abruptly, appalled at the stark joy that spread across his face and quickly added as kindly as possible, "But, Tony, I only think of you as a friend."

When Tony simply stared at her, the joy gone from his face and his brows drawn down in a scowl Maggie leaned back and swallowed, keeping her eyes on his.

"Well, don't do me no favors, Maggie," Tony spit out, slamming his fist into the dashboard making Maggie jump. With an oath he turned to grab the door handle.

"Tony," Maggie said in a quiet voice and reached out to grasp his arm, pushing away the hurt his response had caused. Tony jerked away from her touch, turning once more to glare at her before he rushed out of the car, slamming the door in his wake.

Stunned, Maggie watched his quickly retreating form before she turned and reached with shaking hands to start the car. The sheer intensity of Tony's anger had shaken Maggie to her core. She'd always believed that Tony was a sweet, shy guy, and would never have believed that he had so much violence in him.

Hours later Maggie still couldn't reconcile the Tony she'd thought she'd known with the angry, hurt man who had scared her that afternoon. Resigned to the fact that she wasn't going to be falling to sleep anytime soon, Maggie pulled herself out of bed with a huff and expelled a long sigh.

She trudged through the darkened living room and made her way to the kitchen, turning on lights as she went. She eyed the full fruit bowl on her counter and, with a roll of her eyes, walked past it to pull open the freezer to grab her emergency stash of her mom's homemade cookies. It was lucky she'd been at her parents' house that weekend otherwise the freezer would have been empty.

Maggie grabbed two cookies from the bag and crossed to snuggle down in the large oversized armchair she had positioned by the front window of her apartment. As she settled in to enjoy her treat, Maggie noticed Steven's beat up work car parked in front of Grant's lit up house.

Well, it doesn't take a rocket scientist to figure out why they were up at almost one in the morning, Maggie thought to herself. Clearly they were working on finding the monster that had murdered Jessie Daniels.

Knowing Steven, they would succeed.

Grant struck her as someone who would not give up easily, either. She prayed that they would find the killer soon—it made her uneasy to think that someone in Hope was capable of such a vicious crime.

Hope wasn't without violent crimes, but something about this one was freaking her out. When Cloë had described what she'd heard about the murder, all the hairs on Maggie's neck had stood on end.

Maggie shuddered as she remembered. Forcing the dark thoughts out of her mind again, she sprang up out of the chair—she was trying to *forget* about this stuff, not dwell on it.

Obviously, this was a four cookie situation.

Maggie grabbed two more cookies and sat back down to read a trashy historical romance novel with a bare-chested man in a kilt kissing a scantily clad peasant woman on its cover. If chocolate and sex couldn't help, nothing would.

113

An hour and a half later the sound of a door closing and a car starting woke her. Maggie stood and stretched before she stooped to pick the book she'd been reading up off the floor from where it had fallen. Maggie turned off the lights, collapsed into bed and immediately sank back to sleep.

And, as she slept she dreamed of a bare-chested man holding her close and sweeping her off her feet, carrying her up a long curving staircase lit by candles in sconces that cast flickering shadows on the walls.

As he placed her on a huge four-poster bed Maggie stared up into deep chocolate brown eyes in a dangerous face. His firm sculpted mouth grinned and descended to ravish her mouth, and when he drew back, the face was Grant's. As he lowered, he pressed her body deep into the lush bedding and gently framed her face with his strong hands.

Slowly his rough hands swept down her hair and neck to caress her breasts causing them to ache and her nipples to tighten under his expert administrations. She moaned and shifted under him sweeping her hands up his broad back to tangle in his tousled hair.

He trailed soft kisses along her jaw line and returned to capture her mouth with his. Their tongues twined as his hands stroked up her slim torso and returned to brush feather soft strokes along her collar bone and around her neck, slowly closing to circle the pale column where her heartbeat fluttered desperately against his palms.

Moans of passion faded to screams as his hands tightened and tightened. Her eyes flew open. Her fingers grasped desperately, uselessly at his hands as her vision darkened. He laughed cruelly, and when she blinked again he is transformed into Tony.

Maggie jerked awake, her heart thundering and her hands reached up to grasp at her throat, while she looked desperately around. Finding herself back in the familiarity of her bedroom her hands dropped limply down onto the tangled bedding and Maggie closed her eyes, swearing shakily under her breath. She brushed still-damp curls away from her face and swung her legs over the side of the bed. Glancing at the clock Maggie noted that it was 5:17.

"Damn."

There was no way she'd get back to sleep again. Maggie sighed deeply and stood on unstable legs to walk into the bathroom to splash some cold water on her face.

Maggie stared into the mirror and saw too-dark eyes staring out from her pale face. She squared her shoulders and said, "Get a grip, Maggie. It was only a dream."

I guess that's what you get for eating cookies in the middle of the night, Maggie thought, and walked back into the bedroom to lay back down, but the sight of the twisted sheets stopped her just inside the doorway. There was *no* way she was going to be able to force herself to get back in.

Resigned to being up for the day Maggie dragged on her running clothes and headed out to sweat off the last of the horror of the dream—and the four cookies she'd eaten the night before.

It was going to be a long day.

FIFTEEN

Two hours later Maggie and Grant both stepped out of their front doors at the same time. They stopped, eyes locked for a long moment, the space between them seeming to heat the cool morning air.

Grant grinned and Maggie smiled back automatically as her stomach leaped and dipped.

"Hi, Neighbor," Grant said, his deep voice carrying across the street and sending a shiver of awareness up Maggie's spine.

"Hi, Grant. You're getting an early start this morning."

"You, too."

"Couldn't sleep," Maggie replied breathlessly.

Grant looked her over from the tips of her stylish brown leather boots and ankle length dark green suede skirt past her soft yellow sweater and brown fitted jacket to her softly curling hair pulled back in a tail at her neck. Even from across the street, Grant noted the dark shadows beneath her dark hazel eyes and the pallor beneath her makeup, but only said, "Me either."

When Grant continued to stare at her, Maggie shifted her large brown leather bag up on her shoulder and brushed a stray curl back from her face.

"Well. I better get going," she murmured. When she simply stood on the step Grant felt another grin lifting his mouth.

As she stood frozen to her top step Maggie was also taking stock of the man who had become so familiar to her in such a short time. He was dressed in a crisp black suit and rich brick red shirt that fit his tall frame and set off his dark looks perfectly.

When she finally lifted her eyes and caught the grin and knowing look in his eyes Maggie blushed and practically ran down the stairs to where her car was parked at the curb.

Mortified—again—she grabbed for the door handle and started when Grant's hand closed over hers. Maggie's head whipped up to find him standing right behind her. They locked eyes again.

Jeez he smelled good, Maggie thought and started to lean forward into him before she caught herself and jerked her hand away as if burned.

"You're in my way, Evans," Maggie ground out, her eyes shooting sparks of indignation at him.

Amused at the anger he heard in her voice Grant *just* managed to hold back another grin. Taking another half step forward he backed her into the car and placed a hand on either side of her, boxing her in neatly.

Fury lit her eyes and Maggie opened her mouth to reply scathingly but Grant simply leaned in and captured her mouth as quickly and smoothly as he'd crossed the street to reach her.

Every thought in Maggie's mind vanished. The hands she'd raised to push him away gripped helplessly, then urgently, at his shoulders. He angled his head slightly, deepening the kiss then sliding his lips over hers to brush tiny kisses on either side of her mouth before recapturing her lips and diving in.

The thunder of her heart deafened her for a long moment and a bolt of pure lust lanced through her system, almost buckling her knees. Maggie heard a low moan, and for a long moment didn't realize that she had made it.

Grant pulled back reluctantly, giving her one last kiss before putting some space between them. His hands remained gripped painfully on her car—he knew if he touched her now, even once, he'd have her. No matter that they were standing outside on a public street for the whole world to see.

Maggie gradually realized though Grant was not touching her, that she was clinging to him and dropped her arms to her sides to lean weakly back against the car. Her blind eyes focused and she looked up into eyes so darkened with passion they looked black.

Taking a steadying breath, she briefly closed her eyes to block the sight before she forced herself to meet the heat of his gaze again.

"Well," she said shakily, "That was…hmmm…"

Grinning once again, Grant relaxed enough to release the car and grab her hands. "Maggie. See me tonight," he demanded.

"But…"

"No. No buts, Maggie. See me tonight," Grant said, looking intently down at her befuddled expression.

Maggie stared up into his confident, smiling face and knew she didn't have the willpower to refuse—and if she was going to be completely honest with herself, she didn't want to.

"All right. What time?"

Grant's grin turned into a blinding smile and he replied, "Seven?"

"Okay. Seven. Where?"

"I'll pick you up at your apartment."

"All right."

Grant leaned close and firmly kissed her before he released her hands and strode back across the street to climb into his SUV. Maggie watched him back out of his garage onto the street and drive away before she simply dropped into her car.

For several minutes, Maggie sat there, waiting for her heart rate to drop back down to normal, and for her hands to stop shaking. *What were you thinking?* she thought and banged her head down onto the steering wheel.

"Nothing. Absolutely nothing," she muttered, "How's a girl supposed to *think* when tall, dark and dangerous is blowing the top of your head off?"

Maggie rolled her eyes at herself, then, on second thought, reached up to make sure that the top of her head *was* intact. She'd read that phrase in romance novels before and always scoffed at its use, but she could actually understand what the characters in those books were describing after kissing Grant Evans. Letting out a huge breath she reached out and started the car.

Blocking all thoughts of how stupid it would be to even think about getting involved with someone only a week after breaking up with Bradley Maggie turned on the radio and blasted it.

Instead, she focused on how amazingly *good* it had felt to let go and enjoy herself—even if it was only for a few short moments. A wide grin played across her face and Maggie pictured Grant's beautiful mouth as it had looked just moments before—delicious, dangerous.

Maggie glanced down at the clock on the dash and swore. She was going to be late again.

It had totally been worth it.

Even thinking about how much trouble she could be in for being late for the hundredth time this month couldn't diminish the smile that spread across her face.

Yes, it had totally been worth it. But just in case, she'd stop for coffee.

SIXTEEN

When Grant swung through the station door in his dark suit he sent a blinding smile and a cheerful "Good Morning, Ms. Shirley, Officer Jones" over to where Mrs. Larson sat talking with the sharp looking redhead Steve had told him was Officer Bethany Jones. Both women's eyebrows raised and both smiled at his quickly retreating back.

Momentarily struck dumb the women turned back to face each other, a bemused look on their faces. Bethany rolled her eyes and Shirley fanned her face and said, "I swear that boy could melt ice he's so hot."

"Shirley!" Bethany exclaimed, laughing.

"What?" Shirley asked and leaned forward to pat Bethany's hand, "I may not be in the first bloom of youth, my dear, but I haven't withered and dried up just yet."

Bethany just laughed again and shook her head before she asked, "What were you saying?"

"I was just letting you know that the Chief has set up a duty list for the funeral on Friday. It's up on the board."

All traces of humor gone, Bethany said, "All right. Thanks, Shirley."

"Such a shame. Jessie was such a sweet girl. I go to church with her grandmother, Mabel Stuart, and she's absolutely distraught."

"Do you know her parents, too?" Bethany asked.

"I know her mother, Rosemary, she lives here in town. Her father lives in the Cities—they divorced several years back. Apparently he was seeing someone on the side," Shirley had lowered her voice conspiratorially, tutting softly and shaking her head again. "Anyway, Rose would have let it go, but Mabel wouldn't let her. She talked Rose into filing for divorce. Mabel says they haven't seen hide nor hair of him since he moved away six years ago."

"Didn't he ever come back to see his daughter?"

"Never. He had a *terrible* temper, and he threatened Mabel—he blamed her for talking Rose into getting the divorce— and even destroyed some of Mabel's prize rose bushes. He hacked them up with garden shears the night before he left town. Not that they ever caught him, but Mabel *knew* that it was him that had done it." Shirley shuddered once before continuing, "He never forgave Mabel or Rose and refused to even discuss anything with them. He gave up custody of Jessie and refused to talk to her or meet with her. I guess he said something about her taking her mother's side and betraying him. I'm telling you, the man was crazy."

"Do Evans and Sullivan know about this?"

"I don't know. Do you think I should say something to them? It happened an awful long time ago," Shirley said, a troubled look on her face.

Bethany nodded sharply and said, "Absolutely. Every detail in a murder investigation is important and it may be pertinent to their case. Some of the smallest details have broken cases, and this is one case that needs a break."

Alarmed, Shirley said, "I'll make sure I tell Detective Sullivan as soon as possible. He's meeting with the Chief and Detective Evans right now, and they don't want any interruptions."

"I think that's a good idea. Don't wait too long, Shirley. Every hour counts at the beginning of an investigation."

McKenzie walked in the door, nodded at Bethany and headed straight to his desk. With a tired sigh Bethany said, "Well, I have a stack of paperwork and about a dozen interviews I need to transpose waiting on my desk. I better get in gear." Smiling grimly, she turned and headed over to where McKenzie was slinging a black leather jacket over the back of his chair.

"Morning, Mac. How's it hangin'?"

"Good Morning, Jones. I see you're as charming as ever this fine morning. When are you going to start acting like a lady?" McKenzie asked, a twinkle in his dark eyes.

"Why, when you start acting like a gentleman, Mac," Bethany sang out sweetly, a wicked gleam in her eye and a sharp smile on her face.

McKenzie's booming laugh filled the squad room, and both officers sat down to begin their day.

Behind Chief Banyon's closed door Grant and Steve sat facing the Chief over several open files and a stack of grisly crime scene photographs. Clad in faded denim pants, a crisp white dress shirt and a black bolo tie, the Chief rested his elbows on the desk staring intently at Grant over steepled fingers. A dark brown blazer hung from the coat rack behind him.

Chief Banyon said, "Explain again why you feel it's necessary to bring some stranger into our investigation."

Grant had known that it was a long shot that the Chief would let them do what he had proposed to Steve the night before, but he couldn't quite stop the feeling of disappointment from filling him when he heard the antagonism in Chief Banyon's voice. He'd really wanted this new chief to be supportive and open to his ideas. Instead, it looked like the Chief was simply another political appointee more obsessed with keeping his job than in doing it correctly.

Grant sighed quietly and began, "Look, Chief Banyon..."

"Chief," Steve cut Grant off and gave him a quelling look before he turned to face their boss, "Chief, we've spent most of the past twenty-four hours looking at these murders, and we think that it's undeniable that all three are connected. Evans has had experience on a case like this in Seattle. I trust his judgment, Chief," Steve ended quietly, his eyes never veering away from Chief Banyon's steady blue gaze.

Chief Banyon was pleased to see that his opinions about the two men sitting across from him were right on and that it had been the right thing to pair them up, but he still had doubts.

"Steve, I respect that you are convinced, and that goes a long way with me, but we're not just talking about me. I, and to an extent, you, have to answer to the Mayor and to the people of Hope. I admit that what you've presented me with here is extremely compelling. But I have to know what experience you base these conclusions on, Evans. There's nothing in your jacket that mentions a psychology degree or specific training to deal with these situations. I need more than just your opinion to back up these conclusions, no matter how persuasive they may be."

"Fair enough, Chief," Evans said before he continued, "You're right, I only worked one serial case, and I was really only one of a large number of local law enforcement tasked with assisting the Feds—taking statements, verifying timelines, running background checks—you know the millions of details there are on every case, and the bastard we were after had butchered more than a dozen young women before the connections were made."

Grant paused, lost in memories and rubbed the back of his neck before he continued, "I got to know a couple of the fibbies, went out for a few beers with Ralph—Special Agent Ralph Finney—a profiler. He and I discussed the case, how he worked, how he got into the work, how he got into the minds of monsters. He recommended some good books on the subject. You'd be surprised how much you can learn from books.

"I also convinced my old boss to let me go to a seminar put on by the FBI that focused on identifying some of the basic characteristics of serial killers. But, more importantly, they discussed police procedures that can be used in local departments to identify, catch, and successfully prosecute these killers.

"Look, I'm not claiming to be an expert, that's why we're asking for your okay on this. We need to get our theory confirmed—or denounced—by someone who *is* an expert. The agent I want to send it to, Agent Finney, would do it for me if I gave him a call, and he would keep it quiet if I asked him."

"All right. Get in touch with your contact at the FBI and see if he can *quietly* take a look at the case files to give us some kind of opinion as to whether or not this is the same guy. And, if possible, if we can get some type of working profile to use.

"But, until we get some kind of official verification that your hunch is correct I want the cases worked both ways—as individual cases, and as a single case—so that we cover all our bases."

"You got it, Chief," Steve said. "Who do you want working the case with us?"

"Take Simmons, Donovan, Jones, and McKenzie and start looking at everything again with the idea that a single perp has committed all three crimes. I'll handle the press," Chief Banyon paused and smoothed back his hair, "But I want absolutely no leak of the word serial—don't even *think* the word—until this is confirmed."

Chief Banyon rubbed a weary hand over his forehead and continued, "If your contact does confirm it, I have no problem calling in anyone and everyone who can help us catch this son-of-a-bitch. Any questions?"

Steve shook his head no and Grant looked down for a moment before he lifted his head to meet Chief Banyon's direct blue gaze.

"Thanks, Chief. Thanks for listening, and for believing," Grant said quietly.

"Don't thank me yet, son. I'm still not one hundred percent convinced you're right, but I can't take the chance that you *are*. These women deserve better, and I shudder to contemplate what could happen if we ignore any connection and he kills again."

"All right, Chief," Grant replied, "I appreciate you listening."

Chief Banyon nodded once and turned to answer his intercom when Mrs. Larson beeped through.

"Sorry to interrupt, Chief, but Mayor Grady is on line one. He's called four times already and he's demanding to speak with you at once."

Grinning briefly at the put upon tone of his receptionist's voice Chief Banyon replied, "All right Shirley—it's okay. I'll take care of it."

Letting go of the intercom button, Chief Banyon turned to face the two detectives again and said, "What are you waiting for, gentlemen? Get moving. I can stall Grady for a short while, but he's been calling looking for answers since Jessie Daniels's body was found."

"We're on it, Chief," Steve stood while Grant gathered up the case files and both men walked out of the office. As they crossed the squad room Steve called out to the officers he passed by on the way to his desk, "Rusty, Donovan, Jones, and Mac, I need you guys in the Big Room in fifteen minutes."

Grant watched silently as all four officers nodded their acknowledgement to Steve before they began wrapping up whatever they were working on.

"The Big Room?" Grant asked.

"Yeah, the large conference room behind the Chief's office," Steve answered distractedly while shuffling through his phone messages. Throwing the stack of messages back down on his blotter, Steve heaved a big sigh and dropped into his chair before he asked bluntly, "Can you call your guy now, or do you need to wait until after hours?"

Grant dropped the case files onto his desk and sat facing Steve. "No, I'll call him right away. The sooner he can get a look at these," he tapped one finger on the stack of files, "the better."

"Great. While you do that I'll get Shirley started on making a copy of all the case files to send out."

Grant grinned sheepishly and pulled a large padded manila envelope marked "urgent" from his desk drawer. It was already addressed to Special Agent Ralph Finney, 935 Pennsylvania Ave, NW, Washington, DC 20535. "I got here early, and put it together hoping the Chief would give us the okay."

"And if he hadn't?"

"Then, I'd have crossed that bridge when I came to it," Grant replied evenly.

Steve looked at Grant for a long moment before he reached under a pile of loose papers on his desk and pulled out a completely filled-out form requisitioning the case files from records and another stating the reason he would be copying said files.

"I stopped by on my way home last night," Steve said and shrugged.

Grant leaned back in his chair and grinned over at Steve. As he bent forward to grab the phone receiver, Grant said, "Why don't you get started filling in the guys? This won't take long, and then I'll be in."

Steve agreed and grabbed the files and headed to the Big Room to get started while Grant punched in his friend's number. He heard the phone ring twice and then a voice answered.

"Finney."

"Ralph? It's Grant Evans."

"Grant! How the hell are you? You're living in Michigan now, right?" Ralph boomed over the line.

"I'm doing fine, and it's Minnesota."

"I knew it was one of those cold ones in the middle. Man, it's good to hear your voice," Ralph's voice turned serious, "You had me worried for a while there, Grant. How are you doing, really?"

"Actually, I'm doing good. Jake and I are loving small town life so far. I bought a house, I'm back on the job. Things are going great."

His voice uncertain, Ralph asked, "You're sure?"

"Jesus, Finney, what are you, my mother? I'm *fine*. How are Abby and the kids?"

Taking his cue Ralph went along with the change of subject, "They're great. Abby's back teaching and the kids are in school. Ethan got his license a couple of weeks ago and Abby and I have been praying for the general public every night since. Christine is in the school play and is dating an eighteen year old."

Grant held back a laugh and asked, "So, how's his record?"

"Clean."

"I bet she loves having Daddy check up on her."

"What, do you think I'm an idiot? She has no idea I did it, and I don't ever want her to find out!"

Grant coughed to cover up his laugh, but Ralph heard it. "Laugh it up, Evans. Someday it will be *your* little girl going out with some slick, randy teenage boy and you'll be taking your gun out to clean when he comes to pick her up."

"You're probably right."

"Well, I know you didn't call to discuss my misery over Christine's dating life, so what's up?"

"I need a favor."

Instantly serious Ralph said, "Go on."

"I'm working a case and I think that it may be tied to two others, but I'm not sure. My boss wants more than my lowly opinion before we take things further, so I was wondering if you had the time to look over the cases and give me your opinion."

"I'm guessing since you're asking me directly that this isn't an official FBI request?"

"Not at this time."

"Okay. I can take a look if you send me the case files. But if you want an accurate profile, I'm going to need everything—crime scene photos, toxicology reports, autopsy reports, interviews, everything you've got."

"Not a problem. I can get you a copy of everything by tomorrow."

"It might take me a few days to get to your guy, but I promise I'll be keeping an eye out for it."

"I really appreciate it, Ralph. Thanks, Man."

"No problem. Just promise me one thing."

"What's that?"

"Don't wait another six months to call, okay?"

Grant chuckled and replied, "I think I can give you that promise. I really appreciate your help on this one. Give Abby my love."

"You got it. I'll be in touch."

After making sure the package would be sent out that day Grant made his way into the conference room.

As he walked into the spacious room Grant noted the soft green walls and muted carpet. Like the rest of the station, the room was far more inviting than any he'd previously seen in other stations.

In the center of the room was a large conference table surrounded by at least a dozen chairs, four of which were occupied with officers listening intently to Steve. Steve stood in front of a large dry erase board outlining the details they'd discussed in the Chief's office earlier that morning.

As he made his way around the table Grant caught Steve's eye and nodded when Steve raised a questioning eyebrow. Grant leaned against the back wall and crossed his arms, letting his thoughts wander as Steve began to flesh out the three cases and how they were connected.

With no effort at all, Grant found his thoughts turning to Maggie and their kiss that morning. Without even trying, he could taste her intoxicating flavor on his tongue—warm and darkly rich. As he pictured the sweet, innocent look of confusion on her face—a direct contrast to the flare of passion he had seen burning in her eyes when they had pulled apart—the desire he had managed to bank that morning flared to life again as he thought of the many ways in which he wanted to break her control, to release her hidden desires, to make love to her as he had been dreaming of doing since he'd first laid eyes on her.

If he thought about her long enough, Grant could recall exactly how she smelled—like lavender and vanilla with something deeper, more elemental, underneath. He could remember exactly how she felt pressed against him and could hear the tiny whimpers she'd let out when she'd finally surrendered completely.

With a start Grant was pulled back to the present in time to hear Mac's deep rumble of a voice ask Steve a question and, shaken,

Grant returned his attention back to the meeting. *What in the name of holy hell was wrong with him?*, he thought, shocked at the direction his thoughts had taken. He had no time to daydream like some lovesick boy with a crush.

Grant straightened against the wall, letting his arms fall to his sides and walked around the table to join Steve in front of the officers. It was time to focus on his job.

He would focus on Maggie later tonight.

SEVENTEEN

By the time six-o-clock rolled around Maggie was more than ready to be headed home. Not only had she been late to work that morning, but Tony had emailed rather than called to let her know he wouldn't be coming in. On top of that, Holden had been a bear all day. He'd rearranged his entire week's lectures, and in the process, made about thirty hours of work she, Cloë, and Tony had done the week before useless. As a result, she'd been forced to scramble to find everything he would need for his new topic in time for his classes.

If that hadn't been enough, Bradley had called three times and had actually caught her the last time he'd called because she'd been so distracted she'd not been paying attention.

Maggie blew out an exasperated sigh and shut down her computer. She stacked the files she'd need first thing in the morning neatly on her desktop and thought back over the brief conversation she'd had with her ex.

When Maggie had answered the phone and heard Bradley's haughty voice on the line, she had simply closed her eyes and sat back in her chair. *How could I have ever thought his voice was distinguished*, had been her last frivolous thought.

"Hello, Margaret."

"Bradley"

"It's about time you talked to me. I have called several times before this, Margaret, and your childish behavior is really quite inappropriate."

Stunned at his *gall*, Maggie had sat there fuming in silence, which he had taken as embarrassed agreement. Encouraged to continue he had said, "I really don't appreciate your attitude about this entire unfortunate situation, Margaret. However, we do need to sit down to discuss this in person. I understand you were shocked at my little indiscretion with Trixie the other day, but I'm sure we can work this out satisfactorily."

"*Little*...Your *little* indiscretion?" Maggie sputtered faintly.

Bradley continued as if she had not spoken, "I've taken the liberty of making reservations for us at 7:30 tonight. Wear

129

something nice—maybe the black cocktail dress I picked out for that client's dinner last spring..."

"Excuse me," Maggie interrupted loudly, her voice higher than usual, "Did you just refer to you *screwing* your slut of a secretary in your office in front of me as a 'little indiscretion'?"

"I don't appreciate that tone, Margaret, and I can hardly believe you are using such vulgar language in the workplace. Now calm yourself down. We can discuss any problems calmly and rationally over a nice meal tonight."

Struck dumb again, Maggie had actually pulled the phone away from her ear to look at it before putting it back to her mouth and said as calmly and rationally as she could, "Go screw yourself, Bradley," before she had hung up.

Thankfully, everyone she worked with had been out of the office for classes or lunch and hadn't overheard the disastrous conversation with Bradley.

Even now, more than six hours later, Maggie could still feel her face flame with anger at the idea that that brainless moron had actually believed she would forgive and forget. Truly, she couldn't understand why she'd ever thought he could possibly be someone she could love.

No. That's not true, she thought. *You wanted someone successful, someone take-charge, to do all the work in the relationship for once.* She'd wanted to feel completely feminine, and Brad had taken control and romanced her from the start.

Inwardly cringing, Maggie thought about the many times in which she'd ignored the signs that were warning her that something was wrong—from the simple ways, like how Brad had constantly suggested how she dress or wear her hair—the way he'd done on the phone earlier—to the more important ways, like how he was always coming up with reasons to not come with her to different family functions.

If she were completely, and painfully, honest with herself, no one in her family had ever really liked him. Oh, sure, her parents had always been polite and gracious, but all four of her brothers had made comments to her about him. Steven had actively disliked him.

She'd ignored them, telling herself that they just didn't like him because he was too different, too sophisticated, for her brothers to really understand.

They fished and hunted, loved football and beer—Bradley had loved opera and theater, fine wine and classical music. With no common ground it had not surprised her that her brothers and Bradley hadn't become close friends.

And, in the end, it had been simpler, and more comfortable, for Maggie to attend family events by herself, to make excuses for Bradley to her family.

As she grabbed her purse and jacket and headed out of the office, the image of Grant standing and laughing with her father and brothers popped into her mind. Followed by the memory of the way her mother had gushed about how thoughtful and sweet Grant had been to bring a gift.

Maggie smiled to herself and locked the office door. As she stowed her keys in her purse she turned to find a man standing just a few feet behind her. Maggie jumped, stifling a scream and pressed a hand to her heart.

"Mo. You startled me. I didn't hear you come up behind me," Maggie said breathlessly.

"Sorry, Miss Sullivan. I did say hello a couple a times but you didn't hear me. Everything okay?" Moses' face crinkled in a look of concern, his dark eyes questioning.

"Yes," Maggie smiled, "It was just a long day. Thankfully it's over now," she replied, her voice steady again. "You're in early today."

"I've been working different hours lately to be home more often with my mother," he said.

"She's no better?" Maggie asked, her voice filled with sympathy.

"No. The sickness just won't go away, and doctors said it wouldn't be too long—a matter of weeks, maybe months now, so we're taking care of her at home now."

"We?"

"My little brother, Abe, is home from college to help out."

"I'm so sorry, Moses, but I'm glad your brother is able to help out. Is there anything I can do?" Maggie asked and reached out

131

to place her hand on one of his work-roughed hands where it gripped the handle of a large push broom.

"Just keep praying."

"I will. Good night, Mo."

"Night, Miss."

As Maggie walked away, she thought of how terrible it would be if her own mother were dying, and immediately decided that she would put together a casserole and some cookies to bring over to Mo's house. They wouldn't make up for the fact that his mother was dying, but at least he wouldn't have to worry about dinner for one night.

As she walked up to her car, she glanced down at her watch and swore. If she was going to be ready for dinner with Grant by seven, she'd better get moving.

EIGHTEEN

Dinner was on Grant's mind as well. After hours of going over interview transcripts and making hundreds of phone calls, the case was not any further than it had been when he'd walked through the door of the station—unless you counted eliminating the only likely suspects they had.

There were still several avenues of investigation that were ongoing, but the phone call he'd just completed had confirmed their primary suspect's alibi and eliminated their best hope of quickly closing their investigation.

Jessie Daniel's father was in the clear.

After hearing Mrs. Larson's story that morning he and Steve had spent much of the day running down the people involved and interviewing them. While the story had been confirmed, in the end it was clear that the father—Greg Daniels—had been out of state at a convention the night his estranged daughter had been murdered.

"Daniels is in the clear," Grant said when Steve walked back to his desk.

"The hotel manager was sure it was Daniels? He confirmed he was there?" Steve asked.

"Oh, yeah. It seems Mr. Daniels got a little lit up the last night of the convention and busted up one of the hotel's bars when he punched out another attendee—a Mr. James Oliver, whom I also spoke with. According to the manager, the two were fighting over a football game and things got physical. Daniels had to pay for the damages."

"Well, I guess that's that. Anything else come in while I was gone?" Steve asked.

"Nothing. Jones and McKenzie are still running down the last of the people who said they saw someone in the neighborhood that morning. Simmons and Donovan are wrapping up the interviews of the apartment inhabitants.

"I pulled the investigation report on the fire bombing in the apartment downstairs from Ms. Daniel's apartment," Pausing, Grant held up a small file, "Do you want to go over it tomorrow?"

"Sounds good," Steve said and started to shut down his computer, "Interested in grabbing a beer and some dinner over at O'Neil's tonight?"

"I'd love to, but I've already got dinner plans tonight," Grant said and sat back watching Steve closely.

Surprised, Steve's eyebrows flew up and he asked, "Oh. Is it one of the guys? Just bring him along."

"It's not one of the guys."

"What, do you have a hot date?" Steve asked with a wicked gleam in his eyes.

When Grant didn't reply Steve grinned, leaned his chair back on two legs, and prepared to roast his new friend.

"Jeez, Evans you've been in town, what, less than three weeks? And you've already got a live one? Where'd ya meet her? You've spent almost every waking hour working on your house or with me."

When Grant still didn't reply Steve's grin slowly faded.

"Actually, Steve, I asked Maggie out."

With a thud, Steve's chair fell to the floor. "Maggie? *My* Maggie?"

"Yes," Grant replied and waited for the reaction that could cement—or destroy—not only his working relationship with Steve, but the first, and best, new friendship he'd had in years.

"But, I thought she turned you down," Steve said and Grant had to smile at the genuine bewilderment he heard in Steve's voice.

Laughing, Grant said, "She *did* turn me down, but we've run into each other a couple times since then, and, I don't know, Steve, we just clicked. I asked her again and she said yes."

At a loss for words Steve blew out a long sigh and ran his hand through his hair.

"Steve, I know you've been worried about her lately but it's just one dinner. I'm not looking to hurt her," Grant said quietly and held his partner's gaze for a long moment before he added, "You can trust me not to be careless with her."

Steve was silent for another moment before he seemed to come to a conclusion. He nodded and gave Grant a half smile before saying, "You realize that if you *do* hurt her I will have to seriously kick your ass, right?"

When he heard the humor in his friend's voice Grant laughed, relieved that the tense moment seemed to be over. "I know. If you hadn't threatened me at least once, you'd have been derelict in your brotherly duties."

Steve let out a bark of laughter before he motioned to the pile of paperwork still stacked in front of Grant, "I'll take care of the rest of that. Go."

"Are you sure?"

"Yeah. I know my sister, and you had better be on time or she'll make you pay. Get going."

"I owe you one," Grant said as he pulled on his jacket.

"More than one, Evans," Steve cracked, before his face turned serious once again and he added, "Treat her right."

"You have my word," Grant said and turned to rush through the quiet squad room and out the front door, his mind already on Maggie.

NINETEEN

By the time Maggie finally crashed through her front door it was already after 6:30. She kicked off her shoes and rushed through her quiet apartment to her bedroom taking off pieces of her suit on the way. She dumped the pile of shed clothes onto her armchair as she swept open the door to her closet. There was no time to shower, but she could at least put on something a little sexier than what she'd worn to the office.

After five fruitless minutes, Maggie resigned herself to the fact that no spectacular new clothes had magically appeared in her closet and pulled out her trusty little black dress. After all, it was a cliché for a reason, and this particular L.B.D. *did* look damn good on her, if she did say so herself.

Deceptively plain, the simple silk sheathe appeared shapeless on the hanger, but once on, it clung in all the right places. More importantly, it never failed to make Maggie feel sexy and feminine.

After refreshing her makeup and attempting to tame her unruly curls by jabbing dozens of hair pins into it, Maggie was ready with seven minutes to spare. She picked up her favorite perfume and dabbed it in a few strategic places before she turned to search the bottom of her closet for just the right pair of black heels.

When someone rang the buzzer her head whipped up in surprise and Maggie glanced at the clock before she walked to open the door to buzz Grant in. She stepped to the side of the doorway to do one last quick check in the mirror she'd hung there for this very reason when she heard footsteps coming down the hall.

"Come on in—you're right on time. I'm impressed, Evans. I thought..." Maggie stopped abruptly, the welcoming smile sliding from her face to be replaced by an angry scowl.

"Bradley. What are you doing here?"

"Despite your rude behavior on the phone earlier today, we *do* have an appointment for dinner tonight. I'm willing to overlook your outrageous language and ridiculous temper tantrum this once and give you one last chance to come to your senses."

"Do you want me to tell you where you can shove your 'chance'?"

"Margaret, really. Must you be so crude?"

Maggie closed her eyes at his outraged tone of voice before she turned away for a moment to get composed. Turning back to face him she said, "Bradley, I am going to say this as slowly and clearly as possible one last time. I. Am. Never. Going. To. Forgive. You. Ever!

"I do not want to see your smug face or hear your pompous voice again. You are no longer welcome here." Sighing again, Maggie held up both hands and entreated, "Please just leave."

"Margaret, you can't just throw away everything we had over one little problem. Now come along, darling, we'll be late if we don't leave immediately." Bradley reached out to put his hands on her shoulders as he spoke.

"Take your hands off of me," Maggie said in a low voice and used both hands to shove him away from her. Anger slashed across Bradley's face, transforming his normally handsome features into something ugly and cruel.

Maggie took one instinctive step back before Bradley advanced to grab both of her arms in a bruising grip and said, "Listen, you little bitch, *you* don't get to leave *me.*" With a jerk he pulled her forward up onto her toes so that their faces were almost touching.

Eyes wide, Maggie stammered out breathlessly, "Let me go, Bradley," before hauling back one foot and kicking him in the shin as hard as she could.

Bradley bellowed incoherently and reared back, lifting his right arm to strike her. Maggie ducked and tried to jerk away when all of a sudden she was free and the momentum of her movements sent her flying back into the wall and down onto the floor, driving the breath from her lungs.

"I believe the lady asked you to let her go."

Maggie recognized Grant's voice and she looked up from where she'd landed to see Grant standing over Bradley holding his hand in a crushing grip. Bradley was face down on the floor, his arm pulled up and behind his back at a painful angle with Grant's knee pressing him into the floor.

"Are you all right?" Grant asked Maggie, and when she didn't respond he tried again, "Maggie. Are you hurt?"

Maggie dragged her eyes away from her ex's prone figure to meet Grant's worried gaze and replied, "I'm fine. I just lost my balance for a moment there..." Maggie trailed off and her breath caught in her throat when she saw the wild fury in Grant's eyes—a direct contrast to the gentleness of his voice when he asked, "Do you want to press charges?"

"What? No," Maggie shook her head.

"Are you positive?"

"I'm sure," Maggie said and pushed her way to her feet.

With a jerk, Grant yanked Bradley to his feet, out the front door, and face first into the hall wall. He leaned in and growled directly into Bradley's ear, "I ever see you hanging around here again and I guarantee you will severely regret it. Understand?"

Bradley nodded and Grant released his arm to step away. Bradley grabbed his shoulder and, sending a look of pure hatred at both Maggie and Grant, whirled away to retreat down the stairs.

Grant turned to look at Maggie, "Are you sure you're okay? It looked like you hit that wall pretty hard."

Smiling, Maggie replied, "Yes, I just got the breath knocked out of me. I'm sorry you got dragged into all of this, Grant, but I sure am glad you showed up when you did. I had no idea Bradley was capable of...well, of a lot of things," she said ruefully before continuing with a bright voice, "If you don't mind, I need to just freshen up a little bit before we leave?"

"Are you sure you still want to go out tonight?"

"Absolutely. I won't let him ruin this for me, too. I've been looking forward to this all day."

Looking into her candid face Grant felt his heart take another stumble before it raced forward again. He stepped forward and lifted one hand to cup her face. Rubbing one thumb softly back and forth across her cheek, he said simply, "Take your time—I'll wait for as long as it takes for you to be ready."

Maggie drew in one shaky breath before she stepped back and walked towards her bedroom. At the last moment she turned and met his eyes again. She gestured towards the couch and said, "Make yourself at home. I won't be long."

Grant watched her go through the doorway before he closed the apartment door and, rubbing a hand against his heart walked over to sit on the couch. Not letting himself think about the possible significance of her words, he pulled out his cell phone to call the restaurant and change their reservations.

In the bedroom Maggie pressed two shaking hands to her stomach and lifted wide shining eyes to look at her face in mirror. Surprised that she looked no different than she had ten minutes ago Maggie wondered at the fact that her entire world could change and there could be no outward signs of it.

Grant had said he'd wait for her to be ready, and she'd known immediately that he had not simply been referring to her combing her hair or putting on a fresh layer of lipstick, although that is just what she would do.

No. Just as easily as he'd thrown Bradley out of her apartment, he'd stolen her heart.

"Well, you've done it now. You've gone and fallen in love with him," she whispered out loud before she slapped both hands over her mouth to stifle the laugh of pure joy—and terror—that wanted to burst out of her. That's just what she needed, for Grant to think she was hysterical, or worse, crazy.

No time to worry about it now, she'd just have to put thoughts of love and possible insanity out of her mind for now—she was sure she'd have plenty of time to think it over while she tossed and turned tonight. For now, she was going to keep things light simply enjoy being with Grant. And, more importantly, she could enjoy just being herself again.

Grant was bent over reading the titles of her extensive movie collection when she walked back into the room just a few minutes later.

"All set?" Grant asked and straightened, hands in his pockets. Hiding the relief he felt at seeing her looking composed and happy with a grin he stepped forward to take her hands.

When he'd come in earlier Maggie hadn't taken the time to fully appreciate his appearance, but she took the time to do so now. Although he was still in the same gorgeous suite he'd worn that morning, he'd clearly taken the time to re-shave; otherwise she was sure he'd have the start of a beard by now. From the top of his curling hair to the tips of his shiny shoes he was simply delicious to look at. *And he's mine, all mine—at least for tonight,* Maggie thought, then grinned and said, "All set."

Grant released her hands and together they turned to go out the door.

"So, where are we going?" Maggie asked.

"Well, I still don't know too many places in town, but one of the women I work with recommended The Shack, so I thought if you'd like we could try going there. Have you been?"

"Many times. It's a favorite of mine, and it sounds like just the right place for tonight. Are those for me?" Maggie raised her eyebrows and nodded her chin at a small bundle of daisies sitting on the dining room table.

Grant chuckled and grabbed the slightly crushed flowers to hand them to her. "Yes. In all the commotion I dropped them. Hopefully they aren't too mangled."

"They're perfect. Let me just put them in some water and we can go."

"Maggie," Grant's low voice stopped her as she walked away, "I also forgot to tell you that you look beautiful tonight." Grant's steady gaze shot a lightning bolt of heat straight through her, and for a long moment Maggie could only stand there, hopelessly caught in his gaze.

Unconsciously, her tongue slipped out from between her lips to moisten them slightly, and Maggie blushed when she saw his eyes darken and drop to follow the movement. She cleared her throat and said huskily, "Thank you. I'll just be a moment," and fled the intensity of his look and hurried into the kitchen.

Once safely out of sight Maggie pulled the flowers up to bury her face in them before getting out a vase from under her sink to put them in. Blowing a stray hair out of her face Maggie sagged limply back against the counter.

So much for keeping things light.

Maggie hurried back out and as they walked out the door Grant stepped in close behind her and placed a hand on the small of her back, sending tingling warmth up her spine and out to her fingertips and back again. Maggie glanced up and caught his eye and thought, *the hell with light. Who needs light?*

TWENTY

Maggie spent much of the drive to the restaurant silent. Grant assumed she was still upset over the events of the evening—and although that was true, it wasn't in the way he believed.

"Are you sure you still want to go out to eat tonight, Maggie? We could reschedule," Grant said.

Pulled out of her reverie at the sound of his concerned voice Maggie shifted her attention back to the present from where her thoughts had been since she'd been in the kitchen and the realization that she'd finally fallen in love—with a capital L—had forever altered her world.

"No. That's not necessary. Really. I'm fine, and I've been looking forward to going out tonight all day," she said.

Grant smiled in response, relieved that her voice sounded so normal, and that she was recovering from the earlier confrontation.

"As long as you're sure," Grant said as he glanced over to her.

"I'm not only sure, I'm starving," Maggie laughed. When Grant turned his attention back to the road Maggie briefly closed her eyes and thought *I need to get a hold of myself—I can figure out what the heck to do about falling in love with a man I barely know later.*

Brushing aside all thoughts of love, Maggie grabbed the first topic she could think of and said, "How's the case going? Are you and Steven having any luck so far?"

Grant sighed once and replied, "Well, we are pursuing several lines of investigation at the moment."

"You sound *exactly* like Steven," Maggie half laughed and shook her head, "I don't know if that should make me laugh or make me run for the hills."

"I'll take that as a compliment since I know how close you two are," Grant said and grinned.

"Close, yes. But that doesn't keep him from driving me crazy most of the time," Maggie joked.

"I could drive you crazy, too, Red—If you'd let me," Grant said smoothly.

"Hmmm. Well. I'll keep that in mind," Maggie managed to choke out before saying brightly, "Translating your cop-speak, there've been no breaks in the case?"

"All right, safe subjects. For now. No, we've had no major breaks in the case so far. We had a couple of hopeful leads that didn't end up panning out, but there are plenty more that need to be followed up on."

"That must be discouraging."

"Not really. That's just the job. One of the first certainties I discovered when I became a cop was that most cases are not solved by a single clue. Real life is nothing like movies or books.

"Most cases are broken by asking hundreds of questions, following up on countless pieces of information and painstakingly building a case out of the answers that are found. And while it's not nearly as glamorous as it is in fiction, there's nothing more rewarding than when you solve a crime, or more fulfilling when you prove that the faith that victims and their families put in you is justified," Grant stopped suddenly, his face burning before saying quickly, "At least, that's how I feel."

Cringing inwardly at the way he'd practically poured out his thoughts and feelings, Grant thought *Cripes sake, Evans, why don't you just break into song.* If he wasn't more careful, Maggie really *would* go running for the hills—or worse, see too much about how Grant was beginning to feel about her.

"Well. Now I know how you understood my love for art so well—just like being an artist and being surrounded by art is a part of who I am, of what makes me *me*, being a cop is what makes you who *you* are. It's what makes you complete," Maggie murmured warmly.

Surprised that she could see what no one—not even his own mother or sister—had ever seen, or perhaps never wanted to see, and that she accepted it as right, Grant pulled the car to a stop in the restaurant's parking lot. The shock of someone understanding him on that level swept away the remnants of embarrassment he had been feeling about pouring out his emotions.

He turned to look at Maggie through the darkness of the silent car. Light splashed out from the restaurant's windows to bathe

142

her features in a warm glow and revealed the look of complete understanding that shone out from her eyes and covered her face.

Emotion filled his chest as he reached across the small space between them, and in a gesture she was beginning to almost expect, cupped her jaw and swept his thumb softly along her velvety cheek.

"You know. You understand," he said quietly.

Pressing her face into his hand she whispered one word. "Yes."

For a long moment they just sat until the sound of a car door slamming closed had their eyes and his hand dropping.

"We should get inside," one of them said, and together they turned and exited the car to walk inside.

Grant's first impression of the restaurant was that of warm light and deep colors. The warm gold of the round oak tables contrasted with the rich green of the walls and the deep wine red of the leather booths that ringed the room. Candlelight flickered softly from the walls and in the center of every table lending an air of welcome to the small space.

As a hostess led them to a booth along the back wall Grant was pleased when he noted several familiar faces seated throughout the room—many of whom nodded or even called out greetings to Maggie and occasionally even to him. Once there were seated and had ordered drinks Grant spoke, "So what's good here?"

"Pretty much everything, but I'd recommend the shrimp, or really any of the seafood. If you're in a particularly carnivorous mood, though, the prime rib is superb."

"Hmmm. I'm definitely in a carnivorous mood tonight," Grant quipped silkily as he flashed a killer grin at Maggie before turning his attention back to his menu.

Maggie's delighted laugh rang out and she shook her head before dropping her eyes to her menu in an effort to slow down the racing of her traitorous heart.

"You are going to be trouble, Grant Evans. Trouble with a capital T."

"Scared, Red?"

"Terrified."

"Good."

"Good?" Maggie laughed as the waitress came up to take their order, and shaking her head again, turned her attention to the waitress.

When they were alone once more, the moment Maggie had been dreading arrived.

"Maggie, I know I haven't known you very long and you may feel this is none of my business, but I think you need to report what happened earlier tonight—officially."

Maggie sighed and took a long sip of her wine to give herself a moment to compose the right answer. "Look Grant, I'm really glad that you were there for me today. If you hadn't gotten there when you did, things would have been even uglier than they were. I'm sure that I would have been able to handle things without a problem, but you being there simplified things."

Sighing again, she continued, "I just don't want to go through reporting something that I'm sure will go no farther. Bradley's just not the type to do anything violent."

Hard brown eyes in a serious face met her determined gaze. "He looked plenty violent to me when he was shoving you down. And he looked downright nasty when he was raising his arm to hit you, Maggie."

Waving her hand Maggie shook her head again, "I just bruised his overlarge ego, that's all. I'm sure…"

"Maggie," Grant cut her off and reached forward to gently, but firmly grasp her wrist, "Maggie, I cannot tell you how many times I've heard the same thing from women in abusive relationships. No. Don't shake your head, Maggie. I have seen this situation, or variations of it, too many times *not* to say something. Almost every one of those situations escalated to physical violence. And, in far too many cases, the women ended up dead.

"I know that this is not what you wanted to talk about over dinner, but I've talked to too many grieving families and friends who saw the signs, but never pushed the issue because they didn't want to make their loved one upset or mad."

When she simply sat there, an obstinate look on her face Grant added, "I already care too much *not* to say something Maggie."

For a long moment Maggie was silent. Ignoring her first instinct to get mad and stomp out, Maggie carefully pulled her hand from Grant's and leaned back. "I'll think about it, Grant. Okay? It's not as simple as you make it sound. I have my family to think about, too, and something like this would really upset them. When I picture my brothers' reactions..." Shuddering she trailed off and clenched her hands together in her lap.

"If you won't listen to me as a cop, please listen to me as your friend. I won't bring it up again tonight, but I really want you to do this. If not with me, get Steve to come over and do it."

"I don't want him involved."

"Maggie, you have to know that Steve's already suspicious about what went on with the two of you. I just don't see how you can keep it from him. I doubt that it will be much longer before he goes directly to Bradley."

"I know, I know," Maggie blew out a breath and looked up at Grant again, "All right. I'll talk to him tomorrow, but I'm trusting that you will not say anything to the rest of my family. There's no reason they have to know."

"I won't say anything to them. But Maggie, you're wrong not to tell them, to trust them. They love you and only want what's best for you."

"I *do* trust them, Grant, but I won't worry them about this— especially since I don't believe it will go any further. Please. You have to let me deal with this as I see fit, okay?"

"Okay. Let's talk about something else."

Relieved when he dropped the uncomfortable subject, Maggie relaxed back into her chair before saying cautiously, "What did you have in mind?"

"What's your favorite movie?"

Maggie laughed at his lightning quick change in mood and answered without hesitation, "That would depend."

"On what?"

"On the genre."

"For example?"

"Well, my favorite classic is *Notorious*; comedy: *Caddyshack*; thriller: *Dead Again*; horror: *The Exorcist*; romance:

Return to Me; musical: *Rocky Horror Picture Show*…Should I go on?" she cocked one eyebrow up and waited for his response.

"I deduced the fact that you were a movie aficionado from your impressive DVD collection, but I clearly underestimated the extent of your…"

"Obsession?" Maggie broke in and laughed.

"Passion. I was going to say passion," Grant replied and grinned.

"What about you? Are you a movie fan?"

"I am, but I have a ways to go before I could keep up with you. Maybe you could help me bridge the gap a bit."

Amused at the hopeful look on his face Maggie nodded and said, "Sure, I'd love to, but you may come to regret asking me—I am known for my love of movie marathons."

Grant's grin flashed again and, with a wicked gleam in his eyes, he replied, "Anytime you want to spend several hours in the dark with me, just let me know, Red, and I'll be sure to be there."

Blushing, Maggie shook her head and said with mock sadness, "Yep, you're trouble with a capital T, Evans."

Before Grant could reply their dinners were served and for several moments neither spoke. As their meal went on they spoke of movies they'd recently seen, sports they liked to watch and play, books they loved, what kinds of music they listened to—everything and anything light and fun.

Maggie was surprised by just how many of the same things they both seemed to enjoy. She had wondered if they would have any common ground. She would have liked him if they hadn't, but it was definitely a big plus that they appreciated so many of the same things.

Too full to eat another bite, Maggie sat back and pushed her half-empty plate of shrimp towards Grant. She was not surprised to see him reach for it despite the fact that he'd eaten all of his prime rib, most of the appetizer and an entire basket of bread. She'd watched her brothers eat as much, and more, too many times for her to be shocked.

Leaning forward to rest on her forearms, Maggie settled in and asked, "So why does a man whose lived his entire life as an urbanite decide to pack up his worldly possessions and move to a small town in the middle of Nowhere, USA?"

Grant finished the last bite of shrimp and took a long pull of the water he'd started drinking after finishing his second glass of wine before responding in a neutral tone of voice.

"I wanted a fresh beginning somewhere new and completely different from what I'd always known."

Something important there, Maggie thought before she took the not-so-subtle hint and changed the subject. Just because *she* was falling in love with him didn't mean he felt the same, and clearly the subject was a tender one yet.

"You can't get much different from Seattle than Hope," she said lightly before she asked, "How is Jake settling in to the new house?"

Relieved that she hadn't pressed Grant smiled and said, "He loves it. The apartment we used to live in was nice, but there was no real yard to run around in. I tried to get to the park a few times a week, but I never knew when a case would hit or when I'd have to stay late. This set-up is so much better. I can leave Jake in the backyard during the day and he can get as much exercise as he'd like."

"What will you do when it gets really cold out?"

"I'm not sure yet—I don't have a lot of experience with really cold weather. Just how bad will it get?"

Maggie's eyes twinkled, "It gets *bitterly* cold in the heart of winter. January and February spend most days with highs in the single digits—often with wind chills well below zero. It's not unusual to have a week or two of subzero weather with wind chills of more than fifty or sixty degrees below zero."

"That's definitely cold. Should make running interesting."

All humor fled from Maggie's face and she said, "Seriously, Grant, when it gets that cold out, you have to watch out for yourself and for Jake. You can get frostbite in as little as ten minute's exposure."

"I've read about that, but I guess we'll just have to wait and see how it goes." It's already been pretty cold in the morning and it's only October."

Maggie laughed out loud and shook her head, "You're in for a rude awakening, Evans, if you think weather in the forties is cold. Don't worry. You just need to get one good Minnesota winter under your belt and we'll thicken up that thin blood of yours."

"As long as it doesn't freeze solid," Grant quipped and held the door of the restaurant open for Maggie to walk through. Maggie glanced back over her shoulder and met his eyes for a quick moment before a flash of heat shot through her system and had her quickly turning forward again.

"Oh, I don't think freezing is going to be your problem, Evans," Maggie said wryly and muttered almost silently under her breathe, "A heat wave, maybe."

Hearing, Grant grinned again, appreciating her more and more.

Once they were settled in the car and headed back to her apartment Grant continued their conversation.

"If the weather is going to get as cold as you say, I'm going to have to come up with a solution. I can't just stop running for a month or two."

"I know—I have the same problem every winter. Usually I get a temporary gym membership at the U, but I've been seriously considering investing in a treadmill. I just wish running on one wasn't so incredibly boring."

"Yeah, but they are the simplest solution. Maybe we can check out a few together."

"Maybe we could."

When Grant pulled into his driveway and cut the engine Maggie turned to look over at Grant's profile in the darkened SUV, considering.

"Want to come in for a while—maybe get started on your new movie education?"

"Tempting—you don't know just how tempting that is, Red, but I have a really early morning. I will come in for a quick drink if you're interested."

"All right. Come on up."

Twenty minutes later, they were seated on Maggie's couch, glasses of wine in hand.

"So. Steve is crawling under the window when my mom opens it and tosses the entire tub of dirty water right on top of him."

"Seriously?"

"Oh, yeah. And he's lying down on the ground trying not to yell or swear so she won't notice he's there and not up in bed where he's supposed to be. Meanwhile Seth and Dillon are hanging out of their upstairs windows trying not to laugh and give him away and at the same time Jack runs and grabs some dry clothes so he won't drip all over the stairs and give himself away. So they're whispering instructions and Jack drops the clothes out the window and down to him—except…"

She paused to snort back a laugh before she managed to choke out, "Only not quite *all* of his clothes made it down to the ground."

Grant found himself smiling broadly, "I think I can take a guess about what was lost."

"Right," Maggie said and turned mischievous eyes towards him, "He had to change in the bushes next to the garage and hope that no one would find his jockeys before he had the chance to find them in the daylight."

"And where were you during all this?"

Smirking Maggie said, "Who do you think was lookout? I had my Barbie walkie-talkie clutched in my sweaty little hand, peeking out into the hallway from my bedroom and praying that my mom wouldn't come up the stairs."

"Barbie?"

"Don't judge—I was only eight, what do you want?"

"I'm sorry. Continue."

"Right. So, the next morning we're all still in bed when we hear Mom start screaming for Steve and yelling. Here she'd gone out on the back stoop to grab something from her garden and she walked right into a pair of bright red jockey shorts hanging from the roof of the porch."

Laughing, Maggie set down her wineglass to wipe a tear from her eye.

"Bright red, huh? I'm going to have to give Steve *such* a lot of crap about this," Grant said, a bright gleam in his eye.

149

"Oh, yeah. He's never lived that one down. You should have seen him scrambling to come up with an excuse for *why* his underwear was hanging outside."

"What did he end up saying?"

"I still don't know. He and my mom disappeared into his room and when they came back out again not a word was said, but he didn't use the car for a month. The funniest part? I was outside in the side yard playing when I heard this weird choking noise coming from the front of the house. So I snuck around the corner and hid behind the bushes, and I'll never forget what I saw—Mom was sitting on the front porch swing crying—or what I *thought* was crying. I remember thinking that I would *never* sneak out of the house and make momma cry that way. It wasn't until many years later that I finally figured out that she had been trying to cover up the fact that she had been laughing so hard she was crying."

Maggie smiled softly, her eyes fixed on some image from the past, before continuing, "The memory of that night and my mother kept me from misbehaving for a long time."

"Your mother is a truly remarkable woman. You're lucky to have someone who so clearly loves and *enjoys* each of you.

"There was this one moment during the picnic that I saw her stop what she was doing to just *look* at the four of you standing there talking and laughing. And it was so clear—so obvious to me that she got such a big kick out of you—that she was proud of you. That's an amazing gift."

Oh, you poor man, Maggie thought as she looked over to where Grant sat on the sofa looking down at his drink, *why do you sound so sad? What did your mother look like when she looked at you? Did she see the sweet boy you must have been? Does she see the extraordinary man that you've become?*

But all she said was, "I know. She's always been there for us. Always shown us how much she loved us—even when my brothers and I were in deep trouble there was never any doubt that we were adored.

"That base, the strength and confidence I received as a result from having it, has made me all that I am today. I can only pray that I give my own children the same foundation of love and support some day."

150

"You will," Grant said confidently, his eyes lifted to meet hers.

"How can you be so sure?" Maggie asked and tipped her head to one side, curious to see what he would say.

"I'm sure because I can see how you are always thinking about the people you care about. I can see how you shield and protect those whom you love—whether they need to be protected or not," he ended wryly before draining his glass and setting it down.

Embarrassed, Maggie blushed and raised her own wine glass to her mouth before she realized it was empty. Flustered, she set the flute down with an audible click. Crossing her legs, Maggie raised her chin and turned turbulent eyes the color of a rising storm on Grant, daring him to comment.

Fascinated by the tell-tale flush that deepened her creamy white skin to a delicate rose, and by the spark of temper brewing in her eyes, Grant flashed a knowing smile but said nothing.

"Well," Maggie cleared her suddenly dry throat once before she asked coolly, "Can I get you another drink?"

"No thanks. I better get going," Grant said and continued in his head, *before I decide to quench my thirst another way.*

They both stood and walked to the door. Maggie reached for the handle and lifted her head with a jerk when Grant's hand descended onto hers and he angled his hard body to cage her between it and the door. Wide hazel eyes flashed up to meet dark brown eyes and all the air in the room seemed to evaporate in a blaze of heat.

Unable to move, Maggie merely stared, lost in the moment. And as she stared she saw his eyes darken with desire. Shaken by the intensity of what she saw, Maggie felt a tremor pass through her body and her mouth opened slightly on a soft sigh.

Shaking herself mentally Maggie said in a husky voice she barely recognized as her own, "Thank you for a lovely dinner. Despite the rocky start, I really enjoyed myself tonight."

"Let's see if we can't end it on a better note," Grant said and eased forward to place his lips on hers.

Maggie sighed again and closed her eyes. She had expected him to kiss her—had counted on it if she were as honest with herself as she always prided herself on being—but she'd been expecting an assault on her body. Instead, Grant began toppling the walls she'd built around her heart with a single tender kiss.

Not an onslaught, but a precision strike. And without a single shot fired, she surrendered, body and soul. Later she would be shaken at how easily, how quickly it had happened, but in that moment there was only the press of his lips on hers, the pressure of his warm hand enclosing hers.

They stood there like that, joined by those two points, and the sweetness of the moment made Maggie's heart ache, her breath catch.

And then she opened for him.

With a fierce groan Grant changed the angle of his mouth and dove in. With her free hand, she hooked her arm around his back and over his shoulder to cling, while his banded around her torso, lifting her to her toes.

The hand still gripping hers on the doorknob seemed his only anchor to reality. He understood that if he let go—even for a second—he would be lost.

It had been by sheer will alone that he'd kept his first touch gentle, his kiss light, in the face of the immense need he seemed to have for her. He knew if he didn't stop now he never would, and that couldn't happen. Not tonight. After all that she'd been through, not to mention the promise he'd made to Steve, Grant couldn't let anything happen.

And, despite her ardent response, her sweet surrender, Grant also knew that Maggie just wasn't ready yet. So he stepped back.

With a soft moan of protest Maggie swayed forward before opening eyes blurred with passion to meet Grant's gaze. Staggered by what he saw in them Grant lifted a shaky hand to run it over her tousled hair and down her arm to grip her hand loosely.

"Sweet dreams, Red," he said lightly before he kissed her briefly and released her hand to open the door.

"Good night, Grant," Maggie replied quietly, soberly.

"Make sure you lock up tight."

"I will."

With one last look, Grant turned and walked quickly down the hall before he could throw her over his shoulder and drag her into her bedroom. Maggie watched until he disappeared down the staircase then shut the door to collapse weakly back against it and let her head fall back with a soft thump.

"Sweet dreams…Yeah, right," she muttered under her breath then shoved upright to head into the bedroom to get ready for bed. Halfway there she detoured into the bathroom.

If she were going to get any sleep at all tonight, she'd better take a long shower—a nice cold one.

TWENTY-ONE

Two hours after leaving Maggie's apartment Grant took a break from working on the case files to walk around to the front of his house. He paused in the center of the large three-paneled window that faced the street and shoved both hands into the back pockets of his favorite pair of comfortably ratty jeans.

Staring blankly at the window he saw his own reflection slouched in the dark glass. Letting his thoughts wander Grant found himself thinking back over his evening with Maggie and he smiled as he remembered all the crazy things they'd ended up talking about.

If nothing else, the evening had definitely not been dull. Not that he'd expected it to be. Somehow Grant thought that spending time with Maggie would never be boring. She was too vital, too full of life, to ever be anything but interesting.

What had surprised him most was just how much they had in common with one another. As far as he could see, they'd grown up in completely different worlds. Their families seemed light distances apart. And yet the more he got to know about her, the more he liked her.

Like how she was so devoted to her family—even when she was arguing with one of her brothers or complaining about how over-protective they were, the affection she clearly felt for them was as obvious as her annoyance with them was.

He and his sister Valerie had fought often enough, as brothers and sisters were wont to do, but he could count on one hand the number of times he'd felt genuinely close to her. He loved her, but they had never been friends.

When their father had been killed, he and his sister—as well as his mother—had just drifted apart until they were like separate islands living side-by-side, but somehow never able to shift any closer to one another.

And when he'd gotten accepted into the academy what little affection he'd shared with his mother and Val had been destroyed in a flash of bitter fear on his mother's part and blind fury on his sister's.

Weary at the memory of their reactions to his chosen career, Grant sank down onto the arm of his new couch and remembered back to the day he'd gotten his acceptance to the academy—how thrilled he'd been, how proud to finally be doing something that would bring him closer to the father he'd revered as a boy and had lost to the same calling he found himself irrevocably drawn to as well.

Grant remembered with perfect clarity tearing up the acceptance letters from UCLA and the University of Washington—the same letters his mother had cried over when he'd received them—and carefully smoothing the letter he'd received from the Seattle Police Academy.

He'd lied to his mother, made up any excuse possible to take and pass the written and physical tests needed to apply to the academy. He'd passed the required background investigation, a polygraph, a medical exam, and a psychological exam, and had waited anxiously to find out whether or not he'd gotten in. And here it was—the culmination of all his efforts. What he'd hoped for, dreamed about for years, could finally happen.

Just as soon as he worked up the nerve to tell his mother.

Yes, Grant vividly remembered how happy and terrified he'd felt that day before he'd gone to talk to his mother. And he also remembered how the last spark of hope he'd felt that she could ever understand him, could ever just believe in him, had been extinguished.

God, he'd been so young then. Not as young as friends his same age were—he hadn't been that young, that innocent, since the day his father had been shot and killed when he was twelve—but still green yet, still tender.

Shaking off the memory Grant focused on the present and looked past his own reflection, past the quiet, moonlit street to the apartment building beyond.

His gaze went unerringly to Maggie's windows, and noting they were still lit, he had to stifle the urge to grab his coat and go striding back across the street to beat down her door. He knew if he gave in to his needs and did that, they'd both enjoy it, but he couldn't chance that she may also regret it later.

"Shit," he groaned and rubbed a hand over weary eyes. He was, to put it mildly, completely screwed. How in *hell* had he gotten in so deep, so fast? He was like the bloody Titanic—running full speed ahead into an immovable object and going under before anyone knew what the hell had happened.

And the most pathetic part? He was happy to be doing it. And not only that, he'd do it all again—he'd turn the stupid ship around and aim it for that bloody iceberg and sink under with a sappy smile on his face.

As he watched Maggie's lights turned out. Grant turned away from the view of the now-dark apartment and headed back to the dining room table where he'd spread out his case notes.

He needed to get some kind of dry erase board to use for his case board here at home. They had a main board going at the station, but he really liked to keep his notes at home as well—it made it easier to keep his thoughts organized. To that end, he'd already made a copy of the case file and neatly arranged it in a large black three-ring binder.

But he knew that he always absorbed information more quickly and clearly if it was taken in visually, and as a whole. The best chance he had of solving this case was to lay it all out on a working board. Having everything laid out that way not only kept the case organized, it would help him keep his thoughts in order as well.

Grant rubbed a hand down his face again before he turned away from the table and walked down the hall to his bedroom. He was so tired there was no way he was helping by working on the case any further. In fact, in his current state he was more liable to miss some vital connection, some small fact that could help break the case wide open.

No, he wouldn't risk it. Couldn't afford to. So, he'd sleep.

Grant shed his jeans and t-shirt and eyed the bed longingly, but the memory of Maggie's mouth pressed hotly to his, of how it had felt to hold her in his arms flared to life, as it had been doing ever since leaving her apartment.

With a sigh, Grant resigned himself to the truth—it was going to be a long night, and he seriously doubted that sleeping would be a part of it.

Grant collapsed onto the bed, hoping that, by some miracle of God, he'd drop off to sleep immediately, but it wasn't meant to be.

Instead, memories he was able to keep at bay during the daylight hours, when he was alert, started slipping through the cracks that stress and too little sleep had caused. Memories of his childhood, of losing his father, of his mother and sister, and, of course, of the night he lost his partner and was shot all whizzed around the merry-to-round that was his mind.

Disgusted, Grant punched his pillow twice, preferring to believe it was his pillow that was making him uncomfortable instead of his troubling thoughts. When that didn't work he resigned himself to a sleepless night as the memories and thoughts he normally avoided filled his mind.

As each memory flashed through his mind, playing like a fast-forwarded movie that paused on the moments he most wanted to remember—or forget—he rolled over onto his back, his hands beneath his head to cradle it.

He was eight years old playing catch in the back yard on an ordinary summer day made special because his father was there as he so rarely was.

He was running off the dock at the beach and leaping out into his father's outstretched arms. Ten years later he jumped off that same dock, hand-in-hand with Sarah Lyn, his first love.

He was sitting at a baseball game with his father and grandfather—eating a giant hotdog, drinking an enormous pop, and knowing, even at the age of eleven, that life couldn't get any better than that.

That terrible day in September when he was twelve. He was listening to his father explain that he couldn't take Grant to the station like he'd promised, that something had broken on a case and he had to go in to work instead.

When Grant had kept his head down, not responding, his father had squatted down in front of him and laid a large hand on Grant's skinny shoulder.

"Now, Grant, I know it may not seem fair to you, but I have a responsibility to more than just you, your mother and your sister. I have a responsibility to the people that are counting on me to help them, to protect them, and it's a responsibility that I don't take lightly. Of course I would rather be spending time with you, with the people that I love, but evil does not rest, Grant."

Grant's head had shot up at that, confusion replacing the anger and hurt on his face.

His father had continued, "Now there are those that believe that evil only exists in fiction, but believe me, Grant, it *does* exist. One of my favorite sayings goes something like this: All that is necessary for evil to triumph is for good men to do nothing. Now, I really have to get going, but I'll try to be home early enough so that we can surprise your mom and sister with a trip out for ice cream. Okay?"

"Yes, sir," Grant had replied, smiling once again.

"Good. Now don't forget to get your chores done," he'd said before squeezing Grant's shoulder one last time and turning to walk out the door.

"Yes, sir," he'd said again, and then he'd run out the door to wave good-bye.

What Grant wouldn't do to go back to that day, to hug his father and tell him he loved him, to keep him from walking out of that door.

It had been just a couple of hours later and he'd been raking the leaves in the front yard when the squad car had pulled up in front of the house. His initial excitement over having his dad come home so early in the day had turned to a cold, hard dread that weighed down in his belly when only his father's partner, Detective Daniel Ryan, had gotten out of the car.

Ryan had walked slowly up the path to the door, never looking up when Grant had called out a greeting. The rake had slid soundlessly from his nerveless fingers as he ran across the yard in time to hear his mother's screams.

As he had slowly climbed the three worn stairs that led to his front porch he remembered staring at those stairs, thinking that he'd have to pick up a gallon of paint to fix them up.

When he'd finally dragged his gaze away from the peeling paint he'd looked through the screened door at the scene that would forever be burned onto his mind. Like a nightmare he couldn't wake up from, Grant saw his mother, his sister and Ryan fixed in that moment of anguish.

From then on, whenever he remembered that day he would see them in that same way—frozen like play actors on the stage, waiting, waiting for the curtain that would never drop.

Ryan was crouched over, trying to help his mother get up from where she'd fallen to her knees on the front hall floor, from where she'd collapsed when Ryan had come to the door to tell her that her husband was gone, and would never again come home to her and the two children they'd made together.

Valerie stood motionless halfway down the stairs, one hand on the railing, and tears pouring out from eyes so huge they seemed to swallow her face. She shook her head slowly back and forth, over and over again, whispering, "It's not true," again and again.

Grant remembered thinking that he had to pull himself together because if his father was truly gone it was up to him to take care of his mother and sister now.

He'd pulled open the screen door and stepped through, meeting Ryan's eyes, not knowing how the shattered look in his own shook the older man, as did the way he'd squared his small shoulders and turned to face his mother.

Grant remembered the way his mother had clung to him, sobbing out, "What do we do?" before Ryan had helped him steer her into her bedroom where she'd collapsed onto the bed and curled into a ball.

And, he remembered the terror and grief and blind trust in Valerie's eyes when he'd told her that everything would be all right, that somehow he would make it all right.

Ryan had assured him that he wasn't alone as he'd turned to go, but even at twelve Grant had known exactly how alone he now was, and that life, as he'd known it, was over.

"We'll be all right Ryan," Grant had declared.

And Ryan, taken aback at the way Grant had called him by his last name instead of the usual "Uncle Dan", had only smiled sadly and shaken Grant's hand for the first time with a look in his eyes Grant had not understood at the time.

He understood that look now. Now that he'd lost his best friend, his partner. Now that he was old enough to know the many things that adults do not—or perhaps can not—reveal. He now knew that it had been not only sadness and regret, but also pity and guilt in Ryan's eyes that day.

Sadness and regret that his friend was dead, pity that Grant had to bear the burden of the loss—and the burden of his mother's and sister's losses—and guilt that he'd survived when his partner had not.

Oh, yes. Grant understood, only too well, the full meaning of the look Ryan had given to him that day. And now, more than twenty years later, he appreciated it.

But on that day he'd known little beyond the fact that his father was dead and that somehow, some way, he had to make sure that they would be all right.

And they had been.

Grant had made sure of that. He'd made dinner when his mother couldn't get out of bed to do so. He'd helped his sister with her homework and made sure she'd gone to college. He'd done everything from painting those peeling porch steps to doing the laundry, to doing the countless unending chores needed to hold his family together.

And except for days he spent at his grandparents' house, childhood had ended for him.

Grant shook off the old memory and once again found himself thinking about the day he'd received his acceptance letter to the academy. He'd been so excited, so sure that his mother would see past her fears and understand how right joining the force was for him.

He'd grabbed the precious letter and gone to look for her. He'd found her, as he often did, kneeling in her ruthlessly ordered gardens.

He'd stood above her, awed at how crisp and cool she managed to look on a hot afternoon with a large straw hat tied with a silk scarf shading her face and perfectly manicured hands encased in immaculate gardening gloves.

His heart raced as he waited for her to finish putting in another plant before she shifted back on her heels and looked up into his face.

"Hello, Darling. What brings you out here? I hope you aren't going to disrupt my gardens again?" she'd asked, referring to his attempt to plant his own wildflower garden a few years earlier.

He'd loved the chaos of the jumbled blooms, but his mother had been so appalled she'd razed it and put in a small pond within a month.

"No, Mother. I got some great news today," Grant had grinned and held out the acceptance letter. Her face had lit up.

"Stanford?" she'd exclaimed as she snatched the letter from his hands. The moment she had begun to read, her face drew down into a frown. She'd raised her furious, glittering eyes and said in a clipped tone, "Is this some kind of joke?"

Taken aback by the coldness of her voice, Grant had felt the small spark of hope he'd harbored that she would be proud, if not entirely happy, wink out. In its place, all that remained was a numb determination not to let her needs, her fear, to take this dream away from him as it had with so many others.

He'd be damned if he would give in to her even one more time.

And he hadn't.

There had been furious fights, fear-filled tirades and bitterly angry tears on his mother's part. But, no matter how hard she had begged, pleaded or badgered, Grant had held firm.

Even when Valerie had joined forces with his mother against him, her anger blinding her to how he felt, he'd never wavered. Though he'd tried time and again, any argument or explanation he'd attempted had simply fallen on deaf ears.

Finally, his mother had told him she would no longer support him if he continued down the route he'd chosen and had given him an ultimatum: go to college or move out.

He'd moved out.

Though he'd felt even more alone than when his father had died, Grant had stood his ground, understanding on some level that if he gave in, if he did as they demanded, that he would lose who he was—or perhaps even more important, he would lose who he was meant to become.

So, he'd moved out by the end of the first month after graduation. At first he'd rented a room over Ryan's garage until he'd gotten through the academy and started his first job. He'd always be grateful to Ryan for his support—not once in the years since Grant's father was killed had Ryan failed to be there for him when he needed him. He'd not only given Grant his first apartment, he'd given him the chance to break away and to stand on his own for once.

In the years since, Grant had worked hard to bridge the chasm that had ripped open between himself and his mother and sister, but without being willing to give up his job, he'd never been able to get them to meet him halfway.

Grant shook off the memories of his family and they were immediately replaced by memories of Lou—of the day they'd become partners; spending time with Lou and his family; countless scenes of them working the job; of the last day off together at a barbeque in Lou's back yard; and then, of course, that awful night when Lou had died.

Grant's hands clenched as the memory engulfed him again, overwhelming him with the memory of the sounds—the rustle of garbage shifting in the breeze, the low moans as Lou lay dying—the scents—rotting food mixed with wet concrete and the rusty smell of fresh blood—the horrifying sights, and the pain from that night.

As the memory faded Grant braced himself for the descent of crushing depression that had always followed.

It never came.

Instead he was suddenly thinking of Maggie. The image of her as she stepped out of her bedroom in that incredibly sexy black dress flowed into his mind and washed away the last remains of sadness and desperation that always seemed to coat his mind after reliving Lou's death.

He still felt extremely sad and angry over the loss of a good man—his closest friend. But for the first time in, well, ever, he felt like himself again. The relief that coursed through him was so immense it would have sent him to his knees had he not already been lying down.

The hands he'd clenched relaxed once more and as he let his thoughts wander back to his evening with Maggie he drifted off to sleep.

And in sleep he dreamed. And when he dreamed it was of hazel eyes dark with passion, of bodies pressed together, joining and moving in perfect rhythm, of sweat-slicked skin sliding, sliding.

TWENTY-TWO

While Grant slept through the night Maggie spent a great portion of her night and early morning thinking. Thinking about Bradley, thinking about Grant, and even thinking about how and what she was going to talk to Steven about.

Despite the fact that by the time she'd fallen asleep it was well after three in the morning, Maggie hadn't come up with any perfect solutions or conclusions to her many problems. All she'd managed to do was to worry about what she already knew.

One, she'd never loved Bradley and he was a complete and utter bastard. Possibly—and she still wasn't convinced about this—a dangerous one.

Two, she was not only falling for Grant, she was completely head over heels for him despite the fact that she still had so much that she needed to learn about him.

Three, she was sure that she didn't want to tell Steven about any of this, and she was equally sure that she'd have to or he'd use some other method to find most of it out on his own.

Her last thought before she'd finally fallen asleep was, *Way to keep your life simple and uncomplicated, Mags.*

When her alarm went off less than four hours later, Maggie slammed her hand down on the button and lay back down onto her pillows to take stock.

She'd spent far too many mornings these past few weeks waking up as tired as when she'd gone to bed. Even though she'd gotten even less sleep than she'd been averaging since breaking up with the Creep, she felt surprisingly good.

Happy even—at least as long as she didn't think too hard about talking to Steven.

Maggie blew a breath up at the hair hanging in her face and sprang up—she might as well get her day going. It was going to be a long one, and the sooner she got it started and her conversation with Steven over, the sooner she could relax and just be happy again.

She glanced at the clock and calculated how long she would have to wait before she could safely call Steven without scaring him and decided she had just enough time to take a shower and fix some coffee.

Although she thought it would probably get rid of some of her nervous energy, a run was out. Which, Maggie thought ruefully, was probably for the best. If she *did* run, she'd probably not only burn off her nervous energy, but burn up the rest of her energy in the process. And, she had a strong feeling that she would need as much of it as possible to deal with Steven's reaction to what she needed to tell him.

By the time she'd showered, dressed and poured her first cup of coffee she judged that it was late enough to call. She wasn't surprised that Steven answered on the first ring, but she was amazed at how wide-awake he sounded.

"Hey Mags, what's up?"

"Morning, Steven. You're sure chipper this morning. What's up with that?"

"I got up an hour early today to get a workout in. I've got to pick Evans up, we got a meeting set up for this morning and we need to go over some stuff ahead of time. So, why are you calling me so early, Maggie? What's wrong?"

"Cripes sake, you sound like Mom, Steven. Can't I just call to see how my big brother is doing?"

"No."

Maggie blew out a big breath and blurted out, "Fine. I was wondering if you could stop by this morning or if we could meet for lunch or dinner today. I need to talk to you about a couple of things."

"So talk."

"I'd rather do it face-to-face."

Steve was silent for a long moment before he replied. "Are you okay, Mags?"

"I'm fine, Steven. Honestly. But I do need to talk to you."

"Alright. I'm not sure how nuts today will be so why don't we have dinner tonight?"

"Great. Just give me a call on my cell when you're done for the day and I'll whip something up for us to eat, or we could order in if you prefer."

Knowing how little Maggie's job paid Steve quickly said, "Why don't I stop and grab something. That way I won't worry that

I'll ruin your meal if I end up being a little late. Chinese sound good?"

Relieved, Maggie said, "Perfect. Thanks a lot, Steven. I know how busy you are with your case right now."

"No problem, Maggie. I'll see you tonight."

"All right. Bye," Maggie said and hung up. For a long moment she simply sat there thinking. If she knew Steven, and she did, she knew he was furiously thinking up scenarios for why she needed to speak to him. She also knew that he was bound to have put it together that what she wanted to talk to him about was either about Bradley or Grant, or about both.

"That's what I get for having a cop for a brother," Maggie muttered, then froze when she considered that not only was she related to an ultra-perceptive cop she was now dating one.

Could her life get any more complicated?

Sighing, Maggie glanced up at the clock. No more time for self pity. If she hurried, she had *just* enough time to grab something to eat before she had to leave for work or she'd be late. Again. And this time she really would lose her job.

TWENTY-THREE

When Grant walked into the station the next morning he found Steve hanging up the phone with a concerned look on his face.

"Is everything all right?" Grant asked as he shrugged out of his jacket.

"What? Yes. I think so."

Grant laughed and sat down across from his partner. "If you say so. Anything new come in since last night?"

"Not a thing."

Grant nodded and said, "There's something that's been bothering me about the morning we checked out the Daniels murder scene. Dusty said that the apartment downstairs had been burned out and that there hadn't been any suspects in that case so far. I don't know why, but I keep getting this twinge…"

Grant trailed off before he shook his head once and continued, "Maybe it's nothing, but I think we should look at it a little more closely."

By the time Grant had finished speaking Steve had already dug through the pile of files on his desk to pull out the case file on the fire. He held it up in the air and grinned.

"I pulled it last night to go over it with the officers originally assigned to the case. It's a pretty slim possibility that the two incidents are connected in any way, but I agree that we should definitely take a look—if only to eliminate it as a possibility."

"I guess great minds really do think alike."

"Yeah—either that or crazy minds do," Steve cracked before his expression turned serious, "And speaking of crazy, whoever did set fire to the Beekman's apartment was either a very cool customer, or a crazy one.

"Fire report shows that the fire was lit in all five rooms of the apartment. Which means the guy, or guys, had to be in there while the other four rooms were already burning to light the last starter fire, and considering the accelerants that were used, it had to be blazing pretty hot by the time he got out."

"So how do you know so much about fires?" Grant asked.

"Didn't you know? Jack's a fireman. I took the file over to show to him last night and he gave me the low-down."

167

"Handy. I guess I never did hear what he did at the barbeque. Seth's a teacher and Dillon a paramedic, right?"

"Yep. And Jack has always wanted to be a fireman."

Grant reached for the file, noting that Jones and McKenzie were the case officers before he flipped it open to quickly read through the report from the fire investigator. When he finished, he raised troubled brown eyes up to meet Steve's and said, "I'm guessing that you haven't spoken with Jones and Mac yet?"

"Nope. Jones is in the Big Room, but Mac isn't in yet— dentist appointment—so I figured we'd talk to them after the progress meeting we've got in…" Steve paused to glance at the watch on his wrist before he continued,"…eight minutes."

"Sounds good. Maybe we should pull reports for other unsolved crimes around the same time period as the first two murders.

"If this is connected," Grant tapped the file in front of him before he continued, "there may be others connected, too."

Steve blew out a breath and said, "We better get in there." Steve rose and grabbed another pile of files and papers. He watched as Grant did the same and the two men fell in step together and headed down the hall.

"So. How was dinner last night?" Steve asked, his overly casual tone making Grant grin before he turned his head towards his friend, struggling to keep his face serious.

"The prime rib at The Shack was excellent. I'd highly recommend it."

"I've had it," Steve growled out as the two men entered the room, making Grant smile again at Steve's obvious frustration.

Grant struggled for a long moment to keep his face straight, but once he knew he could keep it that way he said as nonchalantly as possible, "Yeah. Maggie really enjoyed her shrimp, too. We had a nice time—dinner, drinks, and then early to bed."

Steve's head whipped up and Grant nearly lost his control at the sight of blood in Steve's eyes before he managed to add innocently, "Alone."

Grant patted Steve once on the back and dropped into one of the comfortable chairs sitting around the large conference table.

"Very cute, Evans," Steve said and dragged the chair beside Grant out and threw himself down into it. "You're absolutely hilarious."

When Grant merely looked at Steve, a huge smile on his face, Steve gave in and grinned back, muttering "asshole" under his breath before he turned to get the attention of the five other officers sitting around the table talking amongst themselves.

As Steve began going over the latest developments in the case, Grant sank back in his chair, relieved that another major hurdle to dating his partner's baby sister was over and that he and Steve were still on good terms.

Grant knew that it was a gamble to risk his relationship with Steve this way, but there was no way—especially after the time he'd spent with Maggie recently—he could or, more correctly, would turn back now. He'd have to lay it all on the line—his friendship and working relationship with Steve, his newfound happiness, and more importantly, his heart—if he were going to have any chance at winning.

And he had to win. The stakes were too high to lose.

Grant pulled his attention back to the meeting when Mac slipped in through the door and joined Jones at the far end of the table.

Steve finished filling the rest of the officers in on what he and Grant had discovered about Greg Daniels's alibi.

"So, Daniels is in the clear. Dusty have you managed to talk to the last of the occupants from the surrounding apartments and houses?"

Dusty cleared his throat and flipped open his notes, rustling the pages of his file back and forth briefly before clearing his throat again and answering.

"Almost. I cleared all but one tenant of the apartment complex that backs up to the victims building. A Samuel Wolffe. He left for Phoenix, Arizona, on a business trip early the morning of the murder and won't be back until tomorrow night.

"I managed to get ahold of someone in his office and have calls in to his hotel and the conference he's attending. I'm hoping for a call back this morning, and a face-to face interview tomorrow evening. If I don't hear from him, I spoke with Detective Don

Matters of the local police and he's agreed to go over to the convention center to track him down for us.

"As for the remainder of the occupants, there wasn't much there. I have a report that I'm finishing up typing for you guys as soon as this meeting is done."

"Donovan?" Steve turned towards an extremely tall, thin cop dressed in a plaid sports coat and a pair of khaki chinos.

Donovan ran one hand over gray hair slicked back over an ever growing bald spot he attempted to camouflage with several greasy strands of overlong hair, and cleared his throat once before he began.

"After canvassing the neighborhood I've got three different people who said that they saw someone walking down the vic's street about the time of the murder and four who said they saw a strange truck parked or driving on the street, but none of them can say much about it.

"The first, Mrs. Gloria Deluca, was letting her dog, Sparky, that she says has a bladder issue, out at about 4:17 a.m. and spotted a large dark truck parked across the street from her house. She thought it was strange because it hadn't been there at 2 a.m. when she'd been out with the dog, and it was gone by the time she let Sparky out again at 5:45 a.m.

"She also looked out her window around 5 a.m. when Sparky began barking to yell at him to be quiet when she noticed what she assumed was a man walking by on the opposite side of the street. He was dressed in dark clothes and had the hood of his coat up, so she has no real description other than he was 'thinish' and moved quickly.

"Our second witness, Charles Avery, works the night shift at the Seven Eleven over on Grand. He was just getting off the night shift and coming home at 5:40 a.m. when he turned onto his block and saw a dark blue late model Ford truck driving about a block ahead of him. He said he noticed it because the driver was driving without the headlights on.

"Third and fourth witnesses—Donald and Joey Granger, father and son, were delivering newspapers when they heard an engine start up the block. The father, Donald Granger, noticed the truck immediately. Says he's been driving his son along his route for more than a year now, and he knows the cars that belong on the block. Says he's never seen the truck in question before and remembers thinking that the idiot driving it should turn on his headlights or he was going to cause an accident.

"The kid, Joey, also noticed the truck. Said he thought it was pretty old looking, but he noted that there was a large dog kennel in the bed of the truck. Apparently he's been begging for a dog at home."

"What kind of dog?" Jones asked, a twinkle in her eye.

"Maybe he could call it Sparky," Mac added in an undertone.

"Well, he's debating between a retriever and..." Donovan broke off at the round of muffled laughter. He shot the now-grinning redhead a glare before he continued, "Anyway," he added loudly over the snickering, "The kid noticed the kennel."

Steve managed to swallow his own laugh before he interrupted to get them back on track, "Thanks Mikey. What about the second witness you had who spotted someone walking?"

Donovan turned to Bob Sylvester, his partner, a nondescript man sitting next to him in a gray suit, with dark gray buzz cut hair, and dark black round glasses.

"Bob?"

"Yes. Maria Suarez is a nurse at the University Hospital and she had just come out of her house to go into her garage to head in to work when she noticed a man walking past the end of her driveway."

"Was she able to give you a description?" Steve asked eagerly.

Sylvester and Donovan both smiled and nodded before Sylvester continued.

"She was. She got a good look at his face as he passed by."

"Did he see her?" Grant asked, trying to hide the concern he felt.

"She doesn't think so. She was already in the garage, and was looking out the window towards the street when he passed by. It was still pretty dark out, but he passed under the streetlight in front of her neighbor's house. She gave us a pretty detailed description and I have her coming in this afternoon to sit with the sketch artist to work on a composite drawing."

Up until this point in the meeting—and in the meetings that

had led up to this one—Grant had let Steve take the lead, knowing that direction coming from a trusted friend, someone that the other officers had worked with day after day, for years in some cases, would be easier to accept.

But at some point, Grant had to see if they could—or would—trust him. He cleared his throat and began to speak.

"When the sketch is completed we need to make sure we bring it back around to the other witnesses. Dusty, can you show the sketch to all the people in the area around the Daniels apartment?

"If he is our guy, he will have been in the area many times over the past few weeks, possibly months, and people will have seen him. Some may even remember doing so. Donovan and Sylvester, I'd like you two to do the same with the Roberts neighborhood. Mac and Jones with the Martin neighborhood.

"Steve and I are going to probably be talking with all of you over the next couple of days about any unsolved vandalism, arson, break-ins, etcetera, that took place in the three neighborhoods around the times of the murders."

Grant stopped talking and turned to Steve, cocking one eyebrow, to ask if he'd missed anything important. At Steve's subtle head shake, Grant turned back to his team and said, "Any questions?"

When no one said anything Grant said, "Good work everyone. Let's get out there and catch this bastard."

After Dusty, Donovan and Sylvester had filed out of the room and only McKenzie and Jones remained with Steve and Grant, Steve dug out the case file on the arson. Grant got up and walked over to close the door before he walked back to the small group to sit down again.

"So, what can you tell us about the Simpson case?" Steve asked.

McKenzie and Jones glanced at each other. McKenzie inclined his head slightly and Jones began, "Last Tuesday night Gil Bellows, the apartment manager, phoned in the fire and break-in at 11:18 p.m. He and his wife, Jennifer, live across the hall from the Simpson place. The two were watching the late show when they heard a window breaking and smelled smoke. Mrs. Bellows ran upstairs to make sure Jessie Daniels got out of her apartment while

Mr. Bellows called 911. The other apartment upstairs was empty, the family on vacation, and the Simpson's—Rebecca and Simon— had gone out to a friend's house for dinner and a meeting."

Jones paused and glanced down at her notes briefly, but Grant had the distinct impression that she didn't really need the notes to recall any of the details she was relating.

She continued, "The meeting was for their church group— they're planning a mission trip to the Appalachian area of Kentucky and Tennessee this next spring—and the meeting had run late. Lucky for them.

"The fire department responded within seven minutes, but by the time they got to the scene the apartment was completely involved. They were able to keep the fire from spreading to any of the other apartments, but much of the Simpson apartment was destroyed.

"As you have already read, the fire inspector reported that the fire was not accidental. In fact, they found five separate sources with common accelerants and fuel trailers—there were lighter fluid-soaked rags in the center of each room," Jones said, then paused and McKenzie took over, his deep voice filling the room.

"The rest of the apartment complex was cleared and occupants were given the go-ahead to return to their apartments by Friday morning. The Simpson's have relocated to a family member's house. The address is in the file. They were completely shocked, had no ideas of who could have done this, and could think of no reason why.

"That would normally suggest simple vandalism gone out of control, degenerate kids, you know, something like that. But the viciousness and the professional nature of the job led us to believe that this is something nastier—and more targeted."

At McKenzie's words, Grant felt a lead weight settle in his stomach. The picture McKenzie was painting was a grim one. Grant only hoped that this arson was committed by their killer.

If what he hoped were true, then the killer might have made a mistake somewhere. And if the killer had made a mistake, then they would uncover it and use it to nail him.

Grant's gaze met Steve's before they both turned their attention back to McKenzie and Jones.

Jones took over the recitation again. She said, "We have another interview with the Simpson's set up tomorrow. We'd planned on doing it Monday, but the murder investigation took precedence."

Steve nodded his understanding and before he could say anything Jones said, "We spoke with several people in the area about the arson, but we hadn't gotten very far. What do you think about talking with Dusty to see if he can ask the people he interviews today about the sketch to ask them about the time around the fire as well?"

Grant spoke up again, "I think that's a great idea. You guys are definitely on the right track. Something's there."

"Agreed," Steve said, and then continued, "If you guys don't mind, I'd like to talk to the Bellows about a possible connection, and if you two are all right with it, I'd like one of us to tag along with one of you guys when you speak with the Simpson's tomorrow."

McKenzie nodded, agreeing, and said, "Sure, Sully," before he turned to Jones and raised his brow. She flashed a lighting quick grin and said, "I'll take Ace here with me tomorrow while you and Sully talk to the Bellows, Mac."

Grant grinned crookedly at her name for him and almost laughed before he responded, "You got it Jones."

Looking back and forth between the two, Steve frowned once before he cleared his face and added a neutral, "Okay. That's settled. Thanks, Mac, Jones."

McKenzie nodded and stood up while Jones walked around the table to lean against it next to Grant and said, "So, did you get the chance to go to The Shack yet?"

"Officer Jones, if you don't mind, I need to speak with Detective Evans. The two of you will have to discuss your social plans later," Steven said stiffly.

Jones straightened her spine and came up on her feet, green sparks shooting from her eyes. But she only said, "Yes *Sir,* Detective Sullivan," in a voice cold enough to freeze boiling water before she turned back to Grant and added warmly, "I'll catch you later, Ace," and turned sharp green eyes briefly towards Steve before she turned away and strode quickly out of the room, closing the door sharply.

McKenzie looked back and forth between a clearly bewildered Grant and a furious Steve and holding back his own smile he cleared his throat once and said neutrally, "See you guys later."

After McKenzie had closed the door, leaving Grant and Steve alone, Grant turned to his partner and opened his mouth to speak but closed it with a snap when he caught the dangerous look in Steve's eye.

"What's the story here, Evans?" Steve snarled out.

"Story?" Grant asked, confused.

"Yeah. The story. What's the story between you and Bethany?"

"Bethany?" Grant turned towards Steve, eyebrows drawn down, and then realization dawned and his face changed from bewilderment to amusement in a flash, "You mean *Jones*?"

"Yeah, Evans, who did you think I was talking about? You went out with my sister less than twenty-four hours ago and you're here *flirting* with another woman."

All amusement fled and Grant took a moment to remember that as Maggie's big brother, Steve was just looking out for her. He took a big breath and said, "Steve, there's nothing going on with Jones and me. I barely know her. She was nice enough to recommend a restaurant to take Maggie to last night, that's all.

"I know we haven't known each other for a very long time, but you trusted me enough to go out with Maggie, now trust me enough not to worry that every girl I'm nice to or joke around with is not of interest to me romantically."

While Steve sat there thinking Grant added smoothly, "Besides, anyone with eyes can see Jones is only interested in you."

When Steve's mouth fell open, his expression completely transformed to shock, Grant sat back, satisfaction on his face.

A full minute later, Steve managed to sputter out, "M-me?"

"Yes, you. You're a trained investigator, an expert in understanding what motivates other people and in looking for signs of how people are feeling underneath the surface. You can't honestly tell me that you've never noticed the way that she looks at you."

Steve shook his head sharply once as if to clear it then said, "Listen Evans, we're not talking about me, we're talking about you, here."

"Steve," Grant interrupted quietly, his humor gone, "I give you my word that Maggie is the only woman that I am interested in romantically. I can't promise to not talk with or be friends with other women, but I don't cheat on the women that I date—I'd never deliberately hurt someone I care about. And I do care about Maggie, Steve."

Steve nodded and said, "All right, Grant. I know I can get nuts, but I'm kinda worried about Maggie right now. She called me and wants to have dinner tonight, and my instincts are saying that there's something behind it. Do you know what this is all about?"

Sighing Grant ran his right hand through his hair before he crossed one ankle over his knee and said slowly, "Steve, I think you should let Maggie talk to you about this. I don't want to get in the way of how she wants to deal with the situation."

When Steve opened his mouth to speak, Grant held one hand up and shook his head again. "Don't ask me to betray her trust, Steve. I understand why you're asking, and I would tell you if I could, but believe me, she would *not* understand my interference with this."

Struck at the depth of Grant's understanding of his sister, Steve nodded once, "Fine. I'm meeting her in a couple of hours and I'll find out then, but Grant if this is about you, then I *will* be talking to you again."

"I wouldn't expect anything else," Grant grinned over at his friend, and then said, "Now let's get started on reviewing those files."

TWENTY-FOUR

"Earth to Maggie."

"Huh?"

"Maggie, are you okay?"

Maggie surfaced from her thoughts to look up and see a concerned Cloë hovering over her.

"What did you say?" Maggie asked, a baffled look on her face, making Cloë laugh.

"Sweetie, I've been trying to get your attention for almost a minute now. I hope that whatever has you so distracted has nothing to do with work and everything to do with Detective Delicious."

Maggie blushed and threw the invoice she'd been trying to read for the past fifteen minutes down onto her cluttered desk. "Detective Delicious?" she asked.

"Mmm hmm. Mr. Tall, dark, and dreamy. Mr. 'he makes me laugh', Mr...."

"I got it, Cloë," Maggie glanced at Holden's closed office door and held up a hand to stop her friend before she could continue, then she said, "And to answer your question, no. I'm not thinking about work even though I definitely *should* be."

"Hot tamale!" Cloë punched the air in victory and threw herself down onto her chair.

"No. No hot anything. I wasn't thinking about Grant either—at least not directly," Maggie said, then hesitated to lift worried eyes to meet Cloë's for a brief moment before she tucked an errant curl behind her ear and continued, "I was thinking about Steven and..."

"And?"

"And Bradley."

"*Tell* me you are not having second thoughts about that jerk, Maggie. He's a serious creep."

Maggie shook her head and replied quickly, "No, no. It's nothing like that. It's just I had a little run-in with him last night right before Grant picked me up for our dinner date." Maggie trailed off again, unsure of how much to reveal to her friend, but before she could second-guess herself she took a big breath and blurted out,

"And things were getting…ugly…when Grant showed up and saved the day."

After describing the night's events Maggie paused again and glanced over at Cloë in time to see her shoot out of her chair to plant both fists on her hips, looking for all the world like an oversized, outraged, pixie.

"He did *what*? That…He…What a…"

"Exactly," Maggie grinned and leaned back in her chair to enjoy the show. Cloë was one of the biggest sweethearts Maggie knew, but when she was really upset, once she really got going, her temper was something to behold.

In a whirl of motion Cloë began pacing swiftly around the small office, gesturing her arms out wide, shaking her small fists and muttering a series of words that Maggie rarely heard come out of her sweet-tempered friend's mouth.

Cloë stopped directly in front of Maggie's desk, and pointed her index finger at Maggie's nose and said sharply, "You reported that, that…soulless, spineless, scum didn't you?"

When Maggie didn't immediately respond Cloë's arm dropped slowly before she said in a voice all the more affective for its quietness, "Maggie, you have to report him. Now."

Maggie looked away from the outrage and the fear she saw in her friend's eyes and dropped her head down onto her hands. In a muffled voice she said, "I know."

Cloë heard anger and humiliation in Maggie's voice, but it was the hint of despair beneath the other emotions that had Cloë banking her own feelings and reaching out to lay her hand on Maggie's shoulder.

At her friend's comforting touch Maggie lifted her head and said, "I called Steven this morning and he's coming over for dinner. He doesn't know why yet, but I'll be filling out an official report with him."

Clearly relieved, Cloë collapsed back onto her chair before she said, "Well, that's *something* at least. Please tell me that you're going to press charges."

"I'm not sure."

"What?" Cloë yelped, interrupting.

Maggie held up one hand and continued, "I'm filling out a report, mostly because Grant insisted that I do so, but I seriously doubt that a few offensive words and a shove are going to result in any type of official charges."

"Hmph. Well, you be careful, and don't see him again."

Grateful that the worst of the storm had passed, Maggie's eyes twinkled merrily, "Oh, I doubt that Bradley wants to see me again—especially after the way Grant swept the floor with him last night."

"Oh, my. Details, please!"

Maggie felt a satisfied grin stretch across her face as she remembered the night before. "I was arguing with Bradley and things were getting pretty nasty when Grant came up behind him. He had Bradley on the floor so quickly, I barely saw what happened, and then he practically threw him out the door and down the hallway."

Maggie paused to fan herself, knowing that Cloë was always an excellent audience. The perfect listener, Cloë could always be counted on to ooh and aah and call names exactly when Maggie needed to hear them—and her reaction this time didn't disappoint.

Cloë sighed dramatically, one hand on her heart.

Maggie continued, "I must say, it was positively…stimulating."

"Stimulating?" Cloë repeated doubtfully.

"Exciting."

"Exciting?" Cloë said derisively.

"Sexy?" Maggie questioned.

"Sexy," Cloë nodded emphatically, "Definitely very sexy."

For one long moment both women sat there silently before both burst into laughter.

And that is how Holden found them when he opened the door of his office to talk to his always efficient office manager—two women laughing so hard that tears rolled down their cheeks.

The sight of Maggie, her head thrown back, cheeks flushed and eyes bright made him forget what it was he had come out to ask her. He smiled involuntarily before he remembered what it was he wanted to say.

Holden cleared his throat and said, "Ah, Maggie? Do you have a minute?"

Maggie smiled at his hesitant tone and stood up, saying, "Sure, Holden. Cloë and I were just finishing up. I'll see you tomorrow, Cloë, okay?"

Cloë managed to swallow back another chuckle before she nodded and said, "Sure. You can fill me in on how everything goes tonight then."

Holden glanced at his watch, his eyebrows drawing down, and said, "I didn't realize it was already after five, Maggie. We can do this in the morning if you have plans for the evening."

Confused at the formal tone in her usually amiable boss's voice Maggie said, "No, that's not necessary. I'm just having Steven over for dinner. He's probably still at work, and I told him I'd call him once I was headed home so that neither of us would need to worry about holding things up."

Holden smiled, relieved. He'd caught the tail end of the women's conversation and had felt a bolt of unease shoot through him at the thought that Maggie might be seeing someone else already.

When Cloë turned to shut her computer down he held the door to his office open for Maggie. As she swept past him to sit in front of his desk Holden drew in a deep breathe, letting the sweet scent of lavender and vanilla fill his senses as she walked past him.

For a brief moment the longing he felt for her transformed his face before he schooled his features and rounded the desk to face her.

Blissfully unaware of his roiling emotions, Maggie settled into the chair and pulled out her planner and pen. "What can I do for you, Boss?"

Holden sat down in his chair and folded his tanned forearms on his blotter before he said, "I've been talking with the Dean, and I agreed to put together a short seminar, just three weeks long, for next quarter. It would be an evening class, meeting once a week, starting in just over a month."

"That's not much notice," Maggie said sympathetically, "I'll help you as much as you need, Holden."

Holden leaned back in his chair and smiled, "I'm glad you feel that way, Maggie because I want you to put together a series of lectures based on, but not limited to, the themes and information used in your article."

Maggie's hand fell limply into her lap and she stared at Holden, shock covering her small features. He grinned again before he continued, "I'd want you to choose all the slides and prepare the necessary quizzes and the final exam."

Maggie automatically wrote down his instructions, and once she recovered her voice she said, "Holden, I'm flattered that you'd trust me with that, and I'll be happy to do it, but I know how you like to choose the slides you use for your classes yourself."

"That's true. But I won't be teaching this class."

"Who…"

"You will be—if you agree to," Holden said before he smirked at striking his normally self-possessed assistant dumb for a record two times in less than five minutes.

When Maggie drove home forty-five minutes later, the shock and the brief moment of terror that she'd initially felt at Holden's proposal had mostly worn off, leaving a growing excitement. Here was the chance she'd been looking for to branch out and contribute in a more hands-on capacity.

As ideas for the lectures raced through her mind she itched to write them down. She eyed the bulging planner she'd set on the passenger seat and, with her mother's—and Steven's—disapproving voice in her head, immediately dismissed the thought of jotting them down while she was driving.

Steven. She'd forgotten all about Steven.

Maggie fumbled as she reached into her purse, and after several attempts, managed to pull out her cell phone.

"Hey, Mags."

"Hi, Steven. I'm on my way home."

"All right. I'll wrap up what I'm doing and head on out."

"Sounds good. See you in a bit."

"See ya."

Maggie closed her phone and dropped it back into her purse as she turned onto her block. Instead of parking she drove past her apartment—there was one more stop she needed to make.

By the time Steve rang the buzzer, Maggie had run her errand, changed her clothes, set the table, and put the finishing touches on the special dessert she'd whipped together before she'd left the apartment that morning.

After she'd buzzed him in she waited, one hand on the doorknob, with her eye to the peephole. When she saw Steven she unlocked the door. One close call was enough, and it would be a while before she felt completely secure about leaving her door open again.

"Hey, Steven."

"Hi, Mags. I see you're finally being more careful and not leaving your door standing wide open like I told you you shouldn't."

Maggie rolled her eyes and shut the door a little more firmly than necessary before she followed Steven into the apartment. Trust Steven to immediately pick up on the one thing she didn't want to talk about. She'd hoped to put off her discussion about last night's run-in with Bradley as long as possible.

"Oh, you know I always listen to you, Steven," Maggie said sweetly and batted her eyes at him. Steve grinned and said, "Yeah, right, Mags," but he noticed the tension in her shoulders and the worry in her eyes and made a mental note to push the subject later.

Maggie noted his casual attire—a ratty pair of jeans, white at the stress points, and a black T-shirt under a leather jacket—and deduced that he'd had time to go home and change before she'd called. And she wondered if Grant was home, too.

"Where do you want to eat," Steve asked, holding up a bag filled with Chinese take-out boxes.

"At the table," Maggie pointed at the small round oak table her brother, Seth, had passed down to her when he'd married Sybil, before continuing, "Beer or pop?"

"I'll take a Coke if you've got one."

Maggie nodded and went to grab a Diet Pepsi for herself and one of the Cokes she'd stopped to get on her way home for Steven.

Neither spoke as they ate their way through several different containers of steaming food. After emptying her plate and eating a second cream cheese wonton Maggie sat back, weighing the pleasure of eating a third against the extra mile she'd have to run in the morning before she shrugged and reached for the third wonton anyway.

Steve grinned, amused at his petite sister's constant battle to balance her love of food with her need to be fit. He could never understand why she worried so much. She was tiny, and if their mother was any indication, she had nothing to worry about.

"So, to what do I owe this honor?" Steve asked as he filled his plate a third time.

Maggie pushed her empty plate away and grabbed her napkin to wipe nervously at her fingers. She blew out a breath and met Steven's eyes.

"I needed to talk to you. About Bradley."

Now, it was Steve's turn to push his plate away, all humor gone from his face. "What happened?" Steve asked in what Maggie termed his cop voice.

"Who said something happened? Did Grant say something to you?" Maggie said, hoping to stall for just a little more time.

That small hope was immediately dashed when Steve said, "Maggie. You invite me over because you had something to talk about. You left the door shut and locked, and you won't look me in the eye," Steve paused, and when she didn't reply he added, "Tell me what happened, Maggie, because Grant sure as hell didn't tell me a thing."

Maggie sighed again and raised her eyes to meet his. She said, "I want you to promise me that you'll stay calm, that you won't go do anything crazy."

Now it was Steve's turn to simply sit there, face completely blank, eyes shuttered. Maggie rolled her eyes again and said, "At least promise me you'll listen to everything I say before you do anything."

"Fine. Tell me. You can start with why you broke up with him."

"He cheated on me, that's what happened, Steven." Maggie stopped and grinned in appreciation at the word her big brother spat out before she went on, "I'd gone to show him my article and I found him with his secretary. Anyway, I told him to stuff it and left, but he's been calling and emailing me several times a day, at home and work, ever since.

"Well, I've been ignoring him, but I forgot to screen yesterday at work, and he got through to me. He's all 'you're acting immature' and telling me that we need to see each other so he'd made a reservation at a nice restaurant for dinner. But I told him it was over and that he could take his reservations and…Well, you get the picture.

"Anyway, I was getting ready for my date with Grant when the buzzer rang, so I just pushed the button and left the door open like always. Only this time it backfired on me and instead of it being Grant it was Bradley.

"Bradley kept insisting that we go to dinner and things were getting pretty nasty verbally when Grant showed up and threw him to the ground."

Steven's eyes narrowed and he held up a hand to stop Maggie as she opened her mouth to hurry on.

"Back up there, Mags. Tell me *why* Grant had to throw that asshole to the floor if you were just talking."

Maggie wrinkled her nose and, cursing his ability to pick up on the smallest detail, said, "I was hoping you'd miss that."

"Nope."

"Fine. He was grabbing my arm," Maggie pulled the sleeve of her shirt up to reveal an ugly line of purple bruises ringing her bicep. Steve hissed between clenched teeth. Ignoring him Maggie quickly continued. She wanted to simply get it all out before her seemingly calm brother blew.

"And when I said some less than flattering things he almost hit me. If Grant hadn't grabbed his arm he would have," Maggie trailed off as Steve leapt to his feet and paced away from the table and back, his motions jerky.

Steve sat down next to Maggie again and gently held her hand. "Are you okay, Mags?"

Tears stung her eyes as she gripped his hand harder for a moment. "I'll be okay. I was more shook up than hurt or frightened. I wouldn't have even said anything, but Grant talked me into at least talking to you."

Gratitude for his partner's ability to influence his hard-headed sister into talking with him warred with the sharp slash of fear and rage that had flashed through him at her words.

The rage won.

It took every ounce of his control to bank that blind fury, to stow it away until he could aim it at a more deserving, more *appropriate* target, but he did it—barely.

He was silent for a full minute before he managed to pull himself together enough to speak calmly. Finally he said, "You're going to do a hell of a lot more than just talk Maggie. You're going to file charges against the bastard."

"No. No, just wait," Maggie held up a hand when she saw his mouth open again, "I don't want to file any charges—just like I told Grant when he said the same thing. I can't file charges for a few nasty words and an almost hit. No. I won't file any charges, but I'll fill out an official report of the incident on the off chance something else happens—which I do *not* expect to happen."

"Damn straight nothing else is going to happen," Steve growled out.

Maggie's eyes shut briefly before she said sharply, "This is *exactly* why I had no intention of telling you any of this. You promised me you wouldn't do anything, Steven. And you can *not* tell any of the guys or Mom and Dad."

"Maggie…"

"I'm serious, Steven. You tell any of them and I will not forgive you. I swear. I won't have any of them worried about me. It's bad enough *you* know."

Steve eyed his irate sister for a long moment, considering, before he nodded slowly and said, "Okay. We'll do it your way."

Relieved, Maggie slumped back in her chair, and then stiffened again at his next words.

"*If* you file a restraining order against him."

Maggie shook her head and said, "C'mon, Steven, what's the point? A piece of paper will prove nothing, and I really do not believe that Bradley cares enough about me at this point to do anything else."

"Well then filing it won't hurt anything, will it?" Steve said in such a reasonable tone of voice that Maggie had the sudden urge to kick him.

She blew out a long breath that lifted a stray lock of curling hair from her forehead and eyed him, considering. "Is that *really* necessary?" she said in a wheedling tone.

"It's non-negotiable, Mags. You file, or I start talking."

"You wouldn't," Maggie said, her voice quiet with disbelief.

"Not only would I, but after your little rose bush threat I'd feel absolutely no guilt doing it either."

Maggie looked over at Steve's face with its smug expression and serious eyes and knew she was sunk. But, she thought, there was no reason *he* had to know that she was ready to give in.

Oh, no.

She would make him suffer a little bit first. He needed to work for it, she decided, and she knew that he'd expect no less from her, and *she* would be more than happy to oblige.

So, she narrowed her eyes, crossed her arms and proceeded to do just that.

When Steve walked out of Maggie's apartment, tinfoil-covered-plate of double chocolate caramel brownies in hand, he was feeling extremely pleased with himself. He'd finally out-argued his hard-headed little sister.

He'd not only gotten her to agree to fill out a restraining order, he'd managed to distract her before she could make him promise not to go have a little "discussion" with Bradley.

Steve smiled, and if anyone had been walking by at the moment they would have been alarmed, perhaps enough to stop or even to cross the street at the sight of the vicious glee that crossed his face.

He stopped to unlock his truck and glanced across the street at the lit windows at Grant's house, and for a moment considered stopping in. He immediately dismissed the idea—not only would he be seeing Grant bright and early in the morning but, more importantly, he was still far too angry about what Maggie had told him to socialize in any civilized manner right now.

Steve climbed into his truck and drove off, still planning exactly how and when he would have his little chat with Bradley.

Mercifully oblivious to her brother's dark thoughts, Maggie stood in her window and watched until Steve pulled away from the curb and drove out of sight before she collapsed onto her big, comfy chair.

A huge smile crossed Maggie's face—she'd finally out-argued her stubborn older brother.

Dealing with any of the men in her life when they were furious was always exhausting, but for once Maggie knew that she'd held her own with her overprotective sibling. More than held her own, in fact.

Sure, she'd agreed to fill out the restraining order, but she'd known she would have to do something to appease Steven. In the end, she'd gotten what she wanted—Steven would file the report for her and her other brothers and her parents would never have to know, to worry.

And, if she'd never really gotten a promise from Steven not to harm Bradley, she wasn't worried. Not *really* worried, anyway. After all, Steven was a law enforcement officer.

Okay, so maybe she was a *little* worried.

Maggie's smile faded from her face as she pictured some of the things her infuriated brother was capable of doing. But, surely, he wouldn't do anything drastic.

She hoped.

Pushing aside the worry Maggie closed her eyes and tried to regain some of the satisfaction that she'd just been feeling.

When she was younger her mother had always told her that timing was everything. It was an adage that Maggie had never fully understood at the time, but as the years had passed she'd come to see the wisdom of her mother's simple words and acted accordingly.

Hence the Chinese food, ice-cold Coke (Steven's favorite), and the pan of double chocolate caramel brownies. They weren't much, but Maggie had known that the setting, and the timing, could make the difference between dealing with an enraged, completely unreasonable Steven and a coldly furious, rational Steven.

And it had worked—at least as well as anything *could* work with her hot-tempered brother.

Knowing that there was absolutely nothing else she could have done to make the situation any better helped to ease the anxiety that had begun to seep over her. With a sigh Maggie pushed her way up and out of the deep chair to take care of the few dishes she'd used. She knew herself too well to believe that she would get to them first thing in the morning, and they'd be so much easier to handle tonight than whenever she eventually got around to dealing with them.

With a chuckle and a shake of her head, Maggie walked towards the kitchen and thought, timing really *is* everything.

TWENTY-FIVE

For the next two weeks, life was as close to perfect as Maggie could ever remember it being. When she wasn't working or researching for her lectures she was spending every waking moment possible with Grant.

Of course he was extremely busy with the investigation, but whenever they were both free, they were together.

They ran together almost every morning and had dinner out several times. He took her to the movies and she had taken him out on the lake in Seth's boat. They'd spent one memorable rainy afternoon going to antique shops looking for furniture for his house.

They'd gotten completely soaked, but in the end they'd found a china hutch perfect for his dining room, a couple of lamps for the living room, and an enormous stone pig that was so ugly that it had charmed Grant. He'd *had* to have it, and it now stood in his foyer ready to greet visitors as they walked in the front door.

Maggie had never felt more at ease with a man not in her immediate family before.

For Grant, Maggie was a revelation. For the first time since his father had died he was able to be himself—his whole self—with another person.

She understood him almost better than he understood himself. And the miracle was, she accepted him exactly as he was.

The only dark cloud during this time was the constant knowledge that there was a vicious killer on the loose, and Grant and the rest of the force seemed no closer to uncovering who it was.

And, although Grant had talked about the many parts of his life—his childhood, all his many likes and dislikes, his life in Seattle, his grandparents, and his passion for the profession he'd chosen—he never once spoke about Lou or the night they walked into that dark alley together.

He'd opened his mouth to tell her many times, but had always stopped at the last moment. And, although Maggie knew he held back a part of himself she didn't push.

She may not know exactly *what* Grant thought about when he grew pensive and unconsciously rubbed his hand on his thigh as if to sooth it, but she did know that he would share that knowledge with her when he was ready to.

She soon learned that any time she brought up his father or the reasons why he'd moved from Seattle to Hope Grant's face had blanked, his eyes shuttered.

At those moments Maggie pushed aside the hurt she felt and firmly reminded herself that they had only known each other for a few weeks.

As Maggie sat at her kitchen table on a sunny Saturday just a week before Halloween she thought about Grant and the conversation they'd had the night before.

They'd gone to see the latest Bond movie and were arguing over which actor they felt was best in the role.

"Craig?" Grant said incredulously, "You've got to be kidding. It's totally Roger Moore. Now, I would have tried to respect your answer if you'd said Connery, but Craig? No way." Grant shook his head back and forth slowly.

"For the classics it has to be Connery for me. Moore was always a little bit *too* campy for my tastes. But Craig didn't simply slip into an established role. He re-invented one of the most beloved film characters of all time and made him more modern, more exciting, and infinitely sexier."

By the time she'd finished speaking Maggie stood toe-to-toe with Grant, hands on her hips and chin up. The fire of battle burned in her eyes as she raised them to glare at him.

Grant stared, smiling down into her passion-filled face. Slowly the smile slipped from his face and his arms snaked around her to crush her body to his.

Maggie remained stiff for a moment and raised her arms to push him away, but halfway there they shifted to twine around his neck to pull him closer. Every coherent thought slid right out of her head and, helpless to the rising tide of pleasure that swept through her, Maggie simply clung.

Maggie sighed and returned to the present. The powerful memory of their kiss stained her cheeks red and she thought that, yes, the time she'd spent with Grant these last few weeks was definitely some of her happiest.

In the face of that happiness, Maggie was finding it harder and harder to be convinced that falling in love with Grant was a mistake.

With every moment they spent together, the worries and reservations she felt about getting seriously involved with someone so soon after a break-up seemed to no longer matter.

In the face of the strong connection and intense attraction they both clearly felt, her many concerns seemed to just fade away. Maggie knew she should be cautious, go slowly, but things were so happy, so right. She just couldn't seem to care about the timing any longer.

Maggie pushed back from the table. Clearly she wasn't getting much work done. She might as well work on her props and costumes for Halloween. After all, she didn't have much time left to get everything completed. Luckily she didn't have much left to finish.

She'd taken immense pleasure in informing both Jack and Dillon that they would be helping her this year. They'd agreed cheerfully—at least until she'd started measuring them for their costumes. That's when they'd begun to get a little worried.

Little did they know.

Just thinking about the costumes she'd put together for them made her cackle with glee. Maggie turned on the stereo and settled in to sew the last of the sequins on their costumes when someone rang her buzzer.

Maggie set aside her sewing and covered it with a blanket, sure that whoever was at the door was probably one of her brothers or parents. But, when she pushed the button and asked who it was she was surprised and delighted to discover that it was Grant.

After she buzzed him in, Maggie ran to the mirror to make sure her hair wasn't too wild—which, of course, it was. She used both hands to try to tame it as best as possible and grimaced when she looked down and remembered that she'd thrown on some old black cotton yoga pants and an oversized blue sweater to work in that morning.

When Grant's knock came at the door she shrugged and gave her hair one last look before she opened to door to let him in.

"Hey. This is a nice surprise. I thought you were meeting Steven, Jack, and Dillon to play basketball."

Grant flashed a killer grin down at her and leaned down to press a quick kiss to her lips. "I was. I did. We got done a bit ago, and I thought I'd drop by and see if I could spring you from your work for a while."

"Absolutely. Come on in. Are you hungry?"

"No. We ate after the game. Did you get all of your work done?"

Maggie closed the door behind him as he walked into the room and sat down on the couch. "I made a good dent, but I've still got a ways to go before I'll feel like I'm totally prepared. Luckily I've still got a little time before I've got to have it set, and Holden has promised to help me look everything over before the first class.

"So, who won the big game?" Maggie cocked one eyebrow and joined Grant on the couch.

"Jack and I won three out of five, but the last game was really a close one. I'm definitely going to be a little sore tomorrow."

"I thought a big tough guy like you would be in better shape," Maggie teased as she poked a finger into Grant's side.

Grant jerked away, laughing, and swatted her hand, "Cut it out. I meant that your brother, Dillon, has a nasty elbow," he paused to lift his faded blue T-shirt and showed Maggie a line of small, but painful-looking bruises blooming up and down his ribcage and continued, saying, "And I'm gonna be a bit sore later."

Maggie was used to her brothers constant roughhousing and seeing them go at each other. She'd seen her fair share of bloody noses and bruises—had even given a few—but she was appalled at the extent of the damage her normally easy-going brother had inflicted on Grant. Her eyebrows drew down as she reached forward to run her hand gently down his side.

"Oh, Grant," she said sympathetically before her outrage took over, "What was Dillon thinking? When I get a hold of him..."

"Maggie, I'm fine. And to answer your question, I imagine he was probably thinking 'Here's the jerk who's hitting on my baby sister' and he decided he'd make sure I knew he was going to keep an eye on me," he said wryly before he grinned and added, "Not to worry, Dillon's got his own bruises—I didn't meekly stand there and take it, Red.

"Besides," Grant shrugged, "It's basketball," he said so matter-of-factly that Maggie dropped her hand to stare at him for a long moment before she rolled her eyes and said, "Men," in such a disgusted tone that Grant laughed out loud.

Maggie struggled to keep a disapproving look on her face, but she gave in and laughed, too. "You know, you really are just like them. Baboons—all of you." But she reached over to caress his cheek gently before she added, "I don't know whether I should be terrified or thrilled."

Before he could come up with an answer Maggie stood and said brusquely, "Come on, I think I've got something you can put on those bruises that will help."

Grant followed her into her bedroom where she pointed at the bed and said, "Have a seat. I'll grab the salve." She walked into the tiny bathroom just off the bedroom and Grant wandered the room to take it all in.

The walls were painted a rich, deep green that brought to mind a secret, shaded forest glen. A large bed with an iron scrolled headboard and footboard dominated the small space. It was covered with a green and brown satin spread and what looked like dozens of pillows. A large brown velvet chair draped with a beaded green throw sat in the corner of the room and a small, round iron table that made Grant think of Paris sat next to it with a lamp, empty wine glass, and an open book on it.

Shelves loaded with books lined one wall and three large windows dressed in gauzy white curtains faced them. But, what captured Grant's attention the most was the large painting Maggie had hung on the wall above her headboard.

A dirt path twisted through sun-dappled trees, leading further and further into the heart of the forest. Filled with secrets and mystery, and a large helping of passion, the painting spoke to Grant. It seemed to almost call out to him to journey along that mysterious path, to set off on the adventure of a lifetime.

Grant dragged his attention from the framed painting when Maggie walked back into the room and said, "I like your room."

"Thanks. So do I. I always feel at peace when I'm in here. Why don't you have a seat on the bed and take off your shirt."

When Grant raised his eyebrows and leered over at her Maggie blushed and added quickly, "I want to put some of this salve on those bruises before they get any worse."

"Sure, Red," Grant said and stripped off his shirt to reveal his truly amazing body.

Maggie fumbled with the lid of the salve before she was able to unscrew it. She tried to keep her eyes down, but they were drawn upwards to drink in the sight of Grant's perfectly-proportioned chest and flat stomach. Seemingly of their own will, Maggie found her eyes drawn to the line of dark hair that spread across his chest and arrowed straight down and out of sight into the waistband of faded denim.

With a jerk Maggie brought her eyes up to meet Grant's amused gaze. She watched in wonder as she saw the amusement fade as awareness darkened his eyes.

For several heartbeats their eyes locked before Maggie deliberately dropped her gaze to the line of bruises. She leaned down and a curtain of loose hair swung forward to brush Grant's bare chest as she reached out to gently rub the salve in.

Her hand swept slowly up and down his side, learning the subtle dips and curves of his muscled flesh. As her fingers swept across his warm skin Grant's breath caught in his dry throat. When Maggie continued sweeping her hand along his side, he stared down at the top of her head, studying the way the sunlight that beamed in from the window behind them made her hair shine with a rainbow of shades of red—from deep auburn to a soft red-gold, and tried to ignore the effect her touch was having on his body.

He drew in a deep breath and inhaled the sharp scents of mint and eucalyptus. And under them, he smelled the warm scents of vanilla, lavender, and woman that were all Maggie.

When she was almost finished he reached out slowly to grab her hand and, drawing it up to his mouth, he brushed his lips softly across her palm and over her wrist where her pulse beat frantically.

Maggie's eyelids swept down and her brain clicked off as Grant pressed closer to work his way up her arm. He paused to linger at the sensitive curve of her elbow before he straightened and stood before her.

Maggie's eyes dragged open to stare blindly up at Grant. He swept his hand up to cup her cheek before sliding his fingers into her thick curling hair, scattering pins and drawing her hair free from the loose bun she'd arranged it in that morning.

"Grant. I don't think…"

"Don't think, Red," he murmured, "Come away with me— just for a little while."

Taking her silence for consent he leaned forward the last few inches to lay a tender kiss on her parted lips and drank in her soft sighs. Slowly Maggie's arms lifted to join loosely behind Grant's head. The sweetness, the perfectness of the moment filled Maggie, making her heart ache just a little.

Grant drew slightly back, his hands wrapped firmly around her wrists, and said thickly, "Let me have you, Maggie. Be mine."

Maggie knew there should be a reason—several reasons, really—for her to say 'No'. Not a single one of them came to mind.

So she listened to her heart instead.

She pulled back further, her eyes no longer clouded, and said only, "Yes." And with that single word everything changed.

Grant struggled to keep things as tender, as slow, as they had begun, but her acceptance, the absolute need he'd heard in her soft reply, had thrown a switch in him and he could no longer hold back the reservoir of passion that had been building, building from the very first moment he'd seen her barefoot, dressed in cutoffs, framed in her parent's front door.

He dove into her as if she were a cool drink and he were a man who'd been stranded in the desert for days without water. His hands were everywhere at once, stroking, sliding. His lips met hers wildly, hungrily. As his tongue swept against hers his hands ran up her arms and down her sides to mold her body, learning, exploring.

And then those hands were beneath the baggy sweater to find her wonderfully, intoxicatingly bare beneath it. His hands were just a little rough against the satiny smoothness of her skin as they skimmed softly over the flat plane of her stomach, making her muscles bunch and quiver in response.

When those wonderful fingers brushed the undersides of her breasts, Maggie shivered as she threw her head back and moaned in delight.

When he swept the sweater up and off, her arms fell limply to her sides and Grant took a moment to look, to appreciate.

"You're so beautiful, so perfect," he murmured as he drew a single fingertip along her collarbone and down her breast and across one taught nipple before continuing down over her stomach to hook in the waistband of her stretchy pants.

Maggie gripped his shoulders with both hands, trying desperately to remain standing when a shaft of heat arrowed straight to her center.

Slowly he lowered first her pants, and then the triangle of lace beneath them. When she stood naked before him, her eyes dark with passion, Grant reached out both hands to brush through her hair, down along the sides of her breasts, and over her thighs.

A single fingertip lightly swept across her center. Testing, he found her hot, wet, ready.

At her sharply indrawn breath, Grant lowered his head to feast on one small breast, sweeping it with his tongue before turning his attention to her other breast. Maggie's eyes swept closed, her mind dizzy with the intense flood of pleasure.

And before she could recover, could think, his fingers plunged into her driving her up, up and over. Crying out, Maggie felt her knees give out as Grant swept her up and lay her down onto the bed.

The contrast of the cool, satiny feel of the covers against her fevered skin drew another shiver through her as she watched with avid eyes as Grant undressed and rejoined her on the bed.

Once again he possessed her mouth, then nipped and kissed his way along her jaw and down the soft curving line of her throat before he buried his face in the hallow where her neck sloped gently into her shoulder. Drawing in a deep breath, he inhaled the scent that was uniquely Maggie as he growled, "I want to be in you."

"Yes," Maggie breathed out as she swept frantic hands through his hair, across his back, his chest, his thighs to grip his hips. She arched against him, opening. "Now," she whispered.

"Now," Grant said and, lifting her hips, he entered her in one swift stroke.

For one long moment they froze, their eyes locked together, the intense pleasure of their joining overpowering both of them. Slowly his hands reached for hers. Fingers twined, hands gripped, and then they were moving together in a rhythm as old as time.

Lifting and falling, soft sighs and desperate cries. Slowly, slowly Maggie felt the pressure, the pleasure, building once more. Her eyelids began to drop again but Grant demanded, "Look at me. At me, Maggie," and, eyes locked, she flew off the edge of the world. And with a cry, he leapt over the edge to follow her.

"Well…hmmm," was all Maggie could manage after a long moment, her eyes closed and head cradled on Grant's chest. She felt the vibrations of his laughter through her cheek and smiled in response as she lifted her head to look sleepily down at him.

"I couldn't have said it any better myself," he said and used the last of his energy to pull up the covers to keep them warm. He pressed a soft kiss to Maggie's lips before he settled back with a contented sigh.

"So, how are the ribs?" Maggie trailed one hand lightly down his side, and when he jerked back saying, "Cut it out!" mischief lit up her eyes. Maggie cocked her head to the side, taking in the wary expression on Grant's face, and grinned wickedly.

"Ah-ha! Finally, a weakness I can exploit! Big Bad Copper is ticklish."

Grant held up both hands and said, "Now, Maggie…," in a nervous voice, making her grin widen, "Don't do anything you'll regret."

Maggie laughed, raised her eyebrows and said, "A direct challenge. If you knew me as well as my brothers do, you'd know better."

Maggie shrieked, the smug expression on her face gone, as she was suddenly flipped and pinned underneath two hundred pounds of rumpled, sexy man. She sucked in a breath to laugh, but the breath caught in her throat when she looked up into Grant's face as he smiled down at her.

She'd thought that after several weeks she'd gotten over her initial reaction to his almost outrageous good looks, but there were moments, like this one, when she found herself caught unawares, and the pure beauty of his features still had the power to catch her breath.

Grant smiled down at her, oblivious to her thoughts, and a devilish look crossed his face as he said, "Oh, I *do* know that, Red. Why do you think catching you off guard was so easy—I was ready before I opened my mouth."

The laughter in his rumbling voice did nothing to cover up the edginess beneath it, and Maggie was acutely aware of his hard body pressing hers into the mattress. The calm peacefulness their love-making had filled her with drained away to be replaced with a growing excitement.

Grant's teasing grin faded away as he watched the play of emotions cross over Maggie's upturned face. Slowly, slowly he pulled her wrists over her head.

Her eyes widened with awareness and she saw the clear intent on his face, the growing hunger in his eyes. Her already fast pulse skyrocketed, and the knowledge of what he intended had heat pooling once again in her stomach.

Grant dipped his head slowly to nibble back down her jaw to the sensitive lobe of her ear. Maggie's eyelids dropped and her eyes unfocused at the unexpected tenderness.

Grant paused next to her ear and whispered gruffly, his lips brushing softly against her sensitive skin causing a shiver to shoot down her spine, "This time there's no rush, no race. This time there's only you, Maggie. There's only you and me."

He kissed her, but before it could deepen, to speed, he pulled away to travel down, down. His lips and hands learned her body— every dip and curve, every swell and hallow, every texture and scent—as her hands fell limply to the mattress beside her head.

Up and up she built, her limbs so heavy they felt weighted, almost as if she were swimming under water. As she struggled to surface she felt only the softness of his skilled mouth, the subtle roughness of his fingers as they touched her everywhere.

The feeling of his brushing touches seemed to linger until it felt as if she were wrapped from head to toe in him.

Maggie floated on the pleasure as it slowly, steadily built, and for a moment the intensity of what she was feeling, of what she was experiencing, caused her to tense, a small fissure of fear breaking through her bliss. Feeling the tension Grant returned to her lips, and whispered, begged, "Let me. Just...let me."

Maggie fought to surface one last time, but the fear of losing control just wasn't strong enough and she sank back into the pleasure. With one last cry she stiffened, then shuddered as she came. The orgasm rolled through her, drawing out a low moan of satisfaction, and leaving her limp in his arms.

For the space of a heartbeat the tenuous hold Grant had maintained on his need faltered in the face of her absolute surrender, but his need to give her pleasure was too strong, too absolute, and his hold gentled again.

So, with sighs instead of moans, he slipped slowly inside of her and together they began to move. As the pressure built again, slowly, surely, the sweetness of the moment drew on and on until it was simply too much.

With a groan his fingers dug into her hips, tilting her up to sink even further into her warmth. The pace changed and they began to pick up speed. Faster, faster he thrust into her. Harder, harder she ground into him.

Maggie's arms came around his back, her nails biting as she held on tighter, and the tension built and built until neither could hold on any longer.

One of them moaned. Their eyes and lips met. And in the sweetness of that last meeting of lips, they shattered.

TWENTY-SIX

Grant sighed and dropped his forehead to rest it against hers. Maggie's hands came up to rest on either side of his face, and their eyes connected again, leaving Maggie breathless.

"I'm crushing you," Grant said and with one quick move, reversed their positions so that Maggie lay across his chest, her head on his shoulder.

As evening fell, a velvety darkness wrapped them in a cocoon of intimacy. The only illumination, a soft brushstroke of light from a streetlamp, filtered through the sheer curtains she'd hung on her windows.

"Maggie, I'm not sure how to ask this, so I guess I'll just come right out and ask," Grant paused. Wary, Maggie tensed, the euphoria she'd felt ebbing away. She shivered and drew away from his embrace to draw the covers up over them and turned to face him. Deep shadows hid his face, and any clues as to what he was about to say.

"Go on," Maggie said evenly.

"Well, I know that you just broke up with that…with someone," Grant amended quickly, "And I know you may come to regret what just happened—maybe you already do,' Grant finished in a rush.

Maggie interrupted, the hurt and confusion she was feeling clear in her voice, "Grant. Stop. I don't regret what we did—I enjoyed it, and I thought you did too."

"Damn. I'm sorry I'm screwing this up so badly, Maggie. What we just did was absolutely amazing and I don't regret a second of it. I was trying, in my extremely clumsy way, to make sure you were all right with it. I know you told me you wanted to take things slowly, and, well, we pretty much just threw slowly out the window."

Maggie heard more than apology in his voice, she heard a hint of remembered pain and just a touch of concern. And the fact that she did allowed her to box up her disappointment over the loss of their happy moment, and let her focus on finding out *why* it was lost.

"You haven't screwed anything up, Grant. I like that you are worried enough about my happiness that you would bring it up at all," she said sincerely, then added in a teasing voice, "And believe me when I say, when I'm *not* happy, you will *so* know it."

Grant was quiet for so long Maggie thought he was not going to go on, but finally he continued, his voice hesitant, "I guess I let my past create problems where there were none," Grant paused again before he continued, "You see, I was with a woman for over a year and I thought everything was fine, that she loved me—all of me. But she didn't. Everything I thought she was feeling was a lie, and by the time she told me what she was really feeling, it was too late. I'm sorry, Maggie."

Maggie leaned forward, placed one hand on his cheek and laid her lips against his. "Tell me," she said simply.

Grant searched her face, her eyes for any hint that she was upset, and seeing only patience, only acceptance he felt the last shred of wariness slip away and he spoke in a rush.

"She hated what I did for a living. She acted as if she were proud of me, of the work I was doing, but every time I had to cancel our plans, every time something came up and cut our time together short, I could sense her anger and her hurt.

"I dismissed it. I believed that love could overcome anything. I guess I still believe that. But what I didn't realize at the time, or maybe what I didn't let myself see, was that she didn't love me. Not truly. And looking back, I doubt she ever had."

Grant paused to gather his thoughts. "We were happy—or, at least, I was. Then I was offered a promotion that was primarily political. It was a terrific opportunity that I just didn't want. I didn't want to spend my days dealing with the press, with politics. I needed to be on the job.

"I turned it down and it almost ended us. Looking back I should have let it. And then I was shot and she was gone. By the time I left the hospital she'd moved out, and on to someone else."

The entire time Grant had been speaking Maggie's outrage and anger had bubbled and grown until it was ready to boil over. But the weary tone of voice Grant was talking in warned her that there was even more to the story, and that what was left unsaid was in some way even worse, even more difficult for him to deal with.

201

And she just couldn't bring herself to add her anger to the weight he was already so clearly bearing. She wouldn't do that, but she found she couldn't say nothing, so she said simply, "Good riddance."

Grant laughed and some of the weight that he had been feeling lifted from his shoulders, from his heart.

"That's pretty much the same conclusion I came to. Unfortunately, it took a little bit longer for me to get there. It didn't help that I was also dealing with my mother's hysterical panic and my sister's bitter anger at me for getting shot in addition to Shannon's abandonment. But, most importantly, I had to deal with losing my partner, Lou."

Maggie reached out to lace her fingers with his, and the simple show of encouragement was more than he'd received from his family, from his fiancé, when he'd needed it most. Her unconditional support soothed and gave him the strength to tell her all of it.

"We were off duty that night. We'd just closed a major case and we were out celebrating before heading home. We were just pulling up to the bar when the call came in—armed robbery in progress, officer needs assistance.

"We were officially off duty, but there was no question about whether or not to respond. Especially when we found out how close we were—just three blocks.
When we approached, we saw two suspicious people running around the corner and down the alley that ran behind the liquor store that had been robbed. I called it in. Lou was out of the car ahead of me.

"I was only about five feet behind him as we approached the alley." When Grant trailed off, lost in thought, Maggie waited. She rubbed his arm and hand softly, not wanting to interrupt, to rush him.

Lost in his memories, Grant forgot where he was, who he was talking to, as he went back down that alley one more time.

His heart began to pound, his breathing accelerated slightly, and his grip on Maggie's hand tightened painfully as he began to speak once more.

"I saw Lou slow as he came to the end of the corner building and I glanced over to the door of the liquor store as it flew open and a man came out running. It must have only been a matter of seconds for me to identify that the man running was one of ours—a cop. But it was long enough.

I turned back just as Lou started around the building. He glanced back just long enough to place me before he turned forward again, but that was all it took. The two robbers had stopped, panicked because they thought they were blocked in on both ends of the alley. I found out later that a tow truck had pulled into a parking lot a block away, but the flash of lights had been enough to send them back our way. When they saw movement they just started blasting away.

Lou was hit three times before he fell. I remember I dropped to one knee and hugged the wall. It was brick, rough to the touch," Grant paused to shake his head once before he continued, desperate to get the whole story out now that he'd begun.

"I don't remember saying anything, but I was told later that the other cop heard me screaming at them to stop, to drop their weapons. I have no recollection of doing that."

Maggie ached for him as she heard the bewilderment and vulnerability in his voice. She reached out to brush his hair away from his forehead, but didn't speak.

"I only remember seeing Lou on the ground, and then the first one came out firing. And then he was down. Suddenly the second one was just there screaming and firing round after round. Everything slowed down then. Everything became extraordinarily clear as he turned and swung his gun arm up towards me. I can still see the look on his face."

Grant stopped again and closed his eyes before he continued matter-of-factly in a strong, clear voice, "There were several flashes and I felt a tug on my leg. I ignored it. I fired again and again until my clip was empty. I was struggling to get out another clip to keep on shooting, but I was having a hard time getting my hands and arms to work properly. I had no idea at the time, but I was in pretty bad shape—shattered femur, blood loss, and shock all ganged up on me.

"Next thing I remember is laying on the ground and someone saying 'hang in there' over and over again. I remember parts of the ambulance, then nothing until a day and a half later.

"I kept hoping that I would die, and when I woke up I remember the fury, the bitterness that swept me into a deep depression because I hadn't. I had lived and Lou was gone.

"And then Shannon was gone, and so was my family. But none of that penetrated. It was more than two weeks before it even occurred to me to care."

Maggie couldn't remain silent any longer and she said, "Grant you *can't* blame yourself for that. I don't know how anybody could have expected you to be any stronger than you obviously had to be." Especially when your entire world had been ripped out from underneath you, Maggie added silently.

Maggie filed away the horror of the ordeal he had lived through, thank God, and the considerable anger that had built up as he spoke about the way his fiancé, his sister, and even his mother had deserted him when he'd needed them the most.

When she could trust herself to speak again without releasing all that pent up emotion loose she said, "I'm sorry. I'm so sorry, Grant, about your partner, and for what you had to go through alone."

The small fear he'd secretly harbored that she would somehow look at him differently if she knew the truth about his past was gone. The pain he'd felt while telling her faded at the calm acceptance, the sympathetic understanding he heard in her simple words.

With one last shaky breath Grant let go of the remnants of his fear, and the relief he felt was so great he knew that if he hadn't already been laying down, he'd have been on his ass.

He leaned forward to rest his check against hers for a moment before he eased back and said, "I wasn't completely alone. I had Jake and I had Ryan—Daniel Ryan, my father's old partner—in my corner. Without them, I don't know what would have happened, but I do know that I wouldn't be here today."

Maggie shook her head before she replied confidently, "You would have survived, Grant. You're just too strong, too brave, to give up that way. You don't have it in you to be a coward"

Grant felt his heart tremble at the pure conviction he heard in her quiet words. He leaned forward to brush a soft kiss against her lips once, twice, then leaned back and said, "Thank you, Maggie—for listening and for believing."

An hour later they sat facing each other across the kitchen table scarfing down cold pizza and warm wine.

Maggie had pulled on a pair of sweats and an oversized T-shirt. She sat, bare feet propped up on an empty chair, tousled hair trailing over her shoulders as she leaned forward to take a big bite of pizza and grin over at Grant.

He sat in his jeans and T-shirt, both elbows on the edge of her banged up old table. He looked just a little bit dangerous with his hair mussed, and the shadow of a day's growth of beard on his face.

Maggie watched as his white teeth cut through his piece of pizza, her eyes drawn to the sensuous way his lips moved as he chewed. The passion she'd banked began to smolder and fire again, and it was with a great effort that she pulled her gaze away to look down at her plate.

Grant swallowed and wiped his mouth before he leaned back to admire the view of a sexily-rumpled Maggie—eyes slumberous, hair disheveled and, he noted with a smile, a drop of tomato sauce on her chin.

"What?" Maggie stopped eating to wipe at her face.

"Here," Grant leaned forward and brushed his thumb gently across her bottom lip and the skin below it to wipe away the sauce before he absently sucked his finger clean.

Maggie dragged her eyes from his mouth and sighed. How could she want him so badly, so soon after they'd made love? Twice. The need she felt for him was so huge, so deep. It was simply beyond anything she'd experienced before, and she wasn't entirely sure she knew how to deal with it yet.

Maggie sighed again and pushed her plate away before she picked up her wine glass, toying with the stem rather than drinking from it. She set the glass down with a click and leaned back to cross her arms and asked, "So, how's the investigation going?"

Grant watched, fascinated, as the play of emotions crossed Maggie's face, and was once again struck by the thought that so much was going on under the surface that he didn't know or understand. He knew he should be scared, or at least wary, of delving into that unknown sea of emotions.

Instead, he found himself longing to know the thoughts that caused such an array of feelings, to understand her completely. Dismissing his thoughts as ridiculous Grant focused on the question she'd asked for a long moment before he responded.

"It's going alright. Nothing major has come up this week. I can't get too deeply into it, but right now we're using information from an FBI profiler to try to get a better understanding of the motivations behind the killer's actions."

Grant paused to blow out a long breath and to decide how much he could—or should—tell her. "I don't want to scare you, or get too deeply into the details, but I can tell you that this guy is very bad news. Do me a favor?"

"What?"

"Be careful. Make sure you are paying attention to your surroundings when you go out—particularly at night—and please make sure that you are locking up tight at night."

Alarmed, Maggie said, "Do you think I'm in danger?"

Grant reached out to grasp her hand and squeezed gently, "Not really. I'm not saying this to scare you, Red. I just won't feel better until we catch this guy. So, until then, humor me?"

Still uneasy, Maggie said, "All right. I'll be careful."

Grant gave her hand one last squeeze then he cocked one eyebrow up and gave her a fast smile, "So, are you up for continuing my movie education tonight, or do you still have too much to do for your class prep?"

Maggie smiled in response and said, "Oh, I think I could probably squeeze a little movie time into my schedule…for a fee."

"What's the price?" Grant asked, his eyes lit with amusement.

"Let's start with a foot rub and we'll see where it goes from there. Deal?" Maggie asked and wiggled her eyebrows suggestively at him, her face bright with barely contained humor.

"Deal," he laughed.

After they had put their dishes in the dishwasher, they headed back through her little dining room towards the living room. Grant glanced at the laptop, files, slides, and textbooks spread across the surface of Maggie's small dining room table and stopped so quickly Maggie almost ran right into him.

Maggie laughed and placed both hands on the center of his back to get him moving again, but the obvious tension in Grant's body brought her up short. The teasing expression slipped from her face to be replaced with one of concern.

"What's wrong?"

When he didn't answer she slipped around to face him and reached out to grab his hand. "Grant, what is it? Are you all right?"

The concern in her voice penetrated and Grant turned his blank face—his cop face—to look at her.

"I'm fine. What is this?" Grant reached over to pick up a large print showing a woman draped in cloths holding the broken, crucified body of a man.

Maggie studied his serious face for a long moment, looking for a trace of the warm, funny man she'd just spent most of the day making love with, but he was gone, leaving only Detective Evans in his place. Maggie had witnessed similar changes in Steven too many times to be alarmed, but she was confused as to *why* a picture of a five hundred year old statue would warrant his interest.

Slowly Maggie replied, "That's part of the research I've been doing for the class Holden asked me to lead. The picture you're holding is a shot of a sculpture by Michelangelo of the Piéta, or Vesperbild, also known as the Lamentation. It depicts the Virgin Mary mourning alone, the body of her son, Jesus, across her lap."

Grant had to suppress a grin at the lecturing tone her voice took on as she spoke, but he listened silently as she continued.

"I think I told you that I was going to be lecturing on the iconography of the life of Jesus Christ, with a focus on how it was portrayed during the Renaissance period. I've done several studies of the subject, and in particular the Piéta. That's why Holden asked me to teach this class. It's a passion of mine."

Maggie stopped talking and waited for Grant to respond. It was clear to her that his mind was racing, absorbing everything she had said.

Grant snapped his focus to her once again, his eyes intense and said, "Maggie, I have a huge favor to ask."

207

"Ask."

"I need to take a rain check on the movie. I need to find Steven and show him this picture right away." Grant paused, searching her face for signs of upset, and when he found only vague confusion and regret, he felt the weight of dread he hadn't even known was pressing down on him lift.

Maggie pushed aside the burning curiosity over how a picture of a work of art could be related to a series of murders and replied, "Okay. I've got another slide of that image at the office so you can keep that one. Grant, what's all this about? Is it something you can talk to me about?"

"I can't explain right now, but I'm going to need to talk to you about this in greater detail."

Maggie heard the apology in his voice and she leaned forward to kiss him quickly before she said, "All right. Do you want to try calling Steven? My guess is he's probably still at one of my brother's houses."

Grant again searched for, and was unable to find, any trace of anger or sarcasm in her voice. He nodded once and said, "That would be great."

When Maggie made as if to turn back into the kitchen Grant pulled her back around and suddenly Maggie found herself pressed back against the wall by six feet of lean, hard, muscled man being thoroughly kissed.

When Grant stepped away Maggie remained against the wall, grateful for its support. Eyebrows raised, eyes just beginning to cloud with heat again, she cleared her extremely dry throat and said, "Not that I'm complaining, but what was that for?"

Grant reached forward to cup her jaw and placed a soft, whispering kiss on her cheek that made her heart ache before he replied, "For being you, Maggie. Thank you for understanding, for not pressing for more."

Maggie again cursed the woman—women, really—who had treated him so badly that a simple change of plans had him expecting the worst. Out loud she said only, "It's a gift."

Grant's whole face lit with humor and he grinned the devil-may-care grin that always made her breathe catch in her throat.

"It certainly is," he said and pressed one last hard kiss on her lips as he passed by into the kitchen to the counter where her phone sat and picked it up to dial Steve's cell phone himself.

Maggie sighed and pressed a hand against still-tingling lips then headed back through the apartment to take a shower, and to give Grant some privacy to make his call.

Grant leaned back against the kitchen counter and waited for Steve to answer.

"Sullivan."

"Steve, it's Grant."

"Hey, man. You calling to set up a re-match already?"

"No, I...," Grant began, but the sound of the shower being turned on in the background distracted him. His eyes glazed over as he pictured a naked Maggie standing beneath the hot spray of water.

Steve's voice interrupted his ill-timed fantasy, bringing Grant back down to Earth with a thud. He grinned and rolled his eyes—if Steve had any idea the thoughts in his head, Grant would have been a dead man.

"What's up, Evans?"

Grant refocused his careening thoughts and the grin on his face faded, replaced with a look of intensity. "I think we might have caught a break on the Daniel's case."

"What did you find?" Steve asked, his voice now serious.

"Something that may explain, or at least give us a place to start looking for an explanation, the symbols you found on the second body, and the way the last body was displayed."

"Explain."

Grant glanced down at the picture he'd set on the counter and said, "It would be better if I could just show you."

"Okay. When?"

Relieved that Steve wasn't asking any further questions, Grant glanced at his watch and calculated quickly. "I can meet you at my place in about an hour, or if you'd rather, I could come by. But that would take a bit longer."

"No, I'll come over in an hour," Steve paused, thinking thank goodness for Caller I.D., and said dryly, "That should give you plenty of time to say 'bye' to Maggie."

Grant swore under his breath, and then smiled reluctantly. He'd been foolish to believe he could get anything past Steve—particularly when it came to his baby sister.

Damn that Caller I.D.

"Want me to give Maggie a message for you? Grant asked, his voice laced with humor.

"Nah. I'll be seeing her tomorrow at my parents' house anyway," Steve said, waiting to see if Grant had been invited. He was disappointed when Grant said only, "All right, see you in sixty."

A little bit of the good humor Steve had felt when he'd let Grant know exactly how close he was keeping tabs on Grant's relationship with Maggie returned when he thought that Maggie must not have invited Grant back to his parents'—this time as her boyfriend. Pushing aside his guilt over feeling good at Grant's expense, Steve found much of his good mood restored.

Enough so that Steve sounded downright cheerful when he said, "See you soon, Evans."

Grant hung up and crossed his arms, thinking over the information he'd learned from Maggie.

It wasn't huge. Not yet. But it gave them a great place to start.

They may finally have a bit of insight into just *who* this animal was, and maybe more importantly, what motivated him.

Grant was thinking about what he could tell Ralph, and wondering how much it could help flesh out the profile Ralph had promised would be on Grant's desk Monday morning when movement in the doorway had all thoughts of murder being swept out of his mind.

Maggie had pulled on a pair of worn jeans and a soft purple sweater, and had pulled her still-damp wildly curling hair back up in a high ponytail that had Grant remembering the way she'd looked the first day they had met.

After her shower Maggie had dressed quickly, leaving her face clean of any cosmetics, and she had dragged her difficult hair up and away from her face. She had padded softly back towards the kitchen and the sound of Grant's deep, rumbling voice.

For one moment she paused in the living room, unsure. She didn't want to intrude, but the clear sound of the phone being dropped back into its cradle reassured her and she continued.

She paused just inside the dining room to look in at the man she'd just taken as a lover. He leaned, seemingly relaxed, against her kitchen counter, his bare feet crossed at the ankle. His firmly muscled forearms also crossed, the faded blue of the shirt emphasized the golden tan he still had—despite the lateness of the year.

His dark hair was mussed sexily around his serious face. As she watched, his dark brows curved down as he stood, lost in thought. His warm brown eyes were hidden beneath the sweep of impossibly thick black eyelashes that any woman would kill for.

A dark shadow of stubble gave his almost beautiful face a dangerous cast that left her mouth dry. Again.

His soft sculpted lips were pressed together, but as she watched they curved up slightly. Maggie tore her gaze from his mouth to find his eyes on hers. Her lips tipped up in automatic response.

As Grant had stood there thinking, something—a subtle shift in the air, the slightest whiff of her unique scent—drew his eyes up to find hers on him. He had watched as her soft hazel eyes had drifted over him until they'd stopped on his mouth, darkening.

When Grant continued to stare at her, that small smile on his face a contrast to his dark, hungry eyes, Maggie felt her cheeks flame in confused response—passion, embarrassment at being caught staring like a lovesick teenager; they were too tangled up together for her to separate in that single burning moment—and she dropped her eyes to stare blindly at the floor.

Grant straightened and pushed away from the counter to cross the room. He stopped and used a single finger to tip her face up until her eyes met his again. He leaned forward slowly, keeping his eyes open and searching on hers, and brushed a whisper of a kiss on her parted lips before drawing slightly away.

"I need to go," he said with not a little regret, "Steve's going to be at my house in less than an hour, and I still need to shower and get some stuff together before he gets there."

"I understand, Grant. Truly. Besides, I've been meaning to put together a casserole for a co-worker of mine. His mother's very ill, and I should really drop it by his place today. The rest of my weekend is going to be packed."

"I just hate to leave so suddenly. I'd planned on staying," he said in an intimate voice and reached out to grasp her small hand in his.

Maggie grinned, knowing it was what he needed and said cheerfully, "Well, since you feel so bad, Evans, I've got a way you can make it up to me. My parents are having the family over for dinner tomorrow. Wanna come with me?"

Grant smiled, picturing Steve's face when he showed up tomorrow and said, "I'd love to, Red."

Maggie laughed as they turned to walk towards the front door and said, "Don't be too quick to agree, there, Detective. This time you'll be *my* guest, not my brother's, and as you're probably well aware, my brothers can be...a little protective."

"You can't scare me off, Maggie. I'm in. Why don't I give you a call after I'm done with Steve?"

"Sounds good. I had a wonderful day, Grant," Maggie said and tucked her hands in her back pockets before she could grab him again.

Grant leaned forward to press one more kiss on her lips before he turned to go down the hall. "See you, Red."

Maggie sighed and closed the door to lean against it, for a long moment thinking back over the unexpected, and delicious, events of the afternoon before she mentally shook herself. If she was going to get the casserole put together and over to Mo's house before it was dinner time she had to get a move on.

TWENTY-SEVEN

Less than an hour later, Grant sat facing Steve over his dining room table. Steve carefully scrutinized the photograph Grant had gotten from Maggie while Grant waited quietly.

After several minutes of careful examination Steve laid the photo face-up on the table next to an image taken at the Daniels crime scene. In it, Daniels' beaten body sat tied to a chair, a bundle of stuffed clothing draped across her lap.

"It's possible," Steve said finally as his eyes moved back and forth slowly from one picture to the other.

"I think it's more than just possible. I think we may just have figured out what this," Grant tapped the crime scene photo with his index finger, "was supposed to be. I wanted to get your take on it, and if you agree, I want to run it by Ralph."

Steve sat back, his mind racing, looking for alternative explanations. He was sure there were several, but in the weeks they'd been investigating, none of the possible explanations for *why* the body had been posed in such a gruesome and strange manner had been explained.

"Does this tie in, in any way, to the picture on the back of the second victim?" Steve asked at length.

Glad that Steve had made the same intuitive leap he had Grant shook his head once and said, "I'm just not sure. There's a lot I don't understand about what the sculpture represents. It's possible there are meanings that would be obvious to an expert in this type of art that aren't readily apparent to others. I mean, I understand the basic set-up of the figures, but I'm sure there were social implications, significant details in the artist's life, perhaps important connections in the materials used, that I couldn't begin to explain."

Grant paused to gather his thoughts, then shook his head again and continued, "I just don't have enough information at this point. When I saw the image it just clicked, and I wanted to get it to you as soon as I could to see if you saw the same connections I did."

"I do. I guess now we need to find out more. I agree that we also need to get this, and any other information about this development, to your profiler."

213

"I was hoping you would say that. There's something else I wanted to talk to you about," Grant paused to lean forward, his hands clenched together in front of him. He cleared his throat and said, "I'm not sure that you're going to like it, but I think…"

"You think we should bring Maggie in on the case," Steve cut him off.

"Yes. Well, not *in* on the case, but I do think she has a lot of information that could help us with this aspect of the case. I mean even if we have our people spend hours researching this stuff they could still miss important information that an expert like your sister would know."

"What about getting someone else from the department to consult…"

Grant pushed back from the table and shook his head, "From what I've gathered from conversations with Maggie, there are only three other people in the department: a secretary, a grad student and the head. I doubt the secretary would have the depth of knowledge we'll need. As for the grad student and the head of the department, they would probably have the information we'd need, but, well, they're both men within the age range of our killer."

"Do you have a reason to suspect they could be involved?"

"Reason? No. But, I do suspect both would have a full understanding of the significance of both the image and the pose, and I don't think we should take any chances. Obviously they are not the only males that would have that information, but for sure they are two of the most obvious."

Steve closed his eyes and ran a hand up and down his face before he dropped it to the table to look over at Grant. "All right. But I want her involved as little as possible. There's no reason that this ugliness should encroach on her life any more than absolutely necessary."

"Do you think she'll agree to help us?"

"Maggie? Oh, yeah. She knew Jessie a little and the two other girls by name."

Grant nodded. Steve had confirmed what he'd already known about the woman he was getting to know so well. It was a relief to know that his instincts were right on when it came to Maggie, but it was bittersweet.

If there were any other way to get the information they needed quickly he would do it if it meant keeping Maggie as far away as possible from the general ugliness of his job and from the horror of this case in particular.

"All right. Let me give her a call," Grant said and pulled out his cell phone to dial.

Maggie parked her car in front of the small gray ranch house that her directions told her belonged to Martha Swanson. The white trim was peeling and the yard had yet to be raked, but the house seemed to be in good repair.

Maggie got out and rounded the hood of the car to get the casserole dish she'd put on the passenger seat. She turned and walked up the uneven walkway to ring the doorbell. A swatch of lace on a small window to the right of the door twitched and a moment later Mo answered the door, a smile on his face.

"Miz Sullivan, this is a surprise."

"Hi, Mo. I brought this over for you and your mother," Maggie held out the covered dish to Mo and went on, "I hope that she's feeling better."

"Oh, Miz Sullivan, that is mighty fine of you. Mighty fine. Please come in and have a cup of coffee," Mo said and accepted the dish.

"I'd love to stay, but I need to get back home," Maggie said, picturing Grant and hoping he would be able to come back to her apartment that night.

Mo's eyebrows swept down and his voice was filled with disappointment as he said, "That's too bad, I know Mother would love to meet you."

"She's feeling better then?"

Mo nodded and said, "A bit more each day. It's been a long process, but I think we're finally seeing the end of the tunnel up ahead."

"I'm so glad. Now, I put heating instructions right on the top of that casserole. It's ready to eat, or you can freeze it and reheat it when you need it."

"Thank you so kindly, Miz Sullivan. Mother and Abe and I really appreciate a home cooked meal like this."

"Abe?"

"Oh, my little brother is home from college for a short holiday right now."

"That's right. Well the three of you enjoy and I will see you back on campus, Mo."

"Will do, Miz Sullivan. You drive safe, now."

Maggie nodded and smiled again, "I will, Mo. See you next week." Maggie had just turned to leave when the theme song from *Hawaii Five-O* rang out from her purse.

She smiled and hurried down the walkway, all thoughts of Mo and his mother gone as she answered, "Hey, Detective. That was awfully fast. Miss me already?"

"Hey, Red. I'm actually not done yet, but I needed to ask you another huge favor."

"Boy, you just keep racking them up, don't you? Pretty soon I'm going to cash in, Evans, and you are going to be in for it, big time. So what's this big favor?" Maggie asked as she unlocked her car and dropped in to sit behind the wheel.

Maggie put the key in the ignition, but didn't start it. Instead she leaned back with a smile on her face.

"Well, we were hoping that you could maybe come over and give us a little more information on that picture I borrowed from you," Grant trailed off, waiting for her to reply.

Maggie's eyebrows drew in and she thought furiously for a minute before she said, "Sure. I can tell you more about it, but I may have a few questions of my own."

The relief he'd felt at her easy agreement was replaced quickly with wariness. "I'll tell you what, Red, I'll answer any question that I can, as fully and honestly as I can. But there are some things I just won't be able to talk about."

Recognizing a tap dance when she heard one, Maggie chuckled and said, "Nice maneuvering, there, Detective. All right. I'll come. When do you want me there?"

"As soon as you can. If you'd like, we're just about to order in something to eat—you could join us if you haven't eaten already."

Maggie quickly calculated what books and slides she had at home and then decided she'd need to stop at the office for a few additional things. She said, "That sounds fine. I need to make a couple of stops for a few things I should show you, but that won't take me long. Steven knows what I like to eat, so just order and I'll be there as soon as I can."

"Thanks, Maggie. Be careful."

Maggie smiled again and said, "Sure thing, Detective," and hung up the phone. For a full minute she sat staring blindly out the windshield, a goofy smile on her face before she caught sight of her reflection in the rear-view mirror.

"You've got it bad, real bad," she muttered as she reached forward to turn the car on.

Before she drove away Maggie glanced over at Mo's house and was startled to see a face in the window. But before she could get a good look at who it was, the person stepped back out of sight.

Maggie shuddered once, her heart pounding, then rolled her eyes and shook her head. Obviously she was spending too much time thinking about Jessie Daniels.

Over the past week or two, she'd thought many times about Jessie. Everywhere she went, people were talking about her—how she'd lived and how she'd died.

And, thanks to an over-developed imagination, Maggie had found herself checking and re-checking the locks on her windows and doors, being hyper-aware of the people around her when she was walking to and from her car, and had managed to freak herself out on several different occasions when she'd heard a strange noise or when she had had the creepy feeling that someone was watching her.

She dismissed it as being paranoid.

How many times growing up had one of her brother's managed to scare her—especially after she'd heard a scary story or seen a scary movie.?

It was only natural that all the focus on such a brutal murder would do the same thing.

"Get a grip," she mumbled. Here she was freaking out over someone innocently looking out their window when she should already be halfway to the office. She shook her head again and drove off.

She had to get a move on if she was going to make it in to the office, back to her apartment, and over to Grant's before her dinner got cold.

Grant was still smiling when he hung up the phone and turned to face Steve. At the questioning look on Steve's face Grant said, "She's on the way. She has to make a couple of quick stops, but she said that you knew what she liked and could go ahead and order for her."

While Grant talked, Steve carefully studied the goofy look of happiness on Grant's face and thought *he's got it bad*. It took him a moment to identify the strange feeling that surged through him when he saw that look on Grant's face, but when he did, Steve was slightly stunned to discover that it wasn't anger or uneasiness at seeing the man his baby sister was seeing so clearly in love with her.

It was envy.

For the first time in a long time—possibly ever—he wanted to feel that happiness, that connection, to another person.

Steve shook his head to rid himself of the foolish thought as soon as it popped into his head. It was absolutely ridiculous. He was happy with his life exactly as it was.

And he had far too much on his plate right now to even consider looking for a relationship right now.

Steve brought his attention back to Grant and found him staring strangely at him. Steve cleared his throat, and said hurriedly, "Good. Fine. I'll just go order the food. Do you know what you want?"

Grant flashed a grin and said, "Sure. I'll have the General Tso's chicken and a couple of egg rolls."

Wondering just what it was that his partner had been thinking about that had put such a strange expression on his face and distracted him so much, Grant watched Steve pull out his cell phone as he wandered into the living room.

While Steve talked into his phone Grant took out a large blanket to drape over his case board and put away the many pictures and reports he and Steve had spread across his dining room table. He didn't want Maggie seeing the images—not only because the case was ongoing, but because he knew how they would upset her.

He hated to have any part of these terrible crimes touch her life in any way, however small. But Grant also knew that the fastest way to track down this information—and as a result, possibly get that much closer to closing the case and catching the bastard responsible for three girls' deaths—was to talk to Maggie.

Grant was putting the last file back in a box when Steve came back into the room and said, "Food will be here in about forty minutes."

"Perfect. That gives us just enough time to figure out how much, or how little, we tell Maggie and still give her enough information that she can help us."

"I still don't like it," Steve muttered and pulled out a chair.

Grant sank down into the chair opposite Steve and waited for him to sit before he replied, "If it weren't so important, I'd *never* even consider involving Maggie. But I have a very bad feeling that we're running out of time. It's only a matter of time before he strikes again…"

"I know," Steve sighed and rubbed his hand over the back of his neck before he went on, "I don't want her seeing any of the Daniels photos. I think it should be enough for us to describe the positioning of the body and stuffed clothing for her to get the idea.

"As for the drawing and symbols we found on the Roberts girl, I think we can show her close-ups of the drawing without revealing too much. I know she'd never say anything about what we show her, but…"

"But no matter how tough she thinks she is, and how tough she wants everyone else to believe she is, she has a tender heart," Grant finished for him.

Again, Steve was struck forcibly at the depth of understanding Grant seemed to have for his sister after such a short amount of time, but all he said was, "Exactly," then with a swift smirk Steve added, "Just don't let *her* catch you saying anything like that."

Grant barked out a short laugh and said, "I'm the first one to admit that I like to take risks, but I'm not an idiot, Sullivan. I don't have a death wish."

Steve leaned back in his chair and laughed, "Man, do you have *her* pegged, Evans."

Both men grinned, each understanding and appreciating the other.

Turning serious once more Steve continued, "All right. Let's pull together the info we *are* able to show her before she gets here.

Grant agreed, and together the two leaned forward to reach for the few files still left on the table.

Blessedly oblivious to the fact that she was the subject of the men's conversation, Maggie was pulling the last file she needed out of one of the metal filing cabinets crammed into the cramped closet Holden called the file room.

As she slammed the drawer shut she heard the door to the outer office open and shut with a quiet click. She paused then called out, "Hello? Is someone out there?" as she inwardly cursed herself for not turning on a light in the file room.

She'd been in such a rush when she'd gotten to the office, she'd simply headed straight to the file room, leaving the door to the outer office open to shed enough light into the room for her to see.

When no one replied to her call, Maggie's heart started to race. She turned slowly towards the doorway and tried to scream when she saw the large silhouette of a man. With the light at his back, it was impossible for Maggie to make out any features, and for one terrible moment her heart just stopped.

She opened her mouth again to scream, but a wave of terror washed over her and she couldn't get enough air into her constricted chest to make a sound.

When his hand reached out towards her Maggie jerked backwards into the file cabinet. The pain of her back being slammed into the metal handle of the cabinet jolted her out of her panicked state and she drew in a deep breath to scream when light flooded the room, momentarily blinding her.

TWENTY-EIGHT

"Maggie?"

The figure stepped forward, his face now bathed in a wash of light.

"Holy crap, Tony! You scared me half to death!" Maggie exclaimed and pushed a hand hard against her pounding heart as if to hold it in place.

Tony reached up to remove small ear buds from his ears, a look of horror on his face, and said, "Jeez, Maggie, are you okay?"

"Other than having a slight heart attack, yeah, I'm okay. Why didn't you answer me when I called out?"

Tony lifted a hand to point to the now-hanging ear buds. Now that she saw them, Maggie found she could just hear the tinny sound of some rock band coming from them. Still looking upset Tony said, "I was listening to music and didn't hear you. I'm sorry, Maggie. I *never* meant to scare you."

Hearing the obvious regret in his voice Maggie realized that he was no longer only talking about what had just occurred, but also about what had happened the day she'd driven him home and he'd gotten so upset.

Maggie felt the small sliver of unease she'd been feeling since their confrontation diminish at his words. She was so relieved to be back on familiar ground with a man she considered a friend as well as a colleague, she smiled broadly and replied, "Forget about it, Tony. I was just surprised. What are you doing here so late?"

"I wanted to get caught up. Ever since I missed work, I've been trying to catch up, but I haven't been able to during my regular hours. So, I figured I'd come in a couple a nights and get it all sorted out."

Maggie turned back to reopen the drawer she'd opened before Tony had come in and said, "I don't know what we're going to do without you next year, Tony." She pulled the file she needed and pushed the drawer closed as she turned to face him again. "You are the hardest working intern we've ever had. I was just saying to Holden the other day that it was going to be almost impossible to replace you," Maggie smiled warmly and reached out to squeeze Tony's forearm once and continued, "I asked him about possibly

221

trying to keep you on in some capacity next year, but unfortunately he says that it's just not in the budget this year."

"Thanks, Maggie," Tony said as Maggie gave his arm one last squeeze and swept by him to the outer office.

"I need to get going. Don't forget to lock up on your way out."

"Want me to walk you to your car, Maggie?" Tony said. Maggie was so engrossed in her file she missed the longing in his tone as he asked and replied absently, "No, no...I'm fine. See you Monday," and walked out.

"Night, Maggie," Tony replied softly as the door closed with a click.

For a long moment he stood looking at the closed door, saddened by the idea of not seeing Maggie every day at work next year. Somehow he'd convinced himself that that day would never come, that he'd find a way to get a permanent position at the school.

It galled him how easily she'd seemed to accept the fact that he was leaving after this school year. And the thought of her and Holden discussing him, talking about replacing him... Well, he'd seen the way Holden looked at Maggie when she wasn't looking. Tony was sure that one of the reasons there was no room for him was because Holden didn't want him around any longer.

A sharp pain broke Tony's bitter musings, and with a start, he looked down at his hands, surprised to discover he'd been clenching his hands into fists so tightly that his fingernails had dug eight small red crescents into the palms of his hands.

Slowly he relaxed his hands and dropped them to his sides as he walked over to a window overlooking the parking lot. He looked down and could just make out Maggie's form as it walked quickly across the lot towards her car. As he stood in the darkness watching her, Tony saw her stop to talk to Holden.

Finally, the two parted and Maggie opened her car door and got in. The car's interior light flashed on, briefly illuminating the vibrant flash of her bright hair before the door closed and she was once again lost to the deepening darkness of the night.

As she hurried out of the building towards her car, Maggie had already forgotten Tony. She walked quickly, her head down as she dug through her purse for her keys.

She was so focused on thinking about what she still needed to pick up from her apartment before heading over to Grant's she almost ran right into Holden as he rounded the hood of the car he'd parked in front of hers.

"Whoa. Where are you going so fast, Maggie?" Holden asked, his hands grabbing hold of her upper arms to keep her from walking headlong into him.

Maggie's head snapped up in surprise, and she laughed, "Holden! I didn't see you there."

"It's hard to see if your head's buried in a bag, Maggie. What are you doing here so late? And *why*," Holden's voice slowed as his eyebrows drew down, "Why are you walking around a deserted campus after dark, alone?"

Maggie sighed. God save her from overprotective males.

"I needed a couple of files and I'm not nearly as alone as I thought," she added dryly. "What are *you* doing here at this hour?" she asked quickly when Holden's frown deepened and his mouth opened to reply.

"Nice try, Maggie, but you can't distract me. I was meeting with the Dean, but what I want to know is why you are out here alone when some poor girl has just been murdered and her killer is still on the loose.

"You weren't even paying attention to your surroundings, Maggie. If I had been the killer, you would have been easy prey."

Impatient, Maggie glanced down at her watch before she sighed again. She knew he meant well, but she was never going to make it to Grant's at this rate. One look at Holden standing, stone faced, and she knew she wasn't going to get out of there without some kind of explanation.

"I'm fine, Holden. It's not as if there's some crazed serial killer out there targeting women. Jessie was murdered, and I'm sure my brother will find her killer soon. It will probably turn out to be someone she knew who had some grudge against her. Steven has told me many times that almost all murders are committed by someone who knew the victim.

"Besides," Maggie said as she pulled a small canister of pepper spray from her pocket, "I'm not completely helpless."

When Holden still looked unconvinced Maggie blew a gust of breath out in frustration. "Look, Holden, I've got to get going, but if it makes you feel any better, you can chew me out on Monday and I promise I will be suitably chastised when you do," she'd said, humor sparkling in her eyes and voice.

Resigned, Holden's lips tipped up in a slight grin and he said, "I'll make sure I schedule you in bright and early Monday morning—and as long as you're not late…again, you should be able to make it."

Maggie smiled sheepishly, knowing that her stern-sounding boss was really a big teddy bear under his severe bearing. Lifting her right hand in a mock-salute, she snapped to and said, "Aye-aye, Boss."

Forced to smile again, he shook his head and said, "Good night, Maggie. Be careful."

Maggie smiled, her mind already racing forward to Grant once again, and she said, "Right. I will. Night, Holden. See you Monday."

And without another thought about either Tony or Holden, she sped over to open her car door, waving vaguely over her shoulder as she went.

Holden stood, a dark figure alone in the center of the almost deserted parking lot, and watched as Maggie drove away and out of sight before he got into his own car and drove away.

By the time Maggie reached Grant's, her dinner was cold, but luckily neither Steve nor Grant asked what had kept her. If she had to explain to Steven—and perhaps Grant as well—she'd be in for a third lecture, and she just wasn't sure she could listen to another well-meaning male explain to her what a naive idiot she was.

She had had more than enough of over-protective males to last her a lifetime, Maggie thought as she poked the numbers on the microwave to reheat her food rather harder than completely necessary.

Twenty minutes later Maggie pushed her plate away, too full to take even one more bite of her favorite cream cheese wontons.

"So are you guys going to tell me why you need to know about a statue carved hundreds of years ago? What could that possibly have to do with a murder?"

Maggie watched as Steven and Grant glanced at each other, and although she saw no apparent sign of communication, it was obvious the two of them understood each other.

Steve sighed tiredly and began to speak. "Maggie, I know that you understand that anything we talk about is to be kept between us."

Before he could continue Maggie interrupted, a look of incredulity on her face, "Steven. Do you *honestly* believe that I would ever discuss…"

"We *know* Mags. But this is no ordinary case, and if there were any other way to get the info we need quickly, we would do it."

When Maggie just sat, arms crossed, a hurt expression on her face, Steve turned to Grant.

"Maggie. It is not that we don't trust you. We do. We just don't want anyone to know that you are involved with this case. It would be dangerous for you," Grant broke in quietly.

Maggie looked slowly back and forth from Steven's serious expression to Grant's carefully blank face. Her brows drew down and she said, "Steven, what's all this about?"

"Okay, Mags, here's the thing. We need you to tell us about the statue you showed Grant earlier. Anything you know about it or the artist would be helpful to us," Steve said.

"All right," Maggie replied slowly, letting Steve believe—for the moment—that she would ignore the fact that he was changing the subject without answering her question. She continued, "I can probably tell you quite a bit, but Holden would know even more…" She stopped when both Steve and Grant began to shake their heads.

Steve broke in quickly, "We'd rather keep this strictly between the three of us for now."

"Steven, what in the world is going on here? You want to not tell me what a five-hundred-year-old statue has to do with a murder. Fine. But why on Earth can't you talk to Holden about it? You *can't* possibly think that he had something to do with killing Jessie. That's absolutely ridiculous!"

Neither man responded immediately, and once again Maggie watched as the two seemed to communicate silently. Grant sighed deeply and turned slightly in his chair to face Maggie directly.

He said, "What we are going to tell you must be kept between us. You cannot talk about this with *anyone*." Grant paused. Confused, and slightly hurt, Maggie nodded curtly and crossed her arms.

Grant reached over to put his hand on her arm and said, "Maggie. We trust you. But we do *not*, under any circumstances, want to put you in harm's way, and knowing too much or saying the wrong thing to the wrong person or in front of the wrong person, could put you at risk."

Maggie's eyes flew up to meet Grant's and although she relaxed slightly knowing that they did, in fact, trust her she couldn't help feeling alarmed that her safety had been brought up not once, but twice now.

"Great we all trust each other. Now, what the heck is going on?"

When Grant didn't immediately answer she turned to look back at her brother and said sharply, "Steven. Spill it."

"There have been three unsolved homicides in the past two years. All young women. All strangled to death in their own homes. We believe that the three are related, and that the same killer is responsible for all three murders."

"Wait a minute," Maggie said, holding one hand up to stop him, "Are you seriously telling me that there is a...a serial killer in Hope?" Maggie said, unbelievingly, shaking her head from side to side as if to deny it.

"Yes," Steve said softly. He paused until she raised frightened eyes to meet his before going on, "Grant made the connection and we're verifying it through an FBI profiler.

"Maggie, no one has breathed a word about a possible connection between the murders, and we need it to stay that way for now. We don't want to let this bastard know we are on to him, and we absolutely do not want a panic on our hands."

"But, Steven you have to warn the women out there," Maggie gestured sharply and went on her voice outraged, "What if he kills again? What if..."

"Maggie," Grant interrupted her, his quiet, reasonable voice a contrast to her sharp tone, "Chief Roberts has already been on the news several times warning everyone to be cautious—to lock their windows and doors, to take precautions when out alone, to report any suspicious people or activities to the police. To announce more than that would be throwing away any advantage of surprise we may gain, and could, in fact, spur the killer on or scare him into hiding.

"And, as Steve said, if we were to announce that there is a serial killer on the loose in Hope it will surely cause a major panic in the community. Don't think for a second that we would deliberately put anyone at risk."

Abashed, Maggie stared at Grant for a long moment and said softly, "I'm sorry. I didn't mean that. It's just that I can hardly believe it."

Grant relaxed his shoulders slightly at the look of apology he saw in her hazel eyes and the tone of regret he heard in her voice and slowly let out the breath he had been holding. He smiled when she reached forward to squeeze his hand briefly.

"So. How will knowing about the Piéta help catch this guy?" Maggie asked brusquely.

Grant reached across the table to pull a file towards him and said, "The second victim had some symbols drawn on her back that we don't fully understand, and the third victim was posed."

"Posed?" Maggie choked out, her voice filled with horror.

"Yes. She was sitting on a chair with a dummy made out of stuffed clothing draped across her lap. Until I saw the image on your table, we weren't sure what it could possibly represent. But it's my belief—and Steve's—that it was a mimic of that statue.

"It may turn out that the statue has absolutely nothing to do with why the killer is killing or who he may be."

"But you don't believe that," Maggie stated.

"No. I don't believe that. What I *do* believe is that this may just be the break we've been looking for. If nothing else, it could tell us something about him, and any little thing we know will help us, and the profiler, try to understand this guy."

"All right," Maggie said and nodded as she bent down to pull out a glasses case and file from her briefcase before she straightened and pulled on a pair of little reading glasses.

The simple act of pulling on those glasses had Grant fascinated. Suddenly Maggie was transformed from the girl next door to smart and sexy professor in one fast second.

Doing a mental eye roll at the absurdity of his thinking Grant yanked his careening thoughts back to the present.

Maggie opened her files and pulled out her notes and the images she'd collected from the university and her apartment before coming to Grant's house. She began to lecture in a no-nonsense voice that Grant was sure would keep all the kids in her classes in line.

"As I told Grant earlier, the Piéta, which can be translated directly as 'pity' in Italian, is also known as the Vesperbild or the Lamentation. It depicts the Virgin Mary mourning the dead body of her son, Jesus.

"I could give you quite a long history of the piéta, but why don't we start with a brief overview and if you want more information I can get you something more detailed later?"

When both men agreed she continued, "Around 1300, artists developed the pieta in Germany and it reached Italy about one hundred years later. At the time that Michelangelo created this sculpture, there had been a precedent for painted depictions in Italian art, but not in sculpture.

"The particular image you both have seen is of a sculpture carved by Michelangelo in 1499 when he was just 23 years old. That particular sculpture was the first of a number of works done on the same theme by the artist and took him less than two years to create. Commissioned for Cardinal Jean de Billheres' funeral monument, it was moved into St. Peter's Basilica in Vatican City in the eighteenth century.

"Balancing the Renaissance ideals of classical beauty with naturalism, the statue is the most well-known representation of the theme. What's most unusual about his interpretation was that he depicted the Mary as a youthful, serene mother instead of an older, broken-hearted woman. There are many interpretations for why this is so. Now, I can certainly give you some additional information about Michelangelo, but he was one of many artists, known and unknown, who have sculpted and painted the same figures or variations, thereof. Perhaps instead of focusing on the artist's history, a more detailed overview of how and when images of the piéta appeared would be more helpful?"

"You're the expert," Steve said, smiling.

"Well, yes, to some extent, but Holden would have even more information and I'm sure he'd be more than happy to help you out."

Grant leaned back, allowing Steve to answer. "No. I think we'll just keep this all in the family for now. I know that I can trust you, Maggie. I don't know him."

Maggie shrugged and said, "All right. If you say so, Steven, but I'm sure you could trust him."

Neither man replied, and faced with two blank cop faces, she said, "Okaaay, moving on," and proceeded to talk about the history of imagery.

When she finished twenty minutes later, Grant had more than three pages of notes and a headache brewing. With a sigh he leaned back to meet Steve's gaze. Steven ran both hands through his hair before he nodded resignedly to Grant to continue.

Grant again reached forward to pull yet another file from the center of the table towards where he was sitting next to Maggie. Slowly, he opened the file and drew out a small stack of glossy 8X10 photographs and handed them to Maggie. Despite the number of photographs, Maggie quickly realized that there were really only three different subjects photographed from various angles and heights.

It took Maggie several long moments of staring before she realized that what she was looking at were not pictures drawn on paper, but were, in fact, three images drawn in blood on bare skin.

She swallowed once, twice, before she blindly reached for her drinking glass and drank down several gulps of water to moisten her suddenly dry throat enough to speak.

Focusing her thoughts on the pictures rather than the medium used to create them, she was able to return to her former professional mien. She studied each photograph in turn.

The first photograph depicted an apple next to a crudely drawn tree, the second several wavy lines, and the third a bird whose tail feather's seemed to be on fire inside of an oval.

"First of all, let me tell you that what I think these drawings represent is an opinion only. I'm basing my interpretation of what these pictures could represent on the fact that you have told me that the posing of the third victim is directly related to the drawings on the second victim. For that reason I believe that these pictures aren't just drawings, but symbols often found in Christian iconography," Maggie warned, waiting until both Steve and Grant nodded their understanding before she continued.

Laying the first photograph in the center of the table she said, "This first image, I believe, depicts the tree of knowledge of good and evil under which you can see a small circle that I think represents the apple that Eve picked and ate."

She placed the next photograph on the table and continued, "The second image can be interpreted in several ways, but I'm thinking the lines could represent water, which is often representative of purity and cleansing."

Placing the final image next to the other two, Maggie said, "The final image is perhaps the most ambiguous. From the flames apparent on the bird's tail, I would hazard to guess that the bird is a phoenix, which often represents resurrection or rebirth. If that is true, then the oval it appears in could very well be an egg, another symbol of rebirth.

"Holden, and maybe even Tony, who did his graduate thesis on imagery like this, could tell you more. This type of imagery isn't really my area of expertise and I'm sure that someone with more in-depth knowledge could give you further information—and perhaps be more certain that these images actually represent what I think they do."

"This is much more than we knew before, and at the very least, it gives us a starting point. Thanks, Mags," Steve said.

Smiling at the childhood nickname, Maggie gathered her pictures and notes together and put them back into her briefcase along with her glasses.

Grant watched her draw them off with a small twinge of regret as Maggie said, "Not a problem. Let me know if there's anything else you want to know and I'll see what I can dig up for you guys."

Grant glanced down at the several pages of notes he'd written while Maggie had been talking, and looked up at her to say, "Between the two of us, we *should* be able to explain the basics of what you told us to the Chief and our team, but if we have more questions we may need you to come in and help."

Maggie nodded once and said, "Just let me know. I guess I'll let you two get back to it. I need to get some work done on my lectures tonight if I'm going to be able to enjoy myself at all tomorrow. See you at nine?" She turned to ask Grant, oblivious to the look of consternation Steve was giving the two of them.

Grant, who was facing Steve, had *not* missed the look, and he had to bite his cheek to keep from laughing out loud at the look on Steve's face when he heard Grant's reply.

"Nine sharp. I can drive if you'd like—that way Jake can ride along and I won't be worrying about him getting hair all over the inside of your car."

"Great. All right, I'm gonna take off."

"Hang on a sec. Let me get my coat and I'll walk you back."

Maggie smiled and grabbed Grant's arm as he moved to reach behind her to grab his coat. She said, "Don't worry about it. I'm just across the street. Stay and get back to work."

Keenly aware of Steve's eyes boring two holes into the back of his head, Grant stepped forward to place a brief, soft kiss on Maggie's mouth and murmured softly, "Blink the lights when you get inside. Sleep tight, Red."

Too distracted by the tender tone of voice Grant had used to remember that she was supposed to be upset over his obvious display of protectiveness, Maggie just nodded and said, "Okay. Night, Grant."

Maggie turned to leave and at the last moment, looked over her shoulder to where Steve was still standing rooted to the floor and looking anywhere but at the couple in front of him, and said, "Night, Steven," as she walked out the door.

Grant moved to the front window and stood watching until she had disappeared into the front of the apartment building. A minute later, her living room lights blinked twice, then stayed on.

231

Grant turned back to face Steve and found him still standing behind him. Suddenly wary, Grant stood, legs spread, hands in the back pockets of his jeans, and braced for Steve's next words.

Steve stared at Grant for a full ten seconds before he turned and said in a neutral voice, "Let's get this wrapped up. We can pull together something for the Chief and your FBI buddy at the same time, and we can get the info to them ASAP tomorrow morning."

Grant grinned widely, then wiped his face clear again as Steve turned to sit and face him and said in an equally neutral voice, "Sounds good."

TWENTY-NINE

He slipped through the night and stood hidden behind a stand of bushes. It was not in the bright light of daytime, but here, in the deep, dark, velvety shadow-world that he loved, where he was most content.

Oblivious to the chill in the air, he stood, concealed in the blackness, watching until the light he'd stood staring at for hours finally extinguished. Only then did he turn and slink back into the enveloping darkness.

He walked quietly, his sneakers making no noise as they sped quickly down the sidewalk to where he'd left his truck more than four hours earlier. As he drove through the city down deserted streets, he relived his time with his Angel.

He'd watched as she'd entered the darkened office. Alone.

He'd watched as she'd walked across the deserted parking lot. Alone.

He'd watched as she drove away. Alone.

And the longing for her had nearly choked him. Nearly made him reveal his love for her. But he hadn't.

And for that, he was grateful. Because she hadn't been *quite* as alone as he'd first believed. The *other one* had been there.

A bitter fury filled him, making his hands grip the steering wheel so tightly, that his arm muscles ached.

How *dare* the other speak to her, *look* at her with such hunger, when she was his?

He'd waited, waited, until it was clear that she was not doing anything that he would need to punish her for. She didn't care about the other. She'd rushed away with barely an acknowledgment as she'd gone. Clearly the other was not important.

The thought calmed him, but still he would have to punish the other for daring to touch her, to long for her. Only *he* had the right to do that.

He'd followed her back to her apartment and had watched her hurry across the street to a neighbor's house before she'd returned to her apartment. Alone.

It had been more than two more hours before his Angel had gone to bed.

Still innocent.

Never suspecting that he'd watched over her, protecting her from the others who would tempt her to sin. And more importantly, from her own sinful nature.

He let himself through his front door, shutting it silently behind him before he hurried to the locked door under the stairs. After carefully unlocking the door, he slipped through and re-locked the door behind him.

He needed to be alone with his Angel.

Slowly, reverently, he developed the four rolls of film he had taken that night. As the first image of his Angel gradually appeared, as if from a thick fog, onto the photo paper, his heart began to pound.

A flash of the setting sun on hair the color of bright flames. A smiling mouth and flashing eyes staring up off of the page and into his soul.

A side view of an alabaster face half hidden in shadow.

Walking, head-down, looking through her purse, a look of deep concentration on her face.

Washed in the yellow light of her car's interior.

Striding up her apartment building's staircase, wind whipping her loose mane of hair around her face and a strand stuck to her full lips.

They joined the rest on the table. There were hundreds, but he pulled these favorites out and pinned them up on the wall with other favorites that he had taken.

It was several hours later before he was finished, and after he reached out as if to caress her smiling image one last time, he slid back out of his secret place, his temple, and carefully relocked the door before he climbed the stairs to his bedroom and collapsed into bed to dream.

And when he dreamt, he dreamt of her smile and her face, and of her death.

THIRTY

When Maggie had returned from Steven's house, she'd flashed the lights. A day ago—even hours ago—this act would have made her roll her eyes at the idea of checking in like that with someone, anyone, other than her mother.

But tonight, in the face of the knowledge she now had, Maggie had been downright grateful to have not one, but two men she trusted watching out for her safety.

And the fact that they were cops didn't hurt, either.

Though she'd gotten into the habit of locking her door ever since that night with Bradley, tonight she'd found herself walking from room to room, double-checking that every window was closed tight and locked.

She had tried to laugh at her sudden need for security, but the reality of what Grant and Steven had told her was still too fresh in her mind, still too horrifying and terrible for her to feel silly at taking extra precautions.

She suppressed a shiver as she once again fought to not picture the symbols drawn in blood, as she struggled to forget the descriptions of how those three poor women had been murdered. But it was useless.

Maggie rubbed suddenly cold arms vigorously, and resolved to put the details out of her thoughts and instead try to focus on the work she needed to get done tonight if she were going to be able to enjoy the BBQ at her parents' tomorrow with Grant.

Which reminded her, she still had to put together a chicken salad to bring over, and that meant she had to at least boil the noodles and eggs if she were going to throw it together in the morning.

She sighed deeply and set a large pot of water to boil. If she was careful, she could tackle both projects at the same time, and maybe, just maybe, she'd get to bed before dawn.

After settling back down at the table, an egg timer at her side, Maggie concentrated on getting back to work. After struggling for several minutes she succeeded in doing what she had been trying to do for the past hour—she put aside her thoughts of blood and death and once again lost herself in the beauty of art.

Sleep was hard coming for Maggie that night.

Although she'd managed to focus on her work for almost two hours, the small sounds that normally comforted her as she lay alone in bed at night had her jerking and sitting up over and over instead.

With every creak and moan of the old building as it settled around her, her already overactive imagination assailed her with images of the three women whom she had known by name, if not association.

Despite the fact that Grant and Steven had been very careful not to allow her to see any actual photos of the victims, the hurried descriptions of what had been done to the poor girls had been more than enough input to create vivid images of what might have been— and what still could be.

And, though she prayed that the monster who had perpetrated these terrible atrocities would soon be caught, it was nearly dawn before Maggie was able to sink into a restless sleep.

When her alarm clock went off less than three hours later she barely stirred. It wasn't until a steady thumping woke her three more hours later that Maggie finally woke up.

Still half asleep, she rolled over to reach for her alarm clock only to realize that it was already turned off and that the now-furious thumping, newly accompanied by yelling, was coming from her front door.

Her head whipped around to look at the clock, and Maggie noted with a sharp stab of panic the hour—9:08. In less than a heartbeat Maggie's still half-asleep mind clicked into high gear and she swore and leapt out of bed.

As she raced through the dining room she yelled, "Coming!" and ran a self-conscious hand through her untidy hair before she dismissed it as a lost cause and reached out to unlock the front door. She just managed to step back as Grant burst through the now-open door.

"Maggie, are you all right? What's going on? Why didn't you answer? I've been pounding on the door for more than five minutes now…" Grant trailed off as his eyes traveled down from her messy hair to her nightgown-clad body to her bare feet and back again.

236

"You *did* say nine, right?" Grant asked, his voice uncertain, as his brows swept down.

Mortified and trying furiously to keep from laughing somewhat hysterically, Maggie said, "Yes. I'm so sorry, Grant. I overslept."

Assured that Maggie was safe and that he hadn't made a mistake, the look of concern on Grant's face faded to one of amusement and he took a second, longer look at the excuse for a nightgown she was wearing.

Grant stepped forward and closed the door behind them. He reached out and hooked a finger around one of the slim satin straps holding the nightgown up and brushed his knuckle gently over her sensitized skin.

Unnoticed by either of them, the strap slid down her strong shoulder causing the bodice of the nightgown to dip invitingly.

Her gasp was audible, and when he managed to raise his eyes to search her face, Grant watched as Maggie's already bleary eyes glazed and slid half-closed. Her increased breathing caused the already precarious strap to slide a fraction lower and Grant found himself getting lost in her again.

Slowly he lowered his mouth to capture hers. Her mouth opened, but he began to place soft caressing kisses down along her jaw until he reached her ear.

Maggie moaned low in her throat and her head fell back in total surrender, and for a moment Grant tensed, a cocked pistol ready to fire. And then he seemed to gather himself. He sighed and rested his forehead to hers.

"Maggie. As much as I'd like to drag you out of this nightgown and back to bed, I have a feeling your family would miss us, and although it would be a great way to go, I'd really rather not be murdered by your four brothers," Grant said lightly.

Maggie laughed and leaned back to meet his eyes. "All right," she agreed, struggling to level her riotous system and match her calm tone to his, "Let me just quick change, and we can get going. Ten minutes"

Grant smiled and leaned forward to kiss her softly once before he stepped back and let her turn to go back into the bedroom before he settled down onto the couch to wait.

Maggie was as good as her word, and exactly nine minutes later she breezed out of her bedroom. She was dressed in a pair of dark brown trousers and a soft yellow and brown sweater. She'd pulled her tumble of hair up into some twisting knot and secured it with a clip. Small stones glittered at her ears and flashed subtly from her wrist and hands.

If he hadn't known she'd gotten ready in less than ten minutes, he'd never have believed that she could look so put together, so lovely, so quickly. But all he said was, "All set?"

"Yep. Just let me grab the dish I made from the fridge and we can get going."

In less than twenty minutes they were walking up the front sidewalk of the Sullivan's house.

Grant noticed that someone had been busy putting all the flowerbeds to rest for the swiftly coming winter, and knew that it had to have been Elizabeth. He made a mental note to ask her for advice on the best way to winterize the beds around his yard.

A truck pulled in behind his SUV and he grinned when he saw Jack and Dillon getting out and coming up the walk behind them.

"Hey, Evans, that sure is a purty dish you're holding. Did you bake us up a delicious casserole?" Jack grinned and pointed to the large blue container Grant was carrying.

Grant's grin widened into a full smile and he stopped walking and glanced down to eye the small pink and yellow flowers that decorated the container he carried before he raised one eyebrow and said, "I was just giving your sister a hand with her dish, Sullivan. What's that *you're* carrying? You still bringing your dirty laundry home for your Mommy to wash for you, Big Guy?"

Jack flushed as he glanced down at the large duffle he held before he looked at his brother snickering beside him then over to where Grant stood, a sharp gleam of humor in his eyes. Jack shrugged, then smiled sheepishly and said, "Guilty," then muttered loudly, "You damn cops, you never miss a thing."

"That's right, Junior, and don't you forget it," Grant said coolly, then ruined the effect by winking at Dillon before both broke into laughter with Jack joining in a moment later.

While Grant stood talking with her brothers, Maggie walked right up the front porch steps and into her waiting mother's arms.

"Hi, Mom," Maggie said and squeezed her mother tightly for a long moment before she leaned back to grin down into her face.

"Morning, Love. I'm so glad you're here. I know it hasn't been that long, but I miss my baby girl."

Acutely aware of Grant standing a few feet away Maggie rolled her eyes, and then grinned in surrender. She'd always be her Momma's baby girl, and Grant was bound to figure that out for himself before too long—if he hadn't already.

"We missed you at Mass this morning."

Maggie blushed and shrugged before she said, "I overslept."

Seeing that Grant was still talking with Jack and Dillon, and that he didn't need to be rescued yet, Maggie turned to fall in step with her mother, one arm slipped around her mother's waist and the other reached down to grab the large garment bag she'd draped across the porch railing.

"What's in the bag?" Elizabeth asked.

"Costumes," Maggie replied with a gleam in her eye and an evil grin on her face, "For Jack, Dillon and Cloë. Oh, yeah, I invited Cloë to come over, too. Okay?"

"Of course. And what are you up to this year? I'd nearly forgotten that it was almost Halloween when I found your father in the back yard two days ago putting the curtain back together."

"Excellent. Speak of the devil…," Maggie trailed off as she watched her father come down the stairs to join her and her mother in the front hallway. She leaped forward to throw her arms around her father's neck and planted a smacking kiss on his lips.

"Well. Hello, Baby. Not that I'm complaining, but what's all this for?"

"Mom told me you put together the curtain. I was going to ask you for help doing that this afternoon, but you beat me to it. Thanks, Daddy," Maggie said, then leaned in for another hug before she stooped down to pick the garment bag up from the floor where she'd dropped it moments ago.

"Any problems or broken parts?"

"Nope. One of the braces was bent, but I was able to fix it easily enough. So, when are you going to tell us what this year's

239

theme is going to be? Halloween is only a few days away, and I like to brace myself for the event."

"Well, you're in luck. I've got costumes for my three *volunteers* right here," Maggie patted the bag she held and continued, "I have the great pleasure of telling Jack and Dillon all about the special...*help*...they'll be giving me this year. If you're lucky maybe you'll get a sneak peek at them when they try on their costumes."

Maggie waggled her eyebrows up and down, still smiling. Bram pulled the zipper on the bag down a couple of inches and peeked inside. His mouth dropped open and his eyebrows drew up over his twinkling eyes for a surprised moment before he smiled back conspiratorially at his daughter.

"What are you two grinning so evilly about?" Elizabeth asked and reached forward to grab the zipper herself, but before they could answer Jack, Dillon and Grant walked in the door.

Father and daughter looked at the newcomers briefly before their eyes met and both dissolved into snorts of laughter.

"What?" Jack asked, confused.

"You got me," Elizabeth said dryly when neither Maggie or Bram could stop laughing long enough to answer, then went on, "But I think you are going to regret that little dip in the lake you gave your sister." Elizabeth looked away from Jack's scowling face, and Dillon's suddenly nervous one, to face Grant.

Elizabeth had to bite her cheek to keep from laughing, but she managed to say, "Grant, I'm so glad you could come. Just ignore those two loons and come on back to the kitchen. You can finally put that container down and I'll get you something cool to drink.

Grant nodded and smiled, taking in the family dynamics as he passed the still-snickering Maggie and Bram to follow Elizabeth down the hall.

"What was that all about?" he asked as he set the bowl down where Elizabeth pointed on the counter.

"That? Oh, Maggie was just showing Bram the costumes she made for Jack and Dillon for her Halloween show this year. Have *you* seen them?"

Grant glanced back down the hall when he heard yells of outrage from Jack and a loud groan from Dillon followed by renewed peels of laughter from Maggie and Bram before he turned back to face Elizabeth, "No. Maggie wanted it to be a surprise. I *did* manage to catch a glimpse of some pretty crazy sequined material once, but she tucked it away too quickly for me to figure out what it was supposed to be. Do you know what she's making them dress up as?"

"No. But if I know Maggie, it will be something amazing."

Grant grinned at the pride he heard in her voice.

"Now, what would you like to drink—some pop? Iced tea? Coffee?"

"Coffee would be great."

As Elizabeth turned away to pour him a mug, Maggie danced into the kitchen, a large grin on her face.

"Dad said to tell you he was going to get the grill set up. He took Jake with him," she added to Grant.

When Elizabeth turned quickly to look at Maggie, a look of panic on her face Maggie quickly added, "Jack and Dillon are going with him. Can I do anything, Mom?"

Clearly relieved, Elizabeth replied, "No. I've got everything under control for now. Why don't you take Grant out on the front porch and enjoy the peace and quiet while you still can. Your other brother will be here in less than an hour," Elizabeth said and held out two mugs of steaming coffee to Maggie and Grant.

"Thanks, Elizabeth," Grant said.

"Thanks, Mom," Maggie murmured and leaned in to kiss her mother's cheek before grabbing Grant's hand and pulling him back out of the kitchen.

Grant followed Maggie through the now-deserted hallway and back out onto the front porch where they settled down onto the porch swing together.

THIRTY-ONE

"So, what was all that about?" Grant asked.

"You mean the guys?" Maggie cocked one eyebrow up, and grinned again as she took a sip of her coffee before she went on, "I showed them the costumes they have to wear on Halloween. I almost felt sorry for Dillon, but watching that first look on Jack's face…That was priceless."

"I take it they aren't willing participants?"

"Usually they are, and I don't think they had a problem helping until they saw what I'm making them wear."

"I'm guessing it's embarrassing?"

"Oh, yeah. And they *so* deserve every moment of embarrassment they will feel after what they did."

"I'm almost scared to ask…" Grant teased.

Maggie settled back underneath the arm Grant eased around her shoulders and explained. "That first day you were here? The two idiots I affectionately call my brothers got it into their heads that I needed to go swimming in the harbor…in my clothes."

Grant winced and wisely held in the chuckle he wanted to let loose as Maggie continued, "They do it periodically, all four of them, and they always think they're so funny. But, I *always* get them back—whether they know it or not." Maggie said the last sentence so softly Grant almost missed it, but not quite.

Grant couldn't hold back his smile any longer, and Maggie glanced over and caught it. She tried to keep her face serious, but couldn't help an answering grin from spreading across her face.

"You smile, but I'll warn you now, Grant Evans, that if you cross me, I fight dirty. And I always, *always*, get even," Maggie leaned forward and punctuated her words by poking Grant's chest.

Grant was still smiling but he held up both hands in mock surrender and said, "I believe you, Red."

When Maggie relaxed back under his arm he added, "Just what did you mean you get even 'whether they know it or not'? How would they *not* know?"

Maggie grinned impishly and tilted her head to the side as she considered. After a long moment she answered, "All right, I'll give you an example, but if you tell my brothers I *will* find out, Detective, and you will have to suffer the consequences."

"My lips are sealed."

"So, back in high school Jack and I were only a couple years apart—he was a senior the year I was a freshman. He felt he was far too cool to always have his baby sister hanging around, but somehow he still found the time to monitor any kind of social life I tried to have.

"Anyway, there was this one boy, Johnny Freemont. He was a junior, a big time hockey jock, super cute, shy, and totally sweet. Basically a young girl's dream crush. He asked me out and I thought I had died and gone to heaven. I was so excited. We were going to go to the Homecoming dance together. I spent hours looking for the perfect dress, the right hairstyle. I wanted everything to be just right. It was my first real high school date, and it was a big deal that I had been asked because I was only a freshman.

"Well, I was on cloud nine, but when Jack found out he told me that Johnny was a jerk and that I shouldn't go out with him. Of course I ignored him and told him to butt out of my business. He went to my parents and tried to get them to forbid me to go with Johnny to the dance, but they refused. When that failed he dropped it—or I *thought* he had. But then, less than a week before the dance Johnny came up to me and said he was really sorry but he couldn't take me to the dance after all. Somehow he had asked someone else and forgotten, blah, blah. You get the picture.

"My heart was broken, my dreams of the big night crushed, and I didn't know why. It wasn't until the day before the dance that Dillon let slip that Jack had had a *conversation* with Johnny and had pretty much scared him off so badly he'd broken the date rather than go through the trouble of dealing with Jack and the three other brothers Jack had mentioned.

"Long story short, I got even."

"What did you do?" Grant asked.

Maggie sighed once and turned back to face Grant fully as she said, "Well, at first I did nothing. Then there were several small things that I did to torture him. But I never let on that I knew what had happened. Of course Dillon knew that I knew. I'm sure he

243

suspected I must have something to do with Jack's bad luck over the next several weeks, but he could never prove it."

"Give me a for example."

"All right, let's see. The night before a big football game I would hide a lucky sock or move a piece of Jack's equipment. Whenever I could, I hid his car keys. Whenever I knew he liked a girl I would tell her that he liked her. Once I started a rumor that he liked going to the ballet and was spending his weekends learning to crochet with our grandmother.

"I was always careful to make sure that nothing I did was obvious. Nothing could be easily traced back to me, but for a long time that year, Jack had no luck at all. I think that Steven figured out what I was doing, but neither he, nor Dillon, ever ratted me out.

"I had mercy on him after Johnny asked me out for the Christmas Ball."

"Did you go?" Grant asked.

"Absolutely," Maggie nodded, then added, "But not with Johnny. Jack was right about him, he was a jerk. I could never be serious about anyone so intimidated by my brothers."

"Well then, I guess it's a good thing I don't intimidate very easily."

"I don't expect you do, Detective. I guess we'll just have to wait and see."

Hearing the faint wariness in her voice Grant opened his mouth to ask her what was going through her mind when two vehicles pulled into the driveway almost simultaneously and Maggie turned at the sound.

"Maggie…" Grant began, and then closed his mouth. It would have to wait until they were alone.

Unaware of his thoughts Maggie said, "Here come the rest of the crew. You ready to face the gauntlet?"

"I'm ready, Red," Grant said and pulled his arm off of her shoulders to squeeze her hand once before using it to help her to her feet. They stood together at the head of the stairs. Grant slid both hands into the back pockets of his jeans and shifted his weight to one leg while Maggie waited patiently at his side.

Cloë hopped out of a small purple compact, two large paper bags in her arms and a sunny smile on her face, "Hey, Y'all! Isn't it a beautiful day for this late in October? Hi Steven, I haven't seen you in a while," she greeted Steve as he climbed out of his car and rounded the hood of his car to take her bags.

"Hey, Cloë. How're you doing? How's your dad?" Steve asked.

Cloë beamed up at him and replied brightly, "Fine and fine, thank you," before she turned to give Maggie a quick hug and held out a hand to Grant.

"Hi. You must be Grant. I've heard a lot about you. I'm Cloë Sanders," Cloë chattered as she climbed the steps to shake his hand, followed quickly by Steve.

"Guilty," Grant shook her hand and flashed a brilliant smile at her before he said, "It's very nice to meet you, Cloë. Maggie's told me a lot about you, too. Need a hand, Steve?"

Grant shifted his focus from the brown-haired pixie to his partner and missed the exaggerated way that Cloë rolled her eyes and grinned at Maggie, nearly sending her into a fit of giggles.

"Grab the door for me?" Steve said and, as he walked past Grant, added, "Come on back, Man, and I'll get you something decent to drink."

Grant glanced at Maggie and when she smiled and nodded, followed Steve through the door and into the house.

Both women stood staring at the closed door for a long moment before Cloë broke the silence.

"Oh. My. Gawd," she said in an almost awed voice before she added in a mocking voice, "He's pretty good-looking. Talk about a slight understatement, Maggie! He's absolutely beautiful."

"I know," Maggie sighed. She caught Cloë's eye and both women burst into giggles before they collapsed back onto the swing. When she could breathe again, Maggie said, "Listen to us. We sound like we should be back in school, passing notes and sighing over dreamy boys we have crushes on."

"Dreamy…definitely. It's hard to believe that someone *that* delicious is a cop."

Maggie's face turned thoughtful and she turned her head to look back at the door Grant had disappeared though. "I guess so. But if you talk to him at all, you'll see that being a cop *is* who his is. Maybe it's just because I've been around Steven for so many years, but Grant has a certain…something, that makes him so much more than just another beautiful face. I don't know what it is exactly. He's just…*more*."

Maggie trailed off as she turned back to face Cloë again and found her friend staring at her, all vestiges of humor gone. In its place was a look of speculation."

"What?"

"Hmmm," Was all that Cloë said.

"Hmmm? What's that supposed to mean?"

"Well," Cloë began slowly, an earnest look on her face, "In all the months you talked about Bradley, the supposed 'perfect guy', you never once sounded like you did just now."

"What do you mean? How did I sound?" Maggie asked, curious.

"Smitten."

"Smitten?"

"Yep. Smitten, definitely smitten. And if I'm not mistaken, more than a little bit in love."

"Oh, no," Maggie moaned, her eyes squeezing shut as if to deny what Cloë said by blocking even the sight of her friend's thoughtful face.

Cloë reached out to rub a hand up and down Maggie's arm and asked softly, "Why 'oh, no', Mags? Unless I'm completely wrong, I'd have to say that Detective Dreamy is smitten with you, too."

Maggie squeezed Cloë's hand and smiled weakly as she said, "I know. That's just it. I'm more than a little gone on this guy, but that is scaring the crap out of me."

"Why?"

"He's nothing like the guy I always pictured myself being with. Sure, he's gorgeous, sweet, funny, and really smart, but…"

"Yeah, I can see how that would really upset a girl, Mags," Cloë interrupted dryly.

Maggie shook her head and went on, "I know I'm being stupid. I know. It's just that I can't help it. We just come from such different backgrounds and he's so different from the guys that I usually date that I keep thinking that I should be worried."

"Would these guys you usually date be guys like Bradley?"

"Yes. Exactly like him. Grant is more like my brothers than like a guy I would normally be interested in, but it doesn't seem to matter. I can't seem to help myself where he's concerned."

"Well, halleluiah! Grant may not fit into some perfect image you have come up with in your mind of who Mr. Right should be, but I've gotta say that that's a huge point in his favor as far as I'm concerned."

"Gee, Cloë, tell me how you really feel," Maggie said sarcastically, but she was smiling as she said it.

Cloë laughed again, and then turned serious. "Mags, I think that you've had enough heartache and pain recently. I would tell you to let go and just enjoy yourself with Detective Dish in there, but I know better. So promise me that you'll at least not fall all the way in love with the guy until you're *really* ready," she leaned forward and grabbed both of Maggie's hands tightly before she continued earnestly, "Because I know that, for you, love is forever, and I just don't want to see you get crushed."

"How can you say that? That love is forever for me—I've been in love before and it's never lasted."

"You may have been in like, in lust, even infatuated, but I'm talking love with a capital L, here, Maggie. And if you're not careful—or maybe I should say if you're extremely lucky—you're going to fall, and fall hard, for the good Detective for the very reasons you think he's all wrong for you."

Too late was all Maggie could think. But before she could formulate an appropriate reply Seth's car pulled to the curb and her niece, Katie, tumbled out and ran for the porch shouting, "Aunt Maggie! Wait till you hear my news, you're gonna die!"

Katie was followed closely by her brother, Aaron, who was trying hard to appear nonchalant, but he was moving nearly as fast as his sister was as he walked up to where Maggie now stood hugging Katie.

"Hey, Aaron," Maggie said and draped one arm around his shoulders, squeezing hard. "You guys remember my friend, Cloë, right?" Maggie said, trying hard not to smile too much when she saw Aaron blush and duck his head after he nodded and glanced quickly over at Cloë.

247

Unaware of her brother's dilemma, Katie replied cheerfully, "Yeah. Hey, Cloë! Guess what, Aunt Maggie," nearly dancing in place she was so eager to share her exciting news.

"You decided to drop out of school and join the circus as a tightrope walker," Maggie twinkled over at her excited niece before catching Aaron's eye roll out of the corner of her eye and being forced to bite her lip to keep from chuckling out loud.

"Aunt *Maaaaggie!*"

"You met the Jonas brothers and all three of them fell madly in love with you and now you have to choose between them?"

"I wish! But, no…"

"I've got it, I've got it. You and Aaron tried out for American Idol and you're both 'Goin to Hollywood'!"

At this point even Aaron, who was trying madly to keep his composure in front of Cloë, could barely keep his snorts of laughter quiet so Maggie took pity on Katie and at the same time tried to draw attention away from her still-beet-red nephew.

"All right, I give up. What's your big news?"

"We got our report cards and I got all A's and one B, but that was in gym and *I* don't think it should count, and Mom told me if I could keep my grades up like that all year, that she would get tickets for the Taylor Swift concert in May!"

"Wow—all A's, huh? That's amazing, Katie. Good work," Maggie said, giving her niece another hard hug before she turned to raise an eyebrow at Aaron. "And how about you, Mister?"

Aaron glanced up at Maggie, shifted his eyes over to Cloë once before he turned back to Maggie and ducked his head again. He said something too quietly for them to hear.

"What?" Maggie asked, leaning closer to hear better.

"I got straight A's," Aaron said, then he shrugged as if to say 'no biggie' but Maggie had seen the gleam of excitement in his eyes before he'd managed to lower them this time.

"Nice one," Maggie said before she added in a teasing tone, "Are *you* going to see Taylor, too?" as she poked a finger in his side.

Aaron rolled his eyes again, too mortified to do anything but shake his head. Katie hooted with laughter while Cloë stood smiling at her side.

Finally, he was able to speak. "Geez. Give me a break, Aunt Maggie"

"What?" Maggie asked innocently.

"Well, there's no *way* I'd go see that little girl stuff," Aaron sneered over at his sister once before he continued, "Mom told me she'd pay half for that telescope I've been saving up for."

"I think astronomy is so interesting," Cloë said warmly, "I even paid to have a star named. Isn't that so amazing? I named it Sweet Influence after a line in a poem by Emily Bronte that I love that is about the stars. Isn't that beautiful?"

Aaron stood and stared over at Cloë with open admiration and was saved from trying to come up with a coherent response when his parents joined them on the porch.

"Hi, Maggie," Sybil hugged Maggie affectionately before she turned to hug Cloë, too. "Hey, Cloë. I'm so glad you were able to come."

"Me, too," Cloë beamed.

Maggie smiled as she watched the two women she thought of as her sisters of the heart as they chatted together.

Growing up, the one thing she'd longed for more than anything else had been a sister. But no matter how much she had begged her mother for one, or asked Santa for one, or prayed for one, she had been disappointed—until her brother had met Sybil and they'd gotten married.

Almost from their first meeting the two of them had connected, and after so many years, it was hard for Maggie to even remember a time when she'd ever thought of Sybil as anything other than her true sister.

Maggie had felt so lucky, so blessed, and had never imagined that it could, or would, happen again, but it had.

She had known Cloë since they were girls, but it wasn't until she'd gone back to the University to work on her Master's degree and begun to work with Cloë that they'd really clicked. Suddenly, Maggie had had not one, but two sisters.

Beautiful, classy Sybil was the older sister she turned to for advice and support and quirky, sassy Cloë was the little sister Maggie had always wanted to take care of and have fun with.

Seth stepped forward to give Maggie a one-armed hug, his other arm wrapped around a full grocery bag, and broke into her train of thoughts. "Hey, Mags. I hear you brought a date—who's the victim?" Seth asked, a teasing look on his face.

Maggie wasn't fooled by the friendly-looking face, or by the question. She knew that whoever had told him that she was bringing a date would have told him who she had planned on bringing. She had just opened her mouth to reply when she was interrupted again.

"You don't know?" Cloë broke in, her eyebrows so high they disappeared beneath the spiky fringe of her bangs. She grinned quickly, then winked at Maggie before she said, "I think I'll just go see if Elizabeth needs any help in the kitchen. Why don't you two come with me?" Cloë linked arms with an agreeable Katie and a still-blushing Aaron and the trio turned to go through the door.

Seth stared after Cloë and the kids as they slipped through the front door into the house before he skewered Maggie with a dark look and said, "*Should* I know?"

Maggie sighed and looked over at Sybil for help, but when Sybil just grinned and shrugged Maggie returned her attention to Seth and replied, "I brought Grant."

"Grant? As in, Grant Evans? Steve's new partner Grant Evans?"

"Yes, as you very well know. We've been going out for a few weeks now, but I'm sure that you already know that, right?"

Ignoring the sarcastic question Seth turned on Sybil, "Did you know about this?"

Sybil shook her head no and said, "Not officially, but I'm not at all surprised and you shouldn't be either. I want details ASAP, little sister." Sybil wagged her eyebrows at Maggie once before she fell silent.

Maggie blew out another, longer sigh before she replied, "It's not as if it was a big secret or anything. The guys have even played ball with him. I know you were invited…"

When she trailed off, Seth nodded once and said, "I was, Steve called, but I needed to help Aaron out with a school project and didn't make it. But no one mentioned that Grant was trying to put the moves on you."

250

"Seth!" Sybil exclaimed before she smacked his shoulder, and burst out laughing.

Maggie simply shook her head in disgust and said, "Geez, Seth, stop being so romantic, you're embarrassing me here," Maggie said, then rolled her eyes at Sybil and said, "Do you see what I have to deal with?"

Maggie turned to walk away, then she swung back around again to face Seth and said, "*Please* be nice today, Seth. I really like this guy and Steven works with him, so don't do anything annoying or overbearing."

"What do you mean, 'annoying'? When am I *ever* annoying and overbearing?"

"How much time do we have?" Maggie glanced at her watch, eyebrows raised, and said, "Do you *really* want me to answer that?"

A lighting quick grin flashed across Seth's face before he turned serious again and opened his mouth to speak.

Maggie lifted a hand to stop him and said calmly, "Look, I'm not asking you to be best friends with Grant, just try not to act like an overprotective ape this time, okay?"

Seth sighed and said slowly, "I'll try."

"Try real hard, Seth," Maggie said threateningly, and then she leaned forward to kiss his cheek and turned to walk into the house.

THIRTY-TWO

Seth stood for a long moment, his eyes on the door that had closed behind Maggie until Sybil stepped forward to grab his hand.

"Seth?"

"Hmmm?" he murmured distractedly, and then he seemed to shake himself and turned to focus on his wife. "What, Syb?"

"You okay, Honey?"

"Yeah, of course"

"You seem worried about Maggie. Are you?"

"A little, I guess. I'll feel better when I can talk to Steve about it. I just want to see her as happy as we are—especially after whatever happened with that creep. I know she can take care of herself, but, I guess I still have a hard time admitting it to myself, let alone to her."

"I know, Seth. But you've got to try. I think sometimes she's almost drowned by the overprotective men in her life. Maybe if you show her you trust her—even just a little—and that you believe in her, she won't feel like you all think she's a naïve idiot."

"I don't think that," Seth protested as he leaned back to look her in the eye and insisted, "I *don't*," when he saw the clear look of skepticism on Sybil's face.

"Regardless of whether or not any of you think it, that is how you all make her feel." When Sybil saw the look of concern darken his face, she squeezed his hand gently and continued, "All I'm saying is, give her—and Grant—the benefit of the doubt. They may both surprise you."

Seth leaned forward to kiss her and said softly, "I really love you, did you know that?"

Sybil laughed low and smoky as she twined her arms around his neck and said, "Is that so, Mr. Sullivan?"

"As a matter of fact."

"Well if that's true then I think it's safe to tell you that I am completely, madly in love with you. Just don't tell my husband."

Seth leaned his head back and laughed, and then he turned and dropped one arm around her shoulders as they walked up the porch stairs to go into the house.

"All right, Oh Wise One, I'll keep my mouth shut. For now. But you know that if he messes her up, I have an obligation to completely destroy him."

"Understood. If you didn't, I'd have to take care of him myself," Sybil said grimly.

Seth grinned, admiring her all the more for her fierce protectiveness, and together they walked into the chaos of loud voices, ringing phones, a blaring radio, slamming doors, the dog barking, and laughter—the sounds of family.

Grant and Steve swept through the bustling kitchen and out into the backyard to join Bram, Jack and Dillon around the grill.

As they approached the three men Grant caught the tail end of what Jack was saying and had to fight the smile that wanted to spread across his face.

"...can't really expect us to wear that! I mean, there *has* to be someone who could fill in for us or something."

Jack was gesturing wildly with his arms as he paced back and forth between where his father stood trying not to laugh and where Dillon stood looking morose, hands tucked in his pockets.

"What's all this?" Steve asked, eyebrows raised.

Bram glanced over at the approaching men and said very calmly, "Your younger brothers are finding out something they should have learned long ago about your sister—you reap what you sow. And with Maggie, the price tag is always a steep one."

Bram turned from his sons to face the grill again, but not before he grinned and winked at Grant.

"I take it you volunteered to be in Maggie's Halloween show?" Steve asked.

"Volunteered? No. Drafted, forced, *blackmailed*, is more like it," Jack declared dramatically.

Steve glanced over at Grant and the two men exchanged identical, evil grins.

"You've helped out before and it was never a big deal. What's the problem?" Steve asked innocently.

Dillon simply closed his eyes and pretended to shudder while Jack stopped and placed both fists on hips. "What's the problem?"

"Yeah, what's the big deal? Why are you whining like an itty bitty baby, Bro?" Steve asked, enjoying himself.

Ignoring the insult Jack replied, "The 'big deal' is the costumes that," Jack paused looking at his father's back and continued, "that sister of ours made for us to wear. There's no *way* I'm going to wear it."

Genuinely surprised, Steve's eyebrows drew down and he said, "But you love dressing up—the crazier the better..."

Grant had held his tongue during the entire exchange, but he couldn't hold back any longer. He interrupted Steve's comment and said in a too-innocent tone, "Maybe it's the color of the skirt...or maybe you don't think it's short enough. No," Grant shook his head quickly and went on, "It must be the sequins. But, I'm sure if you just *tell* Maggie, she'd be more than happy to add a few more."

Jack stood frowning at Grant. He was so angry Grant imagined he could see steam practically pouring from his ears.

Steve was crying he was laughing so hard and Grant could hold back no longer. Soon, they were both doubled over, laughing, and it took less than a minute for Bram to join in.

Dillon blushed, and then had to smile as he watched his brother, Grant, and his father laughing like a bunch of idiots.

Jack looked furiously from Steve to Grant, and finally to his father before a reluctant grin broke through.

"Ha, ha. You're hilarious, Evans. A real comedian. Maybe you'd like to join us on stage if you like the costumes so much," Jack said.

"No, no. I wouldn't dream of drawing any attention away from your 'performances'," Grant wheezed out, still bent over trying to regain his breath.

"You're all heart, Evans," Jack said, his good humor restored.

"Shit," was all Dillon added.

When Maggie poked her head out the back door two minutes later she was greeted with the bizarre sight of her brothers, Grant, and most unusually, her father, all sitting on the ground laughing.

"Men," she said, but there was more amusement and affection in her voice than judgment. "Hey, Mom, Sybil, you've gotta see this," She called back over her shoulder.

Elizabeth and Sybil got up from the table where the three women had been working on last minute preparations for the barbeque and walked over to look out the screen door.

"Good Lord," Elizabeth said.

"Have they been drinking already?" Sybil asked dryly as she craned to see over Maggie's shoulder.

"At this time of day? It's not even 11a.m.," Maggie exclaimed, "No, they're just acting like fools."

"I wonder what set them off," Sybil murmured as the three women withdrew back into the kitchen to return to their seats around the table.

Cloë bounced into the kitchen at that moment and asked, "What's going on? What are you guys talking about?" as she sat down at the table next to Maggie.

"The guys are all in the back yard sitting on the grass laughing," Maggie said and her eyebrows drew down as she added, "I figured by now the guys would be grilling Grant or giving him a hard time, but he's right in the thick of things, laughing his head off."

"Why do you make it sound like that's bad? Isn't that a good thing?" Cloë asked.

Maggie sighed as she leaned forward to rest her elbows on the table, and then said slowly, "Yeah, it's great. It's just that even though I knew that they got along, I convinced myself that they'd be their usual boorish selves because this is the first time I've officially brought him home as my date. It's strange, that's all, and I'm not sure what to make of it."

Maggie shrugged and picked up the knife she had been using to chop veggies and began to slice another stalk of celery.

"Well, if you ask me, I think it's great," Cloë said cheerfully as she reached for the bag of corn-on-the-cob next to the table. "I'll just take these outside and husk them, Mrs. S."

"Thank you, Cloë," Elizabeth said to Cloë's retreating back. When the door had shut behind Cloë, Elizabeth said, "Hmmm."

255

"Hmmm?" Maggie muttered. When Elizabeth turned Maggie grinned and said "There's a lot of Hmmming going on around here today. Now what are you thinking, Momma?"

Catching herself, Elizabeth just shook her head and smiled, "Oh, nothing important, Baby, just a little of this and a little of that. So tell me, how are things going with Grant?"

Still suspicious, Maggie eyed her friend's back through the screen door, but could find nothing unusual about her. Maggie brought her gaze back to the table and laughed to find both her mother and Sybil watching her, waiting to hear what she was going to say.

"Things are great, Momma. We're having a lot of fun. We go out a couple of times a week, and we never run out of things to talk about. He's so funny and so sweet sometimes. The other day he did the funniest thing...," Maggie trailed off when Sybil and her mother turned to grin at each other.

"What?" Maggie asked.

"Oh, nothing, Dear. You just sounded completely besotted," Elizabeth said, and smiled sweetly at the way Maggie frowned.

Turning back to the peppers she was slicing, Elizabeth had to bite her lip to keep from grinning.

Maggie mentally shrugged as she turned back to the stalk of celery in front of her, careful to keep her eyes focused on the vegetables and not on her mother or sister-in-law. *Besotted? Was she besotted?* Maggie mused to herself. Most definitely. The only question was whether or not she could get away with trying to disguise the fact and buy a little more time before she had to lay it all out on the line for her family, or if she could try to put off that moment until she was more certain of Grant's feelings for her.

Maggie was still debating when Sybil interrupted her thoughts. "All right, Maggie. Spill," Sybil said in a casual voice, but the iron glint in her eyes warned Maggie that her time was up.

Sybil and her mother had not pressed her for details when they had found out that she was bringing Grant to the barbeque. And Maggie was more than certain that they'd both have heard from Steven, or any number of other people, that she'd been going out with him for a while. But neither of them had pressed her for details, or for what Sybil always called the "good stuff", until now.

256

Maggie slowly set aside the stalk she was chopping and raised her eyes to see two avid sets of eyes focused on her face. She spilled.

THIRTY-THREE

Hours later, as Maggie and Grant prepared to leave, Sybil, Elizabeth, and all four of Maggie's brothers stood talking in the hall.

"We better track down Aaron and Jake if we're going to get the kids home and in bed at a reasonable hour, Seth," Sybil said.

"They're right out front. I think that Jake is in doggy heaven after all of the attention he got today," Grant said.

Sybil replied, "The kids simply adore him, and honestly he's the best behaved dog I've ever seen. Well, I guess we better get a move on here, crew. See you all real soon."

As everyone said goodbye Sybil pulled Maggie into a tight hug and whispered, "Be happy," before she pulled back and said in a louder voice, "I'll see you next Wednesday for lunch, okay?"

"It's on my schedule."

"Mine, too!" Cloë said as she leaned in to hug Elizabeth. She continued, "Thanks again for having me, Mrs. S., and thanks for the yummy leftovers."

"You're welcome, dear," Elizabeth said as she squeezed Cloë's hands. Elizabeth turned to face Grant and added, "I'll be by on Tuesday and I'll show you what we talked about. Now give me a hug." She waited, arms lifted, as a delighted Grant leaned forward to scoop her right off of her feet.

"Thanks for everything, Elizabeth. I'll see you Tuesday morning," Grant said as he bent to set her back onto her feet.

"Guy can't even leave the room for a minute before some city-slicker tries to poach his woman out from under him," Bram said loudly as he walked down the hall from the kitchen, a box in his hands.

For a split second, Grant froze, and then he smiled hugely as Bram shoved the box into his hands and winked at him as he grabbed his wife into his arms and dipped her back for a loud smacking kiss.

"For goodness sakes, Bram," Elizabeth fluttered, but it was clear from the bright blush and obvious delight in her voice that she didn't really mind his display of affection.

Elizabeth slipped underneath Bram's arm to wrap her own around his waist. Together, they turned to face Cloë, Maggie and Grant, huge smiles on their faces.

The love was so evident in their every look and gesture that Grant just had to smile watching the exchange.

Shifting his eyes to where Maggie stood next to her parents, grass stains on her tidy pants from playing football with her niece and nephew and hair falling down from her once-tidy hairdo, his gaze softened.

She looked so happy, so content surrounded by the people who loved her. Again and again over the course of the day he had witnessed the many ways in which the Sullivans showed their love and affection for each other—whether with jokes and teasing, simple words, or embraces.

Grant had never seen people so open and easy with one another. He had been punched, squeezed, patted, kissed, and hugged more times in the two days he had spent with this family than he could remember in all the years with his own, the only exception being the times he spent with his grandparents.

Although his grandfather had been more likely to squeeze his shoulder or pat his back, his grandmother had always had a warm embrace for him.

It had been one of the first things he'd noticed about Maggie—her constant habit of touching him. Whenever they were together she seemed to almost need to reach out to him.

They would be just sitting and talking, or watching some movie she would insist he would love and, without seeming to notice it, she would often stretch out her hand to lay it on his or touch his shoulder or back as she walked by. And, of course, there were the many spontaneous hugs and kisses she showered him with.

At first he had been surprised every time it had happened, but more and more lately he had found himself responding in kind without even thinking.

For just a second panic sliced through him: what was he *doing* with this woman? She deserved so much better than the broken, angry man he had turned into. The need to turn and walk away, to permanently remove every possible likelihood of hurting her, was almost overwhelming.

But then she laughed. And standing in that noisy, crowded hallway, watching as Maggie threw back her head to laugh at something Katie whispered to her, he knew without a shadow of a doubt that it was too late.

Maggie had missed the way Grant's face had softened as he'd looked at her, but Elizabeth had not. Neither had Cloë.

When Cloë had trailed off midway through saying goodbye to Steve to smile and sigh, Steve had turned to see what she was looking at to find his tough, street-smart partner staring at his little sister with a look so intense, so intent, that Steve had to grin despite the now-familiar little twinge he felt around his heart.

Steve was still smiling when he turned back around and found Cloë watching him, a satisfied smirk on her face. Her eyebrows rose.

"Bout time, huh?" Cloë said in a low voice.

Steve grinned again and glanced over to look at Maggie's glowing face before he turned back to meet Cloë's eyes once more.

"Yeah, yeah, yeah. Don't make me think about it too hard, okay?" Steve said then, turning serious, he changed the subject and asked, "Do you need a ride home, Cloë?"

"No. I've got my car here."

"If you want, I'd be happy to follow you home to make sure you get there all right."

"Thanks, Steve, but I'll be just fine. Besides, I have to stop on the way home at the grocery store," Cloë said and rolled her eyes playfully. Then, grinning to soften her words, she said, "Now I know why Mags is always complaining about how over-protective you guys are."

Steve had to laugh at the dramatic way she said it, but he turned serious once more as he said, "Just be careful—especially if you are out alone at night, okay?"

"I promise," Cloë said, then added, "It sure is nice having a big brother to look out for you, just don't let Maggie know I said so."

Steve laughed and said, "I won't rat you out, don't worry."

"Thanks. And thanks for the offer, too. I'll see you later, Steve."

"Bye, Cloë."

Cloë turned to wave at everyone else and said, "Bye, y'all. I'll see you tomorrow morning, Maggie."

"Hang on, Cloë, I need to talk to you for just a minute," Maggie said then turned to Grant and said, "I'll be right back, okay?"

Grant nodded and said, "Your mom mentioned something about a book I could borrow from her, I'll just get that and meet you outside in a couple of minutes."

"Perfect," Maggie said and slipped out the door to the front porch.

"So? What do you think?" Maggie asked.

"Weelll…" Cloë drew the word out as she considered and then she grinned broadly, "I've never seen anyone be a bigger hit with your parents, *or* with your brothers. They all got along like he'd been a member of the family for years."

"Oh, God," Maggie groaned dramatically.

"What? That's good right? Don't you want them to like him?"

"Of course I do. Absolutely. It's just that things seem to be going so fast. Cloë, I think I'm in love with him."

Maggie paused and waited for her closest friend to respond to this dramatic statement, and when Cloë only grinned more broadly she said, "Why are you smiling at me like that? Why are *you* so smug?"

"Oh, maybe because I *knew* he was perfect for you the first time you talked about him with that dreamy look in your eyes. All I can say is, you better jump that man's bones sooner rather than later and find out if he's as perfect in bed as he seems to be everywhere else."

Maggie glanced quickly at the front door before smacking Cloë on the arm and laughing. "You shameless hussy! What kind of woman do you think I am?"

"One who's finally and truly in love," Cloë said softly, all humor gone from her voice and a look of satisfaction on her face. She continued, "One who deserves to grab hold of every bit of happiness that she can."

Maggie's laughter died away and tears stung her eyes as she leaned forward to grab her petite friend into a quick hug and replied, "You're the best, Cloë."

Maggie leaned back and a flush of devilish humor danced across her face before she leaned forward, eyes sparkling through the darkness, and whispered expressively, " And since you're *such* a good friend I can tell you that he's not only just as good, he's even better in bed…and out."

"Maggie!" Cloë exclaimed in a shocked voice before both women burst into laughter.

When the front door opened five minutes later and Grant stepped out onto the front porch he was surprised to find Maggie and Cloë both sitting on the top step laughing hysterically.

"Am I interrupting?" he asked slowly and was further surprised when the women simply looked at him and then turned back to each other and laughed even harder.

"I better take off. See you on Monday, Mags. Night, Grant," Cloë said when she could talk again.

"Night, Cloë, and thanks," Maggie said.

Cloë walked down the path and got into her car as Maggie and Grant stood and watched.

"So, is there any chance that you're going to tell me what all that was about?" Grant asked.

"Not a one."

Grant flashed a devilish grin and raised one eyebrow in a now-familiar gesture and said, "You think so, do you? I bet I could get you to spill."

"Not even with all your fancy police tricks, Detective," Maggie said over her shoulder as she turned to go back inside.

"We'll see about that…" Grant threatened as he followed close behind.

THIRTY-FOUR

As Maggie and Grant turned to go back into the house, still arguing back and forth, they didn't see the dark shape of a man shift, half hidden in the shadows of the hedge of bushes that separated the Sullivan's house from their neighbor's.

The killer seethed, his hands slowly tearing apart the branches he held as he thought, *that whore, trying to tempt his Angel to rut like a filthy animal in heat. How* dare *she even imply that his Angel would fornicate with anyone—when she was clearly saving herself for him?*

He hadn't heard the last thing his Angel had said, but he'd seen the brave way she'd laughed off the cruel comments her friend had made. And even more, he'd seen how she'd hugged the undeserving wretch and forgiven her.

His Angel was still pure, still good.

But even the *thought* of another man pawing at her perfect skin, running his greasy hands over her unspoiled body was inconceivable.

It wasn't to be considered, because if it ever happened he would be forced to punish her, to make her pure once more.

The sharp sting of a branch ripping into the palm of his hand brought his twisted thoughts to a halt. He looked down at the dark, wet stain on his hand and closed his fist around it; squeezing so hard drops of blood fell unnoticed to the ground below him.

He allowed his eyes to be drawn up as they followed the fading taillights of Cloë's car as they vanished around a corner in the distance.

Slowly, silently, he slipped from the bushes and down the three blocks to where he'd parked his car, all the while thinking, plotting.

Someone had to pay.

Someone *would* pay.

THIRTY-FIVE

Back inside the house, Grant and Maggie were packing up the last of their things.

Maggie turned to her father and asked, "So what's in the box you brought in earlier, Dad?"

"Oh, yeah, I almost forgot. That's the stuff you said you wanted for the show."

"Thanks, Dad," Maggie hugged Bram again, and then turned to face her brothers, her hands on her hips, "And I will see *you* two here on Thursday night for rehearsal and costume fittings, got it?"

"Yeah, yeah, we got it," Jack sneered as he and Dillon filed out the door.

"We better get going too, Momma, Daddy. Thanks for everything," Maggie said then turned to face Grant. "All set?"

"All set," Grant agreed.

It took three trips to load the SUV with all the props, the container, Jake, and everything else they'd brought with, before they were able to make their final goodbyes.

Maggie sagged back against the cushion in relief. Her family had behaved. For once, she had actually gotten the chance to completely relax with both her family *and* the man she was dating.

While Maggie sat smiling over the way Grant had seemed to be right at home with her crazy family, Grant was also thinking over his day.

Instead of the awkwardness and suspicion he'd expected to experience on his second visit to the Sullivan house he'd been treated as a member of the family.

Sure, the guys had ribbed him some, but it was so obviously good-natured he'd taken it for what it really was—a kind of seal of approval, a blessing.

Grant pulled his attention back to the present and started the SUV. As they turned out of the drive and onto the street he glanced over towards Maggie. She stared blindly out of the car window at the brightly lit houses as they drove by.

Grant turned forward again and said, "That's some awful deep thinking going on over there, Red. What's on your mind?"

Maggie mentally shook herself and turned her head to face him as she replied, "Oh, I was just thinking about Cloë and all of the other women I know, and well, half of me wants to warn them about the maniac that's out there, and the other half knows that doing so would terrify them and could cause a real panic.

"Don't get me wrong, I would *never* say anything, but it's so hard to *know* that the nightmares you always feared are worse than you ever imagined, and suddenly, very real. Honestly, I don't know how you and Steven do it."

"I'm sorry, Maggie. I knew that it would be hard for you to know about what's been going on, but we really needed your help. And, I guess it may be selfish, but I like that I don't have to hide everything that I'm doing from you. I'm also glad that you will be on the alert and hopefully safer as a result."

"I don't think that's selfish, Grant. It *is* scary knowing what's going on, but I'm glad that I know anyway. I just hope that the info I gave you guys will help."

Grant pulled into his drive and parked the car. "We'll be presenting the information you gave us to the Chief tomorrow, and hopefully be able to map out some kind of plan. If there are questions we cannot answer are you still willing to come in to explain the things you told us last night to the Chief and our task force?"

"Of course. I'll just let Holden know that I may have to leave for a family thing when I get in to the office."

"As long as he doesn't find out you're helping us, tell him whatever you think is best."

Maggie's brow drew down and she said, "You don't really believe that Holden is involved in these murders. There's just no way he would *ever* hurt anyone."

Grant sighed and reached out to brush a stray curl away from her confused face.

"Maggie, you have to understand—even if you could never imagine it, I cannot risk the possibility that he *could* be. Even if it is an almost non-existent possibility."

When she still looked unconvinced he continued, "Judging from what you told us, and information I'm unable to tell you about, we think there's a good possibly that the killer has intimate knowledge of your field of expertise. If that's true, we can't risk you talking with anyone about your knowledge of these cases. Not only would it jeopardize the cases, it would put you in danger. And that is absolutely unacceptable.

"Even if you are one-hundred percent convinced that Holden is not involved, there's no way of knowing if he is in contact—no matter how innocently—with the killer. I cannot imagine that the art history community is that large in a city the size of Hope, even considering non-professional interests."

Maggie nodded once and said, "I understand what you're saying and I won't say a thing, but I don't like lying to a colleague, a friend."

"Well, since you're helping Steve out, too, it *is* technically a family thing."

Maggie had to smile a little as she agreed, "All right. I'll let him know right away in the morning. What time is your meeting?"

Relieved, Grant said, "Right away. I'll give you a call as soon as I know whether or not we'll need you to come in, okay?"

Maggie nodded again and Grant leaned forward to cup her face in his hands.

"Thanks, Red," he said against her lips before he sank into her.

"Mmmm," was all Maggie said as all thoughts of bosses, brothers, and murder flew from her head to be replaced by the warm heat of desire that always seemed to be simmering just below the surface since she'd met Grant.

"Come in. Be with me tonight," Grant murmured against her neck as he kissed slowly down to the collar of her shirt and back up again to the lobe of her ear.

Distracted, Maggie took a long moment to respond. "That sounds inviting, Detective, but…"

"No buts, Red."

"*But*, I have to wrap up my class notes tonight—especially if I'm going to be spending my morning with you at the station."

Grant drew slowly, reluctantly away from her to meet her clouded eyes with his.

"All right, I get the message. Want some company while you work?" Grant murmured as his head descended and his lips worked their way to the fluttering pulse in the vee of her neck.

"Hmmm," Maggie's eyes slid closed again before she pulled back and forced her eyes to open. Using one hand to press firmly against the soft leather jacket that covered his chest, Maggie dragged in a deep breath and said, "No," softly before repeating more firmly, "No. If you come over I seriously doubt I will get anything I need to get done, done."

"As long as you're sure…," Grant said as he lifted the hand pushing against his chest and pressed his lips against the center of her palm, shooting a shaft of heat straight to her center.

Distracted again, Maggie said, "What?"

Grant grinned and repeated, "As long as you're sure I can't help?"

Maggie mentally pulled herself together as she said, "Yes, I'm sure. Thanks for a great day."

"It was my pleasure."

Maggie got out of the SUV followed closely by Grant and Jake. "I'll walk you up," Grant began and stopped when Maggie shook her head as she grabbed her bags from the back of the truck.

"Thanks for the offer, Detective, but I think it would be safer if I went by myself."

Grant had to laugh at her wry tone and he leaned forward to press one last hard kiss to her lips before he stood back, hands tucked into his rear pockets and said, "Do me a favor, Red, and blink your lights, okay?"

"Yes, Mother. See you tomorrow."

"Night, Red."

Maggie smiled back over her shoulder as she made her way across to her building and inside. Grant waited until she'd dutifully blinked her living room lights before he turned and, followed closely by Jake, moved up the walk to his front door, whistling.

Several miles away from where Grant and Maggie stood saying goodnight, Cloë stepped from her car and leaned down to grab her bag of leftovers and the bag of groceries she had stopped to get on the way home. A feeling that she was not alone brought her head up in alarm.

She gripped her keys tightly as she searched the shadowed street for several long moments, and then laughed nervously to herself. She slammed the door to her car and cursed Steve Sullivan for making her jump at shadows and imaginary attackers then cursed herself for not taking him up on his offer to follow her home.

With one last glance around, she sped up the front steps to the tiny house she rented and unlocked the front door with fingers still unsteady enough that it took her two tries before she managed to get the key all the way into the lock.

She was so focused on getting inside and locking the door behind her, she never glanced up. Never noticed the edge of an upstairs curtain falling silently back into place again.

THIRTY-SIX

On Monday morning, Maggie woke up in a fabulous mood.

Bright sunlight streamed through her bedroom window. But the cool floor under her bare feet reminded her that winter was not far away. With a shiver Maggie turned her attention to getting dressed and into work on time.

She breezed into the office fifty-eight minutes later, right on time, and was disappointed to find no one there to witness the event.

Tony and Cloë were always there before her. Holden was less reliable, but he usually beat her as well. Maggie shrugged and hung up her coat before she settled down to boot up her computer.

Before she poured her first cup of coffee for the day Tony came in. He nodded once and mumbled, "Mornin', Maggie," as he hurried straight to his desk.

Maggie smiled and answered in kind, but she sighed silently and wondered if things between her and Tony would ever return to the way they had once been. Much as she liked Tony and appreciated his hard work, she was almost glad that he would not be staying on after this year.

Working day-in and day-out with him on a permanent basis would have been extremely awkward for both of them.

Shrugging guiltily, Maggie turned her attention back to her desk, but not before it paused on Cloë's empty desk chair. *I wonder what's keeping her*, Maggie mused, her brow contracted in concern.

As flighty and impulsive as her friend could be in her personal life, Cloë was one of the most efficient and effective workers Maggie had ever met. She was almost painfully prompt, and rarely—if ever—had she been late.

Maggie glanced at the clock. It read 8:08. Cloë was less than ten minutes late, obviously Maggie was overreacting. There could have been bad traffic, or a power outage, or anything, really. Cloë would be here soon, and she would laugh if she could see Maggie now.

Maggie checked her email and the voicemail on both her desk phone and her cell phone, but Cloë hadn't left a message on either. She had Cloë's number half-dialed when she hung up her phone. She was being ridiculous. Surely Cloë would walk through the door any minute now, and the two of them would hash over their weekends like they did every Monday morning.

This reassured her for about two minutes before she asked Tony, "Have you heard from Cloë this morning?"

He straightened in his chair and turned slowly to face Maggie, "No. I figured she must have the day off, or something. She's never late. Maybe she called Holden?"

"Maybe," Maggie agreed, but the doubt in her voice was mirrored on her worried face.

When the office door opened twenty-six minutes later it was Holden who came in, a tray of four coffees in hand.

"Morning, everyone…What's wrong?" his cheerful greeting tuned to concern at the worried looks on both Maggie and Tony's faces.

"Cloë's late. Did she tell you she wasn't going to be in today?" Maggie asked only to have her last hope crushed when Holden shook his head.

"No," he said as he unwrapped the deep red scarf he had wound around his neck and hung it up with his coat before he turned back to face them.

"Have you tried calling yet?"

Maggie nodded, clearly distressed, and said, "Both her house and her cell. No answer at either. I was just trying to decide if I should try her father or not. I'd hate to worry him over nothing."

Holden leaned against Cloë's desk and ran his hand through wind-ruffled hair before he crossed his arms, thinking. After a pause he said thoughtfully, "Well, why don't we wait a little bit longer before we call anyone. If we haven't heard from her by, say ten, then we can start calling around. She's probably just running late, or having car trouble or something, and her phone is turned off."

"You're right," Maggie replied, "I know I'm being ridiculous, but I just can't get rid of this awful feeling that something is wrong," she paused, then shaking her head again she repeated, "You're probably right—she's probably in the shower or driving with the radio up too high again. I'm always telling her she's gonna hurt her ears if she doesn't start turning that thing down once in a while."

Maggie trailed off, but was distracted from her thoughts when Holden lifted a messily-bandaged hand to pick up the tray of coffees.

"What happened to your hand?" she exclaimed and came round her desk to grab Holden's hand in hers.

"Oh, it's just a cut from a mug I broke this morning. I didn't think and grabbed it. It's nothing. Here's your morning jolt," Holden handed Maggie one of the four cups of coffee from the carrier before handing one to Tony and placing a third on Cloë's desk blotter.

"I better get some work done. Let me know when you hear from Cloë," Holden said and walked into his office, leaving the door open.

The morning seemed to drag by. Maggie stopped work every time someone walked by the office to stare at the door, willing it to be her friend. She tried Cloë's phones again and again with no luck, and after sticking his head out and asking several times if they'd heard anything, Holden finally came out to sit next to Maggie's desk.

At exactly ten Maggie called Cloë's father, but only succeeded in making him as worried as they all were. After assuring him that she would contact him the second she saw or heard from Cloë, Maggie hung up the phone.

"I'm calling Steven and Grant," Maggie declared, looking at Holden as is defying him to tell her she was being silly. "I know that officially we can't report this for forty-eight hours, but I'm just too worried to wait any longer. I know if they ask the Chief will let them at least go and check out her house. I even have a key I can give them."

Maggie yanked her purse out of the drawer and began to empty its contents haphazardly out onto her desk. After searching for a minute she found the small key ring and said, "Here it is."

"I think that's a good idea," Holden said.

Maggie reached for the phone and dialed quickly. Steve answered on the first ring.

"Morning, Mags. Can I call you back in a bit? I'm right in the middle…"

"Steven, I need your help," Maggie interrupted.

"What's wrong? Are you okay?"

"I'm fine. It's Cloë. She late and not answering either of her phones."

"Maggie…," Steve sighed.

"I *know* what you're thinking, Steven, but she's *never* late and if something had come up, she'd have called by now. It's just not like her. And, well, I just have a terrible feeling that something is really wrong."

Hearing near panic in his usually collected sister's voice had Steve reaching out to grab Grant's arm as he walked past his desk. "Let me grab Grant and we'll head over to her house and check it out, okay? She's probably just fine; overslept or something. We'll call as soon as we find out more, okay Maggie?"

Relieved at Steven's calm tone, Maggie sagged back in her seat, "All right. But I do have a key for her house if you want to stop and get it. Or, I could meet you at her house."

"No, no. We'll swing by and nab it on the way. *Do not* go over there, Maggie. Do you understand me?"

"I won't."

"Good. Just give me a couple minutes to wrap up one thing and we'll be right over."

"Thanks, Steven."

"What's up? Chief's waiting," Grant said as he stopped to stand next to Steve's chair to wait for him to get up.

"That was Maggie."

"So I gathered. She okay?"

"She's fine, but she's worried about Cloë and wants us to check in on her," Steve said and grabbed a file folder from his desk, then stood to join Grant as he walked back towards the Chief's office.

"You sound worried," Grant kept his voice neutral while he pictured Maggie's sweet, pixie-like friend and all the things that could have happened to her on her way home the night before. Grimacing, Grant felt his gut clench.

"I *am* worried. This is out of character for Cloë, and it takes a lot for Maggie to get as upset as she was when I talked to her. It just feels off."

"We'll go right after we brief the Chief," Grant replied readily.

Grateful for Grant's easy acceptance, Steve said, "All right," then sighed and continued, "Let's get this done."

Thirty-five minutes later, Grant and Steve pulled up in front of Cloë's small, well-maintained house. It had taken just a few minutes to brief the Chief, but they had spent twice that time trying to talk Maggie out of coming before she agreed not to come with them. Only the realization that her continued arguing was delaying them won out in the end.

As Grant rounded the hood of the car he studied the small one-and-a-half story bungalow with interest. Painted a soft sage green that brought to mind shaded forest glens and meadows, the quiet house was trimmed with crisp white trim and accented by a bright purple door. In the cool, quiet morning the house sat silently amidst a sea of fading flowers and trees stripped of leaves.

"Sure doesn't look like anyone's home," he commented as he looked at the drawn shades.

"That's Cloë's car, there," Steve said as he pointed at a compact purple car parked on the street in front of the house.

Grant had hoped that Cloë had simply forgotten her phone at home and had had car trouble or something as equally innocuous, but the hopes of a scenario like that had just been erased. Now, his best hope, if that's what he could call it, was that she was somehow injured in a common, innocent accident, and not in any way that involved foul play.

Not exactly the outcome he had been hoping for when less than an hour ago he'd assured Maggie that Cloë was probably just fine.

Grant sighed and said, "Well, we better find out what's going on." He pulled out his phone and tried calling Cloë one last time. While Steve climbed the front steps and rang the doorbell Grant walked around the perimeter of the house looking for any obvious signs of either a break-in or Cloë.

He found neither, only a tiny postage-stamp back yard overflowing with flowers and a single lounge chair and table.

When he rounded the corner of the house again he found Steve digging the key Maggie had given him out of his pocket.

"There's no one out back. I couldn't get a good look at the basement window, but there were no obvious breaks. I also didn't get an answer," Grant said as he lifted his phone from his ear and closed it.

"Let's check it out," Steve said as he slid the key into the lock and opened the door.

"Cloë? It's Steve. Are you here?" Grant pointed silently to Cloë's purse where it lay on a small table next to the door. Steve nodded and together they both drew their weapons as they made their way through the living room, dining room and kitchen.

Nodding again, this time towards the closed basement door, Grant reached out and silently opened the door, groping blindly along the wall for a light switch before his hand found a hanging chain and pulled.

They made their way down the stairs to the almost empty basement. Nothing seemed to be disturbed, but the sight of the basement window slightly ajar had the dread in Grant's stomach mounting.

"Steve. The window," he said, pointing.

"Shit," Steve swore, then turned and bounded up the stairs and through the living room calling loudly for Cloë. Grant followed him through the tiny house and up the stairs to the second floor.

As he sped down the hall behind Steve, Grant paused only long enough to make sure that both the bathroom and the empty bedroom that Cloë clearly used as an office and craft room were both secure before he pulled to a stop in the open doorway of the third, and last room—Cloë's bedroom.

"Oh, God," Steve said. "Oh, my God, Cloë? Cloë, are you all right? Call it in!" Steve yelled over his shoulder to Grant as he dropped to kneel next to the prone figure that had been blocked from Grant's sight by Steve.

Grant tore his eyes away from the bloody figure on the floor and looked around the completely destroyed bedroom as he holstered his gun and pulled his phone out to call for the ambulance he prayed Cloë still needed.

He hung up and asked from the doorway, "Is she...?"

"She's alive. Barely. But, I don't know for how long."

"The ambulance is on the way. Do you need me over there?"

"No. There's no way I'm going to try moving her, and it's bad enough that I—and the paramedics—will have been in here. We better get the crew over here ASAP."

"I already called the Chief. He's sending, well, pretty much everyone. I'm going to grab the camera before the ambulance gets here. We need to photograph her before they move her."

Steve glared at Grant for a moment before he nodded reluctantly and his face slid into a hard mask as he knelt, waiting next to Cloë's almost completely still form.

Grant was back before Steve finished his cursory examination of Cloë's injuries.

There were too many to count.

"Here," Grant held out the camera to Steve, careful not to step into the room as they both heard the sirens of the approaching ambulance. "I'll show them in," he said and was gone again before Steve took his first shot.

By the time the paramedics pounded up the stairs Steve had taken more than a hundred shots of her body. He stepped back to let the medical professionals get to Cloë and begin their work.

Despite his years on the job and the terrible appearance of her body as it lay there, nothing prepared Grant for the sight of Cloë's severely beaten face and mutilated body when the paramedics gently turned her over onto her back. It was almost more than he could bear.

Steve simply closed his eyes before he forced himself to get back to work. As he continued to take pictures Steve heard the muffled string of oaths from Grant and Steve turned to see his partner's professional mask crack, and just for a moment, the horror Steve felt was reflected on Grant's face before he managed to get control of his emotions again.

"How is she even alive?" Grant asked, staggered.

"She shouldn't be. And she won't be if we don't get her out of here right now. Let's go," one of the paramedics said as he and his partner transferred Cloë to a stretcher and brushed past Steve and Grant on their way to the ambulance.

"Did you see it?" Steve asked quietly.

"Yeah."

"Then, there's no way this could be someone else?"

"No. No chance in Hell," Grant said, "Better get out of here so the lab guys can get in."

Steve nodded and followed Grant downstairs and out the front door to wait for the rest of their task force and the forensics team to get there.

"I better call Maggie," Steve said, the weariness apparent in his voice.

Grant pulled his thoughts back from the room he'd begun to think of as a crime scene and closed his eyes at the idea, saying, "She's going to be crushed."

"Yeah," Steve sighed again and lifted his hands to rub them over his face before he realized that they were covered in Cloë's blood. "I've gotta wash up. Can you call her?"

"Sure," Grant nodded. Then as Grant watched his partner walk away he saw Steve's shoulders slump as he stared down at his bloody hands. Grant pulled out his phone and typed in Maggie's work number.

He dreaded the terrible news he had to tell her. He was just grateful that, despite the fact that he was going to devastate the woman he had fallen in love with, he didn't have to destroy her with the knowledge that her dearest friend had been brutally beaten and murdered by a sadistic serial killer.

At least, not yet.

Maggie answered on the first ring. "Grant? Is she okay?"

"Maggie. I don't want you to freak out. We found her and she's alive..."

"Alive?" Maggie broke in, panic in her voice.

"Yes. Maggie, Honey, I need you to calm down and listen to me, okay? Cloë's been hurt badly, but she's on the way to the hospital right now. I want so much to be able to bring you there, but Steve and I have to work the scene here. Do you have someone who can drive you?"

"Oh, my God. I've got to get down there, Grant. I need to call her dad. Has anyone called her dad yet? I..."

"Maggie," Grant's calm voice broke through her increasingly panicked babbling and he repeated, "Maggie is there someone there who can give you a ride to the hospital? I don't want you getting behind the wheel when you're this upset."

Maggie's eyes slid closed at his steady, composed tone and she took a couple of deep breaths before she replied in a much steadier voice, "Yes. Holden can drive me. But I'm all right now. Do you know whether or not Mr. Sanders has been told yet?"

Grant was relieved to hear how controlled Maggie sounded again. He said, "Yes. I think Bethany is on her way to his house to tell him in person and give him a ride to the hospital if he needs it. Maggie, I'm really sorry I'm not there with you—I wish I could give you a ride myself."

Especially since he didn't like the way her boss looked at her. Something he didn't add out loud.

He had met Holden when he'd stopped in to the University office to pick Maggie up for lunch about a week ago and had immediately noticed how possessive Holden was of Maggie. Grant had made the mistake of mentioning it to her, but she'd laughed it off, saying that she thought of Holden as a big brother or mentor, and that Holden felt the same way towards her.

Grant focused his attention back to the present when Maggie replied, "I understand. No matter how much I need you to be with me right now, Cloë needs you and Steven even more. I know that you will find the monster who hurt her and make him pay."

"You can count on it. The bastard really screwed up this time," Grant said, satisfaction coloring his voice.

"This time? Do you mean…was it the…was it the thing we talked about at your house?" Maggie asked cautiously, conscious of the fact that both Holden and Tony were listening.

"Yes, I think so. But I can't discuss it now."

"I understand."

"Maggie, I'm sorry but forensics is here and I need to get to work. I'll come see you as soon as I can, all right?"

"Okay. I'll be at the hospital and then…I don't know."

"I'll find you, Red. Don't you worry about that. I'll find you as soon as I can," he repeated, then hung the phone up.

Maggie closed her eyes for a moment before focusing on Tony and Holden's faces. She hung up the phone and turned to face them, saying, "Cloë's been attacked. She's on the way to the hospital."

"Is she going to be okay?" Tony asked.

"I don't know. When I asked, all Gra... Detective Evans could tell me was that she was still alive."

"That's bad," Tony said, his eyes huge.

"That's really bad," Holden said as he hurried to grab his coat from where he'd hung it just a couple of hours earlier. "I'll drive. Tony, call the Dean. He'll take care of canceling my classes. I'll pull the car around and you can meet me downstairs in five minutes."

As the door closed behind Holden, Tony picked up the phone to call and Maggie shut everything down, her mind still focused on what Grant had told her.

THIRTY-SEVEN

Four minutes later they were all piled into Holden's car, racing towards the hospital. By the time Holden dropped them off at the emergency room entrance most of the calmness Grant had helped her achieve had faded. Instead, the descriptions Grant and Steven had given her of the killer's three previous victims kept flashing through her mind, interspersed with images of Cloë less than twelve hours earlier.

Banishing the images, Maggie rushed through the doors followed closely by Tony, only to be met with the reality of emergency rooms everywhere. Until Cloë was evaluated, there was nothing anyone could tell them beyond the fact that she was critical, but still alive.

When Holden came in a few minutes later he found Tony sitting in a chair, staring blankly at the floor while Maggie filled out what paperwork she could.

"How is she? Is she going to be all right?"

Maggie looked up into Holden's concerned face and felt tears sting her eyes, "She's still alive. She's critical, and they are going to be sending her to surgery as soon as they stabilize her."

"Oh, my God."

Maggie sighed and looked back at the form in front of her, the words blurring. "They said they'd tell us when she's moved into surgery so we can move to the surgical waiting room. But other than *this*," Maggie gestured at the forms, "There's nothing we can do but wait. And pray."

Holden reached out to squeeze her shoulder and nodded before moving to sit in a chair next to Tony.

Maggie brushed angrily at her tears and turned her attention back to the questionnaire.

She felt so darn helpless.

At least on the way to the hospital she'd been focused on getting here, on helping her friend in some way. But now, there wasn't a thing she could do to help Cloë. Whether she lived or died was in someone else's hands, and the lack of control was an almost physical pain.

279

Maggie handed the completed forms to the nurse behind the check-in desk and collapsed into a chair across from where Tony and Holden sat looking miserable, her thoughts swirling.

The fear and helplessness she felt turned to anger as she focused on the monster who had tried to kill her best friend, then to guilt for not finding some way to warn Cloë about what Grant and Steven had told her about, and then back to fear; what if Cloë died? Who would be attacked—even killed—next?

Fear, anger, guilt, and back to fear. Over and over again until she thought she'd lose her mind. She was so wrapped up in her thoughts it took a moment for Holden's quiet warning to get her attention.

"Maggie."

Maggie looked up to see a doctor walking towards them. The doctor spoke calmly, her face completely neutral. "Miss Sullivan? I'm Dr. Erickson. We managed to stabilize Miss Sanders. We almost lost her once, but we were able to stabilize her enough for surgery. She's on her way upstairs right now. Is her family here?"

"No. Someone is trying to contact her father now. Is she going to be okay?"

Dr. Erickson sighed and said, "It's hard to say right now, we're doing the best we can to help her, but your friend has been severely beaten. In addition to multiple lacerations and contusions, she also has several fractures and internal bleeding. We'll know more after surgery."

"Thank you, Doctor," Holden said as he steered a shocked Maggie to a nearby chair. The doctor nodded and said in a sympathetic tone, "There's a waiting room for surgery on the third floor. When Miss Sanders is out of surgery someone will come see you there. Her surgeon, Dr. Jankowski, is one of the best."

"Thanks," Maggie said softly. As the doctor walked away Maggie buried her face in her hands before she scrubbed her face brusquely and stood up suddenly.

"We better go up to that waiting room. They'll have a phone I can use to try calling Mr. Sanders."

Holden met Tony's eyes, his own bleak, as they stood to follow Maggie towards the elevator. When they reached the waiting room Holden registered with the check-in desk while Maggie tried calling, but got the answering machine again.

They settled into a quiet corner of the room to wait, each consumed with their own thoughts. Ron Sanders came into the room twenty minutes later looking shell shocked and confused. Maggie rushed across the room towards him.

"Mr. S."

Mr. Sanders focused on Maggie's face and he hugged her, "Maggie. What's going on? I talked to Cloë yesterday and she was fine. Then this morning there's a police officer knocking at my door telling me she's on the way to the hospital, that someone attacked her…"

Maggie put her hand behind his elbow leading him to the corner where they were sitting. "Come and sit down, Mr. S. Did they tell you anything about Cloë's condition?"

He nodded as he sank down into the chair she had lead him to, and he said, "Yes. When I came in they told me she was beat up and in surgery. Who would want to hurt Cloë? Everybody loves her…" As he trailed off, his voice caught and he broke into sobs.

Maggie struggled to hold her own tears back and she said a silent prayer, *Oh, Lord, please help me say the right thing. Please don't take my friend. Her father needs her and so do I.*

She leaned forward, trying to smile, and said, "Mr. S. Cloë is so strong. She is going to be fine. She's a fighter, but right now she needs us to be strong for her."

Mr. Sanders nodded and struggled to pull himself together. After several tries, he was able to ask, "Maggie, what happened to her? All the police officer would tell me was that someone broke into her house and attacked her. Why would anyone do that?"

Maggie debated how much she could say, knowing that Tony and Holden were sitting next to them, listening.

"I'm not completely sure. Cloë didn't show up for work this morning, and she wasn't answering her phone. We were really worried," Maggie gestured to Holden and Tony, and then continued, "After a couple of hours I called my brother, Steven, and asked him and his partner, Detective Evans, to check in on her. I have a key.

"They went to her house and found her unconscious in her bedroom and called the ambulance. All they told me was that

281

someone broke into the house and attacked Cloë. They didn't know anything else yet, but I promise you, Mr. S., they *will* find out who did this to Cloë."

Mr. Sanders reached over to squeeze her hands and nodded, unable to speak before he leaned forward to put his head in his hands.

Maggie looked helplessly at Holden before she stood and paced to a nearby window to stare blindly out at the gunmetal gray sky.

Holden and Tony both stared at her slumped form silhouetted against the window, neither man noticing the other had the identical look of longing in his eyes.

When Grant walked through the doorway some time later, he took in the scene before him with a single glance, his jaw clenching and eyes narrowing as he looked from Tony to Holden and then over to where Maggie stood.

Grant hesitated, torn between his duty and the almost overwhelming need he felt to go to Maggie, to comfort her.

Steve had come in on Grant's heels and took it all in as quickly as Grant had. Steve leaned forward and said quietly, "Go. I'll talk to Mr. Sanders. She needs you. Go."

Grant cast one grateful glance at Steve and hurried across the room to where she stood.

"Maggie."

Maggie whirled around, her face pale and wan and eyes filling with tears again at the sound of his voice.

"Oh, Grant," she said, and moved into his arms. Grant ran one hand down her hair and back as he murmured softly in her ear, "It's going to be okay, Maggie. It's going to be okay."

"Grant I'm so scared for her. They wouldn't tell us if she would be okay, and she is so hurt."

Grant pulled away to cup her face with both hands and he looked her in the eye. "You have to believe she is going to be okay. You need to be strong, all right?"

Maggie nodded and Grant brushed away the tears that rolled down her face and leaned forward to brush a soft kiss on her forehead before letting his hands fall to grasp hers. He squeezed and said, "I need to go help Steve. Are you going to be all right?"

Maggie drew herself up and nodded, squaring her shoulders before answering. "Yes. I'll introduce you to Mr. S."

Grant gave her hands one last squeeze and nodded, glad to see a touch of color back on her face.

Together they turned and walked past Tony and Holden over to where Steve and Mr. Sanders were now sitting, talking quietly. As they got close Maggie overheard the tail end of what Steve was saying.

"…notice anything strange over the past few days? Weird calls, strange noises, anything."

Mr. Sanders shook his head, a bewildered look on his face, and said, "No. Nothing. We spoke yesterday morning around 8:30 and made plans to have dinner together tonight, but she never mentioned anything upsetting to me."

Maggie sank down next to Mr. Sanders and he grabbed her hand. She gestured towards Grant as he sat down next to Steve and said, "Mr. S., this is Detective Grant Evans."

Grant nodded his head and said, "Mr. Sanders, I'm very sorry about what happened to Cloë."

Mr. Sanders nodded back briefly and said, "Thank you."

Maggie watched Grant and her brother exchange a glance and, without saying a word out loud, managed to have a conversation. Steve leaned forward again and asked another question as Grant eased back slightly, letting Steve take the forefront. Seeing them together, it was as if they had been working together for years rather than weeks, and Maggie was struck all over again how perfectly and easily that Grant had slid into their lives.

Steven's voice brought her back to the present, "…either of you know of anyone who was upset or angry with Cloë? Or if she'd had any run-ins with anyone lately?"

"Nobody. Everyone loves Cloë," Maggie said.

"Mr. Sanders?"

"No. Cloë was the same—happy, busy…"

"I want you both to think over the last week or two, if there was *anything*, no matter how small, that was strange or just felt off to Cloë or to either of you."

Mr. Sanders shook his head and Maggie started to shake her head again, then stopped.

Grant, who'd been watching them both closely, noted the look as it crossed her face and said, "What is it Maggie?"

Steven and Mr. Sanders both turned to look at her, too, and Maggie folded her arms and looked at all three before she answered, "It's probably nothing…"

"Mags," Steve said in a low voice, his eyes never leaving hers.

Maggie blew out a breath and said, "About five days ago Cloë told me that her neighbor's dog disappeared and how upset they were. The dog had never run away before, and they couldn't figure out *how* it had gotten out of the yard. I don't see how that would have anything to do with someone hurting Cloë, though."

"Everything helps us get a picture of what was going on in her life. I'll need the neighbors' names," Steve said.

"Well, I'm not sure about the husband, but the wife's name is Kathleen. I never really paid attention to their last name and I only met her once. They live in the green house on the left. There's something else, too. About a week after I broke up with Bradley, I guess he stopped by Cloë's house and tried to get her to talk to me. Needless to say Cloë told him to, well," Maggie stopped and looked at Mr. Sanders apologetically before she continued, "Let's just say that she refused to help him. Vehemently. She told me that he was yelling and cursing at her, but that when she told him to shove off, he did."

"And you never told me this because…?" Steve asked, his voice completely bland.

"Steven, I completely forgot about it. I mean after Grant took care of him that night at my apartment, I pretty much just wanted to forget everything about the guy."

Steve held her gaze for a long moment before he said, "All right. Do you know what Cloë was working on in the office?"

Maggie knew him too well to believe that he'd actually dropped the subject for good, but for now she pushed the matter aside and answered, "Sure. I can show you if you'd like, but it was mainly working on the quarterly reports for Holden and entering the latest grades into the computer, doing some research for Tony and me. All pretty routine things that she handles—nothing out of the ordinary."

"Anyone failing or having a problem with the department?"

"Not that I know about. Holden would know more about that. I'm sure if you ask him, he can tell you."

Steve glanced over to where Holden and Tony sat quietly talking together several feet away. "Okay. We'll do that. Listen, if either of you think of anything else—no matter how small or insignificant you think it is—call me."

Steve handed Mr. Sanders his card and stood. He leaned forward to give Maggie a hug when she stood as well, and said softly in her ear, "I'll talk to you more, later. Stay out of trouble, Maggie. Don't go anywhere alone."

Maggie wanted to be able to tell her brother that he was being overprotective again, but the thought of her sweet friend lying on an operating table somewhere nearby, fighting for her life had Maggie quickly nodding in agreement.

"Mom's probably on her way by now," Steve added as he pulled away and walked over to speak with Tony and Holden briefly.

Grant said goodbye to Mr. Sanders while Steve and Maggie talked, then he moved forward to give her one last hug. He said, "We'll find the person who did this, Maggie. I promise. Just be careful, okay? Will you do me a favor? Will you please stay at your parent's until I can pick you up tonight?"

"Grant," Maggie began, then stifling the urge to say no automatically, she took a deep breath and looked past the demand on Grant's face to the concern and fear behind it in his eyes. She went on, "All right. But just for tonight."

Relieved that she'd given in so easily Grant gave her another quick hug and said, "Thanks, Red. I'll call you when I can."

"Be safe."

Grant turned to walk over to where Steve was waiting and the two of them walked out of the waiting room. Maggie followed their departure with her eyes and when they were out of sight she turned to sit down again, only to find both Holden and Tony staring at her.

Holden glanced away as soon as she met his eyes, but Tony continued to look at her, his intense gaze sending a shiver down her spine. Finally, she was forced to look away in discomfort, only to find Mr. Sander's concerned gaze on her.

"Is everything all right, Maggie?"

Maggie glanced back over to Tony and then back to Mr. Sanders again and sighed. "Yeah. Everything's okay, Mr. S."

"It doesn't look like everything's okay to me. If you need help, you ask for it, Maggie. If not from me, then from your brother or your young man."

Maggie's eyebrows shot up and she almost smiled, "My young man?"

Mr. Sanders leaned back, a tired smile on his face, and said, "Detective Evans. A blind man could see the two of you are involved, and despite how distracted I am, I'm far from blind, Maggie."

Maggie laughed and squeezed his hand once before saying, "You got me, Mr. S. You're right, I have been seeing Grant, but I'm not sure that I would call him mine."

"Trust me, when a man looks at a woman the way that he looks at you? He's definitely yours."

Maggie blushed and looked down.

"What concerns me," Mr. Sanders continued in a low voice, "is how those two are also looking at you."

"Tony and Holden? Tony has a little crush on me, but we talked about it and things are fine now. Or they will be soon. As for Holden, he's just a concerned friend looking out for me."

Troubled at her dismissive tone, Mr. Sanders looked over to find both men looking at Maggie again. His eyebrows drew down and he tried again. "Maggie, Honey…"

"Don't worry about it, Mr. S. They're harmless, like two more overprotective big brothers. They're just looking out for me."

Mr. Sanders had heard the stubborn tone of voice Maggie was using too many times to try to talk about it with her any longer right then. He would just have to mention the situation to Bram or Steven the next time he talked with them.

"I'm going to grab some coffee, Mr. S. Would you like some?"

Pulled from his thoughts Mr. Sanders said, "Some what?"
"Coffee."

"Sure, coffee would be good."

After Maggie left, Mr. Sanders got up to walk back over to where Tony and Holden both sat reading magazines and sat down.

286

"Where's Maggie going?" Holden asked.

"To get us some coffee."

"I'll go help her," Tony said as he quickly got up and hurried after her.

Holden looked after Tony, trying to keep his face as neutral as he could only to glance over and find Mr. Sander's knowing eyes on him. Holden shifted uncomfortably in his chair and looked back down to stare blindly at the open magazine as he struggled to keep his emotions from betraying him any further.

Maggie and Tony returned a few minutes later and the four of them sat without speaking for the next four hours, during which time Maggie's mother came and joined them in their silent vigil.

Finally, after more than five hours had passed since Cloë had gone into surgery, a surgeon came into the room. He inquired at the info desk and was pointed in their direction.

Mr. Sanders stood, flanked on either side by Maggie and Elizabeth, and waited for the doctor to reach them.

Maggie clenched her hands together as the doctor began to speak.

"Mr. Sanders? I'm Dr. Jankowski, the surgeon who worked on your daughter. We were able to stabilize her. She suffered two broken ribs, a broken arm, a fractured cheek bone, and a bruised larynx and kidney. In addition, her skull was fractured in two places.

"We think we managed to stop all of the internal bleeding, but we won't know for sure for at least twenty-four hours. We also were able to relieve the pressure in her skull. Right now, she has been put in an artificial coma as a precaution. The swelling on her brain and the bleeding are what we were most concerned about, and both have been successfully addressed. Now we need to wait.

"It may be several days before she is strong enough to be able to regain consciousness, and there is a small chance that she won't. I don't believe that to be the case with Ms. Sanders, but with brain injuries, there is just no way to be one hundred percent sure. She's being moved into ICU right now."

"Will she live?" Mr. Sanders choked out.

The doctor sighed wearily and said, "If she makes it through the next thirty-six hours she has a very good chance. For right now, we will be monitoring her closely and giving her strong antibiotics to help fight off any possible infections that could slow or prevent her healing. I just can't say for sure at this point. It's lucky we got to her when we did. Any longer before she was found and treated, and she would have died."

"Thank you, Dr. Jankowski," Maggie said and she steered a stunned Mr. Sanders back down into the chair that he'd been using.

It was another hour of waiting before Cloë was settled into ICU and they were allowed in to visit her. While Maggie waited for Mr. Sanders to come out of Cloë's room so that she could go in, she sat with her mother and Tony. Holden had left to teach his evening classes with the promise to stop in the next morning to see Cloë before he had his first class.

Elizabeth sat watching Maggie as she stared down at the floor. She reached over to rub Maggie's back and said, "Honey. I want you to come home tonight. Your father is making stew for dinner."

When Maggie didn't immediately refuse, Elizabeth added, "I know that you want to be here for Cloë, but I doubt that they will allow her to wake for at least a day or two. You haven't eaten at all today, and you need to get some sleep tonight if you're going to be able to face tomorrow."

Maggie scrubbed her face with her hands and leaned back in her chair to face Elizabeth before saying, "I know you're right. It's just...I feel like I have to *be* here in case anything happens."

"Ron will be here with Cloë and he'll call if there is any change."

Knowing that her mom was right, Maggie finally nodded and said, "All right. Grant said he would pick me up at your house as soon as he was able to tonight. I just need to see her, to tell her...I don't know, *something* before I can leave."

Elizabeth just nodded and reached over to grasp Maggie's hand in hers. When Maggie lapsed back into silence, her mind far away again, Elizabeth turned her attention to the silent man sitting across from them. She said in a kind voice, "Tony, how are your studies going?"

Tony tore his attention away from Maggie and he focused on her mother instead. He shifted in his chair and cleared his throat before he managed to say, "F-fine. I'm pretty close to finishing my thesis."

As he spoke Tony picked nervously at a small bandage on his left hand. Maggie, who had been listening to their conversation, noticed the movement.

Maggie asked, "Tony, what happened to your hand? Are you all right?"

Tony looked down at his hands and pulled the sleeve of his sweater down as far as he could. "I'm fine. It's just a little cut." He shrugged and fell silent again, his face slightly flushed.

Maggie glanced over at her mother and Elizabeth took her cue and changed the subject. While her mother talked to Tony about his paper and the weather, and a myriad of other safe subjects Maggie wondered to herself how long it would be before she would be able to ask Tony a seemingly simple, friendly question without embarrassing him.

Or worse, somehow inadvertently encouraging his crush on her.

Again, the unwanted thought that perhaps it was a *good* thing that he would be leaving the department in the spring flashed through her mind only to be immediately dismissed as selfish.

Mr. Sanders came back into the waiting room at that moment, his face lined with fear and sorrow. Concerned at how pale and fragile the man looked, Maggie stood and walked over to again lead him to a chair next to Elizabeth. If anyone could comfort him, it was her mother.

"How is she, Ron?" Elizabeth asked gently.

Mr. Sanders simply shook his head and said, "They have her hooked up to some machine that's breathing for her. Her hair...," his voice cracked and broke off. For several moments he struggled for composure, his hands clenched into fists, and he continued in a stronger voice, "They shaved her beautiful hair off. Maggie, if you're determined to go in...beware. She looks..."

Again, he stopped, then he looked directly into Maggie's face and said bleakly, "It doesn't even look like Cloë, she's so black and blue and swollen." Shaking his head, Mr. Sanders fell silent and then stood and said, "I need to make some calls," and walked away.

Forty-five minutes later, when the next visitor was allowed in to see Cloë, Maggie stood frozen in front of her door.

As she stood there Maggie prayed for the strength to face her friend, and the courage to overcome the dread she was filled with at seeing Cloë so horribly hurt.

Shoving aside her feelings, Maggie pushed through the door to Cloë's room and walked quickly over to the slight form that seemed lost in the sterile white expanse of the bed.

For several minutes the only sounds in the quiet room were the rhythmic whooshing of the machine forcing oxygen into Cloë's lungs; the beeps and clicks of the many other machines tasked with keeping her alive; and Maggie's choked gasps as she looked at the unrecognizable mass of tubes, bandages, and bruised flesh that she knew was her friend.

Nothing Mr. S could have said would have prepared her for seeing Cloë like this.

"Oh, Cloë. I'm so sorry," Maggie whispered as she looked to find some part of Cloë's battered arm that she could touch without causing her any pain. Slowly, gently, Maggie lifted one scraped hand to hold loosely in her own trembling hands.

All Maggie could think was that she should have *said* something—anything—to Cloë before letting her drive off alone.

She was still standing there, just holding Cloë's hand, when the nurse standing quietly in the corner told her that her five minutes were up. Maggie nodded and turned back to lean down close to Cloë's ear and said, "I'll be back, Cloë, and your Dad is right outside. Love you, Sweetie."

She gently lowered Cloë's hand back down onto the bed and brushed the tears from her cheeks before she turned to go.

When she came through the door Maggie found Bethany Jones sitting in a chair next to Cloë's door, a carryout-cup of coffee on the small table next to her and a romance novel in her hands.

Surprised, Maggie stopped short and said, "Hey, Bethany. What's going on?"

"Hi, Maggie. Not much. Steve just asked me to come down."

Maggie glanced between the policewoman sitting, casually reading with her gun just barely visible in its holster under her coat, and Cloë's closed door.

Her eyes widened and Maggie felt a spear of fear stab through her making her heart stop for a beat before it began to pound furiously.

"You think he's going to try to finish what he started," Maggie stated in a voice so low, Jones could barely hear it. For a long moment Bethany held Maggie's gaze, her sharp green eyes hard, and she said firmly, "I'm just here to keep an eye on my friend. I was worried about Cloë and wanted to be here. *Nothing* else will happen to Cloë."

Maggie nodded, understanding. Although she believed she knew the real reason that the police officer was there, Maggie did not want to call attention to Bethany—especially since she knew it would upset Mr. Sanders even more than he already was.

Maggie turned and walked back out to the waiting room to find her mother and go home. It had been a long day, and it wasn't over yet.

THIRTY-EIGHT

After leaving the hospital that morning Grant and Steve had driven back to Cloë's neighborhood to see if they could find her neighbors to talk to them about their missing dog. On the surface, the missing dog seemed an anomaly, unimportant and not something two experienced detectives should be investigating.

Or so Grant told himself several times as Steve drove back across town towards the anomaly's address.

Try as he might, Grant could not just dismiss the feeling that the dog's disappearance was important, perhaps vital, to understanding what had happened to Cloë.

And since it had taken Steve less than a second to agree to the trip, it was apparent that he was also thinking the incident could be significant.

After spending close to a decade on the job, Grant had learned to listen to his hunches, to trust his instincts even when common sense would dictate that he was following a wild goose chase.

And sometimes that was the case. But all too often, those hunches had led to something real, something tangible, and over the years he had learned to never ignore his instincts. The few times he had, he'd regretted it—most notably, the night Lou had been shot, Grant had had a terrible feeling, but before he could act on it, Lou had headed down that alley.

No. Even if it ended up being completely unrelated to the case, they had to follow through on it. But he really didn't believe that would be the case. And judging from Steve's easy agreement neither did he.

Steve pulled over to the curb in front of Cloë's neighbors, the Severson's, small green house.

"How do you want to handle this?" Steve asked as he turned the engine off and turned to take a good look at the house.

The small house was set back from the street, its yard enclosed by a wooden fence. The patchy yard was covered in leaves still waiting to be raked and several discarded toys that clearly told him that at least one small child lived here.

Grant thought for a moment and then said, "Just a standard questioning about what they saw or heard last night. The dog thing will come up."

"Okay. You call Dusty to let him know we were going to question the Severson's?"

"Yeah. He and Mac are working their way down the houses across the street and will come back up this way. So we'll be speaking to them first."

"Good. Let's go."

Both men got out of the car, and for the second time that day, made their way up the sidewalk. Only this time they walked past Cloë's house—now covered in crime scene tape—and headed through the neighbor's gate and up to their door.

Grant reached out to ring the doorbell, but the door opened before he got the chance to push it. A small boy, big brown eyes bright with excitement, peeked out through the screen door, one hand clutching a small plastic police car and the other a battered fire truck.

Steve grinned and said, "Well, hello."

"Hi. Are you a stranger? If you're a stranger I can't talk to you. My Momma said so. Not even if you have a puppy or candy or a toy or are lost or anything."

Steve thought for a moment before he said, "Well, Your Momma is right, but I'm a police officer. It's always safe to talk to a police officer, but since I don't have my police uniform on, I should probably show you my badge so you know for sure, huh?"

Eyes huge, the boy nodded vigorously.

Steve grinned and flashed his badge.

"Cool! Are you a police ocifer, too?" the boy turned towards Grant.

Grant smiled and pulled out his badge, "I sure am."

The boy smiled broadly and said again, "Cool!"

Steve said, "Why don't you go tell your Momma that we're here, we need to talk to her."

The boy's face fell serious and he whispered, "Is she in trouble?"

"No. She's absolutely not in trouble, but we need to see if she can help us."

293

"You mean with catching a bad guy? Are you guys going to catch the bad guy who hurt Cloë?"

Steve and Grant exchanged glances but before either of them could reply a harried-looking woman with a baby in her arms stepped into the hallway behind the little boy and said, "What's going on here? Henry Michael Severson, get away from that doorway right now! I told you never to open that door."

"But Mommy, it's the police. They showed me badges and they're not strangers so I talked to them, and they catch bad guys just like on T.V."

As Henry spoke the woman stepped up to him and placed a protective hand on his shoulder and said, "We'll talk about this later, now go inside while I talk to the policemen."

Henry's face fell at her sharp voice and he turned to go. Before he'd taken two steps he stopped and turned to say, "I didn't open the second door, Mommy, I was real careful."

Her blond hair pulled back in a ponytail, the pretty young mother sighed and smiled down at the eager blond boy and shook her head. "Go on in now," she said, her voice soft.

She turned her attention to Grant and Steve and said, "Sorry about that. Can I help you?"

Steve and Grant both showed her their badges and Steve said, "Good evening. Mrs. Kathleen Severson?" The woman nodded and Steve continued, "I'm Detective Sullivan and this is Detective Evans. We're investigating the attack on your neighbor, Cloë Sanders. Could we ask you a few questions?"

Looking troubled, she nodded and unlocked the screen door to let them in and said, "Come on in, can I get you anything to drink?"

After both men had declined, she led them into a toy-strewn living room, and after setting Henry up in the next room with a Wiggles video and setting the baby in a small playpen, she sat down across from them.

"I heard that Cloë was attacked right in her house. I can't believe it. This has always been such a safe neighborhood, but after the last couple of weeks I'm not so sure."

"How well do you know Miss Sanders?" Steve asked, taking the lead.

"Oh, real well. She's always offering to watch the kids for me and baking cookies or playing cars with Henry. She's a good friend and so great with the kids. Everyone loves Cloë, I just don't understand why anyone would ever hurt her."

Mrs. Severson glanced over to make sure that Henry was still engrossed in his video as Steve asked, "Did you see or hear anything out of the ordinary last night or this morning? See anyone out of place in the neighborhood lately?"

She shook her head and said, "I've been racking my brain all day, trying to remember if I'd seen anything strange but I couldn't come up with anything. We were at my parents' house for dinner last night and came home a little after eight.

"I don't remember seeing Cloë's car when we left at about one, and it was still gone when we got back. It's not the kind of car you'd miss if it was there—it's so Cloë," she said fondly and smiled before she continued, "I put the kids to bed and fell asleep with a book less than an hour later."

"How about your husband?"

"He's out of town this week for work. He won't be back until late on Wednesday, and I really wish he were here. I'm a little scared, what with everything that's been going on—that poor girl being killed and now Cloë."

Again she paused to check on her son before she continued in a low voice, "Normally, when my husband's away I feel safe because of our dog, Jasper, but he's missing."

Steve glanced over at Grant and, suppressing his excitement, he asked, "When did this happen?"

"Six days ago."

"Has he done anything like this before?"

"No. Never. He's a wonderful dog, quiet, great with the kids, friendly. Then, about two weeks ago, Jasper started going nuts every night. He would bark and bark and throw himself at the door, growling, until we'd let him out, and he would tear out and bark at the same part of the yard.

"My husband, Sam, went out the morning after the first night he did it and found a few raccoon tracks. So, we figured a family of raccoons had moved into our back yard, but Jasper kept acting the same way every night for over a week.

"We started leaving him tied up in the back yard at night so he wouldn't wake the kids." Pausing, she sighed and looked down at her hands as she twisted them together in her lap before she said, "Then six mornings ago I went out to let him in for breakfast and he was gone. His collar was still attached to the rope. I don't know how, but he must have slipped out of it somehow.

"We never should have left him outside, but after more than a week of the baby getting woken up at one in the morning...I was just too tired to care."

"Did you report him missing?"

Mrs. Severson shrugged and said, "We called the shelters, put up signs, drove all over town, but we couldn't find him. And, without his collar...," she trailed off again.

"Do you mind if we take a look around outside?"

"Sure, go ahead."

"Thanks for your time Mrs. Severson."

The baby started crying, and when Mrs. Severson turned to pick her up Grant and Steve stood up. Grant said, "We'll just let ourselves out the front."

She nodded and bent to comfort the now-screaming baby.

"Well?" Grant asked as they stepped out onto the front porch and closed the door behind them. Steve stood still, hands deep in his jeans pockets, staring for a long moment over at the crime scene tape that sealed Cloë's front door before he said slowly, "Well, I think we need to take a closer look at those supposed raccoon tracks, and see if anything bigger has been back there."

Together they walked around the house in the gathering dusk. The grass was patchy, littered with the usual toys and equipment a home with small children often had; a swing set, sandbox, and dog house that was obviously empty.

Grant walked over to the dog house where it sat against the wall of the Severson's detached garage. He noted the rope was still attached to the dog house, but that the collar had been removed.

Meanwhile, Steve strode over to the clump of bushes in the far back corner of the property where it bordered Cloë's back yard. A small gate opened to the alley that ran behind both properties. The Severson's garage was accessed through the gate, and Steve noted that a small rock path lead from the gate to the alley.

Steve stepped through the gate and examined the ground around the bushes. There had been a lot of rain lately, but it was obvious to him that something a lot larger than a raccoon had been in the bushes. A small section of grass was completely trampled smooth, and the implications sent a wave of rage through him.

Squatting, Steve peered through the branches over towards Cloë's house and noted that from this vantage point, someone had a perfect view of the back door, basement window, Cloë's bedroom window, and the street in front of her house.

"Son-of-a-bitch," he swore roughly as Grant came through the gate.

"What is it?" Grant asked as he came up to where Steve was now standing. Grant took one look at the expression of banked fury on his partner's face as he simply pointed at the ground beneath the bushes.

Grant bent down to look at the area where Steve pointed, immediately seeing what Steve had. In addition to the flattened grass and ideal vantage point, Grant also saw several broken branches and a small scrap of paper or material almost completely covered in mud—as if it had been dropped, then stepped on.

"Steve," Grant said.

Warned by Grant's tone of voice, Steve immediately leaned over to look where Grant pointed.

"Son-of-a-bitch!" Steve repeated, only this time the rage was replaced with a grim satisfaction. Steve stood again and pulled out his phone. "Chief, we need a couple of the forensics guys back out at the Sanders house. Yeah. I know. But we've got something. How long? Okay."

Steve closed the phone and said, "He's gotta make a call. The guys are already gone, but the Chief said he'd get someone out here within the hour."

Grant opened his mouth to ask why it would take so long and closed it without asking. He had to remember that in a town the size of Hope he should be happy that they had access to a separate forensics team at all.

He knew from that morning when he'd asked Steve about it that the team didn't just work in Hope, but were responsible for the entire county which had more than a dozen small towns.

Luckily, Hope was centrally located within the county, and as the largest town it was where the team was headquartered. Out loud he said only, "Okay."

"Let's take a look around the alley, we may get lucky and find more," Steve said.

Grant nodded and said, "I'm going to go ask Mrs. Severson for the dog's collar and let her know that a team of people will be out here for a while tonight."

It was almost four hours later before Grant and Steve finally left the scene. It had taken about an hour and fifteen minutes for the forensics team to get there, and they'd spent more than two hours carefully combing the grounds of the Severson's house and the ally on either side of Cloë's house.

That morning they'd closely examined Cloë 's house and the grounds directly around it—particularly around the basement window—but at that time they'd had no indication that anyone had been watching Cloë.

The paper had turned out to be a partial receipt from a coffee shop on the University campus. In addition to the paper, they'd also found three small silver beads pressed into the muddy grass next to the alley by the Severson's path.

Grant couldn't imagine what the beads could be used for, and he was a long way from being sure that they were even connected to their case, but the fact that they were still fairly close to the surface and not too dirty led him to believe they had been dropped within the last day or two.

Steve pulled up in front of Grant's house and parked. "Are you going to pick up Maggie?"

"Yeah. She's still over at your parents' house. I'll drive her in to work tomorrow too, so I'll meet you at the station in the morning."

"Don't bother coming back. I'll just meet you at the University and we can hit the coffee shop first, then the Art History Department before our 10:30 appointment with the Dean."

"You finally got ahold of the Dean, huh?" Grant asked.

"Yeah, well, I went to school with Dean Mitchell's son, Craig, so I just gave Craig a call and got his dad's number from him earlier."

"I guess it pays to have the home town advantage," Grant said and grinned over at Steve.

"Welcome to Small Town, Minnesota, where everyone knows everything about everyone else—whether you want them to or not."

"I think I'm beginning to get the picture. Three days ago I was in the check-out at Foodmart and the girl behind the register asked me how Maggie was doing. I can't remember her name—I think it was Mitzi or Marnie, something with an M. Anyway, I'd never met her before."

Steve grinned and said, "Missy Nichols, resident gossip. She knows everyone and hears everything. She works at Foodmart nights and weekends and at the diner in the morning. During the course of a week she sees and talks to a large percentage of the town. She's harmless."

"I'm sure she is, but it was a little strange to have someone I've never met before asking me about my personal life."

"You'll get used to it. It's pretty hard to keep secrets in a small town, and that, my friend, can only help us. Someone somewhere has seen something or heard something about this guy. We just have to figure out who to ask."

"And now we have a place to start—the University, and more specifically the Art History Department," Grant said.

"Right. But not until tomorrow. Take care of my sister, Evans."

Grant flashed a grin over at Steve and jumped out of the car. He said, "Night, Steve," and slammed the car door shut before running up the walk to his house.

Steve watched him disappear into the house and decided that instead of going home, maybe he'd just pick up a sub and some coffee and head over to the hospital to relieve Jones and sit with Cloë for a while.

He'd looked forward to going home for the past three hours of standing out in the damp night, but the image of Cloë's face as he'd seen it the night before—lit with joy as she grinned up at him

299

when they'd shared that moment of watching Grant with Maggie—
then the memory of her almost unrecognizable features this morning,
had Steve turning his car around and heading back across town
toward the hospital.

THIRTY-NINE

After taking care of Jake and grabbing a quick shower Grant jumped into his SUV and drove over to the Sullivan's. The house was brightly lit, and after knocking once, Grant walked in the front door and called out, "Hello?"

He could hear Maggie and her father talking in the kitchen, and after he shed his jacket and hung it up, he made his way down the hall in time to hear Maggie say vehemently, "...No. I'm *not* going to do it, Dad. There's no way I could even think about doing that while Cloë's in the hospital."

"You could have someone else fill in for her. Cloë wouldn't want you to disappoint all the kids."

Maggie shook her head as Bram spoke and said, "It's not just about finding someone else to fill in. I just don't think I could do that while Cloë's still so hurt. We'll just have to do the show next year."

Bram looked at the stubborn set to Maggie's face and her crossed arms and sighed. "All right, Honey. If that's really what you want, I understand."

Grant came through the doorway where he'd stopped to listen and said, "Hi, Red. Evening Bram, Elizabeth."

"Grant!" Maggie whirled and quickly crossed the few steps to where Grant stood and gave him a hard hug. As she leaned back she opened her mouth to question him about the case, but the weariness on his face had her quickly shifting gears.

"Come and sit. Do you want something to drink? Coffee?"

Grant sank down at the table across from Bram and said, "Sure, but I don't think I can drink another cup of coffee today."

"How about some tea or hot cocoa or pop?" Elizabeth asked.

"A tea would be great."

"Bram? Maggie?" Elizabeth asked as she opened the cupboard door and reached in to get down a mug.

Bram shook his head and said, "I'm fine," but Maggie said, "I'll have some cocoa, but I can make it, Mom."

"No, no. You sit with Grant and let me do something." Elizabeth turned to get a second mug out while Maggie pulled out the chair next to Grant and sat down.

301

Grant reached over to absently brush a hand down her loose hair and said, "Steve wanted me to tell you that he'd be over in the morning."

Several minutes of silence later Bram watched Maggie reach over to squeeze Grant's hand.

Elizabeth set two steaming mugs in front of Maggie and Grant and a large plate of sandwiches in front of Grant before she rounded the table and sat down next to Bram. "So, is there anything you can tell us, Grant?"

Maggie immediately straightened in her chair and turned to face Grant and he found himself with three sets of intent eyes gazing intently at him.

Grant considered for a minute, taking a long sip of tea to give himself a chance to stall. As he'd driven over, he'd known that they would want to know what he and Steve had found out, and Grant had thought about what he could—or should—tell them.

Although he still had reservations about telling the Sullivan family about the case, it wasn't because he couldn't trust them.

No. What concerned him was the idea that telling them could endanger them in some way, and that was a risk Grant refused to take. Even if it meant hurting them.

"There's not a lot I can tell you. We canvassed the neighborhood and nobody heard or saw anything out of the ordinary. There were signs that the person who attacked Cloë got into her house through the basement window.

"Though we have no way to know for sure, he, or she, was probably already there when Cloë got home last night and gone long before daylight. The neighbors were gone most of the day and evening yesterday. Until Cloë wakes up, we won't know for sure."

"But that's what *you* believe happened," Maggie stated instead of asking.

Grant looked into her eyes and said without hesitation, "Yes. Steve and I both believe that."

Maggie nodded, and after she glanced over at her parents, she gave Grant a look that warned him their conversation was far from finished.

"So, nobody saw anything?" Elizabeth repeated, clearly distressed. She added, "Poor Cloë. And, poor Ron. I haven't seen him this upset since Angelina left them. He was completely lost for months after she left.

"If it hadn't been for Cloë I don't know what he would have done. She did everything for them for weeks until one day he woke up and realized he had virtually abandoned her, too. And ever since that day, he has been a model father, they are the closest of friends. If she doesn't make it, it will completely destroy him."

"She'll make it. She's a fighter. And Steve and Grant will catch the bastard who hurt her," Bram said quietly, his hand grasping Elizabeth's on the table. The look in his steady gray eyes was so like the look Grant had just seen in Maggie's that he had to smile.

"Yes, we will," Grant said, a note of finality in his voice.

After that, the conversation shifted to lighter topics, and when Maggie and Grant had finished their drinks and refused seconds, they stood to leave.

"We better get going; tomorrow is going to be another long one. Thank you for the tea and sandwiches, Elizabeth."

"You're welcome. Now are you sure that I can't get either of you something more to eat? It would only take a minute for me to wrap up something for you."

"There's no way that I could eat another bite, and I don't think Grant could either. But, thanks, Mom," Maggie said and she hugged Elizabeth and Bram.

"I'll give you a call from the hospital tomorrow. I have to go in to the office for an hour or two, but after that I'll be at the hospital."

"Be careful, Margaret," said Elizabeth.

Wincing slightly at the use of her given name, Maggie replied dutifully, "Yes, Mother," and then, feeling guilty, she hugged her mother again and said, "You be careful, too, Momma. I love you."

Elizabeth framed Maggie's face with her hands and said, "Oh, Baby, I love you, too." Elizabeth dropped her hands and turned to Grant and added, "You take good care of my baby, Grant."

Grant nodded, his face serious, as he promised, "I won't let anything happen to her."

"Mind you take good care of yourself, too."

303

Grant's face broke into a broad smile and the warmth her words gave him spread through him as Elizabeth reached up to hug him, too. It had been a long time since he'd had someone who cared enough about him to tell him to be careful—not since he'd been a boy staying with his grandmother.

His smile eased the weariness on his face and had both women grinning when he replied, "Yes, Ma'am, I will."

Maggie had seen the startled pleasure in Grant's eyes when her mother had hugged him and again she promised herself that she would do everything in her power to never hurt him the way his family had.

She was still thinking about his reaction as they drove the short distance to her apartment building. She'd seen that same look each time he told her he would be late, or when he talked about his work and she didn't get mad at him.

She was startled from her reverie when Grant pulled into his garage and shut off the engine. "Earth to Maggie."

"Hmmm? Oh, I'm sorry, Grant, my mind was a million miles away."

"I know you're worried about Cloë, Mags, but she's being watched around the clock by professionals who can help her, there's nothing you could do if you were there."

Ignoring the sharp stab of guilt she felt, Maggie filed away her dark thoughts about Grant's past and focused on what Grant clearly thought she'd been thinking about, and what she *should* have been thinking about—her best friend lying in a hospital bed, hooked up to life support.

"Speaking of professionals, I noticed that Bethany was at the hospital when I left."

Grant sighed. He'd hoped she would be too distracted to catch the significance of having the officer stationed there— particularly since Steve had asked Bethany to dress casually and had chosen Bethany because she knew Cloë in the hope that most people would assume she was just there to visit a friend.

Slowly he said, "I know that Bethany and Cloë are friends."

"Nice try, Detective. I know why you and Steven asked her to be there. I saw that she was armed."

"Look, come inside while I let Jake out and then I'll walk you home and we can talk about it."

Maggie agreed and fifteen minutes later they were sitting together on her living room couch sipping glasses of wine and listening to the classical music CD that Maggie always pulled out when she was in need of calming.

"So, what were you and your dad talking about when I got to your parents'?

Maggie sighed again and settled more deeply into the soft cushions of the couch. "Halloween. He was saying that I should still go forward with it even though Cloë's so hurt. I just don't understand how he could think that I could act as if nothing has even happened."

"I'm sure that he was just trying to keep your mind off of what happened to Cloë. And maybe he wanted to keep *his* mind off of her, too."

Maggie sighed and said, "I guess I didn't think about it that way, but I just can't do it. Especially when she may not even make it through the night. I…"

Maggie shook her head violently and squeezed her eyes shut tight to hold back another wave of tears. She had cried enough.

Now she needed to be strong for Cloë, and for herself.

"Okay, okay," Grant murmured. He swept one large hand gently down her long tumble of curls and leaned down to press a kiss against her hair. Maggie burrowed into his arms and the tension that had held her so taut all day seemed to seep out of her as his arms drew her closer and wrapped her in a soothing embrace.

For several minutes Maggie said nothing. She simply basked in the peace and comfort she felt in Grant's arms. Never had she felt this at ease, this secure with a man.

And in that small moment of comfort the last barrier to her heart crumbled away, and she allowed the love she'd been fighting to hold back free.

A sharp stab of pure joy filled and expanded inside her until she felt she would burst with the strength of it, it was so painful in its intensity.

She loved him. Wholly. Completely. Undeniably.

And though the fear of risking her heart, totally and without reservation, speared through her it was no match for the fierce joy and intense love she felt rising up in her.

So many times her mother had told her that moonbeams and dreams were wonderful, important even, but that when it came down to it, an open and courageous heart was what was needed for true love.

Maggie had never understood it. What did bravery and courage have to do with romance? Absolutely nothing—at least that is what she'd always believed.

But love? Yes, that, it seemed, needed a great deal of courage.

Maggie turned her face up to press her lips to Grant's before she met his eyes and said, "Thank you, Grant."

Grant grinned down into her upturned face and started to say something light, but the expression in her eyes had him pausing. Unsure of what the intense look meant, he felt his heart begin to speed up. Again, he longed to ask her what she was thinking about, but before he could say anything he saw her gaze drop to his mouth and his breath lodged in his throat when Maggie caught his bottom lip lightly between her teeth.

For one suspended moment, a sound like a roaring wind seemed to rush around and through him as Grant felt a flood of desire crash like a wave over him.

Every coherent thought he might have had immediately evaporated, replaced by the sweet smell, the dark taste, the soft feel of only her. He dragged her to him, desperate, dangerous, wanting only her touch, needing only her.

His hands gripped her shirt, her back, her face, moving, moving, until she felt as if she were surrounded.

She reached both hands up to sweep them through his already tousled hair, scratching softly along his scalp, making him moan against her avid mouth.

Standing, they struggled to remove their shirts, the only sounds gasps of pleasure, moans of delight, the sharp intake of breath as each new bit of flesh was uncovered, explored, plundered.

Maggie's head fell back as he set his teeth on her neck and she cried out in pleasure when he ripped aside her bra to pull her into his mouth. Her hands fell still against his bared chest and in one swift motion he swept her up and back onto the couch.

He yanked her jeans down and threw them to the floor before he lowered to retake her mouth. His rough hands swept down her torso before sweeping aside the flimsy barrier of her panties to find her hot and ready.

He took her up and over so swiftly, her head spun as she lay, arms flung above her head to grip helplessly at the couch cushions behind her. She watched him through half-closed eyes as he shed the final barriers between them and lowered to her again.

He paused, his passion-darkened eyes on hers, and in the silence of the moment that seemed like the long indrawn breath taken in the very eye of a storm, Maggie heard only the thundering boom of her racing heart.

As she waited to welcome him, Grant lay poised above her. In that one critical moment—after the initial rush of passion and before the next wave—Grant stared down into Maggie's face to see a look of utter surrender on her face and he felt his heart contract once. Twice.

And the raw power of his emotions swept them both back into the heart of the storm.

Grant felt his ragged breathing begin to back up in his throat and he managed to growl out, "God, you're beautiful."

With a cry she lifted to meet him as he plunged, once more swept up in the fury of the tempest.

Together they rode the storm of passion as it swept them up and over and replete upon the shore again. Deliciously bruised and battered, they lay sprawled together in a tangle of slick limbs in the soft glow of candlelight.

FORTY

Maggie lay completely still for several minutes, wondering vaguely to herself if she was still alive, or if they'd managed to kill each other. When Grant sighed and shifted to pull her over onto his chest she decided that since she could still hear and feel she must still be alive.

Experimentally, she cracked one eye and was rewarded with the sight of the candle still flickering on the coffee table next to her. Emboldened by her success, she decided to try talking.

"Yum," she sighed and she felt Grant's chest vibrate beneath her cheek as he chuckled.

"I'll see your 'yum' and raise you a 'wow'."

Maggie had to laugh and she snuggled closer and then raised her head to look down at him. As she stared down into his still-laughing face she felt the joy expand so far, so fast, she could no longer contain it.

It was time to be brave.

Slowly her smile faded, but still her eyes shone as she said softly, clearly, "I love you, Grant."

Grant felt the world stop along with his heart. Time froze and Grant's vision narrowed and focused until all he could see was Maggie—the way her skin glowed in the candlelight, the soft tumble of her auburn curls shining around her face, the look of intense joy and hope, and even a bit of fear, that shone out of her eyes as they looked down into his.

And like an engine jump-started he felt his heart begin pounding even harder than it had been just moments before. His breath whooshed out to be replaced with happiness so strong, so powerful he could barely breathe.

While Grant struggled to catch his breath Maggie felt her heart sink at his continued silence. The light in her eyes dimmed briefly as she searched his stunned expression for a sign that he welcomed and maybe even returned her feelings, but she didn't see anything but fear in his eyes.

Slowly she dropped her gaze and turned her face down and away from his. When she made to push up and off of his chest his arm banded around her waist and his hand came up to gently cup her cheek and turn her face back to his.

"Maggie," Grant said, his voice so tender, so gentle Maggie's eyes slid shut as she waited for him to continue.

"Maggie, I love you, too. So much it scares the hell out of me. I think I fell in love with you that first day at your parents' house, but I wouldn't let myself believe it—not really."

"Because of Steven?"

"Partly. And also because of me. I've never met anyone like you before—not even close—and I never had anyone accept me, love me."

Grant shook his head and stopped to think. Absently he ran his hand through her hair and down her still-bare back as he thought about how he could explain what he meant and felt to her before he began to speak.

"I told you once that I was engaged."

Maggie drew in a deep breath and waited for him to continue.

"Her name was Shannon Timmons. I thought I loved her and that she loved me. We met several years after I joined the Seattle force at some official event. I'm not even sure which one anymore, but I know I had gotten some official commendation or other, and looking back I'm sure that was one of the things that she was drawn to.

"Shannon is one of those people who are never happier than when they are in the thick of a big crowd, as long as it was a crowd filled with important people—the rich, the influential, the up-and-comers. But all I knew was that she was beautiful, charming, and that she was interested in me.

"We made a date to go out the next week and we were together from that night until the day she left me almost two years later. At first, she told me how much she loved my being a cop, and after the way that my sister, my mother, and the few women I'd dated up until that point had always acted, it was a relief.

"Looking back now, I can see that I was blind. But even then there were signs that all was not as it seemed. Things I didn't see, or chose not to see. It was little things at first—where we were seen, who I hung out with, things like that. And what was easy acceptance in the beginning grew to be annoyance and anger each time the job interfered with her plans.

"She never liked Lou, but I always dismissed it as just one of those things. I was in love—or at least I thought I was—and I thought that love required sacrifices. So I tried to change for her. I wore the clothes she said looked best on me. I went out with the 'successful' couples she met and decided we should socialize with. I was even thinking about taking up golf, for God's sake, because she felt it was something I could do with the higher ups at the station.

"After a while I could tell she despised Lou and my position at the department, but I refused to give them up. She seemed resigned to that. And then about a month before I was shot I was offered a promotion to a desk job that I turned down and she was furious. We had several screaming matches over it, and I was talking with Lou about what I should do the night we got the call. And then Lou was killed and I was shot.

Grant fell silent and looked away from Maggie's sympathetic gaze before he continued. "I was barely conscious, in and out, for the first couple of days after the shooting. Just dealing with the pain—the pain of the shot, but even worse was knowing that Lou was gone, because I *knew* the moment he got hit, the look in his eyes…I knew…"

Grant's voice shook a little as he trailed off and shook his head again. When he began to speak once more his voice was controlled, almost detached in its coolness and Maggie instinctively ran her hand down his cheek to sooth him.

He reached up to grasp her hand in a grip so hard Maggie knew that what was to come was worse, in some way, than even the loss of his partner and friend had been.

"Shannon didn't show up until after I'd been in the hospital for more than a week. Said she heard I was unconscious or sleeping most of the time so she knew I would understand how boring it would have been for her to just sit there."

Maggie spit out a single word that had Grant grinning in appreciation as he met her eyes again.

"That about sums it up. Anyway, I'd spent the two days prior to her visit arguing with my mother on the phone as she begged me to quit the force because I was putting her through hell with all the worry. And now that I was hurt, naturally I would be looking for a new job."

Maggie listened silently as he spoke, his words dripping with a bitter sarcasm that she knew disguised the pain he thought he had gotten over.

"Shannon had been talking with my mother and was thrilled that I'd finally seen the light and decided to quit the job because, and I think this is how she put it, I was in a dead-end job with no hope for advancement now that I was damaged, probably mentally, and now that 'that partner' of mine was dead, I could move on.

"I remember laying there staring at her making excited plans for us and dismissing Lou's death as if it were some kind of convenient happy accident. Something in me just snapped.

"I have never struck a woman before, but I came closer than I would have believed possible in that moment. I told her to get out. At first she was genuinely surprised. She started to protest but I just kept saying it.

"By the time they finally made her leave they had to sedate me. I was screaming at her and I guess they were afraid that I would hurt her or myself, or even them.

"That was the last time I ever saw her.

"I think you can imagine my family's reaction. I was making the worst possible mistake of my life, throwing away a good woman, an opportunity to finally make something out of myself. It went on and on until the doctors finally stopped allowing them access to me.

"I sank into a clinical depression for several weeks until I clawed my way out of it. I still have days when I can feel that yawning abyss stretch out in front of me, the darkness threatens to descend once more, and it takes every ounce of will that I have not to dive headlong back into it.

"If it weren't for Ryan, my dad's old partner, and Jake, I doubt I would have had the strength to make it as far as I have. It's taken almost two years, but I'm finally back working, and God, I've missed it.

"I never knew how much I loved the job until I was forced to be away from it. I don't know if I would have been able to function, working in Seattle, so when I saw the opening here, I leapt at the chance for a change.

"And it was the best decision I've ever made.

"Maggie, I don't know if I deserve you, or Steven, or your whole family for that matter, but I know that I need you. Without you this would just be another city—an escape, yes, but not the refuge it's become. I know that no matter where I would have ended up I would be on the job—it's too deeply ingrained for me not to. I'm just not able to leave it. But here, with you, I could probably manage it if you asked it of me. I need you, want you, that badly. But what makes me love you so completely is that you already accept that part of me."

Silent tears streamed down Maggie's face as she listened to his words.

"Of course, you're not half bad looking, either," Grant teased as he tenderly brushed away her tears.

Maggie let out a watery laugh before she sobered enough to say, "Grant, you may think that what you've gone through has proven that you are weak, that what your mother or your sister said all those years was true, but you couldn't be more wrong. Not everyone could have made it back from what you did, and leaning on others to help you took more courage and strength of will than simply wasting away ever could have. So, don't ask me to think of you as weak, Grant Evans. You are the strongest man I've ever met."

Struck dumb, Grant leaned forward to kiss Maggie once, then once again before he said, "I do love you, Red."

"As you should, Detective," Maggie grinned down at Grant before she added softly, "I love you, too."

Maggie laughed out loud in pure happiness, but her laugh turned into a surprised squeal when Grant suddenly sat up. He caught her up in his arms and strode down the hall to her bedroom. Maggie clung to his neck while she struggled to catch her breath.

She was utterly charmed and delighted by his romantic gesture. She'd always fantasized about being swept away by a gorgeous man intent on making wild passionate love to her, but this far exceeded anything she could have imagined.

Expecting to be ravished, Maggie was confused, and just the least bit miffed, when Grant laid her gently on the bed before he turned to stride back out of the room again.

She levered herself up on her elbows and opened her mouth to call out to him when he came back in carrying two of the candles she'd lit out in the living room. Her mouth shut with a snap before it curved in a dreamy smile and her eyes went misty as she watched him move slowly around the room lighting the many candles she had scattered over the various surfaces.

While he moved around the room, Maggie watched the play of light and shadow move and shift across his chest, his face, his broad back and muscular arms. He was beautiful, inside and out.

Suddenly she was grateful to the women who had him and lost him because they had been too selfish, too blind, to see that he was loving and strong, funny, caring, and true.

And all she could think was, *Thank God. Thank God he was hers*.

When he'd lit the last wick he turned to set the candle on the small table next to the bed. For several moments he simply stood and looked down at her as she lay naked, her pale skin like burnished gold in the flickering light of the many candles.

Maggie fought the urge to cover herself with her arms as she watched his dark eyes sweep over her body. His gaze was so intent, the look in his eyes so intense, she felt her skin warm and tingle wherever his eyes swept, as if he were actually touching her.

Her head sank back and she studied him out of half-closed eyes as he eased down onto the bed to join her.

"Maggie, you are so beautiful. So soft. So perfect," Grant murmured as he lowered to brush his lips across her shoulder and over her neck. He worked his way up her throat to where her pulse fluttered frantically against his mouth.

Maggie collapsed weakly back down onto the mattress and her eyes slid shut as his lips continued their exploration and swept up her jaw and over her eyelids to her temple before finally, briefly, to her waiting lips before they were gone again.

Maggie tried to think, but her senses were slow, as if wrapped up in cotton. There were only his lips, only his rough hands, as they molded and caressed, brushed and lingered over every inch of her.

He worked his way from the hollow of her throat and down her torso, pausing to pay particular attention to each breast before moving down the soft curves of her waist and hip.

And all the while he used his mouth on her, tongue and lips and teeth, she felt the heat, the emotion, begin to grow once more.

What had been a wild storm was now the steady building intensity of the tides—with each ebb and flow, each gentle touch, growing higher and higher until she was swept away, pulled under, surrounded by only him. They were alone in that moment, alone together on the rising seas.

Where once there had been passion and desire, now there was love.

His hand, followed closely by his creative mouth, swept down her thigh, slowly circling her knee and down to her calf to massage the sensitive arch of each foot.

He thrilled to feel her body tremble in response to his touch. And though it cost him to hold his rising need in check he wanted her to not only tremble, but to be as desperate with desire for him as he was for her. And so he waited, patient and greedy, tender and tormented, as he brought her up and up, until she reached blindly for him, begging, "Grant, please."

Maggie did not know what it was she was asking for, simply that only Grant could give it to her. As she trembled like a leaf tossed and turned on waves as they swept up and down, in and out and in again, she called to Grant to bring her back to safety, back to him.

When he moved back up her leg she tensed, her heartbeat thundering in her ears as he eased back for a moment and she felt only his moist breath as it brushed against her inner thigh.

When at last he lowered his mouth to her she cried out, blinded and deafened to all but the roaring waves of need as they swept her up and over the crest and back down the other side again.

Over and over, she skimmed along the tops of each crest until finally she was swept back to dry land, back to earth once more.

When Grant eased up to capture her mouth with his she felt the surging rise of passion once more, and with a roaring sound like wind in her ears she felt the storm sweep back over them again.

The love they felt made each moment more potent, more powerful, and she felt that she would fly apart at the intensity, the violent uprising of her emotions. Until, finally, neither could fight the tide of emotions that threatened to swamp them, and with one last cry they took the plunge together.

Over and over again, in the darkest hours of the night, they turned to each other for solace, for comfort, for love.

And deep in the darkness of the night, sheltered in the shadows, he stared at the shifting play of light as it illuminated the windows of his Angel's bedroom.

He'd watched in confusion as she had entered first the cop's house, then as they'd walked together across the street into her apartment building. He thought the cop had been walking her to her door as he'd done before, but as the minutes turned into hours...

When he could no longer deny that his Angel had lied to him, that she had betrayed him, the pain and anger began to ooze like a poison spreading through his body, slowly building until it felt as if his entire body was on fire with the burn of his wrath.

When the lights moved from her living room to the windows of her bedroom and the cop *still* didn't leave, his anger turned to a blind fury, and for more than an hour he fought the impulse to go inside and rip their hearts out as his Angel had done to him.

He clawed at the ground, cutting deep furrows into the dirt with his fingers until he scrambled to open the pocket of his coat and withdraw the one object that gave him peace.

Under the harsh intake and expulsion of his breathing the sound of his fervent rubbing and swinging of the object sent a near-silent click, click, click out into the night.

Gradually, the red haze receded from his sight, and his mind began to clear. When he came back fully to himself he was panting, his fingers ached and were covered in dirt as dark as the stain on his soul.

At some point, the last lights in her apartment had gone out, but he had no clear idea of when that had happened. Slowly, carefully he made his way back through the sleeping neighborhood.

His mind raced as he began to plan. And as the first streaks of dawn began to light the night sky, he rounded the last corner to reach his car. As his plans became solid in his mind a terrible smile spread across his face until his teeth were bared in a grimace that would have frightened anyone who saw it.

But as he drove off into the breaking dawn, no one saw. No one knew.

By the time he drove into his garage and walked through his door, he was calm once more. He went directly to the locked room beneath the stairway, and after scrubbing the dirt from his hands, began the process of developing the rolls of film he'd shot that night.

Standing at his work table, he looked down at the sheet of photo paper as he put it into the final chemical bath and saw his Angel's face begin to emerge into full, vibrant color.

As the tears poured down his face he brought the dripping print up to rub against his face. Then with a howl he ripped it to shreds and in his fury he swept the tubs of chemicals across the room where they splashed and pooled on the shrine he'd so carefully constructed.

As he collapsed to the floor to sob he never noticed as the carefully arranged pictures began to warp and streak as the liquid ran over them.

His Angel had fallen. His Angel was condemned and only *he* could save her. Only he could make sure that she would never, ever, fall again. She'd have to be punished first, and severely, only then could he save her so that she would never fall again. Not ever.

It was that *whore's* fault—the one he'd broken, the one he'd punished—and the cop's.

The whore had lived. That had surprised him. There was nothing more he could do about that. She was nothing.

But the cop? He would have to pay for tempting his Angel, for making her fall. If it hadn't been for him she would have listened to his warning. She would have been his forever.

Now the cop had to pay—they both did—for what they had done. For what they had destroyed. And for what? Sex? He felt the fury strain like a dog on a leash to break free once more, but the sound of footsteps on the stairs had him sitting up silently.

He looked to make sure that he'd re-locked the door, and seeing the dead bolt in placed he relaxed once more.

"Moses? Is that you down here?" he heard his mother call out.

Still he stayed silent, and after a long moment he heard her steps retreat back down the hall towards the kitchen.

With one last sigh he lay his head back down on the floor and curled up, knees drawn up to his chest, and fell asleep.

And in his sleep he dreamt of blood and screams and death. And as he dreamed he smiled.

FORTY-ONE

Less than an hour after dropping Grant off Steve strode into the ICU waiting room, a tray of coffees in one hand and a bag of sub sandwiches in the other. The room had emptied out until only Mr. Sanders and Bethany were left.

Steve nodded at Bethany before he walked over to sit next to Mr. Sanders. "How's she doing?" Steve asked as he offered Mr. Sanders a large coffee cup. Mr. Sanders accepted it gratefully and took a sip before he replied, "No change, which they keep telling me is good. She's hanging in there."

"Cloë is strong. She's a fighter."

Mr. Sanders nodded in agreement, but he struggled for a moment with the fear before he focused his attention on the younger man again and asked, "Have you found out anything new?"

Steve sighed silently. He'd known that coming back to the hospital would mean he would be questioned, so he'd already decided how he would answer.

"We are still investigating, Mr. Sanders. We have several good leads that we are looking into, but I don't have any answers for you. Not yet. But I promise you that Detective Evans and I are going to do our very best for you. For Cloë."

Mr. Sanders nodded again. He'd known the chances of catching the animal who'd done this to his baby were not great, especially without Cloë being awake to tell them what happened. He also knew that the pretty young police officer sitting outside his daughter's room was not just a concerned friend. And for that he was grateful.

He knew that he should be angry—furious even—but right now all he could feel was a kind of numb terror. Oh, yes, the anger would come. But for now, he was focusing on Cloë.

"I picked up a couple a subs. Would you like one?" Steve asked.

Mr. Sanders shook his head and said, "Thanks, but I'm not hungry, Steven."

Steve just nodded and replied, "Well, I'll just leave one here, and if you get hungry you'll have something."

318

Steve stood and walked over to where Bethany sat reading a book. She'd known the minute Steve had walked into the room but she'd deliberately kept her eyes down as he talked with Mr. Sanders.

As she listened to their exchange she felt a surge of affection for the gruff man as he tried to put the grieving father at ease. She'd known Steve most of her life, but it hadn't been until after she'd begun working with him that she'd really *seen* beyond the boy to the good man he truly was.

Over the last three years they'd become colleagues and close friends, even, but he'd never once looked at her the way she'd dreamed he would. Jones looked away as he settled into the chair across from where she was sitting.

"How's it been?" Steve asked as he handed over another steaming cup and began to unload two subs from the bag. Bethany reached out to take the coffee and replied, "Quiet. A few others stopped by to sit with Mr. Sanders, but no one went in to Cloë's room."

A companionable silence fell between them as the two settled down to dig into their subs, neither one speaking until the last bites were washed down.

"Thanks. I was hungry."

Steve gathered together the waste papers and threw them into a nearby garbage can before he said, "No problem. Why don't I take over here for a while? Sylvester or Donovan will be coming in at two, and then Mac will be here at six. I'd like you to go back to the station and dig up everything you can on these guys."

Steve handed her a sheet of paper with the names of Cloë's co-workers and the people who worked in the building and interacted with her every day on it. He continued, "And, then go home and get some rest because I need you to be back here by ten tomorrow, okay?"

Bethany nodded and shrugged into her jacket before she said, "You okay here alone, Sully? I can stay till Donovan or Sylvester get here and then go run the names."

Steve smiled distractedly up at her and said, "Thanks, but I'll be fine. Go do that and then you get some rest. Tomorrow's gonna be a long one."

Hiding her disappointment, Bethany nodded and said, "Night," before she turned and hurried out of the room.

Oblivious to the fact that he'd crushed his co-worker's hopes again Steve settled back in his chair and pulled out his notes to start writing up a report for the meeting he had with the Chief in the morning. He knew that Grant had put in a few calls to his FBI buddy with the latest information from both Maggie and what they'd found today before he'd gone to pick her up.

Grant had called Steve and let him know that Special Agent Finney had promised to look it all over tonight and fax over an updated profile ASAP tomorrow. He only prayed that the updated profile will help lead them to the killer before he struck again.

So, other than the ever-present paperwork and keeping an eye on Cloë, there was nothing more he could do tonight. He'd been on the job too many years to let that bother him too much. Steve knew that most cases were either solved in the first few hours, or, like in this case, the work of weeks or even months of tedious questioning, searching, and gathering of evidence along with hours of patient waiting.

Waiting for forensics evidence, waiting for interviews to be made, waiting for the right pieces of information to be seen by the right person, waiting for warrants, waiting, waiting, waiting. Waiting until the day when the waiting was over and they could catch the monster that had been haunting his hometown for more than two years now.

Steve pushed the thought out of his head and focused on writing up his report by hand. He'd have to make sure he got in early enough to type it up and get it to the Chief before he headed over to the University to meet up with Grant.

As he focused and wrote Mr. Sanders went in for another five minute visit with Cloë before he finally fell into an exhausted sleep on the waiting room couch.

Steve waited the required time before he rose, and after making sure Mr. Sanders was asleep, went in to stand next to Cloë's bed.

For several minutes he stood stiffly looking down at her too-still form on the bed. Her beautiful dark brown eyes were closed, surrounded by puffy, blackened skin. Tape sutures held together a deep cut on her forehead. Steve had heard the surgeon say that she would need further plastic surgery to help minimize the scar, but it was something she would always have to live with.

Her soft cap of brown hair with its sassy red streaks had been shaved off along the right side of her head. A large swath of bandages covered most of the little hair she had left, but Steve reached out to gently brush aside a few stray strands that peeked out next to her left cheek.

She had always loved doing crazy things with her hair—changing the color or style on a whim. He remembered one summer, she would have only been nineteen or twenty, she'd spent more than two years growing her hair all the way down her back.

Then she'd heard about Locks of Love, a charity that took donated hair to create wigs for children and adults who had lost their hair due to cancer treatments.

She'd gone straight to the nearest hairdresser and chopped it all off. When she'd gotten back from the salon she'd grinned and said that she'd been sick of it anyway.

He'd always admired her for that.

Alone in the quiet room, he finally allowed the strength of the anger that he'd banked away throughout most of the day to break free. And, as he thought of how her beautiful skin had been marred, her silky hair shaved off, Steve had to force himself to relax.

He looked away from her face to the rest of her. Her left arm was in a cast and her right had several different tubes attached to it, but Steve managed to carefully lift her scraped and bruised hand to set it gently in his.

The horror and rage he'd felt when he and Grant had found her—was it only this morning?—swept back over him until his hands shook at the depth of his emotions. He carefully set her hand back down, afraid to hurt her any more than she had already been hurt, and collapsed into the chair next to her bed, head resting on his clenched fists as he again struggled to push back the rage seeing her battered body had filled him with and the guilt he felt at not being able to keep her safe.

When he was finally able to rein his feelings in, he sat back and once more reached for her hand. This time holding it loosely in his while he talked softly about the gossip he'd heard that morning before Maggie's worried call, about the weather outside, and even about how Maggie and Grant seemed to have fallen in love with one another.

And as he spoke he wondered whether or not either Maggie or Grant had told the other how they felt—or if they'd even admitted their feelings to themselves.

Anything and everything he could think of he talked about to her. He stayed until a nurse finally found him still there an hour later and told him he had to leave.

Steve stood and leaned over to press a careful kiss on an unmarred section of skin right below the bandage on her head and murmured softly, "I'll be right outside, Cloë. You're safe."

He returned to his spot outside the door, but his mind stayed focused on the girl he thought of as his surrogate little sister in the room behind him.

Steve was still wrestling with his thoughts and Mr. Sanders was still asleep when Donovan and Sylvester came through the door at ten minutes to two.

Steve tossed aside the two-year-old, dog-eared copy of *Field and Stream* he'd been trying to read and stood to meet them.

"Hey guys, thanks for coming. I know it's already been a really long day for you. Which one of you is staying?"

"We both are," Donovan said.

Sylvester brushed a stray piece of lint off of his gray trench coat before he removed it and folded it neatly over the back of a chair. He sat down across from Steve, his gray suit still crisp and fresh despite the hours Steve knew he must have been wearing it.

In sharp contrast, Donovan sprawled next to his partner in a wrinkled tan coat that looked as if he had balled it into a pile and thrown it into the corner of his car for a week before he put it back on over an equally creased pair of Dockers and a partially tucked plaid shirt.

Steve had to smile at their markedly different appearance. He always pictured the opening credits for *The Odd Couple* whenever he saw them together—and together is the way they always were. In his many years on the force he could count on both hands the number of times he'd seen one of them alone.

Most days he was able to banish the thought right away, but the day had been too long, too emotional, and he felt a broad grin split across his face before he could stop it.

"What?" Donovan asked as he brushed a self-conscious hand over his thinning comb-over.

Steve managed to hold back the chuckle that wanted to burst out and kept his face serious as he replied, "Nothing. I'm just glad to see you guys."

"No problem, Sully. What's the situation?" Donovan drawled as he pulled a half-eaten candy bar out of his coat pocket and took a large bite.

"Jesus, Donovan, are you trying to clog *all* of your arteries? I don't understand how you can eat that crap, especially since you *just* finished eating that greasy excuse for real food in the car," Sylvester said.

"McDonalds is food. Crissake, you're starting to sound like Marie. What the hell else I'm supposed to eat this late at night? There's no place open. And besides, I *like* McDonalds."

Steve smiled as he silently watched the exchange, and broke in when he saw Sylvester's eyebrows draw down and his mouth open to reply. Steve had heard this argument, or one much like it, many times between the two men, but no matter how violently they argued they were completely loyal to each other.

"If you ladies are finished?" Steve paused and waited for both of them to turn back to him before he continued, "Everything's been quiet. No visitors since I've been here. Mr. Sanders is sleeping over there," he gestured towards the couch on the other side of the room.

"Mac will be here at six to take over, okay?"

"Sounds good, Sully," Sylvester said, "We'll take real good care of Miss Sanders."

"I know you will. I'll see you in the morning," Steve said as he shrugged back into his jacket. He tucked his notes and file under one arm and headed out of the hospital to his car. He needed to catch a couple hours of sleep if he was going to be able to function the next day.

Cloë's face swam before his eyes again as he drove out of the parking lot. And with his jaw clenched he swore to himself that this time, the bastard would not get away with it.

This time Steve was going to personally see to it that that monster was stopped.

Permanently.

FORTY-TWO

Maggie woke from a very pleasant dream involving Grant, a fur rug, and a glass full of champagne that he'd poured over her and then licked up in a most delightful manner. The dream had been so real she could swear she still felt the fur rug under her left hand and could still feel the soft lick of Grant's tongue along her arm.

"That's nice," she sighed, her mind still hazy and her eyes still stubbornly closed.

"What's nice?" Grant murmured against the back of her neck and his hands began to wander down her body.

If Grant was kissing the back of her neck, then who—or what—was licking her hand? With an almost audible snap Maggie's eyes flew open to be greeted by the sight of two adoring brown eyes and a large wet, black nose.

Her surprised gasp turned into a giggle as Jake pushed his cold nose against her face and tried to lick her cheek. She'd forgotten that Grant and gone over to bring Jake back to her apartment somewhere between the dead of night and the crack of dawn.

He'd been so sweet, worried that Jake would be happier here with them, that when he asked if he could run and bring Jake back over she couldn't say no.

Grant levered himself up on one elbow to see what was so funny, and a large grin nearly split his face. His big goofy dog was trying to snuggle up to Maggie while she laughed and rubbed his furry head.

"Am I interrupting?" Grant asked dryly, and then laughed when both woman and dog seemed to look over at him and give him the same give-me-a-break look. "All right, all right. It's time we got up anyway."

"Up? It's barely light out. Are you trying to kill me, Detective?" Maggie said dramatically as she pulled her pillow over her head.

Grant found himself smiling again as he reached to pull the pillow away from her face and said, "Nope, but we need to get a move on if we're going to run before I have to head into the office."

325

"How can you even *think* of running? I think we can safely call what we did all night exercise," she grinned lecherously up at him, her hazel eyes half closed with remembered passion. She reached out to rub against his chest and said coyly, "Wouldn't you rather stay right here, all warm and cozy, with me?"

Maggie watched as his already dark eyes deepened with desire. His brown hair was tousled around his face, and a rough stubble marred his otherwise beautiful face just enough to make him appear dangerous in the dim light of the room. When he replied, his voice was light and teasing in direct contrast to his appearance.

"I've got your number, Red. You just don't want to get out of bed and you're trying to seduce me so you won't have to."

"Is it working?" she asked hopefully.

"Well," Grant said casually as he slipped inside her, making her gasp out loud in surprise for the second time that morning. She was so wet, so warm, he almost groaned aloud as they slowly began to move together. Then, as he leaned down to gently worry her full bottom lip with his teeth he whispered a single word, "Yes."

FORTY-THREE

By the time they were showered and dressed Grant had just enough time to drop Jake off at home before they had to leave to get Maggie to her office and himself to his meeting with Steve, on time.

"Do you know when you'll be heading over to the hospital?"

"Probably around 9:30 or 10 at the latest. I really just have to pick up some things and clear up any messages, problems, stuff like that."

"And then you'll stay at the hospital the rest of the day?"

Maggie smiled and rolled her eyes before she looked over at him, "Yes. I'll be there the rest of the day. Cloë could wake up at some point late today and I want to be there when she does."

Grant nodded as he pulled up to her building's parking lot. He noted a younger man in the attendant's booth at the entrance to the lot. "Do I need to park somewhere else?" he asked.

"No," Maggie replied and pulled a small window tag out of her purse, "This is my back-up permit. You can use it today. I'm not technically supposed to use it in any car but mine, but I'm sure that the new attendant wouldn't mind. He's a nice guy. Just pull up to the booth and I'll let him know, okay?"

Grant pulled to a stop and Maggie leaned over to talk to the attendant through Grant's window. "Morning. How are you doing?"

"Fine, Miss."

"I just wanted to tell you that I needed to use my friend's car this morning. Professor St. John drove me over to the hospital to see Cloë and I left my car here. Anyway, I brought my permit to put in his car. It will only be for a couple of hours"

"I'm sorry, Maggie, but I can't let you park a second car here. It's against University policy. There's a visitor's lot about a half mile down the road your friend can use."

Taken aback, Maggie swallowed her surprise and said, "Oh. Well, okay. I don't want to get you in trouble."

He nodded and closed his window and Maggie sat back into her seat. "I'm sorry, Grant, I didn't think it would matter."

"That's okay, I need to meet Steve at the coffee shop anyway, and I think that's closer to the public lot he was talking about, right?"

"Yes, I guess so."

"Don't worry about it. Seriously. I'll just pull up over here and let you out by the front door and try to find a spot near the coffee shop."

"The shop is over in the Student Union on Maple Street, so the closest public lot is over on Walnut. Do you want me to show you where it is?"

"No, that's okay. I know you need to get to work and it will only take me a minute to drive over."

Unsure, Maggie gathered her purse and bag together before she leaned over to press a kiss to Grant's mouth and said, "Thanks for driving me in. I'll see you at the hospital later, right?"

"Right. And tonight you can come over and I'll make you dinner."

"Wow, you cook, too?" Maggie asked her eyebrows raised over twinkling eyes.

"Well, I don't know if I'd call it cooking, exactly, but I do have one or two dishes I can throw together that are pretty good, and after being at the hospital all day you'll be ready for a hot meal."

Maggie reached out to brush her hand over Grant's rough cheek—there hadn't been time for him to shave that morning, she'd kept him too busy—and she said, "You've got a date, Detective. Good luck today."

"Thanks, Red," Grant said and then he leaned over to press a soft kiss to her lips and he said softly, "Be careful today. Love you."

Maggie kissed him a second time and then smiled over at him as she climbed out of the car. At the last moment she leaned down to grin over at him and called out, "Love you, too," before she closed the door and ran across the frost-crusted grass to the front door of her building.

Grant watched until she was safely inside before he glanced at his dash clock, swore, and drove off to try to find a parking spot and meet Steve.

By the time he had parked and walked the quarter mile to the Union he was running almost ten minutes late, and he hoped that

Steve was running late, too. When he spotted the coffee shop he had the impression of a small café on a busy Paris street—all wrought iron and flowers.

There was a long line of people stretched out in front of a counter manned by a small man who looked remarkably like a ferret and a tall, thin girl with hair dyed dark black and completely dressed in black clothes. Above the counter there was a sign with a large steaming cup of coffee cup with the words Caffeine 101 written across it.

He also saw a scattering of people sitting at small round tables that, again, brought to mind Paris—or one of the several hundred coffee places he'd seen daily in the trendy neighborhoods of Seattle. He smiled at the memory—not because he missed it, but because he didn't.

He was happy, really happy, exactly where he was, and it was a relief to be able to be sure, really sure, that he was exactly where he belonged. And where he belonged was in Hope, on the job, with Maggie, and with the relaxed-looking man looking up at him from one of those ridiculously small tables with a questioning look on his face.

"What are you grinning like an idiot for, Evans?"

He'd seen the telltale humor in Steve's eyes and knew that his partner approved of his dating Maggie—even if he hadn't said as much out loud. If Steve had truly disapproved of their relationship he would have said so.

Loudly and clearly.

And if Grant had ignored him, painfully.

But he hadn't, and for a man like Steve, that was tantamount to a blessing. Blessing or not, Grant wasn't foolish enough to tell him the other reason he was late was because he'd had an interlude with Steve's little sister in the shower that had put him fifteen minutes behind time.

Even friendship as good as theirs shouldn't be tested *that* far.

So, all he said was, "Sorry I'm late. It took me forever to find a parking spot and hike it over here."

Grant sank down across from where Steve sprawled, looking far too big to be comfortable in the small chair. Grant eyed the line of people to judge how long it would be before they could talk to the manager.

Steve pushed a cup of coffee over the table towards Grant and said, "How come you didn't just park in Maggie's lot?"

"Squirrely parking attendant wouldn't let her park a second car there so I had to find a public lot. Strange little guy. Has the moon eyes for Maggie."

"Sounds like someone else I know," Steve said dryly.

Grant just smiled again and asked, "So, were you able to talk to the manager yet?"

"Briefly. He said he'd join us out here once the morning rush is over. He said it should be done in about five minutes," Steve said as he glanced at his watch before he continued, "I typed up the report and talked to the Chief first thing this morning. He's anxious to see fast results on this, but he was happy with the updated profile your pal faxed over early this morning."

Steve handed over a sheaf of papers and waited while Grant scanned them.

"Yeah, he called me last night to tell me he'd already read over what we'd sent and would get to it before he went to sleep. He musta worked all night. This is great.

"Have you heard from forensics about the beads or footprints we found yet?"

Steve nodded and said, "They're still trying to place the beads, but they were able to tell us that they are not steel. They're silver and worn from a constant friction—like rolled or rubbed repeatedly. They're still trying to get a fingerprint, but the exposure to the elements has made that all but impossible. As for the footprints, if they belong to our guy forensics place him somewhere between 5'11" and 6' and about 180 pounds, which happens to coincide with our eyewitnesses on the Daniels case."

Grant mused over the information for a minute before he opened his mouth to reply, "You know…I've been thinking…" But, before Grant could finish his thought the coffee shop manager walked up to the table.

"Detective Sullivan, I'm free for about thirty-five minutes before the next class lets out and we'll be swamped again. How can I help you?"

330

"Mr. Franklin, this is my partner, Detective Grant Evans."

"You're the new police detective from Washington?" Franklin asked as he shook Grant's hand.

"Yes, sir. Thanks for helping us out."

"Well, I haven't helped you yet. What can I do for you gentlemen?" he glanced at his watch before he looked expectantly over at Steve again.

"We are trying to find the customer who received this receipt from your shop," Steve handed over the badly wrinkled slip of paper enclosed in a clear evidence bag.

Mr. Franklin frowned and picked up the bag to stare down his nose through his glasses at the paper. He was silent for a long moment before he set it down slowly and said, "Well…I can tell you that it was Caroline Jennings on the register who rang up this drink at 7:54 a.m. The receipt is from last week, so I doubt she'd remember a specific face or person, unless it was a regular customer, and even then…this is a very common drink. Medium cappuccino, plain. I can give you her number and address, or you can come back this afternoon. She's on from two til six. Other than that, there's nothing else I can tell you just from this paper."

"Do you have any surveillance cameras in your shop?"

"Unfortunately, no. I know that the University has a few around outside and the Bookstore down the hall has several, but I don't believe any of them directly cover the shop."

Steve and Grant exchanged a glance then Steve said, "We would like to speak with Ms. Jennings, if you give us her info we'd greatly appreciate it."

When Franklin had gone back to his office to retrieve the information they needed Grant turned to Steve and said, "Why don't I talk to the University security and get copies of those security tapes sent over to the station while you talk to Dean Mitchell. Even if we can't see the shop at the time of the purchase, we can do a scan for guys who fit the approximate age and build entering or leaving the building just before and after the time on the receipt."

Steve agreed as he pulled out his phone. "I'll call the Chief and have him send someone over to get the tapes and they can start reviewing them while we talk to the art history department staff and graduate students.

"After you're done with security, look over these files Jones put together on the department staff. She also looked at all the other university staff that worked in or around the building—it's a fairly small number, so it shouldn't take too long. Then I'll meet you back here and we can go talk to them together."

Grant glanced at the neat stack of files and nodded once before asking, "How was Jones able to pull all these files together so quickly?"

"Oh, well, I saw her at the hospital last night when I went to see Cloë and I asked her to run them then. She went back to the station and got us the files before she went home for the night," Steve replied as he dialed the station.

Steve had just hung up from speaking with the Chief when Franklin came back out of the office with a small piece of paper in his hand. "Here's Caroline's information. I have to get back in there," he gestured to the line that was once again forming outside the shop.

"Sure. Thanks for the help Mr. Franklin."

Franklin nodded and hurried back to help the girl with the impatient line of caffeine-deprived coeds. Steve glanced at his watch and said, "All right, I've got to head over to the Dean's office for that meeting. I'll see you back here when I'm done."

"Okay. I'm off to find security."

"The office is downstairs next to the bowling alley and arcade."

"Thanks. And thanks for the coffee." Grant walked down the hall towards the stairs, whistling a jaunty tune while Steve shrugged back into his coat and shook his head at his clearly happy partner.

If he'd only thought it before, now Steve was certain. His partner was head-over-heels in love with his sister—and, Steve suspected, she with him.

It was nice to see. It had been weeks since he'd seen Grant get withdrawn or moody as he had when he'd first moved to Hope. And Maggie practically glowed she was so cheerful.

At first he had been worried about the relationship, not wanting Maggie—or Grant for that matter—getting hurt when they were both so clearly still recovering from bad situations. But now he was just glad that while they were still hunting down this killer, his sister had one more person looking out for her and keeping her safe.

The attack on Cloë had been far too close to home, and what with Maggie's knowledge of, and contribution to, the case, Steve was worried about her. At least with Grant there in the evenings, and probably the nights he admitted grudgingly to himself, he knew she was much safer.

Of course, he would feel a lot better once the killer was locked up—or dead.

With those grim thoughts, Steve quickened his pace as he walked across the campus in the gray light of the late-October day. Dark clouds were blowing swiftly across the darkening skies. Steve tried to push aside his rising feelings of unease as he hurried on his way, but he could not help thinking that trouble was on its way.

He glanced up at the darkening sky and thought grimly, a storm was coming.

FORTY-FOUR

By the time Steve's meeting with the Dean was over it was close to eleven. He found Grant already back at the table they'd sat at earlier.

"How'd it go?" Grant asked as Steven sat down across from him.

"Great. Dean Mitchell had a list of people with access to the Art History Department all ready for me and he told me we had *full* access to the staff for interviews. He even gave us a list of students—names only—and said that if we had any problems, to let him know."

"I guess it *does* pay to know everyone in town. Something like this happened in Seattle, it would be completely political. There's no way they would have given us student names without warrants."

"Oh, it probably would be here, too, but the Dean is Cloë's godfather, and he's really upset about it. Don't get me wrong, he would have helped us anyway, but we would probably have had to work a little harder for the type of access he's given us. For sure we would have needed to give him a warrant *before* he handed over the student list.

"I promised him we'd get one to him so he's covered legally, but he didn't want to hold up the investigation at all. Here are the employee and student lists," Steve handed over two sheets of paper.

Grant took the sheets and glanced over the three documents before he said, "Looks like there are just a handful of names we need to add to the list you already gave to Jones, Grant paused and looked up at Steve, excitement on his face, "I'm willing to bet we will be able to eliminate most of the student list due to sex and age. The grad student list only has seven names on it and five are women."

"Yep. I'll have the guys look into everyone on the student list, but I'd like you and me to focus on the male staff members and grad students."

"All right. I got the security tapes sent over to the station. Chief said he'd get a couple of guys to start looking at them right away. It's a long shot, but you never know, we could get lucky.

"So how do you want to handle the interviews?"

334

Steve considered the lists for several minutes, then glanced at his watch before he answered, "Jones is already at the hospital, so I'll call Mac and see if he can take a look at the names we don't already have files on.

"Both St. John and Malone are supposed to be in the office, so we can talk to them today. This Randy Ellison, the other grad student? We'll have to see if St. John will give us his contact info."

Grant nodded and he said, "There are only about eight or nine guys on the undergrad list, and it looks like there are three university employees that work in and around the building who we should also talk to: the janitor, Moses Swanson, whom we already had on the list; Sylvester Booker, the gardener; and Abraham Swanson, the kid in the parking lot booth I told you about this morning. Think he and Moses Swanson are related?"

Steve replied, "Yes. Dean Mitchell said they're brothers. Moses—or Mo, as the staff calls him—has worked here for more than ten years, but the brother was just hired. He's just home from finishing college and Mo got him the job in the hopes that he will get into the grad program here in the spring."

Grant raised his eyebrows and shook his head. He still couldn't get over the volume of information Steve could get in less than an hour's conversation. He reminded himself that small towns worked differently than cities—just look at how easy it had been to get the university security to hand over the security tapes—no argument, no warrants, just a quick call to the Dean and Grant had been assured that the tapes would be at the station within the hour.

Just one more thing to like about small town living. If this were the norm, he figured he could get used to everyone knowing, practically before he did, all about his life.

"Well we know the attendant is here, we can talk to him, too. As for the gardener, I can't imagine he'd have much left to do this late in the year."

"You'd be surprised," Steve smiled as he replied, "Mom spends almost as much time in the fall getting her beds ready for winter as she does planting in the spring. We may be able to track him down."

Grant agreed and together they stood to leave. Grant had been in such a rush to get to the Union that morning he hadn't had the time to really look around at the campus. As they walked through the chill weather Grant took the time to look around.

Beautiful brick buildings covered in climbing vines dotted the picturesque campus. The wide open spaces between the buildings were filled with curving walking paths lined with gardens and trees. They seemed to invite long meandering strolls, and Grant noted that there were several students doing just that.

Instead of rushing from class to class he saw couples and single students walking around, seemingly enjoying the chilly day.

Grassy areas were dotted liberally with large trees—maples, oaks, pines, even birch—that lifted their bare branches up into the gray sky, their leaves long stripped from their branches by the strong winds and driving rains common to Minnesota in the autumn.

Soon, he knew, the grounds would be blanketed with the winter snowfalls he'd heard so much about. Then, the many students he saw walking between the buildings would be bundled into layers of outerwear until he imagined they would resemble an army of bright colors moving against a barren white landscape.

Amused at the directions of his thoughts, Grant brought his attention back to Steve.

"What's so funny," Steve asked.

"Hmmm? Oh, nothing. I was just trying to picture everything with a couple of feet of snow on it."

"It looks pretty cool. The snow makes everything look clean and bright—at least until late winter, and then it gets pretty grungy.

"So, what's the story for tomorrow night? Do you know if Maggie's going to do her show, or do you think she'll really cancel it?"

Grant sighed and thought about how upset Maggie had been the night before. "Well, she's adamant that she cannot do it, she's so worried about Cloë. But, I've been thinking…"

Steve waited a minute before he said, "And?"

"And I think she's going to regret not doing it. I think she's most upset about the idea of replacing Cloë with someone else. Especially while she's still in the coma."

"If there's any chance that someone can step in and learn the routine, she's going to need to do that today."

"She won't. Not until she *knows* Cloë's alright. Which is why," Grant continued with a grin when Steve opened his mouth to argue, "Which is why I need Sybil's phone number from you."

"Sybil? Steve asked, the doubt obvious in his voice.

"Yup. I want to see if Katie can meet with your brothers and learn the song movements. Cloë is so tiny, I couldn't think of anyone else who'd fit in her dress, and Katie seems like she'd have a blast helping out."

Steve's face broke out into a grin and he added, "And Jack and Dillon would love it, too. Here's Sybil's number," Steve held out his phone, a number on the display for Grant to see, "You call Sybil. Katie won't be home from school until 3:30, but Sybil can work out the details with you. I'll call Jack and get him in on the plan. He'll love the intrigue of keeping it from Mags."

As Steve opened his phone to dial it Grant dialed in Sybil's number and listened to Steve's voice in the background.

"Jack? Get your lazy butt out of bed. I've got a job for you…"

Grant smiled and tuned out the rest Steve's conversation when Sybil's coolly professional voice came on the line, "This is Sybil."

"Hi Sybil, it's Grant."

"Grant," all the coolness in her voice evaporated as she greeted him warmly, "How are you? How are Maggie and Cloë doing?

Grant smiled at the concern he heard in her voice. "Good. Cloë's holding her own. We should know more later today, but so far she's staying strong. Maggie's really worried, but she's hanging in there."

"Well that's good. I'm glad you are there for her."

Grant was speechless for a moment, and before he could respond Sybil continued. "So what can I do for you today, Grant?"

Grant grinned again. No one ever said the Sullivan women were slow. "Well, it's about Katie."

"Katie?" Sybil asked, surprised.

"Yep. Maggie is planning on calling off her Halloween show because of Cloë, but I'm trying to put it back on again and that's where Katie comes in."

"You want Katie to take Cloë's place?"

"You guessed it. Steve's calling Jack and I was hoping Katie would want to step in and learn the part. I know it's short notice..."

"That's no problem. Katie will be thrilled. She's been begging to be in the show for years now. But, I take it that Maggie doesn't know about this?"

Yep, definitely not slow.

"No. She's dead set on not putting the show on before Cloë's out of the woods, but I'm banking on Cloë. She's tough. And I know how much the show, and the kids who look forward to seeing it each year, mean to Maggie."

Sybil grinned, delighted by the obvious affection she heard in Grant's voice. *He's got it bad*, she thought to herself. Out loud she said, "I know that Katie will love it. Maggie promised her a starring role when she turned ten, but I think we can make it happen a little earlier. Katie can help right after school."

"Great," Grant said, "I managed to sneak the costume out of Maggie's apartment this morning. I'm a little worried about how it will fit. The top...I don't want you or Katie to feel uncomfortable with it. The skirt should be okay because she's shorter than Cloë, but I think she'll have to wear a shirt or something under the top thingy..."

Grant trailed off, clearly uneasy as he shifted from one foot to another. For God's sake, his hands were sweating. Big, tough cop. Yeah, right.

"You're sweet. Don't worry about the top—I'll make sure I fit it to Katie and we'll figure out something tonight to make sure it's modest. Don't you worry about a thing. Just make sure I get the costume today and I'll take care of it."

Absurdly relieved, Grant blew out a breath and said, "Thanks, Sybil. You're an angel."

Sybil laughed and said, "Grant? Jack's calling on the other line. I better talk to him if we're going to make this happen by tomorrow night. I'll see you later."

"Bye, Syb..." Grant said to empty air, and he shook his head, bemused."

"Everything all set up?" Steve asked.

Grant had to laugh out loud. He said, "Sybil is on the job. All I have to say, Steve, is that the Sullivan women are amazing. I've never met their like before. You sure are a lucky bastard to be surrounded by them."

Steve grinned, then laughed out loud, "Don't I know it. Just don't say that to them, or we'll never hear the end of it."

Grant laughed again and said, "I need to get the costume over to Sybil as soon as we're done here."

"Jack is going to stop by the station to pick it up on his way to pick Katie up after school, we just have to drop it off there," he said.

"I hope I don't get killed for this," Grant said.

"If you do, I hope I'm there to see it."

"Gee, thanks, Dude, you're all heart."

The echoes of their laughter sounded across the campus in the cool autumn air, and when Maggie's car pulled out of the parking lot behind the building they approached, neither she, nor the men who loved her, noticed when a second car followed.

FORTY-FIVE

Together, Grant and Steve climbed the short flight of stairs to the building where the Art History Department was located. Grant glanced up to see the name of the building carved in the stone face of the old building—Hamilton Hall.

"Who do you want to talk to first?"

Steve considered for a moment as they climbed a flight of stairs, their footsteps echoing hollowly in the lofty stairwell. "St. John. According to the schedule I had Maggie write up for us the other day he should be in the office all day. He only has one class today, and it doesn't begin until 6:30. He'll be able to give us the info on the two grad students."

"Sounds good," Grant said and he followed Steve through the department's door.

The first thing he noted was that Maggie was already gone. The second was that someone—most likely Maggie or Cloë, or both—had painted the room recently.

The soft shade of blue was so clearly at odds with the drab gray-green color he'd noted as he'd walked through the rest of the building, it was almost a shock.

The third was that the tall, dark-haired man sitting at a small cramped desk in the back corner of the room glaring at him was the same man he'd seen at the hospital the day before, Tony Malone.

While Steve took out his badge and explained why they were there, Grant thought back furiously over the people he'd met since coming to Hope, but he could come up with no memory of Malone, other than seeing him at the hospital, and no reason for someone he'd never really met before to dislike him.

The sound of Malone speaking broke into Grant's musings. "Professor St. John is in his office. Just knock and go in."

Steve said, "Thanks," and Grant followed Steve through the half-glass office door Malone had gestured at. As Grant pulled the door closed behind them he found Malone's eyes on him once more, and the pure hatred in them had Grant's eyebrows lowering as he turned to stand with Steve to face the professor where he sat behind his desk.

Steve said, "Morning, Holden. I'm not sure if you were introduced last night; this is my partner, Detective Grant Evans."

"No, we didn't actually meet. Detective," Holden nodded at Grant before gesturing at the two chairs facing his desk, "Have a seat, gentlemen," Holden said briefly before he shook Grant's hand.

Grant kept his expression neutral but he was surprised by Holden's appearance. With sun-streaked hair and a golden tan, dressed in worn jeans and a faded printed t-shirt, Grant was reminded more of an aging surfer than a respected college professor. Grant noted a light brown corduroy jacket hanging in the corner of the room and guessed it must be St. John's nod to formality.

When he'd seen him yesterday, he'd mistaken him for another student or friend of Cloë's. And again, he thought that St. John looked better suited for some west coast city than a small Midwestern town.

"What can I do for you, Steve?" Holden asked, his voice weary.

Grant noted the worry in the professor's eyes and the dark circles under them, not to mention the obvious finger tracks in his mussed hair—it was clear that he'd been having a hard day or two.

Grant sat back and let Steve take the lead.

"We're looking at the attack on Cloë and we wanted to see if you had any information about what she was working on, or who she was involved with, that could help us out."

Holden shook his head once before he replied, "I came back here last night and looked over all the stuff on her desk and there was nothing there—she was putting together various things for some of my lectures and typing department correspondence, but nothing that would be worth hurting her over."

He stopped and ran a hand through his hair again before he shook his head once more and added, "I can't think of *anyone* who'd want to hurt Cloë. Everybody loves her. There have never been any problems with students or staff that I've heard of. She dated, but I don't know who they were. Maggie would know if there had been any problems there. The two of them are very close."

Steve nodded and said, "What about with the two grad students, Tony Malone and Randy Ellison? Any problems there?"

341

Holden shook his head then said slowly, "No. She and Tony are friends—go to movies, out for coffee, that sort of thing, but usually with Maggie. He might be able to tell you if there were any other students she hung out with. We are a fairly small department, and everyone knows everyone.

"As for Randy, he's been in Italy for the past six months doing an intense study of Roman architecture and its role in pre and post Renaissance…well, they don't really know each other because he's been gone so often over the past year and a half."

"All right. How about you and Cloë? Are you close?" Steve asked, his tone completely neutral and face bland.

Holden sighed and Grant watched closely, expecting to see anger at the implied suggestion. Instead, Holden simply lifted tired eyes to meet Steve's eyes head on and replied, "Yes, we are close. But only as friends. Cloë is one of the sweetest, nicest women of my acquaintance. I love her like a little sister."

"I find that hard to believe," Grant broke in, deliberately suggestive, keeping his gaze on Holden. As he watched, he saw the flash of anger in Holden's eyes and the subtle clenching of his jaw before he replied.

"As I said, there's never been anything romantic between us. Right from the start we've been colleagues and friends, but nothing more. It's terrible what's happened to her, but I don't think I know anything more that can help."

Impressed at the older man's ability to appear composed, Grant nodded, but remained silent as he listened to St. John's too-pat answers. Then he asked, "Where were you night before last between ten and one a.m.?"

Holden turned to face him, his mouth tightening in anger as he answered, the genial concern gone from his voice, "I was meeting with a student until 10:30 or 11p.m. and then I stopped by the bar for a drink or two. I was there until around 1:30."

"We're going to need the name of the student and the bar," Grant said simply, completely unconcerned with the obvious dislike St. John directed at him.

Holden turned back to Steve and said impatiently, "Is this really necessary, Steve? You know I'd never hurt Cloë."

Steve smiled easily and said, "It helps us establish a timeline. It will help Cloë, and as you said before, you love her like a little sister, so I'm sure you'd be more than happy to help us out, right?"

Flustered, Holden replied stiffly, "Fine. If it will help Cloë. The student's name is Mandy Rogers. She's a fourth year who needed some guidance with her entrance materials for a graduate program. I was helping her choose a possible thesis study."

"Sure, sure," Grant said, a small smile on his face as he noted down the name.

"You know, I resent the implication, Detective, and I don't appreciate being treated in this manner. I expected better from you, Steve, than to allow some buffoon of a city slicker, an outsider who knows nothing about this town or the people in it, to just waltz in here throwing around baseless accusations."

Steve leaned back, the amiable smile on his face doing nothing to disguise the obvious anger Grant saw in his eyes. Steve closed his notebook carefully before he said, "Well now, that's duly noted Professor St. John. I'll be sure to register your complaint about Detective Evans with Chief Banyon. I'll be sure to tell him that our long-term resident, Professor St. John, who's been living here all of, what is it, six years? Six years, thinks our newest detective is an outsider."

"A *buffoon* of a city slicker outsider," Grant interjected solemnly.

Steve nodded and said, "Right. A *buffoon* of an outsider who is taking over the department. But in the meantime, we're going to need the name of that bar."

Holden glared from one of them to another, his face slightly flushed and he mumbled, "It was O'Neil's. Now if you'll excuse me, I need to get some things done before I go to the hospital."

Steve stood and said, "Sure thing, Professor. And thanks for your help."

Grant nodded at the furious man and followed Steve out into the main office area once more.

Malone was back at his desk, a proof sheet in front of him and large glasses on his face.

"Mr. Malone, do you have a minute? We'd like to ask you a few questions."

343

Tony looked up and removed the glasses before he rubbed both hands on his jeans and nodded his head jerkily.

"Great," Steve said and he sat down in a nearby chair and Grant stood off to the side where he could better see Tony's face while he talked with Steve.

"What can you tell us about Cloë? Did she have any problems with any of the students or the other employees?"

Tony shook his head vigorously and cleared his throat twice before he answered, "No way. Everyone loves Cloë. The guys make up excuses to come in just so they can see her and Maggie, and the girls all treat her like a sister. She is always, like, helping them out and talkin' to them and stuff.

"I don't ever even remember anyone even arguing with her. Nothing bad like that—even if they got a bad grade or something, she is the first one they tell and she always listens and finds some way to help them."

"Do you know who she was dating?"

Tony shrugged and replied, "Not really. Cloë never seemed to get serious with anyone. She was always just having fun and she'd always end up friends with anyone she'd dated. You know, she never wanted to hurt anyone so she always went out of her way to let them down easy. Sometimes she'd go out with a guy once and know they weren't meant, but she'd go out with them one or two or even three times more because she could never bring herself to hurt them. Then somehow, she'd keep them all as friends."

"Sounds like you know this first hand," Grant said evenly. Tony glanced over at him and nodded again.

"Yeah. We went out once, but we both knew we would be better off friends."

"That must have been hard," Steve said sympathetically.

"Not really. That was almost two years ago now. She helped me get this internship."

"I see. We're trying to set up a timeline for the day Cloë was attacked. Can you tell us where you were night before last between ten and one, Tony?"

Tony licked his lips and rubbed his palms on his thighs again before he said, "Sure. I was at my aunt's house in Duluth until about nine, and then I left to drive home. It takes about three and a half hours to get here from there. I got home just before 12:30 and headed straight to bed. No. Wait. I checked my email and replied to a couple and then went to bed about 1:15."

"Sounds like you've been thinking about that," Grant broke in again.

Tony glared at him and replied, "Well, sure. I watch T.V. I figured you guys would need to know, so I figured it out. I got a gas receipt from the Hinckley gas station and you can check my computer."

"We will, Tony," Steve broke in, smiling, "Thank you for your time. If you think of anything else that might help us, anything at all, just give me a call."

"Sure," Tony reached out to take the card Steve held out to him. Steve and Grant had almost reached the door when Tony called out, 'Detective?" I'm not sure if it's important or not, but I remember that Cloë did have a run-in with a guy last week. It completely slipped my mind."

Steve and Grant stopped and walked back to where Tony was still sitting, and now looking nervously at them.

"Tell us what happened," Steve said, his calm voice a direct contrast to the obvious tension in his shoulders, as he sat back down across from Tony.

"Right. Sure, it was early last Thursday morning and this guy, Bradley? He swept in to the office and demanded to speak with Maggie, only she wasn't in yet. Cloë told him she wasn't here, but the guy just refused to believe her. He just kept talking and talking and demanding to see her. He even tried to break into Holden's office. Cloë finally had to threaten to call campus security before he left in a huff. He told her he knew she was lying and that he'd make sure both she and Maggie'd pay for treating him that way.

"Guy was a total psycho. I haven't seen Cloë that mad before. She was muttering and slamming drawers for a good half hour after that."

"And *was* Maggie here?"

"No," Tony shook his head, "That's what was so crazy about it all. She had a meeting over in another building that morning so she didn't get back to the office until nearly eleven that day."

"I bet she was upset when you told her about what happened."

"Cloë never told her. Made me promise not to tell her either. She said she was going to tell Holden, but she said she didn't want Maggie upset anymore by that jerk than she'd already been."

"All right, Tony. Thanks a lot. Again, if you think of anything else, just give us a call."

"Sure. You don't think that guy hurt Cloë, do you?"

"We aren't going to assume anything at this point."

Looking slightly panicked, Tony stood up and said, "Maggie isn't in any danger, is she?"

"Nothing is going to happen to Maggie," Steve said soothingly as he glanced over to Grant. Grant raised his eyebrows, his mind racing. Obviously Maggie had another fan. The thought didn't worry him, but it did give him a vague sense of unease. Just how many of the men in her life were in love with her?

"We'll be in touch, Tony," Steve commented as he stood and turned to Grant. "I think we need to have another conversation with Professor St. John," he added grimly.

Grant nodded once and together they walked back to knock on St. John's door for a second time.

They heard St. John's call of "Come in," and Grant followed his partner back into the inner office to face a decidedly annoyed-looking professor.

"Is there something *more* I can do for you?"

"Yeah," Grant said roughly as he braced his hands on the desk and leaned forward into St. John's face to say, "You can tell us why you neglected to mention that Maggie's ex, Brad, was here last Thursday harassing and threatening Cloë."

Taken aback, Holden sat back in his seat and said, "I completely forgot about it."

At Grant's disgusted snort of disbelief Holden turned to appeal to Steve, "You have to believe me, I never thought of it. Cloë told me that he had been here looking for Maggie, but I swear she never said anything about him threatening anyone. She just wanted me to know not to tell the guy where Maggie was or anything like that. If she'd told me that he threatened her I would have spoken with him myself, and I would have called campus security to take care of removing him from the campus."

Grant eased back and after he studied Holden's face for several long moments longer he nodded and said, "Is there anything else you *forgot* to tell us?"

Holden shook his head and Grant said, "Fine. If you think of anything, no matter how insignificant you think it may be, call us," before he turned and pushed out of the room.

Steve followed closely on Grant's heels and was almost to the door when Holden said, "Steve, I'm sorry. I truly didn't know he'd threatened her. I would have told you about something that serious."

Steve nodded once and before he opened the door to join Grant he turned to say one last thing, "Look Holden, I understand the position you're in here, and I can even understand that you can't like Grant because of it, but if there's anything else that you've kept from us it will do more than simply damage any friendship you might have with Maggie and our family, it could very well get her, or someone else like Cloë seriously hurt—or worse."

"Look, Steve, I swear, there's nothing else."

Steve nodded and turned to leave.

Steve caught up with Grant in the hallway just outside of the department door and they walked out together. Neither one spoke as they emerged from the building back out into the cool air of the late morning.

They'd walked in silence for several minutes when Grant swore viciously under his breath.

Steve raised his eyebrows and waited, knowing Grant well enough by now to know that he wouldn't remain quiet for long. He wasn't disappointed.

"Son of a bitch! That asshole has a lot of nerve."

Steve kept his expression neutral and replied, "Which asshole?"

Grant's smile flashed in appreciation and he glanced over to find Steve grinning back at him. Grant didn't let the glib remark or the fast grin fool him. He knew Steve well enough by now to know that he was furious that Bradley was still bothering Maggie.

"Well, now that you ask, all three of them, but I was talking about Bradley. After the little run-in I had with him the first night I went out with Maggie, I never heard another word about him bothering her, or anyone else for that matter. Do you think she even knows about what happened here?"

Steve looked over and rolled his eyes once before he answered, "Probably. Even if Cloë didn't say anything, which she probably didn't, I'm sure Maggie's aware that the guy is still hanging around somewhere."

"Why hasn't she said anything to one of us? I told her to tell me if he bothered her again."

"That was your first mistake, Evans. Trying to *tell* Maggie to do anything. Even if she knows you're right, she'll refuse to go along with it if you demand it of her. And here I was, thinking you knew her so well."

"I do," Grant protested, indignant, "I know that, believe me I figured that out right away, but I guess I just never thought she would put herself, or her friends, at risk this way."

Steve sighed and said, "I'm sure she believed he'd never do anything. And maybe he hasn't. She'd never have risked Cloë, of that I am sure. That's why I'd lay odds that Cloë never told her about Bradley's little visit to the office. I gotta believe that Maggie would have told one of us about that."

Grant rubbed the back of his neck wearily and nodded. "Okay. How do you want to handle this?"

Steve came to a stop in front of his car, "Get in. I'll drive you to your car."

When both men were settled in the car Steve continued, "Why don't you get the costume to the station then track down Mags at the hospital to see what, if anything, she knows about Cloë's run-in with Bradley."

"And what are you going to be doing?"

"I am going to pay Bradley a little visit. I think it's time he and I have a little heart-to-heart."

Hearing the suppressed fury in Steve's tone, Grant grinned again and said coldly, "Why don't we do that together?"

Steve glanced over, considering, and noted the dangerous glint in Grant's eyes before he slowly replied, "No. I don't think that would be a good idea. We'll cover more ground apart."

"I don't like the idea of you being alone when you talk to him," Grant persisted.

Steve pulled to a stop at Grant's car and thought for a long moment before he finally agreed. "All right. I'll meet you at the station. We'll talk to Maggie first and then drop by Brad's office for a little chat. That will give me a chance to get the info we found out this morning to the rest of the team."

"Good. I'll see you back at the station. Thanks for the lift," Grant said as he climbed out of the car to get in his own.

FORTY-SIX

By the time Grant had made his way back to the station and dropped Katie's costume at the front desk for Jack to pick up Steve had filled in Dusty and gotten information about the video tapes. He was waiting for Grant at their desks.

"Well, Operation Katie is underway," Grant said as he strode up to where Steve was seated.

"Great. Let's go," Steve said and started walking back through the squad room.

"Where are we going?" Grant automatically followed.

"Dusty has the video tapes cued up to show us a couple of guys," Steve talked over his shoulder as he led Grant down a hallway that Grant had seen, but hadn't gone down since his initial tour of the station. They stopped in front of an open door and Steve gestured Grant in ahead of him.

Grant stepped through the door into a small, cramped room. A countertop stretched across the entire perimeter of the room completely covered by computer monitors. Several of the workstations were occupied by the part-time officers Grant had seen moving in and out of the station over the past two months. In the corner of the room, Dusty sat hunched over a keyboard, his eyes glued to a grainy gray image as it played on a small monitor.

"All right, Dusty, what have you got for us," Steve stepped up behind Dusty and stood next to Grant, arms crossed. Dusty glanced over his shoulder and nodded at both men before he turned back to the screen in front of him.

"There are several guys that fit the profile description, but only one or two possibilities for guys that are off screen long enough to have stopped and ordered coffee between cameras 22 and 28 that flank the hallway where the café is located. Okay. Let me cue this up for you..."

Dusty muttered under his breath as he tapped one key at a time, at the computer. Steve stood patiently behind him, waiting for the video to be cued up correctly.

"Okay, here's the first guy with the beard and the striped shirt. Time on the tape says it was 7:47a.m. when he goes off screen here and you don't see him again until 7:58 here," Dusty tapped a series of keys and the screen switched to a second view of the same man walking down a different corridor, now holding a coffee cup.

"Not exactly a clear view of the guy," Steve said quietly as he leaned in to look more closely at the form on screen. "Looks like dark blonde hair and wears glasses, but other than that, I don't know what I can see."

Grant frowned in concentration as he leaned forward, too. After several moments he leaned back and shook his head as he met Steve's eyes.

"Can we get a print-out of this frame; see if we can't get someone from the café who can identify the guy?"

"Sure, "Dusty said, "I'll have one of the techs see if they can clean it up and then I'll get him to print it up for you.

"All right, Dusty, let's see the second guy."

"Kay," Dusty went back to his muttering and tapping until his computer screen showed a new group of people walking down the hall leading to the café. Dusty paused the image on screen again and started, "Okay, here's the second guy, can't tell the color he's wearing but it looks like dark blue or green, possibly black. No way to tell hair color with the hat. He comes on screen at 7:50 a.m. and then walks past the second camera at 8:03 carrying a coffee cup. He never looks up, so there's no good shot of his face."

Once again Grant leaned forward to study the blurry figure on the screen. The man was walking fast, his head turned away or down from both cameras and further obscured by the baseball cap.

"Does that look like an M to either of you?" Grant gestured towards the hat.

"Yeah. It kind of looks like a Twins hat to me. Not too descriptive. Can you replay that for us again, Dusty?"

Steve waited as Dusty replayed the scene. "Okay, pause it here. Thanks. Okay, can either of you tell what's sticking out of his back pocket, here?"

Both Dusty and Grant leaned forward to squint at the screen for several moments, the only sound the hum of the computers and the soft clicking of keys being pressed. Finally Grant shrugged and eased back, saying, "It could be anything, really. I mean, it could be work gloves, but it could also be pretty much anything.

"Dusty can you have the guys look through the rest of the tapes to see if you have any other views of these guys on any other cameras? Maybe we'll get lucky and one will have a better view of their faces."

"We've already started to do that. So far I haven't had any luck, but there're still more than twenty tapes left to look at. It's pretty slow going."

Grant patted him on the shoulder and said, "Good job, Man. Thanks to you we may have our first picture—no matter how blurry—of our killer."

"Give us a call if you find anything else," Steve added, "Thanks, Dusty."

Together Grant and Steve headed back through the squad room. They'd made it almost to the door when Mac called out from where he sat at his desk, "Hey Sullivan, are you headed over to the hospital?"

"Yeah, we've got to talk to Maggie and she's over there, now."

"Can I hitch a ride? It would save me an extra trip back here with my car since Jones is already there."

"Sure."

Mac shrugged into a heavily battered leather jacket and wound a black cashmere scarf around his neck as he hurried to catch up with them.

"Nice scarf, Mac. It's so purty," Steve grinned as he pushed the front door open.

"Yeah, yeah. My wife gave it to me for my birthday."

Grant just sat back, a large grin on his face as he listened to Steve continue to tease the large detective. As the two detectives bantered back and forth, Grant's mind wandered back over the conversation he'd had with his sister on the phone night before last.

He'd called to thank her for shipping the contents of his storage locker and, as usual, the conversation had disintegrated quickly despite starting out well.

Happy to get his Grandfather's desk and the rest of his furniture he'd picked up his phone and dialed his sister, "Hey, Val, how are you doing? How are Dick and the girls?"

"Hello, Grant. I'm doing well. Dick is working and the girls are in their rooms. And how is life in a small town?"

Hearing the subtle sarcasm in her voice Grant felt his shoulders stiffening, but he kept his voice pleasant as he replied, "Great. I love it here. You and Mom should try making it out here for a visit some time. I think you would really like it, it's beautiful."

She made a noncommittal noise before she said, "Did you receive the items I had shipped? I was so surprised you had me send them so soon after moving there. I would think that you would need longer than just a few weeks to decide you wanted to stay there. Well, I suppose you can always just get them shipped back, though that seems like a terrible waste of money to me."

Grant sighed and said, "Val, I don't plan on moving back to Seattle. I'm happy here. I bought a house, I'm dating an amazing woman, and I have a job that I love doing."

"That's nice. I ran into Shannon the other day. She looked fabulous, as always. She told me that she's engaged to the new assistant District Attorney, Haden Seavers. I've never seen her look happier. It was nice to see. It's a shame you ever let her go, Grant. If you hadn't taken that silly job, you never would have lost her to an *assistant* District Attorney.

"Oh, well. Once you get this idea out of your system and you move back, there's this other woman I think you would be perfect with. Of, course you'd *have* to find a new job, but I'm sure that Dick or one of his associates could help with that."

He never learned.

As he listened to his sister go on and on about the woman who had cheated on him and left him and then continue on to suggest that his entire life was some kind of joke, that he was simply indulging a whim, he felt the last vestiges of what had been guilt for always causing his mother and sister worry break away.

He'd carried the weight of his family's disapproval and fear for so long, but he'd never really understood just how heavy that weight had been, and how far down it had been dragging him.

Relieved at the realization, he sat, letting the freedom he felt at the discovery wash over him as he heard Valerie's voice calling his name.

"Grant? Are you listening to me? At least have the decency to listen to me when I am talking to you!"

Angry once more, Grant cut her off, "Val, just shut up and listen to *me* for once. I am NOT moving back. I do not want to date one of your friends. I am NOT looking for a new job, I have one that I love already, and if you knew me at all, you'd understand that. Thanks for sending my stuff, I appreciate it. Say 'hi' to Mom for me."

Shocked into an outraged silence, Valerie finally answered, "I cannot *believe* you told me to shut up! Of all the nerve. Here I went out of my way to send you your things and I was simply chatting with you and you viciously attack me! I think…"

Again, Grant cut her off, "I know *exactly* what you, and Mom, have always thought of me and the choices I've made with my life. Why is it so hard for you to just be happy for me? Val, you're my baby sister. I love you, and I want you to be proud of me, happy for me."

Letting out a huff, Valerie replied stiffly, "Well, if this is how I'm going to be treated when I talk to you, maybe it would just be better if I didn't."

"Val, c'mon…" Grant began, but he was talking to empty air, the dial tone loud in his ear.

Slowly he had closed his phone. "That went well," he muttered to himself as he dropped his face into his hands. He had still been sitting there when the phone rang five minutes later.

After checking the caller I.D. he'd sat back and answered wearily, "Hello, Mother."

The conversation that had followed had been ugly. And far too familiar. By the time he'd hung up his mother had been in tears and he'd had a huge tension headache so bad that it had taken three extra-strength aspirin and a shot of Jack to get rid of it.

After so many conversations that had ended the same way, Grant had no idea why he was surprised that his family still had the ability to hurt him with their judgmental comments and unwillingness to accept him. In the twenty years since his father's death they had grown farther and farther apart, until Grant felt he didn't even know them anymore.

The truth was, he felt closer to the Sullivans after just a couple months than he ever had with his own family. And how sad was that?

And the worst of it was that he hardly knew his two nieces at all. Caitlyn had been barely two when he'd been shot and Hayley had been just a couple of months old. And although he'd brought them dolls and toys on their birthdays and Christmas, and had stopped in to visit them whenever he could, his estrangement with Val ensured that they weren't close—not like Maggie was with her niece and nephew.

Well, he'd just have to try harder. The next time he called, he'd make sure he got the chance to talk to the girls *before* he talked to Val, and he'd send them some pictures of Jake and the new house. They adored his dog—hung all over him every time Grant had brought him to visit them. This is why he'd continued to bring Jake with him, despite the many comments and complaints his mother and sister had had.

"Evans."

The sound of Steve's voice broke through Grant's musings and Grant looked over at his partner in time to see that he had pulled off the street into the hospital parking lot.

"What?" Grant replied

"That was some trip you took. What's up?"

"Nothing. Nothing, just thinking about a phone call I got the other night from home. Nothing important."

Steve studied Grant's carefully blank expression and knew that there was more to the story than his friend was letting on, but with Mac in the car he didn't want to push the point.

"I was just telling Mac, here, that I saw this really nice sweater set at the mall he might like, that would go perfect with his fancy new scarf.

"Very funny, Sully. You're hilarious. You *know* my wife would have skinned me if I didn't wear it. And what the hell is a sweater set anyway?"

Grant had to laugh at Mac's disgusted tone of voice, and before Steve could needle Mac further Grant jumped in to say, "Well, Mac, since Steve seems to be spending his free time shopping at the mall, maybe he can explain what it is."

As Mac's deep, booming laugh filled the car Steve tried, and failed miserably, to glare angrily at Grant, but he couldn't manage it. Soon all three of them were laughing.

After Steve parked the car the three men got out and walked into the hospital. By the time they got to the Intensive Care waiting room they were composed again.

Grant automatically scanned the room as he walked through the doorway. He spotted several unfamiliar faces, but no Maggie. No Mr. Sanders. And, more importantly, no Jones.

Steve had come up behind him and had seen the same things. He hurried across the room and out into the hallway on the opposite side to reach Cloë's door. Just as he reached the closed door it opened and Jones came out, followed closely by a beaming Maggie.

"She woke up!" Maggie exclaimed, her eyes shining with unshed tears.

Grant and Steve stopped their rush and relaxed as Mac came up behind them.

"Is she talking," Steve asked, "Is she okay?"

Maggie answered Steve, but her eyes never left Grant's face as she said, "She woke up about ten minutes ago. She hasn't really said much, she just opened her eyes when I was in there and she only said 'tired' when I tried to talk to her. She fell back to sleep right away.

"The doctors came in when I buzzed the nurse and they told me that she is in a natural sleep now, and that her vitals are all much improved. They said they are cautiously optimistic that she'll make a full physical recovery. They're thinking she'll wake up fully this evening or by morning."

Grant noted the fact that the doctors had only said physical recovery, and he hoped for Cloë's—and Maggie's—sake, that she would recover mentally as well. With a head injury as severe as Cloë's had been, Grant knew that wasn't always the case. But as he looked down into Maggie's glowing face, he didn't have the heart to say anything that would steal that joy from her."That's great, Maggie," Steve said, but she never heard him, she was too busy looking at Grant.

Bemused, Steve turned to talk to Mac and Jones. "Anything else happening that I need to know about?"

"Nope. Up until a few minutes ago everything had been completely quiet. Mr. Sanders was here all morning and Maggie had just talked him into going down to grab something to eat. When she went in and found Cloë waking up, she called the doctors and then had one of the nurses try to page him to come back to the room. One of the doctors is still in with Cloë and I think that the other went to talk to the nurse about having someone go down to the cafeteria to get Mr. Sanders since he still hasn't returned."

"Okay. Donovan and Sylvester said they'd come in about four. Are you guys going to be okay here until them?"

"Sure," Jones smiled and Mac added, "Sure thing, Sully. Thanks for the ride."

"Not a problem. Mac can fill you in on what's going on with the case. That's one of the reasons we're here, we have to talk to Maggie about something that came up this morning."

As he was talking Mr. Sanders rushed up to the doorway and Steve broke off to watch as he paused to first talk to Maggie and then continue on into Cloë's room.

"All right, I'll let you guys get settled. I need to talk with Maggie."

"See you later, Steve," Jones said as Steve walked back over to where Maggie and Grant were now sitting.

Steve lowered down into a chair next to Maggie and rubbed his hand down her arm, "Do you two want to grab some lunch? We need to get some info from you Mags, and since we all need to eat, I thought we could do it together."

"Sure. I'm so relieved I may actually be able to eat something," Maggie beamed at both men.

FORTY-SEVEN

Tonight would be the night.

His beautiful, perfect Angel had betrayed him. He'd believed she was the One, better, more special than the rest of them, but she was nothing but a whore. No better than the rest of the Angels that had fallen before her.

She'd been different, always happy to see him, telling him in special little ways that she *knew* that they were destined to be together. Forever.

But now she'd ruined *everything*!

As his fury began to build he started to pace quickly back and forth along the side of the Art History building where he waited and watched. He was breathing heavily as he jammed his hands deep into his jacket pockets.

"Hey, Swanson, what's going on? Everything all right?"

He turned slowly, his right hand gripped desperately around the one thing that could calm him, and he was able to calm down enough to say, "Fine. Everything's fine, Professor. I was just waiting for my brother to get off of work to drive him home."

Holden nodded slowly and said uncertainly, "Well if you're sure you're okay…"

The killer ordered his body to relax and he smiled calmly, "I'm great. Just working out a few things in my head—I like to pace when I think, helps my thoughts to flow more freely, know what I mean?"

"Sure. Right," Holden said, relieved. When he'd first turned the corner and seen Swanson he could have sworn he'd seen rage on Swanson's face, but the minute he'd spoken all traces of anger had disappeared so completely, Holden knew he must have been mistaken.

"Well, I guess I'll see you tomorrow, then," Holden said as he turned to leave. Holden heard a rustle of movement behind him, but before he could turn, he felt a blinding flash of pain and the world went black.

The killer looked around quickly, then grabbed Holden's feet and dragged him over to a line of bushes. Then, as he looked down at the fallen man, considered for a moment, then lifted the large flashlight and struck once more.

After making sure the unconscious form couldn't be easily found he calmly turned and walked back to the building to wait for his brother, pausing only long enough to casually wipe the blood from the flashlight off on the grass.

He felt much better, but his Angel was still going to have to pay for disappointing him so badly. For whoring herself with that cop. He felt the rage begin to build again, but this time he envisioned how he would make her pay, make her repent.

And this time instead of pacing he smiled as he planned the night to come.

FORTY-EIGHT

Once they were settled with trays of food in front of them at a cafeteria table a small distance from the other diners Maggie broke the silence, "Okay, I know cop face when I see it. Spit it out, what's up?"

Grant glanced over at Steve, and then sighed. He'd half-hoped that Steve would start them off, but Grant knew that he was the one who would have to question Maggie.

"Well, you know that we were at the University to talk to the Dean and the rest of your department, right? A couple of things came up and we'd like to talk to you about them."

"Okay," Maggie said slowly, "What do you need to know?"

"All right," Grant shifted slightly in his chair, he knew that Maggie was *so* not going to like what he was about to say, but he also knew that he had to say it. "We talked to Holden. Is it usual for him to meet privately with female students off campus?"

Maggie's eyebrows drew down as she answered, "I guess. I've never really thought about it, but one of the things the students love most about Holden is that he's so accessible to them. He often meets students—males as well as females—at coffee shops, for dinner, even at his house from time to time.

"Why are you asking about that?" she added a little defensively.

Grant kept his eyes steady on hers as he replied, "We are just trying to find out everything we can about the people in Cloë's life right now. We also talked to Tony Malone and he mentioned that Cloë had had an incident with a guy late last week. Did you hear anything about that?"

Completely confused by the intense looks both men were aiming in her direction, Maggie replied, "No. I had no idea. What kind of incident? What day did it happen?"

"Thursday morning."

Maggie's face cleared as she thought. "Well, I had a meeting that morning with another department, so I was out of the office, but it's really strange that she didn't say anything about it to me. Or that Tony or Holden didn't say anything.

"Do you guys think this is the guy who hurt Cloë and those other women?"

Relieved at her obvious confusion and outrage Grant relaxed back into his chair and said, "Cloë never said anything because she didn't want to upset you."

"Well, sure I'd have wanted to tell the guy off for yelling at her, but it's not like I would have gone out of my way to track him down or anything."

"It was Brad."

When she didn't reply, only sat there looking confused, Grant continued, "Tony said Brad came in looking for you and he didn't believe her when she told him you weren't there. He got very upset and was really yelling at her until she finally had to threaten to call security to get him to leave."

"Bradley? But why didn't anyone tell me? That jerk!"

Seeing the anger light her eyes and hearing the indignation in her voice Grant had to fight back a small smile. He said, "Because they knew you'd react exactly like this, and they didn't want to upset you."

"I cannot *believe* that bastard would do that. I mean who does he think he is? I am going to go over there right now and…"

"Maggie," Grant grabbed her arm before she could storm off, "Maggie, we are going to talk to him, believe me, but I don't want you anywhere near this guy."

Maggie's eyebrows dropped again and she opened her mouth to tell him what she thought of him telling her she couldn't talk to the creep who'd possibly put her best friend in the hospital, but Steve broke in before she could say anything.

Steve knew Maggie, and he was sure if he could get her to look past her outrage and knee-jerk response to being told what to do, he could stop her. "Maggie, this guy is dangerous. He could be the guy we're looking for."

When she turned, ready to turn her anger on him, Steve held up one hand and continued, "And if it *is* him, you storming down there could tip him off that we suspect him. And whether he is or isn't the killer, he is clearly not the nice guy you believed him to be. Nothing good can come out of you going down there, baby. You need to stay away from him."

Softened by the rarely-used endearment she replied resignedly, the anger gone from her voice, "Still protecting me, Steven?"

She sank back down across from both men.

"Always," Steve answered cheerfully, knowing the crisis had passed.

Grant released her arm when she sat and instead he reached down to put his hand over the one she had placed on the table. He said softly, "We both just want you to be safe, Red."

Maggie glared over at him, but she turned her hand over to gently squeeze his and he threaded his fingers with hers.

"Okay, if you already knew who was yelling at her, why did you need to ask me?"

Grant wisely kept his mouth shut and let Steve reply.

"Because knowing you as well as we do, and caring about you as we do, we figured that, although unlikely, you *could* have known about the visit and just decided not to tell us interfering, pesky, pushy, overbearing men about it."

Maggie opened her mouth to deny it, but instead she closed her mouth and just smiled before she said, "We'll I'd like to say you're wrong, but I have to admit you're right…you guys *can* be pushy, overbearing, and what was the other one? Interfering, that's right."

Humor twinkled in Maggie's eyes for just a moment before she sobered again. "I'd like to believe that I wouldn't have kept something that important from you. Either of you," she added as she looked back and forth between two of the most important men in her life.

On the surface the men didn't look that much alike. Both men were over six feet tall, but Steve's frame was more bulky, brawnier, while Grant's was more streamlined, like a swimmer's—broad through the chest and shoulders and trim through the waist. Steve's hair and eyes were shades lighter than Grant's dark brown.

But as she studied them she also saw that they both wore the exact same expression—indulgent skepticism—along with just a touch of anger that she knew was directed at Bradley and not at her.

In the two months since Grant had moved to Hope, she had watched the two men grow closer and closer to each other. Perhaps because they recognized on some level that their characters, their morals and ideals, were so alike.

Both men lived by a code of honor that ensured that they would always help the helpless. Always stand between the innocent and the evil she'd recently discovered first-hand existed in the world with the sole purpose of harming those innocents. It was what made them good cops, relentless in their pursuit of the man who'd killed all those women and who'd hurt Cloë. People instinctively trusted them knowing, as she did, that they were good men.

It was also what made it so hard for them to deal with the fact that they hadn't yet caught him. And, she knew, it was what would not allow them to stop until they'd ended him.

But most importantly of all, it was a part of what made her love them.

Aloud she said, "At any rate, I didn't know. Now that I do, tell me what you are going to do about it, because I *know* that you are going to do something. Then, I'll decide if I can live without doing something myself."

Maggie watched as identical looks of frustration passed over both men's faces. This time it was Steve that spoke.

"Maggie, please be reasonable. This guy may be extremely dangerous."

"And even if he hasn't brutally murdered several women, he's still dangerous, Maggie," Grant broke in quietly before he let Steve continue.

"Grant and I are going to go speak with the guy and I think you should stay completely away from him. You've already filed a restraining order, so Grant and I will just make this visit an 'official' one and arrest the son-of-a-bitch."

"Steven…"

"Maggie, this guy had verbally threatened you on at least two separate occasions, he's shown a willingness to physically hurt you, and he is still showing up at your workplace and most likely your home. Telling him you don't want to see or speak with him is not working, obviously the restraining order did not bother him, so maybe a legal consequence will wake him up."

Maggie blew out a long breath and lifted both hands in a gesture of hopelessness before letting them drop into her lap. She said, "All right. You win."

"Good," Steve nodded once, then added, "We really need to get back to work, Mags. Are you going to be okay?"

"I'll be fine," Maggie watched as the two men stood to shrug into their coats before she added, "But, I want to hear about your meeting with Bradley tonight." Her tone of voice made it clear that she wouldn't let this one drop.

"We'll talk tonight" Grant answered noncommittally.

Maggie was unsatisfied, but she knew she would get no further with the men at this point. She also knew she'd have a better chance of learning more *later* if she appeared to be agreeable now. So she only smiled and said, "Okay. Be careful."

Steve leaned down and hugged Maggie. "Stay out of trouble, Mags."

"You, too."

Maggie turned to meet Grant's eyes and Steve made a quick about-face and started to walk to the cash register. "See you later, Detective," she said, the smile in her voice matching the one on her face.

Grant leaned down to place a soft kiss on her lips and said softly, "Don't forget, I'm making you dinner tonight."

Maggie lifted one eyebrow and grinned, "Still trying to protect me, Detective?"

Grant pressed another kiss on her laughing lips, only there was nothing soft or sweet about it. When he shifted back, his desire clear in his eyes, Maggie blew out the breath that had backed up in her throat and sighed. "What time?"

"I'll call you later in case I get hung up at some point and have to work late." He looked down into her face, beautiful despite being pale with the worry and fatigue of the past 48 hours, and into her eyes, still darkened by desire, and he felt a surge of love and protectiveness.

Suddenly urgent, he squatted down to say, "Promise me if you decide to leave the hospital that you'll go over to your parents or one of your brother's places."

Baffled, Maggie agreed, "Okay. But Grant, I can't do this forever."

Satisfied that she'd agreed for today, he stood up and said, "I know, Red. I'll call you later. Love you."

Maggie's smile turned dreamy and her heart leapt at the thrill of hearing the still-new words. "I love you, too," she said, her voice husky with emotion. Their eyes held for several moments, the air charged as the world around them receded.

"Yo, Evans, let's hit it," Steve called from across the room, causing several heads to turn, and in the spirit of small towns everywhere, thoughts and conversations turned to the new policeman who was dating the Sullivan girl.

As Grant walked up to him Steve said, exasperation clear in his voice, "Judist Priest, Evans, shake a leg." Secretly, Steve was thrilled. If he'd tried, he couldn't have handpicked anyone more perfect for his sister. But, that didn't mean he had to let *them* know that, so he added, "I could practically see little floating hearts above your head back there."

Unperturbed, Grant just smiled over at his partner, a gleam of malice in his eye, and said, "C'mon, Steve, let's go pay that asshole a visit."

"With pleasure," Steve said, all plans for needling Grant replaced with anticipation.

Several hours later, Grant was still savoring the look on Bradley Whiteside's face when he and Steve had left him, a quivering mass of fear and resentment hunched behind bars in the station's holding cell waiting to be bailed out. He'd started out belligerent, spouting his rights and talking big, but when Steve had produced Maggie's restraining order and begun to question him about the confrontation with Cloë, he'd paled and begun to cooperate. By the time they'd finished with him twenty-five minutes later, he'd been a different man—resentful and defensive, yes, but clearly shaken.

And handcuffing him and hauling him down to the station to be booked for violating his restraining order had been the icing on the cake. He'd be out in a matter of hours, but it was still personally satisfying to see him pale and shaken behind bars.

It was just too damn bad, Grant thought to himself as he typed up the arrest report and interview, that the bastard had an alibi for the night Cloë had been attacked, and one for at least two of the murders. They'd yet to be confirmed, but Grant had no doubt that they would be.

While despicable enough to push around a woman, and even to hit one when his pride had been bruised, Grant did not believe he had the sociopathic tendencies their serial killer displayed. He just didn't match the profile, which was really a damn shame.

He hadn't even gotten the chance to punch the weasel the way he'd wanted to. What little satisfaction he did have was that he and Steve had made it crystal clear that if he went anywhere near Maggie or Cloë, they would not hold back again.

He'd believed them. Of that Grant was very sure.

On the upside, at least with Whiteside off the suspect list, Grant could be relieved that Maggie was much safer and he could stop worrying as much about her.

As he saved his document and hit print, he heard Steve say, "All right, thank you for your help," before he hung up the phone.

"Whiteside's in the clear. That was the last name he gave us. All of his alibis check out."

"Back to the drawing board," Grant sighed.

"Not quite. Dusty told me they'd have a set of photos for us in the morning. They're more than halfway through the videos and they already have a couple possible matches for the guy in the cap. We can take them over to the University in the morning and see if we can get some kind of positive I.D. for them."

Steve paused to dig through the stack of papers that threatened to topple off the edge of his desk before he added, "And, we've got this." He held up a slim file. "Forensics gave me a report on those silver beads we found in the mud behind the Severson's house. They're sterling silver and they all have drill holes indicating they are most likely all from some piece of jewelry, or possibly a bookmark, though because of the size that's less likely."

When Steve stopped talking abruptly Grant stared over at Steve and said, "What is it?"

Steve was silent for several more moments before he replied to Grant, "There's *something* that I recognize about them, but I still can't remember what it is…..something I've seen before, when I was a kid…" He trailed off again thinking furiously before he shook his head again, clearly frustrated.

"It'll come to you," Grant said as he reached over to pick up the evidence bag with the three small beads in it. "Maybe you should show it to your mom."

Steve raised one eyebrow quizzically before saying doubtfully, "My mom?"

"Sure. If you're sure that you saw it when you were a kid, she's a logical choice to ask. She may remember what it was you saw—or she may own something that's similar to what you are remembering. Couldn't hurt anything, and it won't take up much time."

"I guess I could stop over later."

"Sure, otherwise we'll be seeing her tomorrow," Grant grinned as he pictured Maggie's face when he brought her over to her parent's house and she saw the curtain and everything set up the next day.

"True. All right, I'm going to head over to the hospital for a while, let Sylvester and Donovan get some dinner."

"You wouldn't be stopping in to see Cloë, would you?"

"Sure, I will stop in and see if Cloë is awake again and ready to speak with us yet," Steve added.

Grant eyed him speculatively, but seeing how Steve avoided looking at him he decided to let it go for now. He was all too familiar with the guilt his partner was feeling, the helplessness at not having been able to prevent someone you care about from getting hurt.

So, instead he said only, "Okay. I'll give Maggie a call and if she's still there I'll ride over with you and hitch a ride with her."

Steve agreed, once again relieved that Maggie had someone he trusted looking out for her. A quick call later and the men were on their way to the hospital. Cloë had still been asleep, but the doctors seemed satisfied that she continued to improve.

FORTY-NINE

As Grant and Steve had walked into the hospital to meet Maggie, the killer wove his way through the oncoming dusk to Maggie's block. Slowly, silently he worked his way through the neighbor's back yard until he was hidden in a small line of shrubs that bordered the two properties.

He waited for several minutes, watching for any signs that someone had come home early, or maybe home sick and peeking out the windows at him.

When he was completely confident that he wouldn't be seen he slithered through the shrubs and over to the window he'd been using for the past several weeks. He eased himself over the lip of the sill and confidently retrieved the copy of the apartment key he'd made while his Angel had slept.

He worked his way up to the second floor and let himself into her darkened apartment. Moving quickly, he slipped through the dimly lit living room and over to a window facing the street where he knew she usually parked.

He had no idea when she might return, so he hid his bag in the closet and settled in to wait. When he saw her car turn the corner and pull to a stop less than five minutes later he jerked back from the window, his heart racing.

It wouldn't do for his Angel to know that he was waiting for her. He sped across the room towards the closet, automatically reaching into his pocket to sooth himself.

Click, click, click.
Click, click, click.
Click, click, click.

As he pulled the object out, he never noticed when a single silver bead fell silently to the carpet next to the bed.

Calmed once more he eased back into the shadows of her closet to crouch unmoving to wait. He silently gripped the object in both hands, careful to make sure that it didn't move or make noise in the stillness of the apartment.

It took every ounce of his will to keep that calm as he waited the last few moments for her to walk through the door. To undress and ease into bed.

He could wait. He needed to wait if he were going to get away unseen one more time.

He was a god and death was his disciple. And tonight, his Angel would know it.

FIFTY

Less than half an hour after he'd left work Grant and Maggie were on their way home in Maggie's little car. Maggie glanced over and had to stifle a giggle when she saw that Grant was so tall that his head was brushing the ceiling of her small car.

He was so large he seemed to fill the entire car. In the dim intimacy of the small space the scent of his leather jacket mingled with the warm smell of aftershave and the musky scent that was all man surrounded her.

When she drew in a deep breath Grant glanced over, his dark eyes on hers, and she felt her stomach clench almost painfully with desire.

Grant stared into her eyes and his heartbeat began to speed up. Maybe the dinner he'd planned to make would have to be delayed a bit.

Maybe more than a bit.

He reached to brush a single finger along her lips and she was impossibly charmed, unbearably aroused.

Her lips parted in response and the air around them seemed to thicken, to soften. And the silence of the car was broken only by the sound of her ragged breathing.

"Maggie," Grant whispered only her name, but in that single word she heard the straining need and, more importantly, the gentle yearning in his voice that had her heart stopping and then speeding to a roar in her ears.

Maggie pulled to a stop in front of her apartment building, grateful to be off the road. "Let me just run up and get a few things," she said, her voice husky and her hand on the door handle.

Grant climbed out of the car to walk around the hood, his intense gaze never leaving her face. He stopped to reach down and pull her to her feet before he combed his fingers through her hair and crushed his mouth to hers. When she came up for air all thoughts of clean clothes and toothbrushes had fled. She shuddered once, then nodded and said, "I'll get them in the morning."

He grinned wickedly before he kissed her once, hard, then in a whirl he turned her and pulled her by the hand to race across the street. After he fumbled his key into the lock and they stumbled inside, their mouths fused together as hands scrambled to remove clothing.

Grant managed to kick the door closed before he fell back against it, dragging her up to her toes as he raced to touch her everywhere at once. When her fumbling fingers refused to open a button on his shirt she simply pulled until buttons popped and she could scrape both hands down his chest and across quivering abs and down to work the snap on his jeans loose.

He used his hands and teeth on her and when she stood before him in only two skimpy scraps of lace, he paused to look from her tousled hair and bruised lips, down her softly sloping shoulders and curved torso, to her long, lean legs.

He brushed a single fingertip down her neck to the warm vee between her breasts and said roughly, "God, you're perfect," before he ripped her bra away to take her into his hands.

Maggie's gasp of shock turned to a moan of pure pleasure when he lowered his head to take first one straining nipple, then the other into his mouth. She shuddered and her hands stopped moving, then fell limply to her sides as he slowly lowered her panties and she was standing before him, completely exposed. And then she was flying as he dug his fingers into her hips to lift her and press her back against the door.

Galvanized back into action she plunged her hands into his hair and wrapped her legs around him. Grant pulled her mouth back to his as he ran his hands down her sides to pull her closer, center to center. When she trembled against him he could hold back no longer and raising his head to stare into her eyes he sank slowly into her.

First one, then the other moaned as together they began to move. Maggie gripped his shoulders as he leaned into her, his right arm braced against the door next to her head. When neither could stand it any longer, what had begun slowly, tortuously, sped up until they were racing, racing to the edge and flying over together.

Grateful for the support of the door Grant collapsed against Maggie, pinning her against the smooth, cool wood. He was afraid to move, worried that if he did, they'd both fall down.

Maggie weakly lifted her head and pressed an absentminded kiss to the side of his neck before she let her head rest back against the door, enjoying the reassuring weight of Grant's body pressed against her, holding them both upright.

After several moments Grant shifted to brace one hand against the door and kept the other wrapped securely around her waist. He looked down into her upturned face and leaned down the last two inches to brush a kiss against her forehead, check, jaw and finally her bottom lip.

Maggie sighed deeply and said, "Well, that was interesting," in a husky voice that had Grant's stomach muscles tightening again in response.

She felt his chest vibrate as he chuckled weakly. He knew that he had to ignore his initial physical reaction if he was going to survive the night. So, he ignored his jumping stomach and said, "That was a bit more than just interesting, Red. More like mind-blowing."

"Well, either way I'm starving."

"Boy, talk about a one track mind," he teased. Then, in a quick move that had her squealing, he stood up straight and lifted her into his arms to begin to walk down the hall. "Come on, Scarlett; let's get you something to eat."

Maggie's laughter echoed down the hall. She tightened her grip around his neck and fluttered her eyelashes up at him and quipped, "My hero," in a southern accent.

"Wow, I think that's possibly the worst fake southern accent I've ever heard," Grant joked.

"Oh, yeah?" Maggie asked, her voice overly sweet as she slowly lowered her hand to tickle his ribs.

Grant jerked to the side almost dropping her and yelped, "Hey! Cut it out." Maggie laughed again, this time slipping down out of his arms to use both hands more creatively.

"Oh, do you really want to play it that way?"Grant asked, his face dangerous in the dark hallway.

Maggie laughed and, hunger forgotten, turned to run down the hallway—just slow enough to make sure Grant would catch her.

FIFTY-ONE

She never came.

His whole frame shook with his rage as he made his way back through her apartment, down into the basement and out into the utter darkness of the night.

He'd waited for more than six hours but she'd never come in.

Whore. Betrayer. Slut. Jezebel. He wanted to scream it to the whole world. But he'd managed to hold it in until he had driven several miles away from her apartment. As he'd left he'd noticed a single light burning in the small brick house across the street.

The small brick house where his Angel was screwing someone else.

His hands shook so badly he was forced to pull over because he could no longer control the truck. He pulled to a stop on the shoulder of the road just outside of town next to an empty field. The image of her whoring herself like a bitch in heat, rubbing herself all over that *man*, was unbearable—a physical pain.

For several minutes he lost himself in the rage and when he came to he found himself laying on the ground covered in filth from the dirt he'd clawed up and dug into—first with his knife, and then with his bare hands.

He scrambled unsteadily to his feet and weaved his way back to the truck. And, though his body was exhausted, his mind raced and calculated.

His Angel was lost.

For a single moment he sank to his knees, weeping with despair, his dirt-caked hands covered his face before tearing at his hair, the pain of the violent movement clearing away the last dregs of anguish, leaving behind only the rage.

The ugly feeling spread and grew through his mind like a malignancy until his brain was focused only on the preparation he needed to do before he could properly deal with his misguided little Angel.

If he hurried he could be ready by the next day.

He was done waiting for his Angel to come to him. It was time for her to pay for her sins and only he could save her now.

373

Tomorrow he would make sure they were finally alone together—for the first time.

And the last.

FIFTY-TWO

It had been after three before they'd stumbled half-naked into his seldom-used kitchen to devour leftover pizza cold from his fridge while still standing up.

"Well, it's not exactly the nice dinner I'd planned on making for you…," Grant began but Maggie interrupted as she bit into her second piece of pizza, "S'good," she chewed and swallowed before she grinned wickedly and added, "Besides, you can cook for me tomorrow night instead."

Grant looked over to where she leaned back against a counter dressed in one of his old shirts, munching contentedly on a cold piece of day-old pizza and drinking a glass of warm wine he'd neglected to chill for their dinner earlier.

Even with her hair a mess and the huge shirt that she was drowning in, she looked beautiful. He felt the joy that had been missing in his life and he knew that the future that had seemed so lost, so bleak the past couple of years was standing right in front of him.

If he was lucky enough, and brave enough, he could reach out and grab hold of that future, and the promise it held. And if he were smart enough he'd never let it go.

He could look one or five, or even twenty, years down the line and he could see them just like this. Stealing down to the kitchen in the middle of the night to sneak food and talk and make love for the rest of their lives.

And as he opened his mouth to ask her, to tell her, the memory of her distraught face as she stood next to Cloë's hospital bedside made him pause and consider. Even though Cloë had woken up she was still not out of the woods, and he knew Maggie was still worried about her.

Maggie watched Grant as he leaned against a counter across from her, his legs crossed in front of him clad only in an old pair of baggy sweatpants that were slung low on his hips. He seemed perfectly at ease, but she knew him well enough to know that his mind was working overtime.

She set down the crust of her third piece of pizza and sighed, sated and sleepy after hours of lovemaking interspersed with breaks where they slept and played and talked together. She lifted one hand to brush her hair out of her face and winced inwardly at the thought of how she must look, then shrugged philosophically. He'd seen it all by now, and if he hadn't run screaming in fear already, he wouldn't do so over some bad bed-hair.

After several minutes of silence she crossed her arms, raised one eyebrow and said, "What's up, Detective? You falling asleep over there?"

"Hmmm? What? No, no. I was just thinking."

"Musta been something pretty deep. What's got you so distracted?"

Grant looked at her for several moments, his eyes inscrutable before he said simply, "I love you, Maggie."

Maggie flushed with pleasure, her heart speeding, and she said softly, "I love you, too, Grant," then she walked across the room to slide her hands around his waist and lay her head against his bare shoulder, "I love you, too."

"We better get some sleep if I'm going to be able to function at all tomorrow. Come to bed with me, Maggie."

Maggie grinned wickedly and teased, "I'll come to bed with you, but I can't promise to let you sleep."

Grant grabbed her wandering hands and said, "Judist Priest, woman, have some mercy."

"Poor Detective Evans, did I wear you out?" she asked in a mock-concerned voice.

"Smart ass."

Maggie laughed, unable to hold back any longer, and said, "Okay, Detective, I'll give you at least three hours of sleep, but that's all I can offer." She smiled as she remembered that she'd told Holden she wouldn't be in to work the next day and hospital visiting hours didn't start until ten, so she could sleep in as late as she liked.

"I wouldn't be so smug if I were you, Red. You're getting up and coming running with me in exactly two hours and forty-two minutes."

Maggie's smile slipped and she pouted just a little, "There's no way I'm getting up at six in the morning on my day off, Evans."

Grant ran his hands up and down her arms and smirked just a little too broadly, "Poor baby," he echoed her earlier sentiment, "Look at that pout. I like it."

"I don't pout," she said, her voice stiff with righteous indignation.

Grant had to bite his cheek and he managed to stop smiling long enough to say, "Course you don't. Now, come to bed, Red, we need to get to sleep."

"Fine, fine. But there's no way you're getting me out of that bed before nine, Mister."

Grant just nodded and led her back through the dining room where Jake slept and down the hall to his room. He pushed her down onto the bed and shrugged out of his sweat pants before he slid in next to her and wrapped her in his arms.

Maggie sighed deeply and snuggled into his neck to lay one last kiss against his throat. Within moments she was sound asleep.

As he drifted off he thought that he was right to wait to bring up the future. They had plenty of time—the rest of their lives—for him to tell her how he felt about her.

Tomorrow would be soon enough.

FIFTY-THREE

He'd let her sleep until 6:30 and then dragged her out to run five miles in frigid October morning air that had her wide awake and cursing him when she pictured the warm bed they'd left behind.

The bastard had only laughed at her and insulted her until she'd begun running.

And when they'd finished she'd stalked off to take a long hot shower. Five minutes into it he'd slipped in behind her, claiming he was running late and needed to save time, and had proceeded to melt every bone in her body by taking her against the shower wall as the hot water beat down on them both.

The few aches from their night of lovemaking that were still left after their run were soon gone after the session in the shower. And by the time he dropped her off at the hospital she'd been completely relaxed, feeling thoroughly used and pleasantly tired.

She knew she should be completely exhausted, and she suspected she'd crash later, but for now she felt wonderful.

Sneaky bastard.

She'd planned on being seriously annoyed with him for that little running thing for *at least* an hour or two—maybe even three—but instead all she could feel was deliriously happy. God, he made her happy. She'd never experienced anything like it before. The closest she'd ever come was watching her parents, and maybe her brother Seth with Sybil.

Fears and doubts aside, there was no way she could deny any longer that she'd found the one man she was meant to spend the rest of her life with.

For just one heart-stopping moment last night she'd believed he was going to ask her to marry him. When he hadn't, the disappointment had been so sharp she could no longer pretend, even to herself, that her feelings for him could someday fade away.

She no longer wanted to.

She'd been far too tired to think about the consequences of those revelations last night, but as she sat and sipped coffee in a chair next to Cloë's hospital bed, looking at her friend's badly bruised face now turning sickly shades of green and yellow, she knew that life was too short to be wasted on fear.

And although she wanted to run right to Grant and tell him how she felt, she suppressed the need. She could wait for him.

Now that she'd found him, there was no way she was going to let him go. He would just have to accept the inevitable—he was stuck with her.

FIFTY-FOUR

When Grant walked into the station he was met with a flurry of noise and excitement. He quickly made his way over to where Steve talked on the phone. He waited until Steve hung up and then Grant said, "What's going on?"

"I was just going to try calling you again. We got the Son-of-a-Bitch!" Steve slapped a grainy 8 x 10 picture down onto the desk in front of Grant, a look of triumph on his face.

"Dusty worked all night. Went over every angle and shot of those video tapes and he eliminated all the suspects except the guy with the cap. He searched all the tapes from the surrounding buildings and managed to find this view," Steve stabbed a finger down onto the image and Grant leaned closer to get a better look.

"The lab guys enhanced the image as best they could and there he is. Dusty was so excited he woke me up at quarter to six this morning and pulled me in."

"Why didn't you call me?" Grant asked as he stood back up to look at his partner.

"I did, but by the time I did you must have been out on your run, so I figured you'd be in soon enough anyway. I called the coffee shop clerk, Caroline Jennings, and she'll be at home for the next hour and a half. She's agreed to take a look at the picture to see if she remembers seeing him."

"Well, let's get going then," Grant turned to where Dusty leaned wearily against Steve's desk, a big smile on his face, and said, "Good job, Dusty." Steve shrugged into his jacket and retrieved the photograph from Grant's desk to slide it into a file folder.

"Go home and get some rest, Dusty. You've earned it. Let Becky tuck you in," Steve added lightly, a smirk on his face. Dusty's face turned a bright red and he shook his head wearily.

Grant turned away quickly to hide his grin, and he and Steve started to walk through the bustling squad room towards the door.

Grant followed Steve up the leaf-strewn sidewalk of a rambling, blue two-story house badly in need of a paint job. Steve knocked briskly on a door hung with a cheerily smiling skeleton and flanked by two carved Jack-O-Lanterns.

A woman as round and merry as the two pumpkins answered the door dressed in bright orange and black. Her smile turned quizzical as she asked, "Can I help you?"

"Yes, Ma'am. I'm Detective Sullivan and this is Detective Evans, I called earlier? Is Caroline available?" Steve extended his badge towards the woman.

She gestured the men inside and said, "Yes, of course, Detective. Come right in and I'll get Caro. Just come right in here and have a seat, I'll just be a moment."

"I'm here, Mom," Caroline Jennings walked into the living room, a slim girl of nineteen or twenty dressed in snug jeans and a black sweater. Her long dark hair was pulled up into a sleek ponytail that swung back and forth as she walked over to where they stood with her mother.

"Hi, I'm Caroline and this is my mother, Diane," she said as she extended a hand to shake first Steve's, then Grant's hands.

As they all sat down Grant noted that despite how different their appearance seemed to be both women looked over at them with the same intelligent blue eyes.

"Thanks so much for agreeing to help us out, Ms. Jennings," Steve pulled the photograph out of his folder and handed it over to Caroline. She studied the picture for several moments before she handed it back to Steve and folded her hands in front of her.

"I don't really remember much about the day you asked me about, and I can't say for sure who this is. But, I think that's Mo. Moses Swanson. He comes in almost every morning and orders the same thing. He usually wears a hat and jacket that looks just like these. The picture's a bit grainy so I can't be completely positive, but it sure looks like him to me."

Grant and Steve exchanged a look and then Steve turned back to face the two women. "Thank you Ms. Jennings. You have been extremely helpful. I have to ask both of you to not tell anyone else about our visit today, or it could seriously compromise the case we're working on."

"Of course," Caroline said.

Before they were halfway to the car Steve pulled out his phone to call in the positive identification to the Chief and to call for backup when they went to the Swanson residence.

FIFTY-FIVE

Cloë slowly opened her eyes to see Maggie sitting in a chair next to her staring off into space, a dreamy smile on her face. Cloë studied her friend closely. She noted the dark circles under Maggie's eyes and the weary set of her shoulders, and Cloë wondered just how many hours Maggie had sat in the chair next to her bed.

"Maggie?"

Maggie jerked upright, a radiant smile on her face, "You're awake! How are you feeling? Can I get you anything?"

Cloë smiled slightly, her eyes confused, but alert, and said, "Head hurts, achy. Where am I?"

"Grant and Steve found you unconscious in your apartment. You're in the hospital and you've been out of it for three days now. Can you remember anything about what happened?"

Cloë thought for a moment then shook her head once before she stopped and groaned. "Nothing. Last thing was talking to you at your parents' house. Hurts."

"I know, Sweetie. I'll get the nurse and they can help you," Maggie gently squeezed Cloë's hand and she pushed the call button for the nurse.

Cloë closed her eyes but she opened them again as soon as a nurse bustled through the door, her broad, flushed face breaking into a huge smile when she spotted Cloë awake. "Hello there, Deary. I'm Mrs. Fogarty and it's happy I am to see you awake. And how are you feeling this morning, then?"

The nurse stepped nimbly around the bed, and ignoring the many machines and their bright readouts set her fingers gently against Cloë's wrist and took her pulse. Her gunmetal gray hair was pulled ruthlessly back from her round face, leaving her twinkling green eyes unframed.

Maggie was strongly reminded of her Great-Aunt Margaret, whom she was named after, because Nurse Fogarty smelled of baby powder and peppermint and spoke with an Irish accent.

"Well then, that's all right; a bit elevated, but that's to be expected, now, isn't it? Let's just call the doctor and have him check you out now that you're awake. I can see you're aching and hurtin' a bit, Deary, so I'll be sure to have him let me bring you some of the good medicine, too. All right then, I'll be back in a jiffy. You just rest a bit and we'll set you to rights again before you know it."

Nurse Fogarty bustled around the room patting and adjusting as she went, her voice full of cheer as she steadily and efficiently took full measure of Cloë—and never once stopped to let Cloë answer the questions she asked before she whirled out of the room as quickly as she'd come in.

Left slightly breathless, Maggie sat back and looked over into Cloë's laughing eyes and burst out into a fit of uncontrollable giggles that she tried to cover with her hand.

Cloë half-laughed, half-groaned and whispered, "Stop making me laugh. You're going to make my head fall off."

"Might be an improvement."

Maggie's head whipped towards the open door where her brother, Jack, stood grinning, two steaming coffees in his hands.

"Holy crap, Jack! You scared me to death," Maggie exclaimed as he walked over to sit down next to her chair. He handed her one of the coffees as she continued, "Not that I'm not happy to see you, but what are you doing here?"

Jack leaned down to brush a quick kiss on Cloë's cheek before he answered, "I'm checking on Cloë, here, making sure her hard head didn't get too dented," Jack gently squeezed Cloë's hand before he turned back to Maggie, "And, I was looking for you, too. Mom needs you to come over tonight to help with handing out the candy to all the munchkins. She said it's your fault that so many kids come to her house every year and just because you cancelled the show doesn't mean that you get out of handing candy out."

"What do you mean, the show's cancelled?" Cloë broke in, her eyes moving back and forth between the siblings' faces.

Maggie sighed and said, "I cancelled the show. I was too worried about you and I'm down a dancer, so I'll just do it next year—no biggie."

"You should do it anyway. Get someone to fill in," Cloë argued, a little breathlessly.

"I'll take care of it, Cloë. Don't get yourself all worked up," Maggie patted Cloë's arm and glared over at Jack.

Jack managed to look contrite until Maggie turned back to Cloë, then he grinned and winked at Cloë as he said, "I'm *sure* we can work *something* out."

Maggie had heard that mischievous tone of voice too many times to not be instantly suspicious, but when she turned to say something to Jack his face was completely sincere and he had a look of such obvious regret on his face she reconsidered.

She was just opening her mouth to tell him there was nothing to work out when the doctor and Nurse Fogarty came back into the room and all thought of Jack and the many possible schemes he was probably working on flew out of her mind.

Cloë relaxed back against her pillows, confident that Jack had the situation well under control, and turned her attention to the doctor's questions. She would get Jack alone later and make him spill.

"We'll wait outside," Maggie stood and followed Jack out into the waiting room to give the doctor the room he needed to take a better look at Cloë.

"I need to call Mr. S and Grant and Steven to let them know Cloë woke up. Can you tell Mom and Dad?"

Sure. I'll call Seth and Dillon, too."

"Thanks, Jack. And you can let Mom know that Grant and I will both come over to help out tonight, so she doesn't have to worry about it."

Jack smiled and said, "Good. She'll be relieved." *Mission accomplished.* He'd promised Grant he would get her over to the house and Grant had promised to get into Maggie's apartment to pick up her costume and the music at some point before tonight. He and Dillon had already gotten theirs, and of course Grant had pilfered Cloë's outfit and gotten it to Sybil the day before. So, all they needed was Maggie's.

Out loud he said, "Does Grant know he's been volunteered to help hand candy out to several hundred kids?"

Maggie grinned wickedly and replied, "No. But he doesn't want me going anywhere without him or someone else with an abundance of testosterone, so he'll drive me over. I'll tell him that I volunteered him to help...*after* we get there."

She laughed picturing his face and Jack joined in, knowing it was Maggie who was in for the surprise, not Grant. "All right, Mags, I'll let the family know the good news about Cloë. You better call Mr. S. Why isn't he here, anyway?"

"He had an appointment with the hospital social worker, but he'll be here in a few minutes, I think. I'll call his cell phone, just in case."

Jack gave her a hug and said, "See you later, Mags."

"Bye, Jack. And thanks for the coffee."

Jack waved and left as Maggie quickly walked over to the guest phone to dial Mr. S.'s phone, and then Steven's. While she was at it, she'd call Holden and Tony, too. She knew they were really worried.

She got a hold of an ecstatic Mr. Sanders and a surprisingly restrained Steven, but she wasn't able to get to either Holden or Tony—which was strange. They both had cell phones, and she knew they almost always picked up when she called. Holden must be in a meeting or running late this morning.

As for Tony, who knew lately? Maggie shrugged philosophically. Oh, well, they'd get her messages soon enough.

FIFTY-SIX

Tony stood outside the art history building, his phone ringing, unheard, in his jacket pocket. He watched as paramedics lifted Holden's limp body onto a waiting stretcher. Horrified by the sight of his boss's seemingly lifeless body covered in blood Tony didn't hear the detective speaking to him for several moments.

"Mr. Malone," Detective Donovan glanced over to meet Sylvester's eyes and tried again more loudly, "Tony."

Tony turned to focus on the two mismatched men who stood in front of him. "Sorry. What?"

"Mr. Malone I'm Detective Mike Donovan and this is my partner Detective Sylvester. Can you tell me about what happened here this morning?"

Tony rubbed one shaking hand down his face and said, "Sorry. Yeah. Um, I got here about a quarter to eight like I always do and I saw a group of kids over next to the bushes," he pointed vaguely to where several crime scene techs were cordoning off a section of bushes and grounds.

Nervously Tony rubbed both sweaty hands on his pant legs before he continued, "Um, I went over and these two guys were totally freaking out and saying that they'd found a dead guy. They had already called 911, but that girl," he pointed to a short blonde dressed in jeans and a hooded sweatshirt speaking with a sharp-looking redhead as he said, "She told us to all get back from the body and wait for the cops and we could hear the sirens already so we all figured she was right."

"Did anyone touch the Professor?"

Tony shrugged and shook his head as he said, "The girl, Lindsey? She made everyone stay back. She kinda went around back and reached in to feel for a pulse, but other than that I didn't see anyone else go near him. It wasn't until the paramedic guys got here and moved him out of the bushes that I saw the blazer and figure out that it was Professor Holden."

Tony's voice cracked and he said, "First Cloë and now Professor Holden…"

"Mr. Malone," Donovan reclaimed Tony's attention, "Do you know how late Professor St. John was here until last night?"

"Um, well he was still here when I left about 5:30, but that's pretty normal for him. He usually has office hours from 3-6 on Thursdays and then he either heads home or over to the Union."

"Why the Union?"

"He sits and grades papers and talks with anyone who has questions about their homework or class. All the students love him because he goes out of his way to make sure that everyone who tries hard in his classes can pass. It's one of the reasons I tried so hard to get an internship and TA position with him."

"Did you see anyone or anything out of the ordinary when you left here last night?"

Tony considered for a moment before he shook his head. "Not really. There weren't too many people around because it was getting kinda dark and it was pretty cold last night. Just a couple of students across the parking lot and a few people that work here."

"Do you remember the employees?"

"Sure. Professor Richards was getting into her car and I saw Mo Swanson talking to the parking attendant guy before he headed into the building."

"Anyone else?"

"I can't think of anyone else I recognized. Like I said, it was getting dark and I wasn't really paying that much attention. I just wanted to get to my car and warm up."

"Okay. If you think of anything else, no matter how small, give us a call, all right?" Donovan held out a business card and Tony stuffed it into his jacket pocket.

"Sure, Man. Okay. Can I go now? I need to track down Maggie and let her know..."

When the detective nodded Tony wandered away towards the art history building to call the Dean and Maggie.

"Strange guy," Sylvester grunted out as he and Donovan turned to walk over to the cordoned off area.

"Yeah, but helpful enough. What do you have?"

Sylvester glanced down at his note pad and reeled off what he'd learned so far. "A student, the aforementioned Lindsey O'Grady, found the Professor at about 7:40 a.m. Said she noticed a metallic flash in the bushes and went over to investigate. She saw the body and says she ascertained that it had been shoved or kicked into the bushes to hide it."

"Let me guess," Donovan broke in with a smirk on his face, "She study law enforcement?"

"Bingo. She dialed 911 at 7:41 and the first black and white got here at 7:47, right after the paramedics did. They pulled the body out, but not before our aspiring Nancy Drew took several pictures with her camera phone of the body in the position she found it in. She was also smart enough to not trample the crime scene and kept all but the paramedics from getting too close to the body. She went all the way around to the other side of the bushes to take his pulse and it was a miracle he had one.

"Looks like he was hit over the head with a blunt object, and as Detective O'Grady guessed, shoved or kicked under the bushes presumably to try to keep the professor from being found too quickly.

"Ground froze up hard a couple nights ago, so there's not much in the way of footprints or impressions. We can try the surveillance cameras in the area, but they are most likely all pointed at the car lots or the building entrances."

Sylvester closed his notebook and slapped it against his thigh and Donovan said, "All right. Let's get the rest of the witnesses interviewed. Forensics should be done in an hour or so. In the meantime, I think we better brief the Chief and fill in Sully and Evans."

"Agreed."

"I'll fill Jones in and she can talk to the campus security guys about the videos."

"I'll call the guys."

While Donovan and Sylvester stood talking to Tony, Grant and Steve headed back to the station to fill the Chief in, and to request the warrants they'd need to search the Swanson residence.

As they drove, Grant's phone rang and he opened it, "Evans. Where? Is he still alive? Okay. Yeah. Any witnesses? Swanson? We're on our way back to the station now. We got a hit on the surveillance photo that Dusty found. The café worker thinks it's Mo Swanson. Yeah, sure. Okay. I'll see you at the station. Later."

Grant closed his phone with a snap and Steve said, "Who's dead?"

"No one. Yet. Professor St. John was attacked and left for dead last night or early this morning on campus. They're not sure yet if he'll live. Jones, Sylvester and Donavan are interviewing the kids who found his body, and of course, Tony Malone. I'm sure they'll be talking to Maggie, too."

Steve nodded once and asked, "Did anyone see anything?"

"Not really, but apparently when Malone left work last night just before St. John usually leaves he spotted Swanson near where the professor was found."

"Call the Chief and make sure that Swanson's truck is included on the search warrant."

Grant was already dialing by the time Steve stopped talking. When they got back to the station they found the Chief waiting for them, warrant in hand.

"Here's the warrant, it includes his workplace, residence and any outbuildings on said residence, and any vehicles he drives regularly."

"Thanks, Chief," Steve said.

"Are you guys sure this is the guy?"

"Sure? Not completely, but enough to get the warrant and bring him in for questioning."

Banyon stared at the floor for several moments. Grant braced himself for an argument, but before he could say anything Banyon looked up again and said, "All right then. Are you going over to the University first?"

"Yeah. We figured Swanson would be at work by now, and we can take a look through his on-campus locker and work areas and pick him up before we head over to the residence. Hopefully Sylvester and Donovan will be done with their crime scene and able to come with us when we head there."

"All right. Keep me briefed."

"Will do, Chief."

FIFTY-SEVEN

By the time Maggie was allowed back in to see Cloë she was fast asleep again, so Maggie settled in to read the romance paperback she always kept in her bag. She was still reading an hour later when Dusty poked his head through the door.

"Hey Maggie, how's she doing?"

Maggie set aside her book, a huge smile on her face as she softly answered, "Much better. She's sleeping again, but this morning she was awake and talking."

"That's great," Dusty said, sincere relief in his voice. "Maggie can you come out for a couple of minutes? I need to talk to you and I don't want to wake up Cloë."

Concerned by the obvious nervousness on Dusty's face Maggie nodded and quickly followed him into the deserted waiting room and over to a pair of couches that sat facing each other. They sat down and Maggie clenched her hands together when Dusty stared at the floor instead of looking at her.

"Is everything okay, Dusty? Are Steven and Grant all right?"

Hearing the panic in her voice Dusty quickly looked up and raised one hand, "They're fine, Maggie, I just got off the phone with them and they're both fine."

Maggie slumped back into the faded cushions and closed her eyes as the fear drained away.

"Has anyone from the University called you this morning?"

Maggie opened her eyes to fix them back on Dusty's face as she answered, "The University? No. I have the day off. If anything really important came up Holden would take care of it. What is it? What's going on? Are Holden and Tony okay?"

Dusty sighed and said, "Tony's fine, but Holden was attacked last night outside the Art History building."

"Is he…" Maggie couldn't make the rest of the words come out and Dusty swiftly jumped in.

"He's alive. Barely. The paramedics picked him up about an hour and a half ago and brought him here."

"I need to go see him," Maggie said as she leapt to her feet. Dusty stood and reached out to grab hold of her arm.

"Maggie, wait. He's in surgery right now in critical condition. I just got done talking to the nurse. He'll be in the O.R. for at least another hour, maybe longer." Dusty gently steered Maggie back down onto the couch and sat next to her this time with his arm around her shoulders supporting her.

Quietly he continued, "Maggie, he's probably not going to make it. Someone caved in his skull and then left him for dead underneath some bushes. He wasn't found for several hours, and with the weather we had last night," he paused to shake his head before he continued, "It's a miracle he made it at all. Even if he wakes up, the doctors aren't sure if there will be any lasting damage. The silver lining is that the freezing temperatures and hypothermia can work to stop brain damage."

Dusty waited as Maggie processed all that he'd said before he continued gently, "Do you think you could talk? Maybe answer a couple questions?"

Maggie forced herself to nod and push past the grief that was fighting to close her throat to choke out a reply, "Okay."

"Okay. Can you tell me when you saw or talked to Holden last?"

Maggie nodded again and gripped both of her arms tightly, as if to physically hold herself together as she answered in a low voice, "I saw Holden yesterday morning. I worked for just a couple of hours and left early to come here to be with Cloë…"

Maggie trailed off into silence for several moments before she continued, "Holden always understands if I need to go to an appointment or work from home. He was just as worried about Cloë as I was, so he was happy to let me leave as long as I called him with updates."

"And did you?"

Maggie nodded and said, "I called him three times. Once when I first got to the hospital to give him an update. The second time was probably about two in the afternoon. I called to tell him Cloë had woken up briefly. And I called him the last time at about 6:15. I knew he'd be done with his office hours and wanted to catch him before he left for the day. He was just finishing up an article for an art history periodical he occasionally wrote for and he told me he was looking forward to going home and getting to bed early because he had big plans for today."

"Do you know why he had to be up so early?"

Maggie shook her head and smiled sadly. "Not exactly, but every year on Halloween I take the day off and for the past several years, he has tried to surprise me. Last year he sent me a hundred black and orange balloons. Two years ago he hired a couple of high school kids to help him T.P. my apartment's yard.

"It was always something silly and fun. With everything that had happened with Cloë I had completely forgotten it, but after that last call, I figured that he was going to do something after all. He's been teasing me and hinting about doing something big this year, but I guess he never got a chance to do it, because nothing's happened today."

Maggie paused and glanced over at Dusty before she added hastily, "Well, actually, I'm not really sure. I wasn't home last night."

When Dusty didn't say anything, just sat and waited for her to continue, a look of sympathy on his plain, lovable face, she relaxed again and said, "There wasn't anything on my car or outside my place anyway."

Dusty said, "All right," as his mind raced. It looked to him like the Professor had never left campus the night before. "All right, can you tell me anything about what the Professor was working on? Did he have any recent problems with students or the staff?"

"None. Holden gets along with everyone on the staff and his students adore him. The only thing that I can even think of is that we had to tell Tony that we weren't going to be able to have him back again next year because of budget cuts."

"And how did Tony handle that?"

"Well, Tony was upset to begin with, but he understood that our hands were tied. I know him and he'd *never* hurt Holden—he revered him."

Dusty squeezed Maggie's shoulders once as he said, "Okay, okay. Do you know if the Professor was seeing anyone in particular?"

Maggie shook her head and said, "No. He spent almost all of his free time with his students or with a few of the other professors.

I think they had a weekly poker game, but I'm not completely sure. I can give you a couple of names of the professors he hung out with."

"Thanks, Maggie. And thanks for talking to me. I know it's been a hard week for you. If you can think of anything else, don't hesitate to call me. And if you need anything, anything at all, just call, okay?"

Maggie's eyes filled at the compassion she heard in Dusty's voice and she leaned over to give him a hug, "You're a good man, Dusty, and Becky is lucky to have you."

Dusty's face flushed and he cleared his voice before he gave her one last squeeze and stood to go. "Bye, Maggie."

Maggie stood, a small smile on her face, and she said, "Bye, Dusty." She watched the flustered officer leave before she hurried back into Cloë's room to dig her cell phone out of her bag to see why Tony hadn't called her.

When she saw that she'd forgotten to turn it on that morning she said, "Crap!" and quickly turned it on.

She had five messages.

"Everything all right?" Mr. Sanders asked from his chair next to Cloë's bed.

"Sure, Mr. S. Everything's fine. I just need to return a few calls. I'll be back in a bit."

Maggie eased out of the quiet room to listen to her messages. When she did she found three messages from a frantic Tony, one message from the Dean and one from her mother. Ignoring all of them she swiftly dialed Grant's number, then Steven's. When they went directly to voicemail she left messages on both.

As she closed her phone with a snap she thought furiously for several moments before she sighed and squared her shoulders. She'd have to call the Dean and Tony back, but first she needed to go downstairs to the emergency room and see what she could find out about Holden.

FIFTY-EIGHT

Mo hadn't been at work.

After spending more than two fruitless hours combing all the areas of the campus where Mo Swanson regularly worked and meeting up with Donovan and Sylvester, Grant and Steve headed to the Swanson residence, warrants in hand.

According to the schedule the Dean had given them, he wasn't due to come in to work until late afternoon most days. Which made sense, Grant thought, if he needed to clean up after most of the students and staff had left for the day.

If they were lucky, they'd be able to catch him still at home.

And since the forensics team had completed processing the campus crime scene they would be able to come with.

Jones had returned to the station to fill the Chief in and then was planning on heading over to the hospital to meet up with Mac. And, as an added bonus, Grant thought, be on hand to keep an eye on both Cloë *and* Maggie.

Steve pulled to a stop behind two black-and-whites parked in front of the Swanson's house, closely followed by the car holding Detectives Donovan and Sylvester.

As Grant and Steve got out of their car a young blonde officer walked out the front door and walked down the front walk to meet them, saying, "Hey, Sully"

"Hi Sean. Grant, do you know Sean Williams?"

Grant nodded and shook Williams' hand, "Sure."

"Right, then. What have we got?" Steve asked as all three men, followed by Donovan and Sylvester, made their way back up the walk to the front door.

"Like I told you on the phone, we found some pretty strange stuff inside. The mother is upstairs and appears to be ill and bedridden. She's furious that we are searching the house. Younger brother's at work."

"And Mo?"

"Not here. The mother doesn't know where he is—she was asleep when he left—but I don't think she would tell us even if she did know where he is."

"Okay, show us what you found."

395

"We're going to take a look out back," Sylvester said, and he and Donovan split off to walk around the outside of the house to the back yard.

Meanwhile, Steve and Grant followed Williams through the front door of what looked like a normal suburban house on the outside. Both men stopped short when they stepped over the threshold.

The small entryway opened to a hallway that led to a kitchen. A steep staircase was directly in front of them, and to either side there were small rooms. A cramped dining room completely filled with a large dining set on the left and an equally cramped living room to the right.

The living room was filled with an overstuffed coach, two arm chairs, a coffee table and several side tables that had all clearly seen better days. At first glance Grant could see that the house was extremely clean—every surface gleamed as if just polished.

But the astonishing thing was not that the house was so clean, but that every available surface, every spare inch of wall space, was covered with statues and pictures.

The men walked further into the hall and Grant noted with amazement that instead of the usual family photographs and artwork that each picture depicted the image of the Virgin Mary, as did all the statues and sculptures around the rooms.

"What the…" Grant muttered as he made his way into the living room to peer closely at a shelf filled, not with books, but with statuettes and icons of Mary. He slowly turned around the room, a feeling of unease settling into his gut.

"Sully, in here," Williams called from the hallway.

Grant turned to see that Steve had followed him into the room and was staring, eyebrows raised, at a life-size carving of the Blessed Mother standing in the corner of the room, arms outstretched.

Wordlessly the men's eyes met and together they turned to go back to the hallway where Williams waited.

When he stepped out into the hall, Grant saw that Williams had opened a door to a room, a closet, really, that Grant hadn't noticed when he'd first come in.

'Oh, my God," Steve whispered hoarsely.

What Grant saw when he rounded the door and looked over Steve's rigid shoulder made Grant's blood run cold.

Pictures of Maggie covered every inch of the walls.

Grant's eyes swept from image to image, the sick feeling in his stomach twisting and growing until he felt physically ill. The photographs had captured her face from every angle, from very far away to so close up that Grant felt his alarm increase even further.

"The bastard's been watching her for *months*," Steve's grim voice broke through Grant's horror and Grant turned to see Steve point a hand that shook slightly at a picture of Maggie dressed in shorts and a T-shirt playing softball. "This was the 4th of July barbeque at my parents' place."

"There was a padlock on the door when we got here. The mother said she didn't have the key—said her son was a photographer and used it as a dark room," Williams pointed to the small utility sink in the back corner of the room that had a shelf with a row of dust-coated bottles of developing chemicals on it.

Next to the sink was a desk with a laptop and printer set up to print pictures on it, and next to it, a file cabinet.

It looked like Swanson had switched to digital.

"If you look in the cabinet, you'll see it's filled with files—looks like there's negatives going back more than five years. No photos, but look in the trash can."

Steve bent over and lifted the can so that Grant could see inside. There were crumbling ashes of burned photographs. Steve pulled a pen out of his pocket and sifted gently through the blackened papers, and as he did a partially unburned section of a photograph came into sight.

It took a moment for Steve to realize that he was staring into the smiling face of Jessie Daniels.

"Son-of-a-bitch!"

Grant felt his heart stop as he saw what Steve had in the can. "We need to find this guy, now. I'm going to call Maggie and make sure she stays at the hospital. Mac is still there, right?"

When Steve nodded Grant turned his back on the wall of pictures only to be confronted with a large 8 x 10 of Maggie laughing, a look of utter happiness on her face. Shaken, he moved out of the small room before he took out his phone to dial.

When her phone sent him straight to voicemail, Grant immediately hung up and dialed Mac.

"MacKenzie"

"Mac, it's Grant. Is Maggie still there?"

"I don't think so. Dusty came by to talk to her about the attack on campus so I slipped down the hall to grab some coffee. Dusty came to tell me he was leaving, but the by the time I got back to the room only Mr. Sanders was there."

Grant struggled for several moments to keep the panic he felt rising in his chest out of his voice. When he thought he could speak normally he said, "Mac, I need you to see if her car's still there, and if it is try paging her for me. Jones is on her way, so she can sit with Cloë."

"What's going on, Grant?"

"We found the killer's home base and Maggie's picture is everywhere. Looks like he's been watching her for months. We also found evidence that he was photographing at least one of our other victims and there's a lot more to look through."

Mac swore ripely and reassured Grant that he'd get on it right away. Grant hung up and tried Maggie's cell phone again, and when it went straight to voicemail for the second time he left a message, "Maggie, it's Grant. I need you to call me or Steve right away."

After an internal struggle he added, "Stay away from the University. I'll explain when you call me back. Love you. Be careful!"

After making several more calls and having an A.P.B issued on Swanson he steeled himself to go back into the room where Steve was still working.

"Did you reach her?" Steve asked immediately.

"No. I have Mac looking to see if her car's still there and searching the hospital if it is."

Grant saw the fear in Steve's eyes, and hopeless to reassure him—or himself—he distracted him instead. "Find anything else?"

Steve was silent for a long moment before he focused on what Grant has said and replied, "Um, yeah. There are more than a dozen files of negatives in the cabinet, each of a different woman. There are also journals. I've only glanced at them, but they're pretty sick. Seems like this guy sees himself as some kind of avenging angel tracking and punishing the women for imagined sins.

"Listen to this '*July 23, 9:08 a.m. Blasphemy, July 2; 4:26 Improper breach of dress code; July 23, 8:24 p.m. Unlawful touching and fornication. Slut!*' It goes on for pages and pages. Each one filled with supposed sins that are tallied up on the bottoms of each page. It's sick."

Grant's phone rang and he picked it up, "Evans."

"Grant, It's Mac. I found her car. Talked to the nurse and she said she saw Maggie leaving on the elevator. Called Dusty and he said he told Maggie that St. John was here for surgery so I'm on my way to check the surgical floor and waiting rooms, and if she's not there, emergency."

"All right. Keep me posted."

Grant hung up and answered Steve's questioning look, "Her car's still at the hospital. Mac's looking for her now."

"All right. Let's get back to work."

FIFTY-NINE

Maggie had automatically turned off her phone as she entered the Emergency Room to find out what she could about Holden. It ended up taking her twice as long as she'd thought it would because right as she was walking up to the reception desk, the front doors swept open and a woman clearly in labor was rushed in in a wheelchair by an extremely harried-looking man Maggie had no trouble identifying as the woman's husband.

"Just breathe, Honey, nice and easy," he said in a shaky voice.

"*You* breathe while a head the size of a bowling ball is trying to burst out of your body and tell me how nice and easy it feels!" she yelled at the man. Ignoring her yells, he paused to lean down and continued to rub her back soothingly and murmured something softly in her ear that had her smiling tiredly up at him.

Maggie stood to the side as the receptionist had called for a nurse and quickly registered the couple before they were whisked off towards the elevators, the man still patting and breathing and the woman alternately moaning and cursing and smiling in excitement.

Maggie pictured being pregnant with Grant's child, imagined the names she'd probably call him when she was in labor and for one sweet moment the fear for her friend was lifted as she dreamed about the future she and Grant could have together.

The receptionist returned to her seat after having rushed around to the front of the desk to help the couple, a huge smile on her face. She turned to look at Maggie and said, "Hi, it's Maggie, right? How's your friend doing?"

Maggie brought her attention back to the present and realized that the receptionist was the same woman who'd helped her when Cloë had been admitted.

"Yes. She's doing much better, thanks, Tammy," Maggie glanced surreptitiously at the receptionist's nametag and continued, "I was wondering if you could help me find someone else. My friend, Holden St. John, was admitted this morning and I was wondering if you could tell me where he is, or if I could see him."

Tammy's pert smile shifted to a look of concern and she lowered her gaze to the computer in front of her as she typed in

Holden's name. Her eyebrows drew together briefly before she asked carefully, "Are you related to Mr. St. John?"

Maggie shook her head and said, "No. He's my boss and my friend. Maybe you remember him? He was one of the men here with me when my other friend, Cloë, was brought in. I'm the closest thing he has to family here in Minnesota. His only living family member is a sister who lives in California."

When Tammy still hesitated Maggie felt her eyes swell with tears and added, "Please, Tammy. He's my friend and I need to know if he's going to be all right, I need to see him."

"Okay. Let me see what I can find out…" she returned to her keyboard for another moment or two before she sighed and said, "He's still in surgery on the fourth floor. It looks like he's already been in there for two hours…still listed as critical…

"Why don't you go up to the surgical waiting room—it's on the fourth floor at the end of the hallway on the right. There will be someone there you can check in with, and as soon as he's out of surgery the surgeon will meet with you in a small conference room just off of the main waiting area."

Maggie smiled tremulously and said, "Thank you, Tammy. Thank you so much."

She rushed over to the bank of elevators and had just pushed the up button when someone called her name and grabbed her shoulder. Maggie jumped; she'd been lost in her thoughts again and hadn't heard her name being called out.

Maggie turned and found Mo behind her. Surprised to see him away from campus she said, "Mo! What are you doing here?"

"Hi, Miss Sullivan. I just wanted to stop by to see how Miss Sanders was doing and give her these," he paused and lifted a small clutch of carnations, "But the nurse told me she isn't allowed to see anyone but family."

"That's so nice, Mo. I'm sure Cloë would love to see you."

"She's awake now?"

"Yes. She woke up yesterday and was talking today."

"That's good. Was she able to tell anyone what happened to her?"

"No. She still can't remember, but the doctor thinks there's still a chance she could regain her memories," Maggie said, smiling at the look of relief on his face.

"Well, maybe you could give here these for me."

"Sure, Mo," Maggie took the offered blooms, "I'll make sure she gets them."

Mo had just opened his mouth to ask her another question when she heard her name being called again.

"Maggie!"

She turned to see Mac rushing across the waiting room towards her. Alarmed, she said, "Is Cloë okay?"

Mac nodded but before he could say anything she grabbed his arm and said, "Is it Grant or Steven?"

"No. Everyone's fine, but Grant's been trying to get a hold of you, and when he couldn't, he was worried and asked me to find you."

"Oh! I had to turn my phone off down here, but I'll call him when I get up the waiting room upstairs. This is..." Maggie turned to introduce Mac to Mo, but when she did she saw that Mo was already across the room and walking out the door.

Amused, she said, "Well, that *was* Mo. He's a little shy, I guess."

"Moses Swanson?" Mac asked, his voice sharp.

Maggie turned back to face him, confusion on her face, "Well...yes. But what's wrong? He only stopped by to visit Cloë and see how she was."

"You need to talk to Grant, Maggie. C'mon. I'll go up with you, even."

"Oh. I need to go up to the surgical floor. My boss was brought in and I need to find out how he's doing. You need to stay with Cloë and Mr. S., don't you?"

"Officer Jones is with them. I'll just keep you company, okay?"

Frustrated, but not knowing any way that she could get him to leave, Maggie shrugged once more and replied, "Sure," and together they got onto a waiting elevator to ride it to the fourth floor.

When they got to the waiting room Maggie went straight to the sign-in desk to speak with the helper there and let her know that she was waiting for Holden's surgery to be done so that she could talk to a doctor.

Mac walked up to the doorway with her and stopped, his cell phone already calling Grant. When Grant answered the phone Mac said, "I've got her," then waited as Grant relayed the information on to Steve before he continued.

"She was down in the emergency room checking on St. John and had her cell off. When I found her, she was talking with someone, but before I got over to where the two of them were standing the guy took off.

"It was Swanson," Mac heard Grant swear loudly as Mac continued, "But he was long gone by the time I realized who it was. I figured it was better to stick with Maggie and call to let you know she's safe."

"Thank God. Did you tell her about Swanson?"

"No. She asked why I was upset but I told her that she needed to talk to you. She didn't look too happy."

Amused, Grant replied dryly, "I'll bet. I'll take care of it when she calls. Stick with her, okay? The stuff we found...let's just say I don't want her out of your sight until she's with me or Steve, all right?"

"Got it. I'll be with her in the fourth floor waiting room for now, and then probably back up with Cloë."

"Okay. Tell Maggie I need her to call me as soon as possible. Talk to you later."

"Bye," Mac hung up and walked over to the couch where Maggie had sat down. He settled into a chair directly across from her and asked, "Any news?"

"He's still in surgery, and according to the lady at the desk, the surgeon said it could be another couple of hours. So, if you'd rather not wait..."

Maggie trailed off when Mac shook his head and said, "No. I'll stay. I talked to Grant and he asked me to tell you to call as soon as you had the chance, and that he didn't want you leaving the hospital alone at all."

She knew that things were pretty strange right now, but being ordered around by Grant *through* Mac was one step too far. Hadn't she cooperated so far, letting Grant drive her around, staying with her parents or Grant all the time, not talking to her friends at work?

Wasn't she a mature woman used to taking care of herself? It was bad enough that she constantly had her dad and brothers checking up on her, she didn't need some tyrannical jerk telling her what to do! Ignoring the little voice that told her that Grant cared about her and didn't want her to be hurt, that suggested that she might be over-reacting just the teensiest, tiniest bit Maggie fumed silently as she considered the slightly guilty looking man sitting opposite her.

She let him stew for several moments as she fumed, but in the end she resisted—with admirable self-restraint—the strong urge to take out her frustration with Grant's "orders" on Mac.

Instead she pulled out her phone to turn it on and go right to the source.

SIXTY

He'd been so close to her he'd almost changed his plans and taken her right then and there.

But right as he had taken the first step towards her the cop had showed up and surprised him. Heart racing, he'd changed directions and sped away as quickly as possible. He couldn't afford to be surprised—not today. He just needed to follow the plan.

He took several deep breaths as he sat in his truck, willing himself to calm down. At last, his grip eased on the steering wheel and he was able to breathe normally once more, allowing him to finally let the elation he'd felt at being so close to his Angel wash over him.

As he thought over his plans for the coming night his face relaxed into a contented smile. By the end of the night, his Angel would be with him.

Forever.

SIXTY-ONE

Grant and Steve had been at the house more than an hour before they located the scrapbook.

"Grant, take a look at this," Steve said, the forced calmness of his voice tipping Grant off.

"What is it?"

Steve simply held out the small book he had been holding towards Grant. Slightly larger than a diary, the plain black book looked unspectacular—similar to several other notebooks filled with photo notes that they'd found in the second drawer of the file cabinet. Those books had been filled with listings of lighting conditions, apertures, lenses and F-stops used for various shots.

But, when Grant opened the book Steve had given him to the first page he said grimly, "We got the Son-of-a-Bitch." He flipped slowly through the pages, his face blank once more as he fought the revulsion each new page brought him.

Only half full, each page of the book was filled with photographs and mementos, but not of a special trip or a child's achievements. Instead, each entry was dedicated to a different girl. Gory photographs chronicling the beating and bloody murder of each girl filled the pages.

Atop of the page was the heading Fallen Angel One, Fallen Angel Two… As Grant flipped slowly through the pages, the sick feelings he'd managed to suppress earlier came back stronger than ever.

Looking closely he found that the further he went, the more elaborate the pictures. Eventually he found newspaper clippings carefully cut out and attached next to each picture. Some pages had hair clippings, others, pieces of jewelry the bastard had ripped off his victim's bodies.

By the time he'd reached Jessie Daniels (Fallen Angel Twelve), Grant's face was a stony mask. "Where was it?" he asked.

Steve replied, "In a false drawer in the desk. Looks like this guy's been killing for almost six years."

Grant bent down to look more closely at the pages of the scrapbook and saw tiny dates printed on the bottom of each page.

"Judging from the different paper clippings, he's worked in at least three or four other towns, maybe more."

"Which is probably why no one ever tied the killings together."

"I remember this killing, Olivia Donnelly. It made the national news because she was killed right in the middle of a resort in Florida during Spring Break. Cops arrested her boyfriend for it—he had been so drunk he'd passed out, and the two of them had been seen fighting earlier that evening. He denied ever hurting her, but all the evidence pointed to him.

"It was in the press for more than a month because she came from old money—her dad was some big-wig entrepreneur and he was friends with the governor. The press called it the Spring Break Slaying."

"I remember that one, too. That was, what, over three years ago, right?"

"Yeah."

"But, I don't remember that killing involving anything out of the ordinary—it looked like a simple strangling."

"I think so. We need to take a close look at all of these case files. I'm willing to bet we'll find something that we could use to help tie them together with physical evidence."

"I'd like to call Ralph, see if he'd mind flying in to give us a better idea about Swanson. I'm sure that he could gather a lot of insight from this," Grant tapped the black book.

"Do it," Steve said as he carefully took the book back from Grant and sealed in an evidence bag.

Once again Grant walked out of the small room to go into the quiet of the dining room to dial Ralph's number. When he got off the phone with the excited profiler Grant noticed that he had a voicemail from Maggie.

He listened intently for a couple of minutes, alternatively wincing and chuckling, before he saved the message and closed the phone. He'd call her back—in a while.

He thought it best if she had some time to cool off before he did. And, wearing his first genuine smile since leaving Maggie earlier that morning, Grant turned to go back to that small room and

Steve, then stopped, shocked to find Moses Swanson walking up to the house when he glanced out the dining room window.

SIXTY-TWO

After almost two more hours of waiting, Maggie was abruptly shaken out of the state of semi-stupor she'd sunk into after finishing her book more than an hour ago when someone spoke to her.

"Miss Sullivan?" Maggie looked up to find the helper she'd spoken to earlier standing in front of her, a pleasant look on her gently-lined face.

Maggie had the uncomfortable feeling that this had not been the first time she'd said her name. She sat up straight and said, "Yes?"

"Mr. St. John is out of surgery and Dr. Baglovich will talk with you in the small conference room just over there," the lady paused and pointed to a door in the far right corner of the room.

"Thank you," Maggie said and she stood to quickly gather her purse from the floor and her empty coffee cup before she hurried across the room.

When she walked through the door the aid had pointed to Maggie found a small loveseat facing two overstuffed arm chairs that sat on either side of a small round table with a single lamp on it that looked like it had been stolen from the set of *The Brady Bunch*.

She'd just sat down on one of the chairs when a tired-looking doctor came into the room, still wearing his surgical scrubs. "Miss Sullivan?"

"Yes," Maggie said and she reached up to shake the hand he'd extended to her.

"I'm Dr. Baglovich," he said as he eased down onto the edge of the couch to face her, his elbows on his knees and his hands clasped in front of him.

His olive-skinned face wore the shadow of a beard, and although he looked extremely tired, Maggie noted that his dark brown eyes were alert and filled with something she couldn't quite identify, but that looked a lot like regret.

"Mr. St. John sustained several serious injuries. He had six broken ribs, one of which punctured his left lung. I was able to fix that. He also had a broken arm that was set. But, by far the worst injury Mr. St. John experienced was a massive skull fracture.

"I did what I could to stabilize him, but I'm afraid that there's still swelling and bleeding on his brain. He will be moved into Intensive Care shortly." The doctor paused for a moment before meeting Maggie's streaming eyes as he said, "There is a *chance*, albeit a very slight one, that he can recover. But there's not much more that can be done for him at this point. For now we will be monitoring and working on reducing the swelling and bleeding, but until it goes down there's no way for us to repair his skull."

When Maggie remained quiet he continued, "Do you have any questions?"

"How much time does he have?"

"There's no way of knowing. If they'd found him sooner, he may have stood a better chance, but there's no way to know that for sure either. As it stands…if he does not show signs of improvement within the next few days I don't believe that he will. And if that happens he won't have long.

"If he has any other family, I'd send for them. The sooner the better."

"Do you think he'll wake up?"

"It's difficult to say. With brain injuries this severe, there's no way to predict what will happen. It's highly unlikely—but not completely unheard of."

"When can I see him?"

"He should be settled into ICU within the hour."

"Thank you, doctor," Maggie said softly. He nodded once and after shaking her hand gently and placing a hand on her shoulder he left the room, closing the door behind him to give her a few moments of privacy.

Maggie allowed herself just a minute or two to cry, and then she determinedly wiped her eyes and stood up. Crying wasn't going to help her, and it certainly wasn't going to do Holden any good.

Mac was waiting for her when she came out. He took one look at her puffy red eyes and sighed inwardly before he asked, "What did the doctor say?"

"It's not good. They're moving him to ICU now, but the doctor says there's not much of a chance that he'll ever wake up."

"I'm sorry, Maggie."

She nodded, and then said, "Let's go back up. I need to make some calls and look in on Cloë and Holden before I go over to my parents' house."

"Lead the way," Mac said, thinking of the phone calls he, too, needed to make.

SIXTY-THREE

Grant opened the front door just as Mo Swanson reached out to grab the doorknob.

"Where's my mother?" Mo exclaimed, the worry on his face turning to shock when he saw several uniformed police officers in the hall behind Grant. He continued, "What are you doing in my house? Mother!"

Hearing the sudden panic in his voice Grant stepped back and said, "I'm Detective Evans. Your mother's fine, Mr. Swanson, but we'd like to ask you a few questions if you could just step inside and have a seat."

Grant gestured towards the dining room as he spoke. The living room would probably have been more comfortable, but that room still made him feel uneasy.

"Please, what is this all about? Is my brother all right?"

"Your brother is fine as far as we know. We haven't seen him yet. If you could just sit down, I'll be right with you." Grant leaned his head back into the hall and asked the closest uniform, "Can you tell Steve to come into the dining room, please?"

When the officer nodded his agreement Grant turned back into the dining room and sat down opposite Swanson.

"I really need to go. I'll be late for work—I was just stopping home to change quickly before going back to the University."

"I'm sure we can have someone call the University for you," Grant assured him.

Steve came into the room and settled into a chair next to Grant, saying nothing, but meeting Grant's gaze for just a fraction of a second before he turned his focus on the confused—and obviously nervous—man on the other side of the table.

"Mr. Swanson, can you tell us where you were Sunday night between the hours of eleven and six?"

"Sunday? I…What do you mean? I…I guess I was here. Asleep," Mo stammered, completely unnerved.

"Can anyone verify that?"

"I d-don't know. I was home most of the day—only went out for Mass that morning and after reading to Mother for a couple of hours, I went to the drug store to pick up her prescriptions, and then to the grocery store for the fresh fruit she prefers to have in her salads, and then I went to go see a movie. But I was home by about ten-thirty and in bed less than an hour later.

I checked in on Mother about twenty minutes after I'd gotten home, but she was asleep, so I didn't bother her. Abe wasn't home yet, but I heard him come in close to one. I don't think he came to check on me or anything, but my car was in the drive."

By the time he finished speaking, Mo's voice was a little jerky and he looked back and forth between the two impassive men across from him, unable to read their expressions.

"How about the night of July twenty-third or September fourth? "

Mo wrung his hands together and shook his head before he said, "I...I don't know."

"Mr. Swanson, do you often go to the coffee shop on Campus?" Steve broke in.

At a loss, Mo replied, "Sure, yes. I go in to work for a few hours in the morning and usually stop by the café for coffee before I head out. Then I do the second half of my shift in the afternoons and evenings after most of the classes are over.

"Please, what is this about? What does my morning coffee have to do with...anything?" Swanson's angry voice was overly loud in the quiet room as he finally moved past the fear he'd been feeling.

Grant glanced over at Steve again and Steve nodded once.

"Come with me, Mr. Swanson," Grant stood and waited as Mo stood slowly, unsure again, and followed Grant into the hall to the closet under the stairs.

"That's Abe's darkroom, but it hasn't been used in years. Mother keeps it locked, and only she has the key," Mo said, his voice full of fear again as they approached the almost-closed door.

Grant merely pulled the door open all the way and gestured Mo inside. Mo took one hesitant step into the room and froze.

He stood stock-still, only his head moved as he shook it back and forth, back and forth as if to deny what he was seeing.

"Mr. Swanson, can you explain how these pictures got onto the walls? How this notebook is filled with the pictures of twelve brutally murdered women?"

Mo continued to shake his head as he backed away from the room, his eyes filled with what could have been horror, but with what looked an awful lot like fear and shock to Grant.

"Mr. Swanson, your mother's key is missing, and according to her, you are the only person she allows in her room. She also tells us that you, too, have an interest in photography. So I'm going to ask you again to explain how these photographs came to be in this room."

But all Mo could do was turn away from Grant and the room filled with Miss Sullivan's photographs that he could still clearly see behind the policeman.

Angered all over again at the sight of Maggie's smiling face, Grant pulled his handcuffs out of his back pocket and put them onto Mo's right hand, than his left as he said, "Moses Swanson, you are under arrest for the murder of Jessie Daniels, Natalie Roberts, Amanda Martin, and nine other women. You have the right to remain silent, if you give up that right, anything you say can and will be used against you in a court of law. You have the right to an attorney, if you cannot afford an attorney one will be provided for you. Do you understand these rights as they've been read to you?"

Mo looked blankly at Grant for a moment, but when Grant prompted him again he replied with a faint, "Yes, I understand," and Grant led him towards the front door.

"I'll stay and finish up here and I'll catch a ride with one of the guys and meet you at the station," Steve said to Grant, who nodded as he led the docile Swanson out the door and over to his car.

SIXTY-FOUR

By the time Maggie was able to get in to see Holden it was after four. She would need to really hurry if she were going to stop by her apartment before heading over to hand out candy for the little kids—they were her favorites.

So small and sweet in their miniature costumes, walking door-to-door in broad daylight, one hand held tightly by mom or dad, the other holding on to a giant plastic orange pumpkin head almost as big as they were.

Cloë had slept most of the day which was all for the best. If she hadn't, she would certainly have known that *something* was wrong. And, since Maggie had decided not to tell her about Holden just yet, Maggie was grateful that her friend was still so tired, that Cloë could be protected—if only for another day or so.

She would tell Cloë about Holden after she knew more about what was going to happen with him. It had taken Maggie several hours of praying and sitting and just thinking before she'd truly faced the fact that for all intents and purposes, she'd lost one of her dearest friends.

Not only was it unlikely that Holden would live, but if he *did* live, there was a chance that his brain would be damaged so badly that he'd never again be as he had been.

No, that information could wait until tomorrow. Cloë would be a little stronger, and maybe, just maybe, Maggie would be too.

Maggie had told Mr. S. about Holden, and he'd agreed that it was probably for the best to wait. She'd bid them both good-bye and then walked two doors down the hall to Holden's room.

As she walked, she passed Mac and Bethany as they sat reading magazines—her, *Field & Stream* and him, *Ladies Home Journal*. The absurdity of it all had Maggie cracking a grin and shaking her head as she stopped for several seconds, one hand gripped on the doorknob of Holden's closed door, unable to make herself turn it.

Then, she squared her shoulders, literally and figuratively, to face what she would find inside and she pushed the door open. She stepped swiftly into the semi-darkened room, as if going quickly would somehow lessen the pain of what she were going to face—like

415

that frenzied run she and her brothers did from the steamy heat of the sauna her parents had built on the shores of the lake into the icy cold water of the bay.

Struck with a strong sense of déjà-vu, Maggie stepped over to the bed where Holden lay, still as death. His head was swathed in white wrappings and one arm sat in an equally-bright white cast on top of his sheets.

And, although Holden's face was free of the terrible bruises and cuts that had covered Cloë's face, the extreme pallor and sunken appearance of his features was all the more shocking because his handsome features—framed only by the unrelenting white of his wrappings and sheets—remained un-marred.

He lay so still, that for several wild seconds she had the mad urge to reach out and shake him to wake him up, to make him moan in pain, to move, to do *anything* that would dispel the eerie feeling that he was already gone.

She quelled the urge, horrified by her own thoughts, and checked the readouts of the machines Holden was hooked up to, and depending on to live.

It was amazing, and somehow horrifying, that a once-vibrant, highly intelligent man could be reduced to a series of flashing numbers, moving lines, and high-pitched beeps.

Maggie reached a trembling hand to carefully grasp his uninjured hand in hers as she whispered, "I'm so sorry, Holden. You've always been there for me. As my mentor, my friend. And now *you* need to listen to *me*. You ARE going to fight. You WILL wake up…you have to. I have to go now, but I'll be back tomorrow."

Maggie stopped, tears pouring silently down her cheeks again, and she leaned down to place a kiss on his cheek before she straightened and turned to go.

She hesitated only long enough to brush impatiently at her tears before she stepped out of the room and walked over to Mac.

"All right. I need to go to my apartment and then over to my parents' house. I'm assuming that the good Detective has ordered one of you to stay with me…" Maggie paused and looked at the two officers. Mac and Jones briefly glanced at each other before Mac nodded at Maggie.

"And there's nothing I can say that will convince you to let me go on my own?" Again, Mac simply shook his head. Resigned to the inevitable, Maggie continued, her voice resigned, "Okay, then. Let's get moving."

Maggie was almost to her car, followed closely by Mac, when her cell phone rang. She looked at the display and smiled when she saw that it was Grant, despite her earlier annoyance. She wasn't really even upset anymore—she knew that he'd only been looking out for her, and when she thought about what had happened to Cloë and Holden she could only be grateful that he cared enough about her to risk her wrath to make sure it didn't happen to her.

But there was no reason to let *him* know that just yet.

She flipped her phone open and said, "Calling to check up on your prisoner, Detective?"

Grant heard the smile in her voice and laughed, knowing he was forgiven, and said, "Actually, I was calling to give you your release papers. We have our killer in custody."

"What? Who is it? When did this happen?"

"It just happened a couple of hours ago. And that's one of the reasons I'm calling. I'm not going to be able to help hand out candy tonight. Steve and I are going to be tied up for most of the night, but we'll be able to stop by your parents' around nine for your show."

Grant listened to dead silence and waited for the explosion he knew would follow.

Instead he got confusion. "My show? Grant I canceled that."

"I know…but…well, I sorta *un*-canceled it."

"But, I can't do it without Cloë and she…"

Grant hastily cut in, "Katie's going to fill in."

"Katie? But…"

"I stole Cloë's costume and gave it to Sybil, and she fixed it up to work for Katie. Everything's all set. You just have to stop by your apartment and get your costume."

At a loss for words for several moments Maggie stood still while Grant waited for her response. He was confident that after her initial anger she wouldn't be mad—especially now that Cloë was out of the woods and the killer off the streets.

417

What he hadn't expected was Holden being attacked and seriously injured. He knew how close Maggie was to him.

After what seemed like an eternity she finally chuckled and said, "Pretty slick, Detective. I had no idea."

Relieved, Grant let out the breath he hadn't realized he'd been holding and said, "I had some help." He turned serious again and his smile faded as he continued, "How's Holden? And how are *you* holding up?"

Maggie stopped again, this time to lean against her car, and said, "Holden's not doing too good. The doctor did what he could, but he doesn't seem to hold much hope right now. I called his sister in California, and she's flying in early tomorrow morning.

"As for me? I'm, well, I'm not going to say that I'm fine, but I'm hanging in there. It helps knowing that you've caught the guy who probably did this to him. Who is it, Grant?"

Grant hesitated for just a second before he said, "I'll tell you everything tonight. Right now, I've got to go—Steve is waiting for me. I just stepped out of the interview room for a minute to call you. I think Steve is going to call Mac and let him know, but you'll be on your own again once he does."

"You don't sound too happy about that," Maggie commented.

"No, I'm not happy. Yes, we have someone in custody, but he's denying everything, and...I just don't know, something doesn't feel exactly right to me. It's nothing big—I mean we found extremely damning evidence in this man's home, enough evidence that any jury would convict him, and he has no alibis for any of the murders..."

When Grant trailed off Maggie said, "Sounds like you're still trying to convince yourself. What do Steven and the Chief think?"

"They think we have the right guy, and really, so do I. I just can't seem to shake off this little nagging feeling that something doesn't quite fit. It's all a little *too* easy..." Grant paused before he continued, "I'm sure it's absolutely nothing. I better go, Red. I'll see you tonight, okay?"

"Love you."

"I love you, too, Red. See you later."

Maggie closed the phone again and looked over to where Mac was just hanging up his phone as well.

"Looks like you're on your own, Maggie. Have fun tonight and stay out of trouble."

"Thanks, Mac. Stay safe," Maggie watched the tall policeman as he turned and walked back towards the hospital entrance.

Suddenly nervous, Maggie glanced around the empty parking lot and quickly got into her car. If she had to stop at the apartment before she went over to her parents' house, she'd better get going.

As she drove, Maggie went over her conversation with Grant in her head and she realized that he had managed to tell her almost nothing. Well, that would change tonight. She wouldn't let him get away again without telling her everything.

Before she knew it, Maggie was running up the stairs to her apartment. She hurriedly pushed her key into the lock, and in her rush, dropped her bag. She swore once and bent down to pick up the items that had spilled onto the pretty striped rug she kept right inside her door.

As she quickly shoved her cell phone, lipstick, wallet, and four different pens back into her bag, she saw a flash of light reflect off of something small in the rug. Maggie reached out to pick it up and found a few small round silver beads that looked like they belonged on a bracelet or necklace.

It wasn't from anything she wore—she'd have to remember to ask her mom and Sybil if it was theirs. Maggie shrugged and shoved them into her jeans pocket and closed the front door behind her.

She left her coat and purse on the chair nearest to the door and rushed back towards the bedroom.

She was going to be late.

SIXTY-FIVE

Grant hung up the phone and made his way back to the interrogation room where Steve waited, leaning against the wall next to the door.

"Did you get a hold of Mac?" Grant asked.

"Yep. Caught him right before he left the hospital. I can tell that you talked to Maggie by the dopey look on your face. She still ticked off about being shadowed?"

"Nah. She acts a big game, but she knew it was necessary. I still don't like pulling Mac off of her just yet."

"I know, but we need him in here and she's going over to my parents' house. Jack, Dillon, and Seth—not to mention Dad—will all keep an eye on her until we get there. She'll be fine."

Grant heard the reassurance in Steve's voice, and he *would* have felt better if he hadn't also seen his own concern mirrored in Steve's eyes. He'd just call in half an hour and make sure she made it there okay.

"Ready to go back in?" Steve jerked one thumb at the closed door and Grant sighed as he nodded.

Swanson was denying everything and refused to say much more than "I didn't do it" over and over again, a glassy-eyed look on his face, despite repeated questioning.

"At least he hasn't asked for a lawyer yet," Steve added, "I don't know how much longer he'll go without asking for one."

"Well, he'll crack, hopefully before we're old and gray."

Steve grinned and opened the door to see Moses Swanson still in the same position as they'd left him fifteen minutes earlier— leaning forward, his elbows on the table and his head cradled in his hands. As Steve closed the door behind them, Swanson jerked upright, then leaned back into the hard wooden chair he sat on.

Grant and Steve settled in opposite him and Grant leaned back, arms crossed, and began. "All right, Mr. Swanson, let's start from the beginning."

Half an hour later Grant ducked out of the room to dial Maggie's cell phone, and when it went straight to voicemail again, he swore and quickly dialed the Sullivan's.

Elizabeth answered, "Happy Halloween!"

"Hi, Elizabeth."

"Grant! It's so nice to hear from you. Are you able to come over soon?"

"Not yet. Steve and I are tied up with a case, but we plan on being there in time for the big show. Can I talk to Maggie? She forgot to turn her cell phone on again."

"Maggie? Why, she's not here yet. In fact, now that you mentioned it I was expecting her about twenty minutes ago."

Hearing the worry in her voice Grant squelched the growing concern he felt and reassured her, "I'm sure she's just running a little behind. I spoke with her half an hour ago and told her about tonight. She's probably just picking up her costume and changing at home instead of getting dressed at your house."

"I'm sure you're right," Elizabeth said.

Hearing the worry in her voice Grant said, "How about this, give me or Steve a call if she still isn't there in another half hour, okay?"

"All right, Grant. I'll talk to you soon."

"Bye." Now genuinely worried, Grant slipped back into the interrogation room in time to see Swanson shake his head and say again, "I didn't do it," in a completely expressionless voice.

Steve glanced over and raised his eyebrows. Grant shook his head slightly and settled back down next to him. He saw Steve's hand clench the cup of coffee in front of him for a split second before he leaned back and said easily, "Look, Mo, we can go over this all night long because we are not leaving here until you tell us the truth."

Swanson lifted hopeless eyes to them and said, "I *am* telling the truth. I had *nothing* to do with hurting anyone. I don't even know who any of those girls are."

"But you know Maggie Sullivan, don't you, Mo?"

"I would *never* hurt Miss Sullivan…Never."

Steve and Grant both heard the ring of truth in his declaration, but neither man had missed the flash of fear in the eyes of the man across from them. Neither of them had missed the way Swanson's hands had twitched, then clenched together at the mention of Maggie's name.

More than an hour later and they had made no further progress. The only good news was that they hadn't heard from Elizabeth, so Grant assumed that Maggie had made it safely over to her parents' house.

He and Steve stepped out of the room and into the observation room where Chief Banyon stood, legs wide and arms crossed on his chest as he watched the interview through the one-way glass that separated him from Mo Swanson.

As they walked into the room Banyon turned to face them and leaned his lanky frame against the wall. "Well?" he asked.

"He knows something. He's guilty of *something*. Of that, I'm sure," Grant said and he ran one weary hand through his already mussed hair. He sighed in frustration and continued, "I don't know, Chief. All the evidence points to him and I know he's not telling us everything, but is what he's hiding from us the fact that he's a sociopathic killer? I'm just not convinced."

Grant shook his head and looked over to where Steve had eased down to sit on the edge of a low counter underneath the one-way glass that showed Mo Swanson once again sitting with his head held in his hands.

Steve met Grant's eyes and then turned to the Chief to say, "Agreed."

Banyon nodded once and lifted one hand to rub at the stubble that covered his sharp jaw. He stood deep in thought for several moments before Grant spoke up again.

"Chief, my contact at the FBI, the profiler, he'll be here in the morning. I'd like him to take a look at the scrapbook and notebooks we found in Swanson's house, and to talk to Swanson, too. At the very least he'll be able to update the profile and get us a better read on Swanson."

When Banyon still didn't look convinced Grant opened his mouth to continue, then he snapped it shut again when Steve gave him an almost imperceptible shake of the head.

At last Banyon nodded slowly and said, "All right, Evans. We need to try. I talked to the D.A. and he said that we have more than enough to hold Swanson, but I really want a direct evidentiary link or a confession on this one."

"We'll get it Chief. If it's there, we'll find it."

"In the mean time, what's the story on the brother?"

Steve spoke next. "Mac and Dusty are looking for him right now. The mother said he spends a lot of time with his friends and little time at home. Problem is no one seems to *be* his friend. Mac said he missed him at the University by less than fifteen minutes, but he didn't tell anyone there where he was going.

"According to the people Dusty talked to, he mostly keeps to himself and he doesn't really interact with many of the students and staff beyond when he lets them in and out of the lot. And even then, he rarely speaks. They'll have more in an hour or two, I should think."

Satisfied, Banyon nodded once more and said, "Why don't you guys grab a bite and go see Maggie? He can stew for a while before you go back in. Let's see what an hour or two locked up with Henry Baker can do to jog his memory.

Grant pictured the three hundred pound drunk that slept in the station's holding cell most Fridays and often times Saturdays, and grinned. Baker screamed and yelled and threw things—and on more than one occasion had been violently sick in the cell.

"Are you sure, Chief? We can stay…"Steve began to say but Banyon cut him off, saying, "Go."

"Thanks, Chief. We'll be back in an hour or two."

Steve followed Grant out the door and through the station, pausing only long enough to grab their coats on their way out. The nights were getting downright cold lately.

SIXTY-SIX

By the time Maggie had gotten changed into her costume, secured her curls underneath her wig, and put on all of her make-up she was running almost an hour late.

She crammed the jeans and sweatshirt she'd worn that day into a small canvas tote, grabbed her purse and hurried down the stairs and out to her car. She barely remembered to lock her apartment door behind her.

By the time Maggie walked through her parents' front door, Elizabeth was beside herself with worry. She had just picked up her phone to call Steve when Maggie burst through the door saying, "Sorry, sorry. I'm here!"

Elizabeth's mouth fell open in shock at the sight of the person in front of her. She knew that it was Maggie because it *sounded* like her, but it took her several seconds before she could recognize her daughter under the thick layer of paint on her face.

Elizabeth burst into delighted laughter and said, "Wow! I...wow!"

Maggie grinned, her eyes sparkling under thick, dark false eyelashes. "Thanks. Do you think Dad will like it?"

"He's going to get a big kick out of it. I definitely think you've outdone yourself this year."

"That was my plan. If you like mine, just wait 'til you see Jack and Dillon's costumes. I think they're even more...*special*...than mine is," Maggie said mischievously.

Elizabeth just shook her head, a grin on her face.

"Sorry I wasn't here earlier to help hand out candy to the little kids—I got hung up at the hospital and then I found out that tonight was back on and I had to do a lot of prep work before I could leave. You heard about Holden?" Maggie asked, her voice serious again.

Elizabeth nodded and rubbed a hand up and down Maggie's arm, "Were you able to get in to see him?"

"Yeah. Luckily they already know me on the Intensive Care ward, and of course it helped having someone from the police there to vouch for me, too."

Elizabeth opened her mouth, but before she could ask the question Maggie knew she was going to ask, Maggie continued, "He's not doing very well. The doctors don't have much hope at this point.

"I called Trisha, his sister, but she lives in California and won't get here until tomorrow. Anyway, I've been praying all afternoon, and for now I'm going to focus on the kids and try not to think about it. Where's Dad?"

Worried, but not wanting to push Maggie to think about the terrible things that had been happening, Elizabeth said, "He's out hooking up and testing the last of the lights and speakers."

"I had better get out and help him," Maggie began.

Elizabeth broke in, "I called Jack as soon as your father said he was going outside and he and Dillon are already helping him— and hopefully preventing him from killing himself or someone else."

She rolled her eyes and shook her head, but Maggie could still see worry in her mother's eyes so she said, "I'll just throw these bags upstairs and then go see how far they've gotten."

"What's in them?" Elizabeth pointed to the bags at Maggie's feet.

"The rest of my costume."

"The rest? There's more?"

Maggie just waggled her eyebrows and ran upstairs with her three bags.

Elizabeth simply shook her head, amused at her only daughter's actions. Elizabeth loved her boys so much; Seth with his studious ways, Steve with his protectiveness, Jack with his playful sense of humor, and Dillon with his quiet, gentle disposition. But their lives just wouldn't have been the same without Maggie.

Elizabeth had long given up on having a little girl, and with her four sweet boys, had never regretted it.

And then she'd had Maggie.

She'd come into the world on a wild stormy night and had promptly stolen their hearts—even five-year-old Jack's, who had thought that girls were "gross" and that having a little sister was "totally lame."

425

Growing up the youngest, and only, girl in the middle of four overprotective big brothers had been a challenge and an adventure for Maggie, but she'd given them all a run for their money.

Elizabeth walked back to the kitchen still thinking about the past as she began to finish preparing the snacks and desserts she traditionally put out for the family after Maggie's yearly performance.

They'd had so much fun—she'd loved all of her children when they were babies and just growing, but they'd been so much fun as teenagers. She'd just enjoyed each one of them—sure there had been bickering and fighting and tears and yelling from time to time, but with five teenagers, one an extremely emotional and dramatic girl, that was inevitable.

There had been times when she'd collapsed into bed at night, sure that she was raising a pack of heathens and others when she'd laughed until she'd cried. With the five of them, it had changed on a daily—if not hourly—basis.

The one thing that *had* stayed the same was that they'd loved each other fiercely. Elizabeth was just grateful that they'd finally outgrown their tendencies to call each other names.

Maggie thundered down the stairs and into the kitchen, pausing only long enough to grab a handful of chips as she passed by. She opened the back door and called out, "Hey you dweebs, how's it going?" before slamming the door behind her.

Left alone in the kitchen once more Elizabeth shook her head again and let out a soft chuckle.

Some things never changed.

SIXTY-SEVEN

By the time seven o'clock rolled around Maggie was just putting the finishing touches on Katie's make-up.

"There. You look perfect. Almost as pretty as your Uncle Jack and Uncle Dillon," Maggie added, snickering as she glanced over to where the two men stood. Katie giggled and covered her mouth with one hand.

"I'm going to get even with you for this one, Maggie," Jack said, the clear panic in his voice making Maggie laugh again.

"We *are* even, Jack. Just remember tonight the next time the pair of you decides to throw me into the lake!"

Jack looked over at his reflection in the full length mirror propped next to the door and said, with no small amount of disgust, "Shit. Oh, well. Might as well get this over with."

Dillon stood up and just shook his head, his face pale under the layer of make-up Maggie had forced him to endure.

"It will all be over fast. Just think of the kids," Maggie said and rubbed Dillon's shoulder once, a trace of sympathy in her voice despite the evil grin she couldn't seem to get off of her face. "Let's get on stage. Dad will be cueing up the music in about five minutes."

Katie jumped to her feet; nearly beside herself she was so excited and nervous. She followed closely behind her two uncles as they made their way out of the garage where they had gotten ready and out to the curtained area that Bram had rigged to the stage.

Maggie followed closely behind, and the moment she stepped out into the chill of the evening she heard the steady hum of the crowd that was just out of sight behind the curtain.

Heart racing she patted her headdress one last time before taking her place center stage. Her last thought before the curtain opened was that she hoped that Grant and Steven had made it in time. She knew that Seth would be videotaping it, but it would be so much more fun to see their faces when they saw her—and Jack and Dillon—in person.

She stifled one last giggle and then leaned over to squeeze Katie's small, sweaty hand for just a second. Their eyes met as the

427

music began to pump and through the curtain they heard the crowd begin to yell and clap as the curtain was pulled away.

The crowd went wild. And for a moment the music was drowned out by the wave of noise as it washed over them. Maggie's eyes swept the crowd, searching for Grant. She spotted several people she knew, but it wasn't until she and Katie had finished the first part of their dance and had swept to the side of the stage to make room for Jack and Dillon to take center stage that she spotted him and Steven standing at the back of the crowd near Seth.

All three of them were laughing, and for a split second Grant caught her eye, a huge grin on his face, and then she had to step back up to where her two big, burly brothers danced, clad only in the sequin-covered miniskirts, bustiers, and feathered headdresses like the ones that dancers in Vegas wear.

Katie swept between them and they lifted her up on their shoulders. Her costume, a miniature—and thanks to Sybil's clever addition of a flesh colored leotard underneath—more demure version of her uncles' costumes. The three of them moved back and Maggie danced back to center stage and began to lip-synch as Cher's distinctive voice sang out about believing in love.

The long black wig she wore beneath her own feathered headdress swayed and sparkled beneath the lights, but did little to hide the quite amazing amount of skin her own costume bared. Intellectually, she knew that she wore fewer clothes when she went to the beach, but standing center stage Maggie worried that Grant wouldn't approve.

She found him in the crowd again and saw only humor and love in his eyes. She turned her attention back to the performance as she stepped back into line with her three back-up dancers, and together they began to do their Rockette high kicks to wild applause, wolf whistles, and screams of laughter.

With a few last flourishes Maggie felt her brothers lifting her up on their shoulders as Katie did an impressive pirouette that ended in the splits right as the music ended and the lights went out. The crowd went crazy one last time and Jack and Dillon lowered her to the floor and all three collapsed with laughter.

"Good job, Mags," Jack yelled in her ear. Maggie grinned up at him, grateful she was blessed with such wonderful brothers.

Despite all their whining and complaining there had never been a moment where she thought they'd back out. She'd counted on them seeing the humor of the situation and they hadn't let her down—they never had, and she knew they never would.

"So, who's up for an encore?" she teased.

Dillon groaned but said, "I'm in."

Jack pulled her hair and added, "Let's give 'em a good show. What do you say, Katie?"

"Sure!" Katie's eyes were huge and sparkling. Maggie hugged her and looked over to where her dad stood and nodded. The curtain swept back open and as the music came up the crowd began to clap and sing along.

As Grant stood in the crowd he watched Maggie dance and pretend to sing in front of the large crowd of kids and their parents and just shook his head, unable to keep the smile off of his face.

If he hadn't been stupid in love with her before tonight he certainly would have been after.

She was so vibrant. Even with the bright flame of her hair covered by the long black wig and her glowing skin covered with make-up her beauty shone out from her like a beacon that called him to her more surely than a moth to the flame.

Each time him, their eyes met his stomach clenched with his desire and his heart swelled with his love for her. It was a silly thing, the performance, but it was so typically Maggie—full of fun and humor, and most importantly, it helped others.

He'd found out just that night that she collected food from the crowd each year to give to the local food shelf, and any money that was given went straight to a local charity. This year, Sybil had told him when he asked, they'd collected more than $200 that Maggie planned on giving to a women's shelter. Her brothers would drop off the more than twenty bags of food collected at the food shelf in the morning.

Steve and Seth stood on one side of him laughing. They'd never let Jack or Dillon live tonight down. But Grant also knew that if Maggie had asked—or bribed—either one of them, they would have stepped up to take their place despite the outfits. It was the Sullivan way.

429

Elizabeth stood on his other side, pride and amusement lighting her brown eyes. Eyes that, despite being darker in color than Maggie's, so often reminded him of her. He knew that Bram was somewhere backstage making sure that the whole thing ran smoothly.

And then Elizabeth hooked her arm through his and Grant knew that they had folded him into the family. When it had happened he didn't know, but for the first time in his life Grant found himself part of a family who loved him unconditionally.

All because he loved their incredible daughter and sister and, by some miracle of fate, she loved him back.

And for them that was enough. He only wished that he didn't have to go back to the station tonight. He wanted to stay, to tell her exactly how he felt, what he wanted, and together they could make a start on their future together.

SIXTY-EIGHT

As Grant stood, his eyes fixed on Maggie as he thought about the plans he wanted for their future, not more than ten meters away another stood doing the same thing.

Careful to keep several people between him and the cops he'd spotted when he'd first walked into the yard, the man stood, outwardly calm despite their presence.

When he'd first seen them he'd panicked. His eyes had scanned the crowds to see if Mo had cracked, if this was a trap. His heart rate had slowly steadied as he'd searched and found no other cops, no other people casually staring at him or paying too much attention to him.

Luckily, he'd come in with a large group of teenagers and he'd managed to keep them between him and the men he knew were his Angel's brother and the man she'd ruined herself with. After several extremely tense minutes of seeing nothing, he had grown confident that they were not there looking for him.

Still, the importance of the next hour was so great he had to be careful not to assume anything. As always, he had several contingency plans and he knew that as long as he kept his cool he'd be fine.

When the curtain first swept open he had to choke back his fury at seeing his Angel flaunting herself on stage for the entire world to see. If he hadn't been completely sure that his Angel was in need of saving before, he now had no doubts.

It took every ounce of his will to hide his anger and to keep from spewing the vile stream of curses and condemnation he felt building inside him at the stage where she danced—her skin bared for every man to see, inviting every man there to screw her, to touch what was *supposed* to be for him alone.

When a young teenager next to him gave him a strange look he realized that he was breathing so hard he was almost panting and his forehead was beaded with sweat with the effort to contain his anger. He quickly smiled as he shifted away to get control of his breathing.

He shifted his eyes away from the stage and began to picture what he would do to her for her sins here tonight. Eventually he was

431

able to contain his anger, to channel the rage until he was alone, finally alone, with his Angel.

When the second performance ended and the crowd stood cheering he slipped unseen behind a group of trees near the edge of the yard closest to the garage and curtain. Eventually she'd be alone. And then, she'd never be alone again.

SIXTY-NINE

As Steve, Grant and Seth began to steer the boisterous crowd back around the house and on their way home, Maggie stood behind the curtain hugging Katie.

"You were awesome, Katie-Belle! You even made these two look pretty good."

"Pretty good? We were incredible…amazing…stupendous, we were…"

Dillon sighed once and looked down at his clothes as he interrupted his brother, "Dude, I gotta get out of this costume." He wrapped the robe he'd taken off moments before the curtain opened back around his shoulders and sped out of the curtained area and out into the night leaving Maggie, Katie and Jack shouting with laughter.

Bram stuck his head through the curtain, a broad smile on his face, and asked, "What's the joke?"

Maggie stifled one last laugh and managed to say, "I think Dillon's scarred for life—he's going to have nightmares for years after this."

Bram chucked and said, "Oh, I think he'll survive. All set to go, Katie-Belle?"

"Sure, Gramps. Thanks, Auntie Maggie! I had *so* much fun!"

Maggie bent down to slip her arm around Katie's shoulders as she whispered in her ear, "Thanks for rescuing me, Katie. Without you, I'd have been stuck with only the hairy twins."

Katie burst into giggles again and practically danced over to Bram and out into the night. Maggie straightened to watch her small niece walk towards the house, her hand secure in her grandfather's.

Jack joined her and draped his arm around her shoulders. Maggie hooked her arm around his waist and let her head fall to his shoulder in a gesture at once both familiar and comfortable.

"Good job, Mags."

Maggie smiled and lifted her head to tease, "I didn't scar *you* for life, did I?"

"Nah. It takes an extremely handsome, sexy, confident man secure in his manhood to dance on stage dressed as a Vegas showgirl. I rocked. If Dillon had been as manly as me, he wouldn't be so embarrassed."

"You *did* rock, Jack. Thanks," Maggie said as she reached up on tiptoe to press a smacking kiss on his cheek.

"I better go help the guys get everyone out of the yard and then we can head up to the house to be 'surprised' by the feast Mom's been working on all day."

"I'll just get changed and be right out." Maggie watched affectionately as her big burly brother strode across the darkened back yard, still wearing the silver sequined mini skirt and bustier she'd forced him and Dillon to wear.

She only giggled once when she heard his muffled oath when he caught his knee-high, platform silver boots on the edge of one of their mother's flower beds. Shaking her head Maggie stepped into the makeshift changing room in the corner of the garage that her dad had made out of a couple of heavy blankets and some rope.

The rustle of something brushing against the garage had her pausing as she pulled the long black wig and headdress from her head, but when she didn't hear anything else she shrugged and began to peel off the gold lame mini-dress she'd taped herself into earlier in the day. Her mind wandered back over the past half hour as she pulled an old University of Minnesota sweatshirt over her head and her worn Levi's up.

Dropping down onto a folding chair her dad had placed in front of an old crate holding a small mirror she pictured the expression on Grant's face when she'd finally found him in the crowd. The shock and surprise followed closely by humor and then the familiar flare of heat had set her already racing heart scrambling, and the time that had passed had not diminished the desire that look had stirred in her.

She grabbed a face cloth to scrub the stage make-up from her face and imagined all the ways that she and Grant would celebrate once they were alone together. They had planned on a late dinner, but she knew that both he and Steven would be at the station most, if not all, of the night. Sorry as she was that they couldn't have the quiet dinner they'd originally planned on having, she understood—besides, there was always tomorrow.

Maggie set down the used cloth and bent close to the mirror to check that all of the makeup was off and caught a quick movement in the mirror and jumped.

"Nice try, Jack. Very funny. What are you doing back out here..." Maggie stood, one hand pressed to her racing heart, and a nervous smile on her face. But when she whirled in a circle there was no one behind her. "It was just the wind, get a grip Maggie," she sighed. But, instead of sitting back down, she grabbed her costume and makeup bag and hurried out from behind the blankets and around the curtain into the now-deserted back yard.

She looked all around the familiar landscape and when she didn't see anyone or anything she told herself that it was just her overactive imagination. Instead of feeling better, her instincts were screaming for her to get out of one of the places she'd always felt safe. She could see her mother walk past the lit kitchen window just a few yards away, and telling herself she was being ridiculous Maggie broke into a jog. She had almost reached the stairs when her makeup bag slipped out of her hands and she was forced to stop to pick it up.

As she bent to grab it she heard a quick step and the rasp of material, but before she could turn she felt a blinding flash of pain and then there was only the dark.

SEVENTY

It had taken Grant, Steve, and a laughing, still-costumed Jack almost fifteen minutes to completely clear the back and front yards. They all stepped in out of the now-brisk night air and made their way through the Sullivan house to the kitchen where Elizabeth, Bram and Katie sat with Seth, Sybil and a normally-dressed Dillon.

They walked into the room just in time to hear Seth say, "Hey, Dillon, I think you missed a spot, Buddy."

"What? Where?" Dillon sprang up and headed up the stairs to the bathroom to check his face in the mirror for the spot of makeup he'd missed. Seth let out a muffled laugh that Elizabeth quelled with a single raised eyebrow and the soft declaration, "I'll be sure to let Maggie know that you volunteered to help her out next year, Seth. I'm sure she'll be delighted to come up with an…appropriate role for you."

Seth looked slightly panicked as he replied faintly, "Yes, Mom," missing the slight grin Elizabeth aimed over his head at Sybil and Katie. Grant and Steve glanced at each other, but just managed to hold back their own laughter—neither one of them was dumb enough to get on Elizabeth's bad side.

Jack gave Seth a slap on the back as he passed by him on the way up the stairs after Dillon, careful to keep his smiling face averted.

"That's the last of the people. I turned out the light in front, Ma. The only kids who'll be out this late will be the teenagers," Steve broke the silence.

"Where's Maggie? She said she'd be right in."

Bram said, "I think she was going to change before she came in, so she shouldn't be long now."

"I'll go help her with her stuff," Grant said, uneasy with the idea of her being outside all alone.

"And then we have got to get back to the station, Mom," Steve added.

"You have to go back tonight? You can't wait until tomorrow? You two work too hard, and besides, I have sandwiches and pie," Elizabeth protested.

"We'll take some to go, Mom."

Grant smiled to himself over the concern he'd heard in Elizabeth's voice, and the fact that at least part of that concern had been for him. Grant slipped out the back door as they continued to discuss the food and strode across the quiet backyard, guided by the lone light still shining behind the makeshift stage.

But when he slipped behind those curtains and into the blanketed area that served as Maggie's changing area he found it empty. He glanced around, and seeing that her costume and wig were gone he quelled his instant unease. She had probably just gone into the house before they had and gone upstairs to get cleaned up before she went to the kitchen.

He was almost back to the back steps when he noticed something dark in the grass at the base of a small shrubbery next to the path and he veered sharply over to see what it was. When he saw that it was Maggie's metallic makeup bag the blood in his veins ran ice cold.

Swearing richly under his breath he sprinted back to the stairs and again was stopped by something shining dully in the grass just three feet short of the stairs. He stooped down to take a closer look and his fingers shook as he reached down to pick up two small metal beads that were all too familiar.

His hand fisted around the two small beads and the fear he'd felt when he'd spotted the makeup bag tripled as the reality of what was happening sank in.

He was inside in less than three seconds and conversation stopped cold at the sudden reappearance of a deathly-pale Grant in their midst. Steve's heart stuttered once before his face went blank and he said in a dead voice, "Maggie?"

"Gone."

Steve's face paled perceptively but he remained calm as Bram sprang to his feet and Elizabeth echoed, "Gone?" in a bewildered voice before she continued, "But she must just be upstairs getting changed. Maggie?" she called out as she hurried up the stairs followed closely by Sybil.

"She could have run home…" Seth began but Grant cut him off saying, "No. I found this," Grant held out the makeup bag, "and I found these." Grant opened his other hand to reveal the two small beads.

437

Steve sat down abruptly and Seth looked from Grant's strained face to Steve's uncharacteristically upset one before he said, "Will one of you tell me what the hell is going on? Where's Maggie and what do a couple of beads have to do with it?"

Before either man could answer Elizabeth came back into the room followed closely by Sybil, Jack and Dillon. "She's not there," she said.

"Her car's still here," Sybil added quietly as she came further into the room.

"Steve, you have to tell me exactly what is going on…" Seth began furiously, his hands clenched into fists when Steve only shook his head. He would have continued, but Sybil moved further into the room to rest her hands on Seth's tense shoulders and Bram held one hand up to quiet them.

Bram turned to Grant and said only, "Grant?"

"Maggie's been taken, we think by someone who's left beads similar to these at previous crime scenes."

At this Steve seemed to rouse himself as he reached into his jacket to pull out the evidence bag with several matching beads. He cleared his throat twice before he was able to say, "I was going to show these to you to see if you knew what they were from, Mom."

"Me?" Elizabeth looked surprised and a little scared as she stepped forward to take the small bag he held out to her. Her look of terror turned to a look of concentration as she fingered the beads in the bag. "But, Steven what do a few rosary beads have to do with your sister disappearing?"

Shocked, Steve said, "Rosary beads? Are you sure?"

"That's what they look like to me," she turned to Grant and explained, "My aunt was a nurse at St. Mary's hospital and special-ordered metal rosaries—she said they were easier to disinfect."

"I *knew* that I remembered them from somewhere, "Steve said slowly.

As they spoke Grant's mind raced—the information they'd wanted so badly about the beads would be important tomorrow when Ralph got into town, but for now all it meant was that Maggie was kidnapped, maybe dead, and they had the wrong man in custody or, there was more than one involved. Either way, Maggie's time was already running out.

438

"Steve, we need to go. Now."

"Now wait just a damn minute, you're not going anywhere until somebody tells me what the hell is happening here," Bram said vehemently.

Grant looked significantly over to where Katie stood silently by her mother, her dark brown eyes huge in her pale face and Steve immediately turned to Sybil and said quietly, "Take Katie upstairs."

Sybil nodded and put her arm around Katie's shoulders to steer her out of the tense room. As the sound of Katie's protests faded Bram spoke again, "Now, you need to tell us what's going on."

Although the volume of his voice had quieted, Grant heard the steel under the calm statement and saw the look of fear and fury on Bram's normally laid-back face. Grant glanced over at Steve's stony expression and said, "We think Maggie's been abducted. Elizabeth, are you doing okay?"

When she nodded mutely and grasped Bram's hand in hers Grant continued. "There's no way to know for sure at this point, but what little evidence I found," he indicated the bag of beads still clutched in Elizabeth's other hand, "points to a connection to several cases we're already working on. I know that you realize that we cannot give you specifics, but in situations like this time is of the essence and we really need to call in the rest of the team on this."

Jack's furious voice began, "Screw the rules, Grant! You..." only to be cut off by Elizabeth's quiet, but sharp voice, "Jack Tyler, that's enough. You know that your brother and Grant will not stop until Maggie is safely home again. There's no point in yelling at them and delaying them any further," she paused and turned her eyes to Steve and continued, "Steven, I know you and Grant have certain principles that you cannot bend, even for us, but we need to hear from you as soon as you have information."

Jack nodded curtly and Dillon stepped up to grip his shoulder while Seth and Steve's eyes met. Seth nodded and went to flank Elizabeth on her other side. Steve lowered himself until he was eye-to-eye with his mother and said, "We'll find her, Mom." She nodded and handed him the baggie holding the beads.

Grant stood watching helplessly as the family drew together around Steve. Unable to watch any longer he turned and walked out

439

into the hall, pulling out his phone as he closed the door behind him. He punched in the Chief's number and waited until he heard the familiar voice say "Banyon."

"Chief, it's Evans. I need a forensics team sent over to the Sullivan place. Maggie Sullivan's missing."

Five minutes later he was closing his phone when he heard the kitchen door open and shut behind him. Expecting Steve he turned and was surprised to find Bram instead. Wary now, Grant braced himself for the words of anger he was sure Bram had held back in front of his wife and children.

Grant opened his mouth to say something, anything, to the father of the woman he loved, but before he could come up with a single thing to say Bram stepped forward and reached out to grip Grant's shoulder in a crushing grip as he said, "Find her, Grant. Bring her back to us. And when you find the son-of-a-bitch who has her, you take care of him, too, or we will."

"I will."

Hearing Grant's coldly grim tone of voice Bram took a look beyond Grant's blankly composed countenance, a countenance which couldn't completely mask the terror that flared beyond the cold fury burning in his eyes.

Satisfied, Bram eased his grip and spoke in a low, strained voice, "We wouldn't trust anyone but you and Steven to find her."

Grant felt the extra weight, the new level of pressure settle onto his shoulders, but instead of weighing him down, the burden of trust steadied him. Grant opened and then closed his mouth without saying anything, but Bram nodded in understanding as he squeezed Grant's shoulder one more time and then he dropped it to his side.

Steve came through the door then and the two of them walked out the front door to meet the first of the squad cars as they squealed to a stop in front of the house. The forensics truck pulled up less than ten minutes later and Grant knew that the Chief must not have wasted a moment since they'd spoken.

It took Grant less than five minutes to fill the uniforms in and show the forensics team where he'd found the beads, and then he and Steve were driving well over the speed limit back to the station—and their only link to whomever had taken Maggie.

SEVENTY-ONE

Steve drove blindly, his hands fisted tightly around the steering wheel—as if he let up for even a moment his sister would somehow be lost forever. The weight that had settled so heavily onto his chest when Grant had pulled those beads out of his pocket seemed to grow heavier and heavier until he felt he could barely breathe under the pressure of it.

"Oh, my God, Grant. Oh, God, what if..."

"No," Grant broke in furiously as they squealed into the station's parking lot and stopped with a jerk. "No, we are *not* going to go there, Steve. No 'what ifs', no 'should haves'. Not now. We need to stay calm, to focus..."

"Fuck focus, you cold-hearted son-of-a-bitch! That crazy, psychotic monster has my sister and all you can say is *stay calm*? I thought you had feelings for Maggie or was that just a lie? What are you some kind of fucking cyborg?"

Even seeing the blind terror in his partner's eyes and understanding that Steve's rage was not really directed at him could barely hold Grant back as he felt his own rage, his own almost all-consuming fear swell. For a single moment, one split second they surged up in him, his vision tinged red, and then he pushed them down again, knowing that if he let them loose—even for a moment—it could mean losing the one person who had made his life worth living again.

So, instead of letting loose, he felt the hands he had clenched relax at his side and his eyes and face smoothed back into a mask of calm again, the additional hurt Steve's words had caused buried next to the rest of the emotions he couldn't afford to feel right now. Even as he buried the pain and the fear he knew that he'd pay a high price for doing so later. And despite the knowledge, he also knew he would gladly do so as long as it helped them save Maggie.

And if they didn't, then nothing would matter anymore, he thought bitterly.

Composed again, Grant faced the still-furious Steve over the hood of the car and said dully, "Let's get to work," before he turned and walked away from the car and Steve.

441

Steve watched Grant stalk past and for one second he let himself slump forward, both hands braced on the car as he recalled the play of emotions that had crossed Grant's face—rage, terror, pain, and then blank despair.

Even a blind fool—and that is exactly what he'd been—could not have missed what was really going on. Grant was completely in love with Maggie. And instead of understanding, of supporting his best friend, his partner, his brother, Steve had all but kicked him in the teeth.

"Shit," Steve muttered as he rubbed his face with hands that shook. He had to pull himself together before he let his sister down as badly as he'd just let Grant down. He'd just have to fix it with Grant when this was over. Because Grant was right—if they were going to have a chance to get her back then they both had to focus on the here and now.

Steve straightened from the car and turned, his face back in what Maggie would have called "cop mode", and strode into the station behind his partner. They had a lot to do—starting with Moses Swanson.

His time for thinking was up.

SEVENTY-TWO

The first thing Maggie felt was the pain. The pain was a sharp pounding on the back of her head that, after several confused minutes, she realized was pounding in time with her heartbeat. Spikes of shooting pains radiated from her shoulders down to her wrists and from her ankles up her legs.

The second thing she felt was the fear. Fear that washed over her, almost blocking the pain she felt, when she tried to shift those arms and legs and realized that they were tied together. The last of the cobwebs in her poor hurting head were swept away and she remembered walking in her parent's backyard and hearing someone come up behind her and then just the pain.

Her heart raced, causing the pounding in her head to increase until the pain was unbearable and she sank under into the blessed dark again.

When she surfaced the second time the pain and fear were still waiting for her, but she remembered more quickly and stayed calm enough to try to open her eyes to see where she was. At first all she could see was more blackness, but after her eyes adjusted she realized that she was looking at some kind of metal wall.

The sway under her sore body and the hum of tires on pavement let her know she was in a vehicle. Slowly she took stock of her limbs. Her hands were tied tightly behind her back, wrenching her arms and shoulders painfully backward. Her knees were bent almost to her chest and her ankles were tied as well, but had a little more give than her wrist bonds did.

She lay on her left side; her cheek pressed against something scratchy that she decided must be a blanket or carpet. Slowly she tried shifting her legs and wrists hoping to find some slack in the ropes that bit painfully into the skin of her quickly numbing hands and feet, but she was rewarded with nothing but stabs of pain so sharp they made her gasp.

Forced to stop moving to catch her breath again she took further stock. She was cold and seemingly alone. When she tried to lift her head she got only a few inches off the ground before her stomach heaved with nausea and her head twirled in one slow whirl that made her squeeze her eyes shut again against the surge of dizziness and take deep breaths to keep from being sick.

When her system settled she tried again, this time more carefully, and she was rewarded by the sight of a wheel well and the crack of her head as she banged into something just a few inches above her. When the truck bumped over two large bumps she automatically thought railroad tracks right before she hit her head again. She lowered her head in self defense, breathing through teeth clenched against the renewed pounding in her head.

Certain now that she must be in the back of a truck she curled back into a ball, her knees pressed to her chest as she listened to the tires crunch on what was clearly dirt or gravel. While she'd been trying to get a grasp on her surroundings she'd managed to keep her mind from delving too much further into her situation than ascertaining where she was, but reality finally hit home.

Tears slipped silently down her face to soak into the rough material under her cheek as she thought of her parents and her brothers and Grant, and what they must be going through right now. She had no idea how long she had been unconscious, but it had to have been at least thirty or forty minutes if they were already on dirt roads.

Her mom and dad would be frantic by now, and Sybil and Katie, too. But it was Steven and Grant she was pinning her hopes on. They would understand more quickly what her disappearance meant and they wouldn't rest until they'd found her.

Grant would find her—he would never stop until he did. All she could do was pray that he would be fast enough for it to matter, fast enough for her to be able to tell him how she felt about him, for her to be able to tell him that she wanted nothing more than to marry him and to have his babies, to grow old with him.

What would it do to him if she didn't live? He'd only just begun to recover from Lou's death—would he recover from hers? What would it do to her parents and her brothers?

When the truck slowed to a stop, it's tires crunching loudly on dirt and rocks, Maggie squeezed her eyes shut against her tears and vowed that she would do anything she had to do to give Grant and her a chance to make their dreams come true.

And when she heard the truck's door slam and steadily approaching footsteps, the small bit of calm she'd managed to achieve disappeared and her renewed terror almost claimed her again as she struggled to even her breathing and forced herself to relax her face and body. Quickly she rubbed her cheek against the cloth to erase some of the signs of her earlier tears and squeezed her eyes shut.

And then she began to pray.

The truck bed opened with a harsh squeal and she felt the cool rush of the night air as it bathed her face with a chill breeze. Behind closed eyelids the sudden flash of light almost made her flinch as it flared blood red behind her eyelids, but she managed to remain still, her breathing as even as possible.

She longed to open those eyes just a crack to try to see her abductor, but it took an almost superhuman will to remain frozen as that light stayed steady on her face for several minutes.

Finally the light dropped and the she felt rough hands as they dragged her towards the end of the truck bed. Unable to resist any longer she allowed her left eye to crack open to try to see, but all that was visible was a pair of work boots standing on a dirt road.

She closed her eye again and focused all her will on keeping from crying out in pain and remaining limp as she was abruptly hefted over a strong shoulder. Maggie longed to scream and recoil away from those unfeeling hands, to try something, anything, that would let her escape, but she fought against the strong instinct to flee in an attempt to give herself time—time she knew that would run out soon enough.

In her mind she pictured Cloë's brutally beaten face and the list of murdered women. No, the longer her kidnapper believed she was unconscious, the better. Any time she could give Steven and Grant to find her, to catch him, would be worth the agony her body was going through now.

Beneath her side she felt the man shift before he stepped up three wooden stairs, through a door, and several feet into a room. Without warning she was lowered onto a soft surface and she automatically shut her eyes again, but as she did so she caught a quick glimpse of the room she was in—it looked like a one-room cabin, but she was forced to close her eyes before she'd seen much more than a window and an ancient white stove next to an old, beaten-up couch and matching chair.

Once again Maggie could feel her kidnapper's eyes on her and she was startled when she felt a tug and then her hands were untied. Biting the inside of her cheek she managed to keep the cry of pain from leaving her lips as her arms were jerked forward and then up again above her head. Any fleeting thoughts of possible escape ended with the metallic click of handcuffs as they circled first her right, then her left hand.

"There," the quiet rasp of his voice next to her ear had the terror pumping in her chest again. "Now we'll wait and see, Angel. You cannot sleep forever. You cannot avoid your punishment forever."

Maggie struggled for several moments to keep her breathing even, her body still when she felt those too-cold hands sweep possessively down her arm to caress her face and throat before they trailed down her body. When the pressure lifted and she heard his footsteps retreat from the bed she laid on she risked a quick look only to see the back of a slim man walk out the door.

Maggie swallowed down the bile that had risen in her throat and waited for three long minutes before she attempted to move and look around. She tested the strength of the cuffs and was frustrated to discover she had almost as little movement in the handcuffs as she'd had with the ropes. Already chaffed raw from the rough rope, her wrists ached as they hung suspended above her head attached to a wrought-iron headboard.

Several minutes of pulling and yanking left her winded, her arms screaming, and no closer to being free. Once she'd caught her breath again Maggie lifted her legs to see if there was anything she could do with loosening the ropes on her feet, but with her hands above her head she could do no more than look at the knots that held her ankles together.

Oh, well, she thought, she'd never had much hope of breaking free and escaping on her own. Instead she began a visual search of her surroundings—somewhere there had to be a weapon she could use if he ever untied her hands and feet. After all, unless he was going to kill her right away—and she doubted he would, or why would he have bothered bringing her here—he'd have to let her loose to go to the bathroom if nothing else.

So, she took her time, memorizing where every item was as she looked around the small cabin. Immediately to her left was a small table with a cheap lamp, too small to be used as a bludgeon and a door leading, she supposed, to either the bathroom or another room. A small round table and two wooden chairs stood in the corner and the galley-style kitchen occupied the opposite corner from where she lay. The small couch and chair she'd glimpsed before were in the last corner with the door leading outside between them and her.

Looking closer at the kitchen she was dismayed to see that the shelves were bare and the counters clear of even a single useful item. The loud hum of the ancient refrigerator rattled noisily and almost covered the steady dripping of the rusty faucet in the single-tub sink. Looking to where the couch sat she noted a coat-rack and a badly warped framed painting on the wall—both of which could maybe be fashioned into weapons of a sort.

The heavy tread of boots on the steps outside warned her to lay her head down. She had barely closed her eyes again when the door swung opened, letting a gust of frigid October air in. Her abductor crossed the room whistling cheerfully to himself, and Maggie lay helpless to move. She noted with horror that the song he whistled was "If You're Happy and You know It".

When the bed depressed next to her and she once again felt his breath on her face she couldn't hold back the little moan of terror that sounded in her throat.

"Playing possum, Angel?"

The animalistic need to flee upon hearing his predatory voice overwhelmed the common sense that told Maggie there was nowhere to run and her eyes flew open as she struggled futilely against her bonds. The sight of his distorted face mere inches from hers had Maggie cringing back and she struggled to keep calm as her breath began to hitch.

The quick sting of his slap was both a shock and inevitable. Instinctively Maggie froze, her wide eyes on his face—a face she knew. Finally she was face-to-face with the devil, and it wasn't the faceless monster she'd pictured in her mind, it was the face of a man she'd met, had liked.

When he'd seen that she recognized him his face relaxed into an expression of such cruel satisfaction she shrank back desperately, her head shaking back and forth as if to deny what she saw and she pleaded, "Please don't hurt me. Abraham, please…"

"Don't say that name! You are no longer worthy. You whored yourself and ruined everything!" Maggie watched in horror as his face shifted first to rage, then fury and finally to tears as he softly said, "You were my Angel. Mine alone, but now you have to be punished. Don't you see?" he leaned even closer and Maggie saw the unholy glint of fanaticism in his eyes that scared her more than anything else had to this point.

"Don't you see," he repeated as his face broke into a sweet smile that made her stomach hurt, "You *must* be purified in the burning fire of redemption or you will never be saved, you can never be mine again. I knew you were special—different than all the others—right from the start, and when I saw that you had sinned," he paused and his voice hardened, "you sinned and were disgustingly unfaithful whoring yourself like some kind of bitch in heat! I knew you would have to be punished, to pay the price.

"But now I know that you can be saved. Saved in the purifying fire. But first you must be punished for your transgressions," he stood again and looked down on her, his face now contorted into a mask of rage.

Dear God, she prayed, *help me. Help Grant find me*, she thought helplessly as he stepped forward, his hands raised and hatred and madness shining out from his eyes.

She screamed. But there was no one there to hear her. There was no one there to care.

SEVENTY-THREE

Less than five minutes after they'd gotten Moses Swanson back into the interrogation room they had the *who*. Now they just had to find out the *where*.

Upon finding out that Maggie had been taken Mo had been shocked, terrified, and Grant was sure, genuinely upset. Not that Grant cared about that at this point. Right now, all he cared about was getting Maggie back and capturing the sadistic bastard who had taken her and slaughtered at least twelve other women.

Moses continued to deny any knowledge of the previous victims, but he readily admitted that he let his brother, Abraham, borrow his truck whenever he asked, and that Abraham could easily have borrowed his jacket. He also revealed that Abraham was also the only one with the key for the room beneath the stairs in his mother's house.

When asked again about his location on the days of the previous murders Moses could not give alibis, but when questioned about several of the other suspected cases Grant was convinced were tied to these, he was able to prove he'd been nowhere near the towns in question.

Convinced that Moses was telling the truth, Grant began to slowly, methodically question Mo about the places he thought Abraham could go that were secluded, or where Abraham felt safe.

Other than leaving the room several times to confirm Mo's alibis, Steven remained in the room and paced relentlessly back and forth behind Grant's chair, pausing only long enough to stare daggers at Mo when he stopped talking or tried to deny knowledge of any detail.

Mo's eyes tracked Steve's progress, his voice stuttering with spurts and stops each time Steve glared at him. Like a cornered animal, Mo's eyes flicked back and forth from Steve's prowling form to the man sitting across from him like a giant coiled spring. Despite constantly flicking glances at the obvious threat Steve presented as he paced agitatedly back and forth, Mo intuitively focused his eyes on Grant.

Mo's instincts warned that the seemingly calm man in front of him represented the bigger danger—his tawny eyes drilled deep into Mo's, forcing him to look away over and over again.

"Can you think of anywhere that he could have taken her? A distant relative's place? A favorite campsite? Someplace he felt safe or that he considers his own?" Grant knew it was a long shot, but he refused to believe that Abraham had taken her somewhere random.

Grant *had* to believe that Abraham would keep her alive, that he would take her somewhere he felt safe. If he allowed himself to consider the alternatives—the thousands of places he could have gone in the past hour, or, God forbid, the idea that she could already be dead and lying somewhere waiting to be found—then the remaining thread of calmness he was clinging to would surely snap if that happened. And he was afraid that if it did, he would descend back into the black hole of misery he'd had to climb out of following the death of his partner. He couldn't imagine a future without her.

Mo raised a hand that shook to wipe the sweat from his upper lip as he said, "I d-don't know…"

"Don't tell me you don't know, you son-of-a-bitch," Steve roared as he pounded the table next to Mo's trembling hands, "That miserable excuse for a human being has taken Maggie, has slaughtered at least twelve other women, and all you can say is 'I don't know'?"

As Mo cringed away from the enraged cop Grant reached forward to grip Steve's arm and said in a low voice, "Steve. Back off."

Steve whipped his head around to look at Grant before he shoved away from the table to resume his agitated pacing.

"Moses, I believe that you didn't have any idea that Abraham was hurting these women, but now he's got Maggie, and the longer he has her the less likely it is we'll find her in time," Grant spoke softly, slowly.

Mo swallowed convulsively before he whispered, "I don't know where he is. We were never close. We have no family nearby. Our mother's an only child and grew up out East. We never knew our father or his people. I don't even know his name. We never went camping, never went anywhere but church camp, but that was shut down years ago."

Grant sensed Steve come to attention as he stopped his pacing to listen. Keeping his voice calm despite the small twinge of excitement he felt, Grant said, "What camp?"

Confused, Mo said, "Um, well it was out somewhere near Littleton on the other side of the lake. I'm not sure w-where, exactly, but I only went once when I was fourteen or fifteen. But, Momma sent Abraham three years from when he was around twelve until he was fifteen or sixteen, I think. He always hated going— never wanted to be away from Momma, but she made him. She always said our minds needed clean pursuits during those years of temptation; that our hearts needed to be purified. Abraham begged her to let him stay home and finally she took her belt to him, saying the Devil was making him say so."

For several long moments Steve and Grant were silent. Grant because at last it seemed like they were getting to the heart of why all these events were happening, and Steve because he was appalled, unable to see how any loving mother could treat her sons the way he thought this woman had.

Steve pictured his own mother, and the constant steady knowledge of her love. He felt the stirrings of pity for the two young boys, but the image of his mother's tear-streaked face and the fear in her eyes when she'd heard Maggie was missing flashed into his mind and quickly crushed those stirrings of pity before they were fully formed.

It took another forty minutes of questioning before Grant was fully satisfied that they'd gotten every bit of information out of Mo that they could. It hadn't been until more than thirty minutes had passed after they'd first talked about the camp that Mo had remembered a single weekend camping trip that Abraham had taken with one of the neighbor kids up into the hills north of town.

Mo had been in college by then and hadn't remembered exactly which campground the boys had used, but he had remembered the name of the friend—Sean Martin. When Moses had said his name Steve had once again whirled from his pacing to lean both hands on the table, his face inches from Mo's.

"Sean Martin?"

"Y-yes. I'm almost positive his name was Sean and I think his last name was M-Martin."

451

Steve turned to look at Grant before he pushed up and walked out of the door. Ten minutes later Grant left the interrogation room in search of his partner. He was pretty sure he knew what had gotten Steve so excited—Anna Martin.

The first victim in Hope had had an older brother and although Grant couldn't be sure his name had been Sean, he was willing to bet that it was.

Steve was hanging up the phone when Grant walked up. "Just spoke with Dennis Martin, Anna Martin's father. He says he remembers his son, Sean, going on several different camping trips with various friends during high school, but he didn't remember Abraham specifically.

"Martin also said that Sean and his friends would go over to the campground that his wife's brother, Trent Crawford, owned. Place is called Lakeside Cabins. The family still runs the place, but it closes after Labor Day and the family seldom goes out after then. Mr. Martin also gave me both Sean and Trent Crawford's contact info."

"Evans, Sullivan." At the sound of their names, Grant and Steve looked up to see Chief Banyon tilt his head towards the conference room before heading in there himself. The two men gathered their latest information and quickly made their way through the almost-empty squad room to find their fellow detectives already sitting around the table.

They joined them and Banyon leaned one lean hip against the corner of the table and began, "Okay, while you were finishing up with Swanson I had Sylvester and Donovan track down the current info on that church camp—Camp Omega. I've got most of our part-time guys already out at the Sullivan house and the Swanson place searching for anything that could point us in the direction that Abraham Swanson might be going. For now we are assuming that he is going to be headed somewhere secluded to put Maggie there. I've coordinated with both the State and County boys and they are already canvassing the local hotels, motels, abandoned houses, etc. They will be patrolling all the major and not-so-major roadways in a fifty mile perimeter.

"What that leaves are the six of you to search this campground. Dusty I'm going to want you to stay in town to help coordinate the investigations at the Swanson and Sullivan residences."

"Chief, we have something you need to hear," Steve said and then filled them all in on what he'd found out about Lakeside Cabins. Sylvester spoke next, "We managed to get a hold of the current owner of Camp Omega for Boys. Guy's name is Dan Reddy. He said we were welcome to search the campgrounds, said the place hadn't been used in more than eight years and he only goes out a couple times a year to make sure the buildings are secure and to keep the grounds somewhat up-kept. According to him, there are three main buildings housing the kitchen/dining rooms, activities building and meeting rooms. In addition to that there are twenty small cabins scattered around the property, a boat house, horse barns and various storage sheds."

Banyon rubbed one hand across his forehead and sighed. "Okay. Donovan, Sylvester, Mac, and Jones, head out to Camp Omega. I'll see if I can't get some troopers to come and help you guys look there. Evans and Sullivan, talk to Sean and Dennis Martin and get the info on Lakeside. As soon as they are done with Omega, the rest can join you in searching Lakeside.

"Dusty, I've changed my mind, you go with Evans and Sullivan and I'll take care of the in-town investigations myself. All right, I know we are all raring to get going, but I want you guys to be careful and to check in every hour on the hour. The guy we're dealing with here has proven that he is not afraid to kill, and to take out anyone he thinks is in his way, so watch your backs.

"Steve, I know this is hard on you, and if I could spare the manpower I'd pull you from this investigation. But I can't. So don't make me regret this."

"Yes, Sir," Steve said stiffly and stood to leave. Everyone else stood and began moving, each one slapping Grant or Steve on the back as they went by, or murmuring some word of encouragement. As they filed out of the room Grant was the last one left with the Chief.

"Watch out for him, Evans," Banyon began as he skewered Grant with a long measured look before he added, "and for yourself."

Grant nodded and hurried out to catch up with Steve and Dusty. He walked up just in time to hear Steve say, "Dusty, I need you to go talk to Sean Martin and see which cabin he used to stay in, any details he can remember about the weekend with Abraham, really any details about Swanson he can remember." When Dusty replied, "I'm on it," Steve added, "Call when you know. We'll be at Trent Crawford's."

All three men headed out to the parking lot and split up into their respective cars. When they'd settled into the car, Grant behind the wheel once more, Grant said, "Where to?"

Steve gave him the address and they took off. After several minutes of taut silence Grant brought up the thought that had been on his mind for the past half hour. "Steve, we are going to need more than just the three of us searching this campground. Even if it is only half the size of Camp Omega and we eventually get some help from the State, I want people I know looking for Maggie..."

Steve shook his head and held up one hand as he spoke passionately, "I can guess what you're getting at Evans and the answer is no. There's no way we are going to let anyone else in my family put their lives on the line to find this psycho. They have absolutely no training and I won't put them in a situation that could risk their lives. Absolutely not."

Grant released his breath slowly, but remained silent. He'd known it had been a bad idea, but the hint of desperation he felt was slowly but surely eating away at his resolve to keep his personal feelings for Maggie on the back burner. As a trained investigator he knew that the longer it took them to find Maggie, the lower the odds were that they'd find her alive—if at all.

Every minute counted in a typical kidnapping, and there was nothing typical about this kidnapping. The fact that it had been one at all, and not simply a murder, may be due to the circumstances, but Grant didn't think so. Not after spending most of the morning looking through the journals and photo albums found in Swanson's secret room under the stairs. Not after hearing Moses talk about their mother and the hints of things she'd said and done to them.

No matter what the reasons behind this monster's actions Grant knew just three things—Swanson had Maggie, they were missing, and it had already been over two hours.

SEVENTY-FOUR

When Maggie woke for the third time she had no illusions about where she was or about whom Abraham Swanson was.

Too exhausted to move, too scared to open her eyes, Maggie lay as still as she could, listening, listening for the scrape of a shoe on the dirty wooden floor, the rub of clothing as it shifted, or God, help her, the sound of his breathing close by, watching her as she lay there, helpless.

Rejecting the horrifying thought, she focused her mind on steadying her breathing again. The past hours were a blur of pain and terror and fury, and the certain knowledge that the monster that had taken her from her family was going to kill her.

It was only a matter of time.

How much time before he grew weary of punishing her for the sins his warped mind believed she'd committed? How much time before she no longer wanted to fight the pain and the fear. Already she knew she was weakening physically. Only the bright hope of her family, and more importantly, of Steven and Grant, had kept her from succumbing to the terror completely.

When she had waited several minutes and not heard anything she cautiously cracked one of her eyes to look around the room. When she found it empty she allowed herself to relax slightly as she took stock of her aching body.

She could no longer open her left eye, and even the slightest movement of her mouth sent shooting pain up her bruised jaw into her head. Her arms and legs were almost numb from the constant pull of the bonds that still held them. When Maggie attempted to shift her weight to ease some of the discomfort from laying in the same position for so long, her breath caught in her chest as a searing pain seemed to press on her right side and chest making her think she'd had at least one of her ribs cracked.

Taking shallow breaths to try to relieve the sharp, stabbing pains, Maggie collapsed back onto the bed and tears of frustration filled her eyes. She slowly started to relax her muscles, one by one, knowing that she needed to rest as much as possible if she was going to have any chance of escaping—or even surviving long enough to give Grant and Steven a chance to find her.

455

Her only hope was that he'd have to let her get up to use the bathroom eventually if he didn't want a huge mess on his bed. And when he did she had to be ready to act. So, she would conserve her energy and wait.

Wait for an opening to escape. Wait for Grant to come. And if that failed, she would wait for death.

In the depths of the night in the shadows of the forest surrounding the cabin where Maggie was bound, the killer paced furiously, his arms swinging awkwardly at his sides and his face covered with a sheen of sweat despite the freezing temperatures.

The moon's light, so bright earlier in the evening, was completely obscured by dirty gray clouds that looked inky in the deepening night sky. The faint sounds of a dog that barked and cars that rushed by on a nearby interstate were the only sounds other than the rustle of leaves and occasional snap of a stray twig his agitated pacing caused.

He waited for the dawn. When the last hours of the devil's day ended and All Saint's Day could begin. His Angel had lied to him, had whored herself with the cop, had made him believe—really believe—that he'd finally found an Angel worthy of his attentions, worthy of his love.

She had been his special Angel, the most special of all, and the rush of fury at the mere thought of her betrayal had him screaming out into the quiet night. As his guttural cries and screams faded into the depths of the woods his hands fisted in his hair and pulled as he fell to the frozen ground and began to punch and scrape wildly at the dirt.

As the roaring in his head faded he fell to his side, weeping and clinging weakly to the rosary he kept in his coat pocket at all times. As the soothing feel of the beads and the repetition and ritual of the familiar words calmed him, his breathing slowed and returned back to normal.

He dropped off to sleep, curled into a ball on the cold floor of the forest, the previous half hour lost in the psychotic chaos of his mind. After nearly an hour had passed he rose stiffly to his feet to begin pacing again, a beautific smile on his face and the only evidence of his fit the ripped fingernails and dirt-encrusted hands that once again swung rigidly at his sides.

His earlier rage was forgotten as he began, again, to picture his Angel before she fell. The small night noises that had fallen silent when he'd screamed and cursed slowly started again. As he walked, his pace began to increase, and each time he turned to face the path that would lead him back to the cabin and his Angel he longed to stride down it, to finish the process of purification he had started earlier.

He had punished her for making him want her as she had lain writhing on the bed before him—he'd been horrified that she could make him want her even after she'd fallen. No other Angel ever had.

And for just a moment, he'd almost given into the temptation and taken her body, but at the last moment he'd stopped, horror-stricken that he had almost succumbed to her wonton charms, that the devil had almost tricked him into losing his own soul.

He'd had to beat her severely for that, until the pleading and the crying had fallen silent and she had stopped moving. Exhausted, he had fallen into a deep sleep on the dusty sofa across the room from her, but after less than an hour he'd awoken, his fatigue gone, replaced by the manic energy that had led him to pace and scream into the darkness.

Finally, he could stand it no longer and he turned onto the path that would lead him back to his Angel. It was time for her purification to continue.

Inside the dark cabin Maggie listened to the occasional screams and cries that broke the silence of the night and she prayed.

Prayed for the coming morning's light; prayed for someone, anyone, to hear him and to come; prayed for the strength to face the death she knew would come when he'd worked himself up enough to return. Eventually she fell into a fitful sleep, her body jerking and involuntary moans and whimpers echoing quietly into the empty cabin around her.

And asleep, she missed the tread of footsteps as they climbed the stairs outside.

SEVENTY-FIVE

After less than five minutes of speaking with Crawford, it was clear to Steve and Grant that they were going to need a lot more than the two of them and Dusty to cover the Lakeside Campgrounds.

Located east of town along a five-mile stretch of a small river that fed into Ascension Lake the campgrounds were two miles deep and held twenty cabins spaced out over the entire five mile stretch, each about a half-mile apart from the others and completely isolated.

Grant glanced over at Steve as they bent over a map that Crawford had spread out between them. "In addition to the cabins there are three sheds that hold canoes and fishing supplies and a small house here," Crawford paused to point to a place on the map, "The caretaker lives there five months out of the year."

"Is he there now?"

"Nope. May through September. The cabins aren't heated, just equipped with small wood stoves for cold nights."

"What's this back here?" Grant asked as he pointed at two small, unlabeled squares right on the edge of the campground.

Crawford leaned closer to see what Grant was referring to and nodded, "Those are not officially part of my property. They belonged to two of the landowners whom I bought my property from years ago. When the county redrew the property lines during the sales, they put the edge of my property in front of the cabins instead of in the back."

"Are they occupied?"

Crawford shook his head sadly and said, "No. The land is State park land now and they are planning on tearing them down in the spring."

"Why did that take so long?" Grant wondered.

Crawford shrugged, "I guess they assumed the buildings were mine, too, but they've gotten so out of repair, they finally must of decided to get rid of them once and for all."

"Were they in use ten years ago as part of your campgrounds?"

"No, but back then I still did maintenance work in and around them because the county hadn't finalized the property lines yet."

"All right, thank you Mr. Crawford. If we could, we need to take this map and get the keys from you."

"Sure, I got the keys out after you called. Each key is labeled with the number of the cabin as it's listed on the map. Here's the key for the chain that's across the road entrance and a master key that should unlock all the storage buildings."

"Thanks for your help—we'll get them back to you as soon as possible."

"Keep them as long as you need, I just hope you find the poor girl who's missing."

All three men stood and after taking the large key-ring and shaking hands with Crawford, Steve and Grant hurried out to the car.

Steve put a quick call in to update the Chief and Grant listened as he started the older car. When Steve swore violently and said, "Goodbye," Grant turned, one eyebrow cocked, to hear what had upset Steve.

"There's a major car accident on I-35. A semi hauling milk spilled over on 35. The state guys who we needed to help us have been sent to take charge of the cleanup."

Grant was silent for a moment before asking, "Dusty?"

"Chief said he just checked in. Seems Sean Martin couldn't remember much, he'd thought it was one of the cabins inland away from the river that they stayed in, but he couldn't be sure after so many years. He didn't even remember Abraham at first. Dusty's headed over to the campground entrance now and he'll meet us there in about fifteen or twenty minutes."

"Steve," Grant began, but Steve broke in, "I know. I know. Let's go get them."

Without a word Grant whipped the car in a u-turn and pulled into the Sullivan's driveway less than five minutes later. As he parked he looked up at the house—light spilled from every window, and most of the driveway was still crowded with two police cars and the forensic team's van.

They hurried up the walk and inside without a word. There, they found Seth, Jack, Bram, and Dillon gathered in the living room, armed with flashlights and shotguns, and dressed in their winter hunting gear.

Steve came to a stop, exclaiming, "What the hell!" as Elizabeth came into the room followed closely by Sybil and Katie, each holding two large thermoses.

"Watch your language, Steven Michael.

Steve turned to Grant and said, "I thought I told you before that we weren't going to do this—how did they know we were coming?"

Before Grant could reply Bram said, "Steven, do you really think any of us were going to simply sit by and not at least help look? I talked to Chief Banyon about a half hour ago and he let us know what you were going to be doing. We're coming with."

Steve recognized the steely look in his normally mild-mannered father's eyes as one he'd seen countless times in his stubborn sister's. Steve gave in and said, "I know. I mean, we were coming to get you, but this will save us a lot of time. You two, go with Grant in our car," Steve pointed to Jack and Dillon, "I'll go with Dad and Seth in their car. We'll fill you in on the way."

Elizabeth stepped forward to hug each of her sons and Grant in turn before she clung to Bram. "Be careful," she whispered.

"We'll bring her back to you, Darling," Bram murmured before he turned to leave.

Seth kissed Katie and Sybil before he said to Aaron, "Take care of your mom and sister." When Aaron nodded, a determined look on his young pale face Seth grabbed him into a hug, too, before he followed his father out of the room.

The two cars pulled away into the night and Elizabeth stood, an arm around each of her grandchildren, as she watched her men walk away from her into unknown danger. Silently she prayed, *Please, Lord, bring them all back to me safe.*

Over Katie's head her eyes met Sybil's and in them Elizabeth saw the same fear and worry she felt reflected back at her. Elizabeth drew in one slow breath as the second car rounded the corner and drove out of sight, and she set her shoulders. She steered her exhausted grandchildren back into the warmth and light of the kitchen and settled them each into a chair. She bustled around the room, automatically putting hot cocoa into two mugs and fresh-brewed coffee into two others before she joined them at the table.

As Elizabeth studied their pale, weary faces she longed to send them to bed, but she knew that not one of them would be able to sleep. She knew that she couldn't, either, so she did the only thing she could think to do—stay busy. Out loud she forced as much cheer as she could into her voice and said, "Everyone will be hungry when they get back home, who wants to help me make a gigantic breakfast feast?"

As the children slowly began speaking Sybil took the paper and pen from Elizabeth's motionless fingers and grabbed her hand. Elizabeth looked away from where her grandchildren sat, heads bowed over a growing grocery list and stared out the window until Katie's soft voice brought her back.

"We should definitely make French toast, right Grams? That's Maggie's favorite."

Elizabeth turned her back on the darkness of the night that seemed to beat against the window and focused instead on Katie's face. She straightened her shoulders and said firmly, "Absolutely. Let's write *everyone's* favorite down."

SEVENTY-SIX

By the time Grant and Steve pulled up to the entrance to Lakeside Cabins, they had brought the rest of the Sullivans up to speed. They'd agreed ahead of time to keep the details of the attacks out of the update, knowing that it would just upset them even more than they already were. The basic facts were horrifying enough on their own.

Dusty was waiting by the chain that blocked access to the road and followed them in after Steve unlocked the chains and drove forward down the dirt road. It wound for more than three miles through the woods. The stark outlines of trees stripped bare of their leaves loomed out of the darkness, their limbs oddly twisted in the sudden harsh glare of their headlights, creating shadows that shifted and swept as each car passed by.

After almost five minutes of tense silence, the cars came around the final bend to pull into an open area were a large log building with a sign that said "Lakeside Cabins Check In". Below it, a smaller sign reminded any who had made it past the locked chain that the grounds were closed for the season.

They parked and all seven men got out of the cars to gather around the hood of Grant's car where Steve had spread the large map of the campgrounds out.

"Okay, there are twenty cabins, three sheds, the main lodge and two abandoned cabins that all need to be searched. We'll break into three groups—Seth, Dillon and Dusty, you'll take the lodge, the first five cabins and two canoe sheds. Bram, you and Steve will take these eight cabins and the last shed, here. That leaves the last seven cabins and the two abandoned cabins for me and Jack.

"Everyone take a radio and your cell phones. We need to check in every fifteen minutes with each other and then Steve will check in on the hour with Chief Banyon. Chief said he'd get us some troopers as soon as he could, but with the highway cleanup it will be a while before anyone can come, and I don't want to wait."

Grant straightened and nodded to Steve who said, "Officially, we cannot allow any of you to carry firearms, but…" he stopped as Jack, Dillon, and Seth all burst into speech. "BUT, he continued

462

loudly, "the Chief said he would allow you all to carry your rifles as long as you used rubber bullets."

Steve pulled three large boxes of ammunition out of his heavy coat and dropped them on the hood of the car before he continued, "Now, we've filled you in on this guy, if he's here, if you find them, do *not*, I repeat *do not* try to take him down by yourself. If you try and fail, Maggie's gone."

The men fell silent, the tension palpable as Steve's words sank in. Dillon's eyes dropped and Seth reached over to grip his arm while Jack swore and shifted his weight before falling silent again.

Steve waited and Bram put his hand on Steve's shoulder and squeezed. Steve cleared his throat before he continued, "So. What I'm saying is don't screw up. The moment you find something, or if anything feels off at *all*, radio Grant, Dusty or myself. Be slow. Be careful."

Bram grabbed the top two boxes of ammo and handed them to Seth and Jack before taking the third to split with Dillon. After the four men had reloaded their rifles and all had checked their radios they set out, each peeling off at their designated search areas.

The beam of seven flashlights cut through the darkness and the soft crunch of booted feet on dried leaves and twigs were the only man-made sound as the night sounds around them fell silent at their approach.

Grant and Jack walked swiftly along the northern-most trail towards the back set of cabins for nearly a quarter of a mile, the rest of the searchers long since left behind. The images of Cloë and the other victims flashed through Grant's mind for the millionth time since he'd discovered Maggie missing. Jack's bleak voice broke through his brooding thoughts, "Do you think she's dead?"

Grant sighed and slowed to a stop to face Jack before he reluctantly answered, "I don't know. Statistically…"

"Screw statistics, Evans, that's my sister that monster has not some frickin' number," Jack spat out in a furious low whisper. "I want to know what *you* think. Is she…is she still alive?"

Grant sighed again before he answered, "If he's following his typical pattern, then no. But, and this is a big but, I don't think Maggie is typical for him. There's nothing about her that follows his usual pattern or we'd have found her in her apartment instead of combing these woods at four in the morning. Do I think she's still alive? Yes, I do. But the longer it takes for us to find her the worse her chances are of staying that way."

Grant paused for a moment to let his words sink in before he said brusquely, "Turn off your light. The first cabin is just around the bend and I don't want to risk tipping him off if they're there."

Jack quickly turned off his light and as they waited to let their eyes adjust to the darkness he tried to take comfort in the knowledge that Grant still thought his little sister was alive, and tried to block the thought of what had probably happened to her in the past five hours. Calm again—or as calm as he could manage—Jack stowed his flashlight in his backpack and hitched his rifle up more securely before he followed Grant forward once again.

They turned the bend and saw a completely dark cabin nestled among the trees. Grant paused again and hunched down behind a larger tree to wait and watch silently for several minutes before he seemed satisfied. Grant gestured to Jack to stay where he was and began to circle slowly in a wide circle completely around the cabin before he approached a window.

Jack covered him from the tree line and watched Grant's controlled movements, the tension of waiting making his hands grip the stock of his gun so hard his hands began to cramp up. The waiting was agony. He had to grit his teeth together to keep himself from screaming at Grant to hurry. Only the knowledge that he would be putting Maggie in further danger kept him from giving in to the need.

After what seemed like an eternity, but what was probably more like ten minutes Grant rose from his position under the dirty window to wave Jack forward. Jack jogged over and Grant whispered, "I don't see any signs of them, but I want to look inside, too, just to be sure. Stay on the porch and let me know if you see anyone approach."

"Okay," Jack settled onto the porch behind a large planter still filled with the brown, shriveled remains of summer flowers in it. After only a few minutes Grant was back outside and locking the door.

Jack felt disappointment and relief in equal measures—he'd been sure they would find Maggie here, but when they hadn't seen any obvious signs he'd begun to dread what Grant might find in some closet or back room.

"One down, eight to go," Grant said. He switched on his flashlight and they headed back into the trees towards the next cabin on their list.

The same pattern repeated itself six more times until Jack felt he would burst from the ever-mounting tension followed by increasing disappointment each time they found an empty cabin and no signs of Maggie.

As he walked quietly behind Grant he stared at the other man's back, and wondered how he remained so completely calm. He seemed to Jack as if he could be taking a stroll through the woods instead of searching for a homicidal maniac and the woman he loved. Did he even really love her? Not once in the preceding hour and a half had Grant looked or sounded anything other than professional—even detached.

When Grant stopped suddenly to crouch down Jack almost walked right into him. Jack shook off his mounting doubts and focused his light on the ground at Grant's feet. At first Jack couldn't see why Grant had stopped, but the closer he looked the more he saw the signs that someone had passed through the area—several branches broken on a nearby bush, trampled leaves and just beyond the arc of Jack's light, fresh gouges in the ground where someone or something had tried to dig into the frozen ground.

Jack turned to meet Grant's gaze when Grant stood again and the look of vicious triumph and calculated violence on Grant's face had Jack rethinking his assumption that Grant was completely calm, and reevaluating the idea that he didn't care.

Grant gestured back to where they'd just come from and Jack turned and retraced their steps. After they'd walked for a few minutes Grant stopped and called in what they'd found. He told the Chief that they were going to the first of the abandoned cabins on the campground's border.

By mutual consent they both turned off their flashlights when they had gotten back to where Grant found the first signs that someone bigger than a squirrel had been in these woods recently. After he cautioned Jack to remain silent Grant set forward once more, forcing himself to slow down when he longed to run forward as fast as he could.

Only the thought of what could happen to Maggie kept him moving forward with caution.

Steve and Bram were searching their last cabin when the radio on Steve's hip crackled and the Chief let them know what Jack and Grant had found. Their growing frustration and fear disappeared as hope speared through both men.

Steve told the Chief that they would join the other two men within fifteen minutes and signed off. Bram had already pulled the map of the campground out and spread it out against the side of the cabin to find the area where Grant had found the tracks.

"If we cut through here," Bram pointed to an abandoned logging road that cut through the campgrounds at an angle, "We can come around to approach from the rear."

Steve nodded once and called it in before they took off at a jog through the ever-dropping temperatures of the night. Within minutes they'd found the road and after almost ten minutes of silence Steve slowed down, his hand held up to warn Bram to be cautious as they rounded a slight bend in the road to find a rusted red pick-up parked off to the side of the road.

Steve told Bram to cover him. He quickly approached the rear of the truck and his heart pounded so hard in his chest that for a moment he could hear nothing else. He paused to take several deep breaths and then took the last step around the back to find the rear of the truck enclosed. He peered through the windows of the cab, and seeing nothing out of the ordinary, he debated for several seconds over whether or not to open the rear of the cab before the brother in him won out over the cop and he reached out to open it.

Bram grabbed Steve's hand before he could touch the door and whispered, "Go look at those tracks over there," and pointed about ten feet down the road. Steve met his father's eyes for one long moment before he nodded and turned his back on his father's hand as it reached to grasp the truck's door handle.

He'd only gone three steps when the sharp complaint of rusted steel in need of oil made Steve cringe as he quickly searched the trees for any signs of movement. He could only hope that the trees lining the road on either side would muffle any noises they had made—the cabin couldn't be too much farther.

As he waited for his father to complete his illegal search Steve called in the truck's plate and was told that it was registered to a Sam Sweeny, but had been reported stolen two nights ago.

With another muffled creak, Steve heard the rear of the truck close as he turned to walk towards his father and said, "Well, the truck's stolen. Did you find anything?"

"Some old blankets and a roll of duct tape and rope. Nothing out of the ordinary, really."

But Steve could see the drawn expression on his father's face in the moonlight and knew that he was thinking the same thing that Steve was—that the rope and tape were perfectly ordinary and probably found in millions of trucks, but they were also the most commonly used items that kidnappers used to bind their victims.

Silent again, they started back down the road. They no longer ran, but walked as quietly as possible. After only five minutes they could make out a dark shape that was the rear of the cabin through the trees and they stepped quickly off the path into the trees to squat down out of sight.

Steve said as quietly as he could, "We'll move forward about ten more feet, and then I need you to cover me as I take a closer look. Here," Steve handed over his cell phone, "Call the Chief if something happens and I'm not back in twenty minutes. If you see anyone near me, click the talk button twice on the radio and I'll know."

Bram hesitated only a moment before he nodded and clapped Steve on the back before he took the phone and moved forward to settle as comfortably as he could behind a large tree.

Steve crept forward and as he moved, he placed each foot down slowly and deliberately. Even so, every few steps his foot would rustle through leaves or crunch on a pebble, and the sound would make him pause before he continued, his ears strained to hear anything suspicious.

He was halfway to the northeast corner of the cabin when he heard a very muffled thump from the far side of the cabin, his radio clicked twice and he saw a flash of color in the moonlight between two trees on his right.

He dropped quickly to one knee, his gun coming up as he scoured the trees and searched for the source of movement. His radio frantically clicked again and he heard the sound of a twig snapping directly behind him. The bastard must have circled around through the trees he thought as he pivoted swiftly to find himself looking right into the barrel of a gun.

SEVENTY-SEVEN

The click of the cabin door brought Maggie out of her restless sleep with a start of terror that quickly numbed again. Cautiously, she slit her right eye open.

The first thing she noticed was that the small lantern Abraham had left on earlier was no longer lit. A surge of hope swept through her when she could begin to make out the shapes of the furniture as the utter darkness of the night faded into the deep gunmetal gray of pre-dawn.

Despite the gloom of the faint light she knew what was important—she had made it through the night. Slowly despair settled back over her. How many hours had she been missing now? At least eight or nine, she calculated. It had seemed like days, not hours, since she'd been so happy making plans to celebrate with Grant, to meet for lunch later today with Sybil. Would she ever see them again?

As her thoughts swam sluggishly through her mind, she remained as still as possible. She ignored the pain that seemed to permeate her entire body. Instead she focused on listening for some sign of where he was.

She had finally decided that it was safe and tensed to attempt to shift her weight when a harsh scraping noise behind her had her heart rate skyrocketing once more. Quickly she closed her eyes again and tried to even her breathing.

Soft footsteps approached where she lay and she forced herself not to recoil when she felt a hand brushed gently over her hair. For several minutes she felt his hand petting her as she feigned sleep and prayed that she would not betray herself. Finally she heard his steps retreat and the sound of the door as it opened and shut.

Instinct told her that if he found her awake again he would whip his anger back up to a fury, and somehow she didn't believe that she would survive. The cycle of fury and violence followed by the pacing, cursing and screaming, then a short exhausted sleep and gentle petting had run its course three times now. Each time the fury was worse, the violence longer, and the intervals of calmness grew shorter and shorter.

Her time was running out.

As terrified as she was at times, a blessed numbness, of lethargy, weighed her limbs down and slowed her thoughts. But even through her body's defensive reactions she was aware that her captor was working himself up to kill her. Truly, it was a miracle that he hadn't done it already.

The last time he'd beaten her she had wanted him to, just to end the fear, the terrible pain that had eventually given her the escape she'd needed to fall into peaceful darkness. But the pain was too constant, too great to let her stay there for long, and with her regained consciousness there was also a return of her will to survive.

The images of the people she loved swept through her mind and for perhaps the last time she gathered her strength around her. She had just enough energy for one last effort.

Grant and Steven were searching for her, she knew they wouldn't stop. But she was no longer certain that she could hold out long enough for them to find her in time.

She had given up hope that she could somehow escape the handcuffs that were attached to her wrists, but she *had* managed to work the iron headboard back and forth until a sprinkle of fine red powder fell from the bar to her arm every time she shifted. The bars were rusty, and her best chance at freedom.

The problem was she had only short amounts of time to work in, and the pain from her arms—and what she was pretty sure were several cracked or broken ribs—made the work slow because she was forced to frequently stop to catch her breath and let the pain recede. The only thing that was in her favor was that both hands were attached to the same length of iron.

After working all night, she could finally feel the bar giving, and she frantically pulled with every bit of her remaining strength. She had to bite her lip so hard to keep from screaming at the wrench of pain she tasted fresh blood, but the result was a loud squeal as the bar separated halfway from the frame.

Maggie's head swam and nausea threatened to make her pass out again as she fell still, sweating and panting from her efforts. For the first time in hours she felt a real surge of hope move through her. After she had rested for as long as she dared Maggie willed her body to respond, certain that Abraham would return at any moment.

She struggled to move, but she couldn't do much more than shift her head to once more scan the room for a weapon. Her gaze fell on the framed picture that had been hanging on the wall, but which now lay in pieces on the floor, having fallen there during Abraham's last fit of anger.

For once the bastard had helped her out, she thought grimly to herself as she noted several jagged shards of broken glass on the floor near the door. Slowly she reached up to pull one last time to completely break off the bar when she heard the sound she'd been dreading—footsteps on the stairs.

She had just enough time to place one cuff over the separated part of the bar and slump back before the door opened and she heard his voice sing out softly, "Angel, my Angel…Wake up, wake up, the time for judgment has arrived. Oh, yes, my Angel. It's time."

Jack quickly lost sight of Grant as he moved off into the darkness of the woods, but after only ten minutes Jack noted a gradual lightening of the sky. He pulled up his sleeve and looked at his watch, 5:56 a.m. They'd been in the woods for more than three hours now.

One by one he was able to make out more and more of the trees around him, and about a hundred yards away he could see the dark shape of the cabin. He knew that Grant was probably already on the back side of the building and that he was *supposed* to stay put, but after three hours of waiting Jack couldn't stand it any longer.

There was a very good chance his sister was in the building so close by, and he could not wait any more. He carefully moved forward in a direct line until he was only fifteen yards from the cabin. Grant was still not in sight and Jack could no longer see around the far side of the cabin to see if he was almost done. More than fifteen minutes had passed, so Grant probably would be.

Jack wanted to run forward and burst into the cabin, but Grant's constant warnings made him pause. The clearing in front of him brightened further as he crouched behind a tree, undecided. The hours of constant vigilance and lack of sleep combined with the continuous adrenaline spikes followed by disappointment after disappointment to make him tired. And as he sat there, trying to decide what to do next, that weariness made him just a little too slow to hear, just a little too slow to react.

He never heard him approach, and by the time he sensed the movement behind him it was too late. Jack had barely begun to turn when his whole world went dark on a sickening flash of pain in his head.

And then there was only the darkness.

As the killer stood over Jack's crumpled body, on the far side of the cabin Steve looked up into the barrel of a gun and heard a familiar voice growl, "Jesus Christ on a crutch, Sullivan, are you trying to get yourself killed?"

"Nice to see you, too, Evans, "Steve whispered, then sank to the ground for a moment as Grant lowered his gun and offered him a hand up.

"I think this is it," Grant said softly, "I've found signs of someone coming through the woods on the far side of the cabin."

Steve nodded and filled Grant in on the truck he and Bram had found and waved Bram forward to their position. "How do you want to do this?" Steve asked.

"How far out are the Chief and the others?"

"Maybe twenty minutes," Steve replied as his eyes met Grant's, understanding on both of their faces.

Bram stopped beside them and Grant said, "I've got Jack stationed on the opposite corner. Bram cover the back and this side of the cabin and warn us if you see anyone approach."

"Same as before, Dad, two clicks."

"Be careful," Bram said quietly. Grant nodded and then met Steve's eyes once more before he said, "I'll take the back—just give me ten minutes to get into position."

Steve smiled grimly and nodded before both men silently headed back towards the cabin. Steve veered off to the left to circle around the front of the building while Grant moved to the right to make a direct approach to the windowless back door he'd seen on his walk around the cabin earlier.

Too late, was all Maggie could think.

If he had only left her alone for five more minutes… But it was useless to think about what could have been when he was already there. She felt his hand move as it gently pushed the hair off of her forehead, but when she continued to feign sleep, his hand tightened until he was pulling her hair so hard her head was arched back on the pillow.

Knowing it was useless to pretend any longer, Maggie opened her eye to stare up into his monstrous face.

"You tried to trick me *again!*" he said, and fury darkened his face as he held it inches from her own, "Haven't you learned you cannot fool me, you ungrateful whore."

Abraham threw her head back so hard it clanged against the headboard with a teeth-clattering bang that left her breathless. Her eye darted around the room as he reared back to pace violently across the small cabin, spewing curses and vile threats about the man she loved as he went.

Maggie gathered the remnants of her strength and braced to fight back, but Abraham suddenly stopped pacing to run to the front window of the cabin and peer intently out into the breaking dawn's light. He swore and raced across the room to where he'd left a small duffel bag Maggie hadn't noticed before.

He pulled out a large knife that looked like the one her brothers used when they went deer hunting and the terror she thought could not grow bigger doubled. She closed her eye to try to stay calm, but it flew open again at his first step. Then, instead of moving towards her, his attention was on the back door as he hurried towards it.

The second he was out the door, Maggie struggled to move, the terror that the sight of the knife had caused gave her one more surge of adrenaline. With one last terrific wrench of her arms she pulled the iron bed the last half inch she needed it to go and she was free.

Not pausing to rest, Maggie rolled onto her side and off the bed to land hard on the floor. She let herself stop for thirty seconds before she tried to push to her feet, only to find her legs wouldn't support her. Crying, she dragged the dirty rag he'd stuffed in her mouth out and started to crawl towards the jagged shards of glass five feet away.

It seemed to take hours, her arms giving out over and over again as she inched her way across the scarred floor, one hand still clenched around the gag she'd removed. When she finally reached the glass she wrapped a long shard with the gag until she could hold it without cutting her hand. She crawled to place her back against the couch and tried to decide which door to use as she sawed through the rope that bound her feet together.

The front was closer, but whatever, or whoever Abraham had seen was out there, and so was he. The back door was so far away, but he could circle back to that door again after he'd finished taking care of whatever had spooked him enough to leave.

Sitting here won't do anything but make sure *he finds you,* Maggie thought as she mustered up the vestiges of her strength and used the sofa to help lever her body up onto legs that were still shaky, but that held.

She hurried forward as quickly as she could, using first the couch, then the kitchen counter to support her weight as she turned to the back door. She reached out her hands to turn the knob, her right still gripping the makeshift weapon, but before she could she felt the knob turn under her hand. Panicked, she felt herself fall forward as the door jerked open and she almost fell into the tall form of a man.

Her scream was cut short when a large, gloved hand roughly covered her mouth.

Steve moved as swiftly through the lightening woods as he dared. He wanted to check in with Jack before he made his way onto the small porch and he knew if he was going to make the ten minute deadline he had to hurry.

The gloomy filter of light through the trees helped him move around the front of the cabin to the large stand of trees Grant had told him Jack should be standing behind. Steve covered the distance in less than five minutes, but when he got there, Jack was nowhere to be seen. Steve paused, his sharp eyes searching the ground with dread, but it wasn't until he'd gotten several yards closer to the cabin that he found what he'd been looking for, and prayed he wouldn't find—a small darkened patch of ground.

He reached out one hand to touch the ground and felt his heart sink when it came back wet with blood. He pulled out his radio and clicked the talk button twice to try to warn his father and Grant that they were not alone in the woods.

Swearing under his breath, Steve moved forward to approach the porch from the far side of the building. He wanted desperately to search for his brother, but he didn't want to risk Maggie or leave Grant without backup to face what was in the cabin. He prayed a silent prayer that Jack was only hurt as he paused, just inside the tree line to search the woods around him for any signs of movement.

Satisfied that there was no one around he began to move forward again, and didn't see the form as it moved silently up behind him. Steve was almost to the porch, running in a crouch, when he heard the shift of gravel under a shoe behind him and then Maggie screamed.

Maggie struggled to free her mouth from the bruising grip on her face and belatedly remembered the glass still clutched in her right hand. She fell forward and threw all of her weight into one last desperate move—she plunged the broken glass right at the heart of the man holding her, only to have his other arm swing forward to knock it from her nerveless fingers.

"Maggie, stop! Maggie, it's me."

For a split second Maggie froze, confused and unable to believe what she was hearing. She'd imagined him rescuing her over and over again in the past several hours, but now that it was happening she struggled to trust her own ears.

"Grant?" she tried to say, but the hand still covered her mouth and instead it came out as a soft moan. Grant didn't need to understand what she said but he watched the recognition come into her eyes. He pulled Maggie forward to hold her for a brief moment and she collapsed weakly into his arms, feeling their reassuring and familiar strength surround and support her.

She heard him swear roughly when her knees gave out and he quickly scooped her up under her knees and carried her back out into the cover of the trees. For just a moment Maggie gave into the need to let her eyes close and her head to fall weakly onto Grant's chest.

"Are you really here?"

Hearing her tremulous whisper Grant held Maggie closer for a moment then quickly gentled his grip when she gasped. "I'm here, Baby, and so are your dad and brothers."

Suddenly Maggie struggled in his arms, her one working eye wide open and filled with terror again. "He's out here—he went out the back door. He had a knife, Grant. Steve? Daddy!"

"Shhh. I don't know where he is but I'm bringing you to your dad right now."

"Hurry. Don't let him hurt them…"

"Hush, Baby, you need to calm down and be quiet."

When she nodded and looked around warily he released her wrists from her handcuffs, then picked her back up to move quickly towards where her father waited.

Bram saw them coming and he sank to the ground when he saw his daughter, unmoving, in Grant's arms, but then she shifted. Bram's eyes closed and he raised one shaking hand to wipe tears of relief from his eyes. He shook himself once and managed to choke back the blinding rage when he saw the blood and marks on his daughter's hands and face.

For one wild moment he envisioned himself running to the cabin to murder the bastard who had done this to his little girl—and then he saw the look in Grant's blazing eyes and hard expression, and Bram knew that he would have to wait in line.

"Maggie, your dad's here. You'll be safe with him," Grant said gently as he set Maggie down on the ground. He shrugged out of his jacket to put it over her shivering form.

"Daddy?" she croaked out.

Bram had to swallow twice before he could reply, "I'm here, Sweetie. Your safe now, you're safe."

"Don't let him get me again…" Maggie murmured as she fell asleep. She never heard her father's fierce reply. "I won't. You go get that Bastard."

Grant didn't bother to reply, he was already up and sprinting back towards the cabin. More than the ten minutes he and Steve had agreed on had passed, and he still hadn't heard from him.

Maggie's scream was abruptly cut off as Steve whirled to find a large tree branch inches from his head.

He twisted to the side, unable to avoid the blow completely, but he moved just enough to change what would have been an incapacitating, if not fatal blow, to a glancing strike on his left shoulder.

He immediately rolled to his right and felt another blow land on his back, forcing the air out of his lungs. Despite the pain he forced himself to keep rolling—knowing that if he stopped his attacker would kill him.

His only consolation was that if Swanson was out here, Maggie would be safe for the moment. He also knew that she was alive, her scream had proven that, and he refused to consider exactly what that scream meant.

Despite having rolled several times, Swanson had managed to land several blows to the back of Steve's legs and his back. Steve braced himself to take one more blow and rolled over one last time, only this time he stayed on his back and reached for his gun with his right arm.

For the first time he got a good look at Swanson as the branch came right at his face. At the last second Steve managed to get his left arm up to block the blow aimed at his head and heard the audible snap of bones breaking in his arm. The pain was so intense Steve almost fumbled the gun he'd managed to pull out of his holster, but he was able to raise the gun and aim it right up into Abraham's face as Swanson swung the branch one last time.

But before he could pull the trigger, Swanson jerked twice, his eyes widening as the look of hatred on his face faded to blank surprise and he dropped the branch to clutch his hands at the ever-widening spread of red on his chest.

Before the echo of the shots faded into the cold morning light Grant was standing over Swanson's still form. He kicked away the branch still clutched in Swanson's hand and then returned to Steve to go down on one knee, "Steve, are you okay?"

"My arm is screwed, but other than that I'm okay. Is he...?"

"Dead," Grant said in a completely neutral tone before his voice changed to inquire, "Can you get up?" When Steve nodded, Grant felt a surge of relief and he helped Steve to sit up.

"Grant, I heard Maggie scream..."

Grant quickly cut him off, "She's safe. She's with your father in the woods."

Steve sagged visibly with relief, unable to do more than close his eyes and nod.

At the sound of approaching footsteps on the gravel at the edge of the clearing both men raised their weapons only to relax when they saw that it Dusty, followed closely by Dillon and Seth, each supporting a slumped, blood-covered Jack as they walked towards them.

"Oh, thank God, I couldn't find Jack earlier and I was afraid...well, it doesn't matter now.

"The Chief should be here any minute. I guess we're going to need an ambulance or three, huh? I don't like the look of that arm, Man," Grant looked down at Steve's arm where it lay at a decidedly unnatural angle.

Steve had a sheen of sweat on his brow but his eyes were not on his arm, but on his brother. "Is he okay?" he asked, worry in his voice.

"I'm fine, where's Maggie?" Jack asked, his voice a little shaky.

"She's okay; she's with your dad just on the other side of the cabin. She's tired and hurt, but she'll be fine," Grant replied, the determination in his voice not quite masking the clear worry he felt.

Seth and Dillon helped Jack down onto the ground next to Steve and both immediately set out around the side of the cabin to see Maggie with their own eyes.

Grant bent over to take a better look at Jack's head before he stood and pulled out his phone to call the Chief.

"Chief, we got her. We need a couple of ambulances. Swanson's dead. Steve's got a broken arm and needs some stitches, Jack Sullivan has a head injury, possible concussion and is also in need of several stitches. Maggie? She's shocky, and I think she probably has several broken ribs, possible concussion, lots of cuts and bruises, but I'd like to get her looked at as soon as possible. How far out are you? Sounds good."

Grant hung up and said to Steve, "Chief will be here in about five minutes, he's already got an ambulance coming about two minutes behind him. I..." Grant stopped talking abruptly when Bram and Dillon, came back around the cabin followed closely by Seth with Maggie in his arms. He waited while Dillon laid his jacket down on the ground between Jack and Steve, and watched until Seth had laid Maggie down.

She was still wrapped in his and Bram's jackets, but Grant could see that she shivered in her sleep. He worried that shock was setting in and prayed that the ambulance would arrive quickly. He longed to wrap her in his arms, to keep her warm and protected, but with Steve injured and Dusty on his way to the road to lead the Chief and paramedics back to the cabin he was responsible for the people and crime scenes both inside and outside of the cabin.

Seth stood a small distance away from them to call his mother and Sybil to let them know that Maggie was safe, and to tell them to meet them at the hospital.

Steve reached out a hand to touch Maggie's arm, not quite believing that she was real until he could feel her for himself. The only problem was finding somewhere to touch her that wouldn't hurt. He *thought* he'd prepared himself for how she would look when they found her, but the shock of seeing his baby sister beaten was much harder than he ever imagined it could be.

The most important thing, Steve reminded himself, was that she was here at all, that she was alive. Maggie had always been a survivor—and he thanked God she had had the strength to do so again. But as he watched her twitch and moan occasionally in her sleep he wondered at what cost had she obtained her freedom.

He only prayed that the price she paid for it wouldn't be too steep.

SEVENTY-EIGHT

When Maggie woke up she froze and listened, trying to tell whether or not Abraham was in the cabin. When she heard the soft hum of voices nearby she was confused—did he turn on a radio?

And then she remembered. She was safe. Grant and her father had found her. She vaguely remembered waking up in the ambulance and seeing Grant's face right next to where the paramedics worked to get her warm. And when she woke up again she remembered her mother as she arrived at the emergency room, tears pouring down her face.

And she remembered when Grant had told her that Abraham Swanson was dead and would never hurt her again.

Maggie opened her eyes to look around the room and the first thing she saw was Grant asleep in an extremely uncomfortable-looking chair on the left side of her bed. His right hand was open on the bed right next to her left hand, and she shifted until she held his loosely in hers and took a good look at the man she loved, the man who'd saved her.

Bright sunlight from the window behind him fell across his sleeping form. His hair fell in an unruly line across his forehead and the stress of the past twenty-four hours had left their mark on him— his closed eyes were ringed by dark circles and his pale face was darkened by two days worth of stubble, but he'd never looked as good to her as he did in this moment.

She looked around the otherwise empty room in search of the voices that had awoken her and found that although she was alone in the room with Grant several people stood outside the open door of her room in the hallway just out of sight. She listened for several moments, but she couldn't quite make out what they said.

She shifted slightly on the bed and a sharp jab of pain on her left side had her catching her breath on a gasp that had Grant awake and leaning forward in seconds.

"Lay still, Baby. Do you want me to get the nurse?" Grant asked as he reached his left hand up to brush it softly over her hair.

Maggie tried to shake her head no, but the quick flash of pain and instant dizziness forced her to immediately stop, eyes closed against the throbbing ache. Instead she said, "No. I just moved too quickly and my side hurt. What happened? How did you find me? Where are Steve and Dad and…"

"Slow down, Maggie. I'll answer all your questions, I swear, and I'm sure that I'll have just as many for you, but for now I want you to get some rest. The doc says you've got three broken ribs, a minor concussion, several broken fingers, at least two cuts that needed multiple stitches, and too many bruises and minor cuts to count."

"Is that all?" Maggie tried to smile and her eyes gleamed with humor before she asked again, "Where is everyone? Are my mom and dad still here?"

"Yes. They're down the hall with Jack, but they wanted me to tell you that he's going to be okay. He suffered from a slight skull fracture and a concussion, and they'll need to keep him here for at least a couple of days."

"A *slight* skull fracture?" Maggie cried.

"Mags, he's okay. The doctor said that it was a simple linear fracture, which means it's a hairline crack, and, although it's serious, it is *not* fatal. They're keeping him in for observation to make sure that there is no bleeding on the brain, which they'd have to help him out with. Steve is also here. He's in surgery right now for a compound fracture on his arm. He is going to be just fine, too. I know this is a lot to take in."

For several moments Maggie couldn't say anything as she absorbed all that Grant had told her. Grant gently stroked her hand and waited patiently for her to speak. "Okay. Okay, I want to know as soon as Steven's out of surgery and I want to see Jack as soon as I can."

"We can do that. Seth, Sybil, and the kids are down in the waiting area for Steve, and they're going to come and tell us as soon as he's out of surgery. Dillon has been back and forth between your room and Jack's. He just left about fifteen minutes ago to see Jack, so he, or maybe one of your parents, should be back in less than an hour. As for you going over to see him, I'm sure you'll be able to do that tomorrow. In fact, if you have a good night, you'll probably be able to go home tomorrow."

"I really want to see them tonight. I'm fine, and I really need to see them, Grant. I know they were all there to help me, but I don't remember seeing them, and I just *need* to see them, all of them. I...I..." Maggie's voice rose until her breath heaved and she choked on the emotions that seemed to build and build until she couldn't speak any longer.

Grant ran his hand down Maggie's hair again as she collapsed into tears. Helpless to do anything other than wait, Grant said, "Baby, it's okay. You're safe. Everything's going to be all right, just let it all out."

When she had cried herself dry, Maggie whispered, "Oh, God, Grant, I was so scared. All I could think of was that I'd never see any of you again. I knew that you and Steven would never give up until you found me, but I was so scared that I wouldn't be able to hold it together long enough for it to matter. I was so scared that I'd never be able to tell you how much I love you, how much you mean to me."

Grant leaned forward to brush a tender kiss against her lips to sooth himself as much as he wanted to sooth her. He eased back into his chair and replied, "It's all over now, and you can see everyone soon," for a long moment he paused and stared into her eyes before he decided to continue, his voice harsh, "I have never been as terrified as I have been the past eighteen hours. When I went outside and couldn't find you...when I realized that that monster had...I'm just so sorry that I wasn't there when you needed me. I should have stayed outside, should have walked you back to the house and driven you home, I should have realized that we had the wrong guy. I..."

Her heart ached at the look of devastation on his face, and Maggie lifted her hand to cup Grant's face as he dropped his head down onto the bed next to her. She said, "Shhh. It wasn't your fault—none of this was your fault. You're right, I'm fine and everything's going to be all right."

Grant raised his head to look at her again and said, "I love you so much, Maggie. You have to know how much you've changed my life, how much you've changed who I am.

"When I first moved here, I was looking for a second chance, an escape from the life I had lived in Seattle and a reason to truly live again after Lou's death. I thought that reason was going to be the job, and on some level that's been true, but more important than the job has been my friendship with Steve, my meeting your family and being accepted by them.

"But most of all, it's you. You've helped me to finally step back from the darkness and to live again. You make me laugh, and make me think, you are my best friend. And when I thought I would never have the chance to tell you that, the darkness almost swallowed me whole. I've never prayed as hard as I did last night, and here I'm going to ask God for something else after He's answered my prayers to find you alive.

"Maggie I love you, I need you. I wanted to do this differently, and definitely not in a hospital—but, well, I can't wait any longer. Stay with me always, love me forever. Marry me, Maggie."

Overwhelmed, Maggie could say nothing but her heart must have been in her eyes because Grant smiled and eased the grip he had on her hands to lean forward to kiss her again. When he leaned away she drew a breath and said, "I love you, too. Do you want to know what I was thinking about, right before I walked out into the yard?" Grant nodded and she continued, "I was thinking to myself that if you weren't ready to love me and marry me, then I would just have to make you. The whole time I was gone, I was scared. But, I wasn't scared of dying. Of the pain, yes, of the...man...yes, but never of dying.

"No, what scared me the most was never being able to see you again, to tell you that you are the love of my life, and to beg you to marry me and be with me always and forever."

Grant grinned and asked, "So, I take it that was a yes?"

SEVENTY-NINE

When Elizabeth walked up to her daughter's hospital room she paused in the doorway to watch the scene before her—her daughter, lost less than twenty-four hours ago, was restored to her again.

When she had first seen Maggie, so battered and bloody, Elizabeth had to struggle to hold on to her composure, but just hours later, her strong girl was smiling and happy, safe from the terrible man who'd taken and hurt her. She lay smiling up at the man Elizabeth suspected would soon be family, and everything *seemed* right again, but Elizabeth knew that there were more injuries than those that she could see with her eyes. However Elizabeth believed with her whole heart that with Grant and the rest of the family to help her, and with Maggie's faith, they could help Maggie deal with whatever lasting wounds that surfaced.

Elizabeth had finally managed to piece together enough of what had really happened in the woods to know that she owed Grant everything for saving not only her daughter's life, but also her son's. She'd always known that, as a detective, Steven would be put in harm's way, and she had prepared herself for that possibility. But having Maggie and Jack hurt as well had almost been more than she could handle. She could only thank God that they had been delivered from danger, and pray that they would all be fully healed.

When Maggie laughed and said, "Yes!" before Grant leaned forward to kiss her, Elizabeth knew her daughter, at least, was well on the way.

Elizabeth smiled secretly to herself, her heart lightened by the happy scene she'd witnessed, and backed away from the door before either of them noticed her. She'd just slip back to Jack's room to make sure he was staying in bed. He always was ornery when he was ill.

Maggie had been out of the hospital for almost a week before both Jack and Steven were released. For the first few days she had never been alone, even when Grant had had to go to work. Grant had settled her into his house and either her mother or Sybil had been there to help her get dressed or take a shower. Sometimes Dillon or

Seth would hang out and watch T.V. with her and Grant was there through the long nights, holding her when the nightmares woke her screaming from what little sleep she managed. And through it all, Jake never left her side.

At times she felt confined, and her emotions were a whirlwind of ups and downs. The days weren't bad, but when the darkness fell, Maggie struggled with feeling closed in and she spent hours outside with Grant and Jake walking the cold streets until she could stand going back indoors.

She slept with the lights on.

But slowly, as each day came and went, she was able to talk more and sleep more, and she knew that although she would never be exactly the same person she used to be, eventually, it would get better.

"Good grief, you sound like a walking, talking, self-help book," Maggie muttered to herself as she tried to get dressed. She wanted to go to the hospital with Grant to pick up Steven. For the first time since she'd come home, she had taken her first solo shower and had felt elated. But as she looked in the bathroom mirror and saw the rainbow of bruising on her body, the sense of accomplishment she'd felt was quickly diminished. And when she struggled to bend over far enough to tie her shoes with her bandaged fingers, the anger that was always so close to the surface in the days since her abduction exploded.

She was still swearing when Grant came into the room, "Maggie? Are you okay?"

"I'm fine I just wish I could have one single second to myself! For goodness sake all I need to do is tie my freaking shoes—a skill which I've had since I was four years old, I might add—and I can't even do it by myself."

Grant waited for her to stop her tirade, his eyebrows raised and Maggie felt even more foolish. A warm flush spread across her cheeks and tears filled her eyes as she continued in a quieter voice, "I'm sorry, Grant. I just get so frustrated with myself and I take it out on you." Maggie sank down onto the bed, her shoe still clutched in her hands. "And I'm still so upset about Holden. It's just not fair."

They'd gotten the news that Holden had woken up the day before—something no one had expected him to do. But, when he had awoken, he was unable to move anything from the waist down. His spine had been damaged in the beating, and it was unlikely that he would ever walk again.

Grant knelt down until they were face-to-face and put his hands over hers, "They don't know for sure that the damage is permanent," he paused and forced some cheer into his voice to say, "Let's get these things on, and we can go pick up Steve."

Hearing the understanding in his voice, Maggie watched as Grant tied first one, then the other of her shoes. When he was done she put her arms around his neck and pulled him towards her. He put his arms gently around her and watched her close her eyes as he held her close.

"I love you, Grant," she sighed.

"I love you, too, Maggie," Grant replied and laid his head down on top of hers.

At the hospital they found out that Steve was waiting on some paperwork before he could be discharged. Maggie left Grant with Steve and went one floor up to visit Holden.

When Maggie knocked once and poked her head into his room, she saw Cloë sitting next to Holden as he slept. Cloë quickly let go of the hand she was holding and threw a guilty look at Maggie before she smiled and limped over to hug Maggie, "Oh, Maggie, I'm so glad you're all right! I wanted to come to see you, but by the time I knew what had happened you were out of the hospital and they won't let me out of here until the end of the week."

"Oh, Sweetie, I understand, you just sit down again and relax. I'm fine. Just some bruises and some cracked ribs," Maggie said quietly as she helped Cloë sit back down next to Holden. "How's he doing?" Maggie asked.

"Pretty well, all things considered. His sister is still here, and she's going to help get him settled once he's ready to go home. The doctors say he has a small chance of recovering some mobility with extensive physical therapy, but there's no way of knowing for sure. Only time will tell."

486

As she spoke, Maggie saw that Cloë never took her eyes off of Holden and Maggie knew that Holden would not be alone in his battle.

Holden's eyes opened and he smiled at Maggie before he turned to look at Cloë. He reached for her hand and as they smiled into each other's eyes, Maggie grinned and raised her eyebrows.

"I just wanted to see how you guys were doing—I'm here to pick up Steven, they're releasing him today."

"I heard what happened to all of you, I'm so glad you're all okay, Maggie," Holden said.

Maggie nodded and said, "I'm really happy that you're doing better, too, both of you," When Holden turned back to look at Cloë, Maggie chuckled silently to herself and added, "Well, I guess I'll leave you two alone, I need to get back downstairs to Steven and Grant. I'll come see you both again tomorrow."

Cloë tore her gaze from Holden's to grin up at her friend, happiness shining on her face, "Okay, see you later, Maggie."

"Bye."

Maggie slipped out of the room and tried to hurry back downstairs, unable to keep the wide smile from spreading across her face as she thought of two of her closest friends together.

By the time she got back to the room, Grant was wheeling Steve out into the hall and Steve was complaining, "I don't see why I can't walk, there's nothing wrong with my legs...Hey, Mags!" Steve's face brightened at the sight of his sister as she walked up to them.

"Hey, Steven," she leaned down to kiss his cheek and whispered in his ear, "If you behave yourself we'll stop for ice cream on the way home."

Steve grinned and brightened, "Ice cream? That works for me."

"It always has," Maggie laughed and turned to say to Grant, "Even when he was a little boy he was the *worst* patient. Mom always had to bribe him with dishes of ice cream to get him to cooperate when he was sick."

"She did not!" Steve said. Maggie nodded and Grant pushed Steve towards the elevators.

"That's not how I remember it," she said and raised her brows at Steve.

He laughed and teased, "Well, you may be right, but you were no better. With her it wasn't ice cream, it was chocolate and books. Mom always knew exactly what would work best for each of us. She gets the worst temper when she's laid up, as I'm sure you've discovered."

Grant laughed and said neutrally, "I have no idea what you're talking about," he paused significantly before he added, "But just in case we'll stop at the book store and get some books and some Godiva."

Maggie huffed out a laugh and said, "I'd be offended but I never refuse books or chocolate."

After they got Steve settled in the car and had stopped for their treats they headed across town. "Where are we going? My apartment is in the other direction."

"You're staying with Seth and Sybil for a few days until you are off your meds and on the mend."

"Mags, I..."

"Don't argue. We got Jack settled at Mom and Dad's last night and Grant is already taking care of me. Dillon offered to help you out, but Seth and Sybil have a bigger guest room you can use."

"It's just a broken arm," he protested grumpily.

"For which you had to have surgery to repair, and the infection you got didn't help. It's only for a few days until you can get around better on your own, don't be such a big baby."

Grant wanted to laugh at the identical mutinous looks he saw on both Steve and Maggie's faces, but he wisely kept his mouth shut and the smile off his face.

"Fine," Steve gave in first, and Grant had to bite his lip to keep his face straight when he heard the clear disgust in Steve's voice.

Maggie grinned and cleared her throat before she said, "But first we're going over to Mom and Dad's for a little welcome home celebration now that all three of us are out of the hospital."

Steve's face brightened again and he sat back, exhausted from trying to appear fine.

Five minutes later Grant helped Steve out of the car and up the steps to the Sullivan's house. Before they'd even reached the door it was flung open and half the family was there to help bustle all three of them into the house, out of their coats and into the living room where the rest of them were gathered around the sofa, where Jack was supposed to be resting, but instead was telling some joke or story to Aaron and Katie.

Grant got Steve settled in a large armchair with his feet up before he joined Maggie on the loveseat her father had gently pushed her onto. Elizabeth swept into the room and hugged all three of them before she moved over to where Bram stood and put her arm around him, and his came around her.

"Well, now that we're all here the party can really begin. Dinner will be ready in just a little bit," Elizabeth said as she turned to go back into the kitchen.

"Mom, wait a minute," Maggie looked over at Grant where he sat next to her and raised her brows, he nodded and Maggie continued, "Grant and I have something we wanted to tell everyone now that we're all home and on the mend," she paused to take a deep breath and Grant reached over to hold her hand and he took over.

"I've asked Maggie to marry me and she's said yes."

In the pandemonium that followed everyone but Jack sprang to their feet and began talking at once. Maggie was gently pulled into Seth's arms and Steve used his good arm to grab Grant's hand to pump it enthusiastically, a huge smile on his face.

"Welcome to the madness, Evans."

Grant grinned and the half hour that followed passed in a blur of hugs, handshakes, loud congratulations and tears. In the midst of it all Grant saw Maggie and Elizabeth smiling into each other eyes and bursting into tears as they hugged, and the pure happiness of the moment guaranteed that he would never forget it.

He only hoped that his own family's reaction was half as great—he knew it wouldn't match the Sullivan's, but he could always hope. That was a worry for tomorrow, today was for Maggie and her family—his family now, too.

In the chaos of the celebrations Grant noticed Jack still lay on the couch, silent. Grant moved over to sit down near him and asked, "You okay, Jack?"

489

Jack looked up at Grant for a long moment, his face serious before he said, "Before last week I was sure that Maggie was on the rebound, and that you were simply along for the ride. But I saw you out in those woods. You love her so much it was almost painful to see. So, yeah, Man, I'm okay. I'm okay with you, I'm okay with Mags, and I'm definitely okay with the two of you together."

Jack reached out to shake Grant's hand, his face uncommonly serious, before he broke into his usual grin and quipped, "Besides, if you hurt her, the four of us will just kill you."

When Grant froze, unsure of how to respond, Jack burst into laughter and said, "Dude, you should see your face right now," Jack continued laughing until he had to hold his head.

"You're hilarious Jack. Thanks for the warning," Grant said dryly and he met Maggie's eyes as she stood across the room discussing something that had both Katie and Sybil giggling, "But you don't have anything to worry about."

Hours later, as Maggie and Grant lay in bed, the soft glow of the bedside lamp washed over them as they curled together under the covers.

"Hey, Red."

Maggie grinned at the return of Grant's nickname for her—he hadn't used it since she'd been taken—and she replied, "Yeah, Detective?"

"Close your eyes."

Maggie smiled and complied. She felt Grant's arm reach around to grasp her left hand and slip something on her finger. "Okay, open."

Maggie opened her eyes and looked down to see a beautiful square-cut diamond in an antique platinum setting surrounded by a ring of smaller stones. Her eyes filled with tears as she held her hand up to the light.

"It was my great-grandmother's. My grandma gave it to me years ago, but I never met anyone I wanted to give it to until you." When Maggie remained silent Grant added nervously, "If you'd rather pick out something more modern, or a different style, I completely understand…"

"No. Grant, I love it," Maggie turned to face him and reached up to run her hand over his cheek, "The fact that it was your great-grandma's makes it even more special. It's so beautiful—I don't think I could have picked out a more perfect ring."

Relieved, Grant leaned down to kiss Maggie gently. When her arms slipped around his neck to bring him closer his heart skipped a beat and then sped into overdrive. His hands fisted in her hair before they ran down her neck and shoulders to press urgently against the sides of her breasts.

Maggie let out a gasp and a moan that was equal parts pleasure and pain and Grant immediately gentled his hold and swearing at himself he pulled away, "Did I hurt you?"

She shook her head once before she captured his mouth with hers again, using her tongue and teeth as her answer as she pressed her body to his. "Don't stop, I don't want you to stop," she murmured urgently as his mouth began a downward journey. Careful not to bruise, trying hard not to harm, Grant ran his hands down her body until he reached the hem of the oversized cotton t-shirt she'd donned as her nightgown.

Slowly, slowly he eased the hem up, taking time to explore each creamy inch of skin as it was bared. Each time he found a faded bruise or cut Grant swept his lips across the marred skin as if to erase any lingering pain, to replace the memory of violence each mark represented with one of love. And when he'd covered every inch of skin, her body hummed with a tingling awareness that had her lying weak and pliant under his relentless attentions, clad only in a tiny scrap of lace and cotton.

Grant knelt above her long enough to pull off his own clothes before he returned to capture her mouth with his again, his kiss deep and his hands soft and patient against her sweat-slicked skin.

"Are you sure you're ready?" he whispered.

In response, Maggie reached up to grab hair, to pull him down and hold him to her. Their kiss went on and on until Grant tore his mouth from hers to trail his lips back down her body. She sighed, her heart swelling at the sweet tenderness in his every touch.

Inch by torturous inch she felt him ease the final barrier between them down her hips and then there was nothing but the feel of him pressed intimately, perfectly against her.

"Now," she said.

"Now," he agreed.

And as he entered her his eyes met hers and he knew that he was home, finally, perfectly home. And the beauty of that single breathtaking moment in time had the tears in her eyes spilling over as they paused, absolutely in sync, completely at one with one another.

And then they began to move, without rush, without speed, until they rose together in utter accord—and together they peaked, and with one heart they were complete.

As they drifted off to sleep Maggie snuggled her head onto Grant's shoulder and pressed a sleepy kiss to his neck and murmured, "I love you."

Grant kissed her head and breathed in her sweet, familiar scent, and he thanked God for bringing this incredible woman—his heart and soul, his saving grace, his hope—into his life, and he said, "I love you, too, Margaret Sullivan. I love you, too."

And together they fell asleep with the promise of that love strong and sure in their hearts. And with the promise and hope of their future together on the hand she curled in his as they slept and dreamt, together.

The End

Made in the USA
Columbia, SC
14 December 2019

84922443R00272

Foundations of Experimental Embryology

Edited by Benjamin H. Willier
and Jane M. Oppenheimer

Second edition, enlarged
and with a new introduction,
by Jane M. Oppenheimer

HAFNER PRESS
A Division of Macmillan Publishing Co., Inc.
New York
Collier Macmillan Publishers
London

HAFNER PRESS
A Division of Macmillan Publishing Co., Inc.
866 Third Avenue, New York, N.Y. 10022

Collier Macmillan Canada Ltd.

Library of Congress Cataloging in Publication Data

Willier, Benjamin Harrison, 1890—1972 ed.
   Foundations of experimental embryology.

   Includes bibliographical references.
   1. Embryology, Experimental—Addresses, essays,
lectures. I. Oppenheimer, Jane Marion, 1911-   joint
ed. II. Title. [DNLM: 1. Embryology—Collected
works. QS605 W732f]
QL961.W5 1974   591.3'3'072   74-11271
ISBN 0-02-849860-7
Printed in the United States of America

Dedicated to the memory of
Ross Granville Harrison

Preface

It is the purpose of this collection of articles, already recorded elsewhere in the literature, to answer a need of those who are interested in the early history of experimental embryology, and to encourage respect for those investigators who blazed the trails we now follow in contemporary embryology. In achieving these aims we tried to abide by two basic criteria in choosing the selections. Foremost was our desire to include only articles of unusual excellence and of both pioneering and enduring quality, namely those that have had a definite influence on the rise of experimental embryology. Secondly, we wished to maintain a balance of areas among the selections. We hope this small volume reflects something of the variety of the ideas, discoveries, and method of some of the beginning experimentalists in embryology and developmental physiology.

Most readers who have delved at all into the older literature of experimental embryology will, in all likelihood, find old favorites absent from this work. Some articles were too long for inclusion in a volume of this size. Such works give place to what it is hoped will be happy new discoveries for some readers. Embryology has not moved forward in a straight line, and as in all anthologies, some of the choices have been arbitrary. If the readers feel, however, that the basic aims of the editors have been achieved on the whole, the time and work invested in the preparation of this book will have been well spent. The editors will be content if others find the reading of the book as rewarding and intellectually stimulating as they did during its assemblage.

All of the articles, save that of Driesch, are reproduced in full without abridgment in any way. The editors feel strongly that it is important for the student to see how various workers have attacked key problems in the past—how ideas led to technical ways of testing their validity—how the results were analyzed and interpreted.

We terminate this preface by an expression of our deep indebtedness to all of those devoted friends of the embryo who have translated or aided in the translation of the articles written in the German language. We are also indebted to John Spurbeck for his care and skill in preparing the photographic reproductions of the original illustrations. To these we have a special sense of gratitude since without their help this work would have been difficult if not impossible. The editors, however, are solely responsible for the text of *Editors' Comments* preceding each of the eleven articles reproduced.

Benjamin H. Willier
Jane M. Oppenheimer

Introduction to Second Edition

For the 1964 edition of this book, the articles chose themselves. The perspective was inadequate, when that edition was prepared, to judge which of the work of the 1940's and 1950's might later prove to be as influential as were our eleven original milestones. Time has improved the perspective and it is now easier to choose three significant milestones from the 1950's, 1960's and 1970's. The three new articles deal with the nerve growth factor (1954), with ionic communication between cells (1969), and with over-all embryonic patterning (1973).

As in the first edition, each of the three new articles is preceded by brief editorial comments concerning the backgrounds and consequences of the work described. This more general introduction to the volume as a whole speculates as to why it may be easier now to look through certain open windows into the future than it was ten years ago. Briefly stated: the investigators up to the 1940's made great discoveries; those of the decades following exploited them. When old paths of thought became overgrown, new ones were carved into unknown areas and beyond. Several, but not all, of the new directions are suggested by the articles added to this edition; space does not permit including more. But since history, like embryology, does not like overgeneralization, at least one of the new highroads begins as a continuation of what might in the 1930's have been considered as a by-lane. And up through the 1930's, as we shall point out, embryology contributed greatly to other areas of biology. Subsequently, it received more than it gave.

* * * * * *

Science builds upon its past. This is particularly true of embryology which during the 1940's, 1950's, and 1960's expressed itself mainly in commentary on what had gone immediately before. Thus the articles in our first edition exemplify and define the lines of thought that were followed into the next three decades.

The early pioneers, Roux, Driesch, and Wilson (Parts One, Two, Three), concerned themselves with the degree to which factors intrinsic or extrinsic to an egg or its parts govern the development of the embryo or of a given portion of it. Investigation into this problem culminated in the work of Spemann (Part Ten). His experiments and his interpretations of them, his discovery of the organizer, his concepts of induction, treated precisely the same problem. Spemann extended his reach, however, by attempting to discover the moment when a particular embryonic structure becomes irrevocably determined in its path into differentiation. The idea of determination, although it was ultimately to be superseded, became for a while a dominating concept, opening the possibility that different brief moments in time might be critical for the development of different parts. Included in *Foundations* (Part Five) is the work of Harrison which demonstrated that the capacity of the neuroblast to form its protoplasmic outgrowth, the future nerve fiber, is an intrinsic property of that cell. He was soon to show that extrinsic factors influence the direction of outgrowth followed by the developing fiber, and when, a little later, he analyzed the development of limb asymmetry, he showed that the limb axes become established one by one, in sequence, in a series of progressive changes. Thus all these analyses formed threads in the same fabric of ideas.

When Spemann, in an article published slightly earlier than the one chosen here to exemplify his work, first gave the organizer its name, he specified as its function the production not of a specific structure but of a field of determination. Among the authors of our first eleven milestones, Harrison as well as Spemann contributed to field theory. Gradients, as vectors within territories, are constituents of fields. Driesch, and particularly Boveri, began to define and develop the concept of gradients. The particular accomplishment of Child (Part Eight) was to try to describe gradients in terms of comparative rates of metabolism: if you live faster, you die faster, but while you are alive you dominate the slower. Child described his results somewhat fuzzily in terms of the utilization of oxygen; the analytical work already begun by Warburg (Part Six) was to usher in the new era of truly precise investigation of intermediary metabolism. Warburg's discovery of cytochrome oxidase, as an outcome of his investigation into the respiration of the sea urchin egg, provides another example of embryological investigation that was to have far-reaching influence on biology.

Lillie's analysis of the free-martin (Part Nine), in demonstrating an effect of hormones on sexual differentiation, was also carrying embryology towards the explanation of developmental processes in terms of chemical constituents of the embryonic body. Steroid sex hormones were soon to be extracted, isolated, chemically defined, then synthesized in the laboratory. Lillie's demonstration that sex hormones could bring about effects hitherto attributed solely to control by the chromosomal balance of the zygote was sensational, and inevitably stimulated further interest in the already developing field of endocrinology. Once again, embryology was facing outwards.

Hormones from the time of their first discovery were thought to act on specific target organs. Lillie did not feel obliged to remark that it was a matter of specificity that the sex hormones affected, directly at least, only characteristics related to reproduction. Lillie's earlier work, related to fertilization (Part Seven), focussed new insights into specificity, by drawing heavily on concepts from immunology. Holtfreter (Part Eleven) approached specificity from a different direction. In returning to an old notion of Roux's on mutual attraction between cells, he demonstrated changes in what he called affinities and disaffinities between isolated and morphologically identifiable cell groups. Holtfreter's explanation of orderly unions, non-unions, and self-isolations of groups of cells *in vitro* on the basis of elective affinities was vaguer than Lillie's analysis, that was based on the postulate that a demonstrable substance, fertilizin, formed by the egg, acts as a sperm-isoagglutinin. Nonetheless, Holtfreter's results were both dramatic and influential, showing, as they did, that affinities and disaffinities change with time—a further, if still mysterious, example of differentiation progressing in time.

And then, genetics? The period covered by the original edition of *Foundations* was the era of the most rapid development of the premolecular gene theory; it encompassed not only the rediscovery of Mendel's work, but also the investigations involving combined cytological and breeding experiments on *Drosophila* that revealed the linear arrangement of genes on the chromosomes. The avoidance of developmental thinking by Morgan and other members of his school was one of the curiosities of early twentieth century biological thought, all the more anomalous since Morgan himself had been a wise and productive experimental embryologist before he made the acquaintance of *Drosophila*. The lacuna between embryology and genetics during the heyday of the *Drosophila* studies accounts for the fact that no work by a member of Morgan's group is found in this collection. None was concerned with development as an ongoing process. But the work in genetics that seemed so separate from embryology at our original 1939 breakpoint had roots in early studies of development, particularly in those by Boveri, one of whose important discoveries, that of the qualitative difference between chromosomes, is described here (Part Four). Boveri excelled in cytology, and it was cytology that linked the old embryology with the new genetics. The connection, hazy to some, was clearly seen by Wilson, who wrote a wonderful synthesizing monograph on *The Cell in Heredity and Development*. The difficulty of finding a concise discussion of cell lineage by others induced us to include Wilson in the *Foundations* as an exponent of this circumscribed subject rather than as a cell biologist with a wide view of both genetics and embryology. Wilson laid the groundwork for the cell biology that was to come later. What the word *cytology* means, after all, is study of the cell.

To return for a moment to the earliest days, when the nucleus seemed paramount in the regulation of cell division and function: Boveri laid strong emphasis on cytoplasmic influences over nuclear activity. In fact, Driesch had postulated such influences in 1894, and had attempted to explain nuclear activity on the basis of enzymes (ferments, in his terminology). But the cytogeneticists of the 1930's were not in a position to foresee that the problems of heredity might soon be soluble through the discovery that a particular substance in the nucleus, long known in some of its aspects to nuclear chemists, presides over the synthesis of enzymes.

* * * * * *

The important themes in developmental thinking up to the 1940's were thus hereditary factors in development, nucleo-cytoplasmic inter-relationships in development, intrinsic versus extrinsic factors in development, inducers and organizers in development, fields and gradients in development, determination in development, hormones in development, specificity in development, metabolism and oxygen consumption in development. Studies on hormones and on embryonic metabolism soon developed a chemical slant and, eventually, investigations attempted to identify fertilizin chemically. But the concept of induction, which dominated embryology, was most influential in carrying it towards the new biochemistry. At the end of the 1930's, into the 1950's and beyond, the possibility that inducers, if not organizers, might be explained in molecular terms seemed the greatest hope of biochemical embryologists. Yet dependence on it proved to be a fatal failing of embryologists.

Already in the 1930's crushed organizers, killed organizers, killed non-organizers, living or non-living tissues from adults of all animal phyla were shown to have inducing properties. Extracts from these, and innumerable other substances, likely and unlikely, of physiological or non-physiological significance (glycogen, fatty acids, digitonin [a protein], methylene blue, steroid hydrocarbons) all were tested. In the 1930's, Needham excited biologists when his work seemed to be pointing to a new generalizing mechanism based on the fact that steroids included molecules acting not only as sex hormones but also as inducers in normal and as carcinogens in atypical differentiation. Towards the end of the 1930's experimental results had suggested that heterogeneous inducers from different mammalian glands induced different amphibian organs, and attempts were made to isolate the active factors from such highly complex organs as mammalian kidney and mammalian liver; even chick blood was similarly utilized. Ultimately, as might be expected, nucleoproteins became favorite candidates as inducers, and controversies arose as to whether the nucleic acid or the protein moieties were the truly active agents. Controversy continues among investigators still concerned with such investigations, even though neither moiety as an essential factor may act in the way that molecules were thought to thirty or forty years ago.

In fact, whether the elusive substances acted as instructors to the responding cells, or as releasers, was never clear in the early days. One hypothesis of the 1920's was that embryonic parts responding to inducers might be already labilely determined, awaiting only a signal from an inducer to become stabilely so. This idea had to be abandoned because transplantation experiments by Holtfreter seemed to prove unequivocally that prospective nervous system cells differentiate nervous tissue only after contact with archenteron roof. When Barth described conditions under which prospective nervous tissue did form nerve tubes when isolated in inorganic salt solutions, his results were not taken seriously until Holtfreter confirmed his experiments. In fact, although Barth's experiments were performed over thirty years ago, their interpretation is still not entirely clear. He has continued to study the effect on differentiation of embryonic parts of inorganic media altered in ionic constitution and balance. His experiments have not yet received the attention they merit, yet when their significance is appreciated they may prove to be among the most important ones of their era.

The first experiments on induction were performed by transplantation methods. Then the materials to be tested were inserted into the amphibian blastocoele. Holtfreter improved the procedure in the 1940's by placing a sandwich *in vitro*: the "bread" was prospective amphibian body epidermis and the "meat" was the agent to be tested. This ploy had the advantage of isolating the test system from possible influences from a host embryo. Recently Grobstein and others introduced a refinement by separating acting and reacting tissues with millipore filters of known thickness and known pore size. In these experiments, prospective glandular tissues have often been used as potential reactors; they become tubular only in the presence of appropriate mesenchyme on the other side of the filter, demonstrating that actual contact between inducing and reacting tissue is not essential for induction. In some experiments, precursors of collagen were shown to pass through the pores of the filter, but their effects on morphogenesis proved to be secondary rather than primary; collagen deposition on specific sites affects the molding of the tubules but not their first formation.

What had seemed most spectacular when induction theory was being developed was not the simple fact that one embryonic part, say an optic cup, could induce another, say the epidermis overlying it, to become a third structure, say a lens. This was of course an important piece of evidence and an experimentally adduced one at that, supporting the principle of epigenesis which had been accepted on and off since the time of Aristotle. The hero of the drama of induction on Spemann's stage was the organizer; the climactic event was the production, after the transplantation of a small piece of the gastrula, of not only a structure, a *something* that would not have been there otherwise, but that of a whole new organized something, even a *somebody*, a whole new living embryo. What was important for the movement of embryology into its biochemical phase was the hope that some magic molecule with both organizing and inducing powers might be found. Perhaps because of the failure to identify, to the satisfaction of all, *any* molecule even as an inducer—something that might have been expected to be experimentally demonstrable—the idea that embryonic organization could be attributed to a single molecule or molecular type gradually lost its force. The concept of organizers as such gradually dissipated, and the word if used at all today would be found in out-of-date textbooks. Organizer theory, however, played a significant role in stimulating a chemical approach to embryology, and its influence on embryology in general was great, equal in fact to that of Haeckel's expression of the biogenetic law and of Roux's and Driesch's first descriptions of the development of isolated blastomeres. The organizer provided excitement not only to embryologists but also to a wider biological and general public; its impact was similar in its own day to that of the demonstration, a generation later, that DNA is the hereditary substance. It was the organizer that attracted to embryology the efforts of many of the best young biologists of the 1920's and 1930's and possibly the 1940's.

As the emphasis on organizers waned, so did that on determination, although some investigators still use the word today. The concept of determination seems to have been supplanted by that of differentiation, which may include determination. Determination seemed to have been considered to be a one-step process, or a two-step one if the validity of the concept of labile determination is granted. Differentiation, a progressive process, may be construed as more gradual and as involving more intermediate steps than the old concept of determination. Differentiation, as a sequential process, may seem easier to describe in molecular terms. This explains, perhaps, the frequent use of the words chemodifferentiation and cytodifferentiation in the textbooks of the 1970's. But causative values sometimes become confused here. The vertebrate lens contains a higher proportion of protein, and an identifiable protein at that, than other vertebrate tissues. The protein develops, however, only after the lens has been formed: not as a condition of its induction, but as a result of it.

Identifiable substances responsible for differentiation, or growth, in animal tissues, are not entirely unknown. The nerve growth factor described below (Part Twelve) is a factor with a selective effect; an epidermal growth factor related to it is another; erythropoetin is a third. Plants are wiser than animals in the use of chemical regulators of growth and differentiation, or perhaps they are less wise and permit their secrets to be easier to fathom by developmental biologists. But in animals what are such morphogenetic factors really? If epidermis is grown *in vitro* in the presence of vitamin A in greater than physiological quantities, it transforms itself into mucous epithelium. Is vitamin A an inducer? A morphogenetic substance? Investigators are still not agreed as to whether adult sex hormones act as embryonic hormones, or as inducers, or as neither, when exerting their effects on the differentiation of embryonic sex glands and ducts. Large questions remain to be answered here, and new ideas are needed.

We shall return shortly to the problem of differentiation, which many biologists, including most embryologists and some geneticists, consider the central problem of biology now that—as they believe—the problem of heredity is solved. Let us remain for a moment with some relatives of organizers and inducers, the fields and their constituent gradients. Serious explanation in depth of egg polarity, in terms of gradients, was begun by Boveri early in this century. He worked on echinoderm eggs, and double gradients, which prove to characterize these eggs, according to the results of strictly embryological experiments, have been studied for over 60 years. No satisfactory biochemical description of the gradients in the echinoderm egg has ever succeeded. Even now, efforts continue to isolate and define *the* animalizing substance, or *the* vegetalizing substance, whereas, more likely, whole patterns of metabolism are at play. In 1941 Child wrote a big book on gradients but it described rather than analyzed. In the years since, references to gradients have proliferated in the literature but still have received no real explanation. That cells can climb gradients to reach other cells—a quantitative description of affinity or chemotaxis—has been shown for cellular slime molds, and one substance that is graded in quantity is 3′-5′ AMP. But analysis of fields and of most gradients has defied manifold efforts, and recently has not been a popular area of investigation. Because most attempts have been unproductive, Wolpert's efforts (Part Fourteen) to discover how a cell knows its place in its cellular surroundings are welcome. Wolpert too invokes the action of some unspecified diffusible substance as essential to his theory, thus raising the familiar unanswered questions. By adding the dimension of time as one of the parameters fixing the cell into its place in an over-all pattern, he notes what all embryologists have known since antiquity, that change occurs in time as well as space. But even if these aspects of his thought are not new, his approach *is* fresh, and may engender interest in the study of over-all pattern in development. By avoiding the over-allness, and by emphasizing positional information that impinges on the cell and its interpretation by the cell, he confines himself to the more empirical problem of how the unit relates to the whole however the latter may ultimately be defined.

Organizers and fields, inducers and gradients, these are tenuous words as applied to the phenomena of development. Biochemical embryologists have made their greatest advances by describing various developmental systems in chemical terms. Some steps that occur in the development of crystallin proteins in the lens, of collagen in the skin, of chondroitin sulfate in cartilage, provide some selected examples. Such investigations, however, remain descriptive rather than analytical.

The most important progress in biochemical embryology has been the identification of the large number and variety of nucleic acids involved in developmental controls and the partial explanation of their roles in the management of differentiation. From the 1950's, when the structure of DNA as the hereditary substance and the manner of its duplication became known, and later when its mode of action in controlling the production of enzymes in bacteria had been worked out, it was clear that a great challenge remaining for geneticist and embryologist alike was to discover the manner in which the substance of the genes controls the differentiation of cells in a multicellular organism. The main problem of life for a population of microbes is to remain a similar population of microbes in a changed environment. The problem that faces a multicellular embryo is to organize its many cells, all containing the same genes, so that the cells express their genes selectively to become different, while simultaneously maintaining the individuality and integrity of the organism as it changes in time and space.

The transplantation of nuclei has confirmed that all the genes are in all the cells. Experiments, especially those performed by Gurdon, have shown that genes which seem to have been silenced during differentiation can speak again when placed into certain cytoplasmic environments. This provides a basis for controls over genes that exert other controls; it opens a wide field for new investigations into genetic self-organization; that is what it is, since the cytoplasm has been made what it is by the genetic complement it contains.

A large number of nucleic acids of differing size and structure has been discovered in eggs and embryos in an unexpected variety. These nucleic acids are involved in long series of transformations consisting of more steps than would be expected to be responsible for a simple change from a non-determined to a determined state. Gene amplification in oocytes exemplifies a new developmental and genetic principle. Much of this new system of changes remains to be analyzed and could become the basis of a new micro-epigenesis. Developmental geneticists are here aided by the new cytologists who can view with their electron microscopists a number of structures important for genetic controls: nuclear pores, large enough to permit the exchange of molecules between nucleus and cytoplasm; the ribosomes and their parts; the structure of chromosomal loops and puffs, and others. Here combined morphological and molecular studies have permitted cell biology not only to describe but also to analyze sequences of events.

The midcentury successors to the cytologists now consider themselves cell biologists, and pride themselves on studying function as well as structure; but in their fashion so did the old cytologists. The new cell biologists see their role as a larger one, encompassing in molecular terms cell structure and function in development and heredity. Likewise, the old embryologists have become developmental biologists, taking as their province cells in development and genes in development. They study changing form and function on a molecular level in a far wider variety of organisms than did many of those whom they considered as mere embryologists.

The electron microscopes of the cell biologists have revealed structure in greater detail than light microscopes. Internal structure of long-familiar organelles, the mitochondria and the Golgi apparatus, for instance, have been viewed in greater detail. Pinocytosis has been revealed as a mechanism enabling a cell to engulf large molecules. The old ground substance of the cytoplasm, once seemingly homogeneous, was called upon to explain the inexplicable. The electron microscope revealed it not as the simple matrix it was thought to be, but as a maze of channels, continuous with nuclear and external membranes, with granules and droplets galore interspersed. But while in some forms some organelles are sparser in younger cells than in older ones, all too little difference is apparent between an oocyte that will become *Homo sapiens* and an undifferentiated somatic cell of a mammal or of many other organisms. Here, electron microscopy confirms the negativity of light microscopy.

On the positive side, electron microscopy has demonstrated unsuspected connections between cells, connections of a number of varied types. What passes through them remains to be fully investigated. One importance of Loewenstein's contribution (Part Thirteen) is that it draws our attention back to basic physiological properties of cells, long known but long neglected. In a number of investigations besides Loewenstein's, also, it is becoming fashionable to return to these again. The ionic currents he describes as passing from cell to cell could possibly be involved only in the maintenance of homeostatic conditions in cells or cell groups, rather than with developmental change *per se.* Wolpert, however, sees possibilities that the passage of signals across low ionic resistance junctions may have meaning for his own theory. Only the future can point up the significance of the ionic currents, but meantime Loewenstein has given us a new question to ask of embryos. Perhaps it could not have been asked until the infatuation with macromolecules had cooled slightly.

The failure to "explain" induction biochemically, the inability of electron microscopy to reveal more than minor changes in cell morphology during the earliest stages of development (except with respect to structures related to the nucleic acids), the success in studying the roles of nucleic acids in the early stages of development, and the vast upsurge of attention to the nucleic acids more generally, have all cooperated to create a pattern of thought that emphasizes the role of the genes in development at the expense of some of the intermediate processes by which the genes exert their action in the differentiation of multicellular cells. In 1907 Warren Lewis transplanted a small piece of the blastopore lip of a frog embryo below body epidermis of a slightly older embryo, and found that neural tissue and somites differentiated; his interpretation was that the graft self-differentiated. When in 1924 Spemann and Hilde Mangold (Part Ten) performed a similar experiment, they proved, using host and graft of different colors, that the neural tissue was most of it formed by the host and thus was induced. So strong is the emphasis now on what is called genetic prepatterning that I should venture to predict that if the experiments were performed today, Lewis's explanation would be preferred over Spemann's. If a mouse may speak of herself in the same paragraph in which she speaks of a mountain, my own experiments involving transplantation of the teleost gastrula's equivalent of the amphibian dorsal lip have recently been reinterpreted in the literature in terms of self-differentiation rather than induction, even though the occurrence of the latter had been documented by an illustration showing that reacting tissue stained with a vital dye of one color responded to the presence of an inducer vitally stained a different color. That genes are responsible for differentiation no one denies, but it seems demonstrated, though the validity of the demonstration is ignored today, that they act through intermediary mechanisms in multicellular embryos, one of which may be induction in the case of some tissues of some organisms. In any event, the concept of prepatterning is hardly so new as some of those suppose who use the word as a slogan. It goes back at least to that old concept of labile determination, a concept which, as mentioned above, developed hand in hand with that of induction.

Scientific pendula have long swings; perhaps when the one that now marks our time returns towards the center of its arc, new concepts, not yet imagined, will explain both inductive and other differentiative phenomena more successfully than the old. It is clearly predictable that the most likely postulates of the near future will involve factors, ranging from ionic to the macromolecular, relating to the structure and function of membranes; these are the cell organelles whose time is now ripe. The embryologists' cell-to-cell affinity, and cell-to-cell interactions of many other kinds too, including the specificity of nerve connections now under active investigation, seem to promise to be intelligible in terms of active sites on membranes exactly as have the immunological and endocrinological phenomena so successfully studied from this point of view.

The fruits of Wolpert's and Loewenstein's investigations remain to ripen. Of the work described in the three new articles added to the new edition of *Foundations,* that of Levi-Montalcini seems to have had the greatest consequence so far, especially if her interpretation is accepted that a new class of integrators has been discovered that operates on a different level from those previously known.

It would be desirable to close this introduction with some imaginative prophecies for the future. The history of the discovery of Levi-Montalcini's nerve growth factor illustrates the futility of searching for futures; they arrive on their own. The studies of the nerve growth factor grew naturally out of the studies started at the beginning of the century on the relationships of nerve centers to the peripheries they innervate. It was a logical step in the analysis to test the effect on the nerve centers of a fast-growing tumor grafted and growing nearby. It was a success of astute observation to notice that ganglia removed in distance from the tumors responded to its presence, thus to recognize that the active agent might be carried in the circulation. The use of snake venom to clean up the proteins that might be involved as the agent was pure expediency; it was accidental that phosphodiesterase then resided in greater quantities in snake venom than in bottles in laboratory refrigerators. That the venom itself should have been a source of the agent was a matter of the wildest possible coincidence, and could hardly have been predicted. To look next for the factor in mammalian salivary glands was intelligent, but might not have occurred to everyone. To study the amino acid sequence of the factor isolated from these glands was possible in the 1970's because the technique had been worked out for insulin first, then applied to other unrelated proteins, in the 1960's. What an off chance, again, that it should be insulin that the nerve growth factor resembles in its amino acid sequence. The telling of this tale covers the major part of this century; it began with the investigation of that old problem of extrinsic versus intrinsic controls over development. Even ten years ago, it was not clear where the story would end. It is not over yet, but the importance of following the work where it leads is evident.

In emphasizing the unknown, these pages may have too strongly accentuated the negative. But in science the known grows from the unknown, so it is in the unknown that the work of the future must take root. We hope that it will develop ideas as original as the work in this volume. While advances of major import have their origins in the past, newly advancing thought follows unpredictable paths, and scientific inspiration like all inspiration remains a will-of-the-wisp.

* * * * * * *

I owe a debt of gratitude to Edward J. Quigley, Anita Kann, and Valerie Klima for their interest and helpfulness with respect to the new edition, and thanks also to James Ebert and Stephen Roth. The second edition of this book is dedicated to Dorothea Rudnick.

Jane M. Oppenheimer

Jerusalem, February 16, 1974

Table of Contents

Foundations
of Experimental
Embryology

1888

Contributions to the Developmental
Mechanics of the Embryo. On
the Artificial Production of Half-
Embryos by Destruction of One of
the First Two Blastomeres, and the
Later Development (Postgeneration) of
the Missing Half of the Body

by W. ROUX

from the Anatomical Institute of Breslau

Roux, W. 1888. Beiträge zur Entwickelungsmechanik des Embryo.
Ueber die künstliche Hervorbringung halber Embryonen durch
Zerstörung einer der beiden ersten Furchungskugeln, sowie über
die Nachentwickelung (Postgeneration) der fehlenden Körper-
hälfte.* Virchows Arch. path. Anat. u. Physiol. u. kl. Med. **114:**
113-153; Resultate 289-291. Tafel II und III. Translated by Hans
Laufer and printed by permission of Springer-Verlag.

* The portion of the article dealing with postgeneration is
omitted in this translation.

During the second half of the nineteenth century it became gradually apparent that descriptive and comparative approaches to the study of how an embryo develops were inadequate for explaining the role of causal factors in the developmental process. The chief and most influential advocate of a new approach by experiment was Wilhelm Roux (1850-1924), a German anatomist. He founded a new discipline, causal analytical embryology, which he called developmental mechanics (Entwicklungsmechanik *in German). He drew up a program for procedure, and established the* Archiv für Entwicklungsmechanik der Organismen, *the first volume of which appeared in 1894-95. It was the first and for several decades the leading international journal for causal analytical embryology and still is important today.*

Roux defined the over-all program of Entwicklungsmechanik *as the resolution of developmental processes into simpler, but still complex, functional processes, and the analysis of these functional processes into really simple ones, which may be identical with those which underlie inorganic or physico-chemical processes.*

With causal analysis his guiding motive, Roux performed a simple type of experiment on the frog's egg at the two- and four-celled stages of cleavage. If he injured one of the two first-formed blastomeres, the surviving blastomere developed a half-embryo; this is the work that is presented here. With a strong predilection for philosophical speculations concerning development, Roux interpreted the facts as suggesting that differentiation might be one of two types, namely self-differentiation *(independent or mosaic development) or* correlative dependent differentiation *(interaction of cells or groups of cells). He felt that the fact that one cell at the two-cell stage develops a half-embryo suggests that each cell develops independently of its neighbor and thus that the total development represents the summation of partial mosaic developments.*

These conclusions of Roux were later shown to be erroneous for the frog's egg (A. Brachet, 1905; McClendon, 1910). However, Roux's work on the production of half-embryos is significant for several reasons. It initiated a new trend in method of attack on embryogenesis and marked a major turning point in its study by shifting emphasis from descriptive to experimental embryology. It pointed to a new direction for embryological thought and theoretical interpretation. It opened the way for a new and experimental attack on the significance of interrelationships between tissues and thus led to new insights into old problems of epigenesis. It is safe to say that all the analytical embryology of the late nineteenth and of the twentieth century has built upon foundations laid by Roux.

CONTRIBUTIONS TO THE DEVELOPMENTAL MECHANICS OF THE EMBRYO. ON THE ARTIFICIAL PRODUCTION OF HALF-EMBRYOS BY DESTRUCTION OF ONE OF THE FIRST TWO BLASTOMERES, AND THE LATER DEVELOPMENT (POST-GENERATION) OF THE MISSING HALF OF THE BODY

The investigations that will be recorded in this article are closely connected with my previous works on developmental mechanics and presuppose therefore a knowledge of their results, at least for full understanding. Since I have noticed that my previous works have remained almost unknown even to many specialists in the field, it appears proper to preface this treatise, meant for a larger circle of readers, with a brief review of the pertinent results.

The following investigation represents an effort to solve the problem of self-differentiation[1]—to determine whether, and if so how far, the fertilized egg is able to develop independently as a whole and in its individual parts. Or whether, on the contrary, normal development can take place only through direct formative influences of the environment on the fertilized egg or through the differentiating interactions of the parts of the egg separated from one another by cleavage.

For the egg as a whole I answered this question by rotating eggs in a perpendicular plane in such a way that, while the centrifugal force did not inhibit their development, the eggs continuously altered their orientation with respect to gravitational force, to the magnetic meridian and to the source of light and warmth. The result was that normal development was neither suspended, altered, nor even retarded by this process. We can conclude from this that the typical structures of the developing egg and embryo do not need any formative influence by such external agencies for their formation, and that in this sense the morphological development of the fertilized egg may be considered as self-differentiation. Nevertheless, several possibilities of external formative influence still remain that have not been tested by this experiment. These are of a very general character, for example His[2] made the hypothesis that many cells have a tendency to move toward the direction from which oxygen enters, thus enlarging the surface of the embryo. It is also conceivable that the blastomeres lying on the surface of the blastula and the gastrula gradually become flatter on their external sur-

[1] Cf. W. Roux, Beiträge zur Entwickelungsmechanik des Embryo. No. 1. Zeitschr. f. Biologie. 1885. Bd. XXI.

[2] W. His, Untersuchungen über die Bildung des Knochenfischembryo (Salmen). Arch. f. Anat. u. Physiol., anat. Abth. 1878, S. 220.

faces only because influences from outside cause their transformation into functional epithelia, thereby producing a mechanical tendency towards the densest concentration possible and toward the minimizing of the external surface, in contrast to the previous tendency towards the greatest possible sphericity for each individual cell. These speculations must still be checked against reality. The fact also must not be overlooked that the influence of external agencies may be a necessary condition for development, even though these influences may have no directly formative effect. For example, no development at all will take place without a certain amount of heat and also, later, of oxygen. But it cannot be deduced from this that such agencies determine which part of the egg produces the eyes, the blastopore, or the neural groove, or that they are the cause for the specific formation of the parts, despite the fact that abnormal formations result from an abnormal rise in temperature according to Panum, Dareste and Gerlach.

It has thus been shown that the development of the form of the fertilized egg, apart from that of several more general structures, occurs without external formative forces. We therefore have to look for the formative forces in the egg itself, which imposes a very pleasant limitation on further investigation.

As the result of this insight, it seems to me necessary to determine first of all whether all or many parts of the egg must collaborate if its structures are to form normally, or whether, on the contrary, the parts of the egg separated from one another by cleavage are able to develop independently of one another, and to show also, if possible, what share in the normal development each of the two principles has—that of differentiating interaction of the parts with one another, and that of self-differentiation of the parts.

As an argument for a certain independence in the development of the individual blastomeres, one could utilize, although not with certainty, the following fact about the egg of the frog, found by myself and shortly thereafter by Pflüger. This is that the first plane of cleavage of the egg represents the median plane of the future embryo, thus separating the material of the right and of the left half of the body, a fact which has been determined independently by van Beneden and Julin[3] for the ascidians. M.v.Kowalewski[4] later made observations that indicate similar conditions in the case of a teleost (*Carassius auratus*). At the same time I found a fact that we will use later on, that the cleavage plane perpendicular to the median plane of the future animal can be formed first

[3] Ed. van Beneden et Ch. Julin, La segmentation chez les Ascidiens et ses rapports avec l'organisation de la larve. Arch. de Biologie. T.V. 1884.

[4] Miecz. v. Kowalewski, Ueber die ersten Entwickelungsprozesse der Knochenfische. Zeitschr. für wissenschaftl. Zool. 1886.

although it normally appears second—and I later succeeded in producing this anachronism artificially.

In addition, it was already known to previous authors that the upper, black hemisphere of the frog's egg always corresponds to a definite side of the embryo, the dorsal side, according to these authors. This interpretation could no longer be considered correct, however, after my investigations and those of Pflüger. I recently have shown by means of certain localized defects on the cleaved egg that the middle portion of the black hemisphere of the frog's egg provides the material for the ventral surface of the embryo, in contrast to the previous view.[5]

I found moreover that the cephalic and caudal ends of the embryo are already determined at the stage of the first cleavage of the frog's egg and that in the case of *Rana esculenta,* the green or water frog, they are already recognizable by an oblique position of the axis of the egg, a condition which had already been determined independently by van Beneden and Julin for the ascidians and later by M.y.Kowalewski for *Carassius* (although the latter author did not take the occasion to mention his predecessors as having observed this fundamental behavior in relatively closely related classes of animals). It is worth mentioning that observations pertinent to this matter had already been recorded in the posthumous papers of G. Newport, published in 1854. These aroused no notice at the time and were not discovered again until later. I showed furthermore[6] that the position of the cephalic and the caudal side of the embryo in the egg is normally determined by the union of the nucleus of the sperm and that of the ovum, the half of the egg penetrated by the male nucleus becoming the caudal half of the embryo, while the opposite half of the egg produces the cephalic half. It was possible to recognize the direct causal connection because I succeeded in fertilizing each egg from an arbitrarily chosen meridian and thereby determined the caudal side of the embryo of the egg at will. In the case of other animals where the side of the egg fertilized does indeed coincide with a definite side of the embryo, but where spermatozoa penetrate into the egg at a typical point, such a conclusion cannot be drawn with certainty but can at most be expressed as a conjecture.[7]

---

[5] Anatom. Anzeiger. 1888, No. 25. Ueber die Lagerung des Materiales des Medullarrohres im gefurchten Froschei.

[6] Beiträge zur Entwickelungsmechanik des Embryo. No. 4. Arch. für mikrosk. Anat. 1887. Bd. 29.

[7] According to my previous investigations the location of the following form changes are normally determined by the arbitrarily selected location of the region of fertilization.

(1) The spermatozoon takes a typically curved course in the vertical meridional plane which passes through the point of sperm entry: in the fertilization plane.

(2) The union of the two sexual nuclei takes place in the fertilization plane.

(3) In *Rana fusca,* on the side of the egg opposite the side of fertilization, the dark

Such is the case with the hen's egg, where it has long been known that the location of the embryo is determined with regard to the axis of the whole egg, even though the exact relation of the median plane to the first cleavage and the exact relation of this to the direction of the nuclear fusion has not been discovered. V. Kölliker[8] had already surmised that that portion of the blastodisc of the hen's egg that divides most rapidly develops later into the posterior part of the blastoderm, in which the first traces of the embryo originate; and His[9] has shown further that in the blastodisc of the hen's egg after it has been laid every region of the external germ layer corresponds to a definite part of the future animal. For the further development of these parts, however, His assumes—in contrast to possible self-differentiation of the individual regions—mechanical interactions of the region of origin with adjacent or more distant regions. For two of these structures, the neural tube and the intestinal tube, I was able to demonstrate,[10] by separation of their primordia from the parts lateral to them, that such interactions are not necessary, since in spite of their isolation the development of the primordia was completed, and even faster than normally. According to this we should look for the formative causes effective in the development of these tubes in the parts which compose the tube itself, while the neighboring regions even offer a resistance to the development of the tubes, which must gradually be overcome. But from these results we must not deduce that all organs acquire their form by self-differentiation of the complex of

---

hemisphere becomes lighter and takes the form of a gray crescent adjacent to the white hemisphere. This crescent is symmetrically oriented with respect to the meridian of fertilization. In the case of the green frog the pigment is likewise displaced, although perhaps in a somewhat different manner, so that the white portion reaches farther up on the same side.

(4) The first plane of division lies in the plane of the meridian of fertilization.

(5) The first appearance of the blastopore occurs in the meridian of fertilization, namely:

(6) On the half of the egg lying opposite to the side of fertilization, approximately at the border of the dark hemisphere and at the margin which subsequently becomes lighter (see No. 3).

(7) The lateral blastopore lips develop symmetrically with respect to this meridian.

(8) Both the neural ridges and the whole later embryo are located symmetrically with respect to the meridian of fertilization, that is to say, the plane of the meridian of fertilization becomes the median plane of the animal.

(9) The side of the egg that is fertilized becomes the caudal side of the animal.

In order to gain insight into the causal relationships upon which these multiple correlations are based, I have made an effort to produce artificial separations of these correlations and have frequently been successful. A further report on this matter will be forthcoming.

[8] A. Kölliker, Entwickelungsgeschichte des Menschen und der höheren Thiere. Leipzig 1879.

[9] His, Unsere Körperform und das physiologische Problem ihrer Entstehung. 1874.

[10] Beitrag 1 zur Entwickelungsmechanik des Embryo. Zeitschrift für Biologie 1885.

parts of which they are composed. On the contrary, each case must be investigated individually, and for many structures it is beyond all doubt that they are produced by mechanical interactions with neighboring parts, for example the shape of the liver, the lungs (His, Braune), bones (A. Fick), paths of many vessels (G. Schwalbe), etc. In connection with this I have shown, by producing an artificial rhomboid fossa on the neural tube which survived the deforming effect, that the embryo possesses vital adaptability to passive deformation to a very high degree; thus the theoretical possibility of such an origin has been demonstrated for the normal rhomboid fossa, which would agree with His' assumption.

In addition, numerous facts of pathology also argue for the self-differentiation of the parts of the egg, for example dermoid encysted tumors, etc., facts which I have collected in the article last referred to. Yet only direct experimentation with the egg can clarify for us with perfect certainty the actual participation of self-differentiation of the parts of the egg in normal development. Years ago[11] I worked along these lines and verified, in general, that operations that produce an extrusion of material from the cleaving and cleaved egg do not prevent development or cause general malformation. The resulting embryos develop rather normally and have only a localized defect or a localized malformation.

In order to acquire more specialized knowledge, I used the portion of the spawning period in the spring of 1887 that remained, after the conclusion of time-consuming experiments, for pertinent investigations on which I will report in the present article.

Although, as will be seen, the results were very extensive, many important questions had to be left temporarily unanswered, questions that could have been easily answered by continuation and a slight variation of the experiments. This present study is therefore only one installment, as it were, of the theme treated, that of self-differentiation.

The plan of the experiments was as follows:

In the first experiment the eggs of the green frog, *Rana esculenta,* were placed individually in glass dishes, and the oblique position of the black hemisphere and the direction of cleavage were sketched during the formation of the first cleavage. Then one of the first two blastomeres was pricked once or more with a fine needle. The present position of the egg was then compared with the drawing. A new sketch was made if there was a difference, and the location of the puncture points was

---

11 "Vorlaüfige Mittheilung über causal-autogenetische Experimente," Vortrag gehalten am 15. Febr. 1884. in der Schlesischen Gesellschaft für vaterländische Cultur. (Lecture delivered on February 15th, 1884 to the Silesian Society for Native Culture.) My neglect in sending in a review resulted in there being no notice of that lecture in the corresponding annual report of the Silesian Society. The report was first published in Beitrag 1 zur Entwickelungsmechanik, Zeitschrift für Biologie 1885.

indicated, along with the position of the egg material exuded through them, the exovates. Unfortunately most of these eggs in the first experiments either did not develop at all or developed normally, in spite of the fact that the punctured blastomere often discharged large amounts of material and became filled up again by a flow of substances from the neighboring cell. As a result, in addition to their loss, an extreme disorder of the egg substances must have been present. Therefore, after the destruction of a single blastomere I could observe the externally visible processes in a few eggs only. In many of the eggs, the unoperated control eggs as well as the experimental ones, occasional malformations were already occurring, as is customary toward the end of the spawning period. I have already described this effect briefly in a previous publication. Since ability of the eggs to develop normally might cease completely at any time, I operated after the formation of the first cleavage on great numbers of unisolated eggs lying together in clusters. After several hours, or the next day, I selected and placed in separate dishes those eggs in which the operated blastomere had not cleaved. Occasionally the second cleavage occurred during the operation on the first egg, and I then pierced two of the blastomeres lying next to one another, or perhaps only one of four.

Even after repeated puncture of a cell with a fine needle, and in spite of considerable exovation, the cell often developed normally. So, beginning on the third day, I heated the needle by holding it against a brass sphere for a heat supply, heating the sphere as necessary. In this case only a single puncture was made, but the needle was ordinarily left in the egg until an obvious light brown discoloration of the egg substance appeared in its vicinity. Some of this discolored material stuck to the needle when it was pulled out and formed a broad slightly protruding cone—a sign that it had become firmer and thus was partly coagulated. As a result of this, exovates no longer issued even out of the puncture points. I now had better results; they were as follows. In about 20% of the operated eggs only the undamaged cell survived the operation, while the majority were completely destroyed and a very few, where the needle had possibly already become too cold, developed normally. I thus developed and preserved over a hundred eggs with one of their halves destroyed, and, of these, 80 were sectioned completely. Eggs that were intended for the latter purpose were taken out and killed from time to time. More were taken from the early stages, those of the morula and the blastula, than from the later stages already provided with the rudiments of special organs.

In each experiment we likewise, although more rarely, observed in the unoperated control egg a failure of one of the two or four first blastomeres to develop as well as other malformations. These eggs were also preserved at various stages and sectioned for comparison with the

operated eggs. The same was done with eggs which did not develop
in spite of their having been placed in seminal fluid.

Since the treatment of the eggs with respect to preservation and
staining is important for the findings in the nuclei, and since it offers
many difficulties in itself, I will briefly report the essential facts about
it and my experiences which depart somewhat from those of previous
authors. In a slight variation of Born's modification of O. Hertwig's
method, the eggs were killed by placing them in water of about 80° C.
for several minutes; this not only kills the egg and makes it rather
resistant due to coagulation, but suffices also to make it easy to cut
off the periblast. Hardening and preservation were done by Born's
method in 70% to 80% alcohol. Staining was done, according to O.
Schultze's method, in borax carmine followed by differentiation in weak
hydrochloric acid alcohol. Then, for the purpose of embedding, the
eggs were transferred into absolute alcohol overnight, placed in toluene
for several minutes and then for several hours, or days if preferred, in
old thick resinous oil of turpentine. The eggs were placed on blotting
paper and freed of excess turpentine with a brush dipped in toluene.
The eggs, perfectly suited for sketching, were stored dry, but one must
be careful not to use too much toluene in rinsing since otherwise not
enough turpentine resin will remain in the specimen to keep it pliant.
After the evaporation of the toluene the eggs become as hard as stone
and are then correspondingly brittle when cut. This happened to me,
unfortunately, with the majority of the preparations I demonstrated in
Wiesbaden at the Naturalists' meeting, due to my efforts to clean the
surface completely of turpentine. Should this happen, however, the
eggs are still not completely lost. I softened them by placing them for
two or three days in a 30% solution of potassium carbonate; then they
were again dehydrated and saturated with turpentine. A portion of
them remained undamaged and proved upon microscopic examination
after sectioning to be well preserved internally also. Some however
were already so softened on the outside, before the inside became sufficiently so, that their outer portions wore off during the following
manipulations and I had only the remains to cut—which fortunately
provided the most important regions anyway.

Using Spee's method, the eggs were embedded in boiled paraffin
which melted at 50°. I found embedding overnight to be better than the
shorter half-hour period, and I also observed no damage in increasing
the temperature to 60° C. I found danger of the eggs becoming hard
only in toluene, that evaporates completely, after which, as has been mentioned, the eggs become as hard as stone if another fluid or soft substance such as turpentine resin or paraffin does not penetrate them immediately.

The preservation and staining of the nuclei was quite good in many of the preparations and the mitotic structures were therefore easy to see. In other specimens that seemed to have been treated exactly the same way, but had perhaps been overheated in the process of killing, defined structural detail of the nuclei was no longer recognizable.

The information reported below on abnormal nuclear structure cannot, because of the latter's very nature, be attributed to possible changes due to the preparation of the eggs. Moreover, the abnormal nuclear structure was found also in preparations which showed well-preserved normal nuclei in other regions. In spite of good preservation of structure of interphase nuclei, so extraordinarily few mitotic figures were perceptible in many embryos that I had to assume, along with Flemming, that the majority of the mitotic figures (which certainly occur frequently in the process of continuous development) had either reverted to the interphase type during the heat-killing of the egg or had rapidly gone to completion.

The experiments themselves consisted, as has been noted, in altering by operation one of the two cells formed after the appearance of the first cleavage plane in the fertilized egg[12] and thus depriving it of its ability to develop. Coming now to the report of our experimental results, we will first present the processes which take place in the untreated egg-half after this crude interference.

In many cases no developmental phenomena were perceptible in this cell. More often the symptoms of death already described were apparent, gray discoloration and the formation of spots.[13] In other cases these blastomeres went through several further cleavages only to die likewise, as I have elsewhere described, with an accompanying maximal flattening

[12] J. Dewitz recently reported (Biolog. Centralbl. 1887. pg. 93) that unfertilized frogs' eggs can be stimulated to the point of cleavage by placing them in mercuric chloride solution. The more detailed report promised has not yet been published. Nevertheless, this assertion has been reported, unquestioned, in various periodicals. I attempted to check it by placing unfertilized frog eggs in a series of 24 dishes with mercuric chloride solutions of varying strengths (from 0.001-1.4 parts per hundred). In the weakest solution a clouding of the jelly coat and the egg water occurred, if at all, only after several hours. Somewhat stronger solutions caused more cloudiness of the jelly coat in a shorter time and flaky coagulation of the egg water. On the other hand, I noticed in 0.5% solution that the eggs often burst open along half or whole meridians. When this happened the edges of the rupture were either sharp, slightly serrated and granular as a result of the strong coagulation of the yolk; or, if the coagulation had not yet penetrated deeply enough at the time that the surface layer coagulated and shrank, fluid yolk forced its way in fine lines out of the split and then coagulated also. Occasionally such fissures were approximately perpendicular to each other and provided on casual observation an appearance similar to one of the first cleavages. In other cases the egg did not burst open along the great circles or even along circular lines at all but in irregular lines oblique to one another. One cannot, however, designate such coagulation phenomena as cleavages, and thus as vital processes of definite importance in developmental mechanics.

[13] Beitr. zur Entwickelungsmechanik No. 1. Zeitschr. f. Biologie. 1885.

of the cells against one another, occasionally leading to the disappearance of the externally visible cleavage planes. On the basis of the third type of behavior, about to be described, we can properly assume that in these first two cases the supposedly undamaged cells had actually been directly affected by the operation and died from its effects and not as a result of the failure of interaction with the other cells.

In the third type of development, which was achieved in approximately 20% of the treated eggs in the last experiments, the untreated cell continued to survive. Various results might have been expected from this: for example, abnormal processes might intervene which would lead to bizarre structures. Or the single half of the egg, which, after all, according to many authors, is a complete cell with a nucleus completely equivalent in quality to the first segmentation nucleus, might develop into a correspondingly small individual. These authors see in the mechanism of indirect nuclear segmentation, on my authority as it were, only a contrivance for qualitative halving. I have repeatedly and clearly opposed this opinion. But instead of the possible surprises as postulated above an even more amazing thing happened; the one cell developed in many cases into a half-embryo generally normal in structure, with small variations occurring only in the region of the immediate neighborhood of the treated half of the egg. These variations will be mentioned in the section on the behavior of this latter half.

By repeated cleavages of the undamaged half of the egg a structure was at first produced which deserves the name of a *semimorula verticalis,* since it is built substantially like the vertical half of a morula. I mean by this that it was a hemispherical structure which consisted, in its upper region, of tightly packed small pigmented cells, and in its lower region of larger unpigmented cells. One component, however, of the normal morula was not properly developed in the eleven *semimorulae verticales* that were sectioned. This was the segmentation cavity. It should have been represented by an approximately hemispherical cavity adjacent to the undeveloped half and delimited by closely packed cells. Instead of this, the internal cells are merely loosely arranged with interstices between them. Sometimes there is a larger but not sharply delimited cavity that is separated from the undeveloped half by a layer of cells. Occasionally there is no indication at all of the formation of the cavity, not even the loose arrangement of the cells.

The next stage, the blastula, is not distinctly separated from the morula stage, since the blastula develops from the morula mainly by a further diminution in size of the cells and an enlargement of the internal cavity. This latter results from a gradual thinning of the roof of the cavity, which can be extremely varied in different individuals.

I found several *semiblastulae verticales* corresponding to this stage and sectioned them. The interesting thing here is that at this stage the internal cavity proves to be well defined, bordered by densely packed cells in the majority of cases, so that in comparison with the condition in the semimorulae the cells must have subsequently rearranged themselves and approximated themselves closely together. The blastocoele thus formed sometimes lies completely enclosed in the developed half, i.e., it is separated from the undeveloped half by a single or multiple layer of cells (Plate II, Fig. 1). Sometimes it borders directly on the boundary surface, which is approximately flat. In one case, however, it extends into this half (Fig. 2) and has thus acquired approximately the shape of a complete blastocoele; this however was caused merely by an abnormally large secretion of fluid by the developing half. In another case there is no indication at all of the formation of a cavity; the cells lie tightly together at all points and therefore border directly on the undeveloped half.

I thought that I had preserved a very large number of half-embryos at the next stage of development, gastrulation. However, after they were sectioned, it turned out that the majority were still at the blastula stage and that, at the first superficial examination, beginning gastrulation has merely been simulated by a slight indentation of the semiblastula toward the operated half of the egg. In contrast, another group of eggs exhibited, on the thickened free edge, structures that actually characterize a still more advanced stage, so that I have among the sectioned eggs only three half-embryos which are really at the gastrula stage.

The median plane can already be clearly distinguished in the normal gastrula as a plane passing through the center of the whole spherical structure and dividing symmetrically both the horseshoe-shaped blastopore and, internally, the cavity of the archenteron that is continuous with it. The cavity of the archenteron is covered on the outside by a thin double layered sheet that is dark on the outside. The horseshoe-shaped rim of this sheet forms, together with the adjacent white yolk mass, the blastopore. The dark sheet develops into the dorsal half of the embryo and I have therefore designated it as the dorsal plate. The middle of the horseshoe-shaped rim represents the head region and the open part of the arc the tail region of the embyro. Later the two halves of the horseshoe-shaped edge of the dorsal plate approach one another, proceeding in the cephalocaudal direction, and then merge. Normally the horseshoe-shaped rim is divided symmetrically by the median plane of the embryo.

As has been mentioned, because of the turning in of the free edge of the living half it is extremely difficult in half-embryos to identify the pertinent structural features by superficial examination and to judge whether the semigastrula is a lateral or an anterior or a posterior one.

Figure 3 represents a rather advanced stage, where one would be inclined to identify the section as a median one through a *semigastrula*

Plates II and III

All these figures represent frog embryos (*Rana fusca and esculenta*).

F   Segmentation cavity
Ec Ectoderm (external germ layer)
En Endoderm (internal germ layer)
Ms Mesoderm (middle germ layer)

Ch Chorda dorsalis (notochord)
Md Neural fold
U   Gastrocoele; in Fig. 12 blastopore
D   Yolk cells
V   Vacuoles

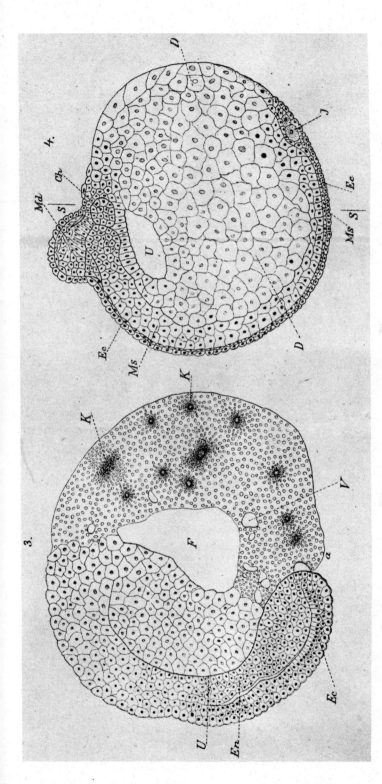

Fig. 1 *Semiblastula verticalis*, vertical meridianal section. The cells are sketched schematically. (a) a cell bounded only toward the developed side of the egg. **Fig. 2** *Semiblastula verticalis*, section of the same. Extension of the cleavage cavity into the undeveloped half of the egg. *KN* nuclear nest. *K'* a very large nucleus with reticular structure. **Fig. 3** *Semigastrula lateralis*, oblique longitudinal section. **Fig. 4** *Hemiembryo sinister*, cross section. *S-S* the median plane. The right half of the egg is already completely cellular as a result of the post-generation of the germ layers which has begun. Notochord has already caught up in its development to the normal size of the cross section. *J* two yolk cells, which have remained young.

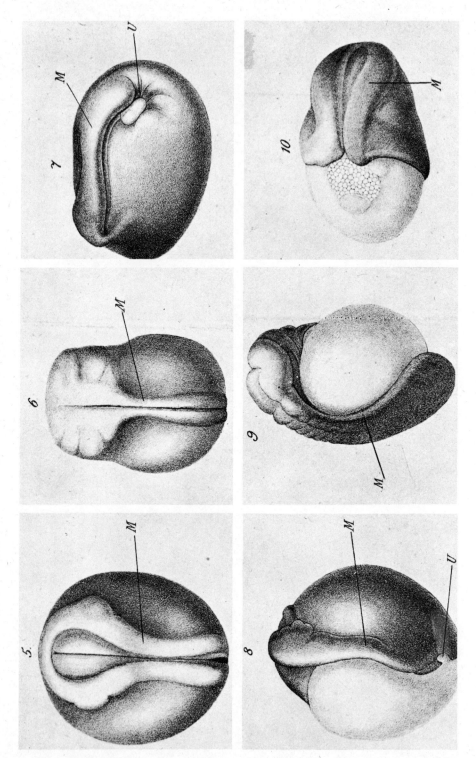

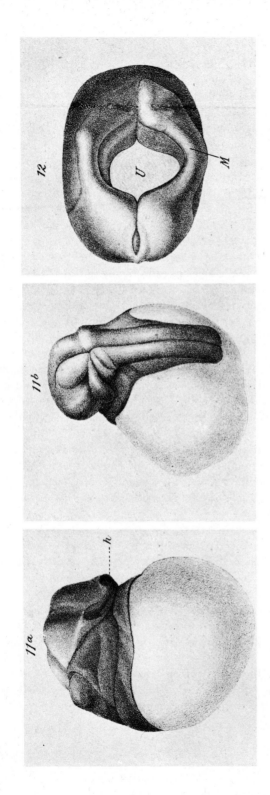

Fig. 5 Dorsal surface of a normal frog embryo with neural folds still separated. **Fig. 6** The same, with neural folds already united. **Fig. 7** *Hemiembryo dexter*, with post-generation of the external germ layer already almost completed. **Fig. 8** The same, older, but with less post-generation. **Fig. 9** *Hemiembryo sinister*, still older, almost without post-generation. **Fig. 10** *Hemiembryo anterior*, already in the process of post-genera-

tion. **Fig. 11** *Hemiembryo anterior*, older. (*a*) ventral side. (*h*) the adhesive gland. (*b*) dorsal side. Post-generation of the neural folds is already far advanced. **Fig. 12** Three-quarter embryo with *asyntaxia medullaris* (Roux). The left half of the head is not developed, the ectoderm is nevertheless already post-generated in its area. (*U*) a part of the blastopore that has remained open.

17

anterior. Since however the direction of the cut is not perpendicular to the surface separating the developed from the undeveloped half, but runs almost parallel to it, and since the dorsal plate is present in almost its entire length, the section figured proves to be one through a *semi-gastrula lateralis*. This diagnosis is easily and certainly confirmed if we mentally integrate the appearance of all the sections. The lumen of the archenteron is still only a slit in spite of its great length. The outer layer, the ectoderm, is clearly distinguishable from the inner layer, the endoderm. The blastula fluid and therefore the blastocoele also is still maintained, which is not normally the case at this time. The incorrectness of the view of previous authors, according to which the side of the egg adjacent to the blastocoele becomes the dorsal side of the embryo, is clearly evident in the more lateral sections where the blastocoele is located on the ventral side of the egg opposite to the dorsal plate. This is true in the developed as well as the undeveloped halves.

The next stage of development normally shows the first external rudiments of special organs, especially the primordium of the central nervous system in the form of a neural plate with both its lateral edges raised as the neural folds. The neural folds are separated from one another by a considerable distance in the cephalic region but gradually approach one another until they almost touch (Plate III, Figs. 5 and 6). The egg can already be called an embryo at this stage. We must now inquire what the unoperated half has formed that may correspond to this stage.

Figures 7 to 9 represent three of the most nearly normal specimens in various degrees of development. These as well as four other similar specimens that I possess all have a single neural fold only, which, however, is developed in its full length and normally shaped apart from inconsequential irregularities.

I must mention in this connection that even in normal embryos the shape of the folds at various ages is not always so constant and stereotyped as in the beautiful models by Ecker-Ziegler so frequently reproduced by later authors. On the contrary, rather high degrees of variation occur that have already been partially described by O. Hertwig[14] and myself.[15] Many of these variations seem to represent reversions to processes that are known in fishes, and that are caused primarily by anachronisms in differentiation and growth of the various parts. Such anachronisms are also evident in the relative delay or acceleration of the development of the individual germ layers. For example, many otherwise normal embryos possessing rather undifferentiated neural folds already show development within the mesoderm, the endoderm and in

[14] O. Hertwig, Die Entwickelung des mittleren Keimblattes der Wirbelthiere. Jena 1883. Taf. V. Fig. 5.
[15] Beitrag 1 zur Entwickelungsmechanik des Embryo. Zeitschr. f. Biol. 1885. Bd. XXI.

the chorda dorsalis that normally does not occur until nearly the time that the neural tube closes. In these cases there is an obvious retardation in the ectoderm as compared with the development of the two other germ layers. Such variations can easily lead to differences of opinion between observers should one of them attempt general deductions on the basis of insufficient material. The rates of development of the two lateral halves of the body also show variations of a lesser degree and provide the advantageous opportunity of permitting two stages of development to be observed in the same specimen.

Such variations, caused by inhibiting factors and the retardation of various processes, occur frequently toward the end of the spawning period, or as the result of an insufficient supply of air. Frequently, however, they are compensated for during the further course of development.

I sectioned six of the *hemiembryones laterales* that were obtained as a result of the above operation. Inspection of the cross-sections shows only half of the neural plate to be present. This is especially noticeable in the more advanced stages where the neural fold is already formed and typical in structure (Fig. 4). The typical arrangement of the cells of the more advanced neural tube is already nicely attained in many preparations but not so obvious in other places. The older embryos show the neural tissue in the cephalic region to be thickened and appropriately shaped. The originally lateral side of the ectoderm (the horny layer) had previously joined with the lateral edge of the neural plate, and in the course of the formation of the neural fold had been raised along with it to approach the midline. In the oldest embryo this horny layer had already separated from the neural part, although there is no opportunity here for it to merge with a similar layer of the other half. For the time being it projects unattached toward the other undeveloped half. This free edge, as well as the dorsal edge of the *semimedulla lateralis,* is curved ventrally, which also occurs in normal embryos.

The cavity of the archenteron has taken form only in the developed half and likewise extends only as far as the chorda. Its lumen is often too narrow and still slit-shaped. In other cases it has enlarged somewhat but is still constricted in the cephalic region by too great a concentration of yolk. The endoderm is normally constituted.

The formation of the mesoderm and the chorda dorsalis is normally a new feature of this phase. Our half-embryos also have formed these parts. I have no specimen in the very short phase in which we could gain clear insight into the origin of the mesoderm. In all the preparations it is already completely separated and in some cases it shows the normal cross-sectional appearance and the normal arrangement of the cells. In the older embryos the separation into lateral plate and somitic mesoderm is taking place or is already completed. In the oldest embryo the latter is already split up into somites. The lateral half of the mesoderm is thus normally developed (compare Fig. 4, Ms).

Since the chorda dorsalis is a median organ, it is of special interest to ascertain whether it is completely or only half formed. In order to judge this, a more exact discussion of its normal development is necessary. The complete separation of the chorda dorsalis from the three other layers takes place later posteriorly than anteriorly. It separates first from the ectoderm, then from the mesoderm, and finally from the endoderm.[16] Occasionally there is a stretch in the middle where it is not completely separated from the endoderm, while farther back it is already completely separate, and then farther posteriorly it again seems to be at an earlier stage of development[17]. Where it is completely separate it is round, oval or oblong in cross-section and is of quite variable thickness at different points along its length, generally decreasing in size from back to front. However very evident exceptions to this rule occur. Occasionally swellings are followed by constrictions in a regularly occurring fashion. Moreover the thickness varies considerably between chordas of different individuals at the same stage of development. The number of cells of approximately corresponding points may fluctuate almost by a factor of two.

Our half-embryos showed the chorda cell layer still connected with the intestinal endoderm in some places, and deflected dorsally as in the normal structure, but corresponding in its extent only to the lateral half of the anlage. Usually, however, the chorda is already completely separated and is round or slightly oval in cross-section. Thus we see that a half-oval has not been formed. The diameters seem to be somewhat smaller in size and number of the cells than is the case in whole embryos, but this could not be determined with certainty because of the normal variation in thickness. Therefore I wish only to mention that the periphery of its cross-section was formed by five cells at its thinnest point, whereas in apparently corresponding stages and regions of normal em-

---

16 I clearly saw metamerism in the separation of the *chorda dorsalis* from the mesoderm. For in each third or fourth section the separation was still hardly recognizable, while, in the sections lying between, the separation was already evident in the completed rearrangement of the cells. This is the case at the time when the chorda still is associated with the endoderm but already lies like a raised strand between the mesoderm halves on both sides, a strand which is still connected with the ectoderm only in a few places, i.e. the strand is not yet separated from the ectoderm by rearrangement of its cells.

17 At the same time it may be seen in this region, where separation from the endoderm has only just been completed, how the latter remedies the defect thus created in its continuity. At first this occurs exactly in the same way as at the beginning of the healing of a wound, by flattening of the epithelial cells at the edge and thus a covering over of the defect only. Subsequently, of course, the epithelial cells multiply and become taller.

bryos the whole chorda consists of eight to ten cells, although sometimes only six.

I wish to remark at this point, however, that I found several clearly recognizable half-chordas, *semichordae,* in preparations which I will describe later. This being so, the finding in the present instance of almost complete chordas must not be attributed to primary formation of the whole but rather to a very early postgeneration of the missing lateral side.

The median plane of the whole embryo, which in our half-embryos is defined only by the surface between the developed and undeveloped halves of the eggs, was represented in many cases by a straight line on the cross-section. That is to say, the dorsal and ventral edge of the *semimedulla,* the center of the chorda, the dorsal and ventral edge of the primitive intestinal cavity, or of the endoderm, and the ventral edge of the ectoderm lay approximately in a straight line. However, in the cephalocaudal direction, as we have said, the *semimedulla lateralis* was bent concavely toward the missing half.

Lateral displacement of the chorda dorsalis, which we observed once, was probably likewise a result of the disturbed mechanical correlation of materials, caused by a missing half. The dorsal part of the endoderm in this case remained against the median line between the semimedulla and the ventral parts. Nevertheless it is interesting that the axial parts can form and develop after such a considerable shift from their normal orientation.

There is a different reason for another phenomenon we also observed repeatedly, the absence of endoderm and archenteron when an approximately well-formed neural fold, chorda, and half of the mesoderm are present. This malformation, which I will call *anentoblastia* and from which an anenteric (gutless) condition will probably result at a more advanced state, cannot be directly related to our present experiments, since I have observed it not only in lateral hemiembryos but also in bilaterally symmetrical embryos, both operated and unoperated. I will describe these in greater detail at some other time. Here I only wish to mention a few points to which I shall refer later. In bilaterally symmetrical embryos the two neural folds are located far apart, occupying the lateral edges of the embryo which resembles an oval plate, almost flat. Under each neural ridge is found a well-differentiated *semichorda lateralis* which is round and easily distinguished in the cross-section by the three or four cells which compose it. A similar though lesser separation of the neural folds is often found confined only to certain regions, especially near the posterior half of the spinal cord. In such a case presence of the endoderm could be demonstrated in the sections. On the other hand, repeated observation of the living egg easily established that the large fissure between the two medullary folds represented the blastopore, at least the remains of it. Now according to other observations of mine, the half neural plate on each side is adjacent to the lateral lip of the blastopore, and the normal symmetrical shape of the neural plate is produced by the approach and fusion of these lips. Therefore if we wish to be exact we cannot designate the absence of fusion confirmed by these observations with the term *spina bifida,* which is customarily used to describe this condition repeatedly observed in higher animals. We must use instead the term *asyntaxia medullaris* (from ἀσυνταξία, non-union) or, simply indicating the result, *diastasis medullaris.* I prefer the first term since it suggests the actual phenomenon.

In cases of *asyntaxia medullaris* in the middle and caudal regions of the embryo I often saw in the course of time the neural folds approach each other caudally. As a result only a hole remained, midway along the length of the neural tube, that later completely closed. What has happened here therefore has only been a retardation of the growing downwards from the equator of the egg of the half dorsal plates from the two sides; qualitative differentiation was not inhibited and produced the neural folds before the fusion of the halves of the dorsal plates. An analogy between the formation of the embryonic anlagen in amphibians and in fishes is quite clearly illustrated by this form of *diastasis medullaris* and by the derivation of the archenteron from the blastopore. The *asyntaxia medullaris* can thus correspond to the "retardation in the joining of the halves of the germ ring to form the middle and posterior parts of the embryo" described by Rauber.[18] Rauber used the term dehiscence of the embryonic primordia to describe this condition, but for the reasons I have stated this does not seem as good a term as the one I have used. Likewise I consider the term *hemididymus* that he used to describe this retardation to have been appropriate only when it was necessary to contrast it with true twinning, which is no longer the case since von Recklinghausen's[19] basic treatment of the problem. Also von Recklinghausen's interpretation of *spina bifida* receives further support from explanation of the *diastasis medullaris* observed in the frog.

In addition to the lateral half-embryos I have now to describe several other imperfect embryos. Some of these also are produced by specimens treated after the first cleavage and are associated with a not infrequent variation in the temporal sequence of the cleavages, which, as we have seen, has a certain importance for the future embryo. Occasionally the actual second cleavage, separating head and tail ends, appears first[20] as I

[18] A. Rauber, Formbildung und Formstörung in der Entwickelung von Wirbelthieren. Leipzig 1880. S. 35 und 123.

[19] v. Recklinghausen, Untersuchungen über die Spina bifida. Berlin 1886, and this Archiv Bd. 105.

[20] My view of this event, that the position of the median plane of the embryo does not coincide with the plane of the first cleavage, and is merely an anachronism,

have proved in opposition to Rauber and Pflüger. It was hoped that such eggs would produce half-embryos of a different character as a result of operations after this first cleavage, provided the untreated cell was capable of development. I tried to achieve the same thing after the second cleavage by puncturing both the two front or the two rear cells. I actually succeeded in this way in producing anterior and posterior half-embryos. One day I produced a substantial number of *semigastrulae anteriores* and set them aside for further development. Beautiful anterior half-embryos developed from these, *hemiembryones anteriores,* the great majority of which were lost during their further development due to an occurrence that I shall describe in the second part. At the present moment I have only four preserved anterior half-embryos. Figures 10 and 11 show the external appearance of two of these anterior hemiembryos; the embryo shown in Fig. 10 has only the front half of the two neural folds. The two normal embryos shown in Figs. 5 and 6 can be examined for comparison, even though they are at a different stage of development. The cross-sections made frontally in the case of the embryo in Fig. 10 and approximately transversely in Fig. 14 reveal the normal internal structure of the neural plate with its neural folds, as well as of the chorda, the mesoderm, and the endoderm. However, this latter encloses only a slit-shaped archenteron cavity that is too narrow cephalically at this stage of development. In both cases the displacement of the yolk, which normally proceeds in a caudoventral direction, was impossible, due to the resistance of the undeveloped posterior half of the egg. The posterior half of the body is missing, just as if it had been cut off; in Fig. 11 we see the subsequent postgeneration of one part of it (see below).

I would like to mention further that the Anatomical Institute here recently received a calf foetus which was developed almost to full maturity. It represented a typical *hemitherium anterius* in its externally visible parts, the whole rump half being absent. The internal organs are at the moment still covered by a translucent membrane originating from the edge of the defect and thus do not permit a more exact judgement. This highly interesting malformation, which is so obviously similar to the experimental results just reported, will be described more exactly by one of my doctoral candidates.

---

gains support from other observations of anachronisms. For example, I have even observed, instead of the first horizontal cleavage, which usually appears as the third cleavage, a third vertical cleavage dividing the whole egg or one half only. Afterwards normal embryos were produced. The third and fourth vertical cleavages are very frequently exchanged, as can be easily established in the case of *Rana esculenta* by use of the cleavage plan which I have given, and this in turn often appears only in parts of an egg. In this year (1887) I caused, by artificial deformation of the egg, the cleavage which forms the median plane to be formed as the third one, and after the horizontal cleavage. This was without harmful effect on later development.

I have no definite example of the corresponding posterior half-embryo. One of the four preserved semigastrulae can perhaps be considered a posterior one, in view of the thickness and shortness of the blastopore lips.

I attempted in several of the eggs which I punctured after the second cleavage to kill only one of the four blastomeres present or to leave only one alive. The latter experiment resulted in several vertical quarter morulas and quarter blastulas, the former in several three-quarter blastulas and two three-quarter embryos. These embryos possess the rear half of the body and one lateral half of the front part. Before the time of the Naturalists' meeting in Wiesbaden I had only seen the embryos soaked with turpentine. Being interested in the first posterior half-embryos that had formed, I overlooked the continuation of one of the neural folds towards the front; moreover this was only slightly elevated. This continuation, after the embryo was completely dried, prepared, and sectioned, turned out to be a true front half of a neural fold. This was the reason that at that meeting both of these embryos were described only as posterior half-embryos.

One of these three-quarter embryos (Fig. 12) is well-developed, and as instructive for us as a pure posterior hemiembryo, because, having seen that the right and left halves of the body can each develop separately, we may assume that the posterior half, which is present only on the left side, likewise develops independently from the blastomere concerned. The neural folds can be clearly seen in this figure. The front half of the right fold is somewhat abnormally shaped externally and a definite *asyntaxia medullaris* can also be seen. In this case this can probably be explained simply by the absence of the front lateral half. Since the lateral lips of the blastopore normally join at the front first and the fusion proceeds from front to rear, that is in cephalocaudal direction, it is easily understandable that an *asyntaxia medullaris* occurs when one of the front lateral halves is missing. The cross-sections through this embryo show that the internal structure of the neural folds is good. Furthermore an indisputable *semichorda dorsalis* is present under the right neural fold. This diagnosis is not subject to doubt, because along a considerable stretch the structure is composed of only three, sometimes four, cells in the cross-section. However, the semichorda is round in cross-section like the questionable semichordas mentioned above. That is to say, half the usual number of cells have joined together and isolated themselves like an epithelium from the environment formed by another germ layer. On the left the chorda is not clearly recognizable. In the rear half the archenteron is present and well formed. In the front the anlage of a half archenteron cavity is present only on the right side, as a narrow interspace.

The persistence of the blastocoele under a typical roof is of special interest in this embryo. The blastocoele lies toward the middle of the embryo lengthwise, and it thus can be seen clearly that the neural folds are located on the side of the egg opposite to the roof of the blastocoele, so that the roof of the blastocoele, which corresponds to the upper and originally pigmented half of the egg, becomes the ventral side of the embryo, contrary to the assertions of previous authors. One can probably properly assume a causal connection between the asyntaxia of the neural folds and the failure of the blastula cavity to be obliterated.

In my last experiment I attempted in several eggs to destroy only the cells above or below the first horizontal cleavage plane. These produced several clear *semiblastulae superiores* in which only the roof of the segmentation cavity is cellular, while the floor of this well-formed segmentation cavity consists of non-cellular matter. The continuation of these experiments will, we hope, provide us with more exact information on the further development of these latter embryos and thus on the exact part played in the formation of the embryo by the blastomeres located above and below the first horizontal cleavage plane.

INFERENCES FROM THESE FINDINGS

In general we can infer from these results that each of the two first blastomeres is able to develop independently of the other and therefore does develop independently under normal circumstances. Furthermore, in the experimental embryos, this happens in a manner which only rarely deviates from the normal development and only in a few conditions which have a surprisingly simple explanation. The progress of this sort of development was followed to the point of the development of neural folds, the primordia of the cerebral vesicles, the primordium of the chorda dorsalis and the formation of the mesoderm as well as its differentiation into somitic mesoderm and lateral plates, even to the point where the somitic mesoderm becomes segmented. Whether with this degree of development we have reached the upper limit of ability to develop independently I cannot say at this time. At this time, however, nothing would indicate that such an assumption is necessary as long as blood is not necessary for nutrition, since the hemiembryo of Fig. 9 which was the furthest developed at the time of its preservation showed no symptoms of death at all—neither the *framboisia embryonalis minor* nor *major,* which I have described as signs of beginning death. Only direct observation will be able to determine what happens after the blood vessels and heart form. This independent development characterizes also the two front and the two rear blastomeres with all their derivatives.

All this provides a new confirmation of the insight we had already achieved earlier that developmental processes may not be considered a result of the interaction of all parts, or indeed even of all the nuclear parts of the egg. We have, instead of such differentiating interactions, the self-differentiation of the first blastomeres and of the complex of their derivatives into a definite part of the embryo. This is valid both for the case when the first cleavage to appear separates, as normally, the right and left half and for the case when it anachronistically separates the cephalic and caudal halves. Each of these blastomeres contains therefore not only the formative substance for a corresponding part of the embryo but also the differentiating and formative forces. The assumption[21] that I had previously made with respect to the significance of cleavage becomes a certainty for the first cleavages. We can say: cleavage divides qualitatively that part of the embryonic, especially the nuclear material that is responsible for the direct development of the individual by the arrangement of the various separated materials which takes place at that time, and it determines simultaneously the position of the later differentiated organs of the embryo. (This applies also to subsequent typical rearrangements of material.) I would like here expressly to remark that this does not mean a prejudgement as to the distribution of such idioplasm as functions only in regeneration and postgeneration with which we will become more familiar later. A more or less complete idioplasm of this kind is present in every cell, that is to say in each nucleus.[22] Nor is the assertion of the importance of the first cleavages, which our experiments had already established, meant to imply that still other processes do not take place in the cleavage stage, for example, the development of many varied qualities in the embryonic substance or the increase in amount of specifically differentiated embryonic material.

Although according to this assertion the first cleavage separates the material of the right and left halves of the body from one another and even though I have introduced the expression "qualitatively halved" embryonic material, still we must not ignore the fact that this material is not morphologically similar although it is qualitatively alike in its chemical and percentage composition. Its arrangement is, after all, such that a right half of the body is produced on one side and a left half on the other. There are several questions in this connection which must be answered separately and which I mention here merely to prevent incorrect views being imputed to me as a result of excessive brevity in my

21 Ueber die Bedeutung der Kerntheilungsfiguren. Leipzig 1883. S. 15 und Beiträge zur Entwickelungsmechanik des Embryo. No. 3. Bresl. ärztl. Zeitschr. 1885. No. 6 u.ff. Separ.-Abdr. S. 45.

22 Thus if the first two blastomeres contain the material for the right and left halves of the body, it is apparent that one of the halves of the body must sooner or later become different, if there is the slightest imperfection of "qualitative halving." If it involves the middle parts, this alteration must extend all the way to the median plane of the individual. We can perhaps thus explain the unilaterality of many variations of development or of maintenance which extend to this plane. For example, premature graying of the hair on one side (particularly when other parts are normal, especially the nerves), *hemiatrophia facialis*, gigantism of one half of the head, etc.

presentation. These concern the arrangements which are the cause of this fundamental dissimilarity, at the time of the first cleavage, on which bilateral symmetry is based. Is it merely in the hemispheric shape of the yolk material and the controlling effect of that shape on the possibly various nuclear components, or is it in their independent arrangement?

It is an obvious further step to extend to the subsequent cleavages the above conclusion regarding qualitative separation of material. I hope to be able to verify by further experiments to what point this extension can be justified. It must similarly be determined whether the derivatives of later blastomeres are capable of self-differentiation or whether the progressive differentiation that forms the embryo is dependent on the coexistence of a whole group, perhaps all the descendants of one of the first four blastomeres. We would then have obtained with each of the first four blastomeres the smallest possible part of the ovum which is capable of self-differentiation. I do not, however, presume this to be the case, in spite of the mechanism of gastrulation which I will describe immediately and which appears to argue for that point.

Let us now proceed to special inferences for developmental mechanics which result from the facts mentioned. First of all it is to be deduced from the normal course of development of the undamaged blastomere that the qualitative division of the cell body and of the nuclear material, which we have just explained and which takes place at the time of cleavage, can proceed properly without any influence from the neighboring cells—and therefore probably does proceed in the normal case without this influence. Secondly, it can be deduced that the nucleus reaches its proper position in the blastomere, so important for the correct arrangement of the separated materials, without being affected by the vital activity of the neighboring cells. The same is true of later cleavages within the region in the neighborhood of the treated cells; therefore this independence can probably correctly be considered general. I further deduce from the dispensability of one vertical half of the egg that the formation of the blastula proceeds without extensive strains in the material, such as far-reaching mechanical interactions of the parts. Because of this I am inclined to attribute the typical formation of the blastula to an active rearrangement of the cells. A contributing factor perhaps is the tendency of many cells to approach the surface as a source of oxygen, which is His' view. The beautiful prismatic form of the epithelia in the roof of the semiblastocoele, which is found in the third (sometimes even the second) cell from the edge and which extends nearly to the rounded and often unattached edge of the cavity, reveals in addition that this shape is also not caused by the crowding together of many cells in a closed surface but by a tendency of the neighboring cells to unite closely and perhaps to extend themselves perpendicularly to the surface at the same time. The stretching may also be just a result of the great intensity of the first tendency.

The anomalous semiblastulas described above, as well as aberrations at later stages of development observed along with normally shaped half-embryos under the same conditions prove that abnormalities can occur more easily in half-embryos than under normal conditions. A task for a later time, which might possibly be very instructive, will be to discover the special causes of these variations and of the predisposition to them created by the incompleteness of the embryo.

The next formative processes cause gastrulation. What I have said earlier, as well as in the last paragraphs, and what I will say further about this process certainly provides sufficient evidence to reveal to the attentive reader the incorrectness of the previous view, most recently presented again by O. Schultze (without giving any real reason), according to which the cavity of the archenteron arises through an upward involution and therefore the originally black upper side of the egg corresponds to the dorsal side of the embryo. However, I will devote a special presentation of my view, along with a refutation of the opposing view, of this process of gastrulation which is of more interest to professional colleagues than my endeavors in the field of developmental mechanics. This is to obviate the necessity of my professional colleagues having to read all my works on developmental mechanics in order to satisfy their curiosity. At this point we will therefore draw only the following conclusions: Gastrulation takes place independently in every antimere and this is the case also in the caudal and cephalic halves. Consequently it is also true for the quarters concerned, and when we take into consideration the further development of these quarters that has been observed we can conclude:

The development of the frog gastrula and of the embryo initially produced from it is, from the second cleavage on, a mosaic of at least four vertical pieces developing independently.

How far this mosaic formation of at least four pieces is now reworked in the course of further development by unilaterally directed rearrangements of material and by differentiating correlations, and how far the independence of its parts is restricted, must still be determined. The well-known rearrangements of the yolk cells during gastrulation are only of secondary importance in so far as these cells represent mere reserve material.

We are further instructed by the *hemiembryones laterales* and the *asyntaxia medullaris* that the lateral half of the notochord also has its primordium in the medial border of the blastopore of the *semigastrula lateralis,* while the neural plate, along with the neural folds, is formed on its adjacent external surface. Furthermore, the primordium of the mesoderm occurs in the dorsal plate. It is of interest that the chorda and the mesoderm are also formed at the places where the intestinal endoderm is missing and even if the intestinal endoderm is missing completely, as is shown by the anentoblasty present in several cases of *asyntaxia medullaris*. It is also illuminating that the lateral part of the ectoderm and the neural plate are separated from one another at the reflected margin, even in our half-embryos, although neither of these two parts of the original ectoderm has the opportunity to unite with its own kind and initially impinges with a free edge against the half treated by operation.

The variant shape of the semichorda of a lateral half-embryo, expressed in a round cross-section instead of a semicircular one, can be easily explained by taking into account the actual process of development. The formation of the chorda of the frog embryo is not accomplished by a constriction from the endoderm cell group concerned, as is usually said, since there are no external parts at the place in question which could produce a constriction. We must rather conclude, in the light of the absence of any device for such a passive transformation, that the separation of the chorda cells from their surroundings occurs through their active rearrangement and transformation. In the lateral half-embryo the surrounding parts are laterally the mesoderm, externally the ectoderm, especially the neural plate, and internally the endoderm, since the chorda epithelium represents here the transition between these two latter layers. After these neighboring parts actively release themselves from one another, the unattached round cells of the chorda, coming from both sides, group themselves together so that their lateral surfaces touch, and thus form a complete strand. This reveals a tendency of the chorda cells to group themselves as closely together as possible and thus to separate themselves from their environment in an epithelium. According to our findings, healing does not take place here by the cells of each half arranging themselves independently in a semicircle but by the closest possible union, and thus isolation from the outside, of cells of the same type. After this the thickening of the semichorda[23] described above takes place very rapidly.

23 This formation of the semichorda simultaneously throws light on the great diversities of origin of the chorda cells from ecto-, endo- or mesoderm. In closely related classes and even orders and families, we must conclude from the variety of statements by numerous conscientious investigators that this diversity actually exists. Since the chorda dorsalis is formed from the epithelium of the lateral free edge of the lateral blastopore lips and since these lips already unite with one another normally during gastrulation, the ectoderm of the one half usually first merging with that of the other and then simultaneously separating completely from the chorda epithelium, the chorda as a result appears in conjunction with the endoderm and forms a groove which opens into the cavity of the archenteron. Since the primordial mesoderm is in the same transitional area of the layers, it is connected in the beginning with the chorda epithelium which then separates off metamerically, as described previously. Not until this has happened does the chorda epithelium separate from the endoderm by rearrangement

On the other hand we have seen more completely in the neural tube how the cells of each half produce approximately, and in its main features, the typical form of the cross-section; we may conclude from this that these cells possess a special formative power for detailed arrangement. This is nevertheless not quite sufficient for the production of a normal cross-section, since we found the semineurula badly collapsed in a dorsal-ventral direction, probably because of the absence of the other half which also serves as support. This is further confirmation for my view, already presented in the introduction, that the elevation of the neural folds on the material of the neural plate does not occur passively from the pressure of lateral parts, since in such a process the lone lateral half of the neural plate would have to be pushed over simultaneously towards the undeveloped side, which was not observable. The jutting out of the median parts mentioned above was at least not such as could be attributed to this cause.

Now that we have become familiar with the behavior of the undamaged blastomere and discussed its significance for developmental mechanics we will turn to the other half of the egg, to the behavior of the cell treated by operation.

The behavior of this half of the egg showed great variety when observed externally and even more when studied internally in successive cross-sections. The diversity of the structures seen implies a whole series of processes which I shall separate into three groups. First of all, there are processes in the material of the treated half of the egg which make this material more or less unusable and which therefore can be designated as decomposition processes, provided one does not object to the fact that progressive processes are also included, such as numerical increase of nuclei. The products of these nuclei, however, must be seen as equally abnormal in their further behavior. Secondly, processes occur that make usable again the changed material of the egg half treated by operation and that prepare it simultaneously for subsequent development. These

---

of its cells, and it unites from both sides in the manner described above. Nevertheless, slight anachronisms occur in this three-fold separation in the frog and then (according to the view of merely descriptive embryology which does not take into consideration the intrinsic nature of the processes) the chorda sometimes "originates" from the endoderm, sometimes from the ectoderm or mesoderm. Even in classes of animals where the mechanism of gastrulation is no longer of this sort, but where, as I have said, a part of the work of gastrulation is already accomplished by the disposition of material during cleavage, even here, as a result of such originally slight differences, there are relatively slight variations which later become typical which will suffice to force the material of the chorda into the ecto-, endo- or mesoderm, either entirely or partially. I quite realize that these thoughts on developmental mechanics diverge to a high degree from the view of descriptive embryology, especially from the predominant dogma of complete evolutionary homology of the germ layers in the vertebrates. Nevertheless, I believe my view will gradually be accepted.

will be grouped together as reorganization processes. Thirdly, processes then follow which by subsequent development replace the missing body parts completely or almost normally. I will call these processes post-generation for reasons to be explained later and will contrast them fundamentally to the regeneration of lost body parts.

I must preface my more special remarks by mentioning that many of the egg cells punctured by the unheated needle developed normally[24] in spite of rough treatment and large exovations. In contrast in other cases no development took place in spite of a very small loss of material. This leads to the conclusion that substances of varied importance for developmental mechanics are contained in the blastomere. First of all, there must be substances that are not essential for development and, secondly, those whose disruption or loss in very slight quantities from the blastomere destroys its ability to develop. At the present stage of our knowledge we shall consider the latter substances preferably as nuclear components. I attempted when operating with the cold needle to disrupt the arrangement of the nuclear parts by manifold movements within the egg; as mentioned above, I was so rarely successful that I preferred to make use of heat as a destructive agent. This then accomplished the desired effect. The cell which had been operated on and partially emptied by the exovate often filled rapidly from the undamaged neighboring cell. This was observed especially clearly when only one of the four first cells after the second cleavage were punctured. The operated cell normally appeared whitish or at least only darkly speckled on the surface instead of being uniformly brown. As an explanation of this phenomenon we will find the pigment on the inside collected around certain structures.

Even when the hot needle was used the operated cells behaved quite variously. Let us first describe those cases in which the treated blastomeres no longer showed any signs of development, because in these cases the first group of processes mentioned above, the decomposition processes, can be seen most clearly. One should not overlook the fact, however, that I was working at the end of the breeding period when development is often abnormal and disruptive influences are less easily tolerated.

The blastomere material certainly did not remain completely unchanged even in these extreme cases, for the cell body as well as the nucleus experienced changes which were the more extensive the later I preserved the egg after the operation, that is to say, the more the unoperated half was already developed. Still, I would not wish to imply by this last statement that a causal connection exists between the progress of the changes on both sides.

[24] With respect to the topographical relationships of the parts of the egg to those of the embryo, it is interesting to note that the stem of the exovate was later on the ventral side of the embryo if it remained attached to the egg and the embryo and if the puncture had been on the black upper hemisphere.

In the cell body proper, that is, the yolk of the operated cell, are located round or oval cavities delineated by a simple but sharp contour. These cavities have a size varying from 10 to 150 μ and may number but a few or several hundred. The content of these "vacuoles" is not stained by borax carmine and is completely unobservable. In this connection I must mention, however, that the sections lie on a finely granulated albumen substrate, so that a similar structure of the unstained vacuole contents would often not be distinguishable in thin sections. Still, I was unable to see the contents even in thick sections placed in Canada balsam. Since these structures answer the definition of a vacuole I will call the process the "vacuolization" of the yolk. This vacuolization is found in the area of the more protoplasmic, formative yolk as well as in the highly granulated nutritive yolk, which are less sharply separated from each other than usually. The vacuolization is often so dense that the individual vacuoles in places are separated from one another in the cross-sections only by a fine protoplasmic thread. Often only the residues of these structures (physically considered, partitioning membranes) are present so that a communication or fusion of the vacuoles is visible. If only a few vacuoles occur, they lie scattered or together in groups. In the latter case the remainder of the yolk then appears normal over large areas.

In addition to this vacuolization there are places in the yolk where the protoplasm forms a coarse or, more frequently, a finely meshed net that lacks yolk granules and is occasionally distinguished by the presence of numerous granules that are brownish black or greenish in transmitted light.

In the operated cell body, further structures are included that I look upon as nuclear. In order to justify this assertion I must first describe the structure of the normal nuclei of the frog embryo as they appear after the treatment mentioned above, that is heating up to 80° C., alcohol, borax carmine, etc. Here, in the various developmental stages of the embryo, the nuclei also show quite a different structure, just as they do in the various highly differentiated cells of the same stage (in accordance with Goette, Ch. van Bambeke and others).

In the blastomeres of the still young morula the nuclei appear as finely granular almost colorless or light-colored masses that are round or oval and from 10 to 30 μ in diameter. These blend into the surrounding protoplasm without a sharp line of demarcation, so that the actual nucleus cannot be separated from an areola of finely granular, unstained material that may possibly enclose it. Because of its size the nucleus extends through several sections and it is therefore easy to overlook several fine dark red granules that represent its extremely sparse chromatin content. Occasionally I have found an equatorial plate consisting of only a few short, clearly granular threads and well-preserved with a regular arrangement of its stained parts. The figures of the other stages

of nuclear division appear, as mentioned above, either to have undergone regression during heating or to have been pushed rapidly to a stage
of completion, since they are only infrequently observed. (It should
be mentioned that granules stained similarly to the chromatin granules
of the nucleus are not infrequently found, in greater or lesser number,
collected between two of the blastomeres.) Sometimes the environment of
the nuclear structure, which is lightly colored and not sharply demarcated, is interspersed with brown granules so that the light-colored
structure is ringed with a dark areola. If the nucleus is undergoing
division, the brown granules, toward the end of the division, are sometimes found only at the two poles, collected on the distal sides in the
protoplasm.

Very infrequently a nucleus of 20 to 30 μ in diameter, consisting of a
finely granular substance uniformly stained rose-red, is found in a cell
surrounded by cells with the nuclei of the type already described. Its
simple and very sharp contour contrasts with the surroundings.

In the blastula stage the nuclei are clearly bordered by a red, double
outlined wall and are like round or oval vesicles of 10 to 20 μ in whose
interior red granules are dispersed or strung together in a sparse, wide-
meshed net of threads. The remaining content is almost colorless and
extremely finely granular so that the whole structure appears only a pale
pink.

At the gastrula stage substantially the same nuclear appearance is
found in the yolk cells as in the blastula, just as pale but a bit smaller,
measuring only 8 to 12 μ in diameter. In the epithelial cells of the germ
layers, on the other hand, still smaller nuclei, merely 6 to 8 μ in diameter, are quickly noticed due to their more intensive red coloration produced by an abundance of chromatin. They are not, however, substantially changed in their structure; but occasionally only a single
boundary line is present instead of the double one and the numerous red
granules in the interior frequently do not show the familiar net-shaped
arrangement.

After the formation of the neural folds in the embryo, we find their
nuclei to resemble those of the epithelia in the gastrula stage. The nuclei
of the yolk cells are still paler and larger than those of the epithelial
cells, however.

In the undeveloped blastomere treated by operation the following
structures are now found, which I would like to consider as nuclear
structures:

1. Round or oval structures of 20 to 30 μ, occasionally up to 60 μ in
diameter, of a uniformly extremely fine granular substance which is
either merely pale or of an intensive red and which is set off from its
environment by a simple but sharp outline. Occasionally these structures
are further separated from the rest of the protoplasm by a sharply defined

colorless crescent or ring-shaped areola. On the other hand, accumulations of brownish-black granules not infrequently form a pigment areola around the nucleus. These nuclear structures are usually solitary and due to their character are associated with the uniformly pale red and simply outlined nuclei which, as reported, we observed on rare occasions in a semimorula.

Secondly, there are structures related to the vesicular nuclei of the next older stage of development, the blastula. They differ from the latter merely in their unusual size of 40 to 60 μ, their common but not invariable size. They have a double-membraned partition of stained substance and show internally a coarse mesh framework of threads composed of aligned red granules. The main portion of their contents is again extremely finely granular and either only pale red or unstained. In addition to these large structures there are frequently identical ones which are only medium in size (16 to 30 μ) and even some which are as small as those of the gastrula and of the embryo, with a diameter of only 8 μ. These differ from the small normal nuclei of these stages only in their low chromatin content and by the fact that they are agglomerated in dense clusters. Such nuclear nests often combine nuclei of very different sizes and may consist of six to thirty nuclei. Some of these nuclear structures also have again the brownish-black pigment areola which surrounds the whole nuclear net.

Both these types therefore conform to normal nuclear structure and vary only in their unusual size and, in the first case, in their coloration that is deeper than that in the normal embryo.

A third group, in contrast, comprises nuclear types which deviate from normal to a greater extent, namely round or oval structures of 8 to 30 μ of a not very granular substance which appears almost homogeneous and is stained a deep dark red. This contains more or less numerous cavities which are apparently empty and rounded like vacuoles. They are surrounded by a simple but sharp outline. Their sharp rounded boundary and their great capacity to absorb dye are in this case the only characteristics that cause me to attribute these structures to the nucleus and not to the cell body. When the granulation of the red material is clearer and its vacuolization of such a high degree that the red material in the interior represents no more than a thin septum, these structures (Fig. 2K') acquire an appearance similar to that of the second type just described. The structures belonging to this third group are also often located closely together in groups of three to six and more, thus creating nests like those of the previous forms, which are occasionally enclosed in more or less abundantly accumulated protoplasm with brown pigmentation or none at all (Fig. 2KN). In many nests the structures of both types occur mixed.

Several times I have found large nuclei of 30 to 40 μ with a double red wall. These nuclei showed internally adjacent to this partition first individual red granules and then, further inwards, numerous randomly oriented rods composed of granules strung together to form a second layer that left a still larger colorless space open internally.

The nuclear structures just described are found in the yolk of the operated cell without any position of predilection being evident. In particular, they are not to be found in large numbers in the vicinity of the developed half of the embryo and are nowhere so near this half that one could assume they had migrated from it.

This being so, the only possibility that remains is that these are derived from the segmentation nucleus of the operated blastomere. The known fact that this nucleus shows a great tendency to reproduce argues also for this assumption. I am not able to affirm anything about the cause of the peculiarities of the nuclei formed in these particular cases.

It is of great interest, on the other hand, and testifies likewise for the correctness of our interpretation of the origin of these abnormal nuclei, that quite the same three kinds of nuclear structures—as well as the vacuolization of the yolk described above—are found soon after the fertilization of eggs which, as a result merely of long-delayed spawning, do not develop after fertilization in spite of not having been operated upon. If it were interpreted that here they are derived from the nucleus of the egg or the sperm, in which a tendency to multiply has not yet been found, then one would have to assume a different origin for the same structure than in the case of blastomeres treated by operation where the nuclei of egg and sperm were no longer present. Further, since in whole developing eggs no opportunity exists for transfer from a developed half, only the segmentation nucleus is common to both cases and can be considered the identical source of the same structures.

Of further interest and importance is the behavior of both egg halves with respect to one another.

Frequently an externally visible demarcation is formed when the developed half becomes larger than the operated half and this contracts toward the latter, so that, even at the blastula stage, a groove similar to the blastopore margin is formed.

In section one sees frequently, even at the early stages, a clear line of demarcation as manifestation of a special demarcation layer. This is a layer, 4 to 8 μ thick, of material which is at times colorless and at times stained slightly red, with a partially blackish-brown pigmentation in the vicinity of the upper edge. It is finely granular, that is, free of yolk granules and can be considered as protoplasm separated from one of the two blastomeres. I surmise that it comes from the treated cell since it is continuous with the latter, while the cells of the living half are separated from it at many points by an angular interspace.

This layer of demarcation usually proceeds from the surface of the egg and penetrates it to various degrees, occasionally up to a third of the diameter of the egg. Where the layer of demarcation is missing, a direct contact is possible, as long as the cells of the developed half are not isolated from the treated one by a fissure. No sharp boundary is recognizable at these points because the cells of the living half are not themselves sharply delimited on the side toward the treated half, although this is definitely true on the other side of their periphery.

This brings us to another type of behavior of the operated cell. The changes of the yolk described above and the abnormal, or at least the abnormally accumulated, division products of the segmentation nucleus are present in only about one-third of all the half-embryos sectioned. (In many cases, to be sure when these derivatives of the segmentation nucleus are absent they are found in the exovate.)

RESULTS

After destruction of one of the first two blastomeres the other is able to develop in a normal way into an essentially normal half-embryo. In this manner we obtained *hemiembryones laterales* and *anteriores,* along with the corresponding preliminary stages of the *semiblastula* and *semigastrula.* Three-quarter embryos with one lateral half of the head missing were also obtained by puncturing the egg after the second cleavage. The following principle could therefore be established: the development of the gastrula and of the embryo initially produced from it is, from the four-blastomere stage of the egg on, a mosaic of at least four vertical pieces each developing substantially independently.

We further saw in the malformation of the *anentoblastia* that the external and the middle layers are able to differentiate their specific structures in spite of the absence of intestinal endoderm, even though the shape of the whole embryo is abnormal as a result of its absence. In the same way the *semichorda dorsalis lateralis* is formed on each side.

The blastomere that is deprived of its ability to develop by the operation can be gradually revived.

This reorganization takes place partially by the transfer of a considerable number of cell nuclei (along with protoplasm?) from the normally developed half of the egg. These immigrated nuclei are distributed throughout the whole bulk of the yolk, wherever the latter is not provided with descendants of its own segmentation nucleus. Both these types of nuclei subsequently multiply. This nucleation of the blastomere treated by operation is followed later by cellularization, as division of the yolk into cells proceeds around each nucleus. Parts that are greatly changed resist this sort of reanimation, and yet they also are made usable later in a somewhat modified manner.

A new supplemental development follows the reorganization of the treated egg half; this is postgeneration, which can lead to a complete restoration of the missing lateral or rear half of the embryo.

This postgeneration does not take place in the same manner as the normal development of the primary half. It is not to be considered therefore as normal but merely belated development. This can be seen from the fact that the postgeneration of the germ layers in the supplementary halves does not take place by independent formation of germ layers as in the case of primary development but only proceeds from the germ layers already formed in the developed half. This can occur only in places where the germ layers of the primary developed half of the embryo are already separated from one another in such a fashion that each germ layer makes contact with the undeveloped egg half through a free lateral edge, an "interruption surface," as in the case of an artificial defect. As a result of this restriction no actual gastrulation takes place during the postgeneration of the lateral half-embryos.

Postgenerative formation of the germ layers occurs in the cell material formed by late cellularization, while the process of differentiation proceeds in resting cell substance. The various differentiations necessary for the formation of a germ layer are here propagated at different speeds in the still undifferentiated cell substance.

Since the various yolk materials and the cell nuclei of the treated egg half are not in their typical location but are situated according to chance determination, it could not be assumed that the typical extent and the typical results of postgeneration are determined by a typical arrangement of specifically characterized substances capable of self-differentiation. We therefore felt ourselves obliged to conclude that specific differentiating influences emanate from the already differentiated material to the still undifferentiated cell substance that adjoins it.

While in our findings the primary development of the first blastomeres and of the complex of their derivatives has proved to be self-differentiation, the reorganized egg parts are capable only of dependent differentiation through the influence of already differentiated parts.

In a new form of malformation, *asyntaxia medullaris,* the failure of the two lateral halves of the neural tube primordia to fuse normally, which is usually related to a corresponding lack of endoderm (*anentoblastia*), the external and middle germ layers showed an independent ability to develop when the internal layer was missing.

1892

The Potency of the First Two Cleavage Cells in Echinoderm Development. Experimental Production of Partial and Double Formations

by HANS DRIESCH

Driesch, Hans. 1892. Entwicklungsmechanische Studien. I. Der Werth der beiden ersten Furchungszellen in der Echinodermenentwicklung. Experimentelle Erzeugen von Theil-und Doppelbildung. Zeitschrift für wissenschaftliche Zoologie 53:160-178; 183-184. Tafel VII. Abridged and translated by L. Mezger and M. and V. Hamburger and T. S. Hall for A Source Book in Animal Biology by T. S. Hall (1951).* Reprinted by permission of Harvard University Press.

* The editors have added Driesch's References, Plate VII, and Explanations of the figures.

One of the first investigators to follow in Roux's footsteps as an experimental analyst of development was Hans Driesch (1867-1941). Driesch, like Roux, studied the development of early cleavage blastomeres. However, he used different material for his investigations, echinoderm eggs, and he performed his experiments by different methods. In the article reproduced here, he reports his first attempts. By shaking the eggs of the sea urchin he was able completely to separate the first two blastomeres from one another. The cell separated from its partner exhibited the same pattern of cleavage it would have followed had it remained in the whole egg, but it formed a ciliated blastula, it gastrulated, and it developed into a pluteus dwarf in size but normal in configuration.

Driesch later (1900) modified his techniques and separated the cells by placing them in calcium-free sea water according to the method of his close friend Curt Herbst, and he carried out his experiments also at later stages, isolating blastomeres at the four- and eight-cell and even later stages. The regulation of partial eggs to form whole embryos led him to conceive of the developing egg as a harmonious equipotential system: equipotential because a part has the potency to form the whole, the implication being that all the parts are uniform (isotropic), harmonious because in forming the whole the parts work so wonderfully together. He defined as the prospective significance of an embryonic cell its fate under the normal conditions of development, but he demonstrated experimentally its prospective potency to be much greater than the significance; he stated that the fate of a cell is a function of its position in the whole. He thus emphasized epigenetic aspects of early development that were underestimated by Roux.

Driesch at first attempted to explain development in mechanistic terms. His Analytische Theorie der organischen Entwicklung *(1894) is a remarkable treatise, and it is couched in terms and expresses concepts that we all use today. He wrote in it, for instance, of position and induction, of contact induction, even of chemical induction. He explained the polarity of the egg in terms of the arrangement of polarized constituents of the cytoplasm. He expressed the strong belief that the action of the nucleus in heredity and development was mediated through ferments, our enzymes.*

As he continued his experimentation and reflection, however, he came to despair of explaining development in such mechanistic terms; he was defeated particularly by its harmonious character. The results of his experiments of separating the blastomeres drove him to vitalism, since he could not conceive of a machine which, when divided, could reconstitute two whole new machines like its original self. He concluded that develop-

ment is regulated by a deus ex machina, *the* entelechy, *a word he borrowed from Aristotle. Subsequently, he completely forsook experimental biology for philosophical vitalism, and became a professor of philosophy. His early discovery, however, and in particular his interpretation of it in epigenetic terms, played a very important role in stimulating interest and progress in analytical embryology.*

THE POTENCY OF THE FIRST TWO CLEAVAGE CELLS IN ECHINODERM
DEVELOPMENT. EXPERIMENTAL PRODUCTION OF PARTIAL
AND DOUBLE FORMATIONS

"Granting that the primordium of a part originates during a certain period, one must, for greater accuracy, describe this by stating that the material for the primordium is already present in the blastoderm while the latter is still flat but the primordium is not as yet morphologically segregated and hence not recognizable as such. By tracing it back we shall be able for every primordium to determine its exact location even in the period of incomplete or deficient morphological organization; indeed, to be consistent, we should extend this determination back to the newly fertilized, even the unfertilized, egg. The principle according to which the blastoderm contains organ primordia preformed in a flat pattern and, vice versa, every point in the blastoderm can be rediscovered in a later organ, I call the principle of organ-forming germ-areas."

In these words, he [His, 1874] formulated the principle so designated by him. Continuing this train of thought, Roux[1] discussed in a perceptive manner the difference between evolution, or the *metamorphosis* of manifoldness, and epigenesis, or the *new formation* of manifoldness; in his well-known experiments on "half-embryos" (of which only the first part concerns us here) he decided the question under consideration, for the frog egg, in favor of evolution.

A not very generally known work by Chabry is the only further investigation of this kind known to me. His specific explanations and figures make it clear that his results are fundamentally contrary to those of Roux. I wish to mention here that I came to know of Chabry's work only after the completion of my own experiments.

As to these, I was interested in repeating Roux's experiments on material which would be resistant, easily obtainable, and readily observable; all three of these conditions are most satisfactorily fulfilled by the Echinoids, which had already served as a basis for so many investiga-

[1] *Beitrage zur Entwicklungsmechanik des Embryo.* I. *Zeitschr. f. Biol.* Bd. XXI. III. *Breslauer ärztl. Zeitschr.* 1885. V. *Virchow's Arch.* Bd. CXIV.

tions. My own experiments were carried out upon Echinus microtuberculatus.

The investigations were made in March and April of 1891. They have led me to many other problems closely connected with the present one, problems whose eventual solution will deepen materially our understanding of the part already solved. Nevertheless, I present my results at this time because they have decided with certainty, for my material, the cardinal point, that is, the potency of the two first blastomeres.

MATERIALS AND METHODS

The first week of my stay in Trieste was lost, inasmuch as I obtained almost exclusively useless material. Whereas the following work follows the above mentioned experiments of Roux in content, the method was taken from the excellent cellular researches of the Hertwig brothers. These investigators, by shaking unfertilized eggs, split off pieces and raised them successfully. It is well known that Boveri used the same method for the production of his "organisms produced sexually without maternal characters," although other factors prevented him from carrying out the procedure exactly.

I therefore went to Trieste with the intention of obtaining one of the first half-blastomeres of Echinus by shaking at the two-cell stage, in order to see, provided it lived, what would become of it.

At an average temperature of about 15° C., cleavage of Echinus eggs occurred 1½ to 2 hours after artificial fertilization. Good material, and only such was used, displayed in only a very few instances immediate division into four cells, an inevitable result, according to Fol and Hertwig, of bispermy.

Shaking was done in small glass containers 4 cm long and about 0.6 cm in diameter. Fifty to one hundred eggs were placed in a small quantity of water. In order to obtain results, one must shake as vigorously as possible for five minutes or more; even then one obtains at best only about ten isolated blastomeres and about as many eggs whose membranes are still intact but whose cells are more or less separated within these membranes.

If shaking is done at the moment of completion of first cleavage, events are, so to speak reversed; the furrow disappears and one obtains a sausage-shaped body whose two nuclei again show connections. In these recombined eggs the furrow reappears in a short time and normal development follows. On the other hand if one shakes too late, the second cleavage occurs prematurely during the shaking. It is therefore necessary to watch carefully for the right moment.

About one half of the blastomeres are, in addition to being isolated, dead; nevertheless I obtained about fifty capable of development. This appears not unfavorable considering the strength of the mechanical treatment, and considering the fact that the isolated blastomeres are in direct contact with the water on at least one side,—a completely abnormal situation. Isolation is obviously possible only where the membrane bursts.

During cleavage the preparations were observed microscopically as often as possible, and during later development usually once every morning and evening.

One more thing about the treatment of the isolated cells. The contents of the glass used for shaking must be poured into fresh sea water as soon as possible since the water has naturally warmed and evaporated.

It was to be expected that the small quantity of water would not be exactly beneficial, nor the bacteria which were especially numerous toward the end of my experiment and were encouraged by disintegrating pieces which had died.

At any rate my method guarantees that one is observing the same pieces on successive days. Unfortunately, Boveri, in his very important experiments, did not succeed in this respect.

But here I anticipate my results. I turn now to a systematic presentation of findings starting with

CLEAVAGE

First a few words about the normal course of events as revealed in Selenka's excellent investigations.

Following two meridional cleavages there is an equatorial one and the germ now consists of eight cells of equal size. Four of these now give off, toward one pole, four smaller cells, and at the same time the others divide approximately meridionally.

The germ now consists of 16 cells and shows a marked polarity with the four small cells, easily recognized, occupying one pole. Further divisions lead to stages with 28, 32, 60, and 108 cells (Selenka). The four small cells which originated at the 16-cell stage clearly indicate the animal pole for a long time. I was unable to establish certainly any differences between the cells of the blastula. At a later stage of development, but before the epithelial flattening due to close union of cells has led to the blastula proper, the Echinus germ, especially in the half containing the smaller-celled pole, consists of cellular rings.

How, then, do the blastomeres of the first division stages after isolation by shaking accomplish cleavage, assuming they survive?

I shall first describe the behavior observed in a majority of cases. Not once did I observe a completely spherical rounding up of the isolated cell. It is true that the normally flat surface tends toward sphericalness but its radius of curvature always remains greater than that of the original free surface of the hemisphere. The cell now divides into two and then, perpendicularly to this, into four parts. Normal controls fertilized at the same time now have eight similar cells the same size as our four. Simultaneously fertilized normal controls have at this time eight similar cells.

In the Echinoids no "gliding" of cells normally occurs either in the four-cell stage nor the ½ eight-cell stage (i.e., my four-cell stage). This is significant because it facilitates considerably the interpretation of the following fact.

About 5½ hours after fertilization occurs, untreated germs have divided into 16 parts, as described above, and isolated blastomeres into 8 parts.

At this point begins the really interesting part of my experiment in that the last-mentioned division brings into existence a typical single half of the 16-cell stage as described; that is, it behaves in the way expected of it according to absolute self-differentiation; it is actually a half of what Selenka's figure shows.

I will now go on to a description of the normal division of my blastomeres, later speaking about the abnormal cases (about 25%).

I carefully followed the formation of a half-germ of 16 cells, i.e., a typical ½ 32-cell stage. Each of the normal concentric cell rings is present, but each consists of half its normal number of cells. The entire structure now presents the appearance of an open hemisphere with a polarly differentiated opening.

In the majority of cases here referred to as normal, the half-germ presented, on the evening of the day of fertilization, the appearance of a typical, many-celled, open hemisphere, although the opening often seemed somewhat narrowed. As especially characteristic, I will mention here a case upon which I chanced in doing the Roux-Chabry experiment. Instead of one of the blastomeres being isolated, it was killed by the shaking. The living one, which had developed in the above manner into a typical half-formation, was in the afternoon attached to the dead one in the shape of a hemisphere; but by evening its edges were already clearly curled inward.

The cleavage of isolated blastomeres of the two-cell stage of Echinus microtuberculatus is accordingly a half-formation as described by Roux for operated frog's eggs.

As already mentioned, this is by far the most frequent behavior. One will not be surprised to find modifications of it in view of damage caused by the strong mechanical insult due to shaking. A few words about these exceptions:

In some cases, germs consisting of about 32 cells (½ 64-cell stage) presented by late afternoon a spherical appearance; development was here more compact, so to speak, though following the typical scheme. This occurs because of a closer union of the cells and is a phenomenon possibily similar to Chabry's "gliding." Normally, the blastomeres of

Plate VII

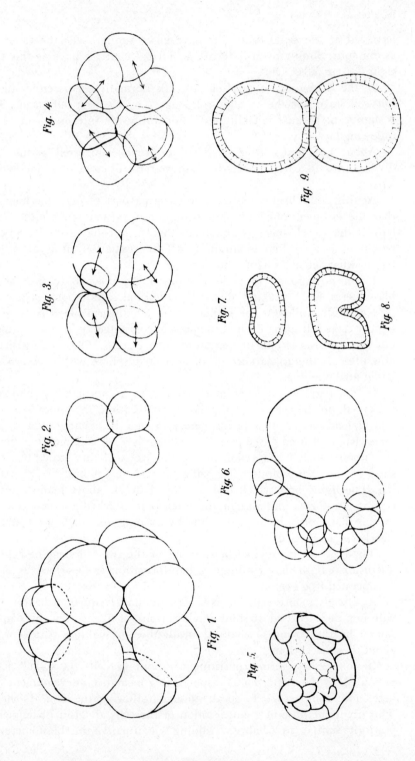

Fig. 4.

Fig. 9.

Fig. 3.

Fig. 7.

Fig. 8.

Fig. 2.

Fig. 6.

Fig. 1.

Fig. 5.

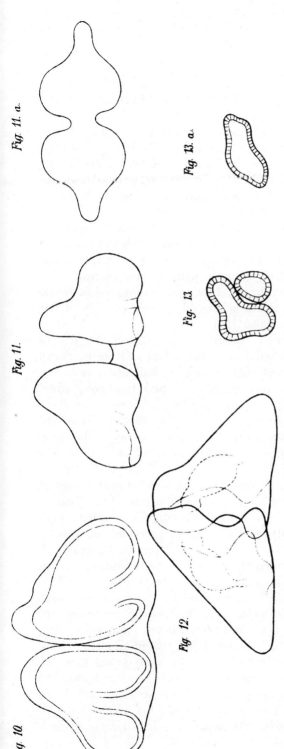

Fig. 1 Sixteen-cell stage, copied from Selenka. Magnification about 400 ×.   Fig. 2 Half-embryo made up of 4 cells (half of an 8-cell stage). Compare with fig. 1. Apochrom. 16 mm. Oc. 8.   Figs. 3 and 4 Half-embryo made up of 8 cells (half of a 16-cell stage). Compare with fig. 1. Apochrom. 16 mm. Oc. 12.   Fig. 5 Half-embryo; cleavage is completed and the half sphere is closing. Apochrom. 16 mm. Oc. 12.   Fig. 6 Half-embryo; one half of the egg is dead. Late cleavage stage. Same magnification as figs. 3 and 4. (The figure attempts merely to give a general impression; only the outlines of the uppermost cells are drawn.)   Fig. 7 Blastula that developed from an extremely distorted 2-cell stage. Although it looks as though it is dividing, it did not form two partial embryos but a single one that was misshapen.   Fig. 8 Blastula in the process of dividing, developed from a very misshapen egg. It formed two partial embryos.   Fig. 9 Blastula in the process of dividing. It formed two conjoined twins.   Fig. 10 The same set of embryos shown as twin gastrulae. Lateral view.   Fig. 11 The same set of embryos shown at the prismatic gastrula stage. Lateral view.   Fig. 11a Seen from above.   Fig. 12 The same set of embryos as twin plutei. The oral fields face toward each other, and the plutei are somewhat compressed and are therefore seen partially from the side. Apochrom. 16 mm. Oc. 8. (From a Canada balsam preparation, somewhat shrunken. The three divisions of the gut may be seen.)   Fig. 13 Blastula from a greatly misshapen 2-cell stage that at the next division separate into ¾ and ¼ blastomeres.   Fig. 13a The fragment from the ¼ blastomere has been constricted off.   Figures 7 to 13a, with the exception of figure 12, were drawn without a camera lucida, but as accurately as possible. Several of them (Figs. 7, 8, 13 and 13a) were drawn at a low magnification, others at higher magnification.

Echinus make contact in only small areas, until shortly before blastula formation.

In other cases—nine were observed in all—there was from the outset (i.e. from the 8 or half 16-cell stage) little to be seen of the usual scheme except as to cell number; specifically, the half germ was spherical from the very beginning, and "gliding" was even more pronounced. I wish to mention especially a case in which the eight cells (half 16) were of almost equal size. Had the role of first cleavage here been different and had I here, to put it briefly, perhaps separated the animal from the vegetal pole instead of the left from the right? By analogy with the experiments of Rauber, Hallez, etc., this seems not unlikely.

The first time I was fortunate enough to make the observations described above, I awaited in excitement the picture which was to present itself in my dishes the next day. I must confess that the idea of a free-swimming hemisphere or a half gastrula with its archenteron open lengthwise seemed rather extraordinary. I thought the formations would probably die. Instead, the next morning I found in their respective dishes typical, actively swimming blastulae of half size.

I have already described how toward the evening of the day of fertilization the, as yet not epithelial, hemisphere had a rather narrowed opening and I have emphasized that tracing of individual cells and hence of the side of the opening corresponding to the animal pole proved impossible. True, I occasionally saw two smaller cells somewhere along the edge but attached no meaning to them. The question as to the actual mode of closing of the blastula must for the time being, therefore, remain unsolved. I may perhaps be briefly permitted to indicate the significance of this.

Now another general question the solution of which I intend soon to undertake: how far does the totipotency of the blastomeres go? That is, up to what stage are blastomeres still able to produce a complete, small organism? In the future I shall call these "part-formations" in contrast to Roux's "half-formations." The polar course of the cleavage, as well as the above hypothesis concerning the closure of the blastula, suggested that perhaps elements of all concentric rings must be present; that would mean, however, that the four-cell stage would be the last from which isolated cells could produce part-formations, since the equatorial cleavage (namely, the third) divides the material into north and south polar rings, so to speak. This is, as stated, for the time being still merely a question; the totipotency of the cells of the four-cell stage seems to me probable in view of the three-quarter + one-quarter blastulae which will be briefly mentioned later. If, on the other hand, the above-mentioned assumption concerning differences in the effect of the first cleavage should prove true, the latter hypothesis, that material from all three rings is necessary for part-formation, would no longer hold.

But let us leave these conjectures and return to the facts. Thirty times I have succeeded in seeing small free-swimming blastulae arise from cleavage as described above of isolated blastomeres; the rest, about 20 cases, died during cleavage or were sacrificed so I could inspect them under higher magnification. Almost all of them at this stage were still transparent and entirely normal structurally though half-sized. I was not, by a method of estimation, able to discover any difference in size between these cells and those of the normal blastula; therefore, the number of cells is probably half the normal number, which is also to be expected from their cleavage behavior.

At the end of the second day, the fate of the experimental cases seemed to be sealed; they showed the effects of strong mechanical insult and of the small amount of water. For germs still transparent at this time, one could count on raising them further; unfortunately, this was the case with 15 specimens only, that is half the total.

The Gastrula and Pluteus

In healthy specimens invagination at the vegetal pole usually begins at the end of the second day; on the morning of the third day little gastrulae swam about actively in the dishes. As stated, I succeeded in observing 15 such specimens.

Three of the formations finally became actual plutei, differing from the normal only in size.

Therefore, these experiments show that, under certain circumstances, each of the first two blastomeres of Echinus microtuberculatus is able to produce a normally developed larva, whole in form and hence a part-, not half-, formation.

This fact is in fundamental contradiction to the theory of organ-forming germ areas, as the following simple consideration specifically demonstrates.

Imagine a normal blastula split along the median plane of the future pluteus; let us now examine one of the hemispheres preserved this way, for instance the left (see Fig. II*). The material at M_oM_u would normally supply material for the median region, that at L material for the left side. But suppose that we imagine the hemisphere closing, as explained above, to form a sphere but still maintaining polarity along BC. Then M_o will come to lie upon M_u, and hence possibly upon the right side of the future part-formation. Or, if in closure the original median areas supplied materials for the median region of the part-formation, then this could be thought of only as the upper or lower median region. If it is thought of as the upper, then the lower would come from a part which would otherwise have formed the left side. However one regards

---

* Editors' note: This text figure replaces an incorrect one in the translation.

it, one cannot escape the fundamental difference in the role which identical material is called upon to play depending upon whether one whole- or two part-formations arise from it,—something which can be brought about artificially. "I'l n'est pas des lors permis de croire que chaque sphere de segmentation doit occuper une place et jouer un role, qui sont assignés a l'avance" (Hallez); not, at any rate, in Echinus.

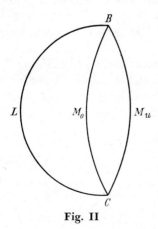

Fig. II

That this is a particularly pleasing result one could scarcely contend; it seems almost a step backward along a path considered already established.

When compared with Roux's, my results reveal a difference in behavior in the sea urchin and frog. Yet perhaps this difference is not so fundamental after all. If the frog blastomeres were really isolated and the other half (which was probably not dead in Roux's case) really removed, would they not perhaps behave like my Echinus cells? The cohesion of the blastomeres, conforming to the law of minimal surface formation, is much greater in the frog than in my object.

I have tried in vain to isolate amphibian blastomeres; let those who are more skillful than I try their luck.

It will not have escaped the reader that the results described might throw light on at least one aspect of the theory of

Double Formation

On this subject, I am in a position to supplement what has already been said. If, from one isolated cell of the two-cell stage, a perfect embryo of half-size is formed (namely a part-formation, in contrast to mere division which yields half-formation as in the case of Roux's frog embryos), it follows unequivocally that both cells of this stage if they are isolated and kept intact will form separate embryos, or twins.

It is highly probable that the separation of blastomeres by shaking was the direct cause of double formation and that without shaking whole-formation would have resulted.

This is certain since part-formations show that an isolated blastomere, provided it lives at all, always develops into a structure which differs from the normal only in size. With other twins, the situation is different, since they are too numerous to be considered accidental formations of this kind, such having never been seen in thousands of larvae observed by the Hertwig brothers and me.

Roux's theory of double formation, must, together with the principle of organ-forming germ-areas previously discussed, be discarded, at least in its general form. I have already remarked that, for our theoretical conceptions, this might be considered a backward rather than a forward step if establishment of facts did not always constitute progress.

Whether or not mechanical isolation or separation of the first two cleavage cells is the only way to obtain twin formation will be left open at this time.

It is an old controversy whether double-formation takes place by fusion or fission; birds and fish would, as mentioned, elsewhere, provide rather unfavorable material for a solution of this problem which in its usual formulation is rather a descriptive than a fundamental one. The observations communicated by other workers as well as my own experiments establish splitting as a cause, to which I may add on the basis of my results, splitting without postgeneration.

Obviously fission- and fusion-double-formation would be two quite different things, hence twinning could be of a dual nature. It is certain that the above mentioned double-fertilization modifies cleavage in such a way that immediate four-cell formation occurs; this is in support of our position, as shown before.

What forces come into play when the blastula closes? Can perhaps part of this process be understood in physical terms? The cell mass takes the form of a sphere, the form, that is, which possesses minimal surface. Further, why is it, after all, that a strong pulling apart of the half blastomeres without destroying them results in two individuals? These and other questions present themselves, but it were futile to indulge in idle speculation without actual facts.

Summary

If one isolates one of the first two blastomeres of Echinus microtuberculatus it cleaves as if for half-formation but forms a whole individual of half-size which is a part-formation.

Therefore the principle of organ-forming germ-areas is refuted for the observed species while the possibility of artificial production of twins is demonstrated.

Addendum: In proof-reading, I will briefly add that I have just succeeded in killing one cell of the two-cell stage of Spherechinus by shaking and in raising from the other half a small pluteus after half-cleavage.

Naples, October, 1891

REFERENCES

1. BORN, Die Furchung des Eies bei Doppelmissbildungen. Breslauer ärztl. Zeitschrift. 1887. Nr. 15.

2. Boveri, Ein geschlechtlich erzeugter Organismus ohne mütterliche Eigenschaften. Sitz.-Ber. d. Ges. f. Morph. u. Physiol. München 1889.

3. Chabry, Contribution à l'embryologie normale et tératologique des ascidies simples. Journ. de l'anat. et de la physiol. 1887.

4. Driesch, Die mathematisch-mechanische Betrachtung morphologischer Probleme der Biologie. Jena, Fischer 1891.

5. Fol, Recherches sur la fécondation et le commencement de l'hénogenie. Memoires de la soc. de phys. et d'hist. nat. de Genève. XXVI.

6. Gegenbaur, Beiträge zur Entwicklungsgeschichte der Landpulmonaten. Diese Zeitschr. Bd. III.

7. Hallez, Recherches sur l'embryologie des Nématodes. Paris 1885.

8. O. u. R. Hertwig, Über den Befruchtungs- und Theilungsvorgang des thierischen Eies etc. Jena 1887.

9. O. Hertwig, Experimentelle Studien am thierischen Ei etc. I. Jena 1890.

10. His, Unsere Körperform. Leipzig 1874.

11. Klaussner, Mehrfachbildungen bei Wirbelthieren. München 1890.

12. Kleinenberg, The development of the Earth-Worm. Quarterly Journal, 1879.

13. Korschelt, Zur Bildung des mittleren Keimblattes der Echinodermen. Zool. Jahrb. Bd. IV.

14. Metschnikoff, Über die Bildung der Wanderzellen bei Asteriden und Echiniden. Diese Zeitschr. Bd. XLII.

15. Plateau, Statique des liquides etc. 1873.

16. Rauber, Formbildung und Formstörung in der Entwicklung von Wirbelthieren. Leipzig 1880. Auch Morph Jahrb. Bd. VI.

17. ―――― Neue Grundlagen zur Kenntnis der Zelle. Morph. Jahrb. VIII.

18. 19. 20. Roux, Beiträge zur Entwicklungsmechanik des Embryo. I. Zeitschr. f. Biol. Bd. XXI. III. Breslauer ärztl. Zeitschr. 1855. V. Virchow's Arch. Bd. CXIV.

21. Selenka, Studien über Entwicklungsgeschichte der Thiere. II. Wiesbaden 1883.

See also references on duplicities (Gegenbaur, Dareste, Lacaze-Duthiers etc.) in Rauber, Klaussner, in Ziegler's Lehrbuch der allgemeinen Pathologie etc.

1898

Cell-Lineage and Ancestral Reminiscence

by EDMUND B. WILSON

Biological Lectures from the Marine Biological Laboratory, Woods Holl, Mass. 1898, pp. 21-42. Reprinted by permission of the publisher, Ginn and Company.

Around the turn of the century Wilson and his contemporaries (C. O. Whitman, E. G. Conklin, F. R. Lillie and others) at the Marine Biological Laboratory (Woods Hole, Mass.) were actively engaged in a study of cell-lineage in a variety of eggs of marine and fresh-water invertebrates by methods that were descriptive, comparative, and experimental. The period has been aptly referred to as "the epoch of cell-lineage at Woods Hole." Broadly speaking the main question the investigators of cell-lineage sought to answer was in what form the potencies of the cleavage pattern exist in the unsegmented egg and how they become realities during the course of development.

It should be noted here that the study of cell-lineage really began with C. O. Whitman's article on "The Embryology of Clepsine" (1878). In that paper Whitman observed bilateral symmetry of the uncleaved egg and traced the individual blastomeres to the principal organs of the body. His general conclusions were expressed in these words: "In the fecundated egg slumbers potentially the future embryo. While we cannot say that the embryo is predelineated we can say that it is predetermined" (p. 263). Although these observations and conclusions were epoch-making, they failed at that time to excite the imagination of some of the foremost embryologists as did the much later studies of Wilson and others on the organization of the egg and its cell-lineage.

With the broad question raised by Whitman in mind, Wilson traced the development of the egg of the marine annelid Nereis in minute detail, cell by cell, from the fertilized egg to the free-swimming larval stage, commonly known as the trochophore. His classical account of the development of this worm, published in 1892, clearly marked him as one of the most outstanding pioneer students of cell-lineage (the name that Wilson gave to this type of study). Thus, he succeeded in demonstrating that cleavage in Nereis is a well-ordered process in which every individual cell has a definite morphological value in the formation of the body of an annelid that has a determinate type of cleavage.

In tracing the developmental fate of the individual blastomeres in Nereis, Wilson put much emphasis upon the mode of origin and fate of the teloblasts, the original stem cells of the mesoderm. His interest in tracing the developmental pattern of these stem cells was initially aroused in an earlier work on earthworm embryology (1890). In this form he succeeded in showing that the mesoderm is formed by teloblasts or pole cells which are large specific cells set aside in early cleavage. From each of the two teloblasts new smaller cells form in orderly succession at a fixed point so as to form long chain-like cords of cells, the so-called mesodermal bands.

By comparing his findings on the earthworm and Nereis with those of other investigators, Wilson pointed out that these annelids and other animals (such as polyclad flatworms and mollusks) belonging to the "teloblastic series," although widely divergent groups, have in common far-reaching similarities in cleavage pattern and in the developmental fate of the different blastomeres. These findings on teloblasts and other blastomeres increased the significance of these features of development for the determination of homologies and in bringing out the important facts of animal relationships.

We are thus brought to the lecture reprinted here, which is characterized by its masterly style of writing and by its cautious analysis of the meaning of the remarkable parallelism in cleavage pattern of widely different forms in terms of which ancestral features have been retained or modified during the course of their evolution.

In his lecture Wilson did not touch upon the far deeper questions of cellular differentiation and of egg organization that were brought into sharp focus by the study of cell-lineage. Nevertheless, he was aware of these problems, for in his 1892 article on cell-lineage he wrote, "It is impossible to reflect upon the complicated yet perfectly ordered events of the cleavage of Nereis without attempting to discover the nature of the causes by which their course is determined" (p. 443). Indeed, in this same article Wilson noted that the developmental fate of the individual cells during early cleavage had been tested by means of experiment by Roux (1888) and Driesch (1892) whose articles are presented in translation on p. 4 and p. 40. The period of the 1890's marks a turning point in the direction of investigation from the morphological to the experimental analysis of cell-lineage and as a consequence indirectly influenced the whole subsequent theory of cellular transformation and differentiation.

CELL-LINEAGE AND ANCESTRAL REMINISCENCE.[1]

Every living being, at every period of its existence, presents us with a double problem. First, it is a complicated piece of mechanism, which so operates as to maintain, actively or passively, a moving equilibrium between its own parts and with its environment. It thus exhibits an adaptation of means to ends, to determine the nature of which, as it now exists, is the first task of the biologist. But, in the second place, the particular character of this adaptation cannot be explained by reference to existing conditions alone, since the organism is a product of the past as well as of the present, and its existing characteristics give in some manner a record of its past history. Our second task in the investigation of any problem of morphology or physiology must accordingly be to look into the historical background of the phenomena; and in the course of this inquiry we must make the attempt, by means of comparisons with related phenomena, to sift out adaptations to existing conditions from those which can only be comprehended by reference to former conditions. Phenomena of the latter class may, for the sake of brevity, conveniently be termed "ancestral reminiscences,"—though it may not be superfluous to remark that every characteristic of the organism is in a broad sense reminiscent of the past.

It is in embryological development that ancestral reminiscence is most familiar and most striking. We all know that development rarely takes the shortest and most direct path, but makes various detours and sometimes even moves backward so that the adult may actually be simpler than the embryo. Such vagaries of development are in many cases only intelligible when regarded as reminiscences of bygone conditions, either of the adult or of the embryo. Sometimes these records of the past are so consecutive and complete that the individual develop-

---

[1] This lecture is based on a paper entitled "Considerations on Cell-Lineage and Ancestral Reminiscence, Based on a Reëxamination of Some Points in the Early Development of Annelids and Polyclades," in *Ann. N. Y. Acad. Sci.*, 1898. In some passages the wording of that paper has been reproduced with only slight change. With the exception of Fig. 4, *the figures are entirely schematic and are designed to show only the broadest and most essential topographical features.* For this purpose the subdivisions of the micromeres have been omitted, and, except in Fig. 4, none of the figures represent the actual condition of the embryo at any given period. While, therefore, very misleading in matters of detail, they are, I think, true to the essential phenomena; and through the simplification thus effected the reader is spared a mass of confusing descriptive detail in no way essential to the broad relation on which it is desired to focus the attention.

ment, or ontogeny, may be said to repeat or recapitulate the ancestral development, or phylogeny. The development of the toad's egg, for example, probably gives in its main outlines a fairly true picture of the ancestral history of the toad race, which arose from fish-like ancestors, developed into aquatic air-breathing tailed forms, and finally in their last estate became tailless terrestrial forms. It was such facts as these that led Haeckel, building on the basis laid by Darwin and Fritz Müller, to the enunciation of the famous so-called "biogenetic" law, that the ontogeny, or history, of the individual tends to repeat in an abbreviated and more or less modified form the phylogeny, or history, of the race. The event has shown that actual recapitulation or repetition of this kind is of relatively rare occurrence. Development more often shows, not a definite record of the ancestral history, but a more or less vague and disconnected series of reminiscences, and these may relate either to the adult or to the embryonic stages of the ancestral type. Thus the embryo mammal shows in its gill-slits and aortic arches what must probably be regarded as reminiscences of a fish-like adult ancestor, while in the primitive streak it gives a reminiscence not of an adult form but of an ancestral mode of development from a heavily yolk-laden egg like that of the reptiles.

If we survey the general field of embryology, we find that ancestral reminiscence in development is most conspicuously shown and has been longest known in the later stages, and many of the most interesting and hotly contested controversies of modern embryology have been waged in the discussion of the possible ancestral significance of larval forms, such as the trochophore, the *Nauplius,* the ascidian tadpole, and many others. It is generally admitted, too, that ancestral reminiscences may occur in earlier embryonic stages. While few naturalists would to-day accept Haeckel's celebrated Gastræa theory in its original form, probably still fewer would deny that the diblastic embryo (gastrula, planula, etc.) of higher forms is in a certain sense reminiscent of the origin of these forms from diblastic ancestors having something in common with existing coelenterates.

It is in respect to still earlier stages, namely, those including the cleavage of the egg, that the greatest doubt now exists; and there is hardly a question in embryology more interesting or more momentous than whether these stages may exhibit ancestral reminiscence, and whether they, like the later stages, exhibit definite homologies, and thus afford in some measure a guide to relationship. None of the earlier embryologists were disposed to answer this question in the affirmative. To them, and it should be added to some of our contemporaries as well, the cleavage of the ovum was "a mere vegetative repetition of parts," the details of which had no ancestral significance, and the ontogeny first acquired a definite phyletic meaning and interest with the differentiation of the embryonic tissues and organs. To these observers the cleavage of the ovum presented merely a series of problems in the mechanics of cell-division, and its accurate study was almost wholly neglected as having no interest for the historical study of descent. And yet it was long ago shown that the blastomeres of the cleaving ovum have in some cases as definite a morphological value as the organs that appear in later stages. Kowalevsky and Rabl traced the mesoblast-bands in annelids and gasteropods back to a single cell, which still later research has shown to have the same origin and fate, and hence to be homologous in the two cases by every criterion at our command. A long series of later researches, beginning with Whitman's epoch-making studies on the cleavage of *Clepsine,* has demonstrated analogous facts in the case of many other cells of the cleaving ovum, and has finally shown that in many groups of animals (though apparently not in all) the origin of the adult organs may be determined cell by cell in the cleavage stages; that the *cell-lineage* thus determined is not the vague and variable process it was once supposed to be, but is in many cases as definitely ordered a process as any other series of events in the ontogeny; and that it may accurately be compared with the cell-lineage of other groups with a view to the determination of relationships.

The study of cell-lineage has thus given us what is practically a new method of embryological research. The value and limitations of this method are, however, still under discussion, and among special workers in this field opinion as to its morphological value is still so widely divided that most of its results should be taken as suggestive rather than demonstrative. Like other embryological methods, it has already encountered contradictions and difficulties so serious as to show that it is no *open sesame*. In some cases closely related forms (*e.g.,* gasteropods and cephalopods) have been shown to differ very widely, apparently irreconcilably, in cell-lineage. In other cases (echinoderms, annelids) the normal form of cleavage has been artificially changed without altering the outcome of the development. In still other cases (*e.g.,* in teleost fishes) the form of cleavage has been shown to be variable in many of its most conspicuous features, so that apparently no definite cell-lineage exists. These and many other facts, less striking but no less puzzling, can be built into a strong case against the cell-lineage program, and I wish to acknowledge its full force. Admitting all the difficulties, I am nevertheless on the side of those who as morphologists believe that the study of cell-lineage has demonstrated its value, and that it promises to yield more valuable results in the future. In this lecture I propose to illustrate some of the more interesting results already attained, and some of the suggestions that they give for future work, by a broad consideration of the cell-lineage of three related groups of animals which on the one hand have been very carefully examined as regards their anatomical and general embryological relationships, while on the other hand their cell-lineage has been more exhaustively studied than that of any other forms. These groups are the platodes (more especially the *Turbellaria*), the mollusks, and the annelids.

That these three groups belong in the same morphological series will probably be admitted by all zoölogists, and most will no doubt further agree with the view of Lang, that in the essential features of their organization the platodes are not very far removed from the ancestral type from which the two higher groups have sprung, the former having remained non-metameric like the platodes, while the latter have acquired metamerism. Accepting this view we should expect, if there be any evidence of race-lineage in cell-lineage, to find in the annelids and mollusks a common type of cleavage, and one which in its main features may be derived from that of the platode. Recent studies in cell-lineage have, on the whole, justified this expectation, and have brought to light some cases of vestigial processes in cleavage which are, I believe, to be reckoned among the most striking and beautiful examples of reminiscence in development. It is especially to these cases that I wish to direct attention.

The cleavage of a number of *Turbellaria* and nemerteans, and of many annelids, gasteropods, and lamellibranchs, has now been shown to conform to a common type which, though complex in detail, is exceedingly simple in its essential plan. A few exceptions there certainly are; but some of these are apparent only (for example, in the acœlous *Turbellaria*), and are readily reducible to the type, while others are undoubtedly correlated with bygone changes in the mode of nutrition of the ovum (as in some of the earthworms and leeches). The most conspicuous exception is afforded by the cephalopods, which have a mode of cleavage entirely unrelated to that of the other mollusks; but the entire development of this group is of a highly modified character. Fully recognizing the real exceptions, we nevertheless cannot fail to wonder at the marvellous constancy with which the cleavage of the polyclades, nemertines, annelids, gasteropods, and lamellibranchs conforms to the typical mode of development. In all these forms the egg first divides into four quadrants. From these at least three and sometimes four or five quartets of cells—usually smaller, and hence designated as *micromeres*—are successively produced by more or less unequal cleavages towards the upper pole. The arrangement of these micromeres (Fig. 1) is constant and highly characteristic, the first quartet being more or less displaced, or, as it were, rotated in a direction corresponding with the hands of a watch (clockwise), the second in the opposite direction (anticlockwise), the third clockwise again, and so on, the spindles of each division being at right angles to those of the preceding and following. In the later subdivisions of the micromeres, also, a most remarkable agreement has been observed; but I shall pass this over entirely in order to focus attention on the broader features of the development.

A large part of the work in cell-lineage during the past ten years has been devoted to a comparison of the morphological value of these quartets of cells in the annelids, mollusks, and platodes; and the remarkable and interesting fact is now becoming apparent that while they do not have exactly the same value in all the forms, they nevertheless show so close a correspondence both in origin and in fate that it seems impossible to explain the likeness save as a result of community of descent. The very differences, as we shall see, give some of the most interesting and convincing evidence of genetic affinity; for processes which in the lower forms play a leading *rôle* in the development are in the higher forms so reduced as to be no more than vestiges or reminiscences of what they once were, and in some cases seem to have disappeared as completely as the teeth of birds or the limbs of snakes. The processes in question relate to the formation of the mesoblast in its relation to the micromere-quartets, and on them the whole discussion may be made to turn.

The higher types—*i.e.*, the annelids, gasteropods, and lamellibranchs —have for some time been known to agree closely in the general value of the quartets. Rabl first demonstrated that in *Planorbis* the entire ectoblast is formed from the first three quartets, while the mesoblast-bands arise from the posterior cell of the fourth quartet, the other three, with the remains of the primary quadrants, giving rise to the entoblast (Fig. 1). The same general result has been reached by subsequent investigators of molluscan cell-lineage, though there are one or two apparent exceptions (*e.g., Teredo,* according to Hatschek) that demand reinvestigation. The same remarkable fact holds true throughout the annelids,[2] the well-determined exceptions being some of the earth-worms and leeches referred to above, in which the typical relations seem to have been disturbed through changes in the nutrition of the embryo. Wherever the typical quartet formation takes place—and this is the case in nearly all the forms that have been adequately examined—the general value of the quartets is the same, the first three giving rise to the entire ectoblast, the fourth giving rise, one cell to the mesoblast-bands and the other three to entoblast, while the remnants of the primary quadrants, including the fifth quartet if one is formed, give rise to the entoblast. This result seems almost too simple and produces an impression of artificiality which may probably account for the reluctance with which it has been accepted in some quarters; but I think it is not too much to say that few facts in embryology have been more patiently studied or more accurately determined. The above statement does not,

[2] See footnote at p. 67 for reference to Eisig's widely divergent account of the development of *Capitella.*

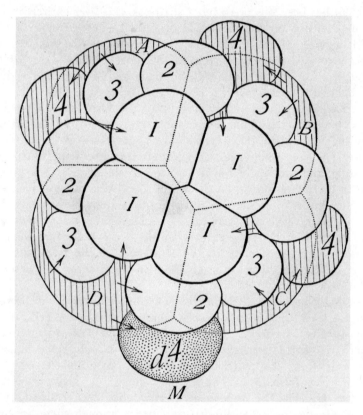

Fig. 1 Diagram of the typical quartet-formation in an annelid or gasteropod; the quartets numbered in the order of their formation; *A, B, C, D,* the basal quadrants. Ectoblast unshaded, mesoblast dotted, entoblast ruled in parallel lines. In many forms (*e.g., Aricia*) a fifth quartet (entoblastic) is formed; in others (*e.g., Nereis*) only three complete quartets and the posterior member of the fourth quartet (d^4 or M).

however, contain the whole truth; but before completing it we may advantageously turn to the development of the *Turbellaria*.

It was long since shown by researches, beginning with Hallez and Götte and culminating in those of Lang, that the cleavage of polyclades shows an extraordinary precise resemblance to that of the annelids and mollusks. Taking Lang's work on *Discocœlis* as a type, we find four quartets of cells successively produced from the primary or basal quadrants following exactly the same law of displacement as in the higher types, assuming the same arrangement, and in their subsequent subdivision up to a relatively late stage following so exactly the plan of the annelid egg that even a skilled observer might easily mistake one for the other (Fig. 4, *A*). Despite this accurate agreement in the form of cleavage, Lang's observations seemed to show that the cell-quartets had a totally different value from those of the higher forms; for he believed the first quartet to produce the entire ectoblast, the second and third to give rise to the mesoblast, while the fourth quartet, with the basal cells, formed the entoblast (Fig. 2, B). Such a result was more than a stumbling-block in the way of the comparison. It was subversive of the whole cell-lineage program; for it seemed to show that the cell-lineage of derivative animals (*i.e.,* annelids and gasteropods), while exactly conforming to the ancestral *form* of cleavage (*i.e.,* that of the *Turbellaria*), differed *toto cœlo* from it in morphological significance. When, some years ago, I first called attention to this difficulty, I felt constrained to the admission that, in the face of such a contradiction, the study of cell-lineage could only be regarded as of very restricted value in morphological investigation; indeed, in a lecture delivered here four years

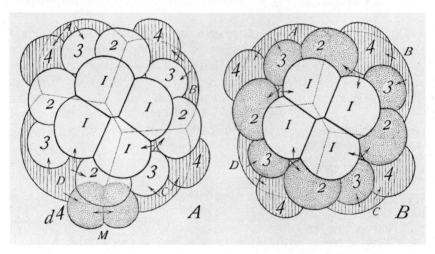

Fig. 2 Diagram contrasting the value of the quartets in an annelid or gasteropod (*A*) with those of a polyclade according to Lang's original account (*B*). Lettering and shading as in Fig. 1. (The true proportions of the basal quadrants and the fourth quartet, which are here misrepresented, are shown in Fig. 4. It is characteristic of the polyclades that the fourth quartet-cells are greatly enlarged at the expense of the basal quadrants.)

ago on the inadequacy of the embryological criterion of homology,[3] I cited this very case as representing a climax in the contradictions of comparative embryology.

[3] "The Embryological Criterion of Homology." Wood's Holl Biological Lectures, 1894, p. 113.

It is not rare in the history of science to find that fuller knowledge may so change the point of view as to transform a seeming difficulty into a pillar of support; and it seems not unlikely that such may be the case with the present one, though some new difficulties have arisen which still await solution. The new evidence relates, on the one hand, to the annelids and mollusks, on the other hand to the polyclades; and since on both sides it tends to bridge a gap which once seemed hopelessly wide, I shall consider it in some detail. In approaching this evidence the two principal difficulties should be clearly borne in mind. The first lies in the fact that the mesoblast-bands of the annelids and mollusks arise from one cell of the *fourth* quartet, while in the polyclade the mesoblast was stated to arise from all of the eight cells of the *second* and *third* quartets. The second difficulty relates to the ectoblast, which in the annelid and mollusk arises from the twelve cells of the first, second, and third quartets; while in the polyclade it was believed to arise solely from the first quartet (Fig. 2). We may consider these two difficulties in order.

As regards the first point, a series of researches during the past three years have shown that in some of the mollusks and annelids the mesoblast has a double origin, a part—and usually the major part— arising from the posterior cell of the fourth quartet, as stated above, while a part arises from cells of the second or third quartet, as in the polyclade (Fig. 3). The major part—which, for reasons that will appear beyond, I propose to call the *entomesoblast*—gives rise to the so-called mesoblast-bands. The minor part, or *ectomesoblast* ("secondary meso-blast," "larval mesoblast," of various authors), apparently does not contribute to the formation of the mesoblast-bands, and in at least one case—namely, that of *Unio*, as described by Lillie—it gives rise to cells of a purely larval character and designated as "larval mesenchyme." The first step in this direction was that of Lillie, just referred to, who in 1895 announced the discovery that in a lamellibranch, *Unio*, one cell of the *second* quartet (a^2 on the left side) gives rise not only to ectoblast, but also to a single mesoblast-cell which passes into the interior, divides, and gives rise to some of the larval muscles ("larval mesenchyme," Fig. 3, *C*). Lillie's discovery was quickly followed by the no less interesting one of Conklin that in another mollusk, the gasteropod *Crepidula*, three cells of the second quartet, median anterior, right and left (b^2, c^2, d^2), likewise give rise to mesoblastic as well as to ectoblastic elements (Fig. 3, *B*),—a process still more forcibly recalling the origin of the mesoblast in the polyclade.

Two years later mesoblastic cells were found, both in the mollusks and in the annelids, to arise from members of the *third* quartet. The first of these cases was observed by Wierzejski (1897) in the case of *Physa*, where the two anterior cells of this quartet (c^3, b^3) give rise to mesoblastic as well as to ectoblastic cells, and exactly similar facts were soon afterwards observed by Holmes in *Planorbis*. Simultaneously with these researches I independently discovered in the annelid *Aricia* two mesoblast cells arising from the two posterior cells of either the second or

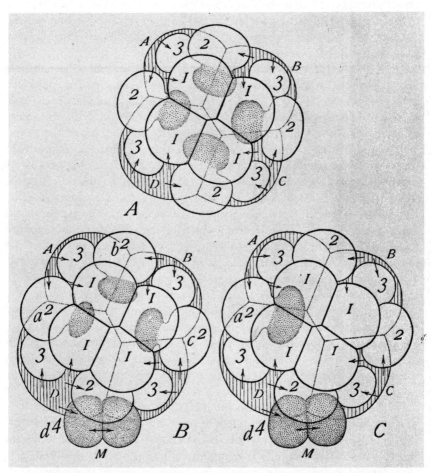

Fig. 3 Diagrams illustrating the value of the quartets in a polyclade (*Leptoplana*), a lamellibranch (*Unio*), and a gasteropod (*Crepidula*). Lettering and shading as in Fig. 1. (For comment on these figures see footnote at first page.) *A, Leptoplana,* showing mesoblast-formation in the second quartet. (Cf. Fig. 4.) *B, Crepidula,* showing source of ecto-mesoblast (from a^2, b^2, c^2) and entomesoblast (from quadrant *D*). *C, Unio,* ectomesoblast formed only from a^2.

the third quartet (*i.e.,* from c^3 and d^3 or from d^2 and c^2), though I could not positively determine which. This was immediately followed by Treadwell's discovery that in the annelid *Podarke* mesoblast cells are formed from three cells of the third quartet, namely, the anterior median and the two lateral cells (a^3, c^3, d^3). It was thus shown that in at least four genera of mollusks and two of annelids a part of the mesoblast has an origin which recalls that of the polyclades, and the view is irresistibly suggested that the formation of this *ectomesoblast* in one, two, or three quadrants in the higher types is a vestigial process or ancestral reminiscence of what occurred in all four quadrants in the ancestral prototype and still persists in the polyclade.

The second difficulty—*i.e.*, the origin of the ectoblast—has entirely disappeared upon a reëxamination of the cell-lineage of a polyclade (*Leptoplana*) which I was enabled to make in the summer of 1897. In this form careful study shows in the clearest manner that the formation of ectoblast is not confined to the first quartet, but that all of the twelve cells of the first three quartets contribute to the ectoblast, precisely as is the case in the annelids and mollusks (Fig. 3, *A;* Fig. 4, for details). A comparison with Lang's figures gives every reason to believe that the same is true in *Discocœlis* and the other forms studied by him, and that on this point he fell into an error which was certainly very pardonable at the time. The quartet-cells from which in the polyclade the mesoblast arises are, therefore, not pure mesoblasts, as Lang supposed, but are *mesectoblasts*, precisely like the cells from which the "larval mesoblast" arises in *Crepidula* or *Unio*.[4]

The researches reviewed up to this point have cleared up the contradiction relating to the second quartet. Passing now to the third and fourth quartets, we find that the newer researches have introduced a new difficulty with respect to each of these quartets; but the new difficulties differ from the old in that they suggest a number of highly interesting problems for future research. As regards the third quartet I was unable to find in *Leptoplana* any evidence that it gives rise to mesoblastic elements such as we should expect to find in the *Turbellaria* in view of the formation of ectomesoblast from this quartet in *Physa*, *Planorbis*, *Podarke*, and probably in *Aricia*. As far as I could find, the third quartet gives rise only to ectoblast cells at the lip of the blastopore (Fig. 4), and Lang's results seem to me inconclusive on this point. Only renewed researches can determine whether this difficulty be real or only apparent. In the mean time it would be well not to lose sight of the fact that the polyclades cannot, of course, be the actual ancestors of the annelids and mollusks, and that the cleavage in the former may differ

---

4 In *Leptoplana* each cell of the second quartet divides off in succession three ectoblast cells before the delamination of mesoblast into the interior occurs at the fourth division (Fig. 4). In *Unio,* according to Lillie, the larval mesoblast is definitely separated at the third division of the micromere (a^2). Professor Conklin informs me that in *Crepidula* the ectomesoblast is formed at about the fourth or fifth division of the micromeres (a^2, b^2, c^2).

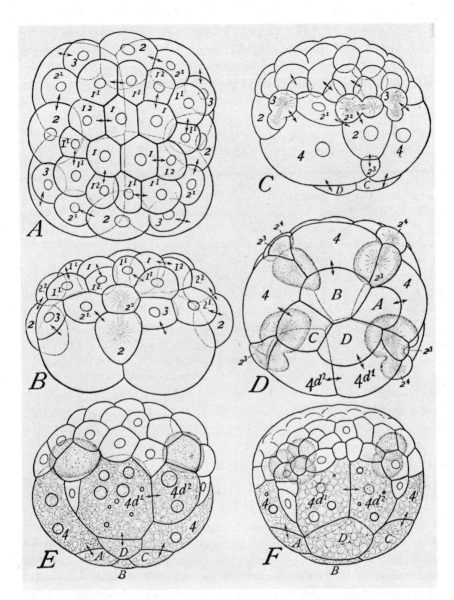

Fig. 4 *Leptoplana.*—(Camera drawings from the transparent living embryos. In these figures the subdivisions of the micromeres are accurately shown.) *A,* 32-cell stage, from the upper pole; *B,* 36-cell stage, from the side, showing second division of 2; *C,* side view approximately 60 cells, showing the third ectoblast cell (2³) derived from 2, the fourth quartet (4), and the basal entoblasts (*D, C*). *D,* delamination of mesoblast in the fourth division of 2 (shaded), from the lower pole, showing the basal quartet of entomeres (*A-D*), and the two somewhat unequal cells (4d¹, 4d²) formed by the vertical division of the posterior cell of the fourth quartet. *E,* posterior view of the ensuing stage, showing the two posterior mesoblast cells (shaded) lying in the interior, and a marked inequality between (4d¹ and 4d²). *F,* later stage; multiplication of the mesoblast cells (shaded), equality of 4d¹ and 4d², as in *Discocoelis.*

very considerably from the common ancestral type. A natural hypothesis is that in the ancestral mode of development all of the first three quartets gave rise both to ectoblast and to mesoblast, and that in all the existing forms the mesoblast formation has been lost in the first quartet and variously reduced or entirely suppressed in one or both of the two succeeding quartets. I think, therefore, that we need not hereafter be surprised to find the formation of ectomesoblast from more than one of the first three quartets, whether in the *Turbellaria* or in the higher forms.

It is when we attempt to bring the foregoing considerations into relation with the history of the fourth quartet in annelids and mollusks that we arrive at a far more serious difficulty; but we can hardly regret a difficulty that is so suggestive of further research. In the polyclade the fourth quartet is relatively very large, the basal quadrants being correspondingly reduced (Fig. 4). All of the eight cells formed give rise, as far as known, to entoblast only. In the annelids and mollusks, on the other hand, only three cells of this quartet—anterior, right, and left—are purely entoblastic, while the fourth, or posterior, cell ("d⁴") divides into symmetrical halves to form the "primary mesoblasts," or pole-cells, from which arise the two mesoblast-bands characteristic of these groups (Fig. 2, *A*). Now, in comparing this mode of development with that of the polyclade, we must choose between the following alternatives. *Either* the mesoblast of the annelid or mollusk, as a whole, corresponds with that of the polyclade—in which case we must assume that in the course of the phylogeny the posterior cell of the fourth quartet has gradually taken upon itself more or less completely the mesoblast formation formerly occurring in the second or third quartet; *or* the mesoblast of the polyclade has dwindled away, perhaps has even disappeared, in the higher forms, where it is represented only by the ectomesoblast, its place having been taken, through a process of substitution, by the mesoblast-bands derived from the fourth quartet. To vary the statement we must assume that a substitution has taken place either in the cell-mechanism by which the mesoblast is formed or in the mesoblast itself, and upon our choice between these alternatives depends the entire point of view from which we regard cell-lineage.

Now, it must be admitted, forthwith, that we have not at command sufficient data to give any certain answer to this question, and we should be careful not to draw premature conclusions in a matter which involves further consequences of such importance. But there are a number of well-ascertained facts drawn from widely diverse sources that point towards the second of the above alternatives; *i.e.,* the view that the mesoblast-bands of the annelid or gasteropod are not as such represented at all in the polyclade, but, phyletically considered, are neomorphs which have more or less completely replaced the ancestral mesoblast. This evidence may be arranged in three lines:—

1. As a result of exact and thorough studies upon the histology and larval development of the annelids, Eduard Meyer was several years ago led to the conclusion that the mesoblast-bands, both in origin and in fate, differed widely from the scattered larval mescenchyme-cells, though the lineage of the latter was then unknown. Developing this idea, Meyer was led to the remarkable conclusion that the mesoblast-bands of the higher types represent the paired *gonads* of the ancestral form—a view nearly related with the earlier one of Hatschek, that the primary mesoblasts were originally eggs, which, in the course of the phylogeny, became in part transformed into peritoneal and other somatic cells, and in part remained as germ-cells. Thus the original mesoblast— *which Meyer definitely compared with that of the Turbellaria*—was gradually replaced, though still persisting in a reduced form as the larval mesenchyme.

I would not at present urge the acceptance of this daring hypothesis; but in the light of later research it has become highly significant, and whether true or false is of great interest as giving a clear picture of how such a process of substitution may have been possible.

2. In the second line of evidence lies Lillie's discovery that the ectomesoblast of *Unio* (derived from a^2) gives rise to purely larval transitory structures; namely, to the adductor muscle and the scattered contractile myocytes of the *Glochidium* larva. In the annelids, too, the same conclusion seems probable, and my friend Professor Treadwell informs me that in *Podarke* there is every reason to believe that the ectomesoblast (derived from a^3, c^3, d^3) is entirely devoted to the formation of the ring-muscle and myocytes of the trochophore, which apparently take but an insignificant part, if any, in the building of the adult body. This result tallies with the view that the ectomesoblast formation in the higher types is a reminiscence of the ancestral process still existing in the polyclade, but in the higher forms relegated to the early stages, and even in them is more or less reduced.[5]

[5] Eisig has very recently (*Mitth. Zool. Station*, Neapel, xiii, 1, 2, 1898) published the results of a study of the cell-lineage and later development of *Capitella*, which are totally at variance with the view here suggested, and the facts on which it is based. Broadly speaking, his results exactly reverse those of all the authors cited above, the mesoblast-bands ("Cœlomesoblast") being derived from the third quartet ($c^{3.1}$ and $d^{3.1}$), while the larval mesoblast ("Pædomesoblast") arises from a portion of M (d^4), the remaining portion giving rise to ectoblast. If well founded, this result is not only fatal to the view I suggest, but is, I believe, nothing less than a *reductio ad absurdum* of the whole cell-lineage program, regarded as a method of morphological research. No one will lightly call in question the results of so conscientious and eminent an observer; and they must be regarded as by far the most serious obstacle that the morphological study of cell-lineage has thus far encountered. I will not attempt to explain away this adverse

3. In the third line lies the evidence, recently obtained, that the pole-cells or teloblasts of the mesoblast-bands of the annelids and mollusks are to be regarded as derivatives of the archenteron, and hence differ wholly from the ectomesoblast in their relation to the primary germ-layers. Kowalevsky, the discoverer of these teloblasts, expressed the

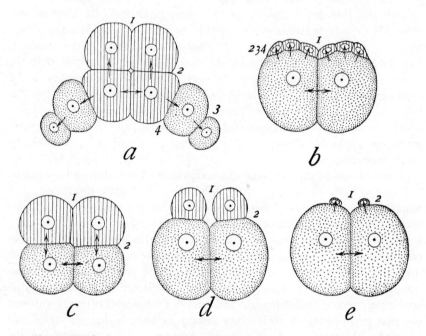

Fig. 5 Diagrams comparing the early divisions of the posterior cell of the fourth quartet (d^4 or M) in Crepidula(a), Nereis(b), Clymenella(c), Unio(d), and Aricia(e). The numerals show the order of the division. Cells destined to form entoblast (their fate as actually observed in Crepidula and Nereis, but only inferred in other cases) ruled in parallel lines, mesoblast dotted. After the divisions here shown, the symmetrical mesoblast-bands are formed from the dotted cells.

opinion, more than twenty-five years ago (1871), that they were to be regarded as derivatives of the archenteron; and a large number of later workers from the time of Rabl (1876) have accepted his view, though

evidence, based on so prolonged and thorough a research. It should not be forgotten, however, that, as Professor Eisig is himself careful to point out, the nature of the material has forced him to contend with great difficulties, since the eggs are normally distorted by pressure (a factor which, as I have experimentally shown in Nereis, may greatly alter the form of cleavage) between the membranes of the tube; and, further, the development cannot be continuously followed in life. A result, based on this material, which stands in such flat contradiction to what is known in other and more favorable forms, must await the test of further research.

only very recently has the full strength of the evidence been developed. In the first place, it was shown through the studies of Rabl, Blochmann, and later workers, that while the posterior cell of the fourth quartet gives rise to the mesoblastic pole-cells the other cells are purely entoblastic. In the second place, the recent studies of Conklin and myself have shown that even the posterior cell of the fourth quartet (d^4) may contain entoblastic as well as mesoblastic material. I showed several years ago that in *Nereis* each of the cells into which d^4 divides buds forth several small cells (Fig. 5, *b*), which do not enter into the mesoblast-bands, though I did not correctly determine their fate. More recently Conklin was able to show that a similar process occurs in *Crepidula* (Fig. 5, *a*), and that the cells thus formed are *entoblast-cells* which enter into the formation of the archenteron. On reëxamining the matter in *Nereis* I found the clearest evidence that the same was true here. In both these cases, therefore, the posterior cell of the fourth quartet is of mixed character, and divides into two mesentoblasts, each of which first gives rise to a number of entoblast cells (two in *Crepidula*, four or five in *Nereis*), the residue constituting the mesoblast. In both these forms, therefore, the ectoblast (and in *Crepidula* the ectomesoblast) are the first completely segregated, and the archenteron which remains gives rise to the mesoblastic pole-cells. The latter are, therefore, of entoblastic rather than ectoblastic origin, and may be designated as the *entomesoblast*.

Further examination of these phenomena brings out some highly interesting facts which seem to constitute a striking case of ancestral reminiscence in cleavage. Several years ago I found in two genera of annelids, *Aricia* and *Spio*, that the small entoblast-cells of *Nereis* and *Crepidula* (*i.e.*, those budded forth from the two mesoblasts derived from the division of d^4 or *M*) are represented by a single pair of quite rudimentary cells, scarcely larger than polar bodies (Fig. 5, *e*), which apparently take no part in the building of the archenteron, and can only be explained as vestiges or reminiscences of such a process as occurs in *Crepidula* or *Nereis*. Later researches have revealed the presence of these vestigial entoblasts in several other forms, and have shown further that they are connected by several intermediate steps with the larger functional cells found in *Crepidula*. Thus in *Amphitrite* (Mead) and *Planorbis* (Holmes) they are quite vestigial, agreeing essentially in size and origin with those of *Aricia*. In *Unio* (Lillie) they are considerably larger (Fig. 5, *d*), in *Clymenella* (Fig. 5, *c*) they are as large as the mesoblastic moiety (Mead); while in *Crepidula* (Fig. 5, *a*) their bulk surpasses that of the mesoblastic part.[6] Such a series creates a strong probability that we have before us a vanishing series like those so well known in adult organs, such as the limbs, the tail, or the teeth. Further, just as the lateral

[6] I am here placing my own interpretation on Mead's and Lillie's observations.

toes of the horse seem to have wholly vanished, even from the ontogeny, so the vestigial entoblasts would seem to have disappeared in some annelids and mollusks, leaving the posterior cell of the fourth quartet purely mesoblastic.

These considerations invest with a special interest the corresponding cell in the *Turbellaria* (*i.e.*, the posterior member of the fourth quartet, $4d$); and this interest is heightened by Lang's discovery that in *Discocœlis* this cell divides earlier than the other cells of the quartet, and into equal halves which lie symmetrically at the posterior end of the embryo. These two cells thus correspond exactly in origin and position with the paired mesentoblasts of the annelids and gasteropods, and the facts naturally led to the suggestion, made by Mead, that they would perhaps be found to give rise to paired mesoblast-bands, as in the higher types. In *Leptoplana* (Fig. 4, *D, E, F*) a similar division occurs, but as far as their fate is concerned my own observations do not sustain Mead's suggestion, on the one hand giving no evidence that these cells give rise to anything other than the posterior cells of the archenteron, on the other showing that they are often unequal or asymmetrically placed (Fig. 4, *D, E*) and only rarely conform to Lang's scheme (Fig. 4, *F*). If, therefore, the polyclades represent the ancestral type in this respect, we must conclude that the entomesoblast was a later development. The remarkable fact is that, if such has been the case, the new mesoblast-formation has been fitted, as it were, upon an old form of cleavage occurring regularly in *Discocœlis* and ocassionally in *Leptoplana*. The two symmetrical posterior entoblast-cells of the polyclade might thus be conceived as the prototypes of the primary mesoblasts or mesentoblasts of the higher forms, which in the course of the phylogeny undertook the formation of mesoblastic as well as of entoblastic elements.[7] The old building pattern was still retained but adapted to a new use, precisely as has been the case with the evolution of larval or adult organs, such as the branchial or aortic arches and the limbs. As the change progressed the posterior cell of the fourth quartet became more and more strictly given over to the formation of mesoblast, its entoblastic elements becoming correspondingly reduced to truly rudimentary or vestigial cells (*Aricia*, etc.), or finally, perhaps, disappearing wholly.

I have endeavored to place these special conclusions in strong relief, not because they can yet be accepted as demonstrated,—and it is quite possible that some other interpretation may yet be placed upon some of the facts,—but because they seem to me highly suggestive of further research in the field of cell-lineage. There are among them two general considerations on which I would lay emphasis.

First, the study of cleavage or cell-lineage in the case of these groups

[7] Lang has pointed out a motive for this form of cleavage in the polyclade, correlating the early and symmetrical division of d^4 with the posterior bifurcation of the gut.

raises a number of highly interesting and suggestive questions in pure morphology. If the mesoblast-bands are a new formation, what is the motive, so to speak, for their origin? Did they perhaps arise through the developments of a new body-region, or a new growth-zone, or bud-ding-region from the posterior part of the ancestral body, as has been assumed by Leuckart, Haeckel, Hatschek, and Whitman in explanation of metamerism? Is the body of the turbellarian homologous to the entire body of an annelid or mollusk, or does it represent only the head or the larval body, to which a trunk region is afterwards added? What is the relation of the entomesoblast to the archenteric pouches of the en-terocœlous types? How do the above results harmonize with the general doctrine of development by substitution? These are examples of some of the morphological questions suggested by the general inquiry. They are admittedly of a highly speculative character, and I, for one, am not prepared to give a positive answer to any of them. But the mere fact that morphological questions of such character and scope are inevitably suggested by studies in pure cell-lineage shows that such studies must not be passed over by the morphologist as having no interest or value for his own researches.

Second, the phenomena we have considered seem to leave no escape from the acceptance of ancestral reminiscence in cleavage, with all that that implies. That the rudimentary entoblasts of *Aricia* or *Spio* are such reminiscences of former conditions seems almost as clear as that the mammalian yolk-sac or the avian primitive streak are such. The forma-tion of the ectomesoblast in annelids and mollusks is nearly if not quite as strong a case. Both these are processes that appear to be vestigial, or, at any rate, approach that character. But the evidence of genetic affinity is no less clearly shown in processes that are not vestigial, such as the formation of the ectoblast in *Turbellaria,* annelids, and gasteropods or lamellibranchs, from neither more nor less than three quartets of micro-meres, or in the origin of the archenteron from the fourth quartet with the remains of the basal quadrants. Between the annelids, gasteropods, and lamellibranchs a far more precise and extended series of resemblances exists. The question has been much discussed of late whether such re-semblances can be called homologies. Probably no one will deny that the ectoblast-cap, arising from twelve cells, is as a whole homologous in the annelid and the gasteropod embryo. Are the individual micro-meres respectively homologous? In the present state of our knowledge this is a question of name rather than of fact; for homologies only gradually emerge during development from their unknown background in the egg. It is for this reason that, as I have urged in a preceding lecture, *the ultimate court of appeal in this question lies in the fate of the cells.* If the structures to which they give rise are homologous, I can find no logical ground for refusing the claim to the cells from which

they arise. Furthermore, this homology must be irrespective of the origin
of the cells, just as the ganglion of a bud-embryo of *Botryllus* is homologous with that of an egg-embryo in the same form, despite the total
difference of origin in the two cases. When, however, we find that the
homologous protoblasts or parent-cells have the same origin as well as
the same fate, the homology becomes the more striking; and it is in the
determination of common origin as well as common fate, as has been
done in so many cases, that the principal significance of recent work in
cell-lineage seems to me to lie. Some of the objections urged against the
reality of cell-homology have, I think, arisen through a failure to recognize among cell-homologies the same distinction between complete and
incomplete homology that was long ago urged by Gegenbaur in the case
of organ-homologies. The posterior member of the fourth quartet in
annelids, for example, is in a broad sense homologous throughout the
group; but the homology is probably not an absolute or complete one,
since this cell may contain functional entoblast *(Nereis)*, rudimentary
or vestigial entoblast *(Aricia)*, or apparently in some cases no entoblast,
as I have described in *Polymnia*. Again, the acceptance of cell-homology
does not, I think, carry with it the necessity of finding a homologue for
every individual cell throughout the ontogeny; for in the case of later
structures no one demands or expects that, in the comparison of related
forms, an exact equivalent shall be found for every subdivision of homologous nerves or bloodvessels or sense organs. Finally, the fact that
cleavage *may* show no constant or definite relation to the adult parts—
as is the case in the teleost fishes—does not alter the equally indubitable
fact that cleavage often *does* show such a constant relation. The probability that the *Nauplius* larva is not a true ancestral form does not
come into collision with the probability that the ascidian tadpole is such
a form. How far in the course of phylogeny the ontogeny has adhered
to its original type and retained the same relation to the adult parts is
a question which stands, as far as I can see, both *a priori* and *a pos-
teriori* on essentially the same basis, whether it be applied to the cleavage
or to the later stages. Let us not forget the difficulties that still beset
us in the application of the biogenetic law to the larval stages and to
general organogeny, and let us not make a greater demand in this regard
upon cell-lineage than on other lines of embryological research. The time
has not yet come for a last word on this subject, and we shall probably
have to await the result of much more extended research before a
satisfactory point of view can be attained.

1902

On Multipolar Mitosis as a Means of
Analysis of the Cell Nucleus

by THEODOR BOVERI

Boveri, Th. 1902. Über mehrpolige Mitosen als Mittel zur Analyse des Zellkerns. Verhandlungen der physikalisch-medizinischen Gesellschaft zu Würzburg. Neue Folge 35:67-90. Translated by Salome Gluecksohn-Waelsch and printed by permission of Prof. Dr. Hans L. duMont, Schriftführer der Physikalisch-Medizinischen Gesellschaft Würzburg.

Embryologists of the mid-twentieth century take so much for granted that an embryo is constructed of cells whose nuclei have become what they are by appropriate processes of meiosis or mitosis that they tend to forget that at the beginning of this century the role of cell inclusions, including the nucleus, in development and heredity was not yet known. Although the role of the egg and sperm in fertilization, and something of the behavior of chromosomes, had been elucidated by Fol (1877, 1879), van Beneden (1883), O. Hertwig (1875, 1878), and others, it was left to Theodor Boveri (1862-1915) to make important contributions to our understanding of the nature and functions of the centrosomes, spindles, and asters, and of the polarity of the egg, and of the influences exerted by the cytoplasm on the nucleus. His most important contributions, however, were those concerning the nucleus itself.

He worked almost exclusively on the eggs of nematodes and echinoderms. He confirmed van Beneden's observation that in Ascaris equivalent groups of chromosomes are furnished by the two parents. He discovered the process of diminution of the chromatin in the germ-cell line in Ascaris and performed an experimental analysis demonstrating that the influence of a particular part of the cytoplasm determines in which cells the diminution occurs. This remains even today the most clear-cut demonstration of cytoplasmic influence on the nucleus that has yet been achieved. He attempted to assess the relative roles of nucleus and cytoplasm in development by fertilizing enucleated egg fragments of one species of sea urchin with the spermatazoon of another species. But his most important contribution of all was his demonstration, on solely embryological and cytological grounds, of the individuality of the chromosomes—a premise independently established by the geneticists and one at the basis of the development of the gene theory as we know it.

Fol and O. Hertwig had shown that echinoderm eggs fertilized by two spermatazoa divide simultaneously, by multipolar mitosis, to form three or four cells, then continue their development, often abnormally. In the paper reproduced here, Boveri related the abnormalities of development to the abnormal distribution of chromosomes. In an analysis that is a masterpiece of induction, he showed that it is not the number of the chromosomes but their abnormal combination that is responsible for the aberrations in development, and by the most ingenious considerations he proved that the various chromosomes differ qualitatively from one another.

This work was the subject not only of the article presented here, but also of an expanded publication, Zellenstudien VI (1907). The illustrations reproduced here are taken from Zellenstudien VI; the 1902 publication contained none. E. B. Wilson, Boveri's peer as a pioneer in the cytological investigation of development, wrote of the 1902 article, in a commemorative essay on Boveri, that "it may be doubted whether a finer example of experimental, analytical and constructive work, compressed within such narrow limits—the paper on multipolar mitosis comprises but twenty pages and is without figures—can be found in the literature of modern biology." Earlier in the same essay he prophesied that Boveri's writings would "long endure as classical models of conception, execution and exposition." History has amply confirmed his judgment. (See Erinnerungen an Theodor Boveri. Ed. by W. C. Röntgen Verlag von J.C.B. Mohr. Tübingen 1918.)

ON MULTIPOLAR MITOSIS AS A MEANS OF ANALYSIS OF THE CELL NUCLEUS

It has been known since the investigations of Fol and O. Hertwig that the penetration of two spermatozoa into the sea urchin egg results in the formation of a tetrapolar spindle and consequently in the simultaneous division of the egg into four blastomeres.[1] Driesch (13) isolated 82 such quadripolar eggs and found that they were unable to develop beyond the stage of an abnormal blastula (the so-called stereoblastula); at the very most, the first beginning of invagination could be observed. "Even an approximately typical gastrula was never formed." I had this same experience three years ago in unpublished investigations in which approximately ten dispermic eggs of *Echinus* were cultured separately. Later I was able to achieve an analogous effect in normally fertilized eggs as a result of suppression of the first cleavage division, a procedure which, as in dispermy, results in the formation of four centrosomes instead of two in the cell. Eggs of this sort cultured in isolation did not develop beyond stereoblastulae.

Several possibilities could conceivably account for this result, and it was possible to subject at least a few of these to experimental tests. I therefore decided to try to ascertain if it were possible to solve the question by means of a most careful analysis of doubly fertilized eggs.

1. Since O. and R. Hertwig (21) had found that damage to the eggs facilitated the penetration of several spermatozoa, it was necessary first of all to consider the possibility that the pathological development of dispermic eggs was caused not by the penetration of two spermatozoa, but by a pre-existing pathological condition of the eggs. The following experiment designed to test this possibility is based on an observation of mine, reported previously (7, p. 439), which indicated that the percentage of doubly fertilized eggs depends largely on the amount of sperm present.

[1] Cf. Boveri (8) concerning exceptions to this rule.

Undamaged eggs of a female were divided into two groups, one of which was exposed to very little, the other to very much sperm; examination of these eggs after the appearance of the first cleavage furrow showed that the first group had very few and the second group very many dispermic eggs. The percentage of abnormal larvae in both groups corresponded to that in dispermy.[2] It was demonstrated therefore that the pathological development of the eggs is a result of the dispermy.

2. Since, as one of the certain consequences of dispermy with resulting quadripolar eggs, each of the four blastomeres contains as a rule a different number as well as a different combination of chromosomes, the next question to be asked was whether this differential distribution of the chromatin might have an effect on the properties of the four cells. The discovery of Herbst (20), who showed that calcium-free sea water separated the individual blastomeres of the sea urchin egg from each other, makes it possible to isolate each single blastomere and to follow its fate. In this way Driesch (17) discovered that quarter blastomeres of normally fertilized eggs are able to develop into normally formed though dwarfed plutei. Whether each one of the four blastomeres is capable of such development was not determined by Driesch. I therefore repeated the experiment in such a way that I separated isolated eggs after the appearance of the second cleavage furrow into their four blastomeres, culturing separately each of these four cells of common origin. As was to be expected, each cell gave rise to a pluteus.

The result is completely different if the four blastomeres of a dispermic quadripolar egg are separated from each other. First of all, such blastomeres will not—except for rare cases—develop into plutei. Secondly, however, many of them develop into at least more or less normal gastrulae in such a high percentage that on the average almost one quarter gastrula is found for every two dispermic eggs; therefore, if we take into account the fate, previously mentioned, of whole dispermic eggs, certain quarters achieve more separately than do all four quarters together. Thirdly and finally—and this is the most significant result of the experiment—as a rule, each of the four blastomeres develops differently. Since development in most of them does not proceed very far, these differences do not ordinarily amount to very much; however, there are also striking cases in which beside one quarter that broke up into separate cells at the blastula stage, or that became a permanent stereoblastula, a more or less normal gastrula is found, or even a young pluteus with segmentation of the gut and skeletal primordia. Whereas, therefore, the four blastomeres of a normally divided egg are equivalent, the properties of the blastomeres of a dispermic egg differ from each other in many respects and to varying degrees.

2 Numerical evidence for this and other statements will be given elsewhere.

3. After this result it was to be expected that different potencies of the four quarters should frequently be demonstrable in the development of whole dispermic eggs also. This indeed turned out to be the case. When the eggs have developed into swollen blastulae with polar differentiation, a stage at which, as a rule, they still appear perfectly normal, one or two of the quadrants of the blastula located between two meridians now begin in many cases to slough cells into the interior. Conse-

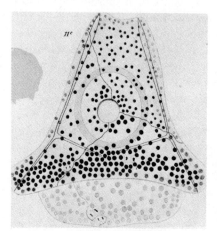   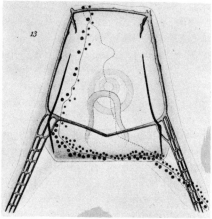

Figure 11c, Plate II   **Figure 13, Plate III**

Two figures from Plates II and III of Boveri's definitive 1907 publication on the development of dispermic sea-urchin eggs. Figure at left, Fig. 11c, Plate II. Pluteus from a *Strongylocentrotus* egg that divided into 3 cells at the first cleavage, viewed from behind. Magnification about 650×. Figure at the right, Fig. 13, Plate III. Pluteus from a *Sphaerechinus* egg that divided into three cells at the first cleavage, viewed from in front. The border of the third containing small nuclei is shown by a line (red in the original figure). A few nuclei on either side of this border, along its course on the front surface, are shown to illustrate the difference in their sizes.

quently, this entire marginal portion appears opaque, or the whole quarter dissolves, shedding its cells to the outside. Finally the remaining part, which is at first still open, closes up again into a vesicle. But there are further events, and here my results differ from the experiences of Driesch mentioned above and from my own earlier ones. Some of the quadrants of the embryo develop into gastrulae and form a skeleton, but now usually in a way that expresses the different potencies of the individual regions, e.g., with an archenteron asymmetrical in degree of differentiation or in location, or with the skeleton present on one side only and even there more or less abnormal.

4. However, even plutei varying from grossly abnormal to completely

normal in structure may develop from dispermic eggs, and here an experimentally obtained variety of dispermic development is particularly
illuminating. In the experiments described above in which the development of isolated blastomeres of dispermic eggs was studied, it was necessary to remove the fertilization membrane, which can be accomplished,
according to Driesch, by shaking the eggs a few minutes after fertilization.
With this procedure, I observed almost regularly the phenomenon which
Morgan (24) already described but whose origin has not been explained,
namely, that some eggs divided simultaneously into three blastomeres.
There are two ways to demonstrate[3] that the three blastomeres are
derived from dispermic eggs in which, as a result of shaking, one of the
sperm centrosomes did not divide; this one gave rise to one pole, whereas
the two other poles were the result of the normal division of the second
sperm centrosome. Morgan studied the development of ten such tripolar
eggs and three of these reached the stage of fully formed gastrulae. I
myself have cultured more than 900 isolated specimens some of which
were whole, some of which were separated into their three blastomeres;
in principle I made the same observations as on quadripolar eggs, noting,
in particular, the same lack of equivalence of the regions originating from
multipolar cleavage. However, the tendency for normal development is
much stronger in the tripolar than in the quadripolar eggs and consequently a quite considerable percentage of plutei, some of them completely normal, are obtained from them. Even the quadripolar dispermic
eggs give rise to plutei in a very small percentage of cases; however, I
never found a completely normal one among these.

5. To explain the facts just reported, we had best start with the
question of the possible origin of the differences in developmental
potencies of the cells resulting from multipolar cleavage. The differential
cannot lie in the cytoplasm. The reason for this is that the tetraster of a
dispermic egg—only these were used for the blastomere separation experiments—and similarly the triaster, are located in a plane (karyokinetic
plane[4]) perpendicular to the axis of the egg. This can be directly observed
in *Strongylocentrotus* by the relation to the pigment ring and can be indirectly concluded from a consideration of the two abnormal cleavage
types studied by Driesch (13) and Morgan (24) in connection with the
axial relations demonstrated by myself. The four blastomeres of the
quadripolar egg are just as equipotential in their protoplasm as those of
the normal four blastomere stage. Similarly, a differential in the centrosomes cannot be assumed. The reason for this is that each two of the
four centrosomes of dispermic eggs correspond to one of the two of the
normally fertilized egg which have identical properties as can be concluded from the study of normal development and all pertinent experi-

[3] In respect to this and other evidence I refer for the time being to the more detailed
description elsewhere.
[4] Cf. my evidence in 9 and 10.

ments. At most in the tripolar eggs the possibility might be considered that the one undivided centrosome differed qualitatively from the two others. However, quite aside from the completely identical behavior of the three cells in the subsequent stages of division, it is specifically the tripolar eggs that may give rise to completely normal larvae. But even different potencies of the centrosomes could not cause what is demonstrated to us by the development of the dispermic eggs, namely, an almost unlimited variability from complete normality to abnormalities of the highest degree, and specifically the so extremely variable and in each particular case so differently combined potencies of the blastomeres derived from simultaneous multiple division. These phenomena could only be explained on the basis of a process which itself is subject to corresponding variability and such a process is presented only in the manner of *distribution of the chromosomes.*

After I realized in 1887 (1) that the karyokinetic figure results from a secondary connecting together of two cell organelles previously independent of each other, on the one hand the centrosomes with their spheres, on the other hand the chromosomes, I was able to demonstrate in 1888 (3, pp. 180 ff), as a result of the first detailed analysis of multipolar division figures, that the distribution of the chromosomes between more than two poles is determined by chance. "Karyokinesis, which in the presence of two poles is a mechanism of almost ideal perfection for the purpose of dividing a nucleus into two daughter nuclei identical in quantity and quality, turns these advantages practically into the reverse as soon as a larger number of centrosomes begins to take effect. . . . Number, size, and—if we have to assign different qualities to the individual chromatic elements—also the quality of the resulting daughter nuclei are determined by chance" (3, p. 185). If we consider our particular case, the number of chromosomes of the mature *Strongylocentrotus* egg is approximately 18, and the identical number is found in the spermatozoon. The first cleavage spindle therefore contains 36 elements each of which divides into half, so that each daughter cell similarly contains 36. The number of chromosomes in the doubly fertilized eggs amounts to $3 \times 18 = 54$. As a result of division of each chromosome into two halves, 108 daughter chromosomes are produced, which are distributed (in the typical case) into four cells. In the case of equal distribution, each of these four cells would contain 27 elements, that is nine less than normal. Actually, such an equal distribution occurs probably only in extremely rare exceptions; the four cells therefore, obtain on the average not only fewer, but also different numbers of chromosomes, and particularly quite different combinations of them. If we designate the individual chromosomes of the dispermic first cleavage nucleus A, B, C, D, etc., then we see that in the case of multipolar cleavage of the egg into four blastomeres only two blastomeres can have a representative of A, or of B, etc., whereas no representative of this particular chromosome gets into the other two blastomeres.

6. Now the question arises: Is the different potency of each individual blastomere of the quadripolar egg based on unequal quantitative distribution or do we have to ascribe different qualities to the individual chromosomes in order to explain this heterogeneity? That a particular number of chromosomes in itself is not required for normal development was demonstrated by myself in experiments, confirmed by Delage (11) and Winkler (32), in which the development of enucleated egg fragments fertilized by one sperm was studied and in which normal plutei developed although they had only half of the normal amount of chromatin and number of elements, that is, only the chromosomes of one sperm nucleus. What was demonstrated here for the sperm nucleus has since been shown to be true also for the egg nucleus as a result of the investigations on artificial parthenogenesis by J. Loeb (23) and E. B. Wilson (30).[5]

We could now also put up the following argument: The number of chromosomes, above a certain minimal limit, does not matter as long as the same number is present in each cell. If the individual regions of the same embryo contain nuclei with different numbers of chromosomes, then abnormalities occur. However, this assumption can also be refuted in two ways. First of all, on the basis of the experiments of blastomere dissociation. Each isolated blastomere of the quadripolar egg has on the average more than the necessary minimal number of chromosomes, and even in the most unfavorable distribution, at least two of the four blastomeres have to obtain more than the minimal number. According to our assumption therefore, each quadripolar egg dissociated into its four blastomeres should yield at least two plutei, which is however not the case.

However, the untenability of this hypothesis may be demonstrated

---

[5] It is irrelevant for this argument whether the normal number of chromosomes is restored in later embryonic stages, a fact which, incidentally, I still doubt on the basis of my investigations. Delage, however, recently extended (12) to artificial parthenogenesis his contention, proposed originally for merogony, that the normal number of chromosomes could be found in later embryonic stages. He was able to count with certainty and in numerous cases, 16 to 19, on the average 18, chromosomes in the cells of parthenogenetic embryos of *Strongylocentrotus*, and thus he considers his earlier statements completely proven. However, it escaped him here that the normal chromosome number of *Strongylocentrotus* is not as he assumes 18 on the average, but 36, as I have found without exception in three different years (1888, 1896 and 1902); the chromosome number of the individual pronucleus is therefore on the average 18, a figure which R. Hertwig (22) actually determined thus (16 to 18) for the egg nucleus in preparation for independent division. According to the hypothesis of the individuality of the chromosomes, therefore we would expect the average number of 18 as found by Delage in the parthenogenetic as well as in the merogonic egg of *Strongylocentrotus;* thus Delage's new counts prove exactly what he believes to disprove, namely, the *failure of regulation of chromosome number.*

in the whole dispermic egg. Also, I had determined previously in my experiments on merogony (5, 7) that larvae from enucleated egg fragments had considerably smaller nuclei than those from nucleated fragments or from whole eggs. This observation I have found to be confirmed in the clearest possible way in a repetition of these experiments just completed, as I shall report in detail in a separate paper. I only would like to mention here the following observation: If one selects from the fragmented eggs of a female on the one hand nucleated, and on the other hand enucleated fragments, and fertilizes these with identical sperm, the larvae developing from the latter fragments contain considerably smaller, and, as I now must add, considerably more nuclei than larvae of the same size[6] and age developing from the former fragments. Thus, the size and number of the nuclei and accordingly also the size and number of cells of a sea urchin larva are respectively—other things being equal—directly and inversely proportional to the number of chromosomes in the mother cell. I was able to determine without doubt, by raising larvae in which I knew with certainty the chromosome number of the individual blastomeres, that this rule holds not only for different larvae but also for different regions of one and the same larva, provided that these regions are derived from blastomeres with different numbers of chromosomes. I cite here merely the not infrequent case of dispermy where only one sperm nucleus unites with the egg nucleus and a normal first cleavage spindle is formed by the chromosomes of these two, whereas the other sperm nucleus comes to lie in a separate spindle which therefore contains only half as many chromosomes. Such eggs almost always divide, as I have described previously (8), into two cells, each with one large and one small nucleus. However, it occurs, sometimes in the beginning, more frequently in one of the later cleavage divisions,[7] that regions with small nuclei separate cleanly from those with large nuclei and consequently, larvae develop whose properties and significance I shall discuss below. Here it may suffice to state that these larvae consist of one part with large nuclei and another part with small nuclei and correspondingly more numerous cells, quite in the same relation that we have estab-

---

[6] This sentence holds true also, even if not quite as strictly, for larvae developing from fragments of different sizes. It is true furthermore, not only for cases with decreased but also for those with an abnormally increased number of chromosomes. I have succeeded in obtaining cleavage of the egg with twice the normal number, that is, in *Strongylocentrotus*, with approximately 72 instead of 36 chromosomes. The larvae contain accordingly much bigger nuclei than those developing from normal control eggs, and, in connection with this, much bigger and many fewer cells. They show only about half the normal number of mesenchymal cells, and never produce, obviously because of this small number of cells, completely normal plutei.

[7] Dr. E. Teichmann will report more details from his own investigations about the variations which occur here.

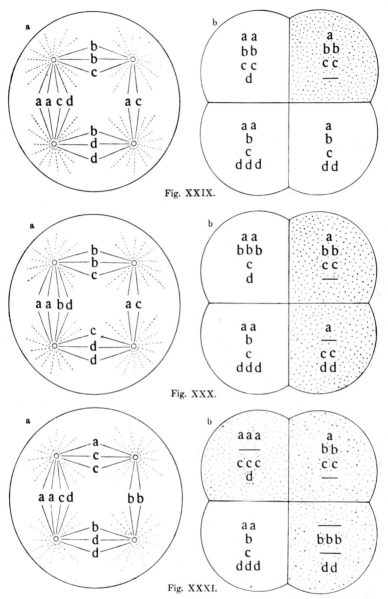

Fig. XXIX.

Fig. XXX.

Fig. XXXI.

Text figures (XXIX, XXX and XXXI) from Boveri's definitive 1907 publication on the development of dispermic sea-urchin eggs, indicating possible random combinations of chromosomes on the spindles of tetrapolar eggs. These figures bore no legends in the original; they were explained in the text. The blastomeres that are unstippled contain chromosomes *a, b, c,* and *d,* and presumably develop normally; those lacking *a, b, c,* or *d,* or several of these, are stippled and would develop abnormally.

lished between larvae developed from nucleated and those from enucleated egg fragments.

Once this is established, the conclusion is unavoidable: since larvae from normally cleaved eggs possess nuclei of equal size in corresponding regions of the organism, those larvae in which regions with different nuclear sizes are found must be derived from eggs in which each of these regions starts out from a blastomere with a different chromosome number. Now, I have found, among the almost normal plutei of the tripolar eggs described above, four in which one-third of the larvae contain very small and correspondingly more numerous nuclei, and the remaining two-thirds contain large nuclei.[8] In the living pluteus, the border at which two such regions meet usually cannot be recognized. Thus it is proven that the different number of chromosomes as it happens to be distributed to the various regions of the egg as a result of multipolar division is not to blame for the pathological development of dispermic eggs.

It should be noted as an important supplement to this statement that I have obtained numerous highly pathological products from tripolar eggs in which size differences between the nuclei could not be demonstrated; in these, therefore, an equal or practically equal distribution of the chromosomes into the three primary blastomeres must have occurred. In this way, the irrelevance of a definitive amount of chromatin has been proven from the opposite direction.

One other idea might perhaps come to mind, namely, that different numbers of chromosomes could occur in the individual cells, but only certain quite definite numbers, namely, those typical for the individual pronucleus and their multiples, but no intermediate numbers. If we consider that it is possible to obtain hybrids between species with different numbers of chromosomes, then such a possibility already becomes highly improbable. However, it also can be disproved more strictly. Namely, if we assume for the plutei described above with a third containing small nuclei, that these small nuclei contain the chromosome number of the individual pronucleus, then it is a necessary consequence that the two other thirds with their nuclei of almost identical size present *intermediate numbers,* thus refuting the hypothesis.

7. Thus, only one possibility remains, namely that not a definite number, but a *definite combination of chromosomes* is essential for normal development, and this means nothing else than that *the individual chromosomes must possess different qualities.* At the moment, we are unable to give a more definite setting to this irrefutable conclusion;

---

[8] It should be noted that this third with small nuclei may belong to different regions of the pluteus. It always, however, represents a region which comprises all zones from the animal to the vegetative pole so that therefore a third of the gut also has correspondingly small nuclei.

only one more exact statement can be made, namely, that all qualities, at least those essential to reach the pluteus stage that can be raised in our aquaria, have to be represented in the dispermic egg at least three times. For according to the experiments on merogony and parthenogenesis the egg nucleus as well as each sperm nucleus contain all qualities.

If we now consider all chromosomes of a dispermic egg to be unselectively mixed in a uniform first cleavage nucleus, and if we suppose that each quality exists in three chromosomes only—in one element from each pronucleus—then the probability that a certain quality is transmitted into each blastomere amounts to 70% in tripolar and 40% in quadripolar eggs. If the individual qualities of each pronucleus are distributed between nine chromosomes (the actual number in *Echinus microtuberculatus*), then the probability that each blastomere of the tripolar eggs obtains all qualities, that is, at least nine chromosomes, representing the whole set, is calculated at 4%, and in the quadripolar egg at 0.0026%.[9]

A strictly absolute value cannot be assigned to these figures. There exist in these distributions conditions which evade all calculations. In addition, it is doubtful what still can be considered a normal pluteus, and particularly it is conceivable that an occasional larva is excluded whose abnormality may be explained in another fashion than by a defect of chromatin qualities. Finally, the number of cases available to me (695 tripolar and 1170 quadripolar eggs) is not very considerable; also, these are derived from three different species. If we take all this into consideration, then we shall find the agreement of the expected with the actual result nevertheless significant. I have found, among the 695 tripolar eggs cultured as wholes, 58 almost normal plutei, that is 8.3% compared with the expected 4%. Among the ten larvae considered to be plutei obtained from the 1170 quadripolar eggs, there was not a single one as normal as the 58 obtained from the tripolar eggs and just mentioned. According to our calculation of course, their occurrence here can hardly be expected.

8. However, not only are the chances for a favorable distribution of the chromosomes greater in the tripolar eggs in general, but there is the additional possibility of a particularly regular distribution which is lacking in the quadripolar eggs. In the case of three poles, it is possible for a complete pronucleus to get into each of the three spindles and from this constellation there could be derived a chromatin complement of the three blastomeres which corresponds almost completely to that of the normal; each cell would possess the normal number of chromosomes and a double set of all qualities, one, that of the egg nucleus and of one of the sperm nuclei, the second, that of the egg nucleus and of the second sperm nucleus, the third that of both sperm nuclei. From this condition,

---

9 This calculation is based on the assumption that all three or four poles are connected by spindles into a triangle or quadrangle.

I would like to derive, in addition to the very interesting asymmetrical forms, the few absolutely normal plutei that I obtained from tripolar eggs and whose nuclei of consistently equal size demand the assumption of an equal distribution of chromatin.

9. If we now examine the abnormal and pathological larvae from the point of view we have reached, they may be usefully divided into three groups:

a) Highly pathological. Here I include all those larvae that had not attained the morphological properties of a normal pluteus in any respect. This group contains, by the way, great variations that will not be considered in detail here.

b) Larvae in which certain pluteus characteristics are missing or appear to have developed abnormally whereas the others are normal. A few examples of this group may be cited: A case where a vesicle-shaped, completely anenteric larva has a perfectly developed skeleton on the left side, whereas the right one is missing completely; furthermore, cases where an otherwise normal pluteus from a tripolar egg lacks completely one or two thirds of the skeleton as though they had been cut away; finally, cases also from tripolar eggs where one third of the pluteus, otherwise practically normal, has no pigment cells. In some of these cases, it was possible to conclude from the nuclear size that the border-line of the defect coincides with the borderline between two regions derived from two different primary blastomeres.

c) Larvae derived from tripolar eggs which though normal within each separate part show the same trait in a different "individual" type on each side, so that they appear more or less asymmetrical. These cases relate closely to my earlier experiments of hybridization of enucleated egg fragments, and if on the one hand they do not operate with differences as great as species differences, on the other hand they are also not open to the objections that could be raised against the hybridization experiments. It is undoubtedly true in the cases just mentioned that different nuclear substance in identical cytoplasm produces a different larval type. These larvae could be explained by the kind of particularly regular chromatin distribution mentioned under 8 where it may happen, for example, that one larval third which contains the right part of mouth and anus contains in addition to the derivatives of all the maternal chromosomes those of one sperm nucleus, whereas the corresponding parts of the other side have obtained in addition to the maternal elements those of the other sperm nucleus. In this case, the individual differences inherent in the two sperm nuclei, differences which otherwise would appear in two different larvae, develop next to each other in the symmetrical organs of one and the same larva. As a matter of fact, I was able to make drawings from the different types of normal control larvae where I combined the right half of one type of larvae with the left half of another one; such pictures corresponded almost exactly to the plutei of tripolar eggs in question.

The experiments just reported appear to me to explain the symptoms of pathological dispermy. We are able to say: double fertilization and pathological development are not related to each other only indirectly in such a way that a pathological condition of the egg leads to pathological development on the one hand, and on the other hand makes dispermy possible, but pathological development is a consequence of dispermy, since the penetration of two spermatozoa ruins the previously perfectly normal egg. However, dispermy does not under all circumstances lead to pathological development, but only under certain conditions which however are almost always present. These conditions are not necessarily inherent in the increase of the number of centrosomes to three or four; for we have found that plutei may develop also from tripolar and quadripolar eggs. And since the *cytoplasm* behaves alike in all cases of multipolar division, it follows from the development of these plutei also, in agreement with the results of E. B. Wilson (31), that simultaneous division into more than two cells is not injurious to the cytoplasm.[10] Rather, the harmful effect of multiple poles is due to the fact that as a rule they cause an abnormal chromatin complement in the daughter cells.

The number of cells is irrelevant in this abnormal distribution. To be sure, the chromosomes as carriers of different qualities have to be present in each cell in a certain minimal number comprising all qualities; but beyond this, their number is irrelevant up to an upper limit harmful for other reasons; and in the reverse sense, a normal chromosome number in all cells, which is possible in tripolar eggs, does not guarantee normal development.

That in spite of the distribution of the dividing chromosomes into more than two cells, all these cells still may obtain all qualities is due to the fact that each quality is represented at least in three different chromosomes in the dispermic eggs. In the case of simultaneous multiple division of a normal first cleavage nucleus each cell could also obtain all qualities; however, the occurrence of such a case would be almost infinitely improbable.

These results on dispermy are in complete agreement with those obtained in studies of cells which for other reasons contain several centrosomes. As mentioned in the beginning, the suppression of the first cleavage furrow has the effect that the two spindles that should belong to

---

[10] Already in 1888 (3, p. 185) the analysis of multipolar mitoses led me to the conclusion "that indeed the cell substance is prepared for a simultaneous multiple division, not, however, the nucleus." However, just now I have reason to assume that this statement does not apply to all egg cells.

the two half-blastomeres come to lie next to each other in the undivided egg. E. B. Wilson (31) recently described cases of this kind, in which this condition led to a direct quadripolar division of the egg, and he obtained normal plutei from such eggs. In my own earlier experiments (8), such eggs divided first of all into two binucleate cells, in which again two spindles appeared and this condition was perpetuated until, sooner or later, the two spindles united into a four-polar figure; then, due to quadripolar division, uninucleate cells resulted which in turn continued to divide regularly. As mentioned above, these eggs did not develop beyond the stage of pathological blastulae. The experiences with dispermy provided the simple explanation for this different development. In Wilson's cases, each of the four simultaneously arising blastomeres obtains the very same chromosomes as in normal cleavage; in the cases observed by myself, the nuclei are also normal as long as they remain separate; however, as soon as a four-polar figure replaces the two separate spindles, the daughter nuclei must, as a rule, just as in dispermy, obtain faulty combinations of chromosomes and thus become pathological.

Closely related to these cases is that type of dispermy where one sperm nucleus remains separate, leading to the formation of two separate, usually parallel, spindles. We reported briefly above (6) about the early development of such eggs. Since the separate sperm nucleus possesses all the qualities necessary for pluteus development, the potentialities of this type of doubly fertilized eggs must be essentially identical to those of the cases just described where the first cleavage furrow is suppressed. If, as in Wilson's experiments, simultaneous division into four blastomeres were to occur, normal, even though not completely normal, development would be expected. In the dispermic eggs isolated by myself with two parallel spindles, such an immediate division into four blastomeres never occurred. However, several underwent a tripolar division into one binucleate and two uninucleate cells. I do not want to elaborate here the rather variable details; we may formulate the result on the basis of the various cases by stating that such eggs maintain the ability of normal development as long as, and to the extent that, the four centers present in the egg or the succeeding cell generations are not combined into one multipolar figure. If, before this happens, a division into uninucleate cells takes place, then the region of the embryo originating from this part has been definitely salvaged for further normal development. Thus, it can be explained that the percentage of larvae reaching a stage beyond that of the blastula is considerably greater in this constellation than where both sperm nuclei have united with the egg nucleus; and it is a beautiful confirmation of all our conclusions that the best developed larva that I obtained from a *tetrapolar* dispermic egg was derived from such a case with a separate sperm spindle.

In general, we may say this for the *Echinus* egg: multiple centrosomes in a cell are harmless for the cell complex that will eventually develop as long as only two poles each unite into one karyokinetic figure and as long as the original nucleus or nuclei were normal. If eventually a cell is formed around each of the centrosomes and around the nuclei resulting from the successive mitotic processes, then all of these will be normal as Wilson actually showed recently in his experiments on the suppression of cell division, and as we have known for some time from a similar process in some cleavage types. Multiple centrosomes have a pathological effect only if groups or more than two divide the available nuclear substance among themselves. In this case, there is no guarantee, or even the possibility, that all cells will be supplied with a portion of all the different qualities represented by the individual chromosomes.

With this we proceed from a consideration of our special case to the general significance of the results just described. A differential value of the chromosomes,[11] as concluded frequently before from studies of the morphology of mitosis, has now been proven and thus a first step has been made towards the analysis of the physiological constitution of the cell nucleus. The difference of our experiments on the nucleus from the previous ones[12] lies in the fact that until now, nothing else could be done but remove the entire nucleus and examine the results of its absence. We supply the cell with a nucleus which lacks certain portions and we follow the consequence of this defect. We have found that such a nucleus is sufficient for certain processes of ontogenetic events but not for others, so that it transmits, for example, the ability of invagination to the derivatives destined to form the gut, but it does not transfer the necessary qualities to the cells destined to form skeleton, or vice versa. We have to conclude from this that only a certain combination of chromosomes, probably no less than the total of all those present in each pronucleus, represent the entire essence of the organism's structure insofar as this is determined by the nucleus.

This recognition leads to the conclusion that the most important aspects of the physiological constitution of the nucleus are completely

11 I myself have maintained until now (4, p. 56), primarily on the basis of my experiences with *Ascaris meg.*, that the chromosomes are essentially equal but individually different formations, and the same opinion I find maintained by Weismann in the recently published "Lectures on the Theory of Descent." This assumption has been refuted for the sea urchin egg by my experiments; and it is clear that therefore the simple considerations which Weismann developed for the reduction division also require at least considerable modification since random distribution of the chromosomes into two groups should in general be equally harmful as a multipolar mitosis. These and related problems, as well as the relevance of this to the results of botanists in studies of hybrids and their descendants, will be discussed separately.

12 My own experiments on fertilization and particularly on hybridization of enucleated egg fragments constitute a certain exception here.

inaccessible to an analysis with the present methods of physiological chemistry. In this respect, Biology has at its disposal means of analysis of much superior resolving power. Even if the biologist is not capable of removing individual chromosomes as would be the ideal case, he possesses, nevertheless, in multipolar mitosis a tool for the production of the most diverse combinations, and embryogeny during which the qualities of the original nucleus unfold themselves provides the analysis of those qualities which are made possible by the various combinations ("Embryonalanalyse" of the cell nucleus).

What could be demonstrated here for the nucleus of the sea urchin egg is valid, with certain modifications, for all nuclei that divide mitotically. For mitotic division itself, however, we may consider as proved what has been assumed for a long time; namely that its goal lies in the transfer of the qualities present in *one* nucleus into many nuclei, and that it is specifically the function of the *bipolar* mitotic figure to multiply successively the nucleus in its totality. These statements, I believe, will from now on be counted among the firm basic principles of general physiology.

If we now consider some details more closely, the experiments offer us the first exact indications about the role of the nucleus in ontogenesis by the certainty with which they permit us to ascribe the disturbances of development exclusively to the chromosomes. It appears that the initial steps up to the blastula stage are independent of the quality of nuclear substance, even though it is essential that the nuclear substance be of a kind capable of existing in the egg.[13] The necessity for particular chromosomes becomes apparent first with the formation of the primary mesenchyme and from then on shows up in all processes as far as development can be observed. But not only do certain chromosomes prove to be essential in this connection; in addition, it appears that with respect to those characters in which we are able to recognize individual variations, the nuclear substance and not the cytoplasmic cell substance imposes its specific character on the developing trait.

Since the dependence of the developmental processes subsequent to the blastula stage on certain definite chromosomes has been determined, and since, on the other hand, it has been demonstrated that the chromosomes of the sperm nucleus, even in the absence of those of the egg nucleus, possess the qualities necessary for the development of all these characters, it may be supposed that the spermatozoon in the normally fertilized egg has an effect on all the processes beginning with the formation of the primary mesenchyme. If this were not the case, then it would have to be concluded in connection with the results of merogony that the sperm chromosomes serve to make possible the development of the

[13] Cf. in this connection, my discussion in 6 (p. 469) and 8 (pp. 14 ff). Incidentally, the statements hold of course for the time being only for Echinids.

traits under discussion, but that the character of these traits is determined not by them but by the egg protoplasm. Actually, Driesch (15) did conclude from his experiments on hybridization of various sea urchin species that all larval characters with the exception of the skeleton were *purely maternal* and not affected by the sperm chromosomes. My own experiments however, demonstrated to me that these statements were erroneous. Not only, as I have shown previously (5, 7), the form and skeleton of the pluteus, but also the shape of the larvae before the formation of the skeleton, the amount and the pattern of the pigments and the number of primary mesenchyme cells may be influenced by the spermatozoon. This means, therefore, that precisely from the time when certain definite chromosomes, known to be present both in the egg and in the sperm nucleus, prove essential for further development, precisely from this point on, developmental processes show themselves influenced in their specificity by both parents equally; whereas earlier stages, for which, according to our results, specific chromosomes are not necessary, demonstrate a purely maternal character (Boveri, 6, p. 469; Driesch, 15). From all these facts, it will have to be concluded that the role of the chromosomes in ontogenesis corresponds rather exactly to the views which have found a brief though not very fitting expression in the designation of these structures as "carriers of heredity."

I would like to ascribe to the cytoplasm of the sea urchin egg only the initial and simplest of properties responsible for differentiation. Polarity and bilateral symmetry depend on the cytoplasmic pattern, and all malformations connected with these axial relations, such as duplications of larvae or the perpetual blastulae originating from fragments of the animal half only and incapable of undergoing polar differentiation, are based on disturbances of defects of the cytoplasm.[14] The structure of the egg cytoplasm takes care, if I may say so, of the purely "promorphological" tasks, that is, it provides the most general basic form, the framework within which all specific details are filled in by the nucleus. Or, the relationship may perhaps also be expressed by stating that simple cytoplasmic differentiation serves to start the machine whose essential and probably most complicated mechanism is located in the nuclei.

I am able to clarify this interpretation still further if I compare it briefly with the opinions that Driesch (18, 19) recently expressed about all attempts to explain ontogenetic events. He says: only a complicated

---

[14] Cf. here my experiments (9). Since that time I have repeated and extended the experiments on the development of purely animal (completely free of pigment) fragments of the *Strongylocentrotus* egg; not one of such cultured fragments from three different females developed beyond the stage of the blastula, whereas all pigmented fragments cultured as controls, and among them considerably smaller ones, developed into plutei.

machine could achieve what we are facing in ontogenesis; however, we are not dealing with a machine here, since a machine would not remain the same if random parts were removed or if parts were transposed in a random fashion, as can be done without harmful effects both in the cytoplasm and nuclei of the *Echinus* egg. The contradiction construed here by Driesch which, in addition to other considerations, leads him to postulate an "autonomy of living processes," appears to me not to exist in reality. I want to disregard completely the fact that the statement that *any part of the cytoplasm* could be removed without harming the potencies of the remaining parts has now had to be restricted very considerably. However, what is more important, also, the assumption that the *cytoplasm could be transposed at random* in the young egg without harmful effects is based on insufficient experience. I have demonstrated earlier (9), and since have been able to determine even more exactly, that minute translocations of the cytoplasm at the vegetative pole lead to the formation of duplications; in the meantime, I have obtained larvae with a duplicated or even triplicated archenteron and others with severe deformations and malformations of the skeleton[15] from clusters of translocated blastomeres provided that the translocations were not corrected, as is often the case. The *Echinus* egg therefore, is nothing less than a harmonic equipotential system. Finally, however, and this is the decisive point, any portion of "nuclei" but not any portion of "a nucleus" may be removed from the young *Echinus* egg. Taking something away from the nucleus has not even been tried in the experiments of Driesch; my own experiments, which did accomplish this, teach us that the nucleus, whose structure may have any degree of complexity, behaves just as Driesch demands from a "machine" in the discussion quoted above.

The conflict that Driesch feels is in my opinion resolved by these facts in a simple manner. It is certainly true that the hypothesis maintained by Roux and Weismann (25, 26, 29) of a differential distribution of that complex structure, postulated now also by Driesch, by way of differential nuclear division, has been disproven, at least for the early development of Echinids, by the experiments of Driesch.[16] However, it appears to me that the quite peculiar interaction of the cytoplasm with its simple structure and differential division and the nucleus with its complex structure and manifold total multiplication may still achieve

---

[15] My colleague Driesch kindly informed me that he also repeated his earlier experiments on the translocation of blastomeres (14, 16) and that he obtained now essentially the same results as I did.

[16] Cf., also, my speculations in 3 (pp. 182 ff), and in 8 (pp. 7 ff) about the difficulties which the development and constitution of multipolar mitoses present for the assumption of a differential nuclear division. The objections raised against these speculations on the basis of the pathological effect of multipolar mitoses are based on a logical mistake.

what Weismann and Roux attempted to explain with the help of differential nuclear division. When the primitive differences of the cytoplasm, as expressed in the existence of layers, are transferred to the cleaved egg without any change in the relationships of the layers, they affect the originally equal nuclei unequally by unfolding (activating) or suppressing certain nuclear qualities, as may be visualized directly in the cleavage of *Ascaris*. The inequalities of the nuclei, in some cases perhaps of temporary nature only, lend different potencies to the cytoplasm, that to begin with was differentiated only by degrees. Thus new cytoplasmic conditions are created which again release in certain nuclei the activation or suppression of certain qualities thus imprinting on these cells in turn a specific character and so on, and so on. In short: a continually increasing specification of the originally totipotent complex nuclear structure, and consequently, indirectly, of the cytoplasm of the individual cells, appears conceivable on the basis of physico-chemical events once the machine has been set in motion by the simple cytoplasmic differentiation of the egg. To explain the origin of normal larvae from isolated blastomeres, as well as from fragments of the egg and the blastula, it is, according to this view, necessary only to propose the assumption—well supported, incidentally—that these fragments obtain from the egg differences such that they release the first nuclear differentiations in the identical manner as does the cytoplasm of the entire egg. The sea urchin egg, apparently one of the eggs with the simplest cytoplasmic structure, teaches us that not every region is able to do this; and we know of other eggs (Ctenophores) in which the releasing egg structure is differentiated so highly that no isolated part of the cytoplasm is able to take the place of the whole.

Whoever has followed the literature on these questions that are under so much discussion knows that various authors have opinions that agree more or less closely in one or the other point with those just expressed. O. Hertwig, Weismann, de Vries, should be cited here. Furthermore, Driesch earlier developed possibilities, which he later rejected again, corresponding in many respects to my own point of view. Also with respect to Roux's doctrine, the common points, such as the interpretation of the nucleus as the real determinant, and that of the differentiation of the cytoplasm as a releasing factor, appear to outweigh by far the difference which lies in his assumption of qualitatively unequal nuclear division. The progress which, as I believe, has been attained by my experiments consists in just this: that now, even though in a field that is still narrow, speculations have been replaced by facts.

Of the manifold relations to other problems inherent in our results, only two points should be considered here briefly; first of all, whether any phenomena are known which appear in a new light as a result of the new insight. In this respect, it appears to me that certain asymmetries, that appear as abnormalities in bilateral animals, particularly in insects, may find a simple explanation on the basis of my results. If a bee has the structure of a drone on its right side and of a worker on its left side, then the right side has developed like a parthenogenetic and the left side like a fertilized egg, i.e., the right side like an egg which has maternal chromosomes only, the left side like one with chromosomes of both parents. On the basis of this consideration, and since it could be demonstrated that in the sea urchin egg asymmetries of a definite kind may be created by an unequal chromosomal composition of different egg regions, the conclusion is almost unavoidable that the reason for asymmetries of insects consisting in a mosaic configuration of male and female areas will also have to be looked for in nuclear differences. In the case just mentioned of purely symmetrical hermaphroditism, it cannot be a question of dispermy. We have to consider a different abnormal chromatin distribution such as I have found earlier in sea urchin eggs (2).[17] Here one half-blastomere contains maternal chromosomes only and the other mixed maternal and paternal chromosomes, i.e., precisely what had to be assumed for the hermaphroditic bees if the reason for this abnormality lies in the chromatin. Due to the peculiar conditions of bee development, the occurrence of such an abnormality is apparently much favored since it appears possible that the egg nucleus is already divided before union with the sperm nucleus as a result of its parthenogenetic potencies, and that the sperm nucleus unites only with one of the cleavage nuclei. This union could even be postponed until later cleavage stages and polyspermy, which is known to occur in bees, could have the effect that sperm nuclei unite with certain derivatives of the egg nucleus and not with others. In this way, the most diverse mixtures of male and female characters could result, as has been actually observed.[18]

Finally, a second question which should be touched upon briefly is that of the consequences of multipolar mitoses in later embryonic stages and in mature tissues. A beginning in this direction may be reported already. In the *Echinus* egg I succeeded in certain individual blastomeres, e.g., in one of the half or quarter blastomeres, to produce multipolar division figures in the macromeres or mesomeres and thus to render

[17] Cf. here also the more detailed demonstration which E. Teichmann (28) gave in this connection based on material preserved by me.

[18] Compare C. Th. von Siebold (27). It could perhaps be objected, against the explanation mentioned above, that a cleavage nucleus capable of division by itself and a sperm nucleus together would cause a quadripolar figure and thus pathological development of the corresponding egg region, similarly to two blastomere nuclei with their two centrosomes in the *Echinus* egg. However, just as the sperm nucleus in the bee egg forms a regular division figure with the egg nucleus capable of independent division, so this will also be possible with a later cleavage nucleus. We are dealing here no doubt with conditions of the cytocenters which deviate from those of the sea urchin egg and probably of most other eggs.

pathological the particular egg region arising from these. The details, interesting in other connections, shall not be discussed here;[19] it is of importance for our considerations that in those experiments which cause pathological conditions exclusively in the derivatives of the macromeres or of the mesomeres, the formation of the pluteus is usually not hindered. The pathological cells frequently enter the cleavage cavity (primary coelom) sooner or later in large numbers, but the normal parts group themselves into a smaller whole, just as in the case of complete removal of portions of the egg.

The fate of the pathological cell clusters that enter the interior cannot be determined in view of the limited life span of sea urchin larvae raised artificially. If, however, we want to classify these formations according to the points of view of pathological anatomy, then we have to designate them as "tumors" and thus arrive at the statement that multipolar mitosis might under certain conditions lead to the development of tumor-like formations. Could not this conclusion throw some light on the riddle of tumors? We are confronted here with quite a peculiar phenomenon, namely that a cell complex loses to some extent the normal qualities of its tissue, and by the maintenance or even occasionally an increase of the ability of the cells to multiply, a departure from the parent tissue and an abnormal proliferation contrary to the plan of the whole occur. It is not disease in the sense of a decrease of vitality, but in the sense of an aim in the wrong direction, that is probably the essential property of the tumor cell. Since it could be shown on the one hand that multipolar mitoses lead to the origin of such cells which have lost their balance, and since on the other hand it is known that simultaneous multipolar divisions are found in tumors, the hypothesis of a connection between these two phenomena seems worthy of an examination. However, it would have to be supposed, in addition, that not only in the developing, but even in the originating tumor, multipolar mitoses occur. What may cause these is a second question and I note that my hypothesis is not irreconcilable with the assumption that the first cause of tumors is of parasitic nature. If I survey reports about the etiology of carcinoma and the many suggestions of physical and chemical insults, and if I consider on the other hand that pressure, shaking, narcotics, abnormal temperatures are precisely the agents with whose help we may produce multipolar mitoses in young eggs, then it appears possible to me that we have before us, in the elements just considered, the entire causal sequence of certain tumors.

[19] It may however be mentioned that the pathological development of one half blastomere always leads to an exclusive defect in the right or left body half, from which one may conclude that the first cleavage furrow determines the median plane, unless stronger influences, such as I have demonstrated in the deformation of the egg (9), inhibit this.

REFERENCES

1. Boveri, Th., Über die Befruchtung des Eies von Ascaris megalocephala. Sitz.-Ber. d. Ges. f. Morph. u. Phys. München, Bd. 3. 1887.

2. Boveri, Th., Über partielle Befruchtung. Sitz.-Ber. d. Ges. f. Morph. u. Phys. München, Bd. 4. 1888.

3. Boveri, Th., Zellen-Studien, Heft 2, Jena 1888.

4. Boveri, Th., Zellen-Studien, Heft 3, Jena 1890.

5. Boveri, Th., Ein geschlechtlich erzeugter Organismus ohne mütterliche Eigenschaften. Sitz.-Ber. d. Ges. f. Morph. u. Phys. München, Bd. 5. 1889.

6. Boveri, Th., Befruchtung. Ergebn. d. Anat. u. Entw.-Gesch. Bd. 1. 1892.

7. Boveri, Th., Über die Befruchtungs- und Entwickelungsfähigkeit kernloser Seeigeleier und die Möglichkeit ihrer Bastardierung. Arch. f. Entw.-Mech. Bd. 2. 1885.

8. Boveri, Th., Zur Physiologie der Kern- und Zellteilung. Sitz.-Ber. d. phys.-med. Ges. Würzburg 1897.

9. Boveri, Th., Über die Polarität des Seeigel-Eies. Verh. d. phys.-med. Ges. Würzburg, N. F., Bd. 34. 1901.

10. Boveri, Th., Die Polarität von Ovocyte, Ei und Larve des Strongylocentrotus lividus. Zoolog. Jahrbücher Bd. 14. 1901.

11. Delage, Y., Études sur la Mérogonie. Arch. de Zool, exp. et gén., 3. sér., T. 7. 1899.

12. Delage, Y., Études expérimentales sur la Maturation cytoplasmique chez les Echinodermes. Arch. de Zool. exp. 3. sér., T. 9. 1901.

13. Driesch, H., Entwicklungsmechanische Studien V. Von der Furchung doppeltbefruchteter Eier. Zeitschr. f. wiss. Zool. Bd. 55. 1892.

14. Driesch, H., Betrachtungen über die Organisation des Eies und ihre Genese. Arch. f. Entw.-Mech. Bd. 4. 1896.

15. Driesch, H., Über rein-mütterliche Charaktere an Bastardlarven von Echiniden. Arch. f. Entw.-Mech. Bd. 7. 1898.

16. Driesch, H., Die Lokalisation morphogenetischer Vorgänge. Ein Beweis vitalistischen Geschehens. Arch. f. Entw.-Mech. Bd. 8. 1899.

17. Driesch, H., Die isolierten Blastomeren des Echinidenkeimes. Arch. f. Entw.-Mech. Bd. 10. 1900.

18. Driesch, H., Die organischen Regulationen. Leipzig 1901.

19. Driesch, H., Kritisches und Polemisches. Biolog. Centralblatt Bd. 22. 1902.

20. Herbst, C., Über das Auseinandergehen von Furchungs- und Gewebezellen in kalkfreiem Medium. Arch. f. Entw.-Mech. Bd. 9. 1900.

21. Hertwig, O., und R., Über den Befruchtungs- und Teilungsvorgang des tierischen Eies unter dem Einfluss äusserer Agentien. Jena 1887.

22. Hertwig, R., Über die Entwicklung des unbefruchteten Seeigeleies. Abh. d. k. b. Ak. d. Wiss., II. Kl., Bd. 29. 1898.

23. Loeb, J., On the Nature of the Process of Fertilization and the Artificial Production of Normal Larvae (Plutei) from the Unfertilized Eggs of the Sea Urchin. Americ. Journ. of Physiol. Vol. 3. 1899.

24. Morgan, T. H., A Study of Variation in Cleavage. Arch. f. Entw.- Mech. Bd. 2. 1895.

25. Roux, W., Über die Bedeutung der Kernteilungsfiguren. Leipzig 1883.
26. Roux, W., Beiträge zur Entwicklungsmechanik des Embryo. III. Breslauer ärztliche Zeitschr. 1885.
27. v. Siebold, C. Th., Über Zwitterbienen. Zeitschr. f. wiss. Zool. Bd. 14. 1864.
28. Teichmann, E., Über Furchung befruchteter Seeigeleier ohne Beteiligung des Spermakerns. Jenaische Zeitschr. Bd. 37. 1902.
29. Weismann, A., Das Keimplasma. Eine Theorie der Vererbung. Jena 1892.
30. Wilson, E. B., Experimental Studies in Cytology. I. A Cytological Study of Artificial Parthenogenesis in Sea-urchin Eggs. Arch. f. Entw.-Mech. Bd. 12. 1901.
31. Wilson, E. B., Experimental Studies in Cytology. III. The Effect on Cleavage of Artificial Obliteration of the First Cleavage-Furrow. Arch. f. Entw.-Mech. Bd. 13. 1901.
32. Winkler, H., Über Merogonie und Befruchtung. Jahrb. f. wissenschaftl. Bot. Bd. 36. 1901.

1907

The Living Developing Nerve Fiber

by ROSS G. HARRISON

Harrison, Ross G. 1907. Observations on the living developing nerve fiber. Anatomical Record, 1:116-118 (Also Proc. Soc. Exp. Biol. and Med., 4:140-143). Reprinted by permission of the Wistar Institute.

Although the cell theory was proposed before the middle of the nineteenth century, it was not yet clear by the beginning of the twentieth century which particular cells in the animal embryo are responsible for forming the axon, the long conducting fiber of the nerve cell. There were then three theories as to the possible origin of the fiber: the cell-chain *theory, first enunciated by Schwann (1839), postulating that the fiber is formed by the chain of cells that form the sheath of Schwann; the* plasmodesm *theory, proposed by Hensen (1864), suggesting the fiber to be formed* in situ *along preformed protoplasmic bridges as a result of functional activity; and the* outgrowth *theory, first postulated by Bidder and Kupffer (1857) and strongly supported by W. His (1886-1890) and S. Ramon y Cajal (1890). This theory maintained that the nerve fiber is an outgrowth of a single cell, the neuroblast, which becomes the nerve cell of the adult.*

In the experiment described in the article reproduced here, Ross G. Harrison (1870-1959) demonstrated the validity of the outgrowth theory by following Roux's precept that independent differentiation may be demonstrated by isolation experiments. Harrison's experiment was crucial. He isolated under aseptic precautions a group of neuroblasts, before the fibers had differentiated, in a hanging drop of frog lymph in which no plasmodesms nor sheath cells were present, and he observed directly that protoplasmic fibers with branched ameboid endings extended from the neuroblasts into the frog lymph. This investigation established the fact that the neurone as a single cell is the developmental, structural, and functional unit of the nervous system and has thus provided the foundation for all subsequent investigation of the nervous system. It was also of great importance in demonstrating the usefulness of tissue culture as an invaluable embryological and biological technique. In 1917 a majority of the Nobel Prize Committee recommended Harrison for an award in physiology and medicine "for his discovery of the development of the nerve fibers by independent growth from cells outside the organism," but the actual award was not made. In 1933 the Committee again considered Harrison's work but decided against an award "in view of the rather limited value of the tissue culture method and the age of the discovery" (Nobel. The Man and His Prizes, by H. Schück, et al., 1951, p. 245). A Nobel Prize was awarded jointly to Enders, Robins and Weller in 1954 for their studies on the growth of human viral infections of embryonic tissues in tissue culture, and the wide application of the technique is now recognized not only by embryologists but by geneticists, virologists, microbiologists, physiologists, and by investigators in many other active fields of biology.

Harrison was also the first embryologist to adopt the grafting method of Born (1897) in the analysis of morphogenetic problems, and he made important contributions to our understanding of the development of embryonic symmetry and asymmetry. His directness of thought, simplicity of approach, depth of perception, and cautiousness of judgment have led to his recognition as an outstandingly great embryologist.

THE LIVING DEVELOPING NERVE FIBER[1]

The immediate object of the following experiments was to obtain a method by which the end of a growing nerve could be brought under direct observation while alive, in order that a correct conception might be had regarding what takes place as the fiber extends during embryonic development from the nerve center out to the periphery.

The method employed was to isolate pieces of embryonic tissue, known to give rise to nerve fibers, as for example, the whole or fragments of the medullary tube, or ectoderm from the branchial region, and to observe their further development. The pieces were taken from frog embryos about 3 mm. long at which stage, *i.e.,* shortly after the closure of the medullary folds, there is no visible differentiation of the nerve elements. After carefully dissecting it out, the piece of tissue is removed by a fine pipette to a cover slip upon which is a drop of lymph freshly drawn from one of the lymph-sacs of an adult frog. The lymph clots very quickly, holding the tissue in a fixed position. The cover slip is then inverted over a hollow slide and the rim sealed with paraffine. When reasonable aseptic precautions are taken, tissues will live under these conditions for a week and in some cases specimens have been kept alive for nearly four weeks. Such specimens may be readily observed from day to day under highly magnifying powers.

While the cell aggregates, which make up the different organs and organ complexes of the embryo, do not undergo normal transformation in form, owing, no doubt, in part, to the abnormal conditions of mechanical tension to which they are subjected; nevertheless, the individual tissue elements do differentiate characteristically. Groups of epidermis cells round themselves off into little spheres or stretch out into long bands, their cilia remain active for a week or more and a typical cuticular border develops. Masses of cells taken from the myotomes differentiate into muscle fibers showing fibrillæ with typical striations. When portions of myotomes are left attached to a piece of the medullary cord the muscle

[1] Read before the Society for Experimental Biology and Medicine at the 23d meeting, New York, May 22, 1907.

fibers which develop will, after two or three days, exhibit frequent contractions. In pieces of nervous tissue numerous fibers are formed, though, owing to the fact that they are developed largely within the mass of transplanted tissue itself, their mode of development cannot always be followed. However, in a large number of cases fibers were observed which left the mass of nerve tissue and extended out into the surrounding lymph-clot. It is these structures which concern us at the present time.

In the majority of cases the fibers were not observed until they had almost completed their development, having been found usually two, occasionally three, and once or twice four days after isolation of the tissue. They consist of an almost hyaline protoplasm, entirely devoid of the yolk granules, with which the cell-bodies are gorged. Within this protoplasm there is no definiteness of structure; though a faint fibrillation may sometimes be observed and faintly-defined granules are discernable. The fibers are about 1.5-3 μ thick and their contours show here and there irregular varicosities. The most remarkable feature of the fiber is its enlarged end, from which extend numerous fine simple or branched filaments. The end swelling bears a resemblance to certain rhizopods and close observation reveals a continual change in form, especially as regards the origin and branching of the filaments. In fact, the changes are so rapid that it is difficult to draw the details accurately. It is clear we have before us a mass of protoplasm undergoing amœboid movements. If we examine sections of young normal embryos shortly after the first nerves have developed, we find exactly similar structures at the end of the developing nerve fibers. This is especially so in the case of the fibers which are connected with the giant cells described by Rohon and Beard.

Still more instructive are the cases in which the fiber is brought under observation before it has completed its growth. Then it is found that the end is very active and that its movement results in the drawing out and lengthening of the fiber to which it is attached. One fiber was observed to lengthen about 20 μ in 25 minutes, another over 25 μ in 50 minutes. The longest fibers observed were 0.2 mm. in length.

When the placodal thickenings of the branchial region are isolated, similar fibers are formed and in several of these cases they have been seen to arise from individual cells. On the other hand, other tissues of the embryo, such as myotomes, yolk endoderm, notochord, and indifferent ectoderm from the abdominal region do not give rise to structures of this kind. There can, therefore, be no doubt that we are dealing with a specific characteristic of nervous tissue.

It has not as yet been found possible to make permanent specimens which show the isolated nerve fibers completely intact. The structures are so delicate that the mere immersion in the preserving fluid is sufficient to cause violent tearing and this very frequently results in the tearing away of the tissue in its entirety from the clot. Nevertheless, sections have

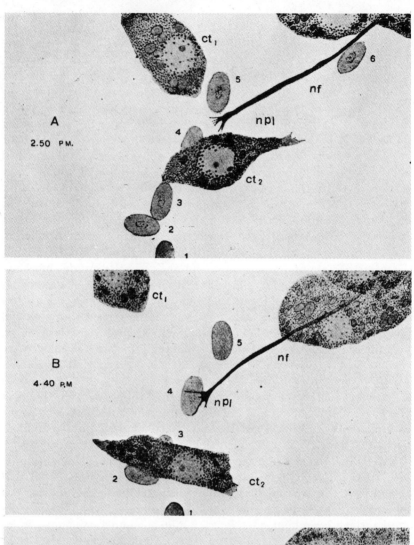

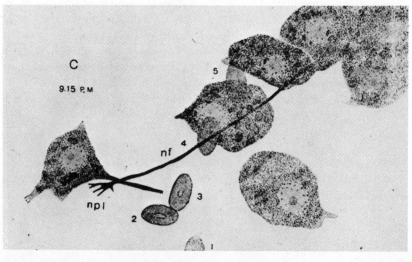

been cut of some of the specimens and nerves have been traced from the walls of the medullary tube but they were in all cases broken off short.

In view of this difficulty an effort, which resulted successfully, was made to obtain permanent specimens in a somewhat different way. A piece of medullary cord about four or five segments long was excised from an embryo and this was replaced by a cylindrical clot of proper length and caliber which was obtained by allowing blood or lymph of an adult frog to clot in a capillary tube. No difficulty was experienced in healing the clot into the embryo in proper position. After two, three, or four days the specimens were preserved and examined in serial sections. It was found that the funicular fibers from the brain and anterior part of the cord, consisting of naked axones without sheath cells, had grown for a considerable distance into the clot.

These observations show beyond question that the nerve fiber develops by the outflowing of protoplasm from the central cells. This protoplasm retains its amœboid activity at its distal end, the result being that it is drawn out into a long thread which becomes the axis cylinder. No other cells or living structures take part in this process.

The development of the nerve fiber is thus brought about by means of one of the very primitive properties of living protoplasm, amœboid movement, which, though probably common to some extent to all the cells of the embryo, is especially accentuated in the nerve cells at this period of development.

The possibility becomes apparent of applying the above method to the study of the influences which act upon a growing nerve. While at present it seems certain that the mere outgrowth of the fibers is largely independent of external stimuli, it is, of course, probable that in the body of the embryo there are many influences which guide the moving end and bring about contact with the proper end structure. The method here employed may be of value in analyzing these factors.

The paper chosen for reproduction in this volume was not illustrated. The figures shown on the facing page are taken from Ross G. Harrison, 1910. The outgrowth of the nerve fiber as a mode of protoplasmic movement. *Jour. Exp. Zool.,* 9:787–846, Figure 2. They represent "Three views of a growing nerve fiber, observed alive in a clotted lymph preparation. 1, 2, 3, 4, 5, red blood corpuscles in fixed position; ct_1, and ct_2, single cells which were seen to wander across the field; *nf,* nerve fiber; *npl,* growing end of motile protoplasm. ×420. *A,* As seen at 2:50 p.m., two days after isolation of the embryonic tissue. *B,* As seen at 4:40 p.m., the same day. Note change in form and position of the loose cells. *C,* As seen at 9:15 p.m., the same day. Movement of cells has covered over the proximal part of the fiber."

1908

Observations on Oxidative Processes
in the Sea Urchin Egg

by OTTO WARBURG

*from the Chemical-Physiological Division
of the Zoological Station, Naples*
(Received 16 July 1908)

Warburg, Otto. 1908. Beobachtungen über die Oxydationspro-
zesse im Seeigelei. Hoppe-Seyler's Zeitschrift für physiologische
Chemie. 57:1-16. Translated by H. Ursprung and printed by permission of the author and Walter de Gruyter and Co.

Early in the twentieth century, at a time when relatively little was known about the role of oxygen in metabolic processes, J. Loeb (1905, 1906), Warburg (1908, 1910), Child (1911) and others were engaged in investigating by physiological methods respiratory metabolism of cells or organisms. It was Otto Warburg (1883-) who, applying the relatively simple techniques then available, first determined oxygen consumption by Winkler's method and estimated nitrogen by Kjeldahl's method in studying the respiratory behavior of cells. In order to have large quantities of cells relatively free of yolk he judiciously selected the sea urchin egg as favorable experimental material. In the 1908 article reprinted in translation below he showed for the first time that fertilization causes a sharp and immediate increase in the respiration of sea urchin eggs. This paper was followed in rapid succession by a series of other important contributions in attempting to analyze the underlying conditions of change in oxygen utilization after fertilization of the sea urchin egg. During the course of these studies on respiration Warburg, on the basis of a chance observation, showed that traces of iron are present in the sea urchin egg. With iron as the cue he then showed in an experimental test that substances from crushed sea urchin eggs to which traces of iron are added form an effective catalyst that accelerates the rate of oxygen consumption. Through an extensive study of oxidation by means of the hemin charcoal model (respiration model) and by crucial experiments he was led to the discovery of the iron-containing Atmungsferment *or respiratory enzyme that is known today as cytochrome oxidase.* "For his discovery of the nature and mode of action of the respiratory enzyme" Warburg was awarded the Nobel prize in physiology and medicine for 1931.*

The pioneer studies of Warburg on respiratory metabolism of the sea urchin egg provoked much interest and research on the nature of the chemical mechanisms involved in cell metabolism. Of particular influence embryologically were his discoveries that the respiratory rate of the sea urchin egg increases after fertilization, continuing to increase up to the time of gastrulation. Although it was found later that these results on the sea urchin egg could not be generalized to cover certain other species, it seems safe to say that Warburg's studies were contributing factors in stimulating the more precise analytical studies that have led to better understanding of biochemical mechanisms in development.

* For Warburg's own account of this discovery see M. L. Gabriel and S. Fogel (eds.). 1955. The enzyme problem and biological oxidations. Great experiments in biology. Englewood Cliffs, N.J.: Prentice-Hall, Inc.

OBSERVATIONS ON OXIDATIVE PROCESSES IN THE SEA URCHIN EGG

Very little is known about the chemical processes that accompany cleavage. The numerous investigations on developmental processes in eggs deal with more advanced stages of ontogenesis; most of them have been carried out on meroblastic eggs, in which the abundance of yolk makes the precise measurement of changes at early stages impossible.

In the sea urchin egg, the amount of living substance is large as compared to the amount of yolk, and the changes after fertilization proceed in rapid sequence, so that within a short time much takes place within little substance. Therefore, I have undertaken some studies on this egg, first on oxidative processes.

Two papers deal with gas exchange in cleaving eggs. Godlewski, Jr.[1] obtained 3.5 cc. CO_2 in 79 hours from 700 frog eggs (760 mm., 0°); the duration of the experiment is so long, and the amount of CO_2 so small that bacteria as well as gases dissolved in the jelly coat and other sources of error could not be excluded. Lyon[2] reports on "rhythmic" excretion of carbon dioxide during the division of *Arbacia* eggs without, however, giving any numerical data.

In chicken eggs cleavage is already in progress in the oviduct. For this reason the paper by Hasselbalch on the liberation of oxygen during the first hours of incubation is not pertinent to our subject.

METHOD

All experiments were carried out on eggs of *Arbacia pustulosa*. In order to measure the intensity of the oxidative processes, I determined the amount of oxygen that disappeared from the surrounding sea water in a given time. For this purpose I collected the eggs according to the method of Lyon[3] and transferred them to a spacious dish in which they sank to the bottom within a few minutes. The supernatant fluid was siphoned off and replaced by water that had been filtered through paper; this procedure was repeated about five times. By this means ovarial fluid, immature eggs, small parasites, bacteria, etc. are removed. Then water is poured on, which was brought to the experimental temperature in the thermostat. The oxygen content of the water had been determined just previously. It is desirable that the water should be saturated with oxygen corresponding to the temperature and pressure of the experiment. After

1 Archiv für Entwicklungsmechanik, Bd. XI. 1901.
2 Americ. Journ. of Physiol., Vol. XI. 1904. Science N.S., Vol. XIX. 1904.
3 Americ. Journ. of Physiol., Vol. IX, p. 308, 1903.

the eggs have sunk to the bottom, the water is siphoned off as completely as possible and they are transferred to the experimental flask, which is filled with water of known oxygen content. In order continuously to renew the water on the surface of the eggs, I fastened the flask on a disc that rotated in an incubator about once every 15 seconds. The temperature was maintained between 20.2 and 20.5° in all experiments. After a certain time the flask—its glass stopper loosened—was immersed in ice water about 2 cm. deep. The eggs soon settled to the bottom, and after exactly one-half hour the water was siphoned off as completely as possible into the determination flask until it was full; necessary precautions were taken to avoid admitting oxygen from the air. The experimental flasks used held 253 or 257 cc., the determination flask 175 or 180 cc. Depending on the purpose of the experiment, water of known oxygen content was again poured on the eggs, or they were immediately incinerated. Oxygen was determined according to the method of Winkler.[4] The solution of thiosulfate used was approximately 1/100 normal. One cc. corresponded to 1.35 mg. iodine or 0.085 mg. oxygen. If organic substances are in solution, the method yields values that are too low. I am convinced that this source of error was not important in my experimental setup. For if oxygen is determined once in the sea water and a second time in the same quantity of sea water in which eggs have cleaved, identical values are found, providing the oxygen content has been made equal. To accomplish this the fluids need only be brought to the same temperature, and shaken vigorously with air for several minutes (while the pressure is kept constant by repeatedly opening the stoppers).

In order to be able to compare the intensity of respiration under different conditions, I did not count the eggs, but rather found it more accurate to incinerate them according to the method of Kjeldahl and to relate the oxygen values to equal amounts of nitrogen. The "respiration" of a known amount of nitrogen, according to expectation, is not constant. For unfertilized eggs the deviations are within the limits of error; for fertilized eggs the largest difference observed is about 20%. If such differences are important, the amounts of nitrogen may be considered equivalent only if obtained from the same batch of eggs. The assumption of the method that in the course of the experiment a measurable amount of nitrogen does not go into solution turns out to be true.

The weight of the eggs, as opposed to their nitrogen content, is probably less meaningful. Since weight varies greatly with the drying temperature, I did not carry out a determination of the water content. Incidentally, data on this question for *Strongylocentrotus lividus* are to be found in the work of Wetzel.[5]

4 E.g., Treadwell, Quant. Analysis, p. 505, 1902.
5 Engelmann's Archiv., 1907, S. 519.

SOURCES OF ERROR

A. Bacteria. The oxygen consumption of the unfertilized eggs is the only concern and not the observed difference after fertilization or other manipulations.

1. 180 cc. sea water from the tap, filtered through paper, did not use any measurable amount of oxygen in 12 hours.
2. If at the end of the experiments the eggs are allowed to sink to the bottom, the bacteria remain in the supernatant water. This supernatant did not use any measurable amount of oxygen in 2 hours.
3. The oxygen consumption per hour is independent of the duration of the experiment.

B. Sperm. Assuming that five of the supernumerary spermatozoa would remain attached to each egg, this would represent an error of 1% (see below). Yet with careful washing only rarely does a single spermatozoon remain adhering to an egg.

C. Oxygen pressure. The experiments were so designed that the oxygen concentration usually did not fall below $3/4$ of the original value. I have convinced myself, however, that absorption takes place regularly even at a concentration as low as $1/4$ of the original value.

D. Development. Cleavage proceeds normally in the rotating flasks. The yield of larvae is as high as in resting dishes. As it is well known, the yield of swimming larvae never reaches 100%, but about 95%. The causes of this developmental arrest are possibly already present in the seemingly normal first stages of cleavage, and oxidation, for instance, may also proceed differently in such eggs. If it is assumed, however, that 5% of the eggs either do not respire at all, or respire twice as much, this irregularity would still fall within the limits of error of the oxygen determination.

The latest developmental stage that I used for the determination of respiration is the 32-cell stage. Experiments in which for one reason or another cleavage was not normal up to that stage are not reported.

Precision: The errors are essentially those in reading the burettes.

EXPERIMENTS

I. UNFERTILIZED EGGS

(Oxygen in cc. thiosulfate; nitrogen in cc. $n/10$ NH₃)

N	Duration of experiment	Oxygen in 180 cc. water		Calculated total decrease of oxygen	28 mg. N consume per hr.
		Before the experiment	After the experiment		
14.6	180 minutes	16.0	14.9	1.6	0.7
22.1	90 minutes	15.5	14.7	1.1	0.7
42.0	90 minutes	15.9	14.6	1.9	0.6
29.5	90 minutes	15.6	14.7	1.3	0.6

Thus 28 mg. N consume from 0.05 to 0.06 mg. oxygen per hour.

These figures are perhaps of some interest in connection with an observation of J. Loeb[6] that unfertilized sea urchin eggs can be kept alive for a week or longer in sterilized water. In seven days, 168×0.06 mg. $=$ ca. 10 mg. oxygen are consumed per 28 mg. nitrogen; without knowing anything about what becomes of the absorbed oxygen we may conclude that the egg is capable of developing even after considerable qualitative or quantitative chemical changes.

II. THE FERTILIZED EGGS

(Oxygen in cc. thiosulfate; nitrogen in cc. $n/10$ NH_3)

N	Duration	Oxygen in 180 cc. water		Calculated total decrease of oxygen	28 mg. N consume per hr.
		Before the experiment	After the experiment		
34.9	1) 60 min.	15.9	11.0	7	4
	2) 60 min.	15.6	10.4	7.4	4.2
16.4	1) 60 min.	15.8	13.3	3.6	4.4
	2) 60 min.	15.6	12.8	4.0	4.9
	3) 60 min.	15.6	12.5	4.4	5.3
31.4	1) 60 min.	15.9	11.5	6.3	4.0
	2) 60 min.	15.9	10.6	7.6	4.8
	3) 60 min.	15.9	10.2	8.1	5.2
20.2	1) 60 min.	15.8	12.9	4.1	4.1
	2) 60 min.	15.8	12.8	4.3	4.3
	3) 60 min.	15.8	12.2	5.0	5.0
23.8	1) 60 min.	15.8	11.8	5.7	4.8
	2) 60 min.	15.8	11.4	6.3	5.3

At the beginning of the experiments, depending upon whether washing was carried out in cooled water or in water at room temperature for one hour, the eggs either had not yet cleaved or had divided into 2 blastomeres.

It becomes evident from the figures that oxygen consumption increases six- to seven-fold after fertilization.

The question arises as to what significance the small increases have although they are definitely beyond the limits of error.

A difference of 0.2 cc. thiosulfate between the first and second hour is due to the method, since the water of the first hour cannot be completely siphoned off, but only to ca. 20 cc.

Furthermore, the respiration that continues until 0° is reached may not be entirely negligible. If the increase arose only from these two sources of error, the oxygen consumption should not show any further increase during the third hour; however this is not the case.

Also it had to be considered whether the treatment of the eggs (cooling with ice, turntable) might cause the acceleration of the oxidations.

6 Vorlesungen über die Dynamik der Lebenserscheinungen, S. 251. 1906.

In order to exclude this possibility and to increase the differences, I divided the eggs from one female into two portions. In one of them the oxygen consumption was determined at the 8-cell stage. The other portion was allowed to stand for several hours in large dishes at room temperature and when the eggs had reached the 32-cell stage they were transferred to the determination flask.

8-CELL STAGE

(Oxygen in cc. thiosulfate; nitrogen in cc. n/10 NH₃)

| N | Duration | Oxygen in 180 cc. water | | Calculated total decrease of oxygen | 28 mg. N consume per hr. |
		Before the experiment	After the experiment		
24.1	60 min.	15.9	12.4	5	4.2

32-CELL STAGE

(Oxygen in cc. thiosulfate; nitrogen in cc. n/10 NH₃)

| N | Duration | Oxygen in 180 cc. water | | Calculated total decrease of oxygen | 28 mg. N consume per hr. |
		Before the experiment	After the experiment		
17.6	60 min.	15.8	11.6	6	6.8

Since the difference amounts to 2.6 cc. thiosulfate, the increase in oxygen consumption is established.

In this experiment the nuclei of the 8-cell and 32-cell stages have been formed at the same velocity. The size of each newly formed nucleus is equal to that of the first cleavage nucleus.[7] If the major quantity of oxygen were consumed in the process of nuclear growth, then the "respiration" at the 32-cell stage would have to exceed that of the 8-cell stage by about three-fold. As can be seen, this assumption, which is often mentioned in the literature, is not at all true.

The differences rather appear to increase with the morphological changes. Yet, I think they are too small to overlook the quantitative relationship that exists here.[8]

[7] As a matter of fact, this is already very probable from morphological findings (O. Hertwig, Morphol. Jahrbuch I, 406; Boveri, Zellenstudien, Heft 5). It was firmly established by developmental-physiological investigations of Boveri and Driesch (see especially: The cell number of "amphikaryotic" half eggs after cleavage and of separated blastomeres of the 2-cell stage).

[8] For this kind of problem it would be necessary to determine at first whether respiration is in fact discontinuous as Lyon supposes. I have not obtained any evidence for this myself, yet it would only concern the small fraction of respiration that is a consequence of morphological changes. With the methods described it will be easy to test

III. FERTILIZED EGGS IN WHICH CLEAVAGE HAS BEEN INHIBITED

J. Leob[9] has found that the division of fertilized eggs can be prevented by putting them into sea water in which the osmotic pressure is raised by a specific amount. If this increase in osmotic pressure is appropriately selected, the nucleus continues to divide though more slowly than in normal sea water. Thus, by this experimental method the morphological changes can either be inhibited (cell division) or retarded (nuclear division). In accordance with the above-mentioned results the oxygen consumption should not change materially under these conditions.

At Naples in order just to inhibit cleavage 1 g. NaCl must be added to 100 cc. of sea water. I divided a batch of eggs into 2 approximately equal portions. One portion was transferred into normal sea water, the other into the hypertonic solution and then the oxygen consumption was simultaneously determined in the two.

IN NORMAL SEA WATER

(Oxygen in cc. thiosulfate; nitrogen in cc. n/10 NH_3)

No.	N	Duration	Oxygen Content Before the experiment	Oxygen Content After the experiment	Calculated total decrease	28 mg. N consume per hr.
1	17.6	120 min.	175 cc. = 15.4	175 cc. = 10.7	6.8	3.9
2	23.8	60 min.	180 cc. = 15.8	180 cc. = 11.8	5.7	4.8

SIMULTANEOUSLY IN HYPERTONIC SEA WATER

No.	N	Duration	Oxygen Content Before the experiment	Oxygen Content After the experiment	Calculated total decrease	28 mg. N consume per hr.
1	14.7	120 min.	180 cc. = 15.2	180 cc. = 11.6	5.1	3.5
2	25.2	60 min.	175 cc. = 14.5	175 cc. = 10.4	5.9	4.7

Comment: The significance of these figures becomes limited by an irregularity which is still unexplained. In the first experiment on May 28, when I transferred the eggs from the hypertonic solution into normal sea water, I found an oxygen consumption of 6.5 cc. thiosulfate per hour and 28 mg. N. I was unable to repeat this experiment until one month later. This time, the eggs (28 mg. N) absorbed an amount of oxygen that corresponds to 5.6 cc. thiosulfate when transferred to normal sea water, as contrasted with 4.7 in the hypertonic solution (experiment 2). However, while in the first experiment almost all the eggs developed into larvae, in the second one the number of larvae formed was very small.

these relations; however, since we are dealing with short periods of time, the eggs would have to be carefully centrifuged and not merely be allowed to sink.

9 Untersuchungen über die künstliche Parthenogenese, Leipzig 1906, S. 1.

IV. EGG AND SPERM CELLS

According to well-founded views[10] egg and sperm cells have the same amount of nuclear substance; yet it is under quite different physiological conditions and, in particular, it "governs" completely different amounts of protoplasm. It seems to me not without interest to compare the respiration of these two cells. I counted the spermatozoa in an Abbe chamber (fixation was with osmic acid, which was most successfully carried out by exposing the slides to osmic vapor for several minutes). The eggs were vigorously shaken at an appropriate dilution; then ½ cc. was quickly taken up into a pipette and allowed to flow out onto a filter paper kept in motion. After a short time the eggs dried onto the paper and then were separated by means of pencil lines so that they could be easily counted with a low power magnifying glass.

Sperm

Experiment 1. The liquid contained 20 million sperm cells per cc. (400 counted) or 3600 million per 180 cc.

An immediate[11] analysis of 180 cc. of this solution by Winkler's method yielded 12.1 cc. thiosulfate; after 70 minutes (20°), the yield was 10.4 cc. thiosulfate.
Decrease per hour: 1.5 cc. thiosulfate.
4000 million sperm cells per hour: 1.7 cc. thiosulfate.

Experiment 2. 33 million sperm cells per cubic centimeter. 5940 million per 180 cc. (400 counted).
180 cc. at zero time: 14.9 cc. thiosulfate.
After 55 minutes at 20°: 12.6 cc. thiosulfate.
Decrease per hour: 2.5 cc. thiosulfate.
4000 million sperm cells per hour: 1.7 cc. thiosulfate.
The error in counting the spermatozoa is ca. 4%; in oxygen determination it is ca. 10%.

Eggs

Experiment 1. Total volume 1000 cc. 850 eggs per 0.5 cc.; 1,700,000 eggs per liter.
N after siphoning off the water: = 9.8 cc. n/10 NH_3.
One million eggs = 5.8 cc. n/10 NH_3.

Experiment 2. Total volume 1000 cc. containing 980,000 eggs. N = 6.1 n/10 NH_3.
One million eggs = 6.2 cc. n/10 NH_3.
Error in counting: ca. 10%.

---

[10] O. Hertwig. Handbuch der Entwicklungsgeschichte.
[11] This eliminates the possible error caused by organic substance.

28 mg. N consume 0.6-0.7 mg. thiosulfate per hour (error of 20%). Consequently, one million eggs consume per hour 0.2 cc. thiosulfate or 0.017 mg. oxygen.

Under the same conditions, one million spermatozoa consume 0.0004 cc. of thiosulfate or 0.000034 mg. of oxygen. In other words, the respiration of an egg cell is 500 ($\pm$ 100) times as high as that of a sperm cell.

V. INFLUENCE ON OXIDATIONS IN THE UNFERTILIZED EGG

1. Hypertonic solutions. In the course of his investigations on artificial parthenogenesis J. Loeb became convinced that weakly alkaline hypertonic solutions have an accelerating action on the oxidative processes of the unfertilized sea urchin egg. He arrived at this conclusion mainly from the fact that hypertonic solutions are no longer active if the oxygen has been expelled.[12]

As a matter of fact, the oxygen consumption of unfertilized eggs can be enhanced up to ten-fold in such hypertonic solutions.

When sea water is used that varies considerably in one way or another from normal composition, the eggs are often damaged; in the case of the pigmented eggs of *Arbacia* this can be easily seen from the color of the supernatant fluid. I never continued such experiments.

I determined the oxygen consumption in three solutions of different hypertonicity:

Solution I: 1 g. NaCl per 100 cc. sea water.

Solution II: 2.3 g. NaCl per 100 cc. sea water.
                Per 100 cc., 1.6 cc. n/10 NaOH

Solution III: 4.3 g. NaCl per 100 cc. sea water, plus 3 cc. n/10 NaOH
                per 100 cc.

The most favorable concentration for obtaining cleavage, after the eggs were returned to normal sea water, was approximately between II and III. However, in these experiments the morphological changes were of less importance to me.

The addition of alkali was carried out according to Loeb's direction. It was not feasible to separate the effects of alkali and salt concentration since each reagent when used alone destroyed the eggs. Yet Loeb was never able to induce parthenogenesis by alkali alone;[13] other observations also support the view that what is effective is the increase in osmotic pressure, and that in this case the alkali plays merely a protective role.

---

[12] Biochem. Zeitschrift, Bd. I, S. 183; Bd. II, S. 34. Pflüger's Archiv, Bd. CXVIII, S. 30. Untersuchungen über der künstliche Parthenogenese, Leipzig 1906, S. 491.

[13] Pflüger's Archiv., Bd. CXVIII, S. 30.

(Oxygen in cc. thiosulfate; nitrogen in cc. n/10 NH₃)

SOLUTION I

N	Duration	Oxygen Content		Calculated total decrease of oxygen	28 mg. N consume per hr.
		Before the experiment	After the experiment		
51.5	60 min.	175 cc. = 14.8	175 cc. = 13.1	2.5	1.0

SOLUTION II

N	Duration	Oxygen Content		Calculated total decrease of oxygen	28 mg. N consume per hr.
		Before the experiment	After the experiment		
11.4	80 min.	180 cc. = 14.4	180 cc. = 12.8	2.3	3.0

SOLUTION III:

(2 experiments)

Date	N	Duration	Oxygen Content		Calculated total decrease of oxygen	28 mg. N consume per hr.
			Before the experiment	After the experiment		
June 7	26.3	80 min.	180 cc. = 14.1	180 cc. = 5.8	11.7	6.7
June 8	10.4	80 min.	175 cc. = 13.1	176 cc. = 10.3	4.1	5.9

The oxygen consumption of the unfertilized eggs amounts to 0.6-0.7 thiosulfate per 28 mg. N per hour. Thus the increase in solution I is only slightly above the limit of error; in solution II the oxygen consumption is raised by four- to five-fold, in solution III by nine- to ten-fold. The increase of oxygen consumption is not proportional to the increase of the osmotic pressure.

Approximate increase of osmotic pressure[14]	In solution	Increase of oxygen consumption
25%	I	0.2 cc. thiosulfate
50%	II	2.3 cc. thiosulfate
100%	III	5.7 cc. thiosulfate

Apparently the increase can be clearly measured only above a certain concentration. This is in good agreement with the observation just reported by Loeb[15] that the osmotic pressure of the hypertonic solution must exceed a threshold value if it is to exert an effect on the eggs.

2. *Hypotonic solutions.* If unfertilized eggs are put in hypotonic sea water for some time and then returned to normal sea water, an increase in oxygen consumption is observed.

[14] Without taking into consideration the degree of dissociation.
[15] Biochem. Zeitschrift, Bd. XI, S. 148.

Experiment I: The eggs were washed first with normal sea water in the usual way, then three times within a half hour in a mixture of ⅗ sea water and ⅖ distilled water (at 24°). They were then returned to normal sea water.

(Oxygen in cc. thiosulfate; nitrogen in cc. n/10 NH₃)

N	Duration	Oxygen Content		Calculated total decrease of oxygen	28 mg. N consume per hr.
		Before the experiment	After the experiment		
20.2	72 min.	180 cc. = 15.6	180 cc. = 14.6	1.4	1.2

A control experiment carried out simultaneously without pretreatment on eggs of the same batch resulted in 0.7 cc. (28 mg. N per hour).

Experiment II. The same as I, except that the hypotonic water consisted of equal parts of sea water and distilled water. The eggs remained in it for 45 minutes.

N	Duration	Oxygen Content		Calculated total decrease of oxygen	28 mg. N consume per hr.
		Before the experiment	After the experiment		
60.8	55 min.	180 cc. = 15.5	180 cc. = 12.6	4.1	1.5

3. Temperature. For the velocity of development of frog eggs[16] and eggs of the ring snake[17] the temperature coefficient is that characteristic of chemical reactions. As was to be expected, this is also true for the oxidations in the sea urchin egg.

(Oxygen in cc. thiosulfate; nitrogen in cc. n/10 NH₃ Temperature 28°)

N	Duration	Oxygen Content		Total decrease of oxygen	28 mg. N consume per hr.
		Before the experiment	After the experiment		
59.2	60 min.	180 cc. = 13.8	180 cc. = 11.0	4	1.4

28 mg. consume per hour at 20°: 0.7 cc. thiosulfate
28 mg. consume per hour at 28°: 1.4 cc. thiosulfate
Increase per 10°: 0.9 cc. thiosulfate

When at the end of the experiment sperm was added all eggs formed membranes.

A rather remarkable feature is the sensitivity to elevated temperature. If eggs are kept at 35° for 20 minutes, they no longer form membranes upon addition of sperm nor do they cleave. Eggs kept for 2 minutes at 40° are already unable to develop; keeping them at 40° for 3 minutes prevents the formation of membranes.

[16] O. Hertwig, Archiv f. mikroskopische Anatomie u. Entwicklungsgeschichte, Bd. LI, S. 319.

[17] Bohr, Skand, Arch. für Physiologie, Bd. XV, S. 29.

4. Negative experiments. I considered the possibility that any movement within the egg might accelerate the oxidative processes. In order to test this supposition, I changed the volume of the eggs 8 times in the course of 80 minutes by putting them alternately in normal and hypotonic sea water. No increase in oxygen consumption was observed than where they had been in the hypotonic solution for 40 minutes.

Besides, I put the eggs upon a machine that shook vigorously up and down. As is known, such treatment may induce the eggs of the starfish to develop. Yet the oxidations in the egg of *Arbacia* were not accelerated.

I am greatly indebted to the staff of the Zoological Station for their constant helpfulness, especially to Dr. M. Henze, the director of the division, and to Professor Herbst who was kind enough to show me how to handle the material.

Heidelberg, July 15.

1913

The Mechanism of Fertilization

by FRANK R. LILLIE

Lillie, Frank R. 1913. The Mechanism of Fertilization. Science 38:524-528. Reprinted by permission of Science.

Lillie's interest in the process of fertilization can probably be attributed in part to the philosophical climate that invested the problem of cell lineage at the turn of the century at the Marine Biological Laboratory (see comments on E. B. Wilson, p. 53) and still more importantly to his own detailed and exact observations on the changing disposition of visibly different particles (yolk spherules and other microscopically visible inclusions) in the cytoplasm of the egg of Chaetopterus (*a marine annelid*) *during the course of maturation and fertilization and their differential spatial distribution during cleavage and subsequent stages. To Lillie such natural phenomena as these give the basis for analyzing the nature of the underlying mechanisms in accord with physiological principles (see comments on Free-martin, p. 137). In his words, ". . . the aim of 'physiology of development' is to discover mechanisms of control of developmental processes" (1932).*

On the basis of this approach, a two-fold experimental analysis of the meaning of the observed cytological phenomena had its origin. First, by the simple method of centrifuging the egg Lillie found that although the visible inclusions were abnormally distributed, typically normal cleavage and development occurred. Out of this analysis came the stimulating concept that the ground substance of the cytoplasm is organized, i.e., it has a definite architecture or ultramicroscopic structure and is the molecular basis of the localization pattern in normal development.

Still more important was the role of the studies on Chaetopterus *in leading immediately to an analysis of the act of fertilization. The changes in the distribution of the particles in the egg cytoplasm, especially upon sperm contact and penetration, were so striking and dramatic that the hunch came to Lillie that the underlying mechanisms involved in the union of the egg and spermatozoon can be analyzed.*

Before the second important paper on Chaetopterus *was published in 1909, he began to study the mechanism of fertilization, a subject that was to engage Lillie and his students for a period of over ten years (1910-1921). The methods used were beautiful in their simplicity, for he had at hand only a microscope, glass slides and covers, finger bowls, test tubes and pipettes. With these tools he soon discovered that the eggs of the sea urchin,* Arbacia (*also* Nereis *eggs) secrete a substance into sea water which causes agglutination of the sperm of the same species.*

The article reprinted here is the seventh of a series of papers published within four years, each one of which was a necessary link in a chain of detailed analyses, the ultimate goal of which, as in all of Lillie's major investigations, was to discover new principles. Indeed, he succeeded in laying down the fundamental truth that fertilization involves the inter-action of specific substances borne by the egg and sperm. Moreover, in this paper he applied for the first time the then current immunological con-cept and terminology of Ehrlich to these interacting substances. They were conceived as linked and reacting with one another in the manner of lock and key combinations. The theory here proposed later became a notable feature of the "Fertilizin Theory," a theory that formulated all of the then known main aspects of the processes of fertilization. A full account of the studies of Lillie was published in 1919 in a small lucidly written book entitled Problems of Fertilization.

In 1912 Lillie summed up with foresight his view of the fundamental problem of fertilization in these words: "The union of ovum and sper-matozoon is not a process in which the sperm penetrates by virtue of its mechanical properties, but one in which a peculiarly intimate and specific biochemical reaction plays the chief role."

In keeping with Lillie's expressed hope, his systematic study of egg-sperm interacting substances and his theories of the mechanism of egg activation, and of the specific adherence of the spermatozoon to the egg and its penetration into the egg, pointed the way for further investigation. During the succeeding four decades intensive investigations by Max Hartmann, Albert Tyler, Lord Rothschild, John Runnström and many others have contributed many new discoveries of significance in the areas of the structural and metabolic changes occuring in the fertilization process, and the immunological nature of the reactions between substances isolated from eggs and sperm. These findings in turn have led to new problems and theories, not to definitive solutions. Much more investiga-tion will be required before the immunological and biochemical aspects of fertilization and initiation of development will be satisfactorily ex-plained.

THE MECHANISM OF FERTILIZATION

In previous papers[1] I have described the secretion of a substance by the ova of the sea-urchin, *Arbacia,* in sea water, which causes ag-glutination of the sperm of the same species. The eggs of *Nereis* also secrete a substance having a similar effect upon its sperm. I therefore named these substances sperm-isoagglutinins. During the present sum-mer I have ascertained that in the case of *Arbacia,* and presumably also of *Nereis,* the agglutinating substance is a necessary link in the fertiliza-tion process and that it acts in the manner of an amboceptor, having one side-chain for certain receptors in the sperm and another for certain

[1] SCIENCE, N. S., Vol. 36, pp. 527-530, October, 1912, and *Journ. Exp. Zool.,* Vol. 14, No. 4, pp. 515-574, May, 1913.

receptors in the egg. As this substance represents, presumably, a new class of substances, analogous in some respects to cytolysins, and as the term agglutinin defines only its action on sperm suspensions, I have decided to name it fertilizin.

My main purpose this summer was to study the rôle of the *Arbacia* fertilizin in the fertilization of the ovum.

1. *The Spermophile Side-chain.*—The first need in such a study was to develop a quantitative method of investigation, and this was done for *Arbacia* as follows: The agglutinative reaction of the sperm in the presence of this substance is, as noted in previous studies, reversible, and the intensity and duration of the reaction is a factor of concentration of the substance. The entire reaction is so characteristic that it was possible to arrive at a unit by noting the dilution at which the least unmistakable reaction was given. This was fixed at about a five- or six-second reaction, which is counted from the time that agglutination becomes visible under a magnification of about 40 diameters until its complete reversal. The unit is so chosen that a half dilution gives no agglutination of a fresh 1 per cent. sperm suspension. It was then found that the filtrate from a suspension of 1 part eggs left for ten minutes in 2 or 3 parts sea water would stand a dilution of from 800 to 6,400 times, depending on the proportion of ripe eggs and their condition, and still give the unit reaction. Such solutions may then be rated as 800 to 6,400 agglutinating power, and it is possible, therefore, to determine the strength of any given solution. This gives us a means of determining the rate at which eggs are producing fertilizin in sea water.

Determinations with this end in view showed that the production of fertilizin by unfertilized eggs of *Arbacia* in sea water goes on for about three days and that the quantity produced as measured by dilution tests diminishes very slowly. Such tests are made by suspending a given quantity of eggs in a measured amount of sea water in a graduated tube; the eggs are then allowed to settle and the supernatant fluid poured off and kept for testing. The same amount of fresh sea water is then added and the eggs stirred up in it, allowed to settle, the supernatant fluid poured off for testing, and so on. In one series running three days in which the quantity of eggs was originally 2 c.c. and the total volume of sea water and eggs in the tube 10 c.c., 6 to 8 c.c. being poured off at each settling, thirty-four changes were made and the agglutinating strength of the supernatant fluid diminished from 100 at first to 20 at the end. Simultaneously, with this loss of agglutinating strength, two things happen: (1) the jelly surrounding the eggs undergoes a gradual solution; (2) the power of being fertilized is gradually lost.

It is obvious that the presence of fertilizin in such considerable quantities in so long a series of washings shows either (1) that solution of the jelly liberates fertilizin, or else (2) that the eggs secrete more fertilizin each time they are washed. Both factors enter into the case inasmuch as (1) eggs killed by heat (60° C.) will stand 14 or 15 such washings, but with more rapid decline of agglutinating power than the living eggs. The jelly is gradually dissolved away in this case also, and is presumably the only possible source of the agglutinating substance. (2) Eggs deprived of jelly by shaking continue to produce the fertilizin as long as eggs with jelly, though in smaller quantities at first, and they are equally capable of fertilization.

The fertilizin is therefore present in large quantities in the jelly, which is indeed saturated with the substance, but the eggs continue to produce it as long as they remain alive and unfertilized. When the eggs are fertilized the production of this substance suddenly ceases' absolutely.

The total disappearance of fertilizin from fertilized eggs can not be demonstrated unless the fertilizin-saturated jelly with which the eggs are surrounded be first removed. This is very easily done after membrane formation by six vigorous shakes of the eggs in a half-filled test tube. Three or four washings then are sufficient to remove the remains of the jelly, and the naked eggs no longer produce the substance.

Such disappearance may be due either to complete discharge from the egg, or to fixation of all that remains by union with some substance contained in the egg itself. That such a substance—anti-fertilizin—exists in the egg can be shown by a simple test-tube experiment: If eggs deprived of jelly are washed 34 times in sea water during three days, they are so exhausted that they produce but little fertilizin; the supernatant fluid may be charged only to the extent of 2 to 10 units. The eggs are now on the point of breaking up. If they are then vigorously shaken and broken up so that the fluid becomes colored with the red pigment of the eggs, it will be found that agglutinating power has entirely disappeared from the solution. The fertilizin present has been neutralized. The same phenomenon may be demonstrated also by treating eggs, deprived of jelly in order to get rid of excess of fertilizin, with distilled water which lakes the eggs and extracts the anti-fertilizin.

It is probable, therefore, that any excess of fertilizin remaining in the egg not bound to the sperm is neutralized by this combination, and polyspermy is thereby prevented.

We have noted (1) the secretion by unfertilized eggs in sea water of a sperm agglutinating substance, fertilizin; (2) the extreme avidity of the sperm for it as shown by dilution tests; (3) in my previous papers the fixation of this substance in sperm-suspensions of the same species (quantitative measurements will be given in the complete paper); (4) the sudden cessation of fertilizin production by fertilized eggs; (5) the existence of an antifertilizin in the egg; (6) in eggs submitted to a series of washings decrease of the fertilization capacity with reduction of the fertilizin. The fact that fertilized eggs can not be refertilized is associated with the absence of free fertilizin in them; (7) I may add that, similarly, eggs in which membrane formation has been induced by butyric acid can not be fertilized by sperm and they contain no free fertilizin.

It is therefore very probable that the substance in question is essential for fertilization.

It may be maintained that these facts do not constitute demonstrative evidence of the necessity of this substance for fertilization, for the presence or absence or diminution of this material associated with presence or absence or decrease of fertilizing power could always be regarded as a secondary phenomenon. However, the second part of this paper dealing with the other, or ovophile side-chain of the fertilizin, strongly reinforces the argument.

Before passing on to this, I may be allowed to note some other properties of the fertilizin: In my previous papers I noted the extreme heat-resistance of the fertilizin, being only slowly destroyed at $95°$ C. I also noted that strongly agglutinating solutions of *Arbacia* may contain a substance which agglutinates *Nereis* sperm and stated that this was probably different from the iso-agglutinating substance. This turns out to be the case and the two can be readily separated. The substance must possess great molecular size, as it is incapable of passing through a Berkefeld filter. It is also non-dialyzable; it does not give the usual protein reactions; a fact for the determination of which I am indebted to Dr. Otto Glaser.

2. *The Ovophile Side-chain.*—Assuming, then, that the union of this substance with the spermatozoon enters in some significant way into the process of fertilization, the problem was to ascertain in what way. The simplest idea, viz., that the union is in itself the fertilization process, was soon shown to be untenable, for the reason that the perivisceral fluid (blood) of the sea-urchin, especially of ripe males and females, often contains a substance which absolutely inhibits fertilization in the presence of any quantity of sperm, but that this substance has no inhibiting effect at all upon the sperm-agglutination reaction. It does not enter into combination with the spermophile side-chain. In other words, the binding of the agglutinin by the sperm may be complete, but in the presence of an inhibitor contained in the blood none of the usual effects of insemination, no matter how heavy, follow.

The details of the experiments upon which the above statement depends are too complex for consideration here. But they showed that the effect is neither upon the egg alone nor upon the sperm alone, for both may stand for some time in the presence of this agent and after washing be capable of normal behavior in fertilization, though there may be some decrease in the percentages. No poisonous effect is involved on either sexual element.

The next suggestion was fairly obvious, viz., that the substance which we had been calling agglutinin, on account of its effect upon the spermatozoa, is in reality an amboceptor with spermophile and ovophile side-chains, and that the binding of the sperm activates the ovophile side-chains which then seize upon egg receptors and fertilize the egg. If this were so, it is obvious that the spermatozoon is only secondarily a fertilizing agent, in the sense of initiating development, and that the egg is in reality self-fertilizing, an idea which agrees very well with the facts of parthenogenesis and the amazing multiplicity of means by which parthenogenesis may be effected. For the agents need only remove obstacles to the union of the amboceptor and egg receptor.

The inhibiting action of the blood from this point of view is a deviation effect due to occupancy of the ovophile side-chain of the amboceptor, either because the inhibitor in the blood is an anti-body to the amboceptor or because it possesses the same combining group as the egg receptor. In such a case, the ovophile group of the amboceptor, being already occupied by the inhibitor, fertilization could not take place.

Fortunately, this idea is susceptible of a ready test; for, if the blood acts in this way in inhibiting fertilization, all that is necessary to neutralize the inhibiting action would be to occupy the inhibitor by the amboceptor (fertilizin) for which *ex. hyp.* it has strong affinity. This experiment was repeated many times in different ways with various dilutions, and the result was always to lessen or completely remove the inhibiting action of the blood.

The plan of such an experiment is this: to divide the filtered blood (plasma) in two parts, one of which is used for control while the other is saturated with fertilizin by addition of eggs. In ten minutes the latter are precipitated by the centrifuge and the supernatant fluid filtered. Fertilizations are then made in graded dilutions of this and the control blood. In some cases the inhibiting action of the blood was completely neutralized, and in all largely neutralized.

The results so far are in agreement with the theory. But if it be true that the egg contains its own fertilizing substance, it might also be possible to induce parthenogenesis by increasing the concentration of this substance to a certain point; though it is conceivable that no increase in concentration would break down the resistance that normally exists to union of the amboceptor and egg receptors. As a matter of fact, Dr. Otto Glaser[2] has shown this summer that a certain amount of parthenogenetic action may be induced in *Arbacia* in this way. I have been in consultation with Dr. Glaser during part of his work and can confirm his statements.

In connection with the assumption that the sperm activates an already existing side-chain of a substance contained in the egg itself, I may be allowed to cite the following statement of Ehrlich:

[2] SCIENCE, N. S., Vol. XXXVIII., No. 978, September 26, 1913, p. 446.

The significance of the variations in affinity will be discussed connectedly at a subsequent time. We shall content ourselves here by pointing out that an understanding of the phenomena of immunity is impossible without the assumption that certain haptophore groups become increased or decreased in their chemical energy, owing to changes in the total molecule. Chemically, such an assumption is a matter of course.[3]

This principle might explain the activation of the fertilizing amboceptor by the sperm.

The question will of course be raised whether there is not another and simpler interpretation of the facts. There are three general classes of these facts: (1) the sperm agglutination phenomena, and the apparent necessity of the agglutinating substance for fertilization; (2) the presence of an inhibiting agent in the blood, especially of ripe males and females; (3) the neutralization of this inhibiting agent by the agglutinating agent (amboceptor). It may be questioned whether these facts have the particular causal nexus that I have given them. But I think it would be difficult to construct a theory taking account of all the facts which would differ essentially from that presented here.

The theory is really extremely simple in its character, and the facts on which it rests are readily tested. It has proven a most valuable working hypothesis; indeed, many of the facts referred to were discovered only after the theory was formed. It has the advantage of offering one theory for initiation of development whether by fertilization or by parthenogenesis. It is capable of explaining the whole range of specificities in fertilization by assuming a specific fertilizin for each species. It furnishes the foundation for the chemical conceptions necessary to any theory of fertilization, and it is susceptible of experimental test.

It will be seen that inhibition of fertilization may occur by block in any part of the mechanism.

1. Through loss of fertilizin by the egg.
2. Through occupancy of the sperm receptors.
3. Through occupancy of the egg receptors.
4. Through occupancy of the ovophile side-chain of the amboceptor (fertilizin).
5. Through occupancy of the spermophile side-chain group.

Of these I have shown the occurrence of the first, fourth and fifth in *Arbacia*. The first in the case of long-washed eggs; the fourth in the case of the inhibitor contained in the blood; the fifth is, I believe, the mechanism for prevention of polyspermy.

The mechanism of fertilization appears to be the same in *Nereis*, though I have not a complete set of data. However, the data that I have are in accord with the theory, and will be described in the complete paper.

[3] "Collected Studies in Immunity," p. 220.

I should perhaps state specifically that the location of the fertilizin is in the cortex of the egg.

It seems to me probable that the activation of the fertilizin is by no means confined to that bound by the single penetrating sperm, but that activation once set up spreads around the cortex. The supernumerary spermatozoa that fail to enter the egg may also play a part by setting up centers of activation. In this connection Glaser's contention that several spermatozoa at least are necessary for fertilization is of great interest. The nature of the effect of the activated fertilizin on the egg is analogous in some respects to a superficial cytolysis, in this respect agreeing with Loeb's theory. But the "lysin" is contained in the egg, not in the sperm, as Loeb thought; if cytolysis is involved, it is a case of autocytolysis. This may involve increase of permeability, the effects of which R. S. Lillie has especially studied. I mention these possibilities in order to point out that the conception contained in this paper is not in conflict with the well-established work of others.

In conclusion, I may point out that the theory assumes a form of linkage of sperm and egg components by means of an intermediate body that may find a place in the study of heredity. The detailed experiments will be published later.

PART EIGHT

1914

Susceptibility Gradients in Animals

by C. M. CHILD

Child, C. M. 1914. Susceptibility Gradients in Animals. Science 39:73-76. Reprinted by permission of Science.

When Child began to apply his theory of axial gradients to the developing egg, embryology had already escaped far from the trammels of evolutionary dogmatism: Curt Herbst and others had viewed developmental phenomena in the light of physiological studies on tropisms; Roux and Driesch and their many followers, including Harrison and Spemann, had proved the egg and embryo to be amenable to microsurgical manipulation. Driesch had stressed the importance of ferments in development, and Jacques Loeb, often erroneously but always with seminal influence on his contemporaries, had considered development in terms of chemistry and physics as he understood them. Most important of all, Otto Warburg had begun his quantitative studies on the respiration of the echinoderm egg that were to lead to the discoveries of the cytochromes and thereby, within a few decades, to transform not only embryology but the whole of biology. But for all this, it was still the studies by Child that exerted the strongest immediate influence in transforming embryology into a physiological science.

Child was not the first investigator to postulate the existence of gradients; the concept had been introduced by Boveri and discussed by him with clarity in 1910. Child's contribution was his attempt to explain gradients on a metabolic basis. His concept of a gradient along an axis, in which anterior regions were dominant to posterior ones, was first introduced in 1911 (in Die physiologische Isolation von Teilen des Organismus als Auslösungsfaktor der Bildung neuer Lebewesen und der Restitution. Vorträge u. Aufsätze über Entw.-mech., herausg. W. Roux, 1911, Bd. 11, 157 S.) to explain certain regenerative and budding phenomena in various invertebrates. He first discussed extension of the concept to cover embryonic phenomena in an article in Science in 1914; the paper reproduced here was the first which presented his embryological data in detail.

Later studies by other workers, utilizing more refined methods, have failed to confirm Child's hypothesis that dominant regions, those first to disintegrate in Child's experiments after the administration of KCN and other poisons, utilize greater amounts of oxygen than do less dominant regions which are slower to die. Nonetheless, Child's attempted explanations of morphogenetic observations on a metabolic basis were of great weight in stimulating the study of the egg and of the embryo as metabolic systems. In its attempt to relate the part to the whole, the gradient theory no doubt exerted its influence on the organizer theory, with which it overlapped to some degree, as Spemann himself realized. It still today remains one of the few general unifying concepts that attempts to account for over-all pattern in the development of the organism as a whole.

SUSCEPTIBILITY GRADIENTS IN ANIMALS

The writer has called attention in several papers[1] to the existence of axial gradients in rate of metabolism in planarians and other forms and their significance in relation to polarity. During the past summer in the course of other work at Woods Hole the opportunity presented itself to examine various forms belonging to different groups and various embryonic and larval stages for the existence of such gradients.

The method used was that of determining the relative susceptibility of different regions of the body to certain narcotics and poisons, KCN, alcohol and ether being chiefly used. To concentrations of these and various other substances which kill within a few hours without permitting any acclimatization the susceptibility varies in general with the rate of metabolism, or of certain fundamental metabolic processes, *i.e.,* the higher the rate of these processes the greater the susceptibility and the earlier death or cessation of movement occurs.[2] Death in these reagents is usually followed very soon, often almost at once, by rounding, separation or disintegration of the cells, so that the time of death can be approximately determined by visible changes of this kind. Results obtained in this manner can be controlled by removing the animals from the solution at different periods and determining when recovery ceases to occur and experience has shown that these two methods of procedure give essentially similar results. In this way the following forms were examined.

In *Nereis virens* the regional susceptibility of developmental stages from the beginning of cleavage to the late trochophore was determined. In the early cleavage stages the micromeres are more susceptible to KCN 0.005 *m.* than the macromeres. They not only disintegrate before the macromeres when the eggs remain in the solution, but if the eggs are returned to sea water at the proper time the micromeres alone are killed and the macromeres recover and resume division, giving rise to defective larvæ.

At the stage when gastrulation is nearly completed the somatic plate region is apparently the most susceptible region of the embryo, and by return to water at the proper time it is possible to obtain larvæ which do not elongate posteriorly and do not form the three larval segments. If the embryos at this stage are left for a longer time in KCN before return to water, both somatic plate and some or all of the macromeres are killed

---

[1] *Jour. Exp., Zool.,* XII., 1912; *Arch. f. Entwickelungsmech,* XXXV., 1913; XXXVII., 1913.
[2] Child, *Jour. Exp. Zool.,* XIV., 1913.

and the intact portion consists of more or less of the ventral portion of pre-trochal and post-trochal ectoderm with or without a part of the macromeres. Evidently the most susceptible regions at this stage are first the somatic plate, and second, the dorsal part of the pretrochal region and the macromeres.

In the developing egg of another annelid, *Chætopterus pergamentaceus,* the relative susceptibilities of different regions are much the same. In the early stages the animal pole shows the highest susceptibility and in later stages a second region of high susceptibility appears in the somatic plate. In still another polychæte, *Arenicola cristata,* the apical region and somatic plate of the young trochophores are the most susceptible regions. The early cleavage stages of this species were not obtained.

In *Nereis* and *Chætopterus* the region about the animal pole is clearly the region of greatest susceptibility, *i. e.,* of greatest metabolic activity in the early stages of development. Later the activity in this region becomes relatively less in *Nereis* as differentiation of the apical larval region advances and the somatic plate becomes the most active region of the egg. But in *Chætopterus* the apical region retains its susceptibility to some extent at the completion of gastrulation, and this region and the somatic plate appear as distinct regions of high susceptibility. In other words, at the beginning of development an axial metabolic gradient exists with the region of highest rate about the animal pole, but as development proceeds this gradient is altered from its primary simple form by the increase in activity of the cells which give rise to body segments and later by decrease in activity in the animal pole region.

In the egg of the sea urchin *Arbacia* in KCN 0.005 *m.* a distinct susceptibility gradient was observed during cleavage, death and disintegration beginning at one region of the egg and proceeding along an axis, but it was not possible to determine whether the region of highest susceptibility was always the animal pole, though in many cases it certainly was. In the later gastrula and prepluteus stages this simple gradient was complicated by the appearance of high susceptibility in the regions where the arms were beginning to develop.

Since in *Nereis, Chætopterus* and *Arbacia* the different susceptibilities of different regions of the developmental stages make it possible to kill with more or less exactness certain parts of the embryo while other parts may recover and continue development, this method may prove of some value in further investigation of the regulatory capacities of the less active regions when isolated from the influence of the more active.

The adult forms of a number of species from various groups were examined for a susceptibility gradient. In the hydroid *Pennaria tiarella* with KCN 0.0025 *m.* and 0.005 *m.* such a gradient appears very clearly in the body of the hydranth, death and disintegration beginning at the distal end of the manubrium and proceeding proximally. A similar gradient exists in the medusa buds of this species. Besides this it was observed that the full-grown hydranths at or near the tips of stem or branches were in general more susceptible than the more proximal. This difference may be due to external factors such as the lower oxygen or higher CO_2 content of the water about the more proximal hydranths in consequence of the greater number of hydranths in a given area, but it seems more probable, in the light of various data concerning the polarity of plants, that this difference in susceptibility of distal and proximal hydranths is the expression of an axial gradient in the colony.

In several other species of hydroids examined at Woods Hole and at La Jolla, California, among them *Tubularia crocea* and *Corymorpha palma* the gradient in the hydranth body is similar to that in *Pennaria*.

The ctenophore *Mnemiopsis leidyi* shows a distinct gradient in susceptibility along each row of swimming plates. The susceptibility of these animals to KCN is very high and most experiments were made with KCN 0.0000375 *m.*—00005 *m.* Rhythmic movement of the plates ceases first at the central end of each row, *i. e.,* the end nearest the apical sense organ, and last at the peripheral end. Before movement has entirely stopped in the apical region the rhythm of the plates in the peripheral half or third of the row becomes different from the central rhythm, being usually more rapid and in some cases irregular or periodic. In two cases a perfectly distinct reversal in direction of the impulse was observed at the peripheral end of a row after movement at the central end had ceased. In this case the impulse started at the extreme peripheral end of the row and traveled some distance in the central direction, finally dying out. This continued for an hour or more before movement at the peripheral end ceased.

This susceptibility gradient is undoubtedly a gradient in the nerve and not in the plates themselves, for the plates do not die in KCN until long after rhythmic movement ceases, and as long as they remain alive direct contact stimulation of single plates produces slight movements of the plate stimulated. However, a slight susceptibility gradient does exist in the plates themselves as is evident from the fact that the plates at the central end of the nerve die first and death proceeds peripherally. The time of death is readily determined, for when they die the plates lose their interference colors and become white and opaque.

As regards the general ectoderm of *Mnemiopsis,* it is difficult to determine the time of death accurately, but observations thus far indicate that the disintegration of the ectoderm proceeds from the apical region.

During the course of my observations on susceptibility gradients Dr. Tashiro called my attention to his discovery of a quantitative gradient in CO_2 production in the claw nerve of the large spider crab, *Libinia canaliculata:* this is a long nerve which readily separates into small strands and is therefore favorable for observation of any structural changes which might occur in connection with death in solutions of narcotics. The nerve is mixed but is believed to consist largely of efferent fibers.

Since there is some evidence in the work of various authors that a gradient of some sort exists in the nerve, the attempt was made to determine whether a gradient would appear in the structural death changes. A number of nerves were observed in various concentrations of KCN from 0.001 *m.* to 0.01 *m.* In these solutions the fibrillæ become after a time irregular in outline and more or less varicose so that the strand appears more or less granular instead of fibrillar like the fresh living nerve. The preparations showed some indications of the progression of the change from the central to the peripheral end of the nerve, but the changes were so slight that the possibility of a subjective factor being concerned could not be neglected. In the attempt to obtain more distinct structural death changes other narcotics were used, and it was found that in ethyl ether the fibrillation almost completely disappeared and the strands became very distinctly granular in appearance in consequence of irregular swelling and varicosity of the fibrils. In 1 per cent ether or somewhat lower concentrations these changes occur, slowly requiring several hours for completion, and a very distinct gradient in their occurrence is visible. The change from fibrillar to granular appearance begins at the two ends of the nerve very soon after it is brought into the solution, and a distinct gradient in this change can be seen extending a few millimeters peripherally from the central end and a shorter distance centrally from the peripheral end. This first change remains limited to the two terminal regions of the nerve and is undoubtedly associated with the stimulation and injury resulting from severing the nerve at these two points.

Later, however, the change begins to progress along the nerve from the central toward the peripheral end, but the change at the peripheral end progresses only very slowly or not at all in the central direction. From this time on a distinct gradient in the change is visible until it has progressed along the whole length of the nerve. Except in the terminal region adjoining the peripheral cut end the death change always progresses in the peripheral direction. The peripheral third of the length may be entirely unchanged at a time when the central third or more has completely lost its fibrillar appearance. When long strands are so arranged that central and peripheral regions are side by side in the same field of the microscope the differences between the two regions are very striking. If the nerve is crushed or injured at any point short gradients appear on both sides of the injury, but do not extend to any great distance before the general change reaches this region in its progress peripherally.

The existence of this centro-peripheral gradient in the death changes of the nerve fiber in narcotics must mean that a gradient of some sort exists in the living nerve and if the action of the narcotics is of the same character here as in other cases we must conclude that this gradient is associated with metabolism and that the rate of metabolism or of certain metabolic processes is in general higher at the central end and decreases peripherally in this nerve.

That metabolic gradients occur very widely if not universally, at least during the earlier stages of development in axiate organisms and structures, is evident from the data of embryology. The so-called law of antero-posterior development must be the expression of an axial metabolic gradient. And as regards plants there is a large body of evidence which indicates that the vegetative tip possesses a higher rate of metabolism than other regions of the same axis. Even in the unicellular body of the ciliate infusoria and in various other cells which show a morphological polarity the writer has observed a susceptibility gradient. In view of the facts it is impossible to doubt that such gradients are in some way closely associated with polarity in organisms, and various lines of experimental evidence which can not be considered here indicate that they constitute the dynamic basis of polarity. There are, moreover, many facts which suggest that the establishment of a gradient of this kind is the first step in individuation in axiate organisms.

1916

The Theory of the Free-Martin

by FRANK R. LILLIE

Lillie, Frank R. 1916. The theory of the Free-Martin. Science 43:611-613. Reprinted by permission of Science.

In 1906 Lillie showed that he had been reflecting on the problem of sex differentiation, for in that year he argued that in the zygote (fertilized egg) we must find the primary cause of sexual differentiation and seek an answer to the question as to "how the differentiated conditions are subsequently produced." To him the old concept of a sexually indifferent stage in the life history "is as necessary and fundamental today as it ever appeared to be, and . . . we cannot depart from it without involving ourselves in absolutely hopeless theoretical difficulties." Thus, Lillie clearly and accurately envisaged that the determining conditions set in the egg at fertilization act so as to direct the course of differentiation of sex characters in either the male or female direction and that such characters arise, like other characters, in an orderly sequence in embryogenesis. Thus Lillie was prepared for a chance event that came about on the family farm northwest of Chicago near the village of Wheeling, Illinois. There, in a prize herd of purebred cattle his attention was first drawn to the "free-martin," a term popularly applied from ancient times by experienced cattle breeders to a barren female which is born co-twin to a normal bull calf. The question naturally arose in Lillie's mind as to whether the sterility of the female was a causal consequence of its association with a male co-twin during uterine life. Was this one of nature's experiments that would test Lillie's hunch that mechanisms in the control of sex differentiation can be analyzed?

Lillie's answer to this question is a model of scientific analysis. In it he displayed during exploration, rigorous logic, penetrating insight and creative interpretation, as you will detect in reading his first published paper on the free-martin as reprinted below. The definitive article, "The Free-martin; a study of the action of sex hormones in the foetal life of cattle" was published in 1917. Somewhat later Lillie learned of a similar analysis of two-sexed twins in cattle by Karl Keller and Julius Tandler, published in 1916 in a veterinary journal, the Wiener tierärtliche Wochenschrift, 3. Jahrg., 513-526. These authors reached the same conclusion with respect to the cause of female intersexuality, as Lillie noted in an appraisal of the work of Keller and Tandler in 1923 (Biol. Bull., 44: 47-78).

Lillie's discovery of sex-hormone action in cattle twins marks a turning point in history of the investigation of the nature, origin and action of sex hormones at a time when very little was known about the subject. It started many researches initially designed to test the sex hormonal theory of the free-martin by experimental means. Further, it furnished a sound basis for the concept of selective response of endocrine receptors to hormonal molecules in the vascular circulation of the embryo.

137

More recent studies have shown that the modification of sex develop-
ment is not the only change that takes place when the allantoic blood
vessels of dizygotic twins are united so as to permit an interchange of
blood (see facing page). In 1945 Owen made the discovery that such non-
identical cattle twins after birth have identical red-cell antigens, and in
1951 Medawar and co-workers found that skin grafts exchanged between
dizygotic twin calves are in the majority of cases mutually acceptable
whereas skin grafts exchanged between individuals of separate birth are
rapidly destroyed by the homograft reaction. Obviously, the mutual
tolerance of the skin and mixture of blood types have the same origin, i.e.,
through an interchange of blood before birth. Initiated by Burnet's
theory of immunological tolerance, Medawar and co-workers succeeded in
reproducing experimentally by injecting living cell suspensions into
embryos and/or new born animals the same state of tolerance to skin
homografts that comes about by natural accident in cattle twins. In
recognition of their work in the elucidation of the development and
nature of the immune response, Medawar and Burnet shared the Nobel
prize in physiology and medicine for 1960.

THE THEORY OF THE FREE-MARTIN

The term free-martin is applied to the female of heterosexual twins
of cattle. The recorded experience of breeders from ancient times to the
present has been that such females are usually barren, though cases of
normal fertility are recorded. This presents an unconformable case in
twinning and sex-determination, and it has consequently been the cause
of much speculation.

The appearance of an abstract in Science[1] of Leon J. Cole's paper
before the American Society of Zoologists on "Twinning in Cattle with
Special Reference to the Free-Martin," is the immediate cause of this
preliminary report of my embryological investigation of the subject. Cole
finds in a study of records of 303 multiple births in cattle that there were
43 cases homosexual male twins, 165 cases heterosexual twins (male and
female), and 88 cases homosexual female, and 7 cases of triplets. This
gives a ratio of about 1♂♂:4♂♀:2♀♀, for the twins instead of the expected
ratio of 1:2:1. Cole then states:

The expectation may be brought more nearly into harmony with the facts
if it is assumed that in addition to ordinary fraternal (dizygotic) twins, there are
numbers of "identical" (monozygotic) twins of both sexes, and that while in the
case of females these are both normal, in the case of a dividing male zygote, to

[1] Vol. XLIII., p. 177, February 4, 1916.

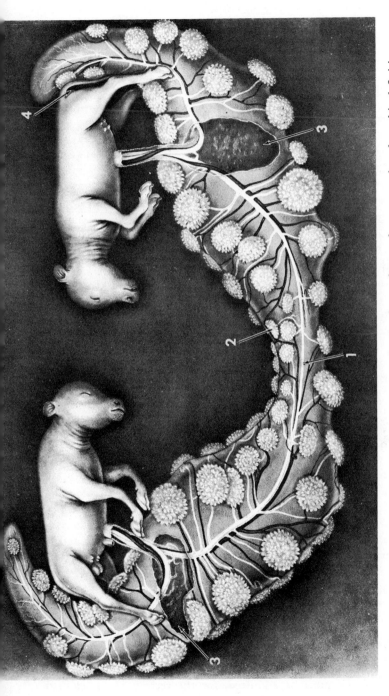

The paper by Lillie reproduced here was not illustrated. The figure shown above was taken from his definitive publication on *The Free-martin; a Study of the Action of Sex Hormones in the Foetal Life of Cattle. Jour. Exp. Zool.*, 23:371–452 (1917). The original legend reads as follows: **Fig. 4** Twin chorionic vesicle of cow; double injection; case no. 47. ♂ 22.75 cm. ♂ 22.25 cm. ×¼. 1, arterial through trunk; 2, cotyledon with venous connection with both sides; 3, amniotic sacs opened; 4, clitoris of free-martin; note female arrangement of teats; cf. with male.

form two individuals, in one of them the sexual organs remain in the undifferentiated stage, so that the animal superficially resembles a female and ordinarily is recorded as such, although it is barren. The records for monozygotic twins accordingly go to increase the homosexual female and the heterosexual classes, while the homosexual male class in which part of them really belong, does not receive any increment.

Cole thus tentatively adopts the theory, which has been worked out most elaborately by D. Berry Hart, stated also by Bateson, and implied in Spiegelberg's analysis (1861), that the sterile free-martin is really a male co-zygotic with its mate.

Cole's figures represent the only statistical evidence that we have on this subject. Let us follow his suggestion and take from the heterosexual class enough cases to make the homosexual male twins equal in number to the homosexual female pairs; this will be approximately one fourth of the class, leaving the ratio 2:3:2 instead of 1:4:2. Which one of these is the more satisfactory sex ratio I leave others to determine; I wish only to point out the fatal objection, that, according to the hypothesis, the females remaining in the heterosexual class are normal; in other words, on this hypothesis the ratio of normal free-martins (females co-twin with a bull) to sterile ones is 3:1; and the ratio would not be very different on any basis of division of the heterosexual class that would help out the sex ratio. Hitherto there have been no data from which the ratio of normal to sterile free-martins could be computed, and Cole furnishes none. I have records of 21 cases statistically homogeneous, 3 of which are normal and 18 abnormal. That is, the ratio of normal to sterile free-martins is 1:6 instead of 3:1.

This ratio is not more adverse to the normals than might be anticipated, for breeders' associations will not register free-martins until they are proved capable of breeding, and some breeders hardly believe in the existence of fertile free-martins, so rare are they.

My own records of 41 cases of bovine twins (to date, February 25, 1916), all examined *in utero*, and their classification determined anatomically without the possibility of error, give $14\male\male : 21\male\female : 6\female\female$. It will be observed that this agrees with expectation to the extent that the sum of the homosexual classes is (almost) equal to the heterosexual class; and it differs from expectation inasmuch as the $\male\male$ class is over twice the $\female\female$ class instead of being equal to it, as it should be if males and females are produced in equal numbers in cattle. The material can not be weighted statistically because every uterus containing twins below a certain size from a certain slaughter house is sent to me for examination without being opened. Cole's material shows twice as many female as male pairs, and the heterosexual class is about one third greater than the sum of the two homosexual classes. I strongly suspect that it is weighted statistically; the possibility of this must be admitted, for the records are assembled from a great number of breeders. But, whether this is so or not, if we add the sterile free-martin pairs of my collection to the male side in accordance with Cole's suggestion, we get the ratio 32♂♂:3♂♀:6♀♀, which is absurd. And if we take Cole's figures, divide his heterosexual class into pairs containing sterile females and pairs containing normal females according to the expectation, 6 of the former to 1 of the latter, and add the former to his male class, we get an almost equally absurd result (18♂♂:23♂♀:88♀♀). On the main question our statistical results are sufficiently alike to show that the free-martin can not possibly be interpreted as a male. The theory of Spiegelberg, D. Berry Hart, Bateson and Cole falls on the statistical side alone.

But the real test of the theory must come from the embryological side. If the sterile free-martin and its bull-mate are monozygotic, they should be included within a single chorion, and there should be but a single corpus luteum present. If they are dizygotic, we might expect two separate chorions and two corpora lutea. The monochorial condition would not, however, be a conclusive test of monozygotic origin, for two chorions originally independent might fuse secondarily. The facts as determined from examination of 41 cases are that about 97.5 per cent. of bovine twins are monochorial, but in spite of this nearly all are dizygotic; for in all cases in which the ovaries were present with the uterus a corpus luteum was present in each ovary; in normal single pregnancies in cattle there is never more than one corpus luteum present. There was one homosexual case (males) in which only one ovary was present with the uterus when received, and it contained no corpus luteum. This case was probably monozygotic.

There is space only for a statement of the conclusions drawn from a study of these cases, and of normal pregnancies. In cattle a twin pregnancy is almost always a result of the fertilization of an ovum from each ovary; development begins separately in each horn of the uterus. The rapidly elongating ova meet and fuse in the small body of the uterus at some time between the 10 mm. and the 20 mm. stage. The blood vessels from each side then anastomose in the connecting part of the chorion; a particularly wide arterial anastomosis develops, so that either fetus can be injected from the other. The arterial circulation of each also overlaps the venous territory of the other, so that a constant interchange of blood takes place. If both are males or both are females no harm results from this; but *if one is male and the other female, the reproductive system of the female is largely suppressed, and certain male organs even develop in the female. This is unquestionably to be interpreted as a case of hormone action.* It is not yet determined whether the invariable result of sterilization of the female at the expense of the male is due to more precocious development of the male hormones, or to a certain natural dominance of male over female hormones.

The results are analogous to Steinach's feminization of male rats and masculinization of females by heterosexual transplantation of gonads into castrated infantile specimens. But they are more extensive in many respects on account of the incomparably earlier onset of the hormone action. In the case of the free-martin, nature has performed an experiment of surpassing interest.

Bateson states that sterile free-martins are found also in sheep, but rarely. In the four twin pregnancies of sheep that I have so far had the opportunity to examine, a monochorial condition was found, though the fetuses were dizygotic; but the circulation of each fetus was closed. This appears to be the normal condition in sheep; but if the two circulations should anastomose, we should have the conditions that produce a sterile free-martin in cattle. The possibility of their occurrence in sheep is therefore given.

The fertile free-martin in cattle may be due to cases similar to those normal for sheep. Unfortunately when the first two cases of normal cattle free-martins that I have recorded, came under observation I was not yet aware of the significance of the membrane relations, and the circulation was not studied. But I recorded in my notebook in each case that the connecting part of the two halves of the chorion was narrow, and this is significant. In the third case the two chorions were entirely unfused; this case, therefore, constitutes an *experimentum crucis*. The male was 10.4 cm. long; the female 10.2 cm. The reproductive organs of both were entirely normal. The occurrence of the fertile free-martin is therefore satisfactorily explained.

The sterile free-martin enables us to distinguish between the effects of the zygotic sex-determining factor in mammals, and the hormonic sex-differentiating factors. The female is sterilized at the very beginning of sex-differentiation, or before any morphological evidences are apparent, and male hormones circulate in its blood for a long period thereafter. But in spite of this the reproductive system is for the most part of the female type, though greatly reduced. The gonad is the part most affected; so much so that most authors have interpreted it as testis; a gubernaculum of the male type also develops, but no scrotal sacs. The ducts are distinctly of the female type much reduced, and the phallus and mammary glands are definitely female. The general somatic habitus inclines distinctly toward the male side. Male hormones circulating in the blood of an individual zygotically female have a definitely limited influence, even though the action exists from the beginning of morphological sex-differentiation. A detailed study of this problem will be published at a later date.

1924

Induction of Embryonic Primordia by Implantation of Organizers from a Different Species

by HANS SPEMANN and HILDE MANGOLD

Spemann, H. und Hilde Mangold. 1924. Über Induktion von Embryonalanlagen durch Implantation artfremder Organisatoren. Wilhelm Roux' Arch. Entwicklungsmech. Organ. 100:599-638. Translated by Viktor Hamburger and printed by permission of Springer-Verlag.

Through an extensive series of exact experiments on the developing newt's egg carried out over a period of almost a quarter of a century Spemann (1869-1941) was gradually led to the discovery of "organizer" effects. The concept may be traced back to his constriction experiments of 1901-1903 in which the blastomeres of the two-celled stage were separated by tightening a human baby's hair around the first cleavage furrow. In some eggs each blastomere developed into a whole embryo small in size (twins), whereas in the majority of eggs one of the blastomeres developed into a perfect embryo and the other one into an unorganized ball of living cells. These differences in results were explained on the basis of variable position of the first cleavage plane with reference to the median plane of the future embryo. In the cases where two normal dwarf embryos developed, the first cleavage plane happened to coincide with the median plane whereas in those cases where only one blastomere gave a whole embryo the first cleavage plane lies at right angles to the median plane, so dividing the egg into dorsal and ventral halves. By constricting eggs during early gastrulation this explanation was proved to be correct. Thus Spemann concluded that as early as the two-celled stage the dorsal half differs qualitatively from the ventral half, the former possessing a quality which enables it to form an embryo whereas the latter lacks such a quality.

In 1918 he reported that small pieces of ectoderm (prospective neural plate and epidermis) exchanged between Triton embryos of early gastrula stages developed in accord with their new position whereas a piece of the dorsal lip behaved in a different manner, i.e., it developed into an embryolike body with neural tube, notochord and somites when transplanted to new positions. From these contrasting results Spemann made the assumption that the dorsal lip was already determined and he suggested that it might represent a "center of differentiation" from which a process of determination gradually spreads forward to the undetermined ectoderm of the gastrula.

It is of historical interest to note here that Lewis (1907) using frog embryos had previously reported that a piece of the dorsal lip grafted to a host embryo develops into nerve tube, chorda and muscle. This he interpreted as indicating that the dorsal lip is determined and undergoes self-differentiation.

Although Spemann had noted as early as 1918 that a graft of the dorsal lip to a host embryo tended to result in the formation of an embryo, the question arose in his mind as to how much of its development was due to self-differentiation, and how much to induction. Lewis had assumed that the transplanted dorsal lip self-differentiated. Concepts of induction had already been developing in Spemann's mind as a result of his earlier studies (1901-1912) on the relationships between optic cup and overlying lens ectoderm, and he recognized that the "organizing" effect of the dorsal lip might be related to inductive action by the archenteron roof on the ectoderm overlying it.

The answer to the question was made possible by grafting a dorsal lip of one species of newt to another species differing in amount of dark pigment. In this way the source of cells which contribute to the secondary embryo could be followed in a precise manner. In a postscript to his 1921 paper on heteroplastic transplantation, Spemann, in referring to experiments made by his student, Hilde Mangold, gave the first description of the dorsal lip as an organizing center which he named the "organizer" (Organisator in German) for short. The experiment described in the 1924 article was a crucial one. It showed that both the dorsal lip and host embryo participate in the formation of a secondary embryo but that the graft contributes the major portion of the chorda-mesoderm and the host the major part of the nervous system. The discovery of the organizer and the analysis of its action was one of the most significant events in experimental embryology; it gave reality to the epigenetic concepts of earlier embryologists, demonstrating experimentally that one step in development is a necessary condition for the next, and won for Hans Spemann the Nobel Prize in Physiology and Medicine in 1935.

INDUCTION OF EMBRYONIC PRIMORDIA BY IMPLANTATION
OF ORGANIZERS FROM A DIFFERENT SPECIES

I. INTRODUCTION

In a *Triton* embryo, at the beginning of gastrulation, the different areas are not equivalent with respect to their determination.

It is possible to exchange by transplantation parts of the ectoderm at some distance above the blastopore that in the course of further development would have become neural plate and parts that would have become epidermis, without disturbing normal development by this operation. This is feasible not only between embryos of the same age and of the same species but also between embryos of somewhat different age and even between embryos of different species (Spemann 1918, 1921). For instance, presumptive epidermis of *Triton cristatus* transplanted into the forebrain region of *Triton taeniatus* can become brain; and presumptive brain of *Triton taeniatus* transplanted into the epidermal region of *Triton cristatus* can become epidermis. Both pieces develop according to their new position; however they have the species characteristics with which they are endowed according to their origin. O. Mangold (1922, 1923) has extended these findings and has shown that prospective epidermis can furnish not only neural plate but even organs of mesodermal origin, such as somites and pronephric tubules. It follows from these experimental facts, on the one hand, that the exchangeable pieces are still relatively indifferent with respect to their future fate; and, on the other hand, that influences of some sort must prevail in the different regions of the embryo that determine the later fate of those pieces that are at first indifferent.

A piece from the upper lip of the blastopore behaves quite differently. If it is transplanted into the region that would later become epidermis, it develops according to its origin; in this region, a small secondary embryonic primordium develops, with neural tube, notochord and somites (Spemann 1918). Such a piece therefore resists the determining influences that impinge on it from its new environment, influences that, for instance, would readily make epidermis out of a piece of presumptive neural plate. Therefore, it must already carry within itself the direction of its development; it must be determined. Lewis (1907) had already found this for a somewhat later developmental stage, when he implanted a small piece from the upper and lateral blastopore lip under the epidermis of a somewhat older embryo and saw it develop there into neural tissue and somites.

It suggested itself from the beginning that effects might emanate from these already determined parts of the embryo that would determine the fate of the still indifferent parts. This could be proved by cutting the embryo in half and shifting the halves with respect to each other; in this case, the determined part proved to be decisive for the direction that subsequent development would take. For instance, the animal half of the gastrula was rotated 90° or 180° with respect to the vegetal half; determination then spread from the lower vegetal piece, that contained just the upper lip, to the upper animal piece. Or two gastrula halves of the same side, for instance two right ones, were fused together. As a result, the half blastoporal lips completed themselves from adjacent material of the fused other half, and in this way, whole neural plates were formed (Spemann 1918).

Thus, the concept of the *organization center* emerged; that is, of a region of the embryo that has preceded the other parts in determination and thereupon emanates determination effects of a certain quantity in certain directions. The experiments to be presented here are the beginning of the analysis of the organization center.

Such a more deeply penetrating analysis presupposes the possibility of subdividing the organization center into separate parts and of testing their organizing capacities in an indifferent region of the embryo. This experiment has already been performed, and it was precisely this experiment that gave the first indication that the parts of the embryo are not equivalent at the beginning of gastrulation (1918). However, this intraspecific, homoplastic transplantation did not make it possible to ascertain how the secondary embryonic anlage that originated at the site of the transplant was constructed, that is, which part of it was derived from the material of the implant and which part had been induced by the implant from the material of the host embryo. The identification of these two components is made possible by heteroplastic transplantation, as for instance by implantation of organizers from *Triton cristatus* into indifferent material of *Triton taeniatus*.

This experiment, that followed logically from its presuppositions, was performed during the summers of 1921 and 1922 by Hilde Mangold née Pröscholdt. It gave at once the expected result that has already been reported briefly (Spemann 1921, pp. 551 and 568). In the following, we shall present the basic facts in more detail.

II. EXPERIMENTAL ANALYSIS

Nothing new need be said concerning the experimental technique; it was the same as in previous experiments (Spemann 1920).

Of the species of *Triton* available, *taeniatus* can best tolerate the absence of the egg membrane, from early developmental stages on; and it is the easiest to rear. Hence the organizer that was to be tested for its capacities was always taken from a *cristatus* embryo and usually implanted into the presumptive epidermis of a *taeniatus* embryo. The place of excision was marked by implantation of the piece removed from the *taeniatus* embryo; that is, the pieces were exchanged.

Experiment Triton 1921, Um 8b. The exchange was made between a *cristatus* embryo with distinctly U-shaped blastopore and a *taeniatus* embryo of the same stage. A small circular piece at some distance above the blastopore was removed from the *cristatus* embryo and replaced by a piece of presumptive epidermis of the *taeniatus* embryo. This *taeniatus* implant was found, later on, as a marker in the neural plate of the *cristatus* neurula, between the right neural fold and the midline, and it extended to

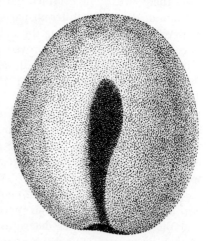

Fig. 1 Um 8 crist. The *cristatus* embryo at the neurula stage. The *taeniatus* transplant is dark and elongated; it is located in the presumptive neural plate. 20×.

the blastopore, slightly tapering toward the posterior end (Fig. 1). One could not see in the living embryo whether it continued into the interior, and the sections, which are poor in this region, did not show this either.

The *cristatus* explant (the "organizer") was inserted on the right side of the *taeniatus* embryo, approximately between the blastopore and the animal pole. It was found in the neurula stage to the right and ventrally, and drawn out in the shape of a narrow strip (Fig. 2). In its vicinity, at first a slight protrusion was observable; a few hours later, neural folds appeared, indicating the contour of a future neural plate. The implant was still distinctly recognizable in the midline of this plate; it extended forward from the blastopore as a long narrow strip, slightly curved, over about two-thirds of the plate (Fig. 3).

This secondary neural plate, that developed in combination with the implanted piece, lagged only a little behind the primary plate in its

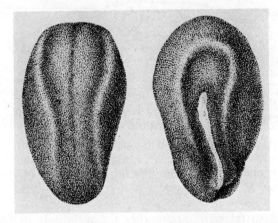

Figs. 2 and 3 Um 8b. The *taeniatus* embryo at the neurula stage, with primary and secondary neural plate; the elongated white *cristatus* implant is in the median plane of the latter. 20×.

development. When the folds of the primary plate were partly closed, those of the secondary plate also came together. Approximately a day later, both neural tubes were closed. The secondary tube begins, together with the primary tube, at the normal blastopore and extends to the right of the primary tube, rostrad, to approximately the level where the optic vesicles of the latter would form. It is poorly developed at its posterior part, yet well enough that the *cristatus* implant was invisible from the outside. The embryo was fixed at this stage and sectioned as nearly perpendicularly to the axial organs as possible.

The sections disclosed the following:

The neural tube of the primary embryonic anlage is closed through the greater part of its length and detached from the epidermis, except at the anterior end where it is still continuous with it, and where its lumen opens to the exterior through a neuropore. The lateral walls are considerably thickened in front; this is perhaps the first indication of the future primary eye vesicles. The notochord is likewise completely detached, except at its posterior end where it is continuous with the unstructured cell mass of the tail blastema. In the mesoderm, four to five somites are separated from the lateral plates, as far as one can judge from cross sections of such an early stage.

Only the anterior part of the neural tube of the secondary embryonic anlage is closed and detached from the epidermis. Here it is well developed; in fact it is developed almost as far as the primary tube at its largest cross-section: its walls are thick and its lumen is drawn out sideways (Fig. 4). Perhaps we can see here the first indication of optic

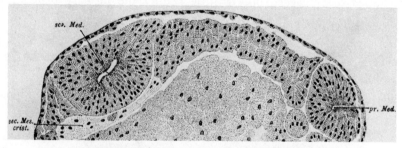

Fig. 4 Um 8b. Cross section through the anterior third of the embryo (cf. Figs. 2 and 3). pr. Med., primary neural tube; sec. Med., secondary neural tube. The implant (light) is in the mesoderm (sec. Mes. crist.). 100×.

vesicles. The central canal approaches the surface at its posterior end, and eventually opens to the outside. Then the neural plate rapidly tapers off; its hindmost portion is only a narrow ectodermal thickening (Figs. 5 and 6).

Although the overwhelming mass of this secondary neural tube is formed by cells of the *taeniatus* host that can be recognized by the finely dispersed pigment, a long, narrow strip of completely unpigmented cells is intercalated in its floor, in sharp contrast to the adjacent regions. This white strip is part of the *cristatus* implant that was clearly recognizable from the outside in the living embryo before the neural folds closed (Fig. 3). The anterior end of this strip is approximately at the point where the thickness of the neural tube decreases rather abruptly; it opens to the outside shortly thereafter. The strip is wedge-shaped, with the pointed edge toward the outside; as a result, only the tapering ends of the cells reach the surface of the embryo (Figs. 5 and 6) or the central canal at the short stretch where they border it.

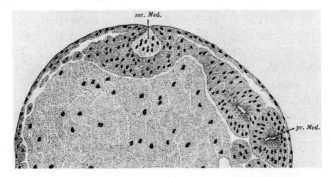

Fig. 5 Um 8b. Cross section through middle third of the embryo (cf. Figs. 2 and 3). pr. Med., primary neural tube; sec. Med., secondary neural tube. The implant (light) is in the secondary neural tube.

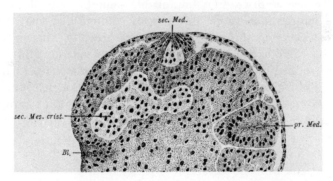

Fig. 6 Um 8b. Cross section in the region of the blastopore (Bl.) (cf. Figs. 2 and 3). pr. Med., primary neural tube; sec. Med., secondary neural tube. The implant (light) has several cells in the secondary neural tube, with its main mass in the mesoderm (sec. Mes. crist.). 100×.

At its posterior end, the *cristatus* strip reaches the blastopore, and it is continuous with a mass of *cristatus* cells that is located between the secondary neural tube and the mesoderm on one side, and the endoderm on the other (Fig. 6). Because of their position one would be inclined to consider these cells as endoderm; but in size they resemble more the mesoderm of the *taeniatus* embryo with which they are associated. At any rate, this cell mass, which extends a bit farther rostrad, has reached its position by invagination around the blastoporal lip. There is yet another mass of *cristatus* cells still farther rostrad. It has the form of a thin plate underlying the anterior part of the induced neural tube, as far as it is closed; at its anterior end and at its sides it coincides approximately with the edge of the tube, and at its posterior end it extends to the ectodermal strip of the implant. This plate is incorporated in the normal *taeniatus* mesoderm (Fig. 4). It is not differentiated further into notochord or somites.

Altogether, a rather substantial part of the implant remained in the ectoderm. This portion was greatly stretched in length; as a result, the circular white disk that was implanted has become a long narrow strip that turns inwards around the blastoporal lip. Shifting of cells in the surrounding epidermis may have played a role in these form changes; the extent to which this occurs would have to be tested by implantation of a marker of indifferent material. A piece from a region near the upper lip of the blastopore could hardly be considered as suitable for this purpose. We know from earlier experiments (Spemann 1918, 1921) that convergence and stretching of the cell material occurs at the posterior part of the neural plate. It is improbable that the cells of the neural plate are entirely passive in this process; rather, they may have an inherent tendency to shift that perhaps has been, together with other characteristics, induced by the underlying endo-mesoderm. This tendency would be retained by the piece in the foreign environment. In this way we might also explain the fact that the piece gains contact with the invaginating region of the normal blastoporal lip, although it was originally far distant from it. Once it has arrived there by active stretching it could be carried along, at least in part, by the local cell shiftings.

Whereas this posterior cell mass is continuous with the cell strip that has remained on the surface, it is separated from the more anterior *cristatus* cell plate by *taeniatus* mesoderm. Therefore, this anterior plate that underlies the neural tube cannot have arrived at its position by invagination around the upper blastoporal lip; it must have been located in the deeper position from the beginning. Undoubtedly it derives from the inner layer of the implant; hence it was originally just under the *cristatus* cells, some of which are now found partly in the neural plate as a narrow strip, and others of which had migrated inside around the blastoporal lip. These displacements carried it along and brought it forward to such an extent that now its posterior margin is approximately level with the anterior end of the *cristatus* cell strip in the neural tube.

Although a piece of presumptive neural plate taken from a region a little anterior to the actual transplant would have become epidermis after transplantation to presumptive epidermis, this implant has resisted the determinative influences of the surroundings and has developed essentially according to its place of origin. Its ectodermal part has become part of the neural plate and the endo-mesodermal part has placed itself beneath it.

Furthermore, not only did the implant assert itself, but it made the indifferent surroundings subservient to it and it has supplemented itself from these surroundings. The host embryo has developed a second neural plate out of its own material, that is continuous with the small strip of *cristatus* cells and underlain by two cell plates of *cristatus* origin. This secondary plate would not have arisen at all without the implant, hence it must have been caused, or induced, by it.

There seems to be no possible doubt about this. However, the question remains open as to the way in which the induction has taken place. In the present case it seems to be particularly plausible to assume a direct influence on the part of the transplant. But even under this assumption, there are still two possibilities open. The ectodermal component of the transplant could have self-differentiated into the strip of neural plate, and could have caused the differentiation of ectoderm anterior and lateral to it progressively to form neural tissue. Or the determination could have emanated from the subjacent parts of the endo-mesoderm and have influenced both the *cristatus* and *taeniatus* components of the overlying ectoderm in the same way. And finally it is conceivable that the subjacent layer is necessary only for the first determination, which thereafter can spread in the ectoderm alone. A decision between these possibilities could be made if it were possible successfully to transplant pure ectoderm and pure endo-mesoderm from the region of the upper lip of the blastopore, and, finally, such ectoderm which had been underlain by the endo-mesoderm. In such experiments, heteroplastic transplantation offers again the inestimable advantage that one can establish afterwards with absolute certainty whether the intended isolation was successful.

In our case, such a separation of the factors under consideration has not been accomplished. Nevertheless it seems noteworthy that the induced neural plate is poorly developed in its posterior part where it is in closest and most extensive contact with the ectodermal part of the transplant; and, in contrast, that it is well developed at its anterior end where it is remote from the *cristatus* cell strip, but underlain by the broad *cristatus* cell plate.

We shall discuss later (p. 174) a second possibility of a fundamentally different nature that is particularly applicable to more completely formed secondary embryonic primordia.

A second experiment, similar to the first, confirms it in all essential points. They both have in common that the implant remains ectodermal to a considerable extent, and therefore later forms part of the neural tube. The situation is different in the following experiment.

Experiment Triton 1922, Um 25b. A median piece of the upper blastoporal lip was taken from a *cristatus* embryo at the beginning of gastrulation (sickle-shaped blastopore). It came from directly above the margin
of invagination and was implanted into a *taeniatus* gastrula of the same
stage in the ventral midline at some distance from the future blastopore.
Twenty-two hours later, when the *taeniatus* embryo had completed its
gastrulation, the implant had disappeared from the surface, which
looked completely smooth and normal. Another 24 hours later, the
embryo had two neural plates whose folds were about to close. The
secondary neural plate starts from the same blastopore as the primary
one; at first it runs parallel to the primary plate, adjacent to its left
side, and then it bends sharply to the left (Fig. 7). Shortly thereafter,
the embryo was fixed; the sections were cut
perpendicular to the posterior part of the axial
organs.

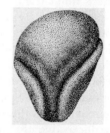

The primary neural tube is completely closed
and separated from the epidermis; its optic
vesicles are protruding. The notochord is separate down to its posterior end which becomes
lost in the indifferent zone. Seven or eight
somites are formed.

The secondary neural tube is also closed
and separated from the epidermis; anteriorly its
walls are broad and its lumen is transverse
(probably an indication of optic vesicles). It
decreases in thickness posteriorly. In its anterior
one-third it is bent sharply to the left and is

Fig. 7 Um 25b. The
taeniatus embryo at the
neurula stage. On the
right is the primary and
on the left the second-
ary neural tube. 20×.

therefore at some distance from the primary neural tube: but more
posteriorly, at its posterior two-thirds, it approaches the latter and
eventually fuses with it; however, the lumina, as far as they are present,
remain separate. This secondary neural tube is formed completely by
taeniatus cells, that is, by material supplied by the host embryo. *Cristatus
cells,* that is, material of the organizer, do not participate in its formation.

The implant has moved completely below the surface. Its most
voluminous, anterior part is a rather atypical mass located directly
under the secondary neural tube (Fig. 8), between it and the large yolk
cells of the intestine. Separate somites cannot be seen, but the contour
of a notochord can be delineated; in the anterior sections, where the
axial organs curve outward it is cut longitudinally, but transversely in
the more posterior ones (Fig. 8). Toward its posterior end, the implant
tapers off; it forms only the notochord and a few cells that merge with
the endoderm (Fig. 9). Thereafter, the notochord disappears also, and

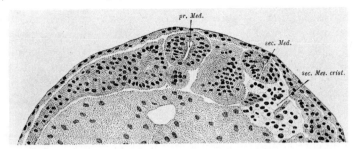

Fig. 8 Um 25b. Cross section in the middle third of the embryo (cf. Fig. 7). In the figure the secondary neural tube is seen to the right of the primary tube. The implant (light) is in the right primary mesoderm (sec. Mes. crist.). 100×.

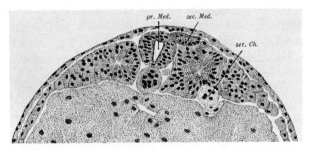

Fig. 9 Um 25b. Cross section in the posterior third of the embryo (cf. Fig. 7). The secondary neural tube is attached to the left side (right in the figure) of the primary tube. The implant (light) forms secondary notochord (sec. Ch.). 100×.

the implant lies entirely in the endoderm and forms the upper covering of a secondary intestinal lumen that extends over a few sections. In its entire posterior part, the implant is separated from the secondary neural tube by interposed mesoderm of the *taeniatus* embryo (Fig. 9). The neural tube extends considerably farther caudad than the implant.

In contrast to the first experiment, the implant in the present case forms a uniform mass; it is not separated into two sections by intervening mesoderm. This must have something to do with the way in which it was shifted to below the surface; however nothing definite can be ascertained concerning this point. The fact that the two embryonic anlagen share the remainder of the blastopore proves that the implant has been invaginated in the normal way around the blastopore. However, it is doubtful whether the implant was entirely passive in this process. It comes from a region whose cells normally participate actively in invagination; and in other instances they have retained this capacity after transplantation. For this reason, the situation becomes complicated.

The implant has formed the entire notochord, also the greater part of mesoderm, which however is not typically segmented, and a small part of the intestinal primordium. It is not clear in the present case whether it has also exerted an inductive effect on the adjacent mesoderm. However, it has certainly evoked the formation of the entire secondary neural tube; but in which way this has occurred remains undecided. A direct influence would be possible in the anterior region where the implant lies directly under the neural tube (Fig. 8); however this explanation is improbable farther back where the implant is displaced by host mesoderm (Fig. 9) or is entirely missing. One would have to assume that this mesoderm has been altered by the organizer and has, in turn, initiated the formation of the neural plate in the overlying ectoderm. However, it could be that the organizer had exerted its entire effect on the ectoderm before it had moved to the interior.

In summary, it is characteristic of this case that implant cells are completely absent in the secondary neural tube, and that the notochord is formed completely by cells of the implant. The same thing is shown, perhaps even more beautifully, in another case (*Triton* 1922, Um 214), in which the notochord formed by the implant, and also the induced neural tube, extend almost over the entire length of the host embryo, and are both near the normal axial organs. But this case again fails to indicate whether the implant can form somites or induce them in host mesoderm. The next case gives information on that point.

Experiment Triton 1922, 131b. The exchange of material was done in advanced gastrulae, after formation of the yolk plug. A large piece of *cristatus*, derived from the median line directly above the blastopore, was interchanged with a piece of *taeniatus* whose origin could not be definitely determined.

The *taeniatus* implant has not participated in the invagination in the *cristatus* embryo; it has caused a peculiar fission (Fig. 10). The neural tube is closed anteriorly; at the point where it meets the *taeniatus* piece, it divides into two halves, one to the left and one to the right. At this point, a bit of endoderm comes to the surface, perhaps as the result of incomplete healing or of a later injury. The cross-sections show a neural tube and notochord in the anterior part back to the point of bifurcation. The two divisions of the neural tube are still distinct for a few sections, but then they become indistinguishable from the surrounding tissue. The same is true, to a greater degree, of the notochord.

The *taeniatus* embryo has reached the neurula stage 20 hours later. The implant is located on the right side, somewhat behind the middle, and next to the right neural fold. Its original anterior half is still on the surface and strongly elevated over the surroundings; its original posterior half is invaginated and appears as a light area underneath the darker cells of the *taeniatus* embryo. The piece is stretched lengthwise and directed from posteriorly, and somewhat above, to anteriorly and somewhat downward. Invagination still continues; a half-hour later, a strip of *cristatus* cells is visible only at the outer margin of invagination. Twenty-five hours later, the neural folds are almost closed; the implant is visible to their right as a long, stretched out pale strip shining through the epidermis. At its posterior end, it continues into an elevation above the surface of the embryo that has the shape of a small blunt horn (Fig. 11). After another 22 hours, the neural tube is note-

Fig. 10 Um 131a. The *cristatus* embryo at the neurula stage. The *taeniatus* implant (dark), in the shape of a triangle with unequal sides, lies in the posterior dorsal half. 20×.

Fig. 11 Um 131b. The *taeniatus* embryo at the neurula stage. The neural folds are closing. The implant (light), in the middle and posterior third, to the right of the dorsal median plane, is visible through the surface layer, and continues into the protuberance.

worthy for its breadth. The implant is still visible at its right side. It apparently participates in the formation of somites; it continues posteriorly into the outgrowth. The embryo was fixed 11½ hours later when a small area of disintegration appeared on the head. The sections were perpendicular to the longitudinal axis.

We shall consider the axial organs, at first disregarding their different origin, and we begin in the middle region, where they show the typical appearance of a duplication (Fig. 14). The neural tube is incompletely duplicated; the upper outer walls and the lower inner walls of the two individual parts merge in such a fashion that their median planes converge dorsally and meet at a right angle ventrally.

There is one notochord underneath each of the two halves. There is an outer row of somites lateral to each notochord, and between them a third row, not quite double in size, that is common to both embryonic anlagen. Also, the intestine shows a double lumen in this region.

We now follow the different organs forwards and backwards from such a middle section.

The left half of the neural tube (at the right on the sections), which already in this middle region is somewhat larger than the right one, becomes relatively larger more and more anteriorly and continues eventually into a normal brain primordium with primary optic vesicles (Fig. 12). Thus the right half becomes reduced to an increasingly more in-

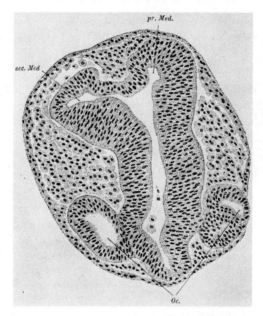

Fig. 12 Um 131b. Section through the head (cf. Fig. 11). Primary and secondary neural tubes are fused and their lumina are continuous. Oc., optic vesicles of the primary neural tube. 100×.

significant appendage and terminates finally without forming optic vesicles. The two tubes continue to have a common lumen; where it seems to be divided into two (as in Fig. 13), we are dealing with a curvature of the tubes resulting in tangential sections through their walls. Toward the posterior region, the two tubes separate from each other; at first their lumina separate (Fig. 15), and then also their walls. As far as one can make out, mesoderm intervenes between them. The larger left tube (at the right in the sections) continues into the normal

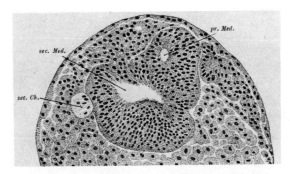

Fig. 13 Um 131b. Cross section in the anterior
third of the embryo (cf. Fig. 11). Primary and
secondary neural tubes are fused but their
lumina are separate. The implant (light) has
differentiated into notochord (sec. Ch.). 100×.

tail bud and the smaller right tube into the secondary tail-bud outgrowth. The greater width of the neural tube had already been observed
in the living embryo; but in the stage of the open neural plate neither
the larger size nor the duplication of the folds, that must have been
present, had been noticed.

The left notochord runs medially, in typical fashion, under the left
part of the neural tube (Figs. 14 and 15, right). The right notochord

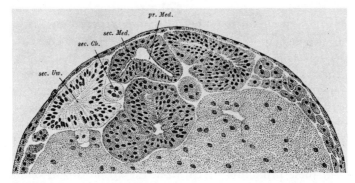

Fig. 14 Um 131b. Cross section in the middle third of the embryo
(cf. Fig. 11). Primary and secondary neural tubes are fused and
their lumina continuous. The implant (light) forms the secondary
somite (sec. Uw.) and the secondary notochord, and in addition
the roof of the secondary gut. 100×.

extends even farther forward than the left one (Fig. 13). It is clearly
delineated (Fig. 14) up to the point where the secondary tail bud begins
(Fig. 15); here its contour becomes indistinct and eventually it disappears
entirely.

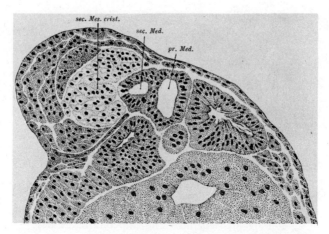

Fig. 15 Um 131b. Cross section at the base of the secondary tail (cf. Fig. 11). The primary and secondary neural tubes are fused; their lumina are separate. The implant (light) is in the floor of the secondary neural tube and forms mesoderm (sec. Mes. crist.) in the secondary tail. 100×.

Of the somites, only the outer left row (Fig. 14, right) is typically developed in its entire length. The outer right row, which is its symmetrical counterpart in the middle region (Fig. 14, left), anteriorly decreases in size considerably. Toward the posterior end it becomes symmetrical within itself, so that the notochord primordium lies approximately in its median plane (Fig. 15). It fades out eventually in the secondary tail bud. The middle row of somites seems, in its middle portion, to belong equally to both sides (Fig. 14). Toward the posterior end, where the right row achieves its own symmetry, the middle row becomes more and more the mirror image of the left row (Fig. 15). The primary plane of symmetry of the duplication therefore no longer bisects the middle row, as is the case in the middle region, but it passes between it and the right row.

Parts of these primordia derive from the *cristatus* cells of the transplant. In the neural tube, there are only a few *cristatus* cells in the median floor of the right half (Fig. 15). Furthermore, the entire right notochord and the entire outer row of somites are formed by *cristatus* cells (Figs. 13-15). In the gut, again, there are only a few such cells, located dorsally, forming the border of a small secondary lumen for a short distance (Fig. 14).

Besides these parts whose *material* derives from the implant, others have received the *stimulus* for their *formation* from the implanted organizer. This is certainly the case with respect to the entire right neural tube. But also the middle row of somites, in its symmetrical portion, has apparently been influenced from both sides, that is, from the normal and the implanted center; and it, in turn, seems to have affected the outer row of *cristatus* somites that are symmetrical to it.

The peculiarity of this case lies in the formation of somites from implanted material and, furthermore, in the interference of the implanted organizer with the normal organization center over a long distance. In the next case, this interference is limited to the anteriormost parts of the two embryonic primordia. Furthermore, the *cristatus* organizer was implanted into the very dark *alpestris* embryo, and the difference in pigmentation is, in part, very sharp.

Experiment Triton 1922, Um 83. The organizer was taken from an early gastrula of *cristatus,* medially, close to the blastopore, and implanted at the animal pole of an *alpestris* embryo in the blastula stage. The *cristatus* embryo disintegrated.

Gastrulation in the *alpestris* embryo begins after 23 hours. The implant is located in the animal half; it is large and curved inwards. Gastrulation is not yet completed after another 23 hours; the implant has disappeared completely into the interior. In its place, a little horn composed of *alpestris* cells protrudes on the dorsal side of the embryo. After another 21 hours, the folds have just begun to form. The little outgrowth is on the right neural fold, at the posterior border of the broad plate. After another 24 hours, the neural folds are in the process of closure; the little horn has disappeared. In the position where it had been visible a small secondary tube branches off the neural tube; it extends obliquely toward the caudal end (Fig. 16). After further development for 24 hours the embryo was preserved and the sections were cut as nearly transverse to the two forks of the neural tube as possible.

Fig. 16 Um 83. The *alpestris* embryo at the neurula stage. Dorsal view. The secondary neural tube branches off laterally from the primary tube and deviates to the right. 20×.

The primary neural tube is closed and separated from the epidermis for almost its entire length (Fig. 18); it is still continuous with the epidermis in the midbrain region where it opens to the outside. The optic vesicles are indicated by compact protrusions of the brain wall.

The primary notochord is delineated in normal fashion for the greatest part of its length (Fig. 18); at the posterior end, it merges with the indifferent tissue of the tail bud.

Of the somites, the left or outer row is normal (Fig. 18, at right); 7

to 8 somites are separate from the lateral plate. The right or inner row (Fig. 18, at left) seems to be somewhat deranged at the anterior end, in front of the bifurcation, as if dammed up.

The secondary neural tube is closed in its middle portion and separated from the epidermis (Fig. 18). It meets the primary tube anteriorly at an acute angle and fuses with it at approximately the level of the future midbrain (Fig. 17); at this point, its lumen opens to the outside.

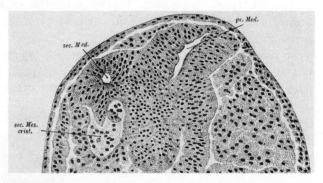

Fig. 17 Um 83. Cross section in the anterior third of the embryo (cf. Fig. 16). In the upper right of the figure may be seen the primary neural tube, from which the secondary tube branches off. The implant (light) is in the mesoderm (sec. Mes. crist). 100×.

Posteriorly, it becomes lost indistinguishably in the surrounding mesoderm of the secondary embryonic anlage, as it would in a normal tail bud.

The notochord is likewise distinctly delineated in the middle portion, (Fig. 18); it lies directly above the wall of the intestine. Anteriorly, it passes without clear demarcation into the mesoderm formed by the implant (Fig. 17), and caudally it merges in the same way with the *alpestris* mesoderm that it has induced.

In the middle region the secondary somites are symmetrically arranged with respect to the secondary notochord and neural tube (Fig. 18). Anteriorly, near the bifurcation point, a mesoderm strip of *cristatus* cells appears between the somites; it connects the lower edges of the somites and separates the notochord from the intestine. In the same region the somites become smaller and indistinct, the left (inner) row earlier than the right (outer) row. Farther back, the somites merge with the unidentifiable tissue in which the notochord and neural tube also lose their identity.

The lumen of the intestine in its middle portion is shifted toward the side of the secondary embryonic anlage, so that it comes to lie in the primary median plane of the duplication (Fig. 18).

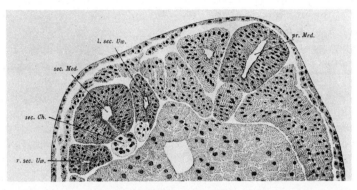

Fig. 18 Um 83. Cross section in the middle part of the embryo (cf. Fig. 16). The primary axial organs are at the upper right of the figure and the secondary axial organs are at the upper left. The implant (light) is in the left secondary somite (l. sec. Uw.) and in the secondary notochord (sec. Ch.). 100×.

In this case, the cell material of the implant participates only in mesodermal structures. The neural tube is composed purely of *alpestris* cells, at least as far as it is delimited from other parts. The notochord, on the other hand, is formed principally of unpigmented cells derived from the *cristatus* implant. But, here and there, distinctly pigmented cells are interspersed along its entire length; they are of the same color as the cells of the neighboring somites (Fig. 18). Since they were never observed in a *cristatus* notochord, they undoubtedly derive from the *alpestris* embryo. Lateral to the notochord, the implant is in an asymmetrical position; in its middle portion it appears in the edges of the *left* somites (Fig. 18, to the right of the notochord), but in its anterior portion, in the *right* somites. In addition, the transplant furnishes the mesoderm strip mentioned above that connects the two sides.

The neural tube and somites of the secondary embryo are definitely induced by the transplant, as far as they are composed of *alpestris* cells.

The pigmentation of the primary and secondary neural tubes is equally deep in both. However, it is surprising how dark the secondary somites are, in comparison to the primary somites (in Fig. 18, however, the difference is exaggerated). It might be assumed that they are formed of different material, that is, of the deeply pigmented cells of the animal half. The experiments of O. Mangold (1922, 1923) have proved that the latter are capable of forming somites. The implant would have carried these cells along with it when it invaginated; this would have been facilitated by the early age of the host embryo (blastula). We shall return to this possibility later. We shall then also discuss the remarkable fact that the implant does not lie in the longitudinal axis of the organs induced by it, but at an acute angle to it.

Experiment Triton 1922, 132. The organizer was taken from a *cristatus* embryo in advanced gastrulation (medium-sized yolk plug). The median region, directly above the blastopore, was transplanted into a *taeniatus* embryo of the same stage. The implant moved inward in the shape of a shallow cup. The *cristatus* embryo, with the exchange implant from *taeniatus*, developed to a larva with primary optic vesicles; it was lost by accident before sectioning. In the neurula stage, the implant had been located medially in the posterior part of the neural plate and extended to the blastopore. Closure of the neural folds was delayed and not quite complete at the caudal end; it was similar to but not quite as abnormal as that in *Triton* 1922, 131b.

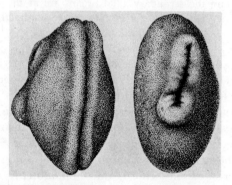

Figs. 19 and 20 Um 132. The *taeniatus* embryo at the neurula stage; the secondary neural folds are viewed from the right side (Fig. 19), and from above (Fig. 20). 20×.

In the *taeniatus* embryo, when this is in the neurula stage, 19½ hours after the operation, the implant is no longer visible. In its place are two short neural folds surrounding a groove. They extend obliquely across the ventral side of the embryo, from left posterior to right anterior in front view. Twenty-five hours later the neural folds have approached each other (Fig. 20). The two folds mentioned above and the groove between them are on the left ventral side of the embryo; they are lengthened, and they approach the anterior ends of the host neural folds at an acute angle (Figs. 19 and 20). After another 22 hours, this secondary embryonic primordium has flattened out anteriorly, but posteriorly it projects considerably above the surface. In this region, somites seem to form. Approximately 28 hours later, the embryo has primary optic vesicles, otic pits and a tail bud. In the secondary embryo, at least on the right side, somites can be quite clearly recognized. After another 20 hours, paired otocysts are seen at its anterior end; they are at the same level as those of the primary embryo. The free posterior end has grown somewhat and is bent toward the primary embryo. Four hours later, a pronephric duct is visible in the induced anlage. The embryo was fixed 6 hours later, when a blister appeared on the dorsal surface; the sections were cut transversely.

Immediately before fixation, the living object showed the following features:

The embryo is stretched lengthwise, but its tail is still bent ventrad (Fig. 21). The optic vesicles are strongly expanded, the otic pits distinct, and a large number of somites is formed. The head is continuously bent to the left, probably due to the secondary embryonic anlage which is on the left side. The latter is rather far ventral, and approximately parallel to the primary axial organs, which it approaches anteriorly at an acute angle. It extends over a considerable part of the length of the primary embryo, from the posterior border of the left optic vesicle to the level of the anus. Its posterior end is lifted up like a tail bud. The central canal of its neural tube is visible through the epidermis, and likewise the lumen of the otic vesicles and of the right somites. The left somites are not recognizable.

Fig. 21 Um 132b. The *taeniatus* embryo shown in Figs. 19 and 20, developed further; viewed from the left side. Surface view of the secondary embryo, with tail-bud, neural tube, somites, and otocysts. 20×.

The evaluation of the finer structures is facilitated by the almost complete independence of the normal and the induced embryonic primordia, in contrast to the two previously described cases.

Of the axial organs of the primary embryonic anlage, the neural tube, notochord and somites are entirely normally developed; so is the right pronephros. The left pronephros, however, which faces the secondary primordium, shows a minor irregularity. In the brain primordium, the primary optic vesicles are already transformed into cups, and the lens primordia are recognizable as slight thickenings of the epidermis. The otic pits have closed to form vesicles, but they are not further differentiated, except for the indication of a *ductus endolymphaticus*. The notochord is separated from the adjacent parts throughout almost its entire length. Between 11 and 13 clearly segregated somites can be counted. Neural tube, notochord and somites pass into undifferentiated tissue at the tip of the tail. The primordium of the pronephros consists on each side of two nephrostomes with associated tubules (Figs. 22 and 23). These open into pronephric ducts, in a normal fashion (Figs. 23 and 24). The left duct has a larger diameter anteriorly than has the right one. The pronephric ducts can be traced far posteriorly, but not to their opening to the outside.

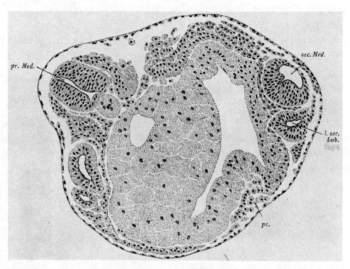

Fig. 22 Um 132b. Cross section at the level of the primary pronephros (cf. Fig. 21). The primary axial organs are at the upper left of the figure and the secondary axial organs at the right. l. sec. Lab., left secondary otocyst; pc., pericardium. 100×.

The secondary embryonic anlage also possesses all the axial organs; they are in part very well formed. The neural tube is closed in its entire length and detached from the epidermis. It is sharply delimited except for its caudal end where it becomes continuous with the undifferentiated mass of the secondary tail bud. In its middle part, the right side is somewhat more strongly developed than the left side (Fig. 24). Toward its anterior end, the diameter increases, and the roof becomes broader and thinner, as in a normal medulla (Fig. 22). At this level, two otocysts are adjacent to it. The right otocyst is shifted forward; it lies at the level of the anterior end (compare the surface view,

Fig. 21), and the left one is slightly more posterior (Fig. 22). They are still attached to the epidermis, and the formation of the endolymphatic duct seems indicated. The notochord extends less far craniad than normally. It is not yet found at the level of the posterior octocyst (Fig. 22); it does not begin until 90 μ behind this section. Otherwise it is well formed, and sharply delimited all the way to its posteriormost part in the tail bud. Somites are formed on both sides; there are more (4 to 6) on the right side facing the primary embryo than on the left side

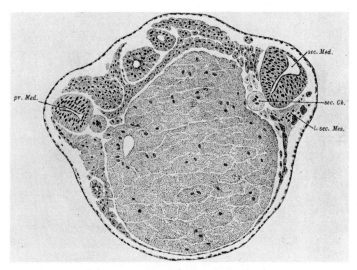

Fig. 23 Um 132b. Cross section in the anterior third of the embryo (cf. Fig. 21). The primary axial organs are at the left of the figure and the secondary axial organs at the right. The implant (light) has differentiated notochord and left secondary somite. 100×.

(2 to 3). On the right side, they extend farther forwards (Fig. 24). A pronephric duct is formed on both sides; again, the left one is longer (about 300 μ) than the right one (about 500 μ) [figures probably erroneously reversed]. Caudally they are not yet separated from the mesoderm, and anteriorly, tubules and funnels are not formed, or not yet. The two adjacent ducts, namely the left one of the primary embryo and the right one of the secondary embryo, are in communication with each other directly behind the second pronephric tubule.

Both embryos share the intestine which is primarily directed toward the primary embryo. It cannot be ascertained with certainty to what extent the secondary embryo has a share in it in all regions. In the pharynx, primordia of visceral pouches may belong to the secondary embryo (Fig. 22); however, they could also belong to the primary embryo and merely be shifted slightly by the secondary embryo. This holds, at any rate, for the heart primordium (Fig. 22 pc, in section through the posterior end of the pericardium). In contrast, a secondary intestinal lumen is distinctly induced beneath the axial organs of the induced anlage, although it can be traced for only a very short distance (about 60 μ; Fig. 24). The anus is somewhat expanded, so that the endoderm is exposed; it is also shifted toward the left side.

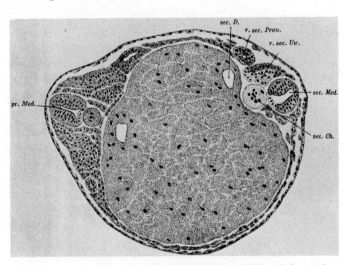

Fig. 24 Um 132b. Cross section through the middle of the embryo (cf. Fig. 21). The primary axial organs are at the left of the figure and the secondary axial organs at the right. r. sec. Pron., right secondary pronephric duct. The implant (light) has formed notochord and part of the right secondary somite. 100×.

The secondary embryonic anlage is again a chimera formed by cells of the host and of the implanted organizer. The two posterior thirds of the neural tube have a ventral strip of *cristatus* cells (Figs. 24 and 25). The notochord is formed entirely of *cristatus* cells. In the somites, the *cristatus* contribution is in the anterior and posterior sections of the left row (Figs. 23 and 25, right) and in the middle part of the right row (Fig. 24, left); there are no somites at all in the middle of the left row (Fig. 24, right). The implant has remained in one piece, throughout its length (Figs. 23-25).

All the other structures of the secondary embryo that are not formed by *cristatus* cells have been undoubtedly induced in *taeniatus* material by the organizer.

Hence, in this case the two embryonic anlagen have interfered with

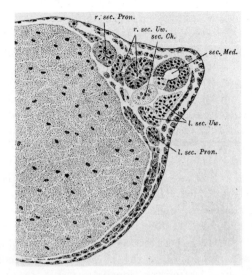

Fig. 25 Um 132b. Cross section through the secondary axial organs, slightly anterior to the secondary tailbud (cf. Fig. 21). The implant (light) is in the floor of the secondary neural tube and in the left secondary somite and has formed notochord. 100×.

each other only to the extent that some of the organ primordia are somewhat more strongly developed on the inner side than on the outer side, and that the pronephric ducts are connected with each other. In other respects, the induced embryonic primordium is entirely independent. This is perhaps one of the main conditions for its complete development.

III. DISCUSSION OF THE RESULTS

1. *Origin and prospective significance of the organizer and site of its implantation.* In all these experiments the organizer was taken from a *cristatus* embryo and inserted into a *taeniatus* embryo, except for one case, where *alpestris* was the host. This combination has proved to be advantageous. The unpigmented *cristatus* cells can be clearly distinguished, over a long period of time, from the pigmented *taeniatus* or *alpestris* cells, and the part supplied by the organizer can thus be sharply delimited from the regions induced by it. Of course, the same would have been true for the implantation of an organizer from the pigmented *taeniatus* or *alpestris* embryo into the unpigmented *cristatus* embryo. This reciprocal experiment would have offered the additional advantage that an organizer could have been implanted into the considerably larger *cristatus* embryo, thus more easily avoiding its

interference with the primary organization center; and, on the other hand, there would have been room for the implantation of several organizers, side by side, and their mutual interference could have been tested. However, several considerable disadvantages cancel out these advantages. For one, the *cristatus* embryos proved to be in general more delicate, as was mentioned above; they seemed, therefore, to be less suitable as host embryos. The larger embryo has probably more difficulty in gastrulation after removal of the vitelline membrane. Furthermore, the neural plate of *cristatus* does not become distinct in early stages, by pigmentation, as is the case in *taeniatus* and *alpestris*. Even after elevation of the neural folds it is much less conspicuous; and for this reason, the small and even less distinct induced neural plates are very difficult to see in the living embryo.

The *region* from which the organizer is taken can easily be ascertained in early gastrulae because the crescent-shaped blastopore gives safe points of orientation. Once the blastopore has become circular, a definite orientation is often no longer possible in the undisturbed embryo. Hence, the piece of host embryo for which the organizer was substituted was implanted in the donor as a marker. This would be an ideal method to determine the normal fate, that is, the prospective significance, of the organizer, if one could be certain that development continues undisturbed despite the operation. As a matter of fact, development is probably somewhat altered (once in a while this can be directly observed), in that gastrulation is impeded. It could be that parts that normally invaginate remain on the surface. The opposite, that is, that more material invaginates than normally, can be excluded almost with certainty. However, this marker is not useless. Even in the most unfavorable case, it will show the position of the organizer with respect to the median plane, whether it was in this plane, or lateral to it; and it will show, furthermore, the *minimal* posterior extent of the organizer. We shall disregard those cases in which a more far-reaching disturbance of development, that is, *spina bifida,* was caused by the implant.

To judge from these markers, or from direct observation, the organizers were all derived from the median plane, closely above the invaginating border of the upper blastoporal lip, or at a short distance from it. They always belonged to the zone of invagination, at least in their posterior part. Accordingly, probably in some cases they would have formed the posteriormost part of the neural plate, but they would always certainly have formed notochord and somites. It cannot be said with the same certainty whether they would have also formed the roof of the intestine. This depends on the lateral extent of the piece, that is, on its width when it was a median piece.

The *age* of the host embryos was variable; it ranged from blastula to advanced gastrula with medium-sized yolk plug. Implantation was always into the animal half of the embryo, but at different places, partly within, and partly outside of the zone of invagination.

Although all this could be determined exactly, the same has not been possible, so far, with respect to the *orientation* of the implanted pieces, since they are exactly circular as is the opening of the micropipette with which they were punched out. This is a disadvantage that will have to be overcome in future experiments. Several different methods suggest themselves, for example, marking the organizer by implanting into it some cells with different pigmentation before it is lifted out; or perhaps an implant with a more characteristic contour can be obtained. Only when the organizer has been implanted in an exactly determined orientation is it possible to establish with certainty the relations between its structure and the direction in which it exerts its effects on its surroundings.

2. *Behavior of the organizer after implantation.* All cases observed have in common the fact that the organizer, which is at first on the surface and level with its surroundings, moves later into the interior, either entirely or in its greater part. The manner in which this occurs differs according to the site of implantation.

If the implant is within the normal zone of invagination, then it passes inwards around the blastoporal lip together with its surroundings. This could be established frequently by direct observation; the piece was seen moving toward the margin of invagination, or immediately in front of it. In other instances, it could be deduced from the result of gastrulation.

Such an invagination of implanted pieces has been observed recently by W. Vogt (1922) and O. Mangold (1922, 1923). In the latter experiments, the implant was indifferent material from the animal hemisphere; it demonstrated its capacity for transformation by becoming mesoderm when carried inside, even though it was presumptive ectoderm. It was also remarkable that an implant taken from a young gastrula seemed to participate more readily in invagination than one from an advanced gastrula (p. 286 ff).

Our experiments cannot be compared directly with these experiments because our implants, derived from the upper blastoporal lip, have brought with them their own invagination tendencies which, depending on the orientation of the piece, might affect the invagination [of the host mesoderm] by either impeding or promoting it. Definite conclusions cannot be expected until it is possible to control the orientation of the implant.

The implant also moves into the interior if it lies outside the zone of invagination. There can be no doubt but that this is caused by forces which the piece brings with it from its region of origin, namely the upper blastoporal lip. Perhaps the first stage in this process is the formation of a depression by the implant; this occasionally appears immediately after implantation and it is frequently still visible on the following day (see p. 164). We have also often observed the gradual disappearance of the implant. The details of this process of independent invagination require more precise investigation. During and after invagination, the implant undergoes a stretching which corresponds approximately in amount to that demonstrated recently by W. Vogt in reimplanted parts of the upper blastoporal lip (cf. v. Ubisch, 1923, Fig. 9). The remarkable protrusion of the piece, which was observed repeatedly (for instance in 1922, 131; cf. p. 157), can probably be ascribed to an obstruction of this invagination which is combined with stretching.

Once arrived in the interior, the implant almost always forms a coherent complex. Only in one case (1921, 8; p. 152) did the mesoderm consist of two portions separated by intercalated host tissue. It was shown that the anterior part probably derived from the deeper layer of the implant.

Even though the process of invagination has to be studied in more detail, the end result is completely clear; it can be read off, directly, from the sections. Depending on its origin and perhaps also on its place of insertion, the implant is brought into the interior more or less completely. That is, part of it remains in the ectoderm and can then be recognized in the neural plate by direct inspection or in sections, where it is found in the wall of the neural tube. Or it is completely sunk into the interior where it forms only mesoderm and perhaps endoderm.

3. *Structure of the secondary embryonic primordium.* The structure of the secondary embryonic primordium is quite complete and can be interpreted most easily when it does not interfere with the primary one. In such cases as that described above (1922, 132), all organ primordia, such as neural tube with otocysts, notochord, somites, pronephros, and perhaps also intestine, can be present and relatively well developed. The only deficiencies are, in the neural tube, the anterior parts of the brain with the optic vesicles; in the pronephros, the tubules and nephrostomes; in the gut, the anus. It does not seem impossible to expect more nearly complete embryos in the course of continued experimentation.

Part of this secondary embryonic primordium always derives from the implant, which can always be sharply distinguished from its surroundings by virtue of its different histological characteristics. The size and position of this component are very variable, depending, undoubtedly, on the size and point of origin of the implant. Host tissue prevails in the neural tube; *cristatus* cells are either absent (e.g. 1922, 25; Figs. 8 and 9, p. 155; 1922, 83, Fig. 18, p. 163), or they form only a narrow strip (e.g. 1921, 8, Fig. 3, p. 149; 1922, 131, Fig. 15, p. 160;

1922, 132, Figs. 24 and 25, pp. 168, 169). This strip is of very different length in the individual cases, but as observed so far, it is always in the median plane; this is of theoretical significance. In contrast, implant tissue predominates in the notochord; in fact, the notochord consisted completely of *cristatus* cells in all cases except one (1922, 83) where small cell groups of the host are interspersed (Fig. 18, p. 163). The somites assume an intermediate position: they can be composed completely of *cristatus* cells (Fig. 14, p. 159), or completely of host cells (Figs. 18 and 25, left); or they can be chimeric, i.e., composed of both (Figs. 18 and 25 right).

The implant as a whole is not rigidly limited to the median plane; this is again of theoretical importance. For instance, in one case (1922, 83) its posterior part extends farther to the left (Fig. 18, right) and its anterior part farther to the right; hence it forms an acute angle with the median plane (pp. 162, 175).

The orientation of these secondary embryonic primordia with respect to the primary axial organs of the host embryo varies considerably. They may be almost parallel to them and nowhere contiguous (1922, 132, p. 164 ff); or they may meet at a more or less acute angle and fuse with them either at the tip, or laterally over a long stretch. To the extent that they are not formed by the *cristatus* cells of the implant, they must have originated from the parts of the host that either were already on the spot, or that came there under the influence of the organizer. This is quite evident for the neural tube; it is formed of cells which otherwise would have formed epidermis of the lateral body wall. The situation is less simple for the more deeply located parts, that is, notochord, somites and pronephros. Sometimes it seems as if they were carved out, as it were, of the lateral plates of the host (e.g. 1922, 132. Figs. 24 and 25). In one case, however (1922, 83; p. 163), the secondary somites were so much more darkly pigmented than the primary ones that the idea suggested itself that they might have been formed by presumptive ectoderm, like the secondary neural tube which they resemble with respect to pigmentation. It would then have to be assumed that the organizer had evoked intensive invagination in the blastula cells of the animal pole where it had been implanted, and had subsequently determined them to form somites. The basis for this possibility is undoubtedly provided by the previously mentioned experiments of O. Mangold. The details of these processes would have to be elucidated by investigations directly aimed at this point.

4. *The causes for the origin of the secondary embryonic anlage.* The causal relationships in the origin of the secondary embryonic anlage are still completely in the dark. The only point that is certain is that somehow an induction by the implant occurs. But even the question of the

stage of development at which this takes place, hence, whether it is a direct, or a more indirect influence, cannot yet be decided.

It is very probable that the inducing action of the implant already begins very early and that it consists at first in inducing its new environment to participate actively in the invagination. That something like this is possible is proved by an earlier experiment (Spemann 1918, pp. 497 ff) in which the bisected blastopore of a medially split gastrula had been fused with material of a different prospective fate and had drawn this latter material into invagination.

The inducing action of the implant could have run its course with this instigation of invagination; everything else could be merely the consequence of this secondary gastrulation. It would then have to be assumed that the general condition imposed on the cells participating in the gastrulation, and by virtue of this process, would in turn provide the stimulus by which further developments are initiated. The different components of the composite chimeric gastrula would then be subjected to this determination process irrespective of their origin. This is actually the case in those chimeras produced by the implantation of indifferent material.

But there is another possibility, namely that after the termination of gastrulation the implant continues to exert determinative influences on its surroundings. For instance, the long, narrow strip of *cristatus* cells in the neural plate could have caused the adjacent cells, which otherwise would have become epidermis, to differentiate likewise into neural plate. And if it should turn out that this is not the correct causal relationship because the development of the neural plate is perhaps evoked by the underlying endo-mesoderm, it is still conceivable that the mesodermal parts of host origin were formed under the influence of the implanted parts.

Both explanations are based on the assumption that the implanted parts have become, by and large, what they would have formed in normal development. According to the first notion, their differentiation would be merely the result of their inherent tendency toward a certain degree of invagination; according to the second notion, the transplants were, in addition, determined with respect to their future differentiation tendency, though perhaps only within the range of a certain degree of variation. These already determined parts would then have the capacity to supplement themselves from the surrounding indifferent parts. It is on this point that the experiments would have to focus that could decide between the two possibilities.

The question of whether decisive facts are already available may be left in abeyance; instead, keeping both possibilities in mind, we shall discuss the factors on which the orientation, the size and the completeness of the secondary embryonic primordia depend.

The first question of interest concerns the *orientation of the secondary primordium* in the host embryo. These are three possibilities: the orientation could be caused entirely by the host embryo, or entirely by the implant, or by a combination of both.

Assuming the first notion to be correct, then the implant would have to be without structure and to behave passively in the process of becoming the substrate [for the neural plate]. Its form and position would be imposed on it entirely by the relations of the host embryo; it would be simply towed along by the cell movements of the latter. Furthermore, the determinative effect would proceed exclusively from this underlying endo-mesoderm; and this effect would be somehow symmetrical with respect to the shape that had been imposed on it from the outside. In this instance, it would probably have to be expected that the secondary primordium would always be similarly oriented with respect to the primary one, and, more specifically, probably parallel to it; but this obviously is not the case. Furthermore, the capacity of the organizer to invaginate autonomously when implanted outside of the normal invagination zone of the host cannot be reconciled with lack of structure within the organizer.

According to the second and third assumptions, the implanted organizer would have a definite structure of its own. On this would depend the direction of invagination and longitudinal stretching and finally, sooner or later, its determinative effect. In this event, the host embryo, in turn, could be either purely passive, or it could participate in the final form and position of the implant by virtue of its own structure or cell movements.

The assumption of an inner structure in the organizer is supported by the fact that the random orientation of the secondary embryonic primordium with respect to the primary one corresponds to the random orientation of the implant. A definite decision will not be possible until the orientation of the organizer can be manipulated at will.

A cooperation of the host embryo seems to be indicated by a peculiarity in the position of the implant to which attention has already been called on p. 164: namely, the longitudinal extent of the implant does not necessarily coincide exactly with the median plane of the secondary embryonic primordium, nor is it necessarily parallel to it; it may form an acute angle with it. This fact would be surprising if the longitudinal stretching of the implant were attributed exclusively to forces residing in it, and if it were assumed at the same time that the implant alone fixes the direction of the determination emanating from it. Under these premises the implant would be expected to stretch exactly in its own sagittal plane and then to supplement itself anteriorly and laterally from adjacent material. It would then be expected to lie exactly in the median plane or at least sagittally in the induced axial organs. The deviation from such a position should probably be attributed to an influence of the host embryo. Either the elongation of the implant is influenced by the cell shifts of the environment, in which event it would then be the resultant of inherent tendencies and extrinsic forces, or the determination itself could be diverted by an inner structure of the host embryo.

These considerations suggest the experiment of destroying the suspected structure of the organizer to test whether the latter can then still have a determinative effect. For instance, a piece of the upper blastoporal lip would have to be crushed, and the attempt would have to be made to place it between the two germ layers of the gastrula by introducing it into the blastocoele of the blastula.

Obviously, the parts of the upper blastoporal lip possess a definite structure by virtue of which they invaginate in a definite direction and perhaps also release stimuli that cause the more indifferent parts to differentiate further in a specific manner. It is irrelevant whether these parts are normally adjacent to the blastoporal lip or brought in contact with it by the experiment. These indifferent parts may also have a directional structure of their own; however this is by no means sufficiently fixed to abolish the influence of the organizer or even to modify it decisively. Depending on the orientation of the implant in the deeper layer of the host embryo, the direction in which its determinative influence pervades the host tissue will differ. For instance, it will pass through the ectoderm in a direction oblique to that of the primary neural plate in cases where the secondary neural plate later forms a more or less acute angle with the primary plate. Whether determination within the induced neural plate, and in the primary as well as the secondary one, is initiated at the posterior or anterior end; that is, whether it progresses cephalad or caudad, as von Ubisch (1923) believes, or whether the entire ectoderm area underlain by organizer is simultaneously affected cannot yet be decided by definite arguments. It may suffice for now to refer to the noteworthy discussions by von Ubisch.

The *size* of the secondary embryonic anlage may depend on several circumstances. The thought immediately comes to mind that it increases with the size of the implant. In addition, its origin, that is, its prospective significance may be of influence and, in this connection, its shape too. It could make a difference whether the implant is short and wide, or long and narrow. Furthermore, the site of implantation could be of importance; and also the age of the implant, either in itself or in relation to the host embryo. These considerations suggest numerous experiments that are feasible; they promise much further insight, quite apart from the surprises on which one can always count from such experiments. One very important factor will be pointed out shortly.

The *completeness* of the secondary embryonic primordium may de-

pend on factors similar to those that influence its size. Again, either
the conditions in the host embryo or those in the organizer could be
of primary importance. With respect to the first alternative, there come
to mind not only the instances of a very obvious interference of the
primordia, where the development of the secondary primordium is impeded by the precocious encounter of its anterior end with·that of the
primary primordium and by its subsequent fusion with it. It could also
be that, despite an apparent independence of the secondary primordium,
the completeness of its formation depends on the primary primordium;
or, more precisely, the primary organization center could co-determine
the mode of action of the implanted secondary center. In this respect,
it is noteworthy, for instance, that in experiment 1922, 132 (Fig. 21, p.
165), the two otic vesicles of the secondary primordium are at almost
exactly the same level as the primary otocysts, and that the secondary
neural tube ends there, blindly. The reason for this could be that the
primary organization center caused the ectoderm at this level to form
the respective sections of the neural tube and the otocysts. And the
reason for the absence of the anterior portion of the secondary neural
tube and the optic vesicles could be that the secondary primordium did
not extend to the level of the optic vesicles of the primary one. Although, according to this version, the primary organization center
would, in the final analysis, also be responsible for the degree of completeness of the secondary primordium, the other assumption could
also be correct, namely that the defect is to be traced back to deficiency
in the implanted organizer. The latter could have been deficient in
certain parts of the organization center which would be necessary for
the induction of anterior neural plate with eye primordia.

Quite similar considerations had been made previously in the discussion of peculiar defects in duplications that originate after a somewhat oblique constriction in early developmental stages (cf. Spemann
1918, pp. 534-536). The neural tube of the deficient anterior end can
be so seriously defective that it ends blindly at the level of the otocysts,
without widening, exactly like the neural tube of the secondary
primordium of the experiment just discussed. It is remarkable that here
again the four otocysts of the two heads are at the same level. The
same possibilities, in principle, were considered as an explanation: the
new method [i.e. of heteroplastic transplantation] will perhaps permit
an exact decision between these possibilities.

Interferences between the two organization centers, the primary one
and the implanted secondary one, are complications that should be
avoided for the time being, as far as possible. Once the analysis has
progressed, valuable information concerning the finer details of the
mode of action of the centers can be expected of them.

Of particular theoretical importance is the question of whether the two embryonic primordia, apart from visible interference, *mutually influence,* or more precisely, limit each other's size. Simple experimental facts show that this is entirely within the realm of possibility. One could have assumed from the beginning that the presumptive neural plate is already determined, in sharp outline, in the ectoderm of the beginning gastrula. This, however, is ruled out by its interchangeability with presumptive epidermis. Then, it could be the size of the organization center which determines the size of the neural plate by the magnitude of its effect. But this is also refuted by the fact that we can remove the ventral half of the embryo without disturbing the organization center and then the size of the neural plate is also reduced to such a degree that it maintains approximately its normal proportion to the reduced whole (Ruud-Spemann, 1923, p. 102 ff). Therefore there must be some retroaction of the whole on the part. We could imagine, for instance, that different primordia require a certain specific degree of saturation which is naturally reached earlier in an embryo of reduced size than in a normal embryo. If something of this sort actually occurs, then we should expect a secondary primordium to exert an inhibitory effect on the first. To test these relationships, more precise measurements would be necessary; these will be tedious but rewarding.

The possibilities that have been discussed presuppose partly one and partly the other of the two basic concepts concerning the mode of induction. It is therefore necessary to find out whether facts are already available to permit a decision in one direction or the other, and to discuss the type of experiments that would have to be designed to bring to light such facts.

It will not be easy to decide by unequivocal experiment whether the process of invagination itself, as the first assumption holds, can create an over-all situation which guides further development in a certain direction. We could try to find out whether passive shifting [of presumptive endo-mesoderm] under the surface has the same effect as active invagination. This could be investigated by implanting endo-mesoderm of a very early gastrula under the ectoderm of another embryo and then observing whether it can produce there the same effect as the endo-mesoderm of a completed gastrula that has already gone through the process of invagination. However, even if the results were clearly positive, the main problem, i.e. the harmonious patterning subsequent to gastrulation, would not be brought much closer to its solution.

As to the other assumption mentioned above, which implies that the implant not only invaginates but also differentiates further by virtue of its inherent development tendencies, a qualifying remark should be made at this time. The possibility was present from the beginning that the implanted piece undergoes pure self-differentiation and develops into exactly the same parts which it would have formed at the place where it came from, and that to form a complete whole it appropriates from the indifferent surroundings the parts that were missing. However, such complete self-differentiation of the organizer almost certainly does not occur, because the implant would then have been too large for the smaller secondary primordium. Insofar as it adapts itself harmoniously to the secondary primordium, its material has been disposed differently than in normal development.

The results of W. Vogt (1922) also argue perhaps against its complete self-differentiation. He found that a piece from the neighborhood of the blastopore becomes ectoderm or endo-mesoderm, depending on whether it remains outside or invaginates inside during the process of gastrulation. The most recent experiments of O. Mangold (1922 and 1923) have shown the same very clearly for the indifferent embryonic areas (i.e. presumptive ectoderm); the experiments of W. Vogt extend this result [namely, lack of rigid self-determination] to the parts near the blastopore.

But complete self-differentiation does not seem to be necessary for the implant to enable it to exert an inducing influence beyond the stimulus for gastrulation. Definitely directed inherent developmental tendency and capacity for regulation are not mutually exclusive. Clarification of this point could be achieved by experiments that would test the effects of different regions of the organization center. If, for instance, a piece taken from its lateral margin should be found later to occupy a lateral position in the embryonic primordium induced by it, then it could be concluded that it was already determined as lateral at the moment of implantation, and that it retained this characteristic after implantation and influenced its surroundings correspondingly. Or, if the degree of completeness of the secondary embryonic primordium should differ according to the exact place of origin of the grafted organizer, this would also indicate differences within the organization center that could hardly have been transmitted to the induced embryonic primordium by stimulation of gastrulation alone.

This much at least is probable: that the possibility exists of a determining effect progressing from cell to cell, not only as suggested by the first assumption, during the period shortly after implantation, when the assumption of an effect on the environment can hardly be escaped, but also during later developmental stages. Among the most recent experiments of O. Mangold (1922, 1923) already mentioned several times, there are some whose continuation could contribute to a decision between the questionable points. If presumptive epidermis, after implantation into the zone of invagination of a beginning gastrula, comes to lie within the somite region, it participates in somite formation. It is not possible to decide when and how the determination of these indifferent cells took place. They could have acquired the characteristics of somites soon after implantation into the upper blastoporal lip, and, on the basis of this first determination, could have participated in all the later destinies of their surroundings. However, this explanation meets with difficulties in the cases where the implant later does not seem to fit smoothly into its environment but forms supernumerary structures. This gives the direct impression that the determining influence emanated from the somite and determined the adjacent indifferent tissue in the same direction. This suggests a new experiment, the implantation of indifferent tissue, such as presumptive epidermis of the beginning gastrula, into an older embryo that has completed gastrulation, so that it reaches its destination without having been part of the blastopore lip. Moreover, the same situation would have prevailed in those cases in which the presumptive epidermis was implanted in the yolk plug, and then moved first into the floor of the archenteron, apparently shifting secondarily into the somite region where it was subjected to determination to form somites (O. Mangold, 1923, p. 258).

If wishful thinking were permissible in questions of research, then we might hope in this case that the second of the previously discussed assumptions would prove to be the correct one. For, if induction should be limited to a stimulus for gastrulation, then the problem of the harmonious equipotential system, which had just seemed to become accessible to experimental analysis, would right from the start confront us again in all its inaccessibility.

Concerning the *means* of the determinative influence, no factual clues are yet available. The experiment proposed above (implantation between the germ layers of crushed organizer that is thus deprived of its structure) could lead us further into this subject.

We would have assumed that the species whose embryos can interact with each other should not be too widely separated in their taxonomic relationship. *Triton cristatus, taeniatus,* and *alpestris,* between which mutual induction is feasible, belong at least to the same genus. However, surprises of great importance seem to be in prospect; Dr. Geinitz in our laboratory has just very recently succeeded (May, 1923) in inducing embryonic primordia in *Triton* by organizers of *Bombinator* and *Rana.* Thus he brought anurans and urodeles into determinative interaction. With this discovery, experimental ideas which seemed to be more dreams than plans (Spemann, 1921, p. 567) have passed into the realm of feasibility.

5. *The organizer and the organizing center.* The concept of the organization center is based on the idea that determination proceeds from cell to cell in the embryo. Such an assumption suggests itself whenever differentiation, that is, the visible consequence of determination, does not start in all parts simultaneously but, beginning at one place, progresses thence in a definite direction. However, pure observation is by

no means sufficient evidence of progressing determination. We might be dealing merely with a chronological sequence in the absence of causal relationship. One way of testing this consists in the interruption of spatial continuity. If such separation does not result in a disturbance, that is, if development that had started on one side of a separating transection continued on the other side, then differentiation in the latter would have been independent, at least from the moment of severance.

A clear example of such a situation in the field of amphibian development is the progressive formation of the blastopore in gastrulation. This begins medially with the formation of the upper blastopore lip; it progresses from there to both sides, and finally reaches the median plane again when the circle is closed at the lower blastopore lip. The observer, quite naturally, gets the impression that the part that is in the process of invagination always draws the adjacent cells of the marginal zone with it. However, if the dorsal half of the embryo including the upper blastopore lip is removed, this does not prevent the formation of the lateral and ventral blastoporal lips, which is not even perceptibly retarded. This holds not only for frontal bisection at the beginning of gastrulation, when determination possibly emanating from the upper lip might already have transgressed the line of transection, but it holds also after frontal ligation in the two-cell stage. Failure of the ventral half to gastrulate would still not have been stringent proof for progressive determination. The fact that gastrulation does occur excludes at least the necessity of assuming such a causal relation.

Braus (1906) followed the same method, in principle, when he analyzed the skeletal development of the pectoral fin of elasmobranch embryos. It is known that the first primordium of fins is a skin fold into which grow muscle buds from the myotomes of the trunk. However, the skeletal rods of the fin differentiate from the mesoderm which fills the skin fold; the rods in the middle form first, then differentiation progresses craniad and caudad. If the tissue that is still indifferent is separated by a cut from the skeletal rods that are already in the process of differentiation, then histological differentiation of pre-cartilage and cartilage proceeds in the former, but organization into separate skeletal rods does not take place. The spatial and temporal progression of this patterning apparently depends on determination that progresses into the indifferent tissue.

We can call this difference in the degree of differentiation at a given moment a differentiation gradient, as does von Ubisch (1923). A gradient is an obvious presupposition for progressive differentiation, although the latter is not a necessary consequence of the former.

This conception of progressive determination leads of necessity back to the conception that there are points in the developing embryo from which determination emanates. It is therefore not surprising to find that this idea has been advocated before. For instance, several sentences in the paper of Boveri on the polarity of the sea urchin egg (1901) hint at an idea akin to ours. Boveri considers the possibility (*op. cit.,* p. 167) that in the sea urchin embryo "every region of the blastula is prepared to form mesoderm or to invaginate and the restriction to one point is effected by the fact that at this point these processes are more readily initiated than at all other points. Once differentiation has started here, then from this point all other regions are determined for their fate by a process of regulation. The existence of such a preferential region is explained by the demonstrable differences in the properties of the cytoplasm in the different regions of the egg." These sentences are qualified later (*op. cit.,* p. 170) in the sense "that beyond a certain zone in the animal region of the egg, the cytoplasmic quality which is necessary for gastrulation is not represented at all, or at least not in sufficient quantity."

Shortly thereafter a similar possibility was considered for the *Triton* embryo (Spemann, 1903, p. 606).

The facts that were known earlier sufficed only to establish the concept of a starting point for differentiation, but not to demonstrate the real existence of such centers. To obtain this evidence, it is not enough to separate the region to be tested, which is believed to be such a center, from its potential field of activity. It must be brought into contact with other parts, normally foreign to it, on which it can demonstrate its capacities. This has apparently been done for the first time in the embryonic transplantations at the gastrula stage. In these experiments the organization center was left in its normal position, and indifferent material was presented to it, so to speak, for further elaboration. A much more penetrating analysis is made feasible by the transplantation of the organization center itself, and of its parts, the organizers. The present investigation makes a first beginning of this analysis. The new possibilities now opened up, particularly in combinations with heteroplastic transplantation, are not yet foreseeable. Several possible approaches to further advances have been indicated in the preceding pages.

For the moment, it is of subordinate significance whether the concepts of organizer and organization center will still prove to be useful when the analysis has advanced further, or whether they are to be replaced by other terms which would be more exact. We can already state that the concept of the organizer is the fundamental one, and that the term organization "center" shall be used only to designate the embryonic area in which the organizers are assembled at a given stage, but *not* to designate a center from which development is being directed. The designation "organizer" (rather than, perhaps, "determiner") is supposed to express the idea that the effect emanating from these preferential regions is not only determinative in a definite restricted direction, but that it possesses all those enigmatic peculiarities which are known to us only from living organisms.

IV. SUMMARY OF RESULTS

A piece taken from the upper blastopore lip of a gastrulating amphibian embryo exerts an organizing effect on its environment in such a way that, following its transplantation to an indifferent region of another embryo, it there causes the formation of a secondary embryo. Such a piece can therefore be designated as an organizer.

If the organizer is implanted within the normal zone of invagination, then it participates in the gastrulation of the host embryo and, afterwards, shares the blastopore with it; if transplanted outside the zone of invagination, it invaginates autonomously. In this case, part of it may remain on the surface and there participate in the formation of the ectoderm and, specifically, of the neural plate; or it may move altogether into the interior and become endo-mesoderm entirely. In this event it is likely that cells of the host embryo can also be invaginated along with the transplant. Indeed, this might be considered already as a determinative effect of the implant on its environment.

In the host embryo, a secondary embryo originates in connection with the implant; it can show different degrees of differentiation. This depends, in part, on whether it interferes with the primary axial organs, or whether it remains completely independent. In one case in the latter category, a neural tube without brain and eyes, but with otic vesicles, and also notochord, somites, and pronephric ducts developed.

These secondary embryonic primordia are always of mixed origin; they are formed partly of cells of the implant and partly of cells of the host embryo. If, in the experiments under discussion, an organizer of another species is used for induction, then the chimeric composition can be established with certainty and great accuracy. It was demonstrated for most organs, for neural tube, somites, and even for the notochord.

There can be no doubt but that these secondary embryonic primordia have somehow been induced by the organizer; but it cannot yet be decided in what manner this occurs and, above all, when and in what way. The inductive effect could be limited to a stimulation to gastrulation, whereupon all else would follow, as in normal development. In this event, the different parts of the secondary zone of gastrulation would be subjected to the determination without regard to their origin. But the induction by the implant could also continue beyond the stage of gastrulation. In this case, the organizer, by virtue of its intrinsic developmental tendencies, would essentially continue its development along the course which it had already started and it would supplement itself from the adjacent indifferent material. This might also hold for the determination of the neural plate; but it is more likely that the latter is determined by the underlying endo-mesoderm. But the development of the implant could not be pure self-differentiation; otherwise it could not have been harmoniously integrated with the secondary embryonic primordium which is smaller than the primary primordium. Apparently the inducing part, while in action, was subjected to a counter-action by the induced part. Such reciprocal interactions may play a large role, in general, in the development of harmonious equipotential systems.

V. REFERENCES

BOVERI, TH., Über die Polarität des Seeigeleies. Verhandl. d. Phys.-Med. Ges. zu Würzburg. N. F. Bd. 34. 1901.

BRAUS, H., Ist die Bildung des Skelettes von den Muskelanlagen abhängig? Morphol. Jarhb. Bd. 35, S. 38 bis 110. 1906.

LEWIS, W. H., Transplantation of the lips of the blastopore in *Rana palustris*. Americ. Journ. of Anat. Vol. 7. S. 137-143. 1907.

MANGOLD, O., Transplantationsversuche zur Ermittelung der Eigenart der Keimblätter. Verhandl. d. dtsch. zool. Ges. Bd. 27, S. 51-52. 1922.

———, Transplantationsversuche zur Frage der Spezifität und Bildung der Keimblätter bei *Triton*. Arch. f. mikrosk. Anat. u. Entwicklungsmech. Bd. 100. S. 198-301. 1923.

RUUD, G. AND SPEMANN, H., Die Entwicklung isolierter dorsaler und lateraler Gastrulahälften von *Triton taeniatus* und *alpestris*, ihre Regulation und Postgeneration. Arch. f. Entwicklungsmech. d. Organismen. Bd. 52, S. 95-165. 1923.

SPEMANN, H., Über die Determination der ersten Organanlagen des Amphibienembryo I-VI. Ibid. Bd. 43, S. 448-555. 1918.

———, Mikrochirurgische Operationstechnik. *Abderhaldens* Handb. d. biol. Arbeitsmethoden, 2. Aufl., S. 1-30. 1920.

———, Über die Erzeugung tierischer Chimären durch heteroplastische embryonale Transplantation zwischen *Triton cristatus* und *Triton taeniatus*. Arch. f. Entwicklungsmech. d. Organismen Bd. 48, S. 533-570. 1921.

v. UBISCH, L., Das Differenzierungsgefälle des Amphibienkörpers und seine Auswirkungen. Ibid. Bd. 52, S. 641-670. 1923.

VOGT, W., Die Einrollung und Streckung der Urmundlippen bei *Triton* nach Versuchen mit einer neuen Methode embryonaler Transplantation. Verhandl. d. dtsch, zool. Ges. Bd. 27, S. 49-51. 1922.

1939

Tissue Affinity, A Means of Embryonic Morphogenesis

by **JOHANNES HOLTFRETER**

*from the Zoological Institute
of the University of Munich*

Holtfreter, Johannes. 1939. Gewebeaffinität, ein Mittel der embryonalen Formbildung. Archiv für experimentelle Zellforschung, **23**, pp. 169-209. Original translation by Konrad Keck, amended by Professor Holtfreter. Printed by permission of the author and Gustav Fischer Verlag.

When Wilhelm Roux carried out the studies so important in transforming embryology from a descriptive to an experimental and analytical science, he was performing his work at a time when experimentation was becoming increasingly important in other fields of biology also. During the 1880's experimental investigations in physiology were burgeoning with particular vigor. Among the experimental studies most important in transforming physiological outlooks were those on tropisms and taxes.

Studies on tropisms influenced the development of embryological concepts in a number of ways (see Oppenheimer in Analysis of Development, *edited by B. H. Willier, et al., W. B. Saunders Co., Philadelphia, 1955, p. 19). These were of particular interest to Roux, who himself published two papers on the behavior of embryonic cells attempting to analyze their relationships to one another in terms of tropisms and taxes.*

Roux's own experiments in this area—as in a number of others—were not very conclusive. It was not until Johannes Holtfreter (1901-) performed the experiments reported in the paper reproduced here that the attractions and affinities (and their opposites) between embryonic cells were again seriously reconsidered.

Holtfreter has been one of the most original and productive of the investigators of amphibian development. In the early period of investigation of amphibian embryogenesis he confirmed, by various methods, including the production of exogastrulae, Spemann's concept that contact between archenteron roof and overlying epidermis is a necessary condition for the differentiation of nerve tissue. After it became apparent that non-living organizer could act as an inducer, Holtfreter demonstrated that tissues removed from members of many phyla from tapeworm to man could act as inducing agents; this investigation has borne its fruits in the work of Yamada and others who are currently fractionating mammalian organs in an attempt to pinpoint chemically the effective molecules. After Barth (1941) performed experiments in vitro *which suggested that under some conditions prospective epidermis might, after all, differentiate nerve tissue in the absence of chorda-mesoderm, Holtfreter (1944, 1945) extended this analysis in such a way as to raise serious doubts as to whether the transmission of a particular substance from inducer to induced could fully explain the induction of nerve tissue. By simply altering the pH of the medium in which the cells were developing, he could influence the direction of differentiation of prospective epidermis or prospective nervous system. He believed that the medium acts on the surface coat of the egg, and in other investigations he pointed out the significance of the surface coat in directing some of the movements of the cells during migration, and he emphasized its importance as an integrative agent during development.*

These represent only a few of his investigations. One of the most important contributions was an exhaustive description of the differentiation of all the various parts of the young amphibian gastrula in vitro *(1938). The key to his success in studying the development of isolated parts of the gastrula lay in his adaptation of the method of tissue culture and to the fact that he devised a satisfactory salt solution which would permit the normal differentiation of the isolated cells.*

These techniques also permitted him to study such recombinations of cells either of gastrulae or neurulae isolated in vitro *as are described in the paper reproduced here. Further, more exhaustive studies of a similar nature on cells of the neurula were reported by Townes and Holtfreter in 1955. Comparable experimental dissociation of embryonic cells and study of their modes of reaggregation is now being carried out on many other kinds of embryonic material, an area in which the focus of interest and emphasis centers on the specific properties of interacting cells. Among the new discoveries are (a) type specific self-sorting of mixed cell populations (Moscona), (b) specificity of interaction between recombined tissue components after isolation from an organ rudiment, e.g., epithelial and mesenchymal components of a salivary gland of a mouse embryo (Grobstein), and (c) self-organization of cells of a functional embryonic organ (kidney, liver) after isolation and random recombination in the reconstitution of the same type of organ once again, i.e., an organ that is morphologically well organized (Weiss and Taylor). These findings in a difficult field of endeavor are of particular interest at a time when immunological concepts are being called upon in the explanation of developmental phenomena. Further, they are of great importance to the understanding of the means by which the cells of the developing organism establish and maintain a harmony of organization.*

It should be remarked here that early in the 1900's H. V. Wilson performed noteworthy experiments in which dissociated cells of sponges and other invertebrates reassembled to reconstitute whole organisms. Although these experiments were masterly in execution they failed, because performed too soon, to excite the imagination of embryologists as did Holtfreter's later but not dissimilar experiments on amphibian embryos.

TISSUE AFFINITY, A MEANS OF EMBRYONIC MORPHOGENESIS

A systematic organizing process, heredity-bound, is recapitulated each time an individual develops. By way of materializing it, new and more specialized agencies come into action successively to bring about new arrangements and differentiations, an event remindful of the construction of a building. These agencies obey their own rules, despite their interdependence and common subordination to the unitarian building plan. Little is known about their nature, but we already know something about their specific accomplishments and their preferred pathways, and we have learned of how, in the course of time, they enhance, supplement, and succeed one another in turn.

Research in developmental physiology since its initiation and orientation by W. Roux has tried to analyze a good number of such agencies, principles or "means" that are at the basis of the formative processes in developing organisms. It remains to be seen whether or not these principles occupy ranks equivalent to each other, and whether an artificial distinction between them will stand up at all to our progressing knowledge. In practice, however, the procedure of separate analyses has proven its value. It has perhaps been unavoidable to deal with the developmental principles of growth, physiological and morphological differentiation, induction, regulation and other phenomena that are manifested in space and time, as though each pursued its own ends. The elucidation of their physico-chemical nature will warrant our interest only after we have sufficiently explored their biological performances. Referring back to the above metaphor: it is not so much the characterization of the laborers but the specifications pertaining to their work, the requirements and rules that they follow while erecting the building, that call for our immediate attention.

The pioneering investigators of developmental physiology were often guided intuitively by considerations of analogy, searching in their own special field for phenomena already known in analogous form in other fields, thus attempting to explain biological phenomena by comparing them with similar ones observed in inorganic systems. Since science depends much on comparing, the heuristic value of such perspectives should not be underestimated. The pioneers were faced by an abundance of unsolved problems. They should not be blamed for the scantiness of their information in this new field, even though they may have been sometimes overconfident in believing that they could explain complicated life processes by pointing glibly to relatively simple processes in nonliving matter. After all, their optimistic materialism has turned out to be more fruitful for research than the resigned attitude of a Driesch who in view of the complexity of developmental events felt compelled to renounce causal analysis *a priori*.

In this era of model experiments, that was epitomized by the artificial cell of Pfeffer and the experiments of Bütschli, Rhumbler and others who attempted to imitate protoplasm, investigators were searching in particular for processes of embryonic development comprehensible in rather crude mechanical terms. Even long before, His (1874), in his treatise on the development of the chick, tried to explain the fundamental events in morphogenesis by "unequal growth" of elastic layers of tissue, although he himself performed no experiments on the live embryo. Organ-forming embryonic regions, endowed with specific rates of growth, represented his point of departure. Forces of pushing, pulling and stretching, graded in space and in time, were considered to play an essential role as means of morphogenesis. To illuminate his concepts, His referred to models of clay, paper, or rubber.

Götte (1875) also considered "growth pressure" to be one of the most important morphogenetic factors. It was not until much later that the capacity for autonomous specific form changes and movements was ascribed to the different cells and primordia (Gurwitsch, Rhumbler, Morgan and others). But it remained for Roux (1894, 1896) to establish a sound foundation for these views by demonstrating such capacities in isolated embryonic amphibian cells. Difficulties arose however in deducing, from observations of the dynamic behavior of isolated cells, rules that would help to explain the formative processes of normal development. Let us discuss these experiments in some greater detail and, proceeding from them, pass on to our own experiments.

I. ISOLATION EXPERIMENTS ON EMBRYONIC CELLS

Even before he started his experiments Roux appears to have had the idea that forces of attraction and repulsion prevail between cells, and that these forces cause groups of the same cell type to aggregate and groups of different cell types to separate during the course of development. He seemed thereby to have come across the track of a morphogenetic factor additional to the growth processes already known, a factor that promised to explain certain processes of gastrulation, germ layer segregation, and organ formation. Evidently, in chemistry, analogous forces were engaged in the synthesis and the degradation of complex compounds; and attraction phenomena of a similar kind, interpreted as chemotaxis, had already been recognized as being involved in bringing the gametes together (Pfeffer, 1873).

The results of experiments carried out with embryonic frog cells, isolated in an artificial medium, seemed to validate this concept. Roux studied the changes in form and position of the ameboid cells; he observed that they would either associate in groups and form spherical aggregates or, in other instances, would migrate away and isolate themselves. It appeared that when the wandering cells approached each other, their random movements became directed. Roux believed that mutual attraction rather than chance movements brought such cells together. He therefore spoke of a positive and negative "cytotropism," which he thought to be operating through the action of cell-specific chemical stimulants which diffuse into the environment in a concentration gradient.

Roux failed to give real evidence for the required elective character of the observed aggregations and separations of the cultured cells. It was even questionable whether the cell movements occurring in the "indifferent" culture media used (chicken egg-white; dilute NaCl solution) were to be regarded as normal and not as atypical and due to adverse properties of the medium.

Even though his evidence was by no means convincing, and only little similarity existed between the cellular movements observed in cell cultures and the formative processes of normal development, Roux advanced the dictum of an elective capacity of self-ordering of embryonic cells. In his opinion the embryo has "the tendency to arrange its cells appropriately according to their qualities, and to rearrange them correspondingly after their qualities have changed during development."

Born (1897) concurred with Roux's ideas on the basis of his results obtained in fusion experiments on parts of amphibian embryos. He concludes that "cells derived from the same germ layer unite to form continuous sheets, whereas cells from different germ layers rather tend to separate from each other" (p. 586). He thought the elective behavior was based respectively upon a mutual active seeking out and separation of the primordial parts. In support of this view, Born pointed out that homologous organ fragments that did not fit together at the time of experimental combination would later heal together into a morphologically harmonious and well-proportioned organ.

In view of the numerous unknown factors involved in such fusion experiments with half-embryos the evidence presented by Born does not appear to be very conclusive. As a matter of fact, in none of the innumerable transplantation experiments which have since been performed on amphibian embryos has anybody found reliable proof of an elective cytotropism.

The experiments of Roux were taken up, after a considerable lapse of time, by Vogt (1913), Voigtländer (1932), and Kuhl (1937). None of these authors was able to find evidence for cytotactically controlled, and still less for electively directed movements of the isolated cells. On the contrary, careful observation of individual cells, especially with the help of time-lapse movies (Kuhl), showed that the direction of migrations was random. Ectodermal cells were found to combine with each other just as well as with cells from other germ layers; they even associated with cells taken from different embryonic stages and from different species. It is interesting to note that experiments involving chemical or electrical stimuli gave likewise negative results with the yolky amphibian cells (Kuhl), although similar experiments performed with ameboid Protozoa and with migratory spleen cells in culture produced positive responses (Kathodotropismus, Péterfi and Williams 1934). In other words, none of the many stimuli tested could bring about directiveness of locomotion among the erratically creeping cells.

Consequently the experiments of Roux that originally seemed so promising must be considered to have been methodologically unsuited for their intended purpose. The dynamic behavior of isolated embryonic cells offered no explanation for the directed cell movements occurring during normal development.

Voigtländer and Kuhl went even further and expressed their doubt as to whether the protoplasmic movements, as observed in the culture medium, can be considered normal vital phenomena. From my own experience I would maintain a less sceptical attitude since I have often observed identical ameboid movements in media that permit the culture of such explants for several weeks and which, therefore, can hardly be considered damaging to cells. We think that simply the release of a cell from its normal tissue environment causes it to move restlessly about and to suffer eventually an early death, as was already observed by A. Fischer (1923) and others on isolated cells of fibroblast cultures. If such cells, however, join in time a cell mass of a certain size, they will readily survive the period of solitary migration.

Thus the only result of these experiments valuable for developmental physiology is the finding that amphibian cells—especially from pre-gastrula stages—roam around restlessly after their dislocation or isolation, until they make contact with a larger group of cells. They then combine with the group to form an aggregate with a minimal, hence spherical, surface. No elective distinction is made between different kinds of cells during this process. But this thigmotaxis is elective insofar as a non-living substrate does not exert the same quieting effect on the ameboid cells as does an organic tissue association. Even though cytotropism, effective at a distance, does not occur, we may go along with Roux in speaking of "Zytarme" [from the Greek meaning cell-junction], meaning a mutual attraction of the living cells *after* they have established contact with one another. This would lead to an intimate but non-elective aggregation. The explanatory value of this phenomenon, however, has its limitations exactly where the isolation experiment was supposed to help, namely, in the analytical interpretation of the directed formative movements beginning at the period of gastrulation.

It is from this junction that our new experiments take their departure. They have shown that there was some truth in Roux's intuitive concepts, even though his and Born's experimental approach did not permit any pertinent conclusions to be drawn. We may list three main reasons to account for the fact that the isolation experiments of Roux and his successors gave such meager results:

1) No strict distinction was made with respect to the origin of the material. Cells were isolated indiscriminately from pre- as well as post-

gastrula stages. It could have been expected, however, that the dynamic response of the cells varies markedly with the stage of the donor embryos.

2) The period of observation was too short (10 to 20 hours). In the normal embryo morphogenetic processes need more time to become clearly recognizable. This was all the more to be expected under the experimental culture conditions.

3) Even during normal development it is not individual cells but whole groups of them—not clearly demarcated from one another—that change their relative positions with kneading movements. In order to detect directed movements, larger cell complexes of homogeneous or mixed composition should have been studied rather than individual cells.

This is what we have done in a variety of experiments on material from embryos of several urodele and anuran species. From the results of these experiments we shall select in a summarizing manner only those that are relevant to the problem of cytotropism. More detailed reports on this material will appear soon in Roux' Archiv. In those reports as well as in some of our earlier papers (1934, 1938a, b) photomicrographs of sectioned material are given as documentation for those processes that we shall illustrate here with slightly schematic drawings.

II. ISOLATION AND RECOMBINATION EXPERIMENTS ON GASTRULA MATERIAL

We too shall begin our isolation experiments with pregastrula stages of amphibian embryos, such as the late blastula; we shall note carefully the origin of the material and follow the fate of the isolated tissue over several days. The cultures are maintained in dilute Ringer's or Tyrode's solution in glass dishes. Let us first observe the behavior of pure endodermal material.

(a) Isolation of pure endoderm. Endoderm which has been excised from the vegetal floor of a blastula or early gastrula consists of large yolky cells which soon increase their surfaces of contact with each other. Within one hour the irregular aggregate becomes a smooth-walled, solid sphere consisting of polyhedrally arranged cells. Within the next 24 hours—sometimes later—no apparent change occurs. If during this time two endodermal spheres are placed in apposition, they will exhibit the same tendency for union that was observed earlier with individual cells (Fig. 1b). The two spheres first join to form a double structure (Fig. 1c) which after approximately one day rounds up to assume the shape of a single sphere (Fig. 1d).

This demonstrates that the ameboid sliding motions of such endoderm cells are maintained for quite some time, and that during this period the cell aggregates retain the capacity for morphological regulation. A similar reconstitution into a spherical shape also takes place when

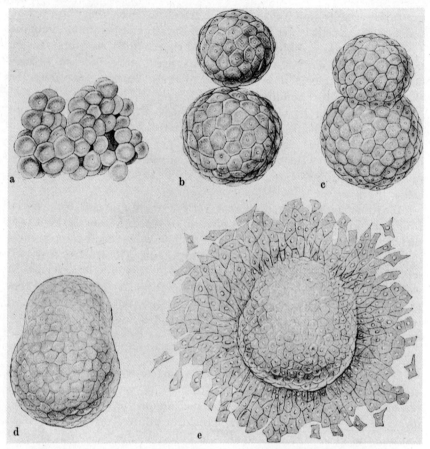

Fig. 1 Behavior of isolated endoderm cells from the amphibian gastrula. (a) The cells shortly after isolation; (b) two aggregates rounded into spheres are placed adjacent to one another; (c) (d) fusion of the two aggregates to form a single sphere; (e) flattening of the sphere and spreading out of the flattened cells.

several spheres are combined, or when a sphere is divided into two halves.

Approximately 20 hours after isolation, a fundamental change takes place in the dynamic behavior of the endoderm cells. Up until then the isolated cells had been nearly spherical in shape, with conical pseudopodia extruding from all sides. When contacting each other the cells tended to become closely associated and thus gave rise to an aggregate with minimum surface. Now the whole mass begins to flatten out shield-like on the bottom of the glass dish, its periphery spreading out like a membrane. Instead of the earlier rounding up, there now appears the tendency in each individual cell, and hence in the whole mass, to increase their surfaces (Fig. 1e). The spreading proceeds radially without favoring any particular axis. Some cells may isolate themselves at the periphery and migrate out a short distance. Within the flattened and two-dimensional cells the centrally located nucleus becomes visible as a clear space among the yolk platelets. Instead of the former lobe-shaped pseudopodia that freely protrude from the cell surface, pointed and occasionally branched processes are now extended over the glass surface. The mode of locomotion changes from an ameboid rolling to a slow sliding motion resembling that of the cells in conventional tissue cultures.

We are obviously dealing here with an autonomous process since in this isolate neither heterologous neighboring tissue nor any other environmental factors are present which could be responsible for the dynamic conversion of the endodermal mass. Endogenous factors must have caused the change in surface tension of these cells. The inorganic substrate is no longer avoided but it is, on the contrary, actively sought out. Even though the cells are generally retained within the peripheral sheet their migratory tendency may none the less lead to their individual self-isolation. The "Zytarme," in Roux's terminology, seems to have changed over to "Zytochorismus," a mutual repulsion [from the Greek meaning cell-separation]. In the present case this change occurs within a homogeneous mass of cells and not, as should have been expected from the concepts of Roux and Born, between cells of different quality. But upon closer examination the term "Zytochorismus" does not quite fit the present situation. It is not so much a mutual repulsion between cells but a tendency to autonomous migration and spreading that has led to the isolation of individual elements, since the cells can return to the central mass as easily as they separated from it. Therefore the dynamic behavior of the cells with respect to each other might rather be designated as indifferent. The original association, once it has been established, is merely tolerated. At any rate, a very firm mutual attraction can no longer be postulated to exist because then the observed self-isolation of the cells could not have occurred.

If such isolates of pure endoderm are cultured for a sufficiently long time, i.e., some 15 to 20 days, the peripheral membrane develops into a sheet of intestinal epithelium while the central mass, though remaining compact, nevertheless also assumes the cytological structures of intestinal cells. In view of this attested adequacy of the culture medium it seems justified to assume that the ameboid movements of the free cells observed in this medium may be considered just as vital as the creeping movements of the cells after they became flattened.

The results of these experiments have significance for the explanation of normal development. It was found that the surface spreading takes place at exactly the stage during which, in the intact embryo, the floor of the invaginated trunk endoderm shifts dorsad where the lateral walls fuse to form the closed intestinal tube. The morphogenetic movements of the endoderm in an explant and in the gastrula and neurula are therefore fundamentally of the same nature.

Still another conclusion may be drawn from this and similar experiments. It has been mentioned above that the environment could not have exerted an initiating effect upon the dynamic conversion of the endoderm. Yet we have to assume that the environment does play a role in the orientation of the spreading movements. Whereas the explanted endoderm spreads centrifugally in all directions along the glass surface, certain laterally and dorsally directed movements occur during the normal formation of the intestinal tube (Vogt 1929). In the embryo rearrangement takes place in three dimensions; in culture it is only in the horizontal plane. When, however, the explanted endoderm has been furnished with the core of a tissue substrate, it will glide over this surface and form an envelope of epithelium facing out. Such inverted intestinal vesicles covered by a peripheral epithelium and enclosing a core of connective tissue have been obtained previously in cultures of intestinal fragments of the chick embryo (Maximow 1925, Fischer 1927, Törö 1930 and others).

Thus the gut primordium merely possesses the tendency to spread indiscriminately over a suitable surface. If, within the intact embryo, the movements of the endoderm become oriented in certain directions, this feature must be due to the particular three-dimensional topography of free surfaces over which the cell material is permitted to glide.

(b) Isolation of endoderm and ectoderm combined. This second experiment deals with the study of the behavior of the endoderm in combination with pure ectoderm. In practice this can be done by excising from an early gastrula the mediocaudal region opposite the blastopore containing presumptive ectoderm and the underlying endoderm. In this operation the accidental inclusion of ventral mesoderm should be avoided.

At first the two types of cells are only loosely interconnected (Fig. 2a). The dislocated white endoderm cells form an irregular heap within the cup of the inward curling ectoderm. If the amount of ectoderm is insufficient to enclose all of the endoderm there soon arises the configuration shown in Figure 2b. The ectoderm has proceeded to encase the rounded-up endoderm, acorn-fashion. The two components establish intimate mutual contact indicating that despite the difference of the tissues the principle of "Zytarme" has been operating.

After approximately one and a half days the aggregate begins to change shape (Fig. 2c). The border zone between the two parts becomes constricted and, within another day, it narrows down to a "wasp waist" (Fig. 2d). Gradually all the endoderm flows out of the ectodermal sac;

the connecting bridge becomes more attenuated until finally the two parts are cleanly and completely isolated from each other (Fig. 2e). If the endoderm mass, now almost spherical, makes contact with a suitable substrate, it can, as described above, spread out and differentiate into intestinal epithelium. If, however, it remains floating freely in the medium, no epithelial sheet is formed, and the whole mass gives rise to a structure of non-polarized but cytologically differentiated intestinal

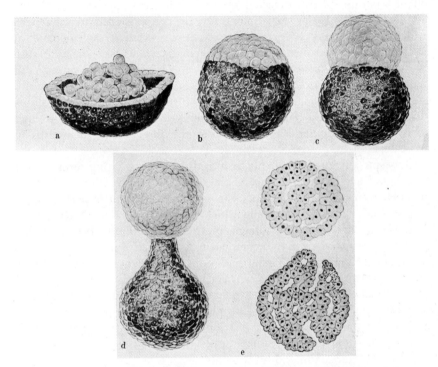

Fig. 2 Combination of endoderm with ectoderm. (a) Beginning of the experiment; (b) the two components have joined together to form a solid sphere; (c) beginning, and (d) almost completed self-isolation of the components. (e) The segregated parts are seen in section to consist of chaotically arranged gut or epidermis cells.

cells, perforated by irregular spaces containing secretion fluid. Isolated pure ectoderm forms a texture very similar to that of pure endoderm (Fig. 2e).

This experiment demonstrates for the first time the process which Roux and his successors tried vainly to find, namely, a definitely active self-separation ("Zytochorismus") of heterologous cell groups that were previously closely associated by "Zytarme." The separation came about neither by differential growth, nor by budding, nor by external push or pull; it was achieved by means of autonomous ameboid shiftings of the cell masses without a significant contribution of growth and cell proliferation. Vogt coined the appropriate term "Gestaltungsbewegungen" (morphogenetic movements) for this type of formative events which are so characteristic of gastrulation.

At first glance the result of the present experiment does not seem to invite further conclusions related to normal development. The rounding off of separate spheres of ectoderm and endoderm appears to be quite atypical. And yet this experiment reveals the existence of tendencies which are probably of great importance for normal development as well. Further experiments have indicated that a whole system of such attraction and repulsion phenomena is operating between various cell types during development and that information on this system will yield valuable information concerning the shiftings and segregations of tissues during organogenesis. Before attempting to relate these findings to normal development let us consider the phenomena themselves in more detail.

It seems advantageous to us to introduce a more fitting term for the forces that are instrumental in these processes of attraction and repulsion. Henceforth we shall apply the term *affinity,* which partly substitutes for the terms of Roux and which may serve as a reminder for the existence of analogous phenomena in chemistry. Affinity may be either positive or negative, it may be graded in its intensity, and may approach the point of neutrality. These gradations may change during development, increasing or decreasing between two cell generations, or they may repeat themselves in cycles. It can hardly be denied that there exists a far-reaching similarity between the phenomena occurring here in tissue associations and the cytotactic relationships between free gametes, such as have been extensively studied under the designation "relative sexuality" by M. Hartmann and his students.

To answer the question as to whether organismic affinity is merely a collective term for a series of subfunctions would require further investigations on an advanced level. Stimulated by the suggestions of Roux and by the experiments with gametes, one feels inclined to relate affinity to the progressively diversified chemodifferentiation of the tissue primordia. Probably the simultaneous interplay of physical forces is equally, if not even more significantly, involved in these phenomena.

(c) Fusion experiments between endodermal and ectodermal isolates. The increasing tendency of endoderm and ectoderm to separate, reported above, can be demonstrated in still other ways. We have mentioned that balls of endoderm may be made to fuse with one another within one or even two days after isolation. In later stages, however, fusion is possible only if the balls are provided with a new wound surface, or if the endoderm is derived from the inside of an early larva. Here a second phenomenon is involved, the arising of a polar property at the outer, nude surface of the peripheral cells; this reduces the ameboid mobility of the cortical layer, and hence its capability of adhesion. We do not wish here to enter any further into the problem of cell polarity, but merely point out that two balls of endoderm placed into contact with each other can exhibit positive affinity as late as two days after isolation, and that these homogeneous aggregates, once fused into a single sphere, never become constricted as do the endoderm-ectoderm composites.

If we now carry out the same combination between endodermal and ectodermal isolates after different intervals of cultivation, we obtain the following results. For example, if in a combination of these two tissues, taken from an early gastrula, the endoderm has been kept in salt solution for one day but the ectoderm is freshly isolated, a complete fusion between them will still take place. But when both isolates are one day old and their outer surfaces brought into contact, no adhesion whatsoever will occur. Only after a new wound surface has been provided will both partners combine though they still will not form a single sphere. The area of fusion will remain still smaller when both tissues are kept isolated for two days and the ectoderm is cut freshly at the site of contact. An isolated piece of ectoderm 3 or 4 days old will not adhere to endoderm, even when the latter is still very young and when some of the outer cells of both partners have been removed.

This experiment shows once more, apart from the problem of polarity which introduces additional complexities here, that in the course of time a negative affinity arises between endoderm and ectoderm. It is manifested by the degree of fusion which the two partners establish when confronted with one another after various periods of time. The shapes of the fused pieces correspond timewise to the constriction phases described above.

It would be feasible to determine by means of additional combinations which of the two cell types plays the more active role. On the basis of the present findings it may already be concluded that although the increasing "antagonism" is mutual, yet it seems to develop earlier in the ectoderm than in the endoderm.

That these phenomena of affinity are quite tissue specific is demonstrated by the following experiment:

(d) Combined isolation of endoderm and prospective connective tissue. We again combine endoderm and ectoderm, but with a thin layer of mesoderm between them. The simplest way to accomplish this is to excise from the gastrula a latero-caudal piece of the marginal zone. In contrast to the previously used caudal sector, this piece contains more elements of the lateral plate giving rise to connective tissue. Indeed, an isolate from the ventral belly region of a neurula would serve the purpose equally well.

As before, the complex mass of cells cultured in physiological salt solution rounds up in a short time into a sphere. Some portion of the endoderm may remain uncovered by the ectoderm because of the insufficient surface area of the latter (Fig. 3a). Here again, one to two days later a protrusion of the endoderm and the formation of a waist-like constriction are observed (Fig. 3b). However, instead of progressing

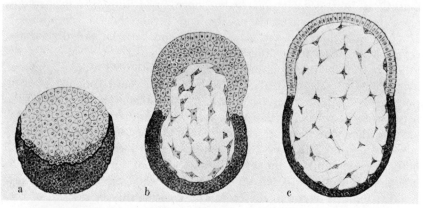

Fig. 3 Combination of endoderm and ectoderm with a layer of prospective connective tissue interposed. Sections. (a) Close union of the cells; (b) protrusion of the endoderm; (c) spreading of the ectoderm and endoderm to form a common epithelial wall around an internal cavity filled with mesenchyme.

further, the constriction regresses in many instances. A vesicle is formed, the interior of which is filled with mesenchyme cells forming a loose network because of the accumulation of secreted cellular fluid. In this instance, endoderm and ectoderm do not remain solid masses of cells but form the epithelial wall of the vesicle (Fig. 3c). The endoderm tends to form a single-celled layer while the ectoderm commonly becomes a layer two cells thick. The two epithelia are neatly delimited from one another and only touch along a ring-like borderline which sometimes appears as a slight fissure. Due to the presence of a common mesenchymal substratum self-isolation of the epithelia does not take place, even if the explants are cultured for an indefinite period of time.

It may be concluded from this experiment that endoderm as well as ectoderm retains permanently a positive affinity for connective tissue. As to intensity, these affinities seem to be even stronger than those between homologous cell material of the same age, since if endoderm and mesoderm are combined after they have been isolated for some time, they still fuse at those advanced stages, which are no longer favorable for homologous combinations.

(e) Endoderm enclosed in an epidermal vesicle. We again combine ectoderm, endoderm and mesoderm. In this arrangement, however, the ectoderm is made to cover completely the other cell types, with the mesoderm lying unilaterally between ectoderm and endoderm (Fig. 4a). The initially tight union of the solid mass of cells loosens up during the following days. It is remarkable that even under these conditions complete

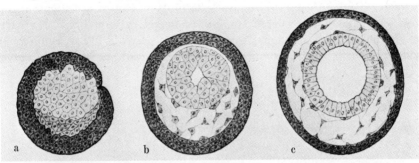

Fig. 4 Endoderm surrounded by ectoderm and mesenchyme separates away from the ectoderm and forms an intestinal vesicle the lumen of which arises by way of secondary cavitation.

detachment of the endoderm from the ectoderm takes place and that a cleft arises between them (Fig. 4b). This takes place autonomously. It is at a later time that this space is invaded and widened by connective tissue.

An epithelial spreading of endo- and ectoderm is facilitated by the hydrodynamic conditions within the vesicle. While the ectoderm produces the external envelope, the inner, initially solid mass of endoderm forms a lumen which ordinarily enlarges due to the accumulation of a secreted liquid, until a single-layered cyst of intestinal epithelium is formed (Fig. 4c).

Thus, here again a self-separation of endoderm from ectoderm is obtained, although, in this case, the endoderm is delaminated into the inside of an epidermal vesicle and both tissues become subsequently cemented together by mesenchyme. The phenomenon of epithelial polarity asserts itself. Under the present conditions, when the endoderm is shielded from the external medium by an epidermal envelope, it develops into an internal cyst with its epithelium facing the central lumen and not the outside as occurred in the previous experiment when the endoderm was lying at the outer periphery of the vesicle. The present arrangement of the three germ layers with respect to one another cannot be regarded as abnormal; in fact it is diagrammatically representative of the normal relationships.

(f) Isolation of combined mesoderm and ectoderm. It is still necessary to investigate the dynamic behavior of ectoderm toward pure mesoderm. We saw that mesoderm, as connective tissue, acts as a binding substance for epithelia and that association with it, once established, is never relinquished. At an earlier stage, however, conditions are slightly different; the affinity first develops in the opposite direction, since the phase of mutual close contact is preceded by a phase during which the ectoderm tends to separate from mesoderm. We can best investigate these relations by choosing a larger amount of mesoderm, for instance, a part of the dorsal marginal zone from an axolotl gastrula. This region provides chiefly chorda and somites, but also almost always regulates to give

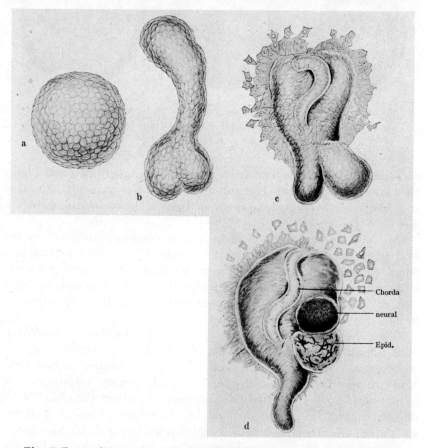

Fig. 5 Form changes in a fragment isolated from the region of the dorsal blastopore. (a) The aggregate rounds up into a sphere; (b) it elongates and forms a hump; (c) the isolate contracts, becomes attached to the glass surface, and begins to separate off a sphere of ectoderm. It segregates notochord and musculature, which is beginning to proliferate peripherally. (d) The ectoderm, which has re-established contact with the rest of the explant, has differentiated into epidermis and neural tissue, and the three axial tissues have grown out to form a tail.

rise to a small portion of ectoderm. Endoderm is absent here. Such explants display a great diversity of form changes and not until a comparison is made of many specimens can the general characteristics of the events be formulated.

At first such an isolate rounds up into a sphere just as does any other isolated fragment of the early embryo (Fig. 5a). Toward the end of the next day it begins to elongate and, after another day, it often takes on the shape of a femur (Fig. 5b). Tissue segregation is not yet apparent, except for a small protruding hump at the lower end of the structure, the histological character of which is not yet clear. On the third day, the upper end has become attached to the glass surface and in doing so contracts and flattens into a shield-like shape (Fig. 5c). The mesodermal character of this part is already indicated by the advancing pseudopodia at the periphery. On the upper surface of this layer a notochord begins to shape up vaguely. The hump of the preceding stage has become set off more distinctly as an almost spherical protuberance which, one day later, can be identified as ectoderm. Its initially pronounced constriction from mesoderm never leads to separation but regresses later on; still later the ectoderm reestablishes a broad contact area with the rest of the explant and differentiates into epidermis or even neural tissue (Fig. 5d).

The subsequent behavior of the tissues need not be of special concern to us in this connection. The chorda becomes more and more prominent as a tortuous rod. The mesoderm gives rise to dorsal musculature and releases at the periphery free myoblasts and connective tissue cells. It is sprouting forth the attenuated cone of a tail which contains, concealed inside, an extension of notochord and neural tube. The ectoderm which at first appears as a homogeneous hump later segregates into epidermis and neural tissue, a process which will be treated in greater detail later on.

The following morphogenetic sequence is characteristic for all such explants of the dorsal marginal zone: 1) general rounding up into a sphere, 2) stretching of the total mass, 3) contraction and flattening of the mesoderm that adheres to the bottom of the dish and a simultaneous incomplete detachment of the ectoderm, 4) further spreading and axial growth of the mesoderm and its partition into muscle and chorda, 5) reassociation of the ectoderm with mesoderm over a widening area of contact and its eventual segregation into epidermis and neural tissue.

During the initial phases, the general changes of shape are produced by means of morphogenetic cell movements whereas the formative principles of cell differentiation, cell proliferation and migrations become significantly engaged only at later stages. When observing such isolates from the dorsal blastoporal region one is reminded of the form changes during the development of a fruiting body in Myxomycetes, that dramatic process which A. Arndt has once demonstrated so impressively in a time-lapse movie. In both instances the material, like a plastic dough, displays all sorts of elongations, transformations, segregations, recombinations, and final differentiations. But whereas in the case of this lower fungus we are dealing with a multinucleate plasmodium, in an embryonic fragment we encounter the remarkable fact that the mass translocations are produced by a multitude of individual cells which nevertheless behave like an organic unity.

Among these processes, the changing dynamic relationship between ectoderm and mesoderm is of special interest, since we recognize therein an expression of affinity relations. At first this behavior resembles, even in its time sequence, the process of constriction in the combination of ectoderm and endoderm. Later on, however, the affinity reverts from a negative to a positive sense, a condition that had existed at the beginning of the experiment. That ectoderm which becomes epidermis will always remain on the surface, while the ectoderm that has been induced to form neural tissue actively penetrates, as neural tube, into the deeper mesoderm layers. To what extent affinity relations play a role in this process will not be discussed further here.

(g) Significance of affinity for the processes of gastrulation. Let us now examine these experimental findings with respect to their significance in developmental physiology. In the first place it should be understood that the phenomena described above are not artifacts introduced by unfavorable culture conditions. The same phenomena have been repeatedly observed under a variety of experimental conditions, as, for instance, when isolates are implanted into the coelom of older larvae, a milieu that may be regarded as eminently suitable for endoderm and mesoderm. We may therefore assume that similar processes, although they cannot be so easily detected, take place within the framework of the whole organism.

We have already pointed out that the epithelial spreading movement of the intestinal primordium is principally the same in both the explant and the gastrula and that the substratum affects the direction of spreading. We also noted that the upward shifting of the invaginated endoderm to form a tube is a natural consequence, on the one hand, of the autonomous and nondirectional spreading tendency of the entoderm, and on the other, of its specific position in a cavity that is only open in a certain direction. The wrapping experiment (p. 200) shows furthermore that an inner lumen of the intestine can be formed subsequently, by way of delamination within an endodermal mass that has been screened against the outer medium by an epidermal envelope. In such a case the pressure of the internal liquid may contribute to a flattening of the endoderm cells into an epithelium.

Ordinarily, connective tissue represents the natural gliding surface and later the substrate of the endoderm. The fact that these associated germ layers, mesoderm and endoderm, comprise a system of such mechanical stability is not due to their accidental, passive apposition but rather depends on their active, permanent combining tendencies. By the way, other mesodermal tissues show the same positive relationship to the endoderm as does connective tissue.

The incompatibility of ectoderm with mesoderm, which is only temporary, and with endoderm, which is increasing, seems to play an important role in the steering of invagination processes. On an earlier occasion we have described a similar process of separation on a large scale, namely, in total exogastrulation (Holtfreter 1933). There, too, a complete stripping off and self-isolation of the ectoderm took place when the endoderm became thinned out to a connecting stalk; however, if some mesoderm was present in the stalk the pinching off process remained incomplete.

Indeed, the normal process of invagination comprises an isolation of ectoderm from endomesoderm during which the connecting zone gradually diminishes. However, there this process does not lead to a moving away of the endomesoderm into the outer medium as in an exogastrula, but to its incorporation within the ectodermal vault. The problem of why invagination and not evagination takes place normally has not yet been clarified. The most likely factors contributing to this result are a mechanical counter-pressure of the vitelline membrane, osmotic conditions and finally an active "tendency" for invagination which first begins at the head-gut region. However, it seems to us important that the second process characteristic of gastrulation, viz., the progressive constriction of the ectoderm, can be carried out independently of invagination. That in this process the epibolic spreading of the ectoderm does not exert an active pushing effect, but rather follows the receding material, was shown in the case of exogastrulation and also in our combination experiment in which an ectodermal epiboly was absent. Furthermore, mesodermal invagination along with a constricting blastoporal rim were observed in embryos that were practically free of ectoderm (Holtfreter 1933, p. 781). It seems to follow that normal gastrulation likewise operates by way of an active moving apart of heterologous tissues. That the connecting zone, in the form of the blastoporal rim, is narrowing down to the anal opening would then be due to the topographical arrangement of the primordial regions. It appears that the driving principle behind the streaming apart of heterologous cell masses has to be sought in a change of affinity between the tissues to a negative state. Let us consider some additional details.

In the intact embryo the ectoderm is everywhere separated from endoderm by a zone of mesoderm, which is, however, very narrow in the ventro-caudal sector, the future anal region, where the mesoderm disappears rapidly during invagination so that ectoderm and endoderm come to border directly on each other. Their epithelial contiguity in the proctodeal borderzone is stable only because in the meantime some mesoderm has shifted underneath and holds them together. In the other regions of the embryo it is probably the temporary incompatibility between ectoderm and mesoderm, observed above in the explants that is instrumental in the involution movements. In addition one must take into account the inherent capability of the mesoderm to stretch itself axially, which it can do independently of any contact with heterologous neighboring tissues; this in itself must lead to a decrease of contact border with the ectoderm. After the mesoderm has moved off the surface of the gastrula and has come to underlie the ectoderm, the phase of attachment between these two layers begins. The strength of adhesion increases progressively, and it becomes particularly pronounced between chorda-somites and neural plate. In a late gastrula the underlying mesoderm can be peeled off easily from the ectoderm; in a late neurula however, this requires much more patient skill, and in the larval stage it cannot be done without severely damaging the cells. If this strong adhesion had already prevailed during the gastrula stage, the gliding movements of the invaginating mesoderm would surely have been arrested.

While, in the dissection of an advanced neurula, many of the mesoderm cells remain stuck to the epidermis, this does not happen in the liver region. In this mesoderm-free region the endoderm is contacting directly the ectoderm (Vogt 1929). This localized non-adhesion between superimposed endoderm and ectoderm may very well be ascribed to the emergence of a negative affinity between them: the advanced neurula corresponds in time to the phase in our combination experiment when the constriction between the two tissue types was almost complete.

Certain phenomena met with in the blastoporal region can also be explained on the basis of the above experiments. It may happen sometimes that beyond the neurula stage a considerable portion of the endoderm remains protruding in the anal region as a yolk plug. Such plugs never fuse with the adjacent epidermis and therefore do not cause an obstruction of the anal opening. They are later either constricted off or become overgrown by the advancing skin. Once the intestinal primordium has invaginated, a mesodermal layer develops everywhere between it and the ectoderm; this binds them together mechanically and causes both of them to elaborate an epithelium whose surface is oriented toward a liquid medium.

Special conditions prevail in the mouth and gill regions that shall not be discussed here in detail. Thus the head endoderm retains adhesiveness toward the ectoderm much longer than does the rest of the endoderm. It is by this means that the inductive origin of the various ectodermal mouth structures becomes possible.

III. ISOLATION AND COMBINATION EXPERIMENTS WITH NEURULA MATERIAL

The preceding experiments and their interpretation have helped us in gaining new insight into the morphogenetic processes, especially those occurring during the period of gastrulation. Now another series of isolation experiments shall be presented which deal with the dynamic relations between epidermis, neural components and mesoderm. They may serve to explain some of the important processes of neurulation.

The most striking feature of a neurula is the appearance of the neural plate, which narrows progressively, involutes into a tube and separates from the epidermis. This is not the place to offer a comprehensive causal analysis of these morphogenetic processes. We shall merely present a few impressive experimental results which will show that in this process also, local growth by cell proliferation, or outer factors such as pressure, push or pull of neighboring tissues are only insignificantly involved, whereas the formative capacities inherent in the cell material proper and physiological influences of the environment are of much greater importance.

(a) The morphogenetic capacities inherent in the neural plate. The histological capacity for self-differentiation of isolated pieces of the neural plate has been demonstrated frequently in transplantation or isolation experiments. In connection with our problem it seems important to examine, first of all, to what extent the amount of neighboring tissues can be reduced without deranging the typical process of neural plate development. Later on we plan to examine in some complex isolates the specific influence of various neighboring tissues upon the neural formative processes. Let us first confine our attention to the brain region.

It is known that the subjacent cephalic endomesoderm does not merely exert a single inductive stimulus on the prospective neural material but that it continues participating in the modeling of its shape. The initial stimulus, however, accomplishes very much, if not the essential part. One arrives at the same conclusion if one considers the amazingly complex effects of a dead abnormal inductor, although it does not take part materially in the modeling of the neural tissue which it induced. A variety of brain structures, even symmetrical ones with typical eyes and other sense organs, can be formed in such a case although the contact influence may have lasted only for some 40 hours (Holtfreter 1934b, p. 234).

Once it has become induced, the ectoderm itself acquires the capacities for an extensive, though certainly not entirely typical morphogenesis. It has been hitherto tacitly assumed that in this process mesenchyme and epidermis play merely a protecting and supporting role. This matter, however, shall become the very problem of our subsequent studies. First, it will be shown that typical form changes take place in a fragment of the neural plate that had been isolated without its subjacent inductors but was supplied with an abundance of epidermis.

The explant shown in Figure 6 was excised from the cephalic region of a fully developed neurula; it consists in part of the lateral portion of the neural plate and, to a larger extent, of the adjacent epidermis. Located between them is the neural crest, the source of origin of mesenchyme, pigment cells and also of ganglia and cartilage.

In a short time the epidermis turns upwards and wraps itself around the neural material whereas the latter contracts and sinks in to form a groove (Fig. 6b). The over-all shape thus resembles a very thick-walled bowl. This shape, since it deviates from a sphere, indicates that although the capacity for ameboid movements of the cells and their inclina-

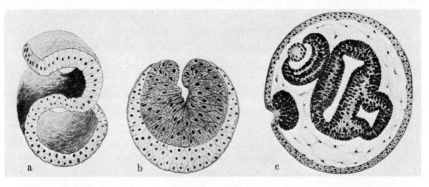

Fig. 6 Isolation of a portion of head neural plate together with a larger piece of adjacent prospective epidermis. (a) Beginning of the experiment: above, neural material, involuted concavely; below, epidermis. (b) The components have tightly united and the neural plate has sunk in to form a groove. (c) Differentiation of a brain with an eye and a nasal pit inside the epidermal vesicle.

tion to establish maximal contact with each other are still present, neural material already possesses formative tendencies of its own. Even under such abnormal conditions it attempts to sink into the depth. Neither a pull by underlying mesoderm, nor lateral pushing by the epidermis can be responsible for this, since mesoderm is absent and the epidermis is initially present only on one side; furthermore this epidermis is deflected in its movements because it attempts to envelop the whole isolate. Yet the involution of the neural primordium takes place nearly concentrically. Moreover, since involution is also observed in pieces completely devoid of epidermis, it must be considered an autonomous process.

On the following day involution is complete and the neural material is fully enclosed by the epidermis. The process of involution usually leads to the formation of a central lumen. Mesenchyme and pigment cells develop from the neural crest; the epidermal vesicle expands and becomes transparent making it possible to see the inner neural mass. The latter develops into a brain diverticulum associated with a typically shaped eye which in turn induces the formation of a lens. Even an olfactory pit may develop in such an isolate. As is brought out by the slightly schematized illustration of Fig. 6c, all the neural material with the exception of the olfactory pit is separated from the epidermis by a layer of mesenchyme. As in a normal brain there arises as fibrous marginal layer and a proximal nucleated layer. If one disregards the obviously fragmentary character of this brain one must admit that its development has proceeded quite typically in the absence of head mesoderm. This is true for the eye and nose as well.

This experiment may serve as a control for a second one which will again raise the question of affinity and may bring us closer to solving the question of the influence of mesenchyme and epidermis upon the configuration of the neural differentiations.

(b) Self-isolation of neural tissue from epidermis. Again we excise from the lateral head region of a neurula a purely ectodermal strip which this time, however, contains relatively more neural plate and less pro-

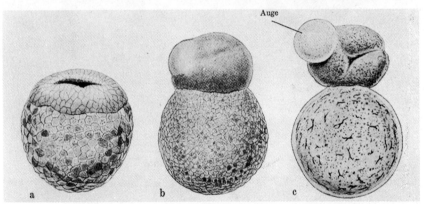

Auge

a   b   c

Fig. 7 Isolation of a portion of head neural plate together with a smaller piece of adjacent prospective epidermis. (a) The conjoined cells have formed a spherical mass, and there is a neural groove. (b) Beginning, (c) progressing constriction.

spective epidermis. As in the previous experiment such a piece immediately bends in such a way that the neural material curves concavely and the epidermis convexly. Both components contract simultaneously and then merge into a compact mass showing a blackish depression (Fig. 7a). This groove disappears at older stages becoming under these conditions covered with neural cells instead of epidermis. Thus the involution of the neural tissue can take place without the assistance of adjacent tissues. If the epidermal component is relatively small, the neural tissue never becomes completely covered by it.

In the course of time a constriction develops, quite similar to that between ectoderm and endoderm with the difference however that here even connective tissue cannot prevent an outward movement of the neural mass. As in the preceding example this mesenchyme stems from the neural crest, i.e., it is of ectodermal and not mesodermal derivation.

One to two days after isolation, the material, now recognizable as neural tissue, begins to slide out of the epidermal envelope (Fig. 7b). The connecting bridge between them becomes narrower with time (Fig. 7c) until complete self-isolation of the neural mass has taken place (Fig. 8a). As the constriction progresses, the exit hole in the epidermis closes.

The brain fragment remains considerably more compact when entirely isolated than when cultured within an epidermal vesicle. Just the

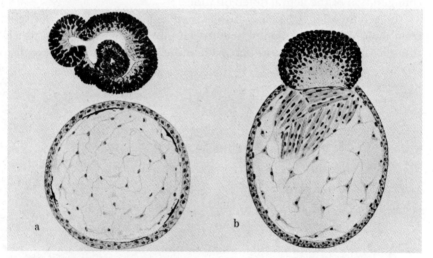

Fig. 8 (a) An uncovered eye has protruded from the isolated neural portion; melanophores and mesenchyme are present within the epidermal vesicle. (b) The neural mass adjacent to the musculature is mushroom-shaped and is not constricted off.

same, an inner, rather slitlike lumen may be formed. However, the nuclei of the neuroblasts are now located at the periphery so that at least a partial inversion of the stratified structure must be assumed. As in the case of the gut epithelium, this inversion of polarity must be ascribed to the absence of enveloping tissues. As regards cytological differentiation, the neural tissue may become quite normal.

In a region remote from the epidermis, an eye has evaginated from the brain fragment. In the living explant it can be distinguished from the other neural parts by its lighter tinge and smooth surface, and in section it appears as a simple hemispherical protrusion from the neural layer.

An identical hemispherical eye protrusion from a solid mass of brain is obtained if, in a whole neurula, all of the epidermis is removed so that the neural tissue is forced to differentiate in a superficial position. These observations prove that the primary eye vesicle is not formed due to mechanical intervention of any neighboring tissues but that its evagination results from active formative tendencies within the eye material itself. Here we find on a smaller scale the same phenomenon of constriction that is exhibited between the whole neural mass and the skin vesicle. Our subsequent experimental results indicate that we are dealing again with the emergence of physiological differences between brain material and eye primordium and thus once more with a show of affinity that causes them to move apart. In an uncovered brain, however, complete isolation of a spherical eye never occurs. Here the significance of the mesenchyme in the development of the eye enters the picture.

The difference between such an exposed eye and one that has formed within a mesenchymal mass, as in our preceding experiment, is very striking. The naked eye primordium does not differentiate into tapetum, multilayered retina, rods and cones, and it fails to fold inward into an eye cup. Differentiation is arrested at the stage of the primary eye vesicle. Therefore, the embedding of the eye primordium in mesenchyme seems to be necessary for the development of all of these organo- and histotypical structures.

In this experiment, all the mesectoderm has remained inside the epidermal vesicle. We find here mainly mesenchyme and pigment cells, but occasionally also small ganglia with outgrowing nerve fibers. The self-isolation of the parts is completed cleanly just as it is in the case of endoderm.

One could argue against the assumption of an active self-separation of the neural mass by postulating that its expulsion may have been caused by a pressure of the expanding mesenchyme. However, this is not supported by a number of other experimental results. It is possible, for instance, to obtain the formation of neural tissue in the almost complete absence of mesoderm by implanting a dead inductor into an ectodermal vesicle. The enclosed neural mass always becomes separated from the ectoderm by a space and, if there is merely a narrow opening to the external medium, it will force itself through it. Correspondingly, negative results are obtained in fusion experiments between ectoderm and neural material that had been kept isolated for a prolonged time.

Thus, even in the absence of mesenchyme, a repulsive action can originate solely in the epidermis. But the mesectoderm also has an inherent tendency to emancipate itself from the neural material which was its former neighbor tissue. For instance, if a piece of neural plate including neural crest is transplanted into the ventral lymphatic spaces of an older host larva, the neural portion develops into a sphere of neural tissue. Mesenchyme and pigment cells, however, derived from the neural crest, migrate away and become widely dispersed in the host tissue. This can be especially clearly demonstrated in xenoplastic combinations (Holtfreter 1929, Bytinsky-Salz 1938). In particular, the cells of the dermis derived from an implant of a foreign species or genus migrate actively underneath the host epidermis; similarly melano- and xanthophores seek out this neighborhood and spread there in their typical manner. A similar "epidermophilic" behavior is shown by the primordial buds of the lateral sensory line (Harrison 1904, Holtfreter 1935).

Thus although these three derivatives of the neural crest sever their connection with neural material, they nevertheless retain the tendency to associate with the epidermis. As is shown by the xenoplastic combinations, the tissue-specific affinities are not confined to tissues of the same species.

From the experiment illustrated in Figure 8b it may be likewise concluded that the extrusion of the neural mass from the skin vesicle cannot be explained as being due to pressure conditions. In this case the isolate included some of the underlying somite material in addition to the ectodermal parts. This material has a much stronger binding power for neural tissue than has mesenchyme. Here too the exposed neural tissue tends to separate from the remaining parts, but is held fast by the muscle mass; it protrudes outward in the shape of a mushroom, its nuclei again located peripherally and the nerve fibers proximally.

Even if there were a pressure exerted by the inner mesenchyme of the skin vesicle, we have never observed this force to be able to cause an isolation of musculature or other mesoderm or endoderm. Thus this segregation phenomenon must be considered peculiar to neural tissue, suggesting that this tissue is not strongly anchored in purely ectodermal mesenchyme.

Likewise, a possibly existing constricting action of the epidermis cannot have played a primary role in this instance, since if this were the case it should also have brought about a separation of the neural material in the experiment with musculature. There, however, the condition as illustrated remains permanent.

Hence we reach the conclusion that the segregation of the ectodermal derivatives must be attributed to the development of a negative affinity between them. This accompanies differentiation since, if prior to the inductive action of the subjacent mesoderm, we isolate a piece—half neural and half epidermal—from exactly the same region, the whole piece retains an epidermal character and no constriction takes place. The relative size of the components is immaterial for the result. The prospective neural mass may be very large and the epidermal portion very small, or vice versa, a further indication that crude mechanical forces such as push and pull cannot play any role.

Finally, still another experimental modification is shown in Figure 9a which illustrates quite strikingly the elective character of tissue affinities.

(c) Positive affinity of eye primordium for connective tissue. The isolate in the present experiment was excised from the median rather than the lateral head region of a neurula; it comprised the primordia of brain-eye and the adjacent frontal epidermis. Although here again the entire brain material slipped out of the epidermal vesicle, the eye remained inside and differentiated into all its typical structures. In the end only the optic nerve retained a connection with the isolated neural mass (Fig. 9).

Why is the eye excluded from the process of isolation? Is it mere coincidence that it remains within the mesenchyme? The fact that there are many similar cases speaks against this supposition. It appears, rather,

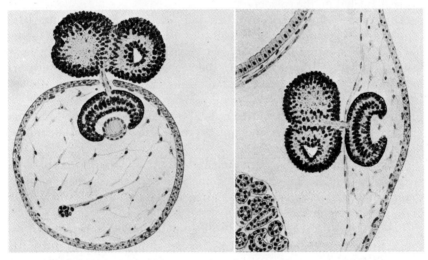

Fig. 9 While the brain material has isolated itself, the eye has remained within the epidermal vesicle.

Fig. 10 Implantation of head neural plate into the abdominal cavity. The eye rudiment has evaginated into the abdominal body wall; the brain portion remains free in the coelomic fluid.

that the eye, in contrast to the brain, has a pronounced preference for mesectoderm. We consider the following experimental findings as a direct proof for this latter view.

We isolate the same piece of neural plate, but this time without any adjacent epidermis and substrate, and then push it through a small slit into the abdominal cavity of an older amphibian larva. There it floats freely between the viscera and the coelomic wall and continues differentiating during the following days. When the host larva bearing the implant is examined microscopically, the following picture is obtained.

If the implant has developed into neural tissue only, it is never found to have established tissue connection with the mesoderm of the host. Such pieces behave exactly like those cultured in physiological saline. Their neural involution may proceed until a tube is formed, or may not pass beyond the neural groove stage. The fibrous layer is always situated centrally, as we have already shown previously in an illustration (Holtfreter 1929, p. 443).

Quite different, however, is the behavior in many cases of the eyes that have evaginated from these brain fragments. They alone, in a remarkably high percentage of cases, establish tissue contact with the coelomic wall, as shown in Figure 10, and they may even become deeply embedded in the host mesenchyme. The attached brain portion always projects freely into the coelom.

Only some definite action on the part of the eye primordium itself can have been responsible for its embedding in mesenchyme. The following course of events must be envisaged. At first, the implant, while temporarily lying still, adhered lightly to the coelomic wall. Then the eye primordium, in contrast to the neural tissue, penetrated the peritoneal lining on its own and invaded the mesenchyme. This process can be explained only on the basis of a specific, positive affinity of the optic material to connective tissue, and not by any pull, pressure or suction on the part of the living substrate.

Thus, in the preceding experimental set-up, it was the result of directed tissue-specific movements of the material rather than of mere chance that the eye became incorporated in the skin vesicle whereas the brain portion emigrated.

The eye gains a remarkable advantage by becoming embedded in the connective tissue of the host. Instead of remaining in the stage of a primary optic vesicle, as do the uncovered eyes in the coelom, it continues its development quite typically, even folding into a cup. A lens is absent because the host epidermis was much too old to form a lens in response to the eye stimulus. It should be mentioned that here the eye has invaded mesenchyme which is of mesodermal and not of ectodermal origin, as it was in the foregoing experiments and as it is predominantly in normal development. Therefore, the age and local origin of the mesenchymatic matrix seem to be immaterial for the embedding process.

Before drawing general conclusions from these observations we should like to introduce a final series of tissue combinations, that will again demonstrate the specificity of these attraction and repulsion phenomena.

(d) Positive affinity of the neural material for mesoderm. From the behavior of neural tissue in the experiment illustrated in Figure 8b it is already evident that this material is attracted by the somite musculature and that it remains permanently combined with it. In this case it had formed a mushroom-shaped cushion because it was only locally attached and it was laterally impeded by the epidermis. If a larger piece of trunk neural plate is isolated from a neurula free of epidermis but including a small portion of the underlying somite primordium, the following result is obtained.

The isolate assumes a nearly spherical shape, and the neural material glides around the mesoderm. In this case rolling in to form a neural tube, such as occurs in pure isolates or in the presence of epidermis, does not take place. A firm adherence to the substrate seems to suppress this inherent tendency. When the somite portion is very small, the neural plate cells spreading over its surface may enclose it entirely and thus form a thick mantle of neural tissue, the fibers of which lie proximally and the cell nuclei distally (Fig. 11a). A neural lumen is absent in this type of

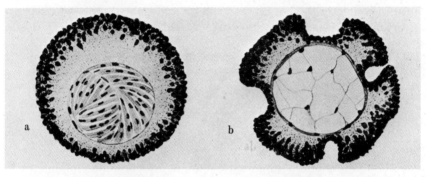

Fig. 11 Polarizing effect of the underlying tissue on neural material. (a) Naked neural tissue adjacent to musculature does not develop a lumen. (b) When adjacent to chorda, the neural layer forms groove-like depressions.

combination. No separation of the two tissues takes place even at later stages.

The tendency for close adhesion of the neural tissue to chorda is even more pronounced. Very striking examples are obtained when, for instance, a fragment of the chorda primordium is isolated from a neurula together with a piece of neural plate, or when a piece of chorda is wrapped in a thin layer of gastrula ectoderm, which is then induced to form neural tissue. Figure 11b illustrates such a case in which chorda is wholly surrounded by a layer of neural cells. This layer does not represent a smooth surfaced, solid cushion as in combination with muscle, but it has formed several groove-like depressions and occasionally even closed lumina.

Thus, whereas neural plate cells in combination with somites tend to accumulate into a thick mass, they tend, in contact with chorda, to spread into as thin a layer as possible. Accordingly, when the chorda surface at their disposal is abundant, the neural cells may adopt an almost epithelial-like arrangement. Local grooves or lumina appear within this layer only when the cells remain piled up because of a limitation of the surface over which they could spread.

In the last two experiments we came upon phenomena that have already been considered elsewhere. Thus Bautzmann (1928) pointed out that the formation of the median groove of the open neural plate might be attributed to a special effect of attraction exerted by the underlying chorda, a view which is supported by considering the firmness with which these two germ layers cling together. Lehmann (1926, 1929) and many subsequent authors have called attention to the peculiar mass distribution and shape of the neural plate material that takes place in response to contact with these inductors. Thus, the part of the neural tube in contact with chorda was always found to be thinned out, whereas it became thickened in its wall that was adjacent to somites. These re-

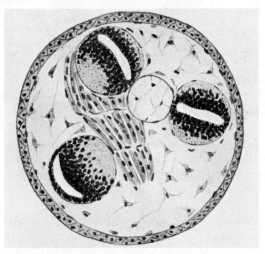

Fig. 12 Morphogenetic influence of chorda and musculature on neural tube, surrounded by epidermis.

lationships are schematically illustrated in Figure 12, assuming in this case that the neural material is surrounded by both mesenchyme and epidermis.

(e) Influence of the inductors upon the shape and arrangement of neural tissue. In the cross-section shown in Figure 12, three neural tubes are depicted which differ from one another by their material arrangement of neural tissue. The neural tube on the lower left, having contact with muscle only, has a distally located transverse lumen. Its basal thickening and the location of the fibrous layer toward the contact surface is in accord with the behavior of neural material that rests directly on muscle in the absence of ectoderm. However, in the present example, the existence of a mantle of mesenchyme and epidermis has permitted the prospective neural material to execute the movements of involution and to form a tube or a cyst.

Somewhat different environmental factors have had a formative influence on the morphogenesis of the neural tube to the right, which rests on chorda. Its surface spreading was prevented and thus a rounded tube was formed with a single lumen perpendicular to the chorda. The basal layer of the neural tube is thin, whereas its lateral walls are symmetrically thickened.

Finally, the uppermost neural tube is unilaterally in contact with muscle and basally with chorda. Both of these tissues have exerted a polarizing influence, since the basal layer is thin, and the wall adjacent to muscle is thickened, whereas the side wall away from muscle is not quite as thin as it would have been if under the unilateral influence of muscle tissue alone. A bilaterally symmetric thickening of both side walls would have occurred only if, as in a normal embryo, the tube had been in contact with somites on two sides.

Let us summarize as follows an evaluation of these last experimental results with respect to their bearing on the problem of affinity.

(1) The mesoderm (chorda and somites), in contrast to the epidermis, exerts a strong attraction on neural plate material, a condition that is retained at least until their histological differentiation has taken place. In this respect chorda is more effective than muscle primordium.

(2) This phenomenon is linked with a tissue-specific polarizing influence of the mesoderm upon the mass distribution of the prospective neural tissue. The contact area is thinned by chorda and thickened by muscle.

(3) In order to form a closed tube the cells of the neural plate while being attracted by mesoderm must be provided with an external supporting matrix. This support, mainly mechanical in nature, is provided in this case by mesenchyme and epidermis. The lack of affinity of both of these tissues for the older neural tissue is probably a contributing factor for the latter to form a rounded cyst or tube, i.e., once the neural material is trapped by these tissues, it tends to reduce its contact surface with them to a minimum.

(f) Significance of affinity for the process of neurulation. In the preceding paragraph it was shown that an insight may be gained into the causal mechanism of the process of gastrulation from the autonomous formative tendencies of the explants and from the dynamic behavior that is exhibited by the germ layers in various combinations with one another. In a neurula the distribution and segregation of meso- and endoderm is completed in rough outlines. Here we are more concerned with the formative processes of the outer germ layer. An attempt will now be made to synthesize the experimental results on neurula material and to relate them to normal organogenesis.

On the basis of the few data presented here in rough outline, a general rule can already be established, namely, that when a morphological segregation occurs in a hitherto undivided cell layer, there is also a change in affinity between the new derivatives. Let us follow the course of events while confining ourselves to the ectoderm and its derivatives.

The gastrula ectoderm is still morphologically and potentially homogeneous, and if fragments from various regions of it are combined together, they show a uniformly positive affinity with one another. In this quality, however, the ectoderm does not differ from the other organ primordia, since, as we have previously seen, all of them at this stage can unite indiscriminately with one another. If the ectoderm remains histologically undetermined owing to the absence of inductive stimuli, it also retains its dynamic homogeneity, a fact which ought not to be taken for granted. If, however, the underlying mesoderm has induced local differences in the developmental capacities of the ectoderm, they will manifest themselves dynamically together with the first appearance of structural differences, if not earlier. The prospective neural plate of an early neurula which is outwardly not yet demarcated will, when isolated, rapidly bend inward, thus behaving like epidermis of the same or even older stages. But when the same material is isolated at a slightly older stage, when the neural folds have become delineated, its edges will bend upward, concavely; and this involution will occur the faster and the more vigorously the later the stage of operation. This concave curling, resulting from a latent state of tension of the neural plate, signalizes the coming of further mass rearrangements of the isolated material which will proceed in the same direction. Even without any support from neighboring tissues, an isolated older neural plate is capable of a concave infolding that leads to the formation of a closed cyst or tube. On the other hand, isolated epidermis, especially if connective tissue is left attached to it, will always curve convexly to form a vesicle.

During the period of involution the neural material loses its capacity to adhere to the ectoderm that is differentiating into epidermis. At the same time it tends to become repellent toward the neural crest derivatives, such as mesenchyme and pigment cells, whereas the latter now tend to combine with epidermis. The active outbulging of the optic vesicle seems to be an expression of a physiological difference arising between it and the brain primordium that forces them to separate from one another. The detachment and complete evagination of the eye are then enhanced by a positive affinity between eye and neighboring mesenchyme. In contact with the epidermis the eye induces a lens with which it will henceforth remain intimately associated. Thus the lens is withdrawn from its generating germ layer. This event does not result from a hypothetical "suction" exerted by the eye primordium, but from an active constriction process similar to that of the evagination of the eye, since it may take place even without the inductive action of an optic vesicle or of any other morphologically defined inductor. Hence it seems that the emancipation of the lens is caused by a physiological estrangement to the epidermis. The lens acquires a positive affinity not only to the eye but also to the nasal pit and ear vesicle.

The following scheme may summarize this intriguing system of affinities of the ectodermal derivatives which comprises sequentially mutual estrangements between parent tissue and its filial primordia and newly arising elective bonds between filial primordia and other tissue derivatives of second or third order. The positive or negative relations between the tissue types are represented by + or − signs:

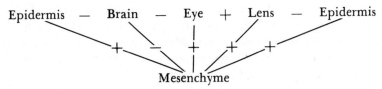

This scheme does not support the viewpoint advocated by Born (1897) that derivatives of the same germ layer attract while those from different germ layers repel each other. The system of relationships is much more complicated. In fact it is precisely the switch from a positive to a negative affinity between organ primordium and parent tissue which becomes the cause of the emancipation and morphogenesis of the derivative. A positive affinity may exist among the derivatives of the same germ layer, as well as among organ primordia of different germ layers. On the other hand, cells of the very same tissue layer may exhibit only a very slight tendency for mutual connections, as for example the mesenchyme. A homogeneous aggregate of either endodermal or epidermal cells, when cultured in the complete absence of a substrate, breaks apart during differentiation into its individual elements. The bonds that hold these homologous cells together are thus much weaker than those which connect them with the mesoderm. Generally speaking then, one finds rather more incidences of positive than of negative affinity between different tissue types.

The initiating stimuli for the introduction of local differences in the ectoderm are derived from the mesodermal and, in part, from the endodermal sublayer. Beginning at the early neurula stage, the prospective chorda, the somites, and the cephalic endomesoderm exert a pronounced attraction for the ectoderm. This leads to an intimate contact between them, which is a prerequisite for the occurrence of induction effects. Varying with the inductive specificity of the underlying tissues, the various neural, mesectodermal and epidermal districts are then physiologically demarcated within the ectoderm. With this stimulation the most important step has been taken, since from then on the newly emerging affinity interrelationships enable the ectodermal primordia to carry out a good number of important morphogenetic processes quite independently of any further cooperation with the inductors. However, under normal conditions, the subjacent heterologous tissues do continue to influence the formative processes and the material disposition of the induced ectodermal derivatives. As an example of this we demonstrated the specifying action which chorda and somites exert upon the distribution of the cellular mass of the neural tube. These secondary formative influences depend likewise on an intimate contact between the modelling agency and the responding pliable material. Correspondingly, the lens primordium requires a prolonged contact with the optic cup in order to acquire and retain its typical structure.

Important though the arising of negative affinities turns out to be for the local segregation of organ primordia from their parent tissue, positive affinities, whether retained or newly acquired, are just as indispensable for the pursuance of an organotypical development. The harmonious intertwining of these phases is assured by the initial disposition of the organ-forming areas of the embryo, as well as by the age- and tissue-specific character of the reactions that are predetermined within the material itself.

There is no need to dwell upon the obvious fact that purely mechanical environmental factors are also engaged in influencing the formative processes of early embryogenesis. This became apparent enough from the explantation experiments alone. But such influences play merely the role of non-specific factors in the realization of these processes and are replaceable to a great extent by non-living structures. In comparison with the physiologically transmitted stimuli, the crude forces of push and pull are of a very minor importance. The blastopore as well as neural tube, optic vesicle, or other organ primordia are not at all molded into shape by extraneous pushing or compressing agencies nor by a pulling from the interior; rather they form themselves by means of active translocations of cell areas that are set in motion by changes of their physiological states. The environment may then guide these autonomous movements in certain directions, and it may thus participate in determining the axiality and over-all shape of the primordial mass. However, the specific morphogenetic tendency inherent in the formative material itself remains the truly organizing principle. We are still far from grasping the physico-chemical processes involved in this "self-mobilization."

In view of the prominence which the study of growth processes has attained in the current work on tissue cultures, it seems timely to emphasize once more that growth is not of primary significance in early embryogenesis. Even the genesis of the disparate organs is mainly achieved by means of morphogenetic cell movements; such as have been strikingly exemplified by the gastrulating pieces of embryos. Only later, when the ameboid mobility of the cells is decreased as a result of differentiation, do the dough-like mass transports of entire cell complexes come to an end. Then locally regulated growth by cell division, by individual cell migration, or by the deposition of intra- and extracellular material takes over as the leading formative principle.

VI. CYTOTROPISM AND AFFINITY

Finally the phenomena of affinity, as treated in this paper, will be contrasted with Roux's cytotropism which provided the starting point for our considerations.

According to Roux, a mutual, dynamic influence between cells may occur in two ways: 1) between freely motile, individual cells (the term cytotaxis would be more appropriate here than cytotropism since we are dealing with the locomotion of free elements), and 2) between cells in cell aggregates (directional movement). The stimulating agents in both cases were supposed to be identical, namely, specific substances emitted by the cells that diffuse away in a concentration gradient and act selectively to bring about either attraction or repulsion. Accordingly the stimulus would act over a certain distance, not only between isolated cells but also amongst the cells in firm aggregates.

Roux's contention of having demonstrated an elective cytotaxis between isolated blastomeres must be considered as disproved on the basis of the aforementioned investigations of Voigtländer (1932) and Kuhl (1937). Nor did the experiments performed by these authors on cell combinations of early embryonic stages yield any evidence for a "self-ordering power" of the cells according to their different qualities.

To what extent these negative findings are also applicable to the cells of more advanced embryonic stages remained undecided. Subsequent investigations dealt with much older, already differentiated single cells of the organism (germ cells, ameboid blood elements). There indeed instances of a chemotactic or cytotactic cellular responsiveness were found. In this connection, attention must also be drawn to the dissociation experiments on sponges, first carried out by Morgan (1900, 1907) and later by Galtsoff (1925). They have shown that harmoniously organized individual sponges can be reconstituted from a mass of completely disorganized isolated cells. More interesting still: when the dissociated cells from one species were mixed with those from another species, only the cells from one and the same species would unite and form a new organism. In this case an actual self-ordering of the free cells seems to have taken place, which suggests that a tissue-specific cytotactic affinity has operated here as the organizing power. Furthermore, in sponges cell affinity seems to be species-specific, which is certainly not the case in amphibians while they are in early embryonic stages.

In an organism, however, it is the mode of movement and the formative changes of integrated cell complexes, rather than the behavior of individual cells, that call for an exploration. Do the cytotropic actions at a distance postulated by Roux exist also between cell complexes as a means of morphogenesis?

The affirmative opinion of Born on this question has not been shared by any of the later experimentalists working on amphibians. However, when tissues from warm-blooded animals were cultured in the usual media consisting of blood plasma and embryonic extract, growth processes were observed that appeared to be based upon cytotropism. This is the well-known bridge phenomenon of growth which often occurred when two explants were placed rather closely together in the same drop of the plasma medium. This phenomenon could be interpreted as the expression of a chemotropic distant action of the explants on one another. Thus a series of experiments on such confrontation cultures has been carried out by Centanni and his co-workers with the aim of ascertaining the elective nature of the stimulus. The results were ambiguous. Tissues of the same as well as of different kinds were able to grow toward each other while in other experiments repulsive effects seemed apparent. Although it was difficult to systematize such findings, Juhásc (1929) believed that they had demonstrated the existence of tissue-specific growth substances acting at a distance; he termed them "cytoblastines."

These interpretations are no longer convincing as a result of investigations by Weiss (1929, 1934). According to him the bridge of cells between two explants can be explained on a purely mechanical basis. As a consequence of dehydration, the plasma around each explant is assumed to undergo local condensation which causes the micelles of the colloidal medium to become oriented along the lines of stress. Since cells proliferate preferentially along such micellar guiding structures, the connecting strand of cells may simply be explained on the basis that a pronounced system of parallel guiding tracks has formed in the zone between the explants. According to this viewpoint, the diversity of experimental results of Juhásc might readily be explained by postulating variations in the dehydrating capacity of the different kinds of tissue.

The concept of cytotropism has found favorable support especially among neurologists since it seemed to provide an explanation for the directed growth of nerves if it is assumed that attracting stimuli emanate from the future effector organ. Some investigators (Kappers, Child and others) considered a difference in electrical potential to be important while others (Cajal, Tello) assumed that specific chemical substances may act as stimulators.

Indeed, several authors interpreted the behavior of the outgrowing axons toward other cells in the explant in terms of chemotropism. There was for instance the observation that when nerve fibers grow into a fibroblast culture in the same plasma medium the path of some of them became apparently deviated in such a way as to make contact with a mesenchyme cell. This was considered proof for the existence of chemotropic relations between the cellular elements (Grigorjeff 1931), even though the nerve fibers would as often as not take no notice of the neighboring cells.

The interpretation of these findings has been rejected by Weiss (1934) on the strength of his counterarguments referred to above. On the basis of further extensive tests in plasma cultures in which neural tissue was confronted with other kinds of tissue, or with extracts of crushed tissues or chemical agents applied to one side, he concluded that the outgrowing nerve fiber does not respond to chemotactic stimulation, and that the direction of its growth is determined primarily, if not exclusively, by mechanical factors.

In commenting on this notion, one could argue, of course, that the conditions in explantation experiments by no means correspond to those prevailing in the organism, and that therefore a negative outcome of such experiments does not permit definitive conclusions as to the processes that occur in normal development. However, such considerations lie beyond the scope of our present topic. What is important here is to point out that on the basis of these investigations of Weiss, which thus far have remained unchallenged, cytotropism has not been experimentally demonstrated for animal tissues. Nevertheless, the notion that side by side with the mechanical factors, there occur intercellular correlations in the nature of physiological stimuli and that they may act as important formative principles, is not put on trial by this view.

To return to our present experiments, let us summarize their principal results, especially in their relation to the foregoing considerations.

In our isolation and combination experiments, carried out on embryonic amphibian material, the question of a chemotropic distant effect between cells has not even been touched upon. All the phenomena here described occurred while the various kinds of cells and tissues were in direct mutual contact. What was actually observed was an orderly union as well as non-unions and self-isolations. The events proceeded in an age- and tissue-specific manner, removed from the embryo as a whole, in a purely protective, indifferent medium and without the participation of a physically structured substrate. We, therefore, called them autonomous events and ascribed them to mutual cell-specific stimulation which we interpreted as an expression of affinities. Their chemical or physical nature was left undiscussed.

These stimulatory affinities share with the hypothetical cytotropism the capacity to bring about gradations of attraction and repulsion between cells, which lead to directional changes in their form and position, even though no action beyond that of direct cell contact has yet been proved.

As a means of the self-ordering of embryonic regions these phenomena are of great significance. They lead to the anatomical segregation of physiologically different organ primordia and to their recombination with other parts of the embryo. They provide a unified explanation for local migration and constriction movements in whole cell complexes, starting with those in gastrulation and being continued during organogenesis. The processes of induction and subsequent formative influences would not be possible without a positive affinity between the reacting material and the inductor. In view of the transparency of the situation and the ready availability of the material there should be no difficulty to explore the problem of affinity by means of further experiments and thus obtain new, well-documented support for a theory of development.

REFERENCES

Born, G., Über Verwachsungsversuche mit Amphibienlarven. Arch. Entw. mechanik **4** (1897).

Bytinsky-Salz, H., Chromatophorenstudien II. Arch. f. exp. Zellforschg. **22**, H. 1 (1938).

Fischer, A., Contributions to the biology of tissue cells. I. The relation of cell crowding to tissue growth in vitro. Journ, exp. Med. **38** (1923).

————, Gewebezüchtung. München, Müller u. Steinicke, 1927.

Galtsoff, Regeneration after dissociation (an experimental study on sponges). Journ. of exp. Zool. **42** (1925).

Götte, Die Entwicklungsgeschichte der Unke. Leipzig, 1875.

Grigorjeff, L. M., Differenzierung des Nervengewebes ausserhalb des Organismus. Arch. f. exper. Zellforschg. **11** (1931).

Harrison, R. G., Experimentelle Untersuchungen über die Entwicklung der Sinnesorgane der Seitenlinie bie den Amphibien. Arch. mikrosk. Anat. **63** (1904).

His, W., Unşere Körperform, Briefe an einen befreundeten Naturforscher. Leipzig, F. C. W. Vogel. 1874.

Holtfreter, J., Über die Aufzucht isolierter Teile des Amphibienkeimes I. Roux' Arch. **117** (1929).

————, Die totale Exogastrulation, eine Selbstablösung des Ektoderms vom Entomesoderm. Roux' Arch. **129** (1933).

————, Formative Reize in der Embryonalentwicklung der Amphibien, dargestellt an Explantationsversuchen. Arch. f. exp. Zellforsch. **15** (1934a).

————, Nachweis der Induktionsfähigkeit abgetöteter Keimteile. Roux' Arch. **128** (1934b).

————, Morphologische Beeinflussung von Urodelenektoderm bei xenoplastischer Transplantation. Roux' Arch. **113** (1935).

————, Differenzierungspotenzen isolierter Teile der Urodelengastrula. Roux' Arch. **138** (1938a).

Holtfreter, J., Differenzierungspotenzen isolierter Teile der Anurengastrula. Roux' Arch. **138** (1938b).

Juhásc, A., Wachstumspolarität bei Gewebezüchtungen in vitro und ihre Beziehungen zur Tuberkuloseimmunität. Arch. f. exp. Zellforsch. **6** (1928).

Kuhl, W. Untersuchungen über das Verhalten künstlich getrennter Furchungszellen und Zellaggregate einiger Amphibienarten mit Hilfe des Zeitrafferfilms. Roux' Arch. **136** (1937).

Lehmann, F. E., Entwicklungsstörungen in der Medullaranlage von Triton, erzeugt durch Unterlagerungsdefekte. Roux' Arch. **108** (1926).

————, Die Bedeutung der Unterlagerung für die Entwicklung der Medullarplatte von Triton. Roux' Arch. **113** (1928).

Maximow, A., Tissue-culture of young mammalian embryos. Publication 361 of the Carnegie Inst. of Washington (1925).

Morgan, T. H., Regeneration in Bipalium. Arch. Entw.mechanik **9** (1900).

Péterfi, T., u. St. C. Williams, Elektrische Reizversuche an gezüchteten Gewebezellen. II. Versuche an verschiedenen Gewebekulturen. Arch. f. exp. Zellforsch. **16** (1931).

Pfeffer, Physiologische Untersuchungen. Leipzig 1873.

Roux, W., Über den „Cytotropismus" der Furchungszellen des Grasfrosches (Rana fusca). Arch Ent.mechanik **1** (1894).

————, Über die Selbstordnung (Cytotaxis) sich „berührender" Furchungszellen des Froscheies durch Zellzusammenfügung und Zellengleiten. Arch. Entw.mechanik **3** (1896).

Törö, E., Das organoide Wachstum der Darmkulturen. Arch. exp. Zellforsch. **9** (1930).

Vogt, W., Über Zellbewegungen und Zelldegeneration bei der Gastrulation von Triton cristatus. I. Anat. H. **48** (1913).

————, Gestaltungsanalyse am Amphibienkeim mit örtlicher Vitalfärbung. II. Teil: Gastrulation und Mesodermbildung bei Urodelen und Anuren. Roux' Arch. **120** (1929).

Voigtländer, G., Neue Untersuchungen über den „Cytotropismus" der Furchungszellen. Roux' Arch. **127** (1932).

Weiss, P., Erzwingung elementarer Strukturverschiedenheiten an in vitro wachsenden Geweben. Roux' Arch. **116** (1929).

————, In vitro experiments on the factors determining the course of the outgrowing nerve fiber. Journ. of exp. Zool. **68** (1934).

PART TWELVE

1954

In *Vitro* Experiments on the Effects of Mouse
Sarcomas 180 and 37 on the Spinal and
Sympathetic Ganglia of the Chick Embryo

by **RITA LEVI-MONTALCINI, HERTHA MEYER,**
and VIKTOR HAMBURGER

Levi-Montalcini, Rita, Hertha Meyer, and Viktor Hamburger.
1954. *In Vitro* Experiments on the Effects of Mouse Sarcomas
180 and 37 on the Spinal and Sympathetic Ganglia of the Chick
Embryo. Cancer Research 14:49–57. Reprinted by permission of
Rita Levi-Montalcini, Viktor Hamburger, and Cancer Research,
Inc.

The concept, originated by the botanist Julius Sachs, that particular morphogenetic substances might be responsible for the form of biological
structure is well over a hundred years old. Few such substances have been
demonstrated to exist; some of the plant hormones might be interpreted
to be compounds of this class. Possibly also classified into this category
may be the nerve growth factor, which acts selectively to increase the size
and number of particular neurones in the nervous system of some vertebrates. Its detection, its chemical identification, and the recognition of
the wide implications of its discovery have been among the most important
achievements of twentieth century biology, and the work on it began as
the outcome of solely embryological studies.

During the first third, approximately, of the twentieth century, investigations of the developing amphibian nervous system, carried out by dele-
tion and transplantation experiments, attempted to ascertain the degree to
which factors intrinsic or extrinsic to the nervous system control the growth
and differentiation of its parts. It was first demonstrated for the developing amphibian that the size of the peripheral field innervated affects the
number of neurones supplying it. This was confirmed by Viktor Hamburger for the chick in the 1930's. In 1948 Bueker, a student of Hamburger's,
at the latter's suggestion, grafted a mouse sarcoma to the limb region of
the chick to test the effects on the nervous system of rapidly growing tissue. As a result of the experiment, the size and number of the sensory
ganglion cells were greatly increased. The work was continued by Hamburger and Rita Levi-Montalcini, who soon observed that not only sensory
but also sympathetic ganglia were enlarged. Further, it was observed that
some sympathetic ganglia at a distance from the tumor and not innervating
it, were also enlarged. Levi-Montalcini's suggestion that the agent might
be a diffusible substance carried in the blood stream was confirmed when
sarcomas transplanted onto extraembryonic chick membranes also exerted
growth-enhancing effects on the sympathetic and sensory ganglia.

The article reprinted here was the first to describe the results of experiments in vitro showing the effects exerted by explanted mouse sarcoma on
the growth of explanted spinal and sympathetic ganglia of the chick
embryo. Ganglia cultured in the proximity of fragments of sarcoma produced dense halos of fibers, and it was concluded that the same diffusible
agent was operative in vivo and in vitro. The possibility of assaying the
effects of the agent in vitro greatly extended the range of new studies of
the growth-promoting agent.

Levi-Montalcini and her colleagues later showed that the factor acts
only on sensory and sympathetic ganglion cells, and only within specified
time limits different for each; it acts on the cells themselves, not on their

fibers. It is found in rich supply in some but not all tumors, in snake venom, and in large amounts in the tubular portion of male mouse submaxillary salivary glands. It is a protein dimer, and the amino acid sequence of the factor produced by the mouse salivary gland has been determined. The molecule bears some resemblance to the insulin molecule, and it has been suggested that the nerve growth factor represents a new type of compound intermediate between inducers and hormones. Many questions about the source and mode of action of the factor remain unanswered, but its discovery may demonstrate the existence of a hitherto undetected integrating system more primitive and more fundamental than the endocrine system of the adult.

Previous experiments have given evidence that mouse Sarcomas 37 and 180 produce an agent which promotes the growth of spinal ganglia (1) and of sympathetic ganglia (12) in the chick embryo. This effect was first observed in experiments in which small pieces of tumor were implanted in the body wall of 3-day embryos, where they grew vigorously. Later, the same effects were obtained when the tumors were transplanted extra-embryonically to the allantoic membrane of 4-day embryos (10, 11, 13). The latter result was considered as conclusive evidence that we are dealing with a diffusible agent.

The response of the nervous system was found to be selective and complex. Only the sensory and para- and prevertebral sympathetic ganglia showed a reaction, whereas all centers in the spinal cord were refractory. The hyperplasia of the ganglia was due partly to an increase in cell number and partly to a cellular hypertrophy. The differentiation of nerve fibers was accelerated, and their number was increased to an extraordinary degree. The supernumerary fibers emerging from the hyperplastic ganglia flooded the adjacent viscera: meso- and metanephros, gonads, spleen, adrenal, thyroid, parathyroid glands, and also the tumor, in cases of intra-embryonic transplantations. Normally, these organs receive only a very scant nerve supply or none at all, in corresponding stages of development.

These results confronted us with two major problems: (a) the chemical nature of the agent and (b) its mode of action. Concerning the latter problem, the previous experiments gave no definite clue whether the agent acts directly on the ganglia or indirectly, by producing complex metabolic changes in the embryo. In this connection, it should be mentioned that the embryos carrying a tumor showed signs of toxic effects (edema, perfusion of the liver by bile, stunted growth) which were eventually fatal to the embryo.

It seemed that the tissue culture method might offer a new approach to the analysis of both problems. This method has several advantages: it permits the direct exposure of the ganglia to the tumor, thus excluding possible influences of the organism; furthermore, extracts of tumors can be easily tested, and other tumors and normal tissues can be screened for possible nerve growth-stimulating effects. Since the behavior of the spinal ganglia of the chick embryo *in vitro,* under normal and experimental conditions, has been studied in great detail (6, 8, 9, 17, 18), one can build on a solid foundation.

MATERIALS AND METHODS

The experiments consisted of the combination of spinal ganglia with fragments of mouse Sarcomas 180, 37, 1, adenocarcinoma dbrB and neuroblastoma C1300. Fragments of embryonic chicken or mouse heart were used as controls. In a limited number of experiments, paravertebral sympathetic ganglia or pieces of spinal cord were exposed to these tumors and to control tissues. Usually, several fragments of the same tumor or of control tissue were placed at a distance of 1–2 mm. from the ganglion; this has been found to be the optimal distance. In no instance were the explants placed in direct contact with each other, but usually the spreading of the tumor resulted in a contact at about 48 hours. In one series, the distance between the ganglion and the tumors was varied, in order to study the range of diffusibility of the tumor agent.

Table 1 gives a summary of all data. It should be pointed out that the number of experiments performed was considerably larger, since, in most instances, several groups of explants were placed in the same hanging drop, at a considerable distance from each other.

The *spinal ganglia* were in most instances lumbo-sacral ganglia of 6- to 7-day embryos. In a few instances, ganglia from 9- and 10-day embryos were used. They were dissected in physiological salt solution under a binocular microscope and explanted *in toto,* that is, surrounded by their capsule.

The isolation of *sympathetic ganglia* is much more laborious than that of spinal ganglia; hence only a limited number of experiments of this type was done. The sympathetic ganglia were obtained from older embryos ranging from 8 to 13 days, since the isolation of younger ganglia is not practicable. Long segments of the paravertebral chain were dissected out and cut into fragments, including one ganglion.

Spinal cord fragments were obtained from 6-day embryos. The lumbo-sacral level was isolated and cut into small square fragments corresponding approximately to one segment. Each fragment was split apart in the median plane, and the lateral halves were explanted separately.

All *tumors* were obtained from the Jackson Memorial Laboratory at Bar Harbor. In the earlier series, the tumor explants were taken directly from the mouse, but they had a strong inhibitory effect on the ganglia. These unsatisfactory results suggested that an adaptation to the chick embryo might be necessary. For this purpose, the tumors were implanted in the body wall near the

TABLE 1

SURVEY OF EXPERIMENTS

(Numbers of Cases)

Combination of	Spinal ganglion	Sympathetic ganglion	Spinal cord	Chick embryo heart	Chick organs
Sarcoma 180	222	29	6	13	21
Sarcoma 37	45	13	20	6	0
Sarcoma 1	32	2	6	0	0
Adenocarcinoma dbrB	30	0	0	0	0
Neuroblastoma C1300	38	0	0	5	0
Heart tissue (from mouse fetus)	99	9	0	0	10
Heart tissue (from chick embryo)	78	26	14	0	0
Miscellaneous chick organs	16	0	0	0	0
Isolated	108	24	3	7	0
Total	668	103	49	31	31

hind-limb bud of 2- to 3-day embryos (for technic see [12]) and allowed to grow there for 4-8 days. They were then used for explantation or transferred to other chick embryos for one or more additional passages. Tumors with at least one passage in the chick embryo proved to be optimally effective. Only the "healthy" peripheral parts of the tumors were selected; the central necrotic and hemorrhagic parts were discarded. The pieces were approximately 1 c. mm. in size.

As *controls,* the following *tissues* were used: heart tissue of 7-day (or in a few instances 8- to 10-day) chick embryos, heart tissue of mouse embryos or fetuses, or of newly-born mice.

The *standard culture medium* was chicken plasma and chick embryo extract. The plasma was obtained by the standard technic of bleeding a rooster through the carotid artery. In all experiments, the extract was diluted 1:3 with Earle's solution. The plasma was ordinarily used undiluted; in a few experiments the plasma was diluted 1:1 with Earle's salt solution.

The *hanging-drop technic* was used throughout; Maximow depression slides with two cover glasses were employed in most instances. Most experiments were discontinued after 48 hours. A limited number of cultures which were carried beyond this period were washed every second day with Earle's solution, and nutrient (serum and extract) was added. In all instances, a set of tumor experiments and a set of control experiments were done on the same day, using the same medium, the same technic, and ganglia from the same embryo.

Fixation.—Most cultures were fixed between 24 and 48 hours and impregnated with silver, following Levi's modification of the Cajal-De Castro technic (8). A few slides were fixed in Bouin's fluid and stained with Ehrlich's hematoxylin.

RESULTS

GROWTH OF ISOLATED SPINAL GANGLIA IN VITRO

Ganglia of 6- to 7-day embryos were chosen for our experiments. In these stages, the ganglia are still in a phase of active proliferation, and some of the neuroblasts have not yet sent out nerve fibers (4). In our previous experiments of *in vivo* transplantations of sarcomas, the spinal ganglia had shown the first responses to the tumor agent on the 7th or 8th day of incubation; hence ganglia of 6–7 days were expected to be in the best condition for reaction *in vitro*.

When ganglia of the lumbo-sacral level are cultivated *in vitro* in the absence of other tissues, they show almost no fiber outgrowth during the first 16 hours. The migration of spindle-shaped cells begins at about 10–15 hours. These spindle cells, whose active migration has been observed by all previous workers, represent a heterogeneous population of Schwann cells, satellite cells, and mesenchyme cells of the capsule. At 24 hours, the migration of the spindle cells is well advanced, and a smaller number of nerve fibers has grown out (Fig. 3).[1] The fibers are distributed irregularly and take a wavy course. Between 24 and 48 hours, the number of nerve fibers increases, but they are still rather sparse (Fig. 7). They have a tendency to fasciculate and to associate with rows and columns of spindle cells. Those fibers which do not join with others follow tortuous routes; occasionally they grow tangentially or in circular paths around the ganglion (8). In accordance with the observations of Levi and Meyer (8), we find that nerve cells do not migrate out of the ganglion, but that the spreading of its surface and the decrease of its density come about by a migration of the spindle cells. Nerve fiber and spindle cell outgrowth continues during the 3d day. After this time, a considerable number of centrally located neurons begin to degenerate. They are disposed of by macrophages which appear in increasing numbers in older cultures. Our observations on normal ganglia are in agreement with the basic studies of Levi and Meyer (8).

EXPERIMENTS WITH SARCOMA 180

Excellent growth of this tumor was obtained after it had undergone one or more passages in the chick embryo. The migration of cells gets well under way during the first 16 hours. At 24 hours, a uniform margin of typical tumor cells surrounds the explant; the cells are large in size and spindle-shaped: they usually adhere to one another, forming long strands. The growth zone appears to be a homogeneous population of

---

[1] Since there is no difference between single ganglia and ganglia combined with embryonic chick heart tissue, with respect to nerve fiber growth and spindle cell migration (see p. 236), only the latter experiments were chosen for illustrations.

sarcoma cells, not contaminated with small-sized fibroblasts of chick origin (Fig. 14, S).

Between 24 and 48 hours, the area of migrating cells is further expanded; the neoplastic cells are healthy. However, the life-span of sarcoma cultures is short, as has been pointed out already by Carrel and Burrows (3). After 48 hours, one finds increasing numbers of degenerating cells and macrophages in the explant and in the growth zone. This occurs even if the cultures are washed and nutritive material is added every other day. The growth conditions could probably be improved by transfer, but in our present investigation, we were particularly interested in the maintenance of the tumor without resection and transfer.

Combination of spinal ganglia with Sarcoma 180.—One or more small pieces of tumor were implanted at distances of 1–2 mm. from a lumbo-sacral spinal ganglion of a 6- to 7-day embryo. The results obtained in a large number of experiments (Table 1) were entirely consistent and uniform. The nerve fiber outgrowth was definitely precocious in the presence of the sarcoma. At 16 hours, few, if any, fibers are present in control ganglia (see above), whereas in the combination experiments with sarcoma, a rather large number of nerve fibers has grown out at that stage; they are limited to the side facing the tumor. Shortly thereafter, fibers begin to sprout from the entire surface of the ganglion. In contrast to control cultures, no spindle cells have migrated out during this period. At 24 hours, the ganglion represents a remarkable picture (Fig. 1). It is surrounded by a "halo" of nerve fibers. They show maximal density and a very straight course on the side facing the tumor. The tips of the fibers branch profusely and form a brushlike border. This phenomenon has never been observed in normal cultures. On the sides not facing the tumor, the fibers become gradually less dense and longer; the direction of their outgrowth is less straight, and some take more winding routes. However, they never wander in all directions nor do they form bundles, as is characteristic of the control cultures. In all well-growing cultures in which the tumor is rather close to the ganglion, the halo of nerve fibers has a very characteristic contour. Toward the tumor, the border of the fiber tips is sharply demarcated and often ellipsoid in outline. One gets the impression that the fibers face an invisible barrier which none of them trespasses. A close inspection shows that the borderline of the fibers is particularly sharp at the interface between cover glass and plasma clot, whereas the fiber length in deep layers of the same culture is somewhat more uneven. The line of demarcation of the fiber tips becomes less sharp with increasing distance from the tumor, the fibers become gradually longer and more wavy and, at the same time, more variable in length. The migration of the spindle cells is greatly reduced, as compared to the control cultures. They are completely blocked on the side facing the tumor, but a few do grow out on the opposite side. This feature becomes more distinct during the following period.

No significant changes were observed between 24 and 48 hours, but all features described above are accentuated. In many instances, the fibers on the side toward the tumor form a very dense, felt-like matting (Fig. 8). When the tumor is close to the ganglion, neoplastic cells reach the nerve fibers and mingle with them. Very few or no spindle cells are found on the side toward the tumor, but they migrate out in increasing numbers on the other side, where they may occasionally form bundles or ribbons combined with nerve fibers. In cultures older than 48 hours, the results were less consistent than in earlier stages, and a systematic study of this material has not yet been made. In general, we have noticed the disappearance of the sharp contour of the fibers on the side facing the tumor; instead, they show a tendency to form weblike networks superimposed on the tumor cells (Fig. 6). The migration of spindle cells is no longer blocked. A strange phenomenon was observed in older cultures which needs further study: The cellular degeneration which is characteristic of control ganglia of 3–6 days does not seem to occur in the presence of the sarcoma, even though the sarcoma itself shows regressive changes.

Combination of Sarcoma 180 with sympathetic ganglia.—These experiments were done in only a limited number of cases and not continued beyond the 2d day. The growth of sympathetic ganglia of 8- to 13-day chick embryos in tissue culture has been briefly described by Levi and Delorenzi (7). Control ganglia show at 24 hours a rather uniform outgrowth of small spindle cells in all directions. The population of these cells is more homogeneous than in the case of the spinal ganglia, probably because sympathetic ganglia can be isolated free of connective tissue cells. A few very fine nerve fibers are mingled with the spindle cells; they do not form bundles, and they grow in a wavy course. On the following days, the number of nerve fibers increases moderately.

The combination with Sarcoma 180 results in a very precocious and exuberant outgrowth of nerve fibers, closely resembling the pattern found in spinal ganglia (Fig. 14). Again, the fibers facing the tumor are shorter than those on the opposite side, and their contour is sharply delimited. The orientation of the fibers is always radial and very straight, and their density is greater toward the tumor. The fibers are much finer than the sensory fibers, and the halo is formed of a very dense, regular matting.

Combination of Sarcoma 180 with chick embryo heart.—The striking inhibitory effect of Sarcoma 180 on the spindle cells of spinal ganglia raised the question of whether fibroblasts of an entirely different origin might also be affected. Fragments of heart from chick embryos of 7–9 days were used. In most instances, no effect of the sarcoma on the growth pattern of heart fibroblasts was observed, even when the sarcoma was actively growing and close to the heart fragment. In a few instances, the migration of heart fibroblasts seemed to be somewhat impaired. The number of experiments is not sufficiently large to establish this point definitely; however, the effect is not at all comparable to that observed in ganglia.

EXPERIMENTS WITH SARCOMA 37

Growth of Sarcoma 37 in vitro.—Consistently good results were obtained with this tumor when it had been grown in the chick embryo for one or more passages. During the first 24 hours, its growth is even more vigorous than that of Sarcoma 180. In distinction to the latter, its cells, which are spherical rather than spindle-shaped, migrate individually and have no tendency to form rows or bands. As a result, the area of expansion of the culture, which increases considerably between 24 and 48 hours, is not as compact as in cultures of Sarcoma 180. After 48 hours, the cultures show signs of deterioration, and an increasingly large number of macrophages is found among the neoplastic cells.

Combination of Sarcoma 37 with spinal ganglia.—The effects on the fiber outgrowth and the spindle cells of spinal ganglia are identical with those observed with Sarcoma 180 (Figs. 4, 10, 12). The density of nerve fiber outgrowth and the demarcation line of the fibers facing the tumor are, if anything, more pronounced than in the case of Sarcoma 180, and the same is true for the inhibitory effect on the spindle cells.

In several series, the distance between the tumor fragments and the ganglion was varied. Maximal effects were obtained when the distance ranged from 1 to 2 mm. At a distance of 3 mm., the effect was somewhat delayed; the fibers were less dense, and their contour toward the tumor was not so sharp as at close distances. However, the general pattern of nerve growth and spindle-cell inhibition was similar to that obtained at shorter distances (Figs. 13, 15). At a distance of 5 mm., a faint effect is still noticeable. On the side toward the tumor, the fibers are distinctly more numerous and longer than on the other sides; however, they are wavy and do not take a straight course.

Combination of Sarcoma 37 with sympathetic ganglia.—This experiment gave exactly the same results as combinations with Sarcoma 180 and therefore requires no separate description.

Explants of spinal cord, alone and combined with Sarcoma 37.—The explants were taken from 6-day embryos. In contrast to cultures of spinal ganglia, no spindle-shaped cells migrate out of the spinal cord (see also [8]). After 24 hours, one finds a limited outgrowth of epithelial sheets which are probably derived from ependymal cells. They are always restricted to some parts of the explant. The nerve fiber outgrowth differs also from that found in sensory ganglia. The fibers are not distributed regularly over the entire surface of the explant, but they are limited to one or a few sites from which they emerge in long strands. Fibers which bridge a localized area of liquefaction show a very straight course, due to passive stretching.

The combination of spinal cord with Sarcoma 37 did not result in an increase of nerve fibers, nor in a change in the general growth pattern. Occasionally,, strands of fibers were directed toward the tumor, but the same behavior of fibers was observed in control combinations of spinal cord with embryonic chick heart, and additional fiber groups were always found emerging from other parts of the explant. Altogether, we consider the spinal cord as completely refractory to the tumor. A small number of experiments with Sarcomas 180 and 1 gave the same results.

EXPERIMENTS WITH SARCOMA 1

This tumor grows *in vitro* even more actively than do Sarcomas 180 and 37. However, there are some differences in the morphology of the cells and in their distribution pattern. The cells are spindle-shaped and much smaller than those of the other two sarcomas. They migrate individually in a radial direction and distribute themselves very evenly, covering a large area in a short period (Fig. 17). During the 2d day, one finds a considerable number of round cells in the growth zone; to judge from their size and cytological characters, they are transformed neoplastic cells. After 48 hours, the explant is almost invariably surrounded by a liquefied area.

Combination with spinal ganglia.—In all cases, the fiber outgrowth is enhanced, as compared to control cultures, and the density of the fibers is increased on the side facing the tumor. However, the results are not consistent. In the majority of cases, the effects were considerably milder than with other sarcomas. The fibers do not show the growth pattern characteristic of the combinations with Sarcomas 37 and 180. They are much less dense, and they do not grow out in a regular straight radial direction nor do they show a sharp line of demarcation in front of the tumor. During the 2d day, the fibers in the area facing the tumor collect in bundles which penetrate into the growth zone of the tumor. The migration of spindle-shaped cells is apparently not affected. In a smaller number of cases, the effects are stronger and more similar to the effects of the other two sarcomas. A typical halo of nerve fibers is present, and, at the same time, the migration of spindle cells is inhibited on the side facing the tumor. Nevertheless, the fiber density never reaches the same degree as in the other tumors. It is perhaps significant that, in the latter group, the plasma had not been diluted and the medium was therefore more dense; no liquefaction occurred in these cases.

EXPERIMENTS WITH ADENOCARCINOMA DBRB

Typical epithelial growth of this tumor was obtained by placing the tumor fragment on the surface of the medium which had been allowed to begin clotting. Since the tumors had gone through one or several passages in the chick embryo before being used for explantation, they contained chick fibroblasts in their stroma, and these cells migrated out along with the epithelial sheets. As has been observed by others, the epithelial growth of adenocarcinomas *in vitro* is delayed in comparison with the growth of sarcomas.

Combination with spinal ganglia.—In all experiments, several fragments of the tumor were placed near one side of the ganglion. The carcinoma did not stimulate the outgrowth of nerve fibers beyond the normal range of controls, and spindle cells migrated out actively in all directions (Fig. 11). In some instances, they were even more numerous than in control cultures. A striking stimulation of the outgrowth of mouse fibroblasts by carcinomas, *in vitro,* has been described by Ludford and Barlow (15).

EXPERIMENTS WITH NEUROBLASTOMA C1300

This tumor is not compact, as are the others, and is rather difficult to grow in tissue culture. However, typical epithelial sheets surrounding the explants were obtained in some cases (Fig. 5, *N*). In addition, a large number of spindle-shaped cells, probably of chick origin, and macrophages were observed in the growth zone.

Combination with spinal ganglia.—In all cases, a number of fragments of different sizes were placed around the ganglion. The results were different from those obtained with other tumors. As a rule, both the fiber outgrowth and the migration of spindle cells were impaired. In a few cases, nerve fibers did grow out, but they were rarely as numerous as in the controls (Fig. 5).

CONTROL EXPERIMENTS WITH EMBRYONIC CHICKEN HEART

The outcome of a large number of combination experiments of spinal ganglia with heart fragments of 7- to 9-day embryos was consistently negative. The presence of the chick tissue did not change the rate, density, and growth pattern of the nerves. The migration of spindle cells from the ganglia was normal in all instances (Figs. 3, 7).

CONTROL EXPERIMENTS WITH HEART TISSUE OF
EMBRYONIC, FETAL, OR NEW-BORN MICE

This tissue grows fairly well *in vitro* (in a medium of chicken plasma and extract), but its rate of growth is much lower than that of mouse sarcoma cells or of chicken heart fibroblasts.

Combination with spinal ganglia.—Toward the end of the first day, the number of nerve fibers on the side facing the mouse tissue is consistently higher than in isolated control ganglia and in ganglia facing embryonic chicken heart. However, the features which are characteristic of combination cultures with sarcomas are entirely missing (compare Fig. 1 to Fig. 2), and the general appearance resembles that of control ganglia. During the 2d day, the preferential growth of nerve fibers toward the mouse tissue is accentuated, and the over-all density of fibers is greater than in controls, but the difference in the growth pattern, between combinations with sarcoma and combinations with mouse heart, is as distinct as it was before (compare Fig. 9 to Figs. 8, 10).

DISCUSSION

Parallelism of tumor effects in vivo *and* in vitro.—The tissue culture experiments had been undertaken with the expectation that it might be possible to duplicate *in vitro* some of the remarkable effects on ganglia which had been observed *in vivo*. The results obtained in the two sets of experiments show striking similarities, but also differences in some essential points. In both instances, the nerve fiber outgrowth is far beyond the normal range, and the fibers begin to grow out at earlier stages than they do normally. In both experiments, the agent acts at a distance, and the tumor does not require contact with the ganglion or with nerve fibers to exert its influence. Furthermore, the specificity of the target, which was one of the essential features of the sarcoma effect *in vivo,* is also characteristic of the *in vitro* experiments; only spinal and sympathetic ganglia show a response, whereas the cells of the spinal cord are refractory. The parallelism between the two phenomena extends to the quantitative aspects of the response. The two sarcomas, 180 and 37, show very strong effects both *in vivo* and *in vitro*. A third sarcoma, 1, which was tested by Bueker and Hilderman (2) *in vivo,* was found to have only a mild effect on adjacent ganglia and none on remote ganglia. *In vitro,* it was likewise much less effective than the other two sarcomas.

The question arises whether we are dealing with a general tumor effect or with a specific sarcoma effect. The results of both *in vivo* and *in vitro* experiments were clearly in favor of the second alternative. Two epithelial mouse tumors were found to be entirely negative. Neuroblastoma C1300 grew intra-embryonically to a considerable size, but it was not invaded by nerve fibers and did not call forth a hyperplasia of ganglia (2). *In vitro,* this tumor grew in an epithelial fashion, though its growth was not very extensive. It did not stimulate nerve growth, but, on the contrary, had an inhibitory effect on both nerve fibers and spindle cells. Mammary adenocarcinoma dbrB, which was first grown successfully in the yolk sac (16), attained in coelomic transplantations a very conspicuous size, exceeding even Sarcomas 180 and 37 (unpublished observations of Levi-Montalcini). Nevertheless, it had no effect on ganglia, and it was not invaded by nerve fibers. This tumor grew well *in vitro;* it formed epithelial sheets mixed with stroma cells, but it was again entirely ineffective as far as nerve fiber stimulation is concerned.

At present, it seems that the agent which promotes nerve fiber growth is restricted to some sarcomas. The parallelism between the tumor effects *in vivo* and *in vitro* is very striking and suggests strongly that we are dealing in both instances with the same agent.[2]

On the other hand, we wish to emphasize some important differences in the mode of response of the ganglia *in vivo* and *in vitro*. In tissue culture, we have found an outburst of fiber growth which begins as early as 12 hours after explantation, reaches a peak between 24 and 48 hours, and regresses during the following days. In intra- and extra-embryonic transplants, the first responses were observed about $3\frac{1}{2}$–4 days after implantation. Following these initial responses, the effects increased steadily until the death of the embryo. It seems that these differences can be accounted for by differences in the experimental set-up. The embryonic transplantations are done when the embryos are 2–4 days old, at which time the ganglia are in early stages of differentiation. The small tumor fragment undergoes an initial regression (5) and does not reach an appreciable size until the embryo is 6–7 days old. After reaching this stage, the tumor enlarges progressively and increases its activity proportionally. On the other hand, the explanted tumor fragment does not undergo regression. On the contrary, cell migration begins a few hours after transplantation, and mitotic figures are present at that time. These features attest to the strong vitality of the tumor explant from the first hours on. The tumor fragment is placed closely adjacent to a ganglion which is apparently in an optimal stage for reaction; therefore, all conditions are given for an immediate response. The rapid decline of fiber growth after 3 days is paralleled by a concomitant regression of the tumor because of the depletion of the medium which was not renewed.

Two other sarcoma effects on ganglia had been observed in embryonic transplantation: an increase in mitotic activity and a cellular hypertrophy of neuroblasts. These two aspects were not studied in tissue culture.

Among the many problems raised—but not resolved—by our previous transplantation experiments was that concerning the *immediate target* of the tumor agent. Two alternative hypotheses were advanced (11, 13): Either the agent acts directly on the potential neuroblasts or indirectly by breaking down the normal resistance of viscera against hyperneurotization, thus inviting an abnormal inflow of pathfinders into the viscera. According to this second hypothesis, the hyperplasia of the ganglia would be the end result of a complex chain of reactions beginning with a change at the periphery. The nerve fibers would mediate the effect from the periphery to the centers.

---

[2] In our previous extra-embryonic transplantation experiments (13) only the responses of the sympathetic ganglia were described in detail. However, responses of the spinal ganglia were clearly manifest both in these experiments (unpublished observations) and in our previous intra-embryonic transplantation experiments (12).

If one admits a basic identity of the tumor effects *in vivo* and *in vitro,* the present experiments can be taken as a strong argument in favor of the first hypothesis cited above. In our experiments *in vitro,* we have observed a precocious outburst of fiber formation almost simultaneously in all parts of the ganglion. The fibers grow straight radially, they do not converge toward the tumor, and, what is most important, they do not establish contact with the tumor until after the peak of the reaction has passed.

The growth pattern of nerve fibers in relation to the culture medium and to other conditions.—All arguments presented so far support the assumption that the main features observed *in vitro,* namely, the conspicuous increase in nerve fiber density and the precociousness of fiber outgrowth, are due to a diffusible agent released by sarcomas. However, in tissue culture experiments, the physical condition of the culture medium cannot be ignored, and the question arises whether some of the strikingly regular features of the growth pattern may be due to this factor. This problem is particularly pertinent in experiments with nerve fibers. Weiss (17) has shown that in many instances where the directional outgrowth of nerve fibres, *in vitro* and *in vivo,* had been attributed to a chemical action at a distance ("chemotropism," "neurotropism"), the "guidance" of nerve fibers was actually achieved by the structural organization of the microscopic or micellar constituents of the ground substance; the fibers do not follow diffusion gradients, but specific pathways or track systems established in the substrate on which they grow ("contact guidance"). The density of fiber outgrowth can also be determined in this way, by the channeling of nutrient supply along preferential lines laid down in the matrix (17, p. 437).

Can any of the sarcoma effects on ganglia be attributed to a structural organization called forth by the tumor in the culture medium? In this connection, it should be pointed out that in our experiments the fiber outgrowth is not directed toward the tumor, but straight radially in all directions (Figs. 10, 13, 14). However, the greater density of the fibers on the side facing the tumor (Figs. 1, 4, 8) could be interpreted in this way. This feature is somewhat reminiscent of the "bridge" phenomenon described by Weiss (17). If two spinal ganglia are explanted adjacent to each other, a large tract of nerve fibers and spindle cells eventually connects the two, whereas fiber outgrowth in other directions remains sparse. It is assumed that the two ganglia call forth a dehydration and thus create lines of tension in the micellar components of the medium. These lines would be mutually reinforced in the area between the ganglia and become a preferential pathway for cells and fibers. A similar explanation may hold in our case; however, the gradual decrease of fiber density with increasing distance from the tumor speaks more in favor of a diffusion gradient set up by the tumor.

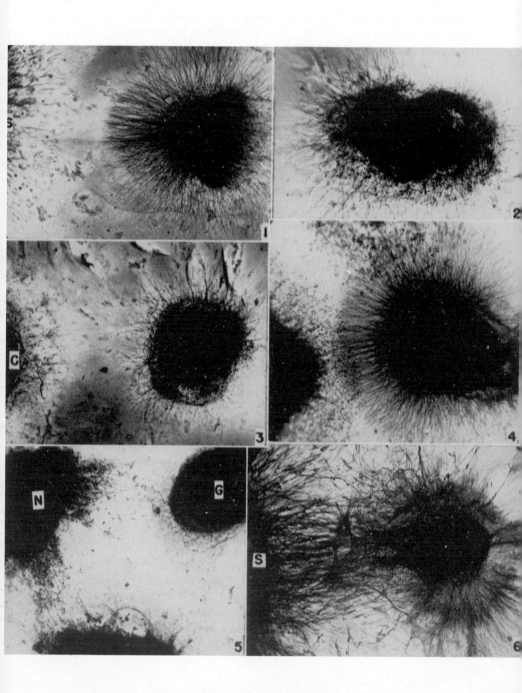

The very straight, radial course of the nerve fibers in the presence of sarcomas is in contrast to the somewhat wavy and bent course which is characteristic of fibers emerging from isolated ganglia (compare Fig. 7 to Figs. 8, 10, 12). It is conceivable that, under the impact of the very actively growing sarcoma, the matrix surrounding the ganglion undergoes a particularly regular micellar orientation in a radial direction which would be reflected in the straight and almost geometric pattern of nerve growth. A liquefaction of the medium which is sometimes responsible for a straight fiber course plays no role in our experiments.

Physical factors could also be responsible for the sharp and very regular line of termination of the fibers in front of the tumor (Figs. 10, 12, 14). This feature suggests the presence of an invisible barrier in the culture medium. No evidence for an interface in the plasma clot along this line was observed, but the possibility remains that such an interface is created by the apposition of sarcoma and ganglion.

The seemingly paradoxical phenomenon that the nerve fibers are shorter on the side facing the tumor than on the other sides (Figs. 10, 13, 14) could be ascribed to the same factor or to a threshold of tolerance for the sarcoma agent.

An analysis of the role of the culture medium in the nerve growth pattern is in progress.

An inhibitory effect of sarcoma on spindle cells.—Sarcomas 180 and 37 had an inhibitory effect on the migration of spindle cells. The inhibition was always complete on the side facing the tumor (Figs. 10, 12, 14). It decreased with the distance from the tumor, and, in cases of mild tumor effects on the nerves, it was barely noticeable on the side opposite to the tumor. A close correlation between the stimulatory effects on nerve fibers and the blocking effect on spindle cells was a consistent feature of all experiments with these sarcomas.

Temperature experiments with spinal ganglia showed a similar relationship (8). When tissue cultures of spinal ganglia of 11-day embryos were reared at low temperatures (32° C.), the spindle-cell migration was inhibited, but the branching of nerve fibers was enhanced.

Magnification of all figures ×55.

Fig. 1 Lumbar ganglion of 7-day embryo, combined with Sarcoma 180 (S). 24 hrs.
Fig. 2 Lumbar ganglion of 7-day embryo, combined with heart of mouse fetus (to the left of ganglion). 24 hrs. Note fiber outgrowth to the left.
Fig. 3 Lumbar ganglion of 7-day embryo, combined with heart of chick embryo (C). 24 hrs.
Fig. 4 Lumbar ganglion of 7-day embryo, combined with 2 fragments of Sarcoma 37. 24 hrs.
Fig. 5 Lumbar ganglion of 7-day embryo (G), combined with 2 fragments of neuroblastoma C1300 (N). 34 hrs.
Fig. 6 Lumbar ganglion of 6-day embryo, combined with Sarcoma 180 (S). 72 hrs.

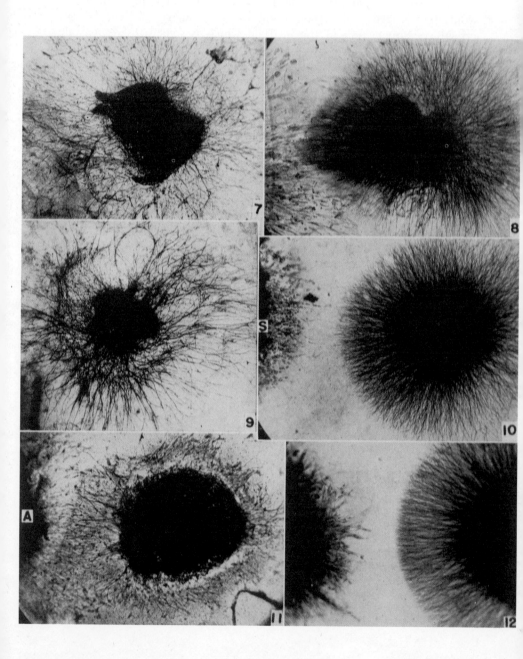

Does a causal relation exist between these two phenomena? And, if so, which is the primary response? Our present material does not permit us to give a conclusive answer to these questions, but a few pertinent observations may be mentioned. It was shown above (p. 232) that the nerve fiber outgrowth in sarcoma experiments is very precocious; in fact, it begins a few hours earlier than the spindle-cell migration in control cultures. This indicates that the response of the nerve cells is independent of the spindle cells. Furthermore, a correlation between spindle-cell inhibition and nerve fiber stimulation does not exist in combination experiments with neuroblastoma. This tumor inhibits both nerve fibers and spindle cells. The relation between these two phenomena deserves further study, both *in vivo* and *in vitro,* since it touches upon the basic problem of the interaction of tumors with host tissues.

Ludford (14) and Ludford and Barlow (15) have also observed slight inhibitory effects of mouse sarcoma on mouse fibroblasts *in vitro.* The same authors found a very strong stimulatory effect of carcinomas on the outgrowth of mouse fibroblasts. Our own carcinoma experiments gave only a slight and not consistent effect of this type.

The effects of normal mouse tissues.—Whereas the combination of chick tissue (from embryonic heart) with spinal ganglia gave entirely negative results, the combination of mouse tissue (from embryonic or fetal heart) with chick ganglia resulted in a consistent increase in the number of nerve fibers on the side facing the mouse tissue (Fig. 2). However, as was pointed out above (p. 237), the growth pattern of the nerves did not show any of the characteristics of the sarcoma effects, but was merely an accentuation of the normal pattern (compare Fig. 9 to Fig. 10). This result suggests that the sarcoma agent may be present in low concentration in normal mouse tissue. However, mouse adenocarcinoma and neuroblastoma were negative, and the question of the distribution of the agent in mouse tissue requires further studies. In this connection, some data of Ludford and Barlow (15) are of interest. These authors reported that kidney tissue of mouse embryos has a moderate stimulating effect on

Magnification of all figures ×55.

Fig. 7 Lumbar ganglion of 6-day embryo, combined with heart of chick embryo (to the left). 48 hrs.

Fig. 8 Lumbar ganglion of 7-day embryo, combined with Sarcoma 180 (to the left). 48 hrs.

Fig. 9 Lumbar ganglion of 7-day embryo, combined with heart of mouse fetus (to the right). 48 hrs.

Fig. 10 Lumbar ganglion of 7-day embryo, combined with Sarcoma 37 (*S*). 48 hrs.

Fig. 11 Thoracic ganglion of 7-day embryo, combined with adenocarcinoma dbrB (*A*). 30 hrs.

Fig. 12 Lumbar ganglion of 7-day embryo, combined with Sarcoma 37. 48 hrs.

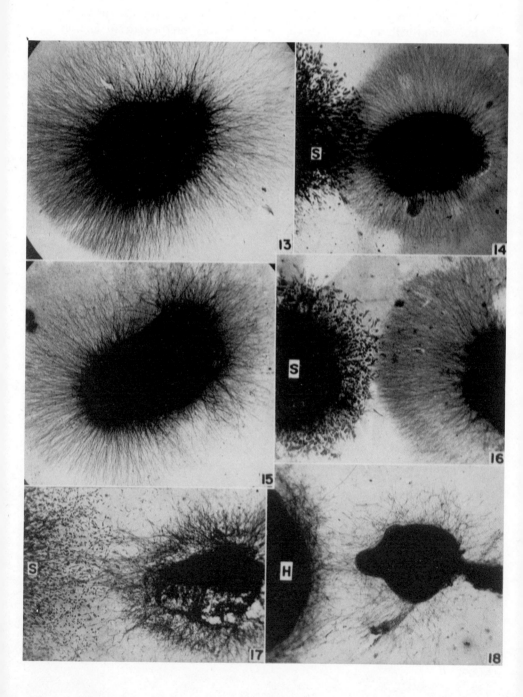

mouse fibroblasts which is comparable to that of some mouse carcinomas, but much milder in degree.

SUMMARY

Small fragments of mouse Sarcomas 180 and 37 were placed at a distance of 1–2 mm. from spinal or sympathetic ganglia of a chick embryo in a hanging-drop tissue culture. Under this condition the ganglion produces precociously, within 24 hours, an excessive number of nerve fibers which grow very straight radially in all directions, forming a dense "halo" around the ganglion. Their density decreases, and their length increases, with increasing distance from the sarcoma. In addition, the migration of spindle cells from the ganglia is inhibited by the sarcomas. Mouse Sarcoma 1 has a similar, but milder, effect. Mouse adenocarcinoma dbrB and mouse neuroblastoma C1300 do not stimulate nerve growth. Control experiments with heart tissue from chick embryos were entirely negative, but heart tissue of fetal mice was found to have a mild stimulating effect. However, in the latter instance, the growth pattern is very different from that found in the presence of sarcomas and very similar to that found in normal, isolated ganglia. Sarcomas have no effect on spinal cord fibers.

It is concluded that the mouse sarcomas tested produce a diffusible agent which strongly promotes the nerve fiber outgrowth of ganglia. The results obtained *in vitro* are compared to previous results obtained by intra-embryonic transplantation of the same sarcomas, and the conclusion is reached that the *in vitro* and the *in vivo* effects on the spinal and sympathetic ganglia are due to the same agent.

ACKNOWLEDGMENTS

The senior author wishes to express her appreciation for a travel grant from the Rockefeller Foundation and for the generous hospitality offered by Dr. C.

Magnification of all figures ×55.

Fig. 13 Lumbar ganglion of 7-day embryo, combined with Sarcoma 37 (to the left). Actual distance between ganglion and sarcoma = 1 mm. (compare with Fig. 15). 48 hrs.
Fig. 14 Paravertebral sympathetic ganglion of 13-day embryo, combined with Sarcoma 180 (S). 24 hrs.
Fig. 15 Lumbar ganglion of 7-day embryo, combined with Sarcoma 37 (located at some distance from the left lower corner). Actual distance between ganglion and sarcoma = $3\frac{1}{2}$ mm. 48 hrs.
Fig. 16 Paravertebral sympathetic ganglion of 13-day embryo, combined with Sarcoma 37 (S). 44 hrs.
Fig. 17 Lumbar ganglion of 7-day embryo, combined with Sarcoma 1 (S). 48 hrs.
Fig. 18 Paravertebral sympathetic ganglion of 13-day embryo, combined with heart of chick embryo (H). 36 hrs.

Chagas, Director of the Institute of Biophysics, University of Rio de Janeiro, Brazil, where the first series of experiments were performed, in cooperation with Hertha Meyer. The experimental work done in St. Louis was supported by grants from the Rockefeller Foundation and the National Institutes of Health.

We wish to express our appreciation of the very able assistance of Mrs. Doris Spruss Fridley and Miss Nancy Starzl. The photographic work was done by Mr. Karl Jacob, Jr., and Mr. A. C. Schewe.

REFERENCES

1. BUEKER, E. D. Implantation of Tumors in the Hind Limb Field of the Embryonic Chick and the Developmental Response of the Lumbo-sacral Nervous System. Anat. Rec., 102:369–90, 1948.
2. BUEKER, E. D., AND HILDERMAN, H. L. Growth-stimulating Effects of Mouse Sarcomas 1, 37, and 180 on Spinal and Sympathetic Ganglia of Chick Embryos as Contrasted with Effects of Other Tumors. Cancer, 6:397–415, 1953.
3. CARREL, A., AND BURROWS, M. T. Cultivation *in Vitro* of Malignant Tumors. J. Exper. Med., 13:571–75, 1911.
4. HAMBURGER, V., AND LEVI-MONTALCINI, R. Proliferation, Differentiation and Degeneration in the Spinal Ganglia of the Chick Embryo under Normal and Experimental Conditions. J. Exper. Zool., 111:457–502, 1949.
5. KAUTZ, J. Differential Invasion of Embryonic Chick Tissues by Mouse Sarcomas 180 and 37. Cancer Research, 12:180–87, 1952.
6. LEVI, G. Explantation, besonders die Struktur und die biologischen Eigenschaften der *in vitro* gezüchteten Zellen und Gewebe. Ergebn. Anat. und Entw., 31:125–707, 1934.
7. LEVI, G., AND DELORENZI, E. Trasformazione degli elementi dei gangli spinali e simpatici coltivati *in vitro*. Arch. It. Anat., 33:443–517, 1935.
8. LEVI, G., AND MEYER, H. Nouvelles recherches sur le tissu nerveux cultivé *in vitro:* Morphologie, croissance et relations réciproques des neurons. Arch. de Biol., 52:133–278, 1941.
9. ———. Reactive, Regressive, and Regenerative Processes of Neurons Cultivated *in Vitro* and Injured with Micromanipulator. J. Exper. Zool., 99:141–81, 1945.
10. LEVI-MONTALCINI, R. Growth-stimulating Effects of Mouse Sarcoma on the Sensory and Sympathetic Nervous System of the Chick Embryo. Anat. Rec., 109:59, 1951.
11. ———. Effects of Mouse Tumor Transplantation on the Nervous System. Ann. N.Y. Acad. Sc., 55:330–43, 1952.
12. LEVI-MONTALCINI, R., AND HAMBURGER, V. Selective Growth-stimulating Effects of Mouse Sarcoma on the Sensory and Sympathetic Nervous System of the Chick Embryo. J. Exper. Zool., 116:321–62, 1951.
13. ———. A Diffusible Agent of Mouse Sarcoma, Producing Hyperplasia of Sympathetic Ganglia and Hyperneurotization of Viscera in the Chick Embryo. J. Exper. Zool., 123:233–88, 1953.
14. LUDFORD, R. J. The Interaction *in Vitro* of Fibroblasts and Sarcoma Cells with Leucocytes and Macrophages. Brit. M. J., 1:201–5, 1940.
15. LUDFORD, R. J., AND BARLOW, H. The Influence of Malignant Cells upon the Growth of Fibroblasts *in Vitro*. Cancer Research, 4:694–703, 1944.

16. TAYLOR, A., AND CARMICHAEL, N. The Effect on the Embryo of Continued Serial Tumor Transplantation in the Yolk Sac. Cancer Research, 9:498–583, 1949.

17. WEISS, P. *In Vitro* Experiments on the Factors Determining the Course of the Outgrowing Nerve Fiber. J. Exper. Zool., 68:393–448, 1934.

18. ———. Experiments of Cell and Axon Orientation *in Vitro:* The Role of Colloidal Exudates in Tissue Organization. *Ibid.,* 100:353-86, 1945.

PART THIRTEEN

1969

Ionic Communication between Early Embryonic Cells

by **SHIZUO ITO and WERNER R. LOEWENSTEIN**

Ito, S. and Werner R. Loewenstein. 1969. Ionic Communication between Early Embryonic Cells. Developmental Biology 19:228–243. Reprinted with the permission of Werner R. Loewenstein and Academic Press, Inc.

Experimental embryology passed through the period of its most rapid ascendency during the half century that ended approximately at the time that Spemann won the Nobel Prize in 1935. Biochemistry was simultaneously undergoing rapid growth, and it was inevitable that embryologists should proceed to explain developmental phenomena in biochemical terms. Joseph Needham's Chemical Embryology, *an extensive monograph that appeared in three large volumes in 1931, provided a strong conceptual framework for the development of what was soon to be called biochemical embryology. Increasing understanding of biochemical mechanisms and the perfection of biochemical techniques permitting the analysis of minute amounts of material has enabled developmental biologists to describe embryonic material in increasingly accurate and quantitative molecular terms. Embryology has thus finally become an exact science. Nonetheless it has not yet been possible to ascertain by solely biochemical studies the constitution of all substances affecting differentiation, and many questions concerning controls of differentiation still remain open.*

The exploitation of biophysical, in contrast to biochemical, methods applicable to the investigation of developmental systems has lagged. Few embryologists in the past have been skillful in performing biophysical analyses of development and differentiation. As early as 1828 Karl Ernst von Baer invoked the possibility that the axiation of the chick blastoderm might be related to galvanic phenomena; Roux performed some inconclusive and not very well conceived experiments testing the effect of electrical current on the position of the first cleavage plane of the frog's egg, and in 1894 Driesch tried to explain polarity in terms of electrical charge. A number of studies have investigated the effects of electrical current on various highly specialized aspects of development, such as nerve fiber outgrowth, but only recently have techniques been developed that are adequate to demonstrate that cells of the young embryo are in ionic communication with each other.

Shizuo Ito, working with N. Hori, showed, in 1966, that ionic current flowing between an intracellular source in a newt morula and the surrounding medium could pass through adjacent cells. Ito and Werner Loewenstein, in the article reprinted here, describe the use of a technique by which an ion current was passed, by the use of a microelectrode, from the inside of one newt morula cell to the ambient medium, or vice versa; by using two additional microelectrodes, they measured the resulting steady state voltage both in the same cell and in an adjacent one. The experiments were performed both in cells in the intact egg, and in cells isolated and recombined in vitro. *These experiments, which demonstrate that the cells communicate by an ionic current passing through permeable junc-*

tional membranes, provide a new direction for developmental studies, leading away from the study of macromolecular structure and function towards the consideration of entities far smaller in dimension. The developmental significance of the results, however, remains to be evaluated.

Among the many examples of tissues now known to present communicating cell junctions (cf. Loewenstein *et al.*, 1965; Loewenstein, 1966), the examples of embryonic tissues (Potter *et al.*, 1966; Ito and Hori, 1966; Sheridan, 1968) are particularly interesting from a developmental point of view. One of the early indications of the presence of communicating junctions in embryonic cells came from the work on newt embryos (Ito and Hori, 1966). In this work, which dealt with embryos at the morula stage, it was found that a large fraction of an ionic current flowing between a point source inside a blastomere cell and the outside of the morula, passed through adjacent blastomeres. This looked like the situation in certain adult epithelial tissues for which it had been shown that the current passed through specialized regions of the cell membrane (*junctional membranes*) with high ionic permeabilities (Loewenstein and Kanno, 1964). The similarity suggested that the cell-to-cell flow of current in the morula reflected such a form of junctional communication too. There is, however, evidence of the presence of a particularly strong ion barrier at the morula surface (Holtfreter, 1943). Thus, if the resistance to ion movement of this barrier is high relative to the resistance of the plasma membranes in the morula, the observed cell-to-cell current flow may have been due to this surface barrier alone, even in the absence of specialized communicating cell junctions. In the experiments to be described here, we examine this question under conditions in which the morula surface is bypassed as a barrier. It will be shown that the blastomeres do indeed communicate through permeable junctional membranes, and that this communication forms rapidly where blastomeres are in contact.

METHODS

Eggs of various developmental stages of *Triturus pyrrhogaster* were collected from ponds and stored in Holtfreter's solution. Immediately before the experiments, the jelly layer surrounding the eggs was dissected away; the vitelline membrane was left in place. This preparation was then set up in a glass chamber filled with Holtfreter's solution, and electrical measurements were begun within 3 hours from time of egg collection.

In the experiments in which the morula surface was broken, pressure was applied onto a pair of adjacent blastomeres with rounded forceps

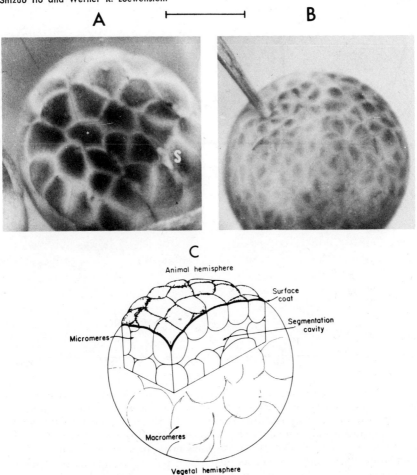

Fig. 1 (A and B) Photomicrographs of morula of *Triturus pyrrhogaster*. (A) Early morula. A crack (*S*) in the morula surface has been produced by applying pressure onto two adjacent blastomeres. (B) Mid-morula into which a hole is being punched with a tungsten needle. Three microelectrodes are seen on top. Calibration ca. 1 mm. (C) Diagram of an early morula.

until a crack appeared between the cells (Fig. 1A); or a hole of about 200 μ diameter was punched into the morula with a tungsten needle or sharp forceps, opening the segmentation cavity to the bathing medium (Fig. 1B). The hole was well away from the cell region where the electrical measurements were made.

For isolation of single blastomere cells (macromeres), mid- or late morulae were cut open along their equators, exposing the macromeres in the segmentation cavity. One or more macromeres were then shaken loose from the blastomere mass and floated to the bottom of the chamber.

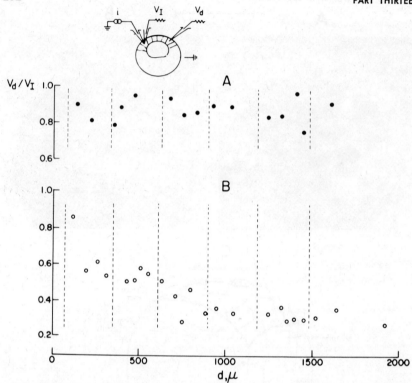

Fig. 2 Voltage attenuation in animal hemisphere of mid- and late morulae. A current i is passed between the inside of one micromere (I) and the grounded bathing medium, and the resulting resistive voltages are measured in this micromere (V_I) and in adjacent ones (V_d) located at varying distances, d, from the current source ($d = 0$). Dotted vertical lines mark approximate location of cell boundaries. Data from different morulae. Each point gives the mean of several measurements in a given micromere. Standard error smaller than size of dots. (A) Intact morulae. Currents are 3–5×10^{-8} A. (B) Morulae with segmentation cavities in communication with bathing medium. Currents are 1.5–3×10^{-7} A. (Current is constant in each morula.)

Many of the macromeres so isolated disintegrated. About a third continued to divide normally. Macromeres of this kind were wedged into the (yolk-coated) cavity formed by the intact surface of the cut egg and the bottom of the bath chamber. The cells were thereby sufficiently immobilized for microelectrode impalement. The work on isolated blastomeres was done in a solution of the following composition: 81.2 mM NaCl; 0.9 mM KCl; 1.2 mM CaCl$_2$; 0.24 mM NaHCO$_3$ ($1.33 \times$ osmolar in respect to Holtfreter's solution).

Intercellular communication was measured by an electrical technique described previously (Loewenstein and Kanno, 1964). The technique consists essentially in passing an ion current with a microelectrode from the inside of a blastomere to the bathing medium (or in the reverse direction) and to measuring with two other microelectrodes the resulting steady-state voltages inside this blastomere and inside a neighboring one (Fig. 2, inset).

For mechanical separation of daughter cells of dividing (isolated) macromeres, the cells were first impaled with the microelectrodes and then slowly pulled apart with the electrodes driven by a micromanipulator. Electrical communication between the cells could thus be monitored continuously during the mechanical separation. In this way, membrane damage could also be detected with high sensitivity by the electrical monitoring. The most suitable stage for cell separation was 40–60 minutes from start of macromere cleavage.

In the experiments in which morulae or isolated blastomeres were exposed to test media of different compositions, late morulae were transferred from Holtfreter's solution into the test medium, washed three times in the medium to eliminate traces of perivitelline fluid, and left in the test solution for 30 minutes before resting potential measurements were made. Blastomeres from these morulae were then isolated in this medium for measurement of their resting potential.

All experiments were performed at room temperatures ranging between 21 and 27°C.

RESULTS

COUPLING BETWEEN BLASTOMERES IN THE MORULA

The blastomere cells of morulae are in ionic communication with each other. The voltage (V) produced by a current from a point source in one blastomere (micromere) is detectable in other micromeres located several cell diameters away. There is little attenuation of voltage with distance in intact morulae. The ratio of voltages[1] in contiguous micromeres (V_{II}/V_I) averages 0.9; the ratio is still above 0.8 in micromeres separated by 1000 μ (V_{1000}/V_I), that is, a distance comprising 3 cell junctions in early morulae or 5 to 6 junctions in late or mid-morulae (Fig. 2; Table 1). The input resistance (for inward current), i.e., the resistance between micromere interior and the bathing medium measured 760 $\pm$ 130 KΩ S.E. (5 cases) in early morulae, and 830 $\pm$ 110 KΩ (9 cases) in mid- and late morulae.

When the morula surface is broken, the input resistance (determined in cells away from the surface break) falls and attenuation of voltage becomes steeper. For instance, the input resistance measured in a macromere of a late morula fell from 1600 to 300 KΩ and the V_{1000}/V_I

---

1 V_I, the voltage in the cell containing the current source; V_{II}, the voltage in a contiguous cell; V_{1000}, the voltage in a cell at 1000 μ from the current source.

TABLE 1

BLASTOMERE INPUT RESISTANCE AND ELECTRICAL COUPLING BEFORE
AND AFTER RUPTURE OF MORULA SURFACE[a]

Stage	Surface	Blastomere input resistance		Coupling[b]	
		Inward current $10^3\,\Omega$	Outward current $10^3\,\Omega$	V_{II}/V_I	V_{1000}/V_I
Early morula	Intact	1200	800	—	0.81
		700	500	—	0.83
		800	600	—	0.82
		357	—	—	0.80
		723	—	—	0.90
		—	583	—	0.90
	Broken	325	270	—	0.38
		325	200	—	0.45
		335	—	—	0.55
		160	—	—	0.44
Late morula	Intact	1620*	—	—	0.87
		667	450	—	0.87
		714	692	—	0.92
		627	—	0.82	0.83
		1138	—	0.88	0.92
		731	—	0.94	0.74
		491	—	0.91	0.84
		759	—	0.93	0.90
		725	541	—	0.80
	Broken	320*	—	—	0.41
		180	—	0.75	0.47
		177	—	0.70	0.38
		365	—	0.86	0.32
		123	—	0.72	0.30
		190	—	0.61	0.34
		243	—	0.68	0.38
		170	—	0.62	0.49
		160	—	0.65	0.33
		476	—	0.51	0.22
		581	—	—	0.22

[a]Data are from different blastomeres in morulae except for data marked with asterisk, which are from the same blastomere, obtained in consecutive runs before and after surface rupture.
[b]For inward currents.

ratio from 0.9 to 0.4, upon opening the segmentation cavity to the bathing medium through a hole of about 200 μ in diameter. Changes of a similar order were obtained with the other two methods for shunting of the morula surface resistance (see Methods). On the average, the input

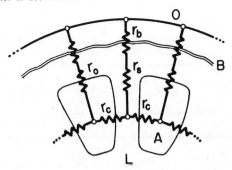

Fig. 3 Equivalent circuit of morula cell system. r_o, resistance of nonjunctional blastomere membrane; r_c, resistance of junctional blastomere membrane; r_s, perijunctional resistance; r_b, component of morula surface resistance in addition to r_o (see text *footnote* 2). All resistances are distributed. *A,* blastomere; *L,* segmentation cavity; *O,* bathing medium.

resistance fell from 760 $\pm$ 130 to 290 $\perp$ 42 KΩ S.E. in early morula (4 cases) and from 830 $\pm$ 110 to 270 $\pm$ 45KΩ in mid- and late morulae (11 cases); and the V_{1000}/V_I ratios fell from 0.84 $\pm$ 0.018 to 0.45 $\pm$ 0.035 S.E., and 0.86 $\pm$ 0.02 to 0.35 $\pm$ 0.026, respectively, upon rupturing the morula surface (V_{II}/V_I fell from 0.89 $\pm$ 0.022 to 0.68 $\pm$ 0.077 in mid- and late morulae). Table 1 summarizes the data.

The morula may be represented by an equivalent circuit of the kind illustrated in Fig. 3, in which r_b is the resistance of the morula surface[2]; r_o, the nonjunctional blastomere membrane resistance; r_c, the resistance of the junctional blastomere membrane; and r_s, the intercellular space resistance. The above results show that r_b is a significantly high resistance and, hence, contributes to the low degree of voltage attenuation. However, it is clearly not a sufficient cause for the high electrical coupling: when r_b is shunted, electrical coupling between blastomeres persists. Hence $r_c << r_s$[3]; $r_c < r_o$; i.e., part of the current flows from blastomere interior to interior through low-resistance junctions. This part reflects the actual intercellular communication in the sense used in earlier publications from this laboratory (cf. Loewenstein, 1966, 1967a).

[2] To facilitate the representation of Fig. 3, the resistive component r_b of the morula surface is drawn as residing in a surface (B) different from the blastomere plasma membrane. In the absence of structural evidence for such a coat, an equally valid representation (and one leading to the same general conclusion above) is one in which the resistive components r_b and r_o are both parts of the structure of the plasma membrane portion facing the morula exterior, i.e., the resistance of this membrane portion is higher than that of the (nonjunctional) membrane portion facing the morula interior and higher than that of the (nonjunctional) membranes in general of the blastomeres not at the morula periphery.

[3] r_s is thus an ion barrier insulating the intracellular compartment from the extracellular one at the level of the cell junction (*perijunctional insulation*) (Loewenstein, 1966).

TABLE 2

MEMBRANE POTENTIALS OF BLASTOMERES *in Situ* AND ISOLATED
FROM MORULA IN VARIOUS MEDIA

Medium (mM) [a]	In situ (mV)	Isolated (mV) [b]	Number of morulae
(1) Holtfreter's solution 61 NaCl, 0.7 KCl, 0.9 CaCl$_2$	−39 ± 1.6 (46)	−29 ± 1.5 (36)	4
(2) 61 KCl, 0.9 CaCl$_2$	−33 ± 1.2 (62)	−2 ± 0.4 (54)	9
(3) 61 KNO$_3$, 0.9 CaCl$_2$	−39 ± 1.9 (30)	−7 ± 0.7 (24)	5
(4) 61 K$_2$SO$_4$, 0.9 CaCl$_2$	−31 ± 1.1 (14)	+3 ± 0.7 (17)	3
(5) 61 NaCl, 0.9 CaCl$_2$	−42 ± 2.5 (30)	−32 ± 1.5 (38)	5
(6) 61 choline chloride, 0.7 KCl, 0.9 CaCl$_2$	−35 ± 1.5 (40)	−27 ± 0.8 (67)	7
(7) 122 NaCl, 1.4 KCl, 1.8 CaCl$_2$	−50 ± 1.2 (72)	−26 ± 1.0 (62)	6
(8) 122 sucrose, 0.9 CaCl$_2$	−46 ± 3.6 (11)	−32 ± 1.5 (20)	3
(9) 10 EDTA, 63 NaCl	−34 ± 25 (23)	−9 ± 1.4 (14)	4

[a] All media contain 0.24 mM NaHCO$_3$.
[b] Mean values with their standard error; sign indicates polarity of blastomere interior with respect to bathing medium. In parentheses, the number of cells on which the measurements were taken. The last column to the right gives the number of different morulae on which measurements were made. Measurements on *in situ* and isolated blastomeres were done in consecutive runs.

In intact morulae, with the current source inside a blastomere, the voltages measured inside the segmentation cavity are comparable to those measured inside blastomeres. This shows that there is no resistance comparable to that of the outer morula surface between blastomeres and segmentation cavity. (Electrode position inside the large segmentation cavity is easily recognized by distance of electrode advancement and by a 30–50 mV potential positive with respect to the bathing medium. Micromeres have resting potentials of 40 mV, negative with respect to the bathing medium.)

The surface barrier is further brought into evidence by differences in the effects of media of different ionic composition and of chelators on the membrane potential of blastomeres *in situ* and in isolation. Whereas media in which K^+ substitutes for Na^+, or media containing the chelator disodium ethylenediaminetetraacetate (EDTA) produce marked fall in the membrane potential of isolated blastomeres, they show little, if any significant effect on the membrane potential of *in situ* blastomeres. Table 2 summarizes the effects of the various media used, including the effects of two hypertonic media.

The high resistive character of the surface of the embryo appears to be retained at stages of development later than that of the morula. Measurements of input resistance, with microelectrodes in extracellular

A   B

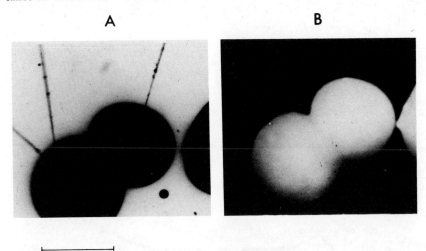

Fig. 4 Photomicrographs of a dividing isolated macromere. (A) The macromere at the end of division (about 90 minutes on the time scale of Fig. 5) in trans-illumination showing the three intracellular microelectrodes used for continuous measurement of electrical coupling. (B) The same macromere in epi-illumination a few minutes later. Note the macromere to the right in the process of adhering to the dividing macromere. Scale ca. 300 μ.

locations in the blastomere mass of late blastulae, give values of the order of $10^6\Omega$; and of $10^5\Omega$ in the neural plate, neural fold, and epidermis of neurulae.

COUPLING AND UNCOUPLING IN ISOLATED BLASTOMERES

The occurrence of junctional communication is shown most clearly in blastomeres isolated from the morula. Figures 4 and 5 illustrate experiments in which electrical coupling is continuously monitored across the cleavage plane of an isolated macromere during division. At the start of cleavage, at the time of broad protoplasmic continuity, V_{II} and V_I are roughly equal and input resistance about 2.25 MΩ. As cleavage proceeds, input resistance falls reaching a minimum of 0.69 MΩ at the time the daughter cells look most separated in the light microscope. Subsequently, input resistance (daughter cell I) rises to 3.75 MΩ and electrical coupling between the cells decreases below a ratio of 1, attaining values around 0.55 by the time the daughter cells are about to cleave in their turn (time, ca. 90 minutes). The V_{II}/V_I ratios of 6 experiments of this kind ranged from 0.33 to 0.87 at this time.

At 40–60 minutes after onset of cleavage, the daughter cells can be separated mechanically. The procedure was to pull the cells apart while probing their electrical coupling. Figure 6 illustrates a continuous sequence. In the course of their separation, the cells remain at first con-

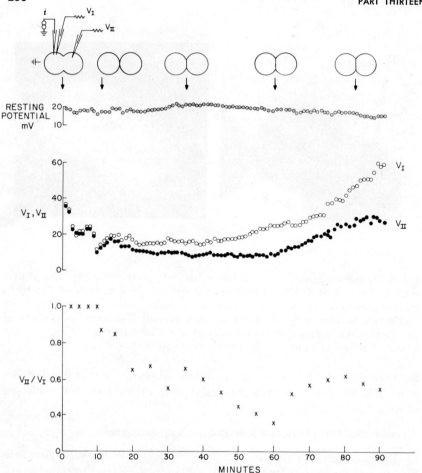

Fig. 5 Intercellular coupling during and after cleavage of an isolated blasto-mere. Microelectrodes are inserted into an isolated macromere (mid-morula stage) at the time the cell shows the first signs of cleaving (time zero). The elec-trodes remain in their intracellular position throughout cleavage for pulsing of current ($i = 1.6 \times 10^{-8}$ A) and for recording of the corresponding voltages V_I (open circles) and V_{II} (closed circles) on either side of the cleavage plane. Before the onset of cleavage, the macromere had a diameter of 440 μ; upon completion of cleavage (time = 80–90 min) the daughter cells had diameters of 320 μ (I) and 400 μ. Temperature 25–26°C.

nected by three "bridges" of cross sections of the order of 1 μ^2 and lengths of the order of 10^{-4}–10^{-3} cm and finally come fully apart (see also Fig. 7). Concomitant with this is a progressive loss of electrical communica-tion: the V_{II}/V_I ratio, which at the beginning of the three-bridge stage is 0.66 (nearly the same as before separation), falls to about 0.22 in the single bridge stage and then to below 0.05, the limit of resolution of the method, as the bridges are cut. The input resistance of cell I increases from an initial value of 3 MΩ before separation to 5 MΩ after full separation. The latter corresponds to a specific resistance of 2.5 $\times$ 10^4 Ω cm^2 (area calculated on the basis of maximal and minimal cell diameter).

When the separated cells are brought into contact again, they adhere to each other; and this is followed by reestablishment of intercellular communication. Figure 8 illustrates a sequence in which two daughter cells of an isolated macromere are first pulled apart causing interruption of electrical coupling (b). They are then micromanipulated together, whereupon electrical recoupling ensues (c).

DISCUSSION

The present results show that the morula surface offers a high resistance to ion flow. The surface resistance is so high relative to resistance of the plasma membranes not in contact with the morula exterior that current injected into a cell is distributed in the morula over considerable distance from the current source. Thus, as is evident from the equivalent circuit of Fig. 3, a rather high V_{II}/V_I ratio would result even in the absense of communicating cell membrane junctions, provided simply that the resistance along the intercellular spaces is high relative to the morula surface resistance. This means only that low voltage attenuation alone is no demonstration of cellular communication through specialized (permeable) membrane junctions. That such junctional communication is indeed present here, and to a degree comparable to that in other communicating tissues (cf. Loewenstein, 1966), is shown by the persistence of a high V_{II}/V_I ratio under conditions in which the morula surface resistance is shunted; and, conclusively, by the occurrence of electrical coupling in blastomeres in complete isolation from the morula.

Rather small areas of cell contact seem to suffice for good communication between blastomeres. At one stage of the experiment illustrated in Fig. 6, the only visible connections between cells were three bridges with cross sections each of the order of 10^{-8} cm^2. Communication was then as good as when the cells were in their normal full contact situation. Even a single bridge was enough to provide clearly detectable communication (Fig. 6). This situation is comparable with that in adult epithelial tissues, such as urinary bladder (Loewenstein et al., 1965), skin (Loewenstein and Penn, 1967), liver (Penn, 1966), and thyroid (Jamakosmanovic and Loewenstein, 1968), and in tissue-cultured fibroblasts (Potter et al., 1966), where rather small junctional membrane areas of the occluding kind (cf. Farquhar and Palade, 1963) appear to furnish cell-to-cell communication.

From experiments of the kind illustrated in Fig. 6, it is also evident that the conductance of unit area, and hence the ionic permeability, of the junctional membrane must be much higher than that of the non-

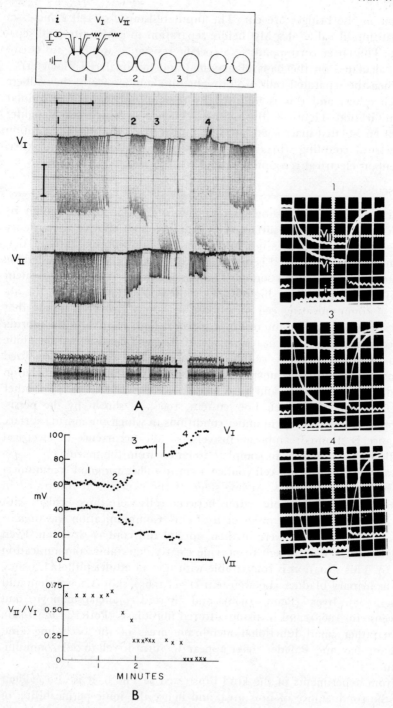

junctional membrane. A rough estimate of junctional resistance r_c may be obtained if we assume that the nonjunctional membrane resistances r_o are equal in the two osculating cells. Then, if $r_s > > r_c$, $V_{II}/V_I = r_o/r_o + r_c$. In the three-bridge situation, $V_{II}/V_I = 2/3$. Thence, $r_c \approx 1/2\ r_o$. Now, the upper limit of junctional membrane area is of the order of 10^{-8}–10^{-7} cm^2 (as against 5×10^{-3} cm^2 of nonjunctional area); and r_o is roughly $5 \times 10^6\Omega$, the input resistance measured in one of the cells after full separation (the change in resistance due to the incorporation of the small former junctional portion into the nonjunctional surface is negligible). Thus the lower limit of junctional membrane conductance of unit area is of the order of 10 to 10^2 mho/cm^2 (as against a 10^{-4} mho/cm^2 nonjunctional membrane resistance).[4] This high value falls within the range of conductances calculated for junctional membranes of a wide variety of other communicating cell systems (Loewenstein et al. 1965) .

A striking phenomenon is the change in membrane permeability occurring during the establishment of communication in artificially dissociated blastomeres. Completely uncoupled cells with membranes of rather low ionic permeability all around, and with negligible intercellular

---

[4] The plain *membrane* conductance is probably even somewhat higher, since the junctional resistance r_c includes here also a *cytoplasmic* contribution due to constriction ("bridges") of the current path at the region of osculation. However, this is unlikely to change the order of magnitude of the estimate of junctional membrane conductance. A cylindrical path of cytoplasm ($100\ \Omega$ cm) with cross section and length of the order of 10^{-8} cm^2 and 10^{-4} cm, respectively, would offer a resistance of the order of $10^6\ \Omega$.

Fig. 6 Interruption of cellular communication. Two daughter cells of an isolated macromere are slowly pulled apart while their electrical coupling is monitored. *1–2*, the cells are mechanically and electrically coupled (they are at a stage corresponding roughly to time 60 min on the scale of Fig. 5); *2*, start of mechanical separation; *2–3*, cells separating but still connected by several thin strands; *3–4*, connection thinned down to a single fine strand; *4*, complete cell separation. (A) Strip chart recording giving i, V_I, and V_{II} pulses as downstrokes from baseline. Baseline of voltage records gives resting potential, which is 20 mV in both cells at *1*. The record is continuous throughout the period of cell separation, except for an interruption of several minutes between *3* and *4*. Time calibration, 1 min; voltage calibration, 25 mV. $i = 2 \times 10^{-8}$ A (200 msec pulse duration) throughout the experiment, except for the period to the right of *4* when i was reduced to one-half. (B) The corresponding plots of the peak values of V_I and V_{II}, and of V_{II}/V_I. (C) Three samples of high speed oscilloscope records (taken simultaneously with the panel A records) displaying the time course of membrane current- and voltage changes corresponding to, from top to bottom, *1*, *3*, and *4* of the panel A records: Calibration: 1 grid division = 50 msec; 14 mV.

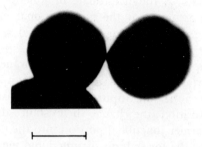

Fig. 7 Photomicrograph of a pair of separated macromere daughter cells from an experiment of the kind illustrated in Fig. 6. Note the connecting strands between the cells. The mechanical situation and the degree of electrical coupling are similar to those in stage *3* of Fig. 6. Calibration, 200 μ.

space resistances r_s, become readily and fully communicating upon contact (Fig. 8). We have no precise data on the time course of the formation of junctional communication; from the scattered data, we have the impression that the establishment of communication takes only seconds. This means that both the formation of the perijunctional insulation (i.e., the becoming of $r_s > > r_c$) and the transformation from low to high permeability at the junctional membranes are completed within this time. This situation is comparable to that in sponge cell junctions which has already been analyzed (Loewenstein, 1967b).

A question of considerable interest concerns the time when junctional communication first arises in the embryo. There is no definite answer

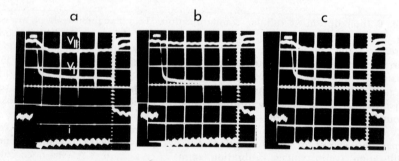

Fig. 8 Establishment of cellular communication. Two daughter cells of a macromere of mid-morula are first separated mechanically and then manipulated into contact again, while electrical coupling between the cells is monitored continuously. (a) Electrical coupling just after normal cleavage of the macromere. (b) Electrical coupling upon complete mechanical separation of the cells. (c) Recoupling following cell readhesion. Current, 3.5×10^{-8} A; 225 msec duration. Voltage calibration, 14 mV per grid division.

yet available. The present results show that many cells, if not all, are intercommunicating at the morula stage. We have not made as yet comparable measurements of electrical coupling at earlier embryonic stages in the newt. But a comparison may be made with the data on electrical coupling at the first cleavage stage of egg cells of starfish (Ashman *et al.*, 1964) and of sand dollar (Ito and Loewenstein, see Loewenstein, 1966). In both cases no junctional communication was found between the first daughter cells on completion of egg cell cleavage, and this correlates with poor mechanical coupling between these cells. However, it is not certain whether the electrical uncoupling here reflects the actual state in this early embryonic cell system. In the starfish experiments the cell system was treated with isotonic urea to soften the fertilization membrane for microelectrode penetration, and in the sand dollar experiments the fertilization membrane was eliminated mechanically by gentle shaking in seawater. Although these treatments were mild, there is no certainty whether they may have altered junctional communication. This possibility must first be investigated thoroughly before a valid comparison can be made, particularly since we know now that junctional communication is easily interrupted by a wide variety of agents (Loewenstein *et al.*, 1967; Politoff *et al.*, 1967, 1968).

SUMMARY AND CONCLUSIONS

Communication between the cells of the morula of *Triturus pyrrhogaster* was examined with an intracellular electrical technique.

Cells in the morula are in ionic communication with each other, and this irrespective of the presence of a strong ion barrier at the morula surface. The membrane surfaces of cell contact (junctional membranes) are much more ion-permeable than the rest of the membrane, and the communicating cell interiors are insulated from the exterior at the level of the junction by a diffusion barrier (perijunctional insulation). As a result, the interiors of most, if not all, of the cells in the morula form a common pool, at least, with respect to their small ions.

When the cells (macromeres) are isolated from the morula and from each other, the former junctional membrane regions are no longer distinguishable in their permeability from the rest of the cell surface membrane; the entire membrane is of low ion permeability. When such cells are manipulated into contact, they rapidly form a communicating system in which junctional membrane regions differentiate into elements of high permeability, circumscribed by a perijunctional insulation. Areas of membrane contact with cross sections of the order of a μ^2, or less, are sufficient for providing a normal degree of communication.

This work was aided by grants from the National Science Foundation and the National Institutes of Health. We thank Dr. S. J. Socolar for valuable discussion.

REFERENCES

Ashman, R. F., Kanno, Y., and Loewenstein, W. R. (1964). The intercellular electrical coupling at a forming membrane junction in a dividing cell. *Science* 145, 604–605.

Farquhar, M. G., and Palade, G. E. (1963). Junctional complexes in various epithelia. *J. Cell Biol.* 17, 375–396.

Holtfreter, J. (1943). Properties and functions of the surface coat in amphibian embryos. *J. Exptl. Zool.* 93, 251–323.

Ito, S., and Hori, N. (1966). Electrical characteristics of *Triturus* egg cells during cleavage. *J. Gen. Physiol.* 49, 1019–1027.

Jamakosmanovic, A., and Loewenstein, W. R. (1968). Intercellular communication and tissue growth. III. Thyroid cancer. *J. Cell Biol.* 38, 556–561.

Loewenstein, W. R. (1966). Permeability of membrane junctions. *Conf. Biol. Membranes: Recent Progress, Ann. N.Y. Acad. Sci.* 137, 441–472.

Loewenstein, W. R. (1967a). Cell surface membranes in close contact. Role of calcium and magnesium ions. *J. Colloid Interface Sci.* 25, 34–46.

Loewenstein, W. R. (1967b). On the genesis of cellular communication. *Develop. Biol.* 15, 503–520.

Loewenstein, W. R., and Kanno, Y. (1964). Studies on an epithelial (gland) cell junction. I. Modifications of surface membrane permeability. *J. Cell Biol.* 22, 565–586.

Loewenstein, W. R., and Penn, R. D. (1967). Intercellular communication and tissue growth. II. Tissue regeneration. *J. Cell Biol.* 33, 235–242.

Loewenstein, W. R., Socolar, S. J., Higashino, S., Kanno, Y., and Davidson, N. (1965). Intercellular communication: renal, urinary bladder, sensory, and salivary gland cells. *Science* 149, 295–298.

Loewenstein, W. R., Nakas, M., and Socolar, S. J. (1967). Junctional membrane uncoupling. Permeability transformations at a cell membrane junction. *J. Gen. Physiol.* 50, 1865–1891.

Penn, R. D. (1966). Ionic communication between liver cells. *J. Cell Biol.* 29, 171–173.

Politoff, A., Socolar, S. J., and Loewenstein, W. R. (1967). Metabolism and the permeability of cell membrane junctions. *Biochim. Biophys. Acta* 135, 791–793.

Politoff, A., Socolar, S. J., and Loewenstein, W. R. (1968). Permeability of a cell membrane junction: Dependence on energy metabolism. *J. Gen. Physiol.* in press.

Potter, D. D., Furshpan, E. I., and Lennox, E. J. (1966). Connections between cells of the developing squid as revealed by electrophysiological methods. *Proc. Natl. Acad. Sci. U.S.* 55, 328–333.

Sheridan, J. D. (1968). Electrophysiological evidence for low-resistance intercellular junctions in the early chick embryo. *J. Cell Biol.* 37, 650–659.

1973

Positional Information in Chick Limb Morphogenesis

by D. SUMMERBELL, J. H. LEWIS, and L. WOLPERT

Summerbell, D., J. H. Lewis, and L. Wolpert. 1973. Positional Information in Chick Limb Morphogenesis. Nature 244: No. 5417: 492–496. Reprinted with the permission of L. Wolpert and Nature.

Among the most pervasive concepts that have imbued the thought of embryologists attempting to analyze development have been those involving embryonic gradients and fields. C. M. Child's efforts to explain axial gradients on a metabolic basis have already been taken up here (Part Eight). Neither gradients nor fields have ever been strictly or satisfactorily defined for embryology. They imply graded quantitative differences along an axis or along a set of axes. A gradient, as linear, is one-dimensional. A field may be construed as two-dimensional, for theoretical purposes, if it characterizes a flat territory, for instance the disc which will later form the limb bud in amphibians; it becomes three-dimensional when the round limb disc becomes a more or less cylindrical limb bud. Gradient and field theory have in the past been more descriptive than analytical. Their appeal has rested on their emphasis on the relations of parts to wholes, on consideration of actions of units as subservient to the surroundings of which they form a part and of the complexities in the over-all patterns of development which embryos excel at elaborating and which are so much more difficult to comprehend than are their separate constituent units.

Lewis Wolpert has been devising a theory to explain how a cell knows its position, to put it anthropomorphically, in a spatial pattern. He postulates that a cell, in a specialized position in space, reacts to the informational cues it receives in a manner dictated by its genome and its past history. In the first developmental systems explored as models, the cues were interpreted as including two gradients, one involving an unspecified diffusible substance, the other involving intrinsic positional values.

In the article reprinted here, Summerbell, Lewis, and Wolpert have analyzed the development of the chick limb as an example of a growing organ. This is an ideal system to have chosen. The work of John W. Saunders, Jr. and of others has shown that the chick limb lays down its skeletal elements successively in proximo-distal sequence. If the apical ectodermal ridge covering the limb bud is removed, distal elements fail to form. If an extra apical ectodermal ridge is added, a new distal axis forms.

Summerbell, Lewis, and Wolpert repeated these experiments on chick wing buds, deleting the ridge or adding a supernumerary one. They also repeated another earlier experiment and exchanged the apical caps of wing buds differing in age. They extended the analyses of the results beyond those of previous studies, however, by measuring the length of the skeletal parts differentiated after the experimentation.

The investigators interpret their quantitative results as excluding the possibility that long-range signals might be operative. They suggest, instead, that positional information may be specified by timing mechanisms, possibly related to the number of mitoses that have occurred. Thus the mechanism they now propose is one in which positional information is based on positional value, positional signal, and a third parameter: an autonomous change of value with time.

These speculations concerning the development of embryonic pattern are totally new, and they are original in that they encourage analysis of data concerning actions and interactions of territories of cells not only in the usual three-dimensional patterns of space, but also in the fourth dimension of time. They have the added virtue of being amenable to quantitative verification.

Spatial patterns of cellular differentiation may be established by a two step process: the cells may first have their positions specified with respect to certain boundary or reference regions, as in a coordinate frame, and may then interpret this positional information by selecting an appropriate course of differentiation, according to their genome and developmental history.[1,2] The idea of positional information has so far been applied principally to regulative systems such as insect epidermis[3] and *Hydra*,[4] where growth is not a prominent feature. For these systems some quite successful models have been developed, involving two gradients, one in a diffusible substance, acting as a signal of position, and another in a more stable cell parameter which may be considered as an intrinsic positional value. The diffusible signal gradient may be maintained, for example, by a source at one boundary and a sink at another.[5] The models embody rules for the interaction between the two gradients.

Here we show how positional information may be assigned and used to pattern a growing organ, the embryonic chick limb. The mechanism is different from those mentioned above, according to which cells read positional information from the local value of a position-dependent signal. Just as navigation can depend on clocks as well as maps, so the intrinsic positional character of cells and tissues may be decided by a combination of spatial and temporal cues. In particular, specification by timing can supplant specification by a graded signal maintained by localized sources and sinks. This is especially true for patterns laid down in the course of growth.

For example, as the limb grows out and lengthens, the more and more distal positional values may be allocated just behind its advancing tip at later and later times. The tissue at the very tip can, through growth, serve as a source of the new distal territories, while its own positional character remains in a state of flux. The tissue that emerges early from the labile tip region, in this type of outgrowth, will be proximal; the tissue that emerges late will be distal. The positional character of a group of cells may therefore be decided by the length of time that they or their ancestors have spent in the labile tip region. Some spatial signal is needed to mark out the extent of that region, but this is the only cue that the surrounding tissues must supply to generate the proper proximo-distal sequence of parts. There is no need for an external signal to specify positional value. The specification may, instead, depend entirely on the timing of the stay in the labile region, if there, and only there, tissue changes spontaneously to become steadily more distal in its intrinsic character.

If the rate of this spontaneous change is proportional to the rate of cell division in the labile region, then the assignment of positional values will always be harmoniously linked with growth; the pattern will be tailored to the size of the system at every stage. This is an important consideration for almost all embryos, both plant and animal, whose growth may often be hastened or delayed by chance variations of temperature. There is some direct evidence that cells in a different type of system, an insect epidermis,[3] can change their intrinsic positional value only when they divide. In the type of outgrowth described here, cell division may continue outside the labile region, but there it will not be associated with a change of positional value. A labile region where new positional values are successively engendered in the course of growth, we shall call a "progress zone." For an idealized system (Fig. 1a) growing out uniformly along one axis with a progress zone at its tip, we obtain, at successive times, the patterns of positional value shown schematically in Fig. 1b.

We shall now argue that the embryonic chick limb does in fact develop by such a mechanism. We shall consider only the proximo-distal organization. There is substantial evidence that the antero-posterior coordinate of positional value is specified in a different way, involving some kind of signalling from a polarizing region close to the posterior border of the limb bud;[1,6] very little is known about the dorso-ventral axis.

THE CHICK WING

The chick wing bud starts as a very small bulge from the flank, and grows out as a tongue-shaped mass, consisting of mesenchyme encased in ectoderm. The ectoderm is even and featureless, except for the apical ectodermal ridge, a thickening running round the distal rim of the bud. Earlier work has emphasized the interactions between the mesenchyme and this ectodermal ridge in relation to limb outgrowth.[6-8] We have suggested that the overall shape of the limb bud may depend on the mechanics of the ectoderm and in particular on the strengthening role of the apical ridge.[9]

We wish here to focus attention on the mechanism by which the skeletal elements along the proximo-distal axis are specified, each with its

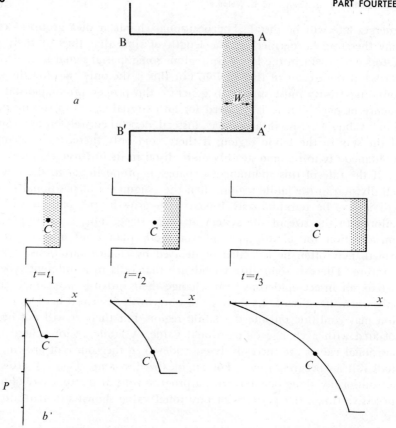

Fig. 1 *a,* An idealized outgrowth. BB′ is its base, and AA′ is its tip. The progress zone, of width *W,* is marked by shading. *b,* The positional value *P* is shown as a function of the distance *x* from the base of the idealized outgrowth at three successive times, t_1, t_2, t_3. *C* marks the mean position of one typical cell lineage followed through the three ages. Inside the progress zone, *P* is taken to change at a rate proportional to the rate of cell proliferation, while elsewhere *P* is fixed so that the pattern of positional values can only spread out by interstitial growth. Note that the size of the progress zone governs the size of the structures that emerge. If the zone were reduced to half its normal width, the full normal range of positional values would initially be crammed into only half the normal expanse of tissue: each anatomical rudiment would be only half its normal length.

own distinctive character. These are laid down within the mesenchyme in a proximo-distal sequence:[10] the primordia of proximal structures begin to differentiate first, while the primordia of more distal structures appear at successively later times and more distal positions. But the tip, that is, the layer of mesenchyme extending inwards from the apical ridge for about 400 μm, remains apparently undifferentiated up to stage 28 or so (Fig. 2), and continues to proliferate relatively rapidly.[11] We find auto-

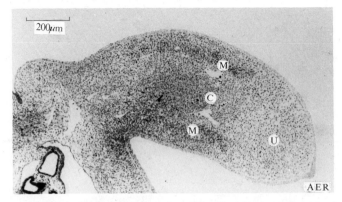

Fig. 2 A stage 23 chick wing bud sectioned in the plane of the proximo-distal and dorso-ventral axes. (Fixed in Karnovsky's fixative, embedded in 'Araldite', cut at 1 μm, and stained with toluidine blue.) AER, apical ectodermal ridge; U, undifferentiated tip mesenchyme; M, pre-muscle; C, pre-cartilage.

radiographically that all the cells there are actively dividing; the distal cells have been reported also to preserve a "morphogenetic potential" at stages when proximal cells have already lost it.[12] We suggest that there is a progress zone located within this mesenchyme beneath the apical ridge, that is, the tip of the limb bud is a region of change, generating tissue with new and progressively more distal positional values. These positional values are interpreted by the cells to give the sequence of distinctive structures.

REMOVAL OF THE APICAL RIDGE

A classical experiment of Saunders[10] shows that the lability of the tip mesenchyme depends on the presence of the apical ectodermal ridge. Saunders found that if the apical ectodermal ridge is cut off, the limb fails to develop distal elements: it is normal up to a certain level beyond which there is nothing. The later the stage at which the ridge is removed, the more nearly complete the resulting limb. Conversely, when a supernumerary ridge is grafted onto the dorsal surface of a limb bud, a secondary distal axis develops beneath it.[6] We have repeated and extended (D. S. and J. H. L., unpublished) Saunders's series of experiments of the former type with a view to providing more quantitative data, and have measured the lengths of the various skeletal elements, using the undisturbed side as control.[13]

In Fig. 3 we show the cut-off level following apical ridge removal between stages 18 and 28. In the terms of our theory, apical ridge removal halts the change of positional value in the apical mesenchyme: when the ridge is removed progress stops in the zone at the tip. The cells there lose their lability prematurely, reduce their rate of prolifera-

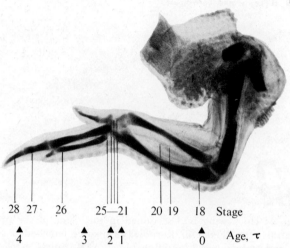

28 27 26   25—21   20 19   18 Stage

4   3   2 1   0   Age, τ

Fig. 3 The mean level of truncation is shown following apical ridge excision at each of the stages indicated. The mean for each stage is derived from measurements of at least seven cases. Beneath the stage numbers we mark the estimated age τ defined as the number of cell divisions that have elapsed in the tip mesenchyme since stage 18, when the limb bud first begins to bulge out. Note the bunching of results at the wrist. This is due to a relatively high cell density and low proliferation rate in that region after it emerges from the apical zone (D. S. and J. H. L., unpublished). The truncated limbs and contralateral controls were fixed in 5% TCA at 9–10 d incubation, stained with alcian green, and cleared in methyl salicylate for measurement.

tion, and start to differentiate according to their current positional value. The resulting limb is therefore shorter, lacking not only the most distal positional values, but also the cells which would have expressed them.

By excising the apical ridge, we assay for the positional value at the tip. If, for example, we halt all changes of positional value at stage 22, and obtain a limb truncated at the wrist, the most distal positional value in the stage 22 limb bud must have been that corresponding to the wrist. The assay is, however, marred by two uncertainties; we do not know accurately the extent of trauma, nor how promptly the positional value stops changing after the apical ridge is removed. Disregarding this correction, we can now reinterpret Fig. 3; it shows, for each stage, S, from 18 to 28, which eventual limb structure has the same positional value as stage S tip tissue. We can use it in conjunction with presumptive fate maps to deduce the width of the progress zone. Our analysis gives 300 ± 100 μm as a rough estimate (D. S. and J. H. L., unpublished) .

GRAFTING OF DISTAL TIPS

There is evidence that the course of the change in proximo-distal positional value which occurs in the progress zone is governed by its internal autonomous kinetics rather than by a level-specific signal from outside, for example from the apical ectoderm or the stump. The elegant and crucial work of Rubin and Saunders[14] has shown that the influence of the apical ridge does not determine the axial level of the underlying mesenchyme. They showed that ectodermal caps can be exchanged between limb buds of different ages, each then developing into a normal limb. In terms of our model, the apical ectodermal ridge is needed to keep the mesenchyme labile at the tip, but it does not direct the path of progress there. The ridge issues a general permit rather than specific instructions.

From experiments in which the tips of two limb buds of different ages are exchanged (Fig. 4a) specification within the progress zone by a signal from the proximal stump can be ruled out. If both pieces of each composite bud develop according to their original presumptive fates, some parts of the resulting limbs will be missing or duplicated. If the stumps signal positional values to the tips, however, the presumptive fates of the tips will be radically modified. Our results, which will be reported in detail elsewhere, show that at least when the grafted tip is more than about 300 μm wide (that is, 300 μm from cut surface to apical ridge), the presumptive fate of the tip is not altered except perhaps in the immediate vicinity of the junction. Deficiencies and reduplications are regularly produced, and the measured size and form of the grafted distal regions resemble those of the donor control limb (Figs. 4a–c and 5). These findings clearly exclude long-range signals controlling either growth or pattern formation in the distal region, and in particular rule out humoral mechanisms and mechanisms whereby elements already formed inhibit formation of further similar elements.[15] Similar results have been recorded by Amprino et al.,[16] but Hampé[17] and Kieny[18,19] have emphasized the regulative capacity of the chick limb bud, and have reported that grafted distal tissue may sometimes be converted to a more proximal character by the influence of proximal host tissue. Their evidence, however, is not compelling, and is not corroborated by further experiments of our own (D. S. and J. H. L., unpublished). The regulation they observe occurs chiefly in grafts of apical slivers so thin that the progress zone due to the apical ridge of the graft can extend into the host, and there bring about considerable regeneration of excised parts without any signalling of positional value. We do not rule out the possibility of some short-range interaction, however, by which cells cooperate to adopt a locally uniform, compromise character. Such a local smoothing interaction may well occur at the time of differentiation, outside the progress zone, and over short distances affect the histological interpretation of positional value. It could also occur earlier, inside the progress zone, and directly affect the assignment of positional value. We do not know how far the autonomy seen on a coarse scale corresponds to autonomy of individual cells.

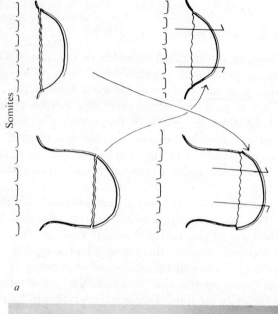

Somites

a

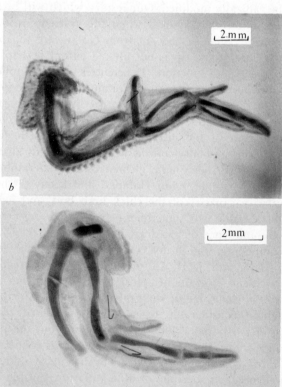

2.mm

b

2mm

c

Fig. 4 *a–c,* The whole of a stage 19 wing bud is exchanged with the distal quarter of a stage 24 wing bud (*a,* dorsal view). The grafts are held in place with pins. The outcome corresponds with negligible regulation. Typically a young bud on an old stump (*b*) gives a humerus and forearm of the same

Doner	Host				
Stage 19/20	20	22	24	24	24
Predicted composite limb					
Observed composite limb					
No. of cases	3	5	8	3	2

Fig. 5 An entire young wing bud is grafted on an older host stump, as in Fig. 4a. The stages of donor and host are as marked on the sketches in the top line. The predicted outcome is derived from fate maps[28] assuming no interaction between host and donor. The observed outcome is a mean, derived from measurements on several composite limbs; the number of measured limbs is shown in the bottom line. Apart from some possible local regulation affecting not more than about half an element, the observations agree with the predictions.

APPLICATION TO OTHER SYSTEMS

The idea that positional information might be specified in growing fields by a timing mechanism, such as the counting of cell divisions in a labile zone, seems applicable to a variety of other systems. It could, for example, explain how positional values are assigned within a blastema so as to follow the rule of distal transformation.[2] If blastema formation involves setting up a progress zone from the cells at the cut surface, then the regenerate will automatically originate at the positional value corresponding to the level of the cut, and from there develop only the more distal levels. Thus, for example, a blastema on the proximal face of the distal half of an amputated structure will yield a mirror image regenerate. This phenomenon occurs in the regeneration of both amphibian limbs[20] and insect imaginal disks.[21] A timing mechanism may also specify positional values in the retina, where they may be used for making the regular pattern of retino-tectal connexions.[22] Up to the stage when the system has its polarity specified, there is uniform cell division,[23] but after this, growth is confined to a relatively narrow ring near the outer edge.[24] Thus cells at the outer edge of the mature retina have divided more

---

length as in the host's contralateral control wing, followed by a humerus, fore-arm and hand of the same length as in the donor's control wing. By contrast, an old tip on a young stump (c) gives a humerus of the same size as in the host's control wing, followed by a hand of the same size as in the donor's control wing. (The photographs in fact show composite limbs from two different pairs of chicks.)

times than those nearer the centre. There may thus be a progress zone during retinal growth which could provide the retinal cells with a radial coordinate analogous to the proximo-distal coordinate in the limb.

SPECIFICATION OF POSITIONAL VALUE

We have proposed a new mechanism, based on autonomous changes of positional value with time rather than on signals from far off, to specify positional information in a growing system. On this basis, a model can be developed to give quantitative predictions of the outcome of various grafts; and these predictions are consistent with the experimental data (D. S. and J. H. L., unpublished). Several questions now require further investigation. For example, how is positional value registered by individual cells and is it a continuous variable? Does it change only at cell division, suggesting an analogy with regulation in the insect epidermis[3] and with Holtzer's "quantal mitosis"[25]? Are individual cells autonomous, or is there local averaging of positional value by short-range communication between cells inside or outside the progress zone? How does the apical ectodermal ridge specify the width of the progress zone; is hyaluronic acid involved, as some recent experiments[26] perhaps suggest?

More generally one can begin to see how positional information may be specified in different systems, using, in different ways, three principal components: a positional value, a positional signal, and cell division. In *Hydra* a new boundary region may be formed when the signal is a threshold amount below the positional value; in the insect epidermis the positional signal sets the positional value at cell division; in the vertebrate limb bud the positional value changes autonomously at cell division; and in intercalary regeneration in the insect limb differences between the signal and the intrinsic value may initiate cell division.[27] Our analysis of the chick limb strongly indicates that one should look for a biochemical correlate to the proposed changes in positional value in the progress zone. While suggesting where to look, and what to look for, it unfortunately provides no indication whatsoever as to how to do it.

We thank Mrs. Margaret Goodman for technical help, and the Science Research Council for financial support.

REFERENCES

1. Wolpert, L., *J. theor. Biol.*, 25, 1 (1969).
2. Wolpert, L., *Current Topics in Developmental Biology*, 6, 183 (1971).
3. Lawrence, P. A., Crick, F. H. C., and Munro, M., *J. Cell Sci.*, 11, 815 (1972).
4. Wolpert, L., Hornbruch, A., and Clarke, M. R. B., *Amer. Zool.* (in the press).
5. Crick, F. H. C., *Nature*, 225, 420 (1970).
6. Saunders, J. W., and Gasseling, M. T., in *Epithelial-Mesenchymal Interactions* (edit. by Fleischmajer, R., and Billingham, R. E.), 78 (Williams and Wilkins, Baltimore, 1968).

7. Zwilling, E., *Adv. Morphogen.*, **1**, 301 (1961).
8. Amprino, R., in *Organogenesis* (edit. by de Haan, R. C., and Ursprung, H.), 225 (Holt, New York, 1965).
9. Summerbell, D., and Wolpert, L., *Nature new Biol.*, **239**, 24 (1972).
10. Saunders, J. W., *J. exp. Zool.*, **108**, 363 (1948).
11. Hornbruch, A., and Wolpert, L., *Nature*, **226**, 764 (1970).
12. Finch, R. A., and Zwilling, E., *J. exp. Zool.*, **176**, 397 (1971).
13. Summerbell, D., and Wolpert, L., *Nature new Biol.*, (in the press, 1973).
14. Rubin, L., and Saunders, J. W., *Devel. Biol.*, **28**, 94 (1972).
15. Rose, S. M., *Regeneration* (Appleton-Century-Crofts, New York, 1970).
16. Amprino, R., and Camosso, M. E., *Arch. Anat. micr. Morph. exp.*, **54**, 781 (1959).
17. Hampé, A., *Arch. Anat. micr. Morph. exp.*, **48**, 345 (1959).
18. Kieny, M., *Devel. Biol.*, **9**, 197 (1964).
19. Kieny, M., *J. Embryol. exp. Morphol.*, **12**, 357 (1964).
20. Rose, S. M., in *Regeneration* (edit. by Rudnick, D.), 153 (Ronald, New York, 1962).
21. Bryant, P. J., *Devel. Biol.*, **26**, 606 (1971).
22. Gaze, R. M., *The Formation of Nerve Connections* (Academic Press, London, 1970).
23. Jacobson, M., *Devel. Biol.*, **17**, 219 (1968).
24. Straznicky, K., and Gaze, R. M., *J. Embryol. exp. Morphol.*, **26**, 67 (1971).
25. Holtzer, H., in *Control Mechanisms in the Expression of Cellular Phenotypes* (edit. by Padykula, H. A.), 69 (Academic Press, New York, 1971).
26. Toole, B. P., *Devel. Biol.*, **29**, 321 (1972).
27. Bohn, H., *Wilhelm Roux' Arch. Entwicklungsmech. Organ.*, **167**, 209 (1971).
28. Amprino, R., and Camosso, M., *Wilhelm Roux' Arch. Entwicklungsmech. Organ.*, **150**, 509 (1958).